Praise for the New York Times
White House Chef Mys...

FONDUING FATHERS

"Hyzy, as always, fills this novel with a clever plot and fascinating behind-the-scenes glimpses of life in the White House. But it's Ollie who carries the series, and never more so than in this moving page-turner."

—*Richmond Times-Dispatch*

"This time [Ollie's] investigation is a personal one, as closely held family secrets are revealed. Scenes in the White House kitchen will appeal to foodies. A touch of romance rounds out this delectable offering." —*RT Book Reviews*

"[A] mystery delight . . . This is a fantastic installment in the series . . . The White House staff is still quirky and interesting, and the recipes at the end range from really easy to needing to raise the spirit of Julia Child as a spirit guide . . . and yes, there is fondue." —*Kings River Life Magazine*

AFFAIRS OF STEAK

"Hyzy shines in this volume. *Affairs of Steak* proves unequivocally that this series burns as bright as the sun during a sweltering D.C. summer."

—*Seattle Post-Intelligencer*

"These are wonderful books, enjoyable to read, hard to put down, and they make you really look forward to the next one in the series." —*AnnArbor.com*

"Fun and intriguing . . . I will keep my eye out for other books in the White House Chef Mystery series." —*Fresh Fiction*

continued . . .

BUFFALO WEST WING

"Hyzy's obvious research into protocol and procedures gives her story the realistic element that her readers have come to expect from this top-notch mystery writer. Adventure, intrigue, and a dash of romance combine for a delicious cozy that is a delight to read." —*Fresh Fiction*

"A captivating story from the very first page until the end. The plot thickens like pea soup, and each character has a different spice to add to it. From the easy-to-recreate recipes in the back to its high-energy, ever-changing story line, this one is good enough to serve to the higher-ups. Ollie is definitely a character worth following. Great job, Julie Hyzy. Another all-around great read!" —*The Romance Readers Connection*

"Ollie Paras is at the top of her game in [*Buffalo West Wing*], as is Hyzy . . . Every White House Chef Mystery is cause for celebration. The daily schedule in the White House kitchen is trauma enough, but Hyzy always ratchets up the tension with plots and danger . . . Julie Hyzy's star shines brighter than ever with *Buffalo West Wing*." —*Lesa's Book Critiques*

EGGSECUTIVE ORDERS

"The ever-burgeoning culinary mystery subgenre has a new chef-sleuth . . . The backstage look at the White House proves fascinating. Recipes are included for Eggcellent Eggs." —*Booklist*

"A quickly paced plot with a headstrong heroine and some recipes featuring eggs all add up to a dependable mystery." —*The Mystery Reader*

HAIL TO THE CHEF

"A gourmand's delight . . . Julie Hyzy balances her meal ticket quite nicely between the glimpses at the working class inside the White House with an engaging chef's cozy." —*Midwest Book Review*

"The story is entertaining, the character is charming, the setting is interesting . . . Fun to read." —*Crime Fiction Dossier* (Book of the Week)

"[A] well-plotted mystery." —*The Mystery Reader*

STATE OF THE ONION

"Pulse-pounding action, an appealing heroine, and the inner workings of the White House kitchen combine for a stellar adventure in Julie Hyzy's delightful *State of the Onion*."

—Carolyn Hart, national bestselling author of *Death at the Door*

"Hyzy's sure grasp of Washington geography offers firm footing for the plot."

—*Booklist*

"[A] unique setting, strong characters, sharp conflict, and snappy plotting . . . Hyzy's research into the backstage kitchen secrets of the White House gives this series a special savor that will make you hungry for more."

— Susan Wittig Albert, national bestselling author of *Death Come Quickly*

"From terrorists to truffles, mystery writer Julie Hyzy concocts a sumptuous, breathtaking thriller." — Nancy Fairbanks, bestselling author of *Turkey Flambé*

"A compulsively readable whodunit full of juicy behind-the-Oval Office details, flavorful characters, and a satisfying side dish of red herrings—not to mention twenty pages of easy-to-cook recipes fit for the leader of the free world."

—*Publishers Weekly*

INAUGURAL PARADE

JULIE HYZY

BERKLEY PRIME CRIME, NEW YORK

THE BERKLEY PUBLISHING GROUP
Published by the Penguin Group
Penguin Group (USA) LLC
375 Hudson Street, New York, New York 10014

USA • Canada • UK • Ireland • Australia • New Zealand • India • South Africa • China

penguin.com

A Penguin Random House Company

State of the Onion copyright © 2008 by Tekno Books.
Hail to the Chef copyright © 2008 by Tekno Books.
Eggsecutive Orders copyright © 2010 by Tekno Books.
Penguin supports copyright. Copyright fuels creativity, encourages diverse voices,
promotes free speech, and creates a vibrant culture. Thank you for buying an authorized
edition of this book and for complying with copyright laws by not reproducing, scanning,
or distributing any part of it in any form without permission. You are supporting writers
and allowing Penguin to continue to publish books for every reader.

Berkley Prime Crime Books are published by The Berkley Publishing Group.
BERKLEY® PRIME CRIME and the PRIME CRIME logo are a registered trademark of
Penguin Group (USA) LLC.

Library of Congress Cataloging-in-Publication Data

Hyzy, Julie A.
[Novels. Selections]
Inaugural parade / Julie Hyzy.—Berkley Prime Crime trade paperback edition.
pages cm
ISBN 978-0-425-27025-7 (paperback)
1. White House (Washington, D.C.)—Fiction. 2. Cooks—Fiction. 3. Washington (D.C.)—Fiction.
I. Hyzy, Julie A. State of the Onion. II. Hyzy, Julie A. Hail to the chef. III. Hyzy, Julie A.
Eggsecutive Orders. IV. Title.
PS3608.Y98A6 2014
813'.6—dc23

PUBLISHING HISTORY
Berkley Prime Crime trade paperback edition / June 2014

PRINTED IN THE UNITED STATES OF AMERICA

10 9 8 7 6 5 4 3 2 1

Interior text design by Laura K. Corless.

CONTENTS

STATE
OF THE
ONION

For Mike . . .
Thanks

ACKNOWLEDGMENTS

What wouldn't I give to be invited to dinner at the White House! Better yet, to spend just one day in the White House kitchen. I'd love to work alongside the women and men there who personify excellence. Just one day. It would be a dream come true.

While no one actually said they'd have to kill me if they told me the truth, researching this novel has presented some interesting challenges. I'd like to thank all the Secret Service personnel and staff at the White House who answered my peculiar questions about how Ollie might "do this or that" as best they could. And I'd like to thank the Department of Homeland Security for not breaking down my door after my many Internet searches of "Camp David," "terrorist," "assassin," "White House floor plan," and the like.

So many wonderful people have helped me to the extent they could without compromising security. Any and all errors with regard to the White House and its protocols are mine.

A sincere thank you to those who helped me with firsthand information: Karna Small Bodman, Tony Burton, and Chris Grabenstein. Thanks also to Paul Garbarczyk, Mitch Bramstaedt, and Marla Garbarczyk, who provided me with a plethora of valuable resources. And to Congresswoman Judy Biggert, whose office arranged for my White House tour.

Enormous thanks to Marty Greenberg of Tekno Books for allowing me to create Olivia and her pals—a true thrill. Thanks also to John Helfers from Tekno for his editing expertise and unflagging good cheer. Also from Tekno, many thanks to Denise Little, who put me on the right path to learn White House lore and whose innovative recipes keep Ollie cooking.

I also wish to express my gratitude to my editor, Natalee Rosenstein, at Berkley Prime Crime, for having faith in me, and for taking time out at Bouchercon to meet and talk. I truly appreciated the welcome.

If it weren't for the Second Amendment Foundation and the Tartaro family, Ollie wouldn't have a clue about firearms. Of course, she's still learning . . . and she needs lots more practice.

My dear friend Ken Rand inspires me every day. And he'd be the first to remind me that Max Ehrmann does, too.

From the moment this project began, my writing partner, Michael A. Black, offered support, advice, and unfailing encouragement. I wouldn't be here without him.

I am exceptionally blessed with a wonderful family and great friends who encourage me to follow my dreams. Thank you to Curt, Robyn, Sara, and Biz. You guys are my life.

Finally, special thanks to the Southland Scribes, Sisters in Crime, Mystery Writers of America, and to the entire writing community. What a privilege it is to belong to such an interesting and generous group.

CHAPTER 1

I SLID MY EMPLOYEE PASS INTO THE CARD READER AT THE NORTH-east gate of the White House, and waited for verification—a long, shrill chirp that always made me wince. The pedestrian gate unlocked with a *click* and one of the guards, Freddie, emerged from the checkpoint to meet me. Like all of the staff here, he was fit, smart, and imposing. But he had a soft spot for those of us in the kitchen. We gave the guys cookies when we had time to make an extra batch.

"Hey, Ollie," he said, looking at the bulky parcel in my hand, "What's that?"

I pulled the commemorative silver frying pan out from its bag and smiled as I ran my fingers over the words engraved on its base. "Henry's retirement gift," I said. "Think he'll like it?" Henry Cooley, the White House executive chef, was formally retiring after many years of dedicated service. All of us who worked in the White House kitchen had chipped in to give him something to remember us by.

"It's cool," Freddie said. "He'll love it."

"I hope so." I eased the pan back into its bag just as the sky rumbled and a crack of lightning zinged from the direction of the Washington Monument. I grimaced. "I practically ran from the Metro to beat the storm. Looks like I just made it."

"Like the Prez says, 'You're helping conserve energy and battle traffic congestion,'" he said, jotting notes on his clipboard. "Be proud of it, Ollie. Or should I start calling you Executive Chef Paras?"

"I am proud. I'm also getting wet," I said. My stomach did its customary flip-flop when Freddie mentioned the executive chef position, and I struggled to quell the excitement that rose every time I thought about being appointed to succeed Henry. "Besides, I don't have the job yet. Nobody knows who'll end up running the kitchen."

A grin split Freddie's dark face. "Well . . . I know who I'm rooting for. Just don't forget us uniformed guys when you get that promotion. We get hungry, too."

"I'll bake a batch of celebration goodies just for you."

Freddie stepped back out of the morning rain and into the well-lit guard post. Shouldering my purse, I gripped the bag to my chest and headed up the walk to the East Appointment Gate, hunching my shoulders against the growing storm. Like many White House employees, I commuted to work via the Metro, but it only took me so far. And in the rain, a three-block walk from the station to the check-in seemed to take forever. Thank goodness I was almost there.

The sky was overcast and the weather wet and cold for mid-May—a perfect day to spend cooking. But I'd snuck out to pick up Henry's gift, and I needed to get back before tonight's dinner preparations began.

Just as I passed the first tri-flagged lamppost, a commotion up on the North Lawn caught my attention. There were no White House tours scheduled today—no one should have been in that area. I turned and watched in disbelief as a man raced between trees from the direction of the north fountain toward the East Wing of the White House, two Secret Service men in furious pursuit.

My breath caught as the intruder pounded across the high-ground lawn. Although my view was skewed—the North Lawn was elevated a good four feet from the east walkway where I stood—I could see that this guy was long-legged and moving fast. He was clearly in excellent physical shape, but I knew he'd never make it. Our Secret Service personnel are the most dedicated and best trained in the world. If he didn't surrender soon, they'd quit yelling at him to stop and would start shooting. But right now the runner, one arm pumping, the other wrapped around a black portfolio, was outpacing the agents by at least two strides.

The guy had to be nuts. Ever since 9/11, anyone with common sense knew better than to try to circumvent the enhanced White House security. A threat to our president's safety meant getting shot almost on sight.

I crouched, scanning upward to see the ever present snipers posted atop the White House roof, their dark silhouettes menacing against the gray sky. They jockeyed for position, taking aim. But the profusion of trees on the North Lawn, in full bloom, apparently provided too much cover.

The man didn't look back, not even when the Secret Service guys bellowed at him to stop. He sprinted faster than I've ever seen a person run before. He zigzagged, staying beneath the cover of the trees, as if he knew exactly what he was doing.

My heart pounded and my limbs tingled as I stared. It was like watching a terrifying movie. But this was real. It was happening right in front of me.

Then the requisite emergency training kicked in.

Don't panic. Think.

I stepped off the pavement and ducked behind one of the tall trees lining the walkway. Digging out my cell phone, I dialed the White House security number, even as I kept an eye on what was going on. Remembering to breathe, I also reminded myself that the best thing to do was to stay out of the professionals' way. They'd have this guy caught in no time. If he didn't slow down, he was in for a nasty tumble down the east embankment. And that would get him nowhere except jammed between the ground's gentle slope and the iron fence that surrounded it.

I could see that he had Middle Eastern features: a dark complexion, full mustache and beard, and shoulder-length black hair, which trailed after him like a short cape. His expression—white teeth gritted in a tight grimace—made him look like a snarling Doberman.

A flat-voiced woman answered the phone. "State the nature of the emergency."

"A man," I said. I told myself to stay calm, but my body rebelled, making my voice tremble. "On the North Lawn. There are two Secret Service agents chasing him."

"Yes," she said. "We are aware." I heard clicking in the background. "Your name?"

"Olivia Paras, I'm one of the assistant chefs."

Another click. "Where are you, Ms. Paras?"

I was about to tell her when the man threw the thick folder to his left. Both agents' eyes followed the item's movement. The man stopped, spun, and launched himself at them. He used his split-second advantage to grab one agent's right arm, twisting it around in some kind of martial arts move—and effectively using the man's body as a shield from the other agent. Cracking his elbow into the captured agent's temple, he knocked the man out cold and snatched his pistol from a suddenly limp hand.

Now he had a gun.

I was frozen in place.

"Ms. Paras?"

I almost couldn't speak.

"He . . ."

The second agent dropped into a shooting stance, his firearm extended. The intruder gripped the first agent and whirled, releasing the unconscious figure like an Olympian throwing a hammer. The second agent fired, but missed. His colleague's body slammed into him before he could get another shot off, knocking them both to the ground.

"The agents are down—he's got a gun!" I said.

The intruder didn't wait to see if either agent would get up. He retrieved his package and sprinted away.

As he ran, he lifted the firearm, pointed it at the sky, and thumbed its side. The magazine fell out of the pistol, tumbling behind him. A second later, the gun followed.

"He just tossed the gun," I said, my words sounding slow and stupid. Not surprising, since my mind was shouting that this couldn't be happening. "He's running again. But . . ."

"Where are you, Ms. Paras?"

I wondered how the woman on the other end of the phone could stay so calm at a time like this. I was having a hard time sorting through the flood of stimuli to give her crucial information. I swallowed hard.

"He's headed toward the East Wing," I finally managed. Then, remembering to answer her question, I added, "I'm on the walkway, just north of the East Appointment Gate. Behind a tree."

"Stay there." I heard her address someone else before she returned to me. "Stay out of the way."

I didn't say anything; I was in perfect agreement with that command.

I peeked around the other side of the tree, going up on my toes to see better, just as more Secret Service agents appeared: Five sentries snapping into action, positioning themselves like the pillars of the North Portico. They stood along the East Wing, firearms drawn. They aimed for the man, who was now close enough for me to hear the wet *splat* of his footfalls in the grass.

The intruder spotted the guards and altered his trajectory, veering in my direction.

Then shots sounded.

And I was in the line of fire.

I dropped to the ground, staying low even as I watched. I told myself that being behind a tree could save me from getting nailed as an innocent bystander.

I hoped to God that was true.

Transfixed by terror, I was powerless to move. The sounds of shouting agents and popping gunfire washed over me like some video game sound track.

But this was real.

The man did a skip-step.

He must have gotten hit.

Then, unbelievably, he doubled his speed, heading right for the sudden embankment decline. He was sure in for a surprise when the ground dropped out from under him.

"Stay where you are, Ms. Paras," the woman said into my ear. "And don't hang up."

The intruder was bent in half and weaving from side to side as he ran, trying to avoid the bullets of the sentries and the snipers. Secret Service agents were racing this way now. But they were so far behind that I worried the guy might get away after all.

A sudden sprint. And then, as if he knew precisely where the embankment declined, he leaped into the air, clearing the ground-drop and the iron fence that surrounded it. It looked like slow motion, though it was anything but. Pedaling madly as he soared above the fence, he landed in a thumping skid, rolling onto the pavement less than fifty feet from my position. He boosted himself upright, and in a couple of hops, cleared two small decorative fences that kept people from walking on the grass. He was headed right for me. As if he knew I was there.

I should have shouted into the phone. I should have screamed.

But I didn't. I realized that I was here, at this moment, with an opportunity. I was the one person in the perfect place to do something just right. I knew he couldn't have seen me. He was too focused on getting away.

I dropped the phone. I looked around. But Henry's retirement gift was all I had.

The man closed the distance between us in a heartbeat.

I grabbed the skillet with both hands and jumped to my feet. As he ran past I slammed him with it, right in the stomach. I heard his grunt of pain, and an exclamation in a language I didn't understand. He sank to the ground.

"Ms. Paras?" a tinny voice called from my discarded phone.

I shouted to the agents, "Here! Over here!" I jumped, hoping they could see it was me—hoping they wouldn't open fire again. "Don't shoot!"

The man's expression, though suffused with pain, softened when he looked up at me. Dark brown eyes met mine. "Please," he said.

As he spoke, he scuttled to his feet faster than I would have thought possible. Not dazed or weak at all.

I didn't think. There wasn't time to think.

I whacked him upside the head with the frying pan—the impact reverberated up my arm and sounded like a melon being dropped into a stainless steel sink. He fell to his knees, grunted an expletive.

After a hit like that, I figured he'd be out cold for sure.

But he turned to face me. Still conscious.

I took a step forward, ready to smack him again.

"Over here," I screamed, panic making my voice shake.

The intruder tumbled sideways, cradling his head in one hand, blood dripping from the top of his scalp. His legs worked like he was trying to ride a bicycle, and this time his words were labored. "Please," he said, "must warn . . . president. Danger."

I stood openmouthed, heart pounding, wielding the pan like a tennis racket, when the man's foot gained purchase and he started to pull himself up again.

"Please," he said. "I . . . must . . . warn . . ."

I cracked him again, this time slamming his shoulder.

From behind me, I heard the welcome sound of running feet.

"Ollie, get back," Agent Craig Sanderson said as they surrounded us in a half circle. "Quick. We've got him covered."

They didn't have to tell me twice.

I had a good view of the man from the side, but he kept his face down. His eyes were clenched shut, and he looked awful. Blood dripped from the gash in his head, pooling in the grass below him. He held his hands out, open and empty, shouting to the agents, "I am unarmed."

I noticed now that he wore shabby clothing, but brand-new, high-end athletic shoes and what looked like body armor. No wonder the shots hadn't stopped him. This intruder had come prepared.

The portfolio he carried was tucked under his leg.

I backed up farther as fast as I could, praying I wouldn't trip.

As I cleared their established perimeter, the Secret Service closed in on the intruder, bending his arms behind his back. With a circle of .357 semiauto-matics trained on the guy, two agents stepped in to put some kind of plastic zip-tie thing on his wrists. Lots more operatives gathered, and Agent Thomas MacKenzie broke away from the group to gently remove the skillet from my white-knuckled fist. "You okay?"

I nodded. But I wasn't. All of a sudden my knees went weak; my hands started shaking. I steadied myself by grabbing his shoulder.

"Better get out of the way." He gestured toward a bench across the walk. He held my arm as we made our way over. "Sit down." In a low voice, he asked, "What the hell are you doing here?"

I knew his irritation had nothing to do with me. He was worried about the president and this situation. "I was picking up Henry's gift," I said. "The skillet." I pointed to it in Tom's hand.

Back in the knot of Secret Service personnel, Agent Sanderson lifted the intruder to his feet. Then Sanderson gave an exclamation of surprise, and I heard the sound of a body hitting the ground. I craned my neck to see better.

The intruder lay flat on his back, his bound hands behind him. He stared upward, his gaze still radiating fierce energy, but his voice was strangely con-versational.

"It's good to see you again, Craig," he said. "How is Kate? And the children?"

CHAPTER 2

TOM'S HAND DROPPED FROM ITS PROTECTIVE PERCH ON MY shoulder and he stared, as we all did, at the bloody man on the grass.

Agent Sanderson said, "Naveen?" then glanced up, saw me and Tom and the skillet. "Oh, Christ. Gentlemen, let's get him out of here."

Brusquely, Tom took me by the elbow, stood me up, and steered me toward the East Appointment Gate. "Let's get you out of here, too."

He handed Henry's dented and bloodied skillet to another agent, who carried it gingerly, held away from his body.

"Hey, I just bought that," I said. "It's a gift."

"Sorry, ma'am," the agent said as he placed the abused frying pan into a large, clear plastic bag, "It's evidence now."

"But . . ." I said, uselessly.

I could feel Tom's arm pressuring me to move on. "Henry's not retiring for a couple of weeks yet," he said, "you'll probably have it back before then."

"Probably?"

He didn't answer. Just kept us walking. Tom was six-foot-four, 238 pounds of muscled Secret Service agent. I'm five-foot-two, 110 pounds of busy chef. I'm very strong for my size—handling industrial-sized pots full of boiling water all day will do that for a lady. But I wasn't anywhere near strong enough to resist Tom. It was no contest.

Twisting, I wriggled around in his grip, trying to watch what was going on inside the tight circle of agents. Although there were women in the Secret Service, there apparently weren't any on duty this morning. All I could see were strong, broad shoulders clad in business suits, forming a cage that the intruder could not possibly escape. Between the agents' legs, I could see the man being pulled from the ground. I heard him talking with Agent Sanderson, but I couldn't make out what was being said.

"Naveen, huh?" I asked. Sanderson had called him by name.

"Come on," Tom said with impatience.

I planted my feet. The hundred tasks I'd been prioritizing as I walked back to work could wait. Even I knew that this morning's excitement would throw the First Family's schedule into a tizzy. "I want to see how this ends, since I was in on the start of it," I said.

"This is a crime scene. You don't belong here."

I put my hands on my hips and stared up at him. The flat, expressionless look was gone from Tom's eyes. He was mad. At me. For what, I had no idea.

"But I'm a material witness."

His lips compressed. "Don't you have work to do in the kitchen?"

"Yes. I do. It'll keep. Craig knows that guy," I said. "It sounded like they were friends."

The storm had passed and the sun was making a welcome appearance—but I could see doubt clouding Tom's blue eyes. He glanced over to the cluster of activity around the intruder and I realized why he was so ticked off with me. He wanted to be part of that group, not the bodyguard who made sure the assistant chef made it to the kitchen safely.

"He's bluffing," Tom said. "Guys like that are pretty resourceful. He must have studied Craig's dossier."

"No." I shook my head. "Craig recognized him."

When Tom took my arm again, I let him lead me the rest of the way. "I'm fine," I said, when we reached the staff entrance. "Go on back. I don't need an escort from here."

He didn't need telling twice.

Before I was through security, he was lost in the sea of agents bustling along the walkway.

ALTHOUGH THE NUMBER OF STAFF OFTEN MUSHROOMED TO twenty for state dinners, the permanent White House kitchen staff numbered only five. Marcel, the executive pastry chef, had agreed to cover for me while I was out picking up Henry's gift. In repose, Marcel's black, aristocratic face could have graced the cover of any men's magazine, but when he was worked up, his large eyes popped, making him look like an alert, dark-skinned Muppet.

"Olivia! *Qu'est-ce que . . .*" he said as I shed my jacket and opened the linen cabinet. "What happened?" Whenever Marcel got agitated or upset, he forgot himself and dropped into his native language for some colorful invective. I'd picked up a lot of French when I studied in Paris, but my vocabulary had more to do with cooking than with street patois. I didn't understand Marcel very well when he really got on a tear, but I sure loved to hear him talk. One of these days I needed to look up the words he yelled so fast. I didn't want to use them in public until I was sure they weren't unforgivable.

Marcel finally wound down enough to lapse back into English. "They have shut down the building," he said.

"I know." I sat. "Secret Service told me."

"What?" he asked. "And you, *mon petit chou* . . . How you say . . . ? You look like three-week-old escarole."

"Thanks a lot." I blew out a long breath. My little adventure had taken a toll on me. Now that I was safe, back in the haven of the kitchen, I could feel cracks working their way through my usually calm veneer. Forcing a smile as I looked up into his worried face, I lied. "I'm fine."

"*Oui*, and I am the pope," he said.

I stood up, but my hands shook so much as I pulled out my white tunic and tall toque that I wondered if I could put my uniform on.

My hesitation to talk wasn't just nerves. I wondered how much I was allowed to say about what had just happened. The less I said, the better, I imagined. But since the attack had happened outside on the North Lawn, where tourist video cameras were always running, I figured the whole thing would be on CNN or Fox News any minute now. Plus, Tom hadn't told me to keep my mouth shut.

Thinking about it, I was pretty sure I didn't need to maintain total secrecy. There were always newscopters hovering around. We lived in an up-to-the-minute world. The incident was probably already on the wires.

"The Secret Service caught some guy trying to get in."

"*Merde*." Marcel strode over to the corridor that connected our busy kitchen with the rest of the lower level, and peered out. "I saw agents running by earlier, but it is quiet now. Where did this happen? Did you see him?"

"I saw him," I said, hoping that would be enough to keep Marcel happy. "And Agent MacKenzie made sure I got back here safely. So, everything's good."

"Yes," Marcel said, with a wry pull to his lips. "If the oh-so-handsome Thomas escorted you up here, then I'm certain everything is quite good. For you."

I ignored his comment. Striding back into the heart of the kitchen, I was all business. "Anything else going on?"

"Quiet as, how you say, a grave."

"I think you mean *tomb*."

Marcel shrugged. "Henry is still at the White House Mess." He made a face. Marcel hated the term we used for the other kitchen, the one run by the navy that serviced the round-the-clock staff. "He will be back shortly. But where is Henry's gift? Was it not ready?"

Shoot, in all the excitement I had already forgotten what I supposed to be carrying. I was about to answer when the chief usher, Paul Vasquez, came into the kitchen. As head of the executive residence staff, Paul dropped by occasionally, usually to confer with Henry over menu decisions. Today his handsome features were strained, and he ran a hand through his salt-and-pepper hair, a gesture I'd seen him use only during periods of stress. "Olivia, may I have a word with you?"

Uh-oh.

I followed him through the corridor and into the China Room. It was one of my favorite rooms, and I couldn't wait until the day my mother finally made the trip out here to visit me. She'd be captivated, as I was, by the gorgeous display—and the wealth of American history it represented. When I was first hired at the White House, I'd poked my nose in here fairly often, determined to memorize which china pattern belonged to which First Family. I'd gotten pretty good at it.

As Paul gestured me into one of the two chairs flanking the room's fireplace—the one with its back to the door—I reviewed the china patterns to myself in an effort to calm my nerves. Whatever Paul wanted probably had something to do with my being outside when I shouldn't have been. News traveled fast around here.

He ran his hand through his hair again before meeting my eyes. "I've just been notified about the disturbance outside. The Secret Service has characterized your involvement in the incident as . . . reckless."

I opened my mouth to protest, but he stopped me with a look.

"You got in the middle of a firefight," he said.

"How was I supposed to know I was walking into it? I was just heading back to work from—"

"I know all about your important errand."

That didn't surprise me. Paul knew everything that went on in the White House.

He sat all the way back in his chair—I sat at the edge of mine, with my hands folded in my lap like a schoolgirl's. I didn't think whacking an intruder with a pan was cause for White House dismissal, but I was pretty sure that interfering with official Secret Service business was.

I kept silent, uncomfortably aware of each inhalation in the quiet room.

"Where is Henry's gift now?" Paul asked.

That surprised me. Paul didn't know? "One of the agents took it."

He nodded; undoubtedly some loose end was tied up for him. "Agent Sanderson is on his way to debrief you. He's understandably . . . upset . . . by the breach in security." Paul stared at one of the bas-relief figures carved into the fireplace surround, but I could tell he wasn't seeing it. "Your actions today will have serious repercussions for all of us. We can't ever afford to do anything that might put ourselves at risk, because to do so puts the White House—and everyone in it—at risk." When he met my eyes again, his expression softened. "But I have to tell you, Ollie, I personally think it was a damn brave thing you did."

When he glanced over my shoulder, I turned. Craig Sanderson crossed the threshold, a dour look on his face.

As he left, Paul patted my shoulder and leaned down to whisper in my ear, "You'll be okay."

Craig strode across the carpeting, emanating anger with every step. He sat and stared at me, waiting a long time before he spoke. The tension in the room grew so tight that the china on display almost seemed to hum.

"Ms. Paras."

Craig and I were on a first-name basis and for the first time, his gentle Kentucky drawl took on a menacing air. The fact that he wasn't calling me Ollie made me feel nervous and small. I didn't like it. "Yes, Agent Sanderson?"

His eyes snapped up, warning me to not take this lightly. I wasn't, but if he had a problem with what I'd done this morning, I wished he would just say so. At least then I'd have a chance to explain what happened.

"We have a tape of your call to the emergency operator."

I waited.

"She instructed you to stay low and get out of the way."

"I did."

His eyebrows rose and he continued, enunciating each word with slow precision. "Then how do you explain the fact that when we reached you, you were attacking an armed intruder with a frying pan?"

"He ran right by where I was hiding. I was the only person in place to stop him. So I stopped him. But you're wrong—he wasn't armed."

"You don't know that."

"Yes, I do. I saw him drop the agent's gun as he ran. I was just inches away from him when I hit him." I thought about the black portfolio the guy had been carrying, and I suddenly realized that I truly had no idea as to whether he'd been armed or not. So, I took a different approach with Craig. "You know, I heard him ask you about your family. Is he a friend of yours?"

For the first time since he'd come into the room, Craig's face registered emotion—I'd surprised him. Before he could answer, I touched his arm. "He really *was* trying to warn the president about something, wasn't he?"

Craig's muscles were taut beneath my hand. I pulled away.

"No," he said. "He was not. He was an unauthorized intruder and he is being dealt with even as we speak. As for you," he said, glaring, "in the future, when you are given a direct order by *any* of the security staff—and that includes uniformed guards as well as the emergency operators—you will follow that order without deviation. Is that clear?"

There was so much more I wanted to say, but this was not the time. "Yes. Very clear."

Nodding as though granting absolution, he continued in a gentler tone, "Now, tell me what happened, from your perspective, and let me know exactly what he said to you."

I went through everything, including my fears and my puzzlement at the running man's quiet demeanor when he tried to talk to me. I tried to read Craig, tried to see behind his blank, professional expression, but I got nothing.

When I finished, Craig stood. "I will direct Chief Usher Vasquez to eliminate all mention of this incident from your personnel files. It will not appear on your permanent record. But don't let it happen again." He fixed me with a look that was anything but friendly, and left.

I wasn't fooled. The only reason my involvement in the skirmish wasn't going on my record was because of how bad it looked to have a little lady assistant chef stop the bad guy that the big macho Secret Service couldn't catch.

I resisted the urge to make a face at Craig's retreating back.

TO KEEP MY HANDS BUSY, I CHOPPED FRESH TOMATOES AND onions for use later in the day. We always needed things chopped. When one of the other assistants, Cyan, came in a few minutes later, she shrugged out of her jacket and donned an outfit similar to mine, jabbering all the while.

"You should see all the network crews out around the perimeter. Lafayette Park is a mob scene. What's going on? I thought the president's news conference was scheduled for tomorrow. Wasn't it? I didn't think it was today—he's not back in residence till this afternoon, right? Did Marcel make coffee?"

"Over there," I said. The coffee carafe sat where it did every day, but Cyan had a powerful need to keep conversation going. She was a few years younger than I. Taller, too, but then again, almost everyone was. Her red hair was pulled back into a half pony, which bounced as she made her way to the carafe.

I thought about what she'd said. The president wasn't due back to the White House till later. The determined trespasser, Naveen, had obviously gotten some bad intelligence if he'd come to warn the president on a day when he wasn't even in the country.

"Where's Marcel?" she asked.

"He went over to the White House Mess to meet Henry."

"Did you pick up the gift? Can I see it before they get back?"

The awareness that I'd lost the commemorative pan during this morning's encounter hit me hard—like I'd been the one slammed in the head. "I don't have it here," I said, not wanting to explain further. Not now, at least.

I bit my lip and kept working. I always chopped onions next to an empty stove burner, with the flame turned high. Cyan, used to my habits, ignored me as she stood before the computer monitor to study the day's schedule. Late last night, Henry and I had updated it.

"What's next?" she asked, clicking ahead on the calendar.

"Getting ready for India's prime minister," I said. "He's arriving this afternoon, and meeting with the president this evening. Remember that menu we worked up a while back?"

"Oh, yeah," Cyan said. "The one you came up with when Henry was on vacation. I hate working so far in advance."

I laughed. "And so you're working here—why?" The meals we designed were so scrupulously planned that we always started weeks in advance, to be certain to get everything just right.

"I'm just saying I like spontaneity."

"Speaking of spontaneity," I said, looking up, "what color today?"

"Emerald green." She blinked wide eyes at me so I could appreciate her contact lenses.

Returning to my chopping, I shook my head. "You change so often that I've forgotten what your real eye color is."

"Blue." She grinned. "Just like my name."

"Good morning," the president said, striding into the kitchen's work area. My hands stopped mid chop.

President Harrison R. Campbell had a boyish face, but a statesman's bearing. He'd taken office in January, upsetting the incumbent by a wide margin, his victory due in no small part to his platform of unity.

"I thought you were in Reykjavik, sir," I said before I could keep the words from tumbling out.

Two Secret Service men in dark suits followed him in. The White House kitchen has relatively narrow aisles running between cabinets, countertops, and our center work area. Although Cyan and I were small, the president's imposing authority and the two giants behind him made for some cramped quarters.

"Nope," he answered—casually, like I had any right to question his whereabouts. "I got in late last night." He pointed to the pile of minced onions on the far end of my cutting board and then to the flame flicking upward from the range's burner. "Cuts the crying, doesn't it?" he asked.

Startled that he noticed, I stammered. "Yes . . . yes. It does."

"My mother used to do the same thing."

I smiled. "Mine, too."

The fact that he'd been in residence last night made me remember my musings about the intruder's erroneous intelligence. The man had been right after all. He'd claimed to want to warn the president—who shouldn't have been here this morning, but was. I tucked away that little tidbit as I shut off the stove and wiped my hands.

President Campbell towered over me, but smiled as he made a small gesture to the two agents behind him. "May I have a word with you, Olivia?"

Like I would say no.

"Sure," I said, then winced at my flip-sounding response. "I mean, yes, of course, sir." I turned to look for a quiet corner, but the two agents had already directed Cyan out of the room.

The moment it was quiet, the president fixed his bright blue stare on me. "I want to thank you for what you did this morning."

Surprised, all I could manage was, "Oh." And despite the worry that I'd say something stupid if I continued talking, I plunged on. "It was an honor. Sir."

Wearing the same expression he did during difficult press briefings, he nodded. "The Secret Service is handling the incident in cooperation with other agencies, and the man has been taken into custody. I just wanted to let you know so that you don't worry about your safety here at the White House."

My safety?

"I wasn't worried." Words raced through my mind, all out of order. I'd never had so much difficulty putting sentences together. "That is . . . not for myself. The man was trying to get to you, sir. He said he needed to warn you."

"You spoke with him?"

"No," I said. I pictured myself standing over the guy, skillet in hand. "It was more like he tried to talk to me."

The president waited.

"He . . . he said you were in danger."

The president's face was grim. "As are we all, in times like these." We both felt the weight of his words. "The security staff might have a few more questions for you. Don't be alarmed if they call you in again."

He must have caught my quick glance at the clock.

"I didn't have a chance to eat breakfast this morning," he said. "Scrambled eggs and toast will be enough for now." He smiled at me. "And Mrs. Campbell informs me that tonight's menu for India's prime minister is your creation."

I nodded.

"Then I'm very much looking forward to dinner."

"Thank you, sir. I hope everyone enjoys it."

"I'm sure we all will."

He stretched out his hand. It was only the second time I'd shaken the president's hand, but this time was just as thrilling as the first. "And, Ollie, one more thing." He fixed me with those intense blues again. "Other than Secret Service personnel, I would appreciate it if you don't speak of this morning's events with anyone else."

CHAPTER 3

"OLLIE, ARE YOU OKAY? WHAT'S HAPPENING?" HENRY WALKED IN moments later, talking up a storm. "I just passed the president in the corridor. Was he in here with you?"

I opened my mouth to speak, but stopped myself as Cyan and Marcel appeared behind Henry. Not thirty seconds before, the president of the United States of America had asked me not to discuss this with anyone, and here I was about to spill the spaghetti with my coworkers.

"Yeah," I said, "he'd like scrambled eggs for breakfast."

Henry glanced in the direction the president had exited and gave me a thoughtful look. "He came down here to tell you that in person?"

I nodded.

Although he was set to retire on his sixty-seventh birthday, Henry was still one of the most vibrant and quick-witted people I knew. He was also the most talented chef I'd ever worked under. It was just in the past couple of years that I'd noticed him taste-testing more often, as evidenced by his expanding waist-line, and delegating the more physically demanding tasks to us. His light brown hair had started to thin and go gray at the temples, but his voice was just as resonant as it had been when I'd joined his staff during the administration immediately prior to this one.

Cyan's eyes widened. "That's all he said? Why did he have to talk with you in person, then? Alone? I bet it had something to do with all the commotion outside this morning. Did it? Hey, you must have been outside when it happened, weren't you?"

Henry picked up on Cyan's comment, but she didn't seem to notice her gaffe. "What commotion? You were outside, Ollie?"

I shook my head, "I forgot my keys down by the staff entrance." I hated lying to Henry, but between the president's words and the need to keep my errand secret if we were to pull off our surprise, I didn't think I had much choice.

He smiled. "Maybe you should tie those keys around your neck." He let out a satisfied sigh. "As for the commotion, I'm sure we'll hear more about it later."

Cyan moved closer. "So, what did the president really say?"

"Not much." I pointed to the computer monitor. "President Campbell said he was looking forward to the big dinner tonight. And that he hadn't had breakfast and he's hungry. We should probably get those scrambled eggs started."

"Oh, come on. He must have wanted something. What was it?" Cyan took a deep breath which, I knew, heralded another slew of questions.

Henry raised his hand, silencing her. "Less talk, more work." To me, he said, "Say no more, Ollie. The president's meals are our first responsibility. Scrambled eggs it is."

We set to work on a second breakfast. The timing was tough because of the official dinner tonight, but it wasn't anything we couldn't handle.

In addition to the scrambled eggs, we prepared bacon—crisp—wheat and rye toast, fruit, coffee, orange juice, and Henry's Famous Hash Browns. More than just pan-fried potatoes, Henry used his own combination of seasonings that made my mouth water every time he prepared the dish. The president and First Lady were so impressed with the recipe that they insisted we serve them at every official breakfast function.

Henry wielded the frying pan with authority, flipping his special ingredients so they danced like popcorn, sizzling as bits landed back in the searing hot oil. "Work fast, my friends. A hungry president is bad for the country!"

After the meal was plated and sent to the family quarters, we cleaned up the kitchen and began preparations for lunch. Then it was time to pull out the stops as we got the official dinner together for India's prime minister. This wasn't as significant an event as a state dinner, where guest lists often topped one hundred, and we were required to pull in a couple dozen temporary assistants to help. This was a more sedate affair; it required a great deal of effort, but it was certainly manageable for a staff of five.

I'd designed a flavorful menu, and the First Lady, after tasting the samples we provided, had approved. We'd feature some of the best we had to offer: chilled asparagus soup; halibut and basmati rice with pistachio nuts and currants; bibb lettuce and citrus vinaigrette; and one of Marcel's show-stopping desserts. We'd done as much as we could in advance without sacrificing fresh-ness or quality, but the time had come to marshal the troops and get everything in the pipeline for the big dinner.

Talk among us turned, as it inevitably did, to the subject nearest to our hearts—the First Lady's choice for Henry's successor.

After months of interviews and auditions, the field had been narrowed down to two: Laurel Anne Braun and me. Laurel Anne was a former White House sous-chef, and host of the wildly popular television show *Cooking for the Best*. She and I had worked together at a top restaurant when I'd just gradu-ated from school, long before my White House days. I'd been promoted over her. She'd never forgiven me. And she made it a point to make sure I knew that. I was hoping to avoid her, if I could, when she came in to prepare her audition meals at the White House.

"She does not have a chance against you," Marcel said, his "chance" sound-ing like "shantz." He deftly arranged chocolate petals to form lotus blossoms. Tonight's dessert of mangoes with chocolate-cardamom and cashew ice cream, would be the crowning glory of the evening's meal. He'd worked late for several nights to create the fragile chocolate pieces, and I held my breath as he assem-bled them. The gorgeous centerpieces came together like magic, without his breaking even one of the delicate petals. "Henry recommended you, *n'est-ce pas*? This is the most important consideration."

Cyan had removed the asparagus from the boiling water after its four-minute bath then waited for it to cool slightly before beginning to slice the blanched stalks for the soup. "Really, Ollie, I don't think you have a thing to worry about—"

She was interrupted by Bucky's arrival. The final member of our permanent staff, he didn't socialize much with the rest of us. That was fine by me. Bucky and Laurel Anne had worked together in the White House kitchen under the previous administration. Henry had never told me the entire story of why she left. All I knew was that my subsequent hiring after Laurel Anne's departure had won me a prime spot on Bucky's hit list.

The four of us stopped talking the minute Bucky walked in. But it bothered me that we did.

I shrugged. What did it matter if Bucky heard us? We all knew that Laurel Anne was the lead contender for the executive chef position. Catching Cyan's eye, I said, "Thanks, but come on." I cut into a segment of grapefruit and expressed its juice into a bowl. "The First Lady's been Laurel Anne's guest on the show . . . what? twice? . . . in the past *four* months. That wins her big brownie points." I diced the remaining fruit, grimacing at nothing in particular. "I don't even know why Laurel Anne needs to audition. The prior First Family ate her meals for years. For crying out loud, Mrs. Campbell's probably already made up her mind. And this is all just wait-and-see . . . for show."

Next to me, Henry prepared the entrée. Since halibut is a lean fish easily susceptible to over- or undercooking, I'd decided on a simple pan-frying method. We'd had the fish flown in from Alaska waters, vacuum-sealed in manageable-sized pieces and kept on ice to maintain freshness, but no flesh ever touched ice directly. Later, we'd brown them on one side in olive oil, then bake them in flavored butter. Henry shook his head as he expertly sliced the flatfish into steaks. "Don't be so down on yourself, Ollie. Mrs. Campbell knows you, too." He graced me with one of his fatherly smiles, the kind I couldn't resist. "And I know you."

"Thanks," I said, smiling back.

Cyan piped in again. "And you know, the TV show might just work against her. The White House doesn't allow that sort of distraction among the staff. Knowing her, she'd never give up the glamour."

Bucky spoke up from his quiet corner. "Laurel Anne gave an interview about her upcoming audition. I saw it on a local channel last night."

I stopped what I was doing. We all did.

"She's from Idaho, you know. The First Lady's home state." Bucky raised his eyes to ensure we were paying attention. We were. "If Laurel Anne gets the executive chef position, she says she'd happily give up *Cooking for the Best* because her new vocation will be 'Cooking for the Prez.'"

When Bucky returned to shelling pistachio nuts, I made a gagging motion for Cyan and Henry to see.

Like he had eyes in the back of his head, Bucky addressed me again. "Just think, Ollie, if Laurel Anne gets the nod, you'll be reporting to her."

"Maybe, maybe not." I bit the insides of my cheeks to keep my voice level. "If she's in charge, I don't see myself sticking around here very long."

Henry gave me an avuncular pat on the back. "Then it would be the White House's loss."

BEFORE THE GUESTS ARRIVED, I STOLE OVER TO THE STATE DINING Room to have a quick look. As always, the sheer grandeur took my breath away.

The staff bustled about, making last-minute adjustments to the placement of water glasses and candles on round tables covered in saffron-colored silk. Our floral designer, Kendra, and her staff snipped and pruned and made tiny changes to the green mums and hot pink roses she'd shaped to resemble elephants in honor of India's prime minister. The entire room, with its magnificent attention to detail, suffused me with pride. I glanced up at George P. A. Healy's portrait of Abraham Lincoln. It hung above the fireplace, and I got the distinct feeling that our sixteenth president was watching over us as we strove to make our current president proud.

What thrilled me most was that I'd designed tonight's menu—the centerpiece of the evening. I'd done it. Me. The lowly assistant chef.

A smile tugged at my lips. The lowly assistant chef with her eye on the executive chef's position. I stood over one of the place settings and ran my finger along the rim of the dinner plate. This was the Clinton china collection, with architectural designs from the State Dining Room, the East Room, and the Diplomatic Reception Room incorporated in its gold band. The north face of the White House graced the plate's center—a first for presidential china. It was one gorgeous design.

I'd worked hard to make tonight's menu sparkle, and with a small sigh of pride, I realized I couldn't ask for a more perfect setting to showcase it.

Just as I made my way out, Craig Sanderson appeared in the doorway with another agent. Though I recognized him as Secret Service, he was not part of the usual Presidential Protection Detail, or PPD, as we liked to call them.

"Agent Sanderson," I said, not sure if he and I were back to first-name friendliness. "I'm surprised you're still here."

Without missing a beat, he turned to his companion. "This is the assistant chef I told you about. Olivia Paras. Olivia, this is the assistant deputy of the Secret Service, Jack Brewster."

The man, a taller, older fellow with a wide-set nose and ruddy complexion, raised an eyebrow as he gave me the once-over. "You were the young woman involved in the altercation this morning?"

"Yes," I answered, suddenly ill at ease.

"And you are employed here as an assistant chef?"

"Yes."

He stared a long moment. Nodded. "We may have more questions for you later."

I scooted away before he decided to question me right then and there.

* * *

AT HOME THAT NIGHT, I TURNED ON CNN, SNUGGLED INTO MY
comfortable red pajamas, brushed my teeth, and spent a few important
moments at the mirror fixing my hair. I poured a glass of wine for myself, and
made sure I had a chilled mug in my freezer and a supply of Samuel Adams in
the fridge.

The official dinner for India's prime minister had gone so well that the
White House social secretary, Marguerite Schumacher, had made a special
effort to visit the kitchen and let us know what a success tonight's event had
turned out to be.

I sighed, contented.

It still amazed me that I was here, in Washington, D.C., working in the
most important kitchen in the world. A far cry from life back in the Chicago
two-flat with my mom and nana.

The sun had gone down two hours ago, and I couldn't believe it'd been just
this morning that the Secret Service had carted away the man . . . Naveen . . . the
guy I'd knocked to the ground. It felt more like a year ago.

I caught a glimpse of the clear, starry night above my balcony, and I wondered if Mom and Nana stared up at the stars and thought of me, as I thought
of them. I would love to have them both relocate here, but Nana was set in her
ways, and my mom would never abandon her. Not even to live near me.

I'd made noises today about leaving the White House if Laurel Anne got
the executive chef position, but I wasn't kidding anyone, least of all myself.
This was my dream job, and I'd fight with everything I had before I'd give it
up to the likes of Laurel Anne.

On a whim, I popped a blank tape into my VCR and started recording the
news. As I expected, they were still running the story. I wanted to know more
about this Naveen. And what danger he had talked about. And how he knew
Craig Sanderson.

Mostly, though, I just hoped to catch myself on-screen. Vanity maybe, but
someday I'd be able to pull out the tape and brag about my participation to my
grandkids.

I settled into my leather sofa and took a long sip of Gewürztraminer. The
German wine fluttered down my throat, filling me with quick warmth.

Tonight's handsome anchorman kept a studious look on his face as he
reported the headline news: A change of regime in the Middle East. Prince

Mohammed of Alkumstan had been overthrown by his brother Sameer, who immediately assumed total control of the country. Sameer claimed to stand for peace.

I sighed. Yet another tale of Middle East unrest and more empty promises. I waited for the juicy stuff. Finally, the anchor introduced the clip. "From Washington, D.C., dramatic footage shows an intruder apparently attempting to gain access to the White House."

The recording showed the man running toward the building. This was a completely different perspective—a view from behind. It looked like it'd been shot from along the front fence. Somewhere in D.C., a lucky tourist was probably counting his windfall tonight. In the tape, the intruder ran away from the camera, dodging the two men in pursuit. Ahead of him, I saw the five agents waiting, guns at the ready.

But something looked off in the picture. Something not quite right.

I brushed the thought away. It had all happened so fast, and I'd been much closer to the action than the camera was. Frightened, too. The scene was bound to look a lot different from that viewpoint.

The running man's figure was small and grainy in the wide-angle shot, and I watched as he threw his package off to his left and turned to face the two agents chasing him. They cut the playback there, and resumed the clip with the man being led away in handcuffs. They shoved him into an unmarked vehicle, his face turned from the camera's prying lens.

The anchorman continued to narrate. "The man, who officials refused to identify, is thought to be Farzad Al-Ja'fari. He threw an object the Secret Service initially believed might have contained a bomb."

Blood rushed from my face. My limbs went weak. A bomb? And he'd picked it back up. He'd had it when I whacked him. What if I'd whacked the bomb instead?

I felt the room grow small as I focused on the television.

"Al-Ja'fari, who is wanted for questioning in connection with several recent bombings in Europe, was apprehended without incident. There is no word yet on whether he actually carried a bomb, or what he intended to do if he had reached the White House."

Nothing about my involvement. I wasn't entirely surprised. How would it look if the intruder evaded our Secret Service only to be smacked on the skull by the mighty chef and her silver skillet? In a way, I was relieved. It looked like I still maintained possession of my anonymity.

I took another sip of wine and half-listened to the remaining commentary. When it finished I stopped the VCR, then changed channels. It was just about time for me to tune in Laurel Anne Braun, master chef and host of *Cooking for the Best*.

Maybe it was masochism on my part, but curiosity compelled me to watch my competition. Just before Henry had publicly announced his impending retirement, he'd told me in private that he'd recommended me to succeed him. I was flattered, honored, and just a little bit starstruck. If named executive chef for the White House, I would be the first female in history to hold the position.

I paid close attention as Laurel Anne canted her head at the camera. It responded by zooming in on her expressive face.

"Welcome again to *Cooking for the Best*, where I always cook for the best. Because I cook for you!" She pointed to the camera and gave a winsome smile.

While the woman was no raving beauty, she certainly had presence. Like an over-the-hill Julia Roberts, she wore a constant little smirk—as if sharing a private joke with her beloved audience—yet always radiating confidence.

By comparison, I was tiny. Short, with dark hair and brown eyes. She had me by half a foot, at least. And even I could see how her height helped maintain an air of power. Still, having worked with the woman, I knew that in real life her mask of self-assurance often dropped, and she became manic at the very times she should've maintained her cool. Mishaps were common in any kitchen. Keeping a level head made all the difference in the success or utter failure of an important meal. Laurel Anne was a control freak who shattered when things skidded out of control.

Watching her depressed me, so I switched it off. Instead of turning CNN on again, I rewound and replayed my tape of the news. My disappointment that I hadn't made it to the small screen had faded. Now I wanted to figure out what was bugging me about that clip. A little voice in the back of my head insisted it was important.

There he was. Again, the long-distance view. But again, something struck me as being not right.

Three replays later I started to catch subtle details. Although the recording was grainy and I couldn't see the man's features on the screen because he faced away from the camera, he had the same flowing dark hair I'd noticed this morning. He seemed shorter, but that could've been due to the camera's angle. He rapidly outdistanced the two agents.

I stopped the playback just as he lofted his package to the left. The purported bomb. As I stared at the screen I tried replaying the real scene in my mind, and all I could recall was that he was getting *away* from the agents. That he'd *chosen* to turn and confront them. Why?

The scene on the screen, frozen before me, mocked my memory: the man's arm held high; the black portfolio spinning, airborne; the two agents running behind him.

The intruder's head had twisted toward the camera as the package flew into the air. On my prior viewings, I'd watched the package. This time I took a look at the man.

I inched closer to the TV screen.

Too close. At this foreshortened distance everything turned into wiggly patches of light.

Backing up, I squinted.

"It's the nose!" I said aloud.

I moved forward and backed up a few more times to get the best angle I could. The tape was fairly clear, but the runner's profile took up only a very small portion of the screen. It was hard to be sure, but the man's nose and chin were all wrong.

I stood two feet from my screen and shook my head. This wasn't the man I whacked.

Despite my panic as he tried stumbling to his feet, I knew I remembered his profile perfectly. I always remembered faces.

And this face was not his face.

I perched on the edge of my couch and stared at the frozen screen, my hands running through my hair, as though my fingers might unearth answers there. This didn't make sense. How could a tourist have the wrong man in the film? It made no sense at all.

Wait a minute.

I rewound the tape and replayed.

The anchorman said that the recording came from an "undisclosed source."

An undisclosed source?

Something was rotten as week-old stew meat.

I wanted to shout, to tell someone. To report it. But there was no one I could talk to.

That is, not until the doorbell rang.

CHAPTER 4

I FLUNG OPEN THE DOOR, EXPECTING TO USHER TOM STRAIGHT to the sofa where I could replay the tape for him. But before I could utter a word, he surprised me by thrusting forth a tissue-wrapped bouquet of flowers. This wasn't a generic pick-'em-up-at-the-grocery-store arrangement, either. This weighty bundle had all sorts of exotic blooms mixed in with the requisite profusion of roses, daisies, and greenery.

"They're beautiful," I said, touching a delicate snapdragon and taking a deep sniff of the fresh-cut scent as he came in and shut the door. Puzzled by the unexpected gift, I opened my mouth to ask what the occasion was, but he interrupted.

"Happy anniversary."

"Anniversary?" We'd been dating for more than a year, and we'd gone out for a special dinner to celebrate that momentous occasion in April. I knew he hadn't forgotten that, which made me feel like a very bad girlfriend for asking, "But, it's been—"

"Thirteen months."

This was not at all like the Tom I knew. While he was always a gentleman, his thoughtfulness generally revealed itself in unusual ways, like the time I mentioned some of my favorite old-time movie stars. That same day, he went out and bought me *Captains Courageous, Roman Holiday,* and *Mr. Smith Goes to Washington.* We snuggled in for the first of many black-and-white movie nights. He could be incredibly sweet. He was always thoughtful. But Tom was not a flowery kind of guy.

"Well, technically," I said, still perplexed, and hoping for a little more clarification, because I sensed that something was up, "it'll be thirteen months tomorrow."

He grinned, stepping forward to snake an arm around my waist. I looked up into those blue eyes twinkling down at me. "True," he said, "but I didn't think it would be very romantic for me to run out on you after midnight to go pick these up."

"Oh," I said, stringing the word out, "so you expect to be staying overnight?"

His arm snugged me in tighter. "That's the basic idea."

I loved being close to Tom. I loved pressing myself against him, feeling those taut muscles, the power in his arms. As one of the Secret Service, and a member of the elite PPD, he was charged with protecting the president of the United States—often referred to as POTUS—the White House, and everyone associated with it. He was a formidable guy and I had to admit, I felt protected when I was with him. Still, I inched away. "We're crushing the flowers," I said.

He let loose, a little. "Got anything to eat?"

I smirked. "What do you think?"

As he rummaged through my refrigerator, I put the flowers in water, thinking about the evening that lay ahead. "There's a mug in the freezer," I said.

"Don't need it."

"Hey!" I snapped my fingers, and spun to face him. "There's something you have to see."

He'd opened a can of Pepsi. Taking a long drink, he gave me a once-over from head to toe and back up again. "Something I haven't already seen?"

I slapped his arm in a playful gesture. "No, really. I taped the news and there's something wrong with what happened this morning." I canted my head. "What's with the Pepsi?"

"I'm on call."

That took me by surprise. "How come?"

Tom shrugged, not looking my direction. "Did you know that *Inherit the Wind* is on tonight? The Spencer Tracy version." He grabbed the clicker and changed channels. Fredric March's face took up the small screen as Tom lowered himself into the sofa's center cushion and placed his Pepsi on the coffee table. He patted the area next to him. "Hurry up. It's one of your favorites."

"Actually, I have to show you this tape of the news," I said. The president had explicitly asked me not to discuss this morning with anyone but the Secret Service. How convenient it was for me to have a Secret Service boyfriend.

I couldn't wait to show him the news program I'd taped. More than that, I wanted him to be as intrigued and excited about the inconsistency as I was.

I reached to take the clicker, but Tom didn't let go.

"Come on," I said, laughing. "We usually fight because neither of us *wants* to hold the clicker. This time I'm willing to take it from you." I tugged again.

Tom tugged back, grabbing me with both hands as he reclined on the couch. He pulled me on top of him and nuzzled my neck. "God, you smell good," he said.

I was a sucker for neck-nuzzling, and I felt my body tingle itself into readiness for what it hoped was to come.

But the discrepancy in the news tape nagged at my brain even as Tom's lips sought mine. Try as I might, I couldn't put the morning's events out of my head until we talked.

I pulled away. "Tom," I said, just a little bit out of breath, "Can I just show you something I taped on TV first?"

"You want to stop now?" he asked, snuffing a laugh against my face so that his warm breath tickled my ear. "You sure?" He pulled me tighter against him and I fought the urge to ravish him right there.

"It's really bothering me."

He took me by the shoulders and pushed us apart, staring up at me. I watched disappointment cloud his eyes. "What's so important?"

The tone of his voice made me hesitate, but I knew this couldn't wait. I slid off him and headed to the VCR. "I taped the news."

"You said that already."

"Yeah, but you have to see this. I think somebody faked the released tape."

I turned to catch his reaction to my pronouncement, but he'd already boosted himself off the couch and was heading back to the kitchen. "I'm hungry," he said.

The tape was all set to play. "Give me five minutes and I'll fix you something."

I heard the sound of the fridge opening. His voice was muffled. "You watch it," he said.

"I've seen it." I raised my voice so he could hear me, but I knew I sounded strained. To keep from shouting to him, I made my way to the kitchen. "What is with you?" I asked.

He stood, shutting the fridge, holding a plate of bacon-wrapped olives speared with little wooden skewers that prevented them from unrolling. Shrugging, he turned to the countertop, his back to me, while he removed the Saran Wrap cover and downed two of the appetizers.

"Those are better warmed up," I said.

He shrugged again. "Guess I better get used to things being cold."

"What is that supposed to mean?"

He still didn't turn, so I got next to him, real close. He popped two more in his mouth and chewed, not making eye contact.

I touched his arm, keeping my voice low. "Tom, what's wrong?"

He took one of the small wooden skewers and stabbed at a wayward olive. "I brought you flowers. It's our anniversary. And all you want to do is watch some news program? I might get called in any time tonight for a big debrief."

My eyebrows raised and he graced me with a glance.

"No, nothing I can talk about," he said, then continued. "But instead of relaxing, you want me to watch some news program that you think is faked."

This took me aback. Tom was never a whiner. In fact, he was one of the most even-tempered souls I'd ever encountered. That's what drew me to him in the first place. The fact that he was complaining like this made my antennae go up. I wondered about this debrief that he mentioned. It must be something big to be working on his emotions like this. "Okay," I said, squeezing his arm. "I didn't mean to ruin the moment. I guess I didn't realize that you really might get called in tonight. But, this isn't a fake news program."

"Oh yeah?" He turned to me now, pointing another little skewer. "What is it then, a scene from one of those silly 'reality' shows you like to watch?"

The jibe against my guilty pleasures bothered me. But what bothered me more was the fact that it seemed he hadn't been listening at all.

"Tom," I said, and this time I waited till he actually looked at me. "Something is wrong, okay? Can you give me that much? I want to get your opinion on something."

"I brought you flowers," he said again.

"And they're beautiful." I was getting angry. What was this? Bribe time? Give the girl flowers and have your way with her? This wasn't the relationship I'd signed on for. "But if you care for me at all, you'll sit on the couch for five minutes and watch something. All I want is your opinion. Okay?"

I couldn't believe it. He actually had to think about it. I watched him slowly come to a decision, even as his eyes slid toward my front door. He was truly considering leaving.

I planted my feet. "Tom?"

His expression shifted. To me it looked like he winced before saying, "Okay. Five minutes."

I sat next to him on the sofa, and pointed the clicker to start the tape. There was Naveen, running. As he prepared to throw his portfolio, I paused. "See? Right there."

Tom ate a couple more appetizers.

Getting up, I stood next to the television, indicating the key spot on the screen, like a teacher with a PowerPoint presentation. "Look," I said with a triumphant smile. "That's not him."

"What are you talking about?"

I fought my exasperation. "That's not the same guy from this morning."

"Sure it is." Shaking his head, Tom returned his attention to the food and Pepsi on the table before him. "Who else would it be?" he asked. "If they caught some other guy running across the White House lawn this morning, somebody forgot to tell me about it."

"Tom," I said, and I waited till he dragged his gaze from the table to meet mine. "Look close. This isn't the guy from this morning. Whoever sent this tape to the networks changed the guy's face."

His blue eyes didn't waver, but I caught the set of his jaw. Something was up.

I set my hands at my hips. "Why would they do that?"

"You're seeing things." He stood, carrying the half-finished plate back to the kitchen. "Quit worrying about stuff that doesn't concern you." When he turned to me again, his expressions crinkled into that skeptical look he often wore when we watched the news. "You know how these media people are. They don't get the footage they want, they create it."

I pointed to the drama still frozen on my screen. "I was there this morning. This footage is real. It's just the face that's fake."

"Give me a break. You're seeing things."

I didn't have an answer to that, and I said so. I hadn't been expecting him to laud my observational skills, but I did expect something more than this abject lack of interest. The derision in his tone hurt.

"But . . ." I persisted, staring at him in disbelief. How he could not be as blown away by this as I was mystified me. My voice went limp. "But I was there."

And then, it hit me. Tom *knew* why the news stations were playing this fake tape because he was in on it. He'd known about it from the start. Hence, the disinterest. Hence, the reluctance to watch the tape.

I stared at the flowers. Hence, the "Happy Anniversary" distraction. Damn it, how could I be so dense sometimes?

"There is no Farzad Al-Ja'fari, is there?" I asked, butchering the name from the newscast. "The guy this morning really is called Naveen, and he really is a friend of Craig's, isn't he?"

Tom rolled his eyes, licked his lips, and otherwise tried to avoid answering me.

"Just tell me why they faked this news coverage," I said. "That doesn't make any sense."

"Nobody faked any news coverage."

That was an out-and-out lie and we both knew it. A swift anger washed over me. I knew there were a lot of things Tom couldn't tell me, but I never expected him to deliver a blatant lie and expect me to swallow it.

"Fine," I said. "Have it your way. Just tell me one thing. Is he okay?"

"Who?"

"Naveen. I hit him pretty hard. I feel bad about that."

"Don't. He was just another loony trying to get close to the president. Maybe he should thank you because you knocked some sense into him."

"Do you guys have him in custody?"

"We turned him over to the Metropolitan Police. He's their problem now."

That very moment, Tom's pager went off. After checking the numbers he glanced up, met my furious glare, and gave a weak smile. "Duty calls."

I kept silent as he kissed me on the forehead and turned to leave.

"I'll call you."

I nodded and followed him, not wanting this argument to end here—not wanting him to leave while I was angry. Mostly just wanting him to stay to work this out. "Be safe," I said.

He raised a hand in acknowledgment.

Two seconds later the door shut and my gaze drifted to the vase of flowers. I didn't understand. I didn't understand at all.

CHAPTER 5

WE ALL APPLAUDED AS PAUL VASQUEZ CONCLUDED THE MORN-
ing's surprise announcement. Thanking us for our time, he turned away from
the lectern to let the buzz begin. Now that the official presentation was over,
everyone relaxed and a few of us stepped forward to meet the most recent
addition to our White House staff family.

Head of the newly created cultural- and faith-based Etiquette Affairs department, Peter Everett Sargeant III wore pride in his position like the perfectly
pressed, bright red pocket handkerchief that contrasted against his dark Armani
suit. Though not especially tall, Sargeant cut an impressive figure. He was just as
polished and dignified as Paul, but Sargeant's deepened crow's feet and
line-bracketed mouth made me believe he had at least ten years on our chief usher.

Shaking hands with Henry, the new guy raked his gaze over all of us kitchen
personnel, and with patent curiosity, we watched him right back.

"Actually," Sargeant said, responding to Henry's greeting, "I would prefer
being addressed as the 'sensitivity director.'" He drew out his syllables in such
careful, round tones that I was reminded of that elocution scene from *Singin'*
in the Rain. Giving a self-deprecating smile, he added. "It's so much less cumbersome when addressing me. Don't you agree?"

Cyan glanced over, lifting her eyebrows and elongating her nose in a hoity-toity
expression. I shot her a reproving look. I knew Sargeant had to be nervous and I
didn't want him to catch Cyan's little joke. I remembered when I'd been presented
to the staff. My debut was done with a lot less fanfare—after all I was an assistant
chef, not the head of a department—but I'd been awestruck, eager, and hopeful
that everyone would like me. I was sure Sargeant felt the same way.

Henry shifted to the side and I thrust my hand forward. "I'm Olivia Paras," I began.

Sargeant cocked his head to one side. "How tall are you?"

Puzzled, I answered, "Five foot two."

He turned to Henry. "Isn't such slight stature a hindrance to keeping the kitchen running efficiently?"

Henry took a moment before answering. His usually jovial face now mirrored the confusion I was feeling, but his cheery demeanor returned in half a beat. He laid a hand onto my shoulder. "When it comes to the kitchen," he said, beaming, "Ollie here outclasses anyone. And I'm talking even the great chefs of Europe. Ollie may be tiny, but she's got what it takes."

Sargeant licked his lips. It was the only movement in his otherwise rigid body. As though he tasted my name and found it bitter, he said, "Ollie."

My hand still hanging out there, I looked to Henry for guidance, but his pointed glance seemed to warn me that I was on my own. I could almost hear him lecture me that if I were fortunate enough to become the next executive chef, I'd be handling much more prickly situations than this one.

"Right . . . Ollie," I said, my voice a little too high, a little too animated. "That's what everyone calls me." With the high-voltage confidence I displayed, I decided Mary Poppins couldn't have done better. And, since Sargeant didn't look like he was about to shake my still-outstretched hand, I took the initiative and grabbed his. "It's a pleasure to meet you."

We shook briefly. He grimaced and dismissed us with a nod.

On the way back to the kitchen, I shook my head. "What were they thinking when they hired this guy?"

"Let's not be too harsh, Ollie," Henry said, but when he glanced back at the gathering, he wore the same expression he had the time we realized we'd accidentally left Limburger cheese out all night. "He's probably just nervous."

"Maybe," I conceded.

Cyan rolled her eyes—violet, today. "Look at the guy. He walks like he's got a pole stuck up his—"

"Cyan!"

She shot Henry an abashed smile. "I'm just glad he doesn't oversee the kitchen." She gave a mock shudder. "Can you imagine having to report to someone that stuffy?"

Marcel wasn't scheduled to come in until the afternoon. I wondered what his take on the new man would be. I suspected I would never get the warm and fuzzies from Peter Everett Sargeant III.

Bucky, trailing behind us, spoke up. "Nothing wrong with running a tight ship."

Henry's neck flushed red.

"Of course . . ." Bucky continued, picking up his pace to make it to the kitchen first, "I'm not saying you don't." He cast a benevolent smile over his shoulder, but his eyes remained expressionless.

I patted Henry's back. "He's just jealous," I whispered. "That Sargeant guy completely ignored Bucky when he went up to say hello. At least I got an insult out of the deal."

Henry winked at me. "That you did."

The president's lunch today was a special affair. He had morning and afternoon meetings scheduled in-house, so he'd opted for a low-key meal with Mrs. Campbell in the residence. With the limited time the couple spent together alone, we knew we wanted to serve up something memorable.

I drew one of my trusty American-made Mac knives from its holder and went to work. As I chopped crabmeat for the first course, a crab-spinach appetizer served with crostini, Bucky stewed cherry tomatoes for garnish, and Henry and Cyan prepared risotto. I had a supply of truffle oil on hand. I'd add that, and a tiny bit of shaved truffle into the risotto just before serving. A little truffle goes a long way, and we knew that this extravagant addition would be just the right touch for today's meal.

A sharp rap pulled our attention to a visitor in the doorway.

Peter Everett Sargeant III reminded me of a grouchy squirrel. With his hands positioned as though he were cradling a precious nut, he canted his head three different ways in the space of two seconds. Alert, wary, eager.

"Welcome to our kitchen," Henry said.

Henry placed emphasis on the word *our*. I liked that.

"Yes," Sargeant said. He smiled, looking as though the effort caused him pain. "I'm availing myself of the opportunity to familiarize myself with the layout of the property." He seemed to take in everything in quick snippets—a tendency that contrasted with the careful cadence of his speech. "And the organizational structure."

His smile faded when it rested on me.

What had I done to incur this man's immediate distaste? His disapproval radiated toward me just like that Limburger cheese aroma.

Henry washed his hands in the sink, raising his voice to be heard over the rushing water. "It's a little tight in here for a tour, but we'd be happy to answer any questions you have about food preparation."

Sargeant scratched the side of his nose. "No tour. I'm here to explain some procedural changes."

Henry shut the water off, dried his hands. "Such as?"

"Effective immediately, all official dinner menus will be vetted through my office."

"But we—" I took a step toward him.

"Ah-ah-ah," he said, holding up the same index finger he'd used to scratch his nose. "I'm not finished."

Cyan and I exchanged a look. Had Paul Vasquez approved this change in the chain of command?

As though he'd heard my thoughts, Sargeant continued. "The chief usher and I have discussed this at length. In view of the administration's commitment to supporting diversity, we've decided that I shall have final say on all menu offerings."

I couldn't stop myself. "*You're* doing the taste-testing?"

He nodded.

Henry stared up at something near the ceiling for a couple of beats before he took a position next to the diminutive Sargeant. Looking down, he addressed him by his first name. "Peter," he began, squaring his shoulders and scratching at his wide neck, "I can't say I'm happy to hear this." Sargeant fidgeted. "We always defer to the First Lady's preferences. It's not only tradition. It's *our* policy. Perhaps I should have a talk with Paul."

Sliding sideways, Sargeant raised both squirrelly hands. "No, you misunderstand."

"Oh?"

"When I said that I had final say, I meant only that I will decide along with the First Lady." He shrugged his shoulders three times as he talked. "That's all."

Henry glanced back at us. It was difficult enough to come up with varied and exciting menus for visiting dignitaries that met their dining requirements while pleasing our decision maker, Mrs. Campbell. She wasn't fussy, but she certainly had her own tastes. We were still in the process of learning them. To also have to clear all choices through Sargeant would make the task arduous at best. I didn't understand why the change had to be made, and said so.

Sargeant graced me with another derisive stare, but didn't answer. "And," he continued, "when you draw up the menus, and provide me with samples, I will want to know which of you"—he allowed his glance to fall on each of us in turn, avoiding Henry's glare—"is responsible for which course."

"What is your reason for that?" Henry asked.

"In addition to being the sensitivity director, I like to think of myself as a mentor." Stepping backward, he nudged his way toward the door. "In time, I'll know which of you are contributing to the kitchen's success—and which of you are simply dead weight." His hand reached up, holding the jamb as though for support. "I enjoy helping people grow."

Then it hit me. I was shorter than he was. I was, in fact, the only one of the chefs whose stature didn't compete with his. It dawned on me at that moment, that Peter Everett Sargeant III had singled me out to pick on—because he thought he could. Because he perceived me as weak.

The man was no better than a playground bully.

Once he was gone, I sidled over to Henry at the computer screen. Unruffled, he clicked to open up a new document. I watched him for a long moment, as I thought about Sargeant's new directive, thinking about all the changes that had taken place since our new president took the oath of office in January. We'd seen a whirlwind of activity in the past few months. This was just one small part of it.

"What's that?"

Henry's large shoulder lifted. "If we are to have a new procedure, I need to set it up."

"How do you do it?" I asked.

He twisted his head to look at me. "You've set up dozens of spreadsheets and documents before. What are you talking about?"

"No, I mean, how do you cope with all the changes? All the time? With each new administration, there are adjustments. I know that. But how do you keep from questioning the wisdom of the decisions?" I glanced at the doorway. "If they're choosing a man like Peter Everett Sargeant III to run an entire department—"

"Ollie," he said, now turning his entire body my direction, giving me his undivided attention, "we are the chefs for the most important home in the world."

"I know that."

"Our country depends on our president. And he depends on us. When we step through the White House gates, we become more than just ordinary citizens." He stared north, as if seeing the endless stream of protestors standing sentry in Lafayette Park. "We leave behind the controversy, the rancor, the turmoil."

His voice rumbled to the crescendo I knew was coming. "We are our country's decision makers when we cast our votes on Election Day. But when we leave the polling place, when we enter our world *here*," he jammed a finger onto the countertop, "we must be focused on the part *we* play in keeping our country great. We are not here to change policy, but in a way, to help promote it. And we must be vigilant to discourage dissension." He lifted his chubby index finger, pointing skyward. "We are here to cook for President Campbell, the most powerful man in the world, and for his guests. If these heads of state are well-fed and content, they will be cooperative. They will make wise decisions."

He broke into a wide smile. "What power we hold, Ollie."

I'd heard his lecture before. I earned a recitation each time I questioned anything, from the president's decision to open trade negotiations with a former enemy country, to what color tie he chose to wear for a press conference. Although Henry and I differed on *how* to put aside our beliefs and convictions, we both did it. We all did. As far as I knew, all White House staff members set aside politics to serve our country in the best way we knew how. For me, and for most of us, it was a point of pride.

Bucky interrupted the sudden quiet with slow applause. "Nice speech, Henry. Do you practice that in front of a mirror?"

Throwing Bucky a look of disgust, I returned to my chopping board, hands on hips. Hiring him was another decision I questioned.

Henry must have sensed my thoughts, because he drew up next to me and whispered in my ear, "A White House chef must be less concerned with the state of the union, and more concerned with the state of the *onion*."

That made me giggle.

He was right, though. Since George Washington's time, when the building of the "President's House" was first commissioned, this center for democracy has held immense stature in the world. The building, designed by James Hoban, was finally completed in 1800, too late for George Washington's use, and almost too late for John and Abigail Adams. They took occupancy shortly before Jefferson's inauguration.

History lived in these walls. And as a member of the staff, it was my duty to ensure the level of grandeur never diminished.

Just then, Peter Everett Sargeant III reappeared in the doorway. "One more thing," he said, his voice ringing high above the kitchen noises. We stopped our activity to hear him better. "I need a curriculum vitae from each of you. Today, if possible. Tomorrow at the latest." Again, he fixed only me with a look of contempt. "I need to know what I'm dealing with."

Bucky snorted as Sargeant left. "What a pompous ass."

Henry looked ready to admonish Bucky, but stopped himself.

"Since when do we report to him?" I asked.

"I'll make an appointment to talk with Paul," Henry said. "We'll get this settled."

I picked up a plate, hefted it in my hands, and eyed the doorway. "I think I'd like to settle this myself," I said, "with a well-aimed smash over the man's head."

"Relax, my dear," Henry said. "With a disposition like that of Peter Everett Sargeant *III*, it is doubtful there will ever be a *Fourth*."

CHAPTER 6

NAVEEN'S NAME SIMMERED ON THE BACK BURNER OF MY BRAIN, bubbling around and keeping me from devoting my complete attention to the tasks at hand. After we finished lunch preparations and the waitstaff served it, we started in on the thousand other items that required attention. I went to the computer screen, knowing I needed to put the finishing touches on the ladies only luncheon Mrs. Campbell would host the following week.

My alert program reminded me to contact our sommelier. He was prepared for tonight, but he and I needed to chat further about the upcoming luncheon.

Next week we'd be serving prosciutto and melon, followed by Chicken Maryland. Mrs. Campbell had requested a menu similar to one Mrs. Johnson had served during her tenure as First Lady. I thought about that now as I stared at the screen.

Security had changed a lot over the years. Before I was born, visitors lined up outside for White House tours, and they were granted free access most mornings each week. Today visitors were required to plan in advance. Submit official requests, provide social security numbers.

I sighed.

Naveen was an example of why the rules had changed. And I'd been the one to stop his unauthorized intrusion. Why didn't I feel better about that?

Henry meandered by to assure me that he'd look into Peter Everett Sargeant's dictum. Little did he know that it wasn't the supercilious little man who'd set me off-kilter—well, not entirely—but the dark intruder from yesterday's skirmish. I wished I could confide in Henry, but he'd be the first to remind me that my top duty was to the president.

Tonight, one of the Campbells' adult children would be present at dinner, and we'd already planned the family favorite—ultra thin–crust pizza. Loaded with artichoke hearts, sun-dried tomatoes, and Italian sausage delivered from Chicago, it was one of our specialties. Cyan was kneading dough even as I tapped at the keyboard.

Pizza was easy. But planning the next several weeks was more of a challenge. It took the remainder of the day to work out logistics for seven "intimate" dinners of less than ten guests each, four larger affairs with guest lists topping twenty, and three luncheons of varying sizes. I studied diet dossiers, made notes on allergies, and juggled entrée, accompaniment, and dessert choices, until the arrangements lined up perfectly like a culinary version of a Rubik's cube.

Twilight kept me company after work as I trudged three blocks to the McPherson Square Metro station. I used the time to check my voice mail. Hearing Tom's voice cheered me at first, but his message—he'd be tied up but would try to call later—chased away my hopes for a cozy evening. He and I hadn't parted on the most upbeat of terms last night and I was eager to see him so that we could make things right.

The stations and the trains themselves were lonely at night. We pulled into Farragut West and I stared out the window—this time of day I rarely had trouble getting a window seat. At the stop, my attention was captured by two Metro Transit Police officers talking with a Middle Eastern man on the platform. He resembled Naveen. Not enough for me to believe it was the same man, of course, but enough for yesterday's incident to jump once again to the forefront of my thoughts.

The transit cops seemed to be unruffled, in control, and even as I wondered what their conversation was about, we pulled out of the station, one stop closer to home.

But . . . the scene jogged my memory. Tom had said that Naveen was the Metropolitan Police's problem now. Which meant there must be a record of his incarceration.

The world whispered by as I put together what I knew.

A man had been apprehended, running across the White House lawn.

This same man was apparently on a first-name basis with one of our Secret Service PPD agents.

The videotape of the man's transgression, however, hadn't made it to the news. Not really. What had been offered for the viewing public's pleasure was a snippet of the scene. Carefully faked. Though obvious to anyone who'd been there.

I made an unladylike snort, which caused the old man sitting across the aisle to glance over. With a smile to convince him I wasn't a commuter loony, I continued my musings.

The Secret Service had been there.

I'd been there.

For some reason, the Secret Service didn't want Naveen's face broadcast across the country. Why not?

The people who usually jumped the White House fence were either mentally unstable or on a mission. Naveen struck me as one of the latter. When an intruder was caught inside the perimeter on an unauthorized jaunt, the incident generally ensured him a few minutes of fame wherein he (and it was almost always a male) used his screen time wisely to shout his vital message to a national audience.

But . . .

Naveen hadn't shouted.

My cell phone buzzed from the recesses of my purse. A quick glance at the number and I knew Tom had managed a little free time. I was still amazed that I could get service belowground.

"Hey," he said when I answered.

"Hey, yourself. Where are you?"

"Driving," he said. A second later I was able to make out the fast-moving car noises in the background. I also heard another voice.

"You alone?"

"Nope."

I guessed. "With Craig?"

"You should have been a detective."

I laughed at that. Tom and I hadn't exactly "come out" with our relationship to our colleagues, although a few of the kitchen folks weren't fooled. I knew Tom's end of the conversation would be as devoid of identifying characteristics as he could make it.

"You're still on duty?" I asked.

"Yep."

"And so you just called to tell me how much you missed me."

"Uh-huh."

"Because I'm the light of your life and you don't know what you'd do without me."

I could almost see him roll his eyes at that. He didn't answer as much as grunt.

"And because you're so crazy about me," I continued in a chipper voice, trying to keep the tone light, but determined to press my point, knowing he'd be forced to respond agreeably because Craig was right there, "you'll tell me more about that faked news broadcast later, right?"

Dead silence.

"I'll call you back later," he said. And the phone went dead.

Damn. Sometimes when I pushed my luck it snapped back to bite me.

I knew there were things Tom couldn't tell me, and I was okay with that. Keeping things classified was part of his job, after all. Part of his sworn duty. But I also knew that Tom often chose to keep things from me when there was nothing classified about them. He didn't appreciate the way I analyzed and picked at things until I understood them. I found the process fascinating. He found my doing so annoying.

Tom was just trying to protect me from too much knowledge, and from knowing things I shouldn't know. I understood that. But this time it felt different.

I watched out the window as the train emerged into the evening light at Arlington cemetery. I thought about my dad, and how I hadn't been out to his grave in a long while. The world was a dangerous place for heroes.

And then, another thought began to grow and take hold.

Maybe Naveen really did have an important message for President Campbell.

Blood rushed from my feet to my face and back down again, heralding a moment of absolute clarity. The look in the man's eyes when he'd stared up at me hadn't been the unfocused, crazed look of a lost soul. He wanted to tell me something. He'd said that the president was in danger.

But Tom hadn't taken Naveen's warning seriously. No one had, apparently. The man had been sent to the D.C. Jail.

My arm reclined against the train's window frame. Not particularly comfortable, but it gave me the chance to tap my fingers against the glass as I pondered all this.

Naveen had been willing to talk with me. He'd been about to tell me of the danger when I'd whacked him in the head.

I grimaced.

The train pulled into my station just as I pulled myself out of my musings.

By the time I made it to my apartment, I knew exactly what I had to do.

CHAPTER 7

"I'M TRYING TO GET IN TOUCH WITH ONE OF YOUR INMATES," I said, wondering if that was the politically correct way to phrase it. I held my cell phone in a grip so tight I thought the plastic casing might crack. "I'd like to talk with him."

The woman's flat, capable tone—uncannily similar to that of the dispatcher who'd warned me to stay out of the way yesterday morning—made me wonder if there was some moonlighting going on here. "I'll need his name," she said.

"He was caught running across the White House lawn. Yesterday."

"I need a name," she repeated.

"Naveen."

"First or last?"

I guessed. "First."

"I need the inmate's last name." This time the tone wasn't so flat. I caught a hint of her impatience.

"It's . . ." Shoot. I had no clue. "Well, you see," I said, "I—he—" My heart raced, making clackety pounds against my ribcage. I knew I was overstepping my boundaries here, knew I had no right to make this phone call. When I first picked up the phone, I'd been nervous. Now I was near panic. I'd foolishly expected my description of "White House Intruder" to be enough to identify him. After all, how many fence-leaping Naveens could there be?

"Ma'am?"

"I'm his girlfriend," I said in a rush.

Where did that come from?

"And you don't know his last name?"

Thinking fast, I decided to go for ditsy bimbo. "Well—" I began, trying to buy time as I came up with a logical explanation that would still provide the information I needed, "—we haven't been together very long, and he has a hard name to pronounce. I'd never be able to spell it."

The woman's irritated sigh *whoosh*ed over the phone line. It gave me hope. "Naveen," she repeated, then spelled it.

"That's right," I said, hoping it was.

With the memory of Craig's anger crawling along my insides, I paced. I crossed my fingers as I listened, hearing the woman tap computer keys. I sure hoped repercussions of this phone call didn't blow up on me like yesterday's call to the dispatcher had. That's why I'd taken the precaution of the cell phone. The jail's caller ID, if they had it, would just show up as numbers, and wouldn't include my name. I was sure the D.C. Jail got hundreds of phone calls for inmates each day. No one would bother to find out who was looking for Naveen. At least I hoped they wouldn't.

Another sigh. More clicks.

"I'm sorry," the woman finally said. "We have no one in our system by that name."

"But, they told me . . ."

"I'm sorry. Whoever gave you that information was incorrect. We have no one incarcerated for trespassing on the White House grounds."

"I—"

"Is there anything else?"

My fingers now uncrossed, I dropped my shoulders. Stopped the anxious pacing. "No. Thank you very much for your time."

The logical portion of my brain, which I occasionally suspected occupied less than its allotted half, ridiculed my efforts. What was I hoping to accomplish by talking with Naveen?

I didn't know, exactly. I just couldn't shake the sense that I'd screwed up somehow and I needed to make things right. I certainly didn't regret playing a part in Naveen's apprehension, but I did regret cracking him in the head with the commemorative pan. He hadn't threatened me in any way—in fact, it had been more like he'd been asking for help.

Resting my butt against my kitchen countertop, I rubbed my eyes. I should just let this go. I knew that.

But.

Just a quick Internet search, I told myself. Real quick. If I didn't come up with anything, I vowed to let it go.

After inputting countless different combinations of "Naveen," "White House," "trespass," "Secret Service," "D.C. Jail," and "Farzad Al-Ja'fari"—the intruder's name from the newscast—I came up with nothing beyond the broadcast pabulum from the night before. I was just about to try a Google image search when the phone rang.

"I was just thinking about you," I said as I picked it up.

Tom made a noise that was half rumble, half laugh. "Good. I was afraid you'd be sleeping."

"But it's not that—" I glanced at the tiny clock at the bottom of my screen. "Holy geez, it's almost two."

"Yeah, I'm finally off for the night." He didn't yawn, but I could hear the weariness in his voice. "Heading home."

"I should probably get some sleep, too," I said. "I have to be up in a couple of hours."

"What're you doing up so late, anyway?"

I opened my mouth, with no idea how to answer. What could I say? Oh, I've been conducting my own investigation—because you won't tell me anything.

I hesitated. And, despite being wiped out from his extended shift, Tom unfortunately picked up on it.

"Ollie?"

"Just surfing the 'Net. You know how I get sometimes."

"What were you looking up?"

A clock-tick went by.

"Just . . . stuff."

He made a noise. Frustration, agitation; I couldn't tell. He knew I was hiding something. That drove me nuts. The few times I'd tried to surprise him—either with a special date or a gift—he always had an inkling of what was coming. Some people might call it a sixth sense, but I knew that Tom was just that good of an agent. He'd been trained to pick up on clues others might miss. Trying to put one over on him was an exercise in futility.

"What were you looking up?"

I pushed out a laugh and said, "You caught me." Using what Tom always told me was the most effective way to lie—the best spies in the world did it—I kept my answer as close to the truth as possible. "I was searching online for news about the guy who jumped the fence." I left out the little tidbit about calling the D.C. Jail.

"For crying out loud, Ollie." A slight scratchy noise over the phone line told me Tom was rubbing his face in frustration. "That's done. Over with. Case closed."

"Did you ever find out what the guy wanted to warn the president about?"

"We found out everything we needed to know."

"What does that mean?"

"It means that the guy was a loony who jumped the fence just like a dozen loonies do every year. We sent him to the D.C. Jail where he belongs. End of story."

I started to protest that Naveen wasn't in the D.C. Jail, but Tom would want to know how I knew that. I took a different tactic. "What's his last name?"

"Why?"

"Because I'm not finding a whole lot online under the name 'Naveen.'"

"Good," he said. "Let's keep it that way. Listen, the Secret Service already handled this. That's what we're here for. We've got lots of experience and we know what we're doing. It was just bad luck that you happened to be there when the intruder got past security. But . . ." He slowed his next words down, emphasizing each syllable. "We have taken care of this. We have handled incidents like this in the past. We don't need help from a White House chef. Understand?"

I wrinkled my nose at the phone.

Perhaps sensing that he had come down too hard on me, he added, "Come on, you wouldn't want me to tell you how to fry a chocolate mousse, would you?"

In spite of myself, I laughed. "You don't fry a mousse, silly."

"See what I mean?"

I knew I should just give it up. Heck, I'd done all the investigation I could. I'd attempted far more than I should have and I'd come up empty. Agreeing to let it go kept Tom happy and made me look good, so I had nothing to lose. "Okay," I said. "I'll drop it. On one condition."

"And what's that?"

"That if any of this gets resolved, you let me know." I added, quickly, "Only if it's declassified, I mean."

I heard Tom yawn and stretch. "You got yourself a deal, little Miss Detective. Now, why don't you get some sleep and I'll see you tomorrow—er—later today sometime."

With a smile, I nodded into the phone. "Can't wait."

* * *

WHEN POUNDING NOISES ROUSED ME FROM SLEEP AT FOUR FIF-
teen, I jerked into that startled state of alertness that everyone dreads. It took
me several seconds to realize that someone was at my door, and my bleary
mind couldn't fathom the reason for the insistent thumping even as habit sent
me scurrying to answer it.

I had a moment of awareness before throwing open the deadbolt and I
remembered to check the peephole first. Tom and Craig stood in the hallway.
Craig's hands were at his side in classic alert stance, his gaze moving back and
forth, taking in the length of the short corridor.

"Ollie, wake up. Open the door."

I blinked and looked out the peephole again. "Tom?"

My voice croaked, but both of them snapped to attention at the sound.

Tom wore an expression I'd never seen on him before. Well, at least not
directed toward me. "Let us in."

Fairly confident they weren't here to shoot me, I swung open the door just
as Mrs. Wentworth across the hall swung open hers. Her arthritic hand clawed
at the doorjamb as though to steady herself and as Tom and Craig pushed past
me, she asked, "Want me to call the police, honey?"

The two men spun to face my elderly neighbor. She didn't flinch.

"No, thanks," I said, trying to force a smile. "These are friends of mine."

They both turned to stare at me, frowning with such obvious effort that
for a moment I doubted my own words. My skin sizzled. Could something
have happened to Henry?

"Well, if I find out in the morning that you're dead, I'm going to give the
police their full descriptions." She brushed at her wispy white hair as she backed
into her apartment, raising her voice. "You hear that, you two goons?"

"Good night, Mrs. Wentworth," I said. Then, shutting the door, I rested
my butt against it. "She looks out for me."

The angry frowns hadn't disappeared. If anything, they'd gotten more
intense. Tom paced my small living room as Craig stood before me, hands at
his sides, eyes glued to mine.

"What's wrong?" I asked. "What's happened?"

"Have a seat, Ms. Paras," Craig began, gesturing toward my kitchen. Behind
him, Tom's hands worked themselves into fists.

Despite the fact that I'm short and relatively petite—and I'll stay that way as long as I keep from ingesting large doses of carbs—I don't back down easily. But I knew these two—one of them intimately—and until I knew what was up, it probably wasn't a good idea to provoke a confrontation.

I sat at my kitchen table.

Craig took the chair opposite mine. Tom continued to pace, staring down at my linoleum as though he were trying to memorize it.

"Are either of you going to tell me what this is about?"

"Jesus Christ, Ollie," Tom said. He stopped moving long enough to flash a look of fire my way.

"What?" I asked, flaying my hands out. But I fought a sinking feeling in my gut. I had a feeling I knew exactly "what."

"Where is your cell phone?" Craig asked.

They had me.

"Shoot," I said. Then, attempting an extremely feeble joke, I added, "I don't mean that literally, of course."

Craig's words were precise, his drawl more intense than ever. "Do I take your reaction to indicate that you comprehend the reason for our visit here at this godless hour?"

Craig talking to me in Secret Service–speak was more frightening than Naveen's performance had been.

Tom kept pacing.

I decided that the old adage about the best defense wasn't applicable only to football. "Have you been tapping my calls? That isn't right. That isn't even legal." A moment's doubt as I turned to Tom. "Is it?"

He stopped pacing. "You ever hear of caller ID?"

"Well, yeah," I began to say, the way some people say "duh," "but how the heck could you guys have done it?" As I spoke, I tried putting the pieces together in my head, but the picture wasn't coming clear. "You have some sort of alert put on all White House employee phone numbers? So no matter where I call, you can tag me?"

Craig's lips moved. But not much else did. "You overestimate your importance, Ms. Paras."

That was a slam. It got my back up. "Apparently," I said, "I'm more important than I thought if you've got nothing better to do than pay me a visit because I happened to dial the D.C. Jail tonight."

"Happened to dial?" Craig repeated. "Are you claiming that you reached the D.C. Jail's number in error?"

My brain finally defuzzed enough to grab hold of the facts and make sense of them. Tom and Craig weren't here because my phone number raised an alert—they were here because they'd been instructed to follow up with anyone who tried to contact Naveen at the jail. Because they were watching the guy for suspicious activity.

When my cell phone number popped up on the jail's caller ID, Craig probably assumed it belonged to another conspirator. Finding out that it was one of the assistant chefs calling on a whim probably made the two men in my kitchen want to throttle me.

"I'm sorry," I said.

"Sorry?" Tom asked. "Didn't I tell you that we were handling this?"

Craig's head perked up. "Agent MacKenzie? Have you been in conversation with Ms. Paras about this subject prior to this visit?"

The last thing I wanted was for Tom to get into more trouble than I'd already put him in. "Craig," I said, pulling his attention to me again. "I'm Ollie, remember? We're friends. Or we were before that Naveen guy ran at me."

To my surprise, he didn't interrupt. So I continued. "*Of course* Tom talked with me about this." Tom squeezed his eyes shut, but I ignored it. "He walked me up to the gate after it happened and he took the pan I had engraved for Henry, too. He said it was evidence." I raised my voice as though addressing Tom, who resumed his pacing. "I haven't gotten that back yet either, you know."

"Why did you call the D.C. Jail?" Craig asked.

Tough question. I worked hard not to look over to Tom as I spoke. "I hit the guy pretty hard," I said. "And then, when he called you by name . . ."

Craig's expression didn't change but for a tiny flinch that deepened the tiny lines bracketing his eyes.

". . . I thought that I might've been wrong to have hit him. And he seemed so sincere when he told me the president was in danger." My words came out in a rush now. "I knew that if he was a bad guy he probably got taken to the D.C. Jail, so that's why I tried to call there. But the woman said he wasn't locked up there, that there wasn't even a record of him being arrested. And so I'm wondering now—did I hurt him? Is he okay?"

Tom and Craig exchanged a look that, to me, appeared to be Tom saying, "Isn't that what we figured she was doing?"

Craig worked his tongue around the inside of his mouth. When he finally spoke, his Kentucky drawl was soft. "Ollie," he began. I felt my shoulders relax at the nickname. "We understand that you have a soft heart. We understand that you found yourself in a situation that you were not trained to handle. But I must take this opportunity to remind you that you cannot involve yourself any further in this matter."

"I didn't mean to—"

He held up a hand. "Tom and I have taken it upon ourselves to talk with you. We are not bound to report your actions, nor take this matter any higher than our conversation here tonight. But I caution you that the jail is under orders to let us know when anyone tries to contact yesterday's uninvited guest. I suggest that you do not try to contact him again."

"So he is at the jail, but they just couldn't tell me?" I asked.

Exasperation crossed Craig's face. "I am not at liberty to disclose that information."

My apartment faced east, and I caught a glimpse of the sunrise, just at that point where the sky is pink and full of promise. Its hopeful brightness helped convince me that tonight's crisis was over.

"I'm sorry to have caused you any problems," I said.

Craig stood, nodded to Tom.

As they prepared to leave, I realized I'd have to hustle to get myself to the White House by my regular time. At the door, Craig turned to me. "No more secret investigations. Are we clear on that?"

"Cross my heart," I said, gesturing across my chest. But I didn't add, "Hope to die."

CHAPTER 8

"DON'T YOU SLEEP ANYMORE?" I ASKED TOM.

He shrugged.

We'd agreed to meet at one of the many hot dog stands interspersed between souvenir vendors along 17th Street NW. Tom ordered a Polish with sauerkraut and I got my usual hot dog with mustard and tomato. If I'd been by myself, I'd have taken onions, too.

As I ducked under a tree to get out of the unseasonably hot sun, Tom gave our snacks a frown. "With all the amazing food you create, how come we eat this junk?"

"A taste of home. For me, at least." I thought about Chicago-style hot dogs, the stuff of which legends are made. "But you're avoiding my question."

He shrugged again.

"You've got some nasty dark circles there," I said. "And you look like you're ready to drop."

"Gee, thanks," he said, rolling his eyes.

"Come on." I touched his arm. "You know I'm just worried about you."

There was a long moment of silence. I took a bite of my hot dog, and Tom stared out to some middle distance. I tried to figure out what he was looking at, but there was nothing unusual out there. I waited. I knew what was coming.

"Just what the hell did you think you were doing?"

A bench opened up and I motioned toward it, buying time. "Let's sit."

Tom grumbled, but complied.

Once settled, he started in again, keeping his voice low enough to prevent strangers from eavesdropping, but yelling at me all the same. "Do you have any idea how much trouble you caused me last night? When the number turned out to be yours, I thought Craig would explode. What would've happened if he decided to then look at all your calls? Huh? Then he would've found my number on your recent call list—and we would've had a lot more questions to answer."

"I thought you said that there's nothing wrong with us going out together. I thought you said that it isn't against any regulation."

He frowned again, looking away, his Polish tight in his hands, still wrapped, apparently forgotten. I glanced down at my hot dog. I was starving, and I could've wolfed it down in three bites, but it felt somehow impolite to eat while I was being chastised.

"That's not the point."

"Then what is the point?"

He turned to me, staring with such intensity that I leaned back. "I told you we were handling this. I know you were involved. It's unfortunate that you were there. But now your only job is to get uninvolved. Do you understand that?"

I nodded.

"Good."

Tom unwrapped his Polish and started in.

I took a big bite of my hot dog. Chewed, swallowed, and then said, "There's just one thing—"

His expression dropped. "What?"

"I just wanted to find out if I'd screwed up or not. And—okay—I was worried about the president. Naveen said—"

"Quit calling him Naveen."

"That's his name, isn't it?"

"Just quit it, okay? It makes it sound like you know the guy. You don't. And you won't."

I decided to take a different approach. "You know how nosy I can be sometimes."

"That's an understatement."

I ignored the dig, and took another bite before continuing. "I caught the guy," I said, allowing just a bit of wheedling to creep into my voice. "I think I'm owed a little explanation."

Tom ate more of his food.

I waited. Sometimes that's all it takes.

"You know I can't tell you anything that's classified."

"And you know I would never want you to."

He nodded. "Craig and I discussed this before we went to see you. We disagreed. I wanted to lay out the information for you, because I know how you can be. How you pick, pick, pick at things till you figure them out." From the look on Tom's face, I gathered that this wasn't one of my more endearing traits. "Craig didn't appreciate that idea at all. He decided to take the hard-ass approach. Figured it would be more effective with a timid assistant chef." For the first time that afternoon, Tom smiled. "Little does he know."

I felt the ice begin to crack. I smiled, too.

Tom continued. "I couldn't very well tell him that I knew how to handle you, so we did it his way."

I tried to disguise my eagerness, but the hopeful lilt to my tone gave me away. "You're saying that the matter has been declassified?"

He glared, but I could tell that his anger was long gone. "Some of it. Only some."

"And are you willing to share that 'some' with me?"

With a twist, he shifted his body to face me. "I'll tell you what I can—it's the same information we would give any White House staffer who asked. But." He held up a finger. "I first need you to agree that you'll drop this little investigation of yours."

I finished off my hot dog. It was better than biting my tongue. If I'd have spoken, I'd have blown it by protesting his exaggeration. I was about to get answers. Arguing now could only hurt me.

"I have no intention of calling the jail again. I swear."

He cocked an eyebrow and waited.

"And I promise not to try to find Navee—I mean, the guy who you guys caught yesterday."

I meant it. I really did.

Tom's fears apparently assuaged, he continued. "I can't tell you where he is right now, but I can tell you that his name *is* Naveen." He held up his hand. "No last name, okay?"

I nodded.

"Naveen is one of ours. Different agency."

I was about to ask if he was CIA, but Tom's look stopped me.

He continued. "And yes, he does know Craig. That's not classified. Neither is the fact that he's uncovered some information that suggests President Campbell may be in danger."

"You mean he thinks someone's planning an assassination?"

"Ollie," Tom said in a voice just shy of warning, "there are always threats against the president. If I knew about a planned assassination attempt, I couldn't tell you. What I can tell you is that the matter is sufficiently grave that we're following up on every possible front."

"If this Naveen fellow is one of the good guys," I said, trying to reason it out, "why was he running across the White House lawn?"

Tom sighed. "He's a talented agent—one of the best—and he's uncovered a lot that other guys might've missed, but he's fanatical. Naveen is always seeing conspiracies. Everywhere." Tom rolled his eyes. "He claims that there are higher-ups in the Secret Service who have been compromised."

"Do you believe him?"

"Right now, we have to believe him. We can't afford not to."

I considered this.

Tom stared off into some middle distance again, then seemed to come to a decision. "There's more," he said, "and this is off the record."

"Gotcha."

"We're eventually sharing this information with everyone on staff, but I figured it won't hurt to bring you up to speed early."

I wadded the hot dog's wrapper into a ball, itching to egg Tom on, wanting him to hurry up and tell me whatever this big thing was. But he was not a man to be rushed. I gripped the little paper ball tighter.

"Information will be disseminated. Soon." He licked his lips, the last bite of his Polish still in his hand. He took a deep breath. Blew it out. "Naveen told us that the Chameleon has targeted someone at the White House."

Targeted. The way Tom looked at me when he said it gave me shivers.

"The Chameleon?"

Almost whispering now, Tom continued. "You know there are paid assassins out there who'll go after anyone if the price is right?"

I nodded.

"The Chameleon is as ruthless, as mercenary as they come. I don't know of a single one of our allies who wouldn't celebrate if the bastard was caught."

"Why is he called the Chameleon? Because of his slimy activities?"

"No." Tom stood up. "Let's walk."

We tossed our trash and headed north up 17th Street. Tom kept watch as we strolled past the Eisenhower Old Executive Office Building, fondly known as the OEOB. We crossed to the west side of the street because of construction.

Whenever anyone came too close, or someone passed us, he stopped talking entirely.

"The guy is called the Chameleon because he blends in, no matter what the circumstance. No one has been able to spot him yet. We don't know his name, what he really looks like, or even where his allegiance lies. If he has any." Tom snorted. As we waited for the light to cross back east at Pennsylvania Avenue, he looked down at me. The smile in his eyes was back. I'd been forgiven for my phone call fiasco. "That's it, okay? Right now you don't need to know anything else."

"I understand."

"And until we bring the rest of the staff up to speed, keep this to yourself, okay?"

"I will."

We started walking again. "But," he said, "I wanted you to know because it'll help us to have another set of eyes. You see anything unusual . . . you get a new delivery boy . . . or anything seems amiss, you let us know."

One thing was bothering me. "If the guy—Naveen—wasn't arrested, and he isn't at the jail, then where is he?"

"We've got him somewhere safe."

I pointed north. "Blair House?"

"No way," Tom said. "Too high-profile. We want to keep this all very quiet. If the Chameleon knows Naveen's been talking with us, then we've got a whole 'nother set of problems to worry about. Right now we've got Naveen covered. We were afraid that his little stunt the other day might've alerted the Chameleon that he's here."

"So that's why you guys faked the news coverage!"

"Shhh."

"I wasn't that loud," I said, but I lowered my voice. "Sorry."

Tom glanced around. Nobody. "It's okay. Just trust me, all right? We agents are trained for this stuff, just like you're trained. We're both working to be the best in the world." He stopped. "We better split up."

"Yeah," I said. Although a few coworkers probably suspected there was more to our relationship than agent and chef, we both felt more comfortable keeping things under wraps for now.

"I guess I better see if there's any trouble brewing across the street." He turned toward Lafayette Square, then stopped. "Hey. When are you going to find out about the executive chef position?"

My stomach flipped at the question. I wished I knew. "The other woman—Laurel Anne Braun—hasn't had her audition yet."

"That the woman with the TV show?"

"Yeah."

Tom grimaced.

Great. Everyone thought that Laurel Anne was the shoo-in. Even my boyfriend. "You'll knock 'em dead," he said, but I wondered if he meant it. "Speaking of knocking 'em dead—you think you'll have any time this weekend to head out to the range? I need to get some practice in." I knew that. Secret Service agents needed to qualify at the range two weeks out of every eight. Before his turn came up for qualification, he always spent time practicing on his own.

"I'd love to."

He gave a quick wave and was gone.

Just as I cleared the northeast gate and passed its accommodating chirp, my cell phone rang. I pulled it out of my purse, smiling because I knew it had to be Tom, calling from across the street. But when I glanced at the number, I didn't recognize it.

"Hello?"

"Ms. Olivia Paras?"

The voice was familiar, but it held an accent I couldn't place. "Yes."

"My name is Naveen Tirdad. I believe you have been looking for me?"

CHAPTER 9

"WHAT?" I SPUN, THEN RAN TO THE MASSIVE BLACK GATE. "HOW did you find me?" I looked out across Pennsylvania, trying to catch a glimpse of Tom in the park. Or of Naveen. For some reason I thought he might be watching me. After all, I was in almost the exact same spot I'd been when he ran past. "Where are you?"

"Before I answer your question, I must know why you attempted to locate me."

"I wasn't. That is, I mean . . ."

"Did you not try to reach me yesterday by telephoning the jail?"

Holy geez. How could he know that? I considered lying, but all of a sudden I was afraid to. Craig and Tom knew I'd made the call. And Naveen was one of ours—so it followed that he knew, too. "Yes," I said, my voice coming out as sheepish as I felt. "I did. But . . ."

But . . . what? I had no explanation beyond my own foolish inquisitiveness. Not for the first time, I thanked God I wasn't born a cat. My curiosity would've killed me years ago.

"You are the young woman whom I encountered near the northeast gate, yes?"

That was a polite way of putting it. I relaxed a little and stopped searching the passing pedestrians. Freddie stepped out of his security booth, looking concerned.

"Hang on," I said into the phone.

Freddie checked me in, still looking puzzled. I faked a smile, and mouthed, "I'm okay," before hurrying toward the East Appointment Gate. To Naveen, I said, "I'm sorry for hitting you with the frying pan."

"Is that what it was? It felt like a sledgehammer."

"It was a gift," I said and realized how silly that must sound. I'd been about to ramble on further about Henry, but I stopped myself. "I hit you too hard. You were bleeding," I said. "I'm very sorry."

"Your apology is unnecessary," he said. "Your actions were precisely right. Your goal was to protect the president—and for that I commend you."

"That's very gracious of you. I know that . . . that . . ." For the life of me, I couldn't figure out how to politely say ". . . that you're a bit of a fanatic." So, I stumbled. "That your intentions were good."

"Ah, so the Service has spoken with you."

All of a sudden it dawned on me that I'd promised Tom not to involve myself further in this affair. Now, here I was, on the phone with the very subject of our most recent conversation. Tom would kill me if he knew I was talking with Naveen.

But I hadn't initiated the phone call. Not that that little fact would make a difference with Tom.

"I can't talk to you."

"Why not?"

"I . . . they . . . I shouldn't have tried to contact you. I'm going to hang up now."

"Wait." He made a thoughtful-sounding noise. "Have they told you about the communiqué I intercepted?"

"No," I said. "Really. I have to go."

"Then why did you attempt to contact me?"

I made it to the East Gate, but I couldn't very well continue this conversation as I cleared security, so I paced in circles outside, talking fast, as though that made my conversation less of a transgression. "I was afraid I had hurt you and I just wanted to make sure you were okay."

He seemed to consider this. "That is what I thought."

"Well, it's been nice talking with you," I said. Lame, very lame. "I'm glad you're all right . . ."

"Wait, do not hang up. I must speak with you."

"I have to get back to work. I'm late as it is."

"Then meet me."

"No!" Tom's angry face loomed in my mind's eye, and my answer came out fast and loud. But then my curiosity reared its quizzical head. "Why?"

"I have information about an—"

He stopped himself. I was sure he was about to say "assassin."

"About?"

"The communiqué I intercepted has vital information that must be conveyed to the president."

"You should tell the Secret Service."

"I believe they have been compromised."

"No way."

"It is true."

I shook my head.

"May I call you Olivia?"

I answered automatically, "Sure," then frowned.

"Olivia, think about it. What if I am right? What if there has been a breach in the Service? Do you really wish to take the risk of not listening to what I have to say?"

This was getting weird. And I needed to get back to the kitchen.

"Listen," I said, beginning to understand Tom's insistence that this guy was a conspiracy freak, "I'm just an assistant chef. I don't have anything to do with this. You should talk with one of the agents you trust."

"I cannot."

"I really have to get going."

"Please," he said.

I heard the word and it was déjà vu. When I'd whacked him he'd said "Please." And then I whacked him again. But Tom said Naveen was one of the good guys. I hadn't listened to him then, but I had the opportunity to listen now. Didn't I owe him that much?

"Okay, what's so important?"

"Not over the phone. We must meet in person."

This was beginning to sound like a bad Internet chat hookup. "No."

"You must. Your actions proved to me that you are trustworthy. After you risked your life to stop me, I knew then that you value the president's life very much. I need to convey a message to someone who is not part of the security contingent. It is imperative that I do so. And right now you are the only person I trust who has the ability to deliver this message."

I opened my mouth, but he interrupted.

"I promise I will not hit *you* with a frying pan."

That made me smile. "I don't know," I said. I knew my resolve was wavering. And I think he knew it, too.

"Tomorrow. Somewhere very public, so you need not be afraid of me."

I was surprised to realize that I wasn't afraid of him. Naiveté or stupidity—I wasn't sure which it was. "Where?" I waved to the guard at the East Gate. "Hurry. I really have to get back."

"At the bench next to the merry-go-round."

I knew where that was. Everyone in D.C. knew the merry-go-round on the Mall just outside the Smithsonian Castle. "What time?"

"Twelve o'clock."

"Midnight?"

I thought I heard him laugh. "Certainly not, Olivia. Noon. Will this work for you?"

"I don't think—"

"Please."

He just had to say that again, didn't he?

I sighed. "I'll be there."

CHAPTER 10

I THOUGHT IF I COOKED UP SOMETHING FAMILIAR I'D BE ABLE to get my mind off my troubles. I planned to start a batch of Crisp Triple Chocolate Chip cookies. My comfort food. But there were more surprises in store for me when I got back.

Peter Everett Sargeant—his back to the door as he addressed our group—prevented my surreptitious return to the sanctuary of the kitchen.

I tapped his shoulder to ease past him. "Excuse me," I said.

He drew back as though slapped. "It's about time you showed up. Where were you?"

I didn't think it would behoove me to tell him I'd been on the telephone with the White House fence-hopper from the other morning, so I said, "Lunch."

Sargeant made a dramatic show of looking at his watch. He still hadn't moved enough out of the way to let me pass and join the rest of the kitchen team. "And how much time is allotted for 'lunch'?"

The way he said it made my skin crawl. As though he somehow knew where I'd been.

Henry answered before I could retort. "If Ollie would have known about this impromptu meeting, I'm sure she would have been here earlier." He waved me forward and Sargeant was obliged to allow me by. "Ollie, Peter here has just informed us about an upcoming state dinner."

Peter. I loved the fact that Henry called this guy by his first name.

"If you'd been here," Sargeant began, as I took a position between Marcel and Cyan, "you would know how important it is for us to make this dinner a success."

I couldn't stop myself. "I think we all realize how important it is to make *every* dinner a success."

Sargeant looked taken aback. He sniffed, settled himself, and continued. "Which brings me to the next item on my agenda: Laurel Anne Braun's audition."

My stomach squeezed, and I felt blood rush up from my chest to flush across my face. As though Sargeant knew exactly how Laurel Anne's name affected me, he took that moment to laser his gaze in my direction. My face grew hotter.

"It is my understanding," the little man said, "that up until now, this kitchen has been unable to schedule Ms. Braun's audition. I know that everyone here is very busy. And that there may be some misguided loyalty afoot"—he made another point of looking at me—"but perhaps, instead of taking extended lunch breaks, we should consider putting the White House's needs first."

Behind me, Henry made a sound that could have been muted anger or a warning for me to keep my cool.

I sucked my lips in and bit down to keep from saying something I might regret later. We'd been in touch with Laurel Anne's people almost every day for the past several weeks. Since she was a television star, with appearance commitments and filming deadlines, we worked through her representatives rather than with Laurel Anne directly.

Twice she'd been scheduled for her audition and twice she'd cancelled out on us at the last minute.

"So," Sargeant continued, "I have taken it upon myself to see that Ms. Braun is provided the opportunity she deserves. She will be here two weeks from tomorrow and I trust that you will all work with her to ensure that her audition goes smoothly."

I was about to protest that, as her primary competitor, it would be a conflict of interest for me to assist her, but apparently Sargeant wasn't finished with his announcement.

"I am particularly pleased to tell you that not only will Ms. Braun bring her *Cooking for the Best* talents to share with us"—Sargeant beamed—"but she will bring a cameraman along as well. Her producers have agreed to film her audition for broadcast purposes."

Henry and I exchanged worried glances. "No one is allowed to film at the White House," he said. "It's not done."

Sargeant shook his head as though he'd expected Henry's protest. "We will make an exception for this. I'll take care of it."

"Have you cleared this with Paul Vasquez?" I asked.

His lips barely moved as he repeated, "I'll take care of it." Without missing a beat, he turned. "If there are no other questions, I'm off to my next meeting." As he left, he tossed us a dismissive wave. "Carry on."

Henry pinched the bridge of his nose. "Just when you think you've seen it all."

Cyan and Marcel made supportive noises as they moved back to the tasks Sargeant had interrupted. Bucky wasn't in today, and I wasn't sure if that was a good thing or not. I patted Henry's back. "So when is this state dinner and who is it for?"

He raised his big head, as though grateful to me for bringing up a topic he could relate to. "It's next Wednesday," he said. "We will host the heads of state from two countries."

"Next Wednesday?" I was aghast. We usually had months to prepare for state dinners. And then the rest of the message made it through to my brain. "And we're hosting two countries? How? Which ones?"

Henry rolled his eyes. His bushy eyebrows arched upward melodramatically. "Peter Everett Sargeant III hasn't deemed it appropriate to provide those specifics just yet."

"What? We have a state dinner to prepare for in just over a week and he won't tell us who the guests are?"

"That's what he says." Henry lowered himself onto the stool near the computer. The way he sat made me believe he carried the weight of the world across those broad shoulders.

"How can we plan a menu that way?"

"A week," he said. "I have prepared state dinners in less than that. But I've always known who the guests are." He shook his big head. "And I also haven't ever had to deal with a prima donna television star and her entourage before."

This was a double bomb. We would be scrambling to get as much prep work done as possible over the next few days. We usually had at least two months' notice before anything this big. I could only imagine the anxiety in the social secretary's office today. This was madness. It ordinarily took weeks to compile a guest list, and even with three calligraphers on staff, they'd be working 'round the clock to get invitations out. I'd heard of these last-minute official events, a rarity around here. The staff still talked about Prime Minister Ehud Barak of Israel's visit in 1999 when a working lunch for eighteen people was transformed into a dinner for five hundred over a matter of five days. Successfully.

If that team could do it, so could we.

But with two heads of state and a "secret" guest list, deciding on a menu would be close to impossible. There was almost no time to schedule a taste-test. "Have you talked with Paul?" I asked. "About the reporting structure, I mean?"

"We're stuck with Sargeant. He's apparently golden. I have no idea why."

That was the worst news yet. "What are we going to do?"

For the first time since I came back from lunch, the sparkle returned to Henry's eyes. "Yes, Ollie. What are we going to do? You want the executive chef position, don't you?"

I bit my lip. Nodded.

"Then this is your project as much as it is mine. The executive chef position is a job like any other. There are ups and downs. You may get this appointment and not like it at all."

"With the way they're rolling out the red carpet for Laurel Anne, there's no danger of that."

"Don't be so sure." He clapped his hands together and stood. "No time like the present. Let's see what menu items we can come up with to submit to the First Lady for taste-testing." He pursed his mouth. "And to our good friend Peter as well."

I STOLE OUT OF THE KITCHEN TO FIND PAUL VASQUEZ. FORTU-nately, he was in his office and not overseeing the million other duties that were carried out by White House staffers on a daily basis.

"Paul, do you have a minute?"

He gestured me in as his desk phone rang.

Thirty seconds later he'd responded in the affirmative twice, the negative once, and he thanked whoever was on the other end before he clamped the receiver back in place and turned his full attention to me.

"How are things in the kitchen?" he asked. The tone was amiable, but the eyes were questioning. We both knew I would never come visit this office unless I had something important to talk about, so I spared him the extraneous chitchat and dove right in.

"I'd rather not be here when Laurel Anne Braun auditions."

His expression tightened. Creases appeared between his dark eyebrows as he consulted some papers on his desk. "She's not due here for two weeks."

"I know, but what with this surprise state dinner, I didn't want to lose sight of the audition issues."

He nodded, as though he'd expected me to say that. "I understand your frustration," he said, "but as soon as we get a menu settled the kitchen should be in good shape." Shaking his head he squinted, as though a thought just caused him pain. "But I have to tell you, our director of logistics is pulling her hair out tonight to get everything arranged in this short time frame."

"Why so little forewarning?"

Paul gave me a cryptic smile. "Circumstances presented themselves. And our president is taking advantage of a unique situation. It's a good move." His index finger traced information on the page as he spoke. "But, back to your request. Why don't you want to be here with Laurel Anne?"

I shifted. "From what I understand, she and I are the final two contenders for the executive chef position."

Paul's silence kept me talking.

"Don't you think it would be a conflict of interest for me to be here during her audition?"

He smiled, a bright flash of white. "You mean like you may be tempted to sabotage her efforts?" The smile widened. "Come on, Ollie, we know you better than that."

"I know," I said, my face blushing to acknowledge his comment. "But for appearances' sake, I thought it might be best—and besides, the kitchen isn't that big," I said. It was stating the obvious, but I desperately wanted out of the place when Laurel Anne and friends showed up. "Especially if she's bringing her television crew."

Paul laughed. "Why on earth would you think she'd do that?"

"Sargeant . . . er . . . Peter Everett Sargeant said so."

Paul sat back, blinking as he digested my statement. No question, that little bomb had come as a surprise. "I will look into that."

It was a crack—an opening. I decided to push my luck. "Chief Sargeant won't tell us who the guests are for the state dinner."

Got him again. This time Paul sat up. "You must be mistaken."

I shook my head. "Henry and I have no idea what to plan for, what to stock. I mean, if we had an idea of even the region they come from—"

"They're from the Middle East," he said sharply. "The prime minister of Salomia and the prince of Alkumstan. I will see to it that the kitchen gets the complete dietary dossier on all our guests by this afternoon."

"Thanks."

Paul looked as though he wanted to grab the phone and get things in motion, so I stood. "One last thing," I said.

He glanced up and I knew I had to take my best shot, one more time.

"I'd be happy to work ahead, as much as possible, for all our commitments. I'll put in as many hours as needed. You know I will." Paul nodded and I could see him waiting for the other shoe to drop. "But I'd really appreciate it if I could be excused when Laurel Anne arrives for her audition."

I could tell I'd won this one. He gave a brief nod. "I'll mention it to the First Lady. She has the final say on these decisions."

"Thanks, Paul."

As I exited his office, I heard him punching numbers into his phone.

I suppressed a smile. Something was finally going my way.

CHAPTER 11

THE NEXT DAY HENRY FINALLY RECEIVED THE DIETARY DOSSIERS. "Salomia and Alkumstan," I said. "I couldn't believe it when Paul told me." Prime Minister Jaron Jaffe of Salomia was a sworn enemy of Prince Sameer bin Khalifah of Alkumstan. The two countries had been at war for decades. Ill will didn't begin to describe the horrors these two populations inflicted on one another. "I'm surprised Prince Sameer is coming here now. Isn't he the guy who just overthrew his brother?"

"One and the same," Henry said. "And he did it without bloodshed."

We went over the dossiers, and read the hastily prepared summary of the purpose of this joint visit. During recent talks, the president had detected an opportunity for truce between the two countries, at least as far as trade agreements were concerned. Logic followed that if they could find common ground in business, perhaps eventually both countries could envision peace between their peoples as well.

"I guess Sameer really meant what he said when he took over Alkumstan," I said finally. "He claims to want peace in the Middle East. This would be a logical first step."

"Apparently so. His brother, Mohammed, and Prime Minister Jaffe haven't ever shared the same soil. This is a major coup. They will be creating history here. And whether or not a final trade agreement is achieved, it is a step in the right direction."

Working in the White House was big. Not just big; huge. I knew it and I remembered it every single day, but the truth was, after being on staff for this long, I'd gotten used to hearing the names of powerful individuals. After all, I'd discussed their preferences for meals, made myself aware of their dietary quirks and eccentricities. I'd gotten to know VIPs in my own way and slowly I'd become used to the idea of playing a part in the big world that was the White House.

But the upcoming state dinner exceeded all. This summit to discuss trade agreements could herald the beginning of a new era.

Delighted by the plethora of information provided about our guests and their nutritional needs, Henry was eager to design a menu that would wow and delight all those present. Immediately after breakfast preparations, he urged me to join him at the computer.

I eased onto the stool next to him, my voice nonchalant. "Oh, by the way, I'm going out for lunch today."

He cocked his head. "I thought we would work through lunch."

"Oh," I said, not knowing what to say. "Um . . . something came up."

"What is it?"

I hated lying to Henry. But I couldn't very well tell him that I was meeting Naveen.

When I hesitated, he asked, "A date?"

"No." Then I thought about it. "Well, kinda."

He rubbed his chin as he stared up at the clock. "Okay, then we'll just move a little faster this morning." His thick finger pointed to the first name on the list, Prime Minister Jaffe's. "I know how much you enjoy bringing the flavors of the visiting dignitary's culture into our American fare. Any ideas for an entrée that will please this man . . ." he moved his finger to the next two names, "as well as these two?"

He indicated Prince Sameer and his wife, Princess Hessa. Again, I realized how significant this was. Almost as momentous as Jimmy Carter's Camp David Accords. I stared at the computer screen, where we always recorded our meal plans, and tapped my lips with my finger. "No," I said honestly. "The two cultures, while close in proximity, are far apart in what they prefer to dine on. This might take some research."

Henry nodded. "Where are you going for lunch?"

The question took me aback. "Um," I said, stalling, "up near the Mall."

He gave me a funny look. "Really? Where do you plan to eat?"

I opened my mouth, but he interrupted.

"None of my business, I know. But I assume you're heading into the commercial area, if you have lunch plans. Can you pick something up for me?" He leaned sideways to write out the name of a book. "Here," he said. "If you don't mind. I ordered this from the bookstore on Thirteenth. They're holding it."

Great. I shouldn't have opened my mouth. I'd planned to zip out to the Mall and back. This detour would cost at least fifteen minutes and we were already pressed for time in the kitchen. Still, Henry rarely asked for favors, so I smiled and said it'd be no problem at all.

"Good," he said. "There are a number of innovative ideas in that book. I've been meaning to get it for months. It will come in handy for this event."

WITH HENRY'S NOTE IN MY CAPACIOUS PURSE, I STRUCK OUT FOR my meeting with Naveen, just about ten minutes before noon. I could've taken the Metro, but I knew I could walk the distance faster. I wore my new Jackie O sunglasses—purchased specifically for today's meeting—and just as I veered off of Pennsylvania, taking a right on 12th Street NW, I pulled the rest of my disguise out from the recesses of my purse.

No one paid any attention to me as I twisted my hair and shoved it beneath a Chicago Bears baseball cap. Still walking, I tugged the cap's brim low so that it almost touched the top of my sunglasses. Within minutes I had the National Mall in sight. I stepped up my pace, pulling out the final items from my stash—a dark blue, very wrinkled windbreaker, and my old 35mm camera. When I pulled the strap over my head and settled the camera into place, I knew I looked like your average eager tourist on a jaunt to the Capitol. The one thing I couldn't do much about was my height. Belatedly, I realized I should've worn something with a heel. Darn.

It was a meager disguise, but a necessary one. I wanted to get this meeting with Naveen over with as quickly as possible—give him the chance to impart his vital piece of information and then get myself out—but I didn't want the Secret Service detail shadowing Naveen to recognize me. Without this disguise, I hadn't a prayer.

I'd done the best I could, under the circumstances, to blend into the sight-seer background. I was still afraid of one thing—Tom. Even with my oh-so-clever appearance manipulations, Tom would know me in a heartbeat. I sure hoped he was on a different detail today.

As the merry-go-round came into view, I slowed my pace. A tourist wouldn't rush to the side of a carousel. Not without a little kid in tow. Plus, the windbreaker's added layer on this unseasonably warm day was making me hot. I drew a finger across my brow between the hat and sunglasses, and came away with a load of perspiration.

Never let 'em see you sweat.

I almost laughed.

Right about now, sweat was the least of my worries.

The sun overhead, the hat, the sticky windbreaker, and my own nerves were working overtime to produce a different kind of heat—that of real fear. But I couldn't stop now. Not until I knew what Naveen wanted to tell me.

Circus music drew me closer. I saw small children on brightly colored, rhythmically rising and falling horses, attentive parents with protective arms around their backsides. Just a normal, pleasant day in our nation's capital.

For me, however, it was anything but.

My feet continued forward, each step bringing me closer to the spinning ride even as my brain argued that this was one of the most foolish things I'd ever done.

I checked my watch. Noon.

Naveen had to be here somewhere. There was an elderly couple on a park bench near the ice cream vendor's cart. They wore matching red shorts, wraparound sunglasses, and white visors. Three people stood in line for ride tickets, but all three had small children with them. There were about a half-dozen other adults surrounding the merry-go-round, pointing cameras or waving at the riders. Not one of them looked like my memory of Naveen.

The carousel began to slow, but it wasn't until its shrill bell rang, signaling the end of the ride, that the passengers were able to get off their horses and make their way to the exit.

I scanned the riders as they filed past me. I checked my watch again. I was certain he'd said noon.

There seemed to be nothing to do but wait. I worried, briefly, about the Secret Service guys noticing my loitering, so I lifted the camera and took a couple of shots of the ride, the Capitol, and the Washington Monument, all of which would've made great pictures if I had any film in the camera. Bringing it along had been a last-minute inspiration but I hadn't had time to pick film up on the way.

Yep, I'd make a great spy, wouldn't I?

I wandered toward the ice cream cart, and eyed the chocolate bar with almond crust. It might be the only lunch I got today, I reasoned, and reached into my purse for some money.

A tap on my shoulder.

"Excuse me, ma'am, but I believe you dropped this."

I turned. Naveen was there, smiling, handing me something. A piece of paper. Folded. Like a note kids would pass in grammar school.

Automatically I took it, thanked him, and felt my mood shift from startled to puzzled when he walked away again.

The red-shorted elderly couple had vacated the bench next to me, and Naveen took a seat there, opening up a newspaper to read. Ignoring me completely. I took my cue from him and walked a few feet away.

Ice cream novelty forgotten, I opened the note, bracing myself for the big important information that Naveen needed to give me.

PURCHASE A TICKET TO RIDE THE CAROUSEL. CHOOSE THE RIDE'S BENCH SEAT. I WILL JOIN YOU THERE.

Not what I'd been expecting. And I was beginning to feel prickly annoyance. The sooner I got what I came for, the sooner I could rush over to the bookstore and pick up the cookbook Henry wanted. Then, I could get back to my normal life and not have to worry about the Secret Service, and more important, Tom, who would be furious with me because of this little adventure.

I decided to cut the silliness right here. I turned, prepared to confront Naveen, prepared to ask him straight out to tell me what was on his mind.

But he was gone.

Maybe the guy was a nutcase. But then again, maybe he was the smart one, here. Secret Service personnel were shadowing him, and the last thing I needed to do was to have one of them scrutinize me too closely.

Fine. I'd play along.

Another carousel ride was ending. I hurried over to the ticket booth.

In my haste, I bumped into a man rushing the other way.

"Sorry," I said.

He locked eyes with me—shooting me a look of such instant, violent disdain, that I was taken aback. The man was blond enough to be mistaken for an albino, but his eyes were a luminescent blue. He shoved me out of his way with the back end of his arm—like an old-time villain clearing a table of debris—and pushed past without a word.

"Well, excuse me," I shouted after him as I regained my footing. Some people were just born rude. I thrust my two dollars into the booth's window and remembered to thank the woman behind the glass as I claimed my ticket.

Last in line, I stood behind a man holding two kids' hands. I tried not to be conspicuous about looking around—looking for Naveen—but I couldn't help myself. What was I doing here but playing a part in someone else's conspiracy fantasy?

I'd gone this far. I'd take my seat on the bright red bench and see what happened.

Just as the ride operator opened the gate for the next set of riders, I felt a soft poke in my back.

"Do not turn around," he said. "I believe we are being watched. I will not join you on this ride."

I started to move away, but his fingers grasped the back of my windbreaker, stopping me. In a voice so low that the shuffling man in front of me wouldn't have been able to hear, Naveen said, "You must ride. I will wait. If it is clear, I will join you on the next ride." He let go and whispered, "Do you understand?"

I nodded, and walked forward, clearing the gate as Naveen took off.

This was getting to be too much.

Faced with the prospect of riding the merry-go-round alone, I made my way toward the miniature bench amid the painted horses. Wouldn't you know, it was already occupied by the red-shorted old folks. Completely annoyed at this point, I made my way to the outer perimeter, and grimaced when a ten-year-old beat me to the bright turquoise serpent. I chose one of the last empty critters, a white horse with a patriotic red, white, and blue saddle.

The ride's shrieking bell sounded the moment we were all in place, and the merry-go-round began its never-ending path to nowhere with me bobbing up and down, feeling more than just a little bit foolish.

I caught sight of Naveen in snippets as the ride turned. He had on sports sunglasses and navy blue running pants. His gray sweatshirt, with cutoff sleeves, revealed very impressive biceps. Looking like every other runner in the area, he wore nonchalance like a second skin. If I hadn't been attuned to his concerns, I wouldn't have given him a second glance.

He pulled his newspaper up, made his way to the bench near the ice cream vendor, sat, and began to read.

There were two round mirrors placed just outside the merry-go-round's fence. Sitting atop tall metal poles, they were placed strategically at about one-third and two-thirds around the perimeter. Their large convex surfaces gave the ride operator a constant view of the entire mechanism.

I tried to catch Naveen's reflection in the westernmost mirror every time my horse turned its back on the bench.

Nothing out of place.

He sat there and continued to read the paper.

Was this all just a hoax? Let's see how far the silly assistant chef will go? Was there a hidden camera somewhere, and a grinning television host ready to leap out and tell me this was all one big joke?

I came around again. Up and down, up and down. Without being too obvious, I watched Naveen as I circled past. No, this was no joke. His body was tense, and his dark eyebrows arched over the black lenses. He'd seen something, or thought he had.

We were slowing. Naveen hadn't yet gotten up to buy a ticket and I wondered if I should ride alone again. It'd be just my luck for some paranoid parent to call security and have me detained for suspicious behavior. Or a kid complain that I was hogging a horse.

The music continued as I whirled past again, but this time I felt a subtle change in speed.

The slowing went on for another several turns. I decided that as soon as I got off, I'd march over to Naveen, sit next to him, and force him to cough up this "vital information." If he wouldn't, I'd leave. Simple as that. I needed to take charge here.

Coupling this ridiculous errand with a trip to the bookstore meant I'd probably be late getting back. I hated to be late.

We were almost stopped now.

Naveen sat up straighter, suddenly alert.

A man approached him. The same man who'd pushed me aside. He was moving too quickly. Oddly fast.

Naveen recognized the guy. Jerked away.

But the guy came in close.

Too close.

This was no Secret Service agent. Even I knew that.

My horse finally stopped, and as I rose in the stirrups to get off, the shrill bell announced the ride's end.

But this time, the bell sounded different—with a cracking background noise.

Naveen toppled off the bench onto the ground.

The blond man stood and began strolling away.

"Naveen!" I screamed.

Facedown in the dirt, Naveen didn't move.

I leaped off the horse and made my way to the exit, realizing belatedly that my shout had attracted the blond man's attention. He turned around. For the second time, we locked eyes. And I read in them a coldness I'd never experienced before.

He changed his direction and came after me. Not strolling anymore.

I had no other option.

I ran.

CHAPTER 12

MY SHORT LEGS WOULDN'T WIN ME THIS RACE. I NEEDED HELP and I needed it now.

I took off as fast as I could, my feet straining for purchase on the gravelly path. With nothing in my mind beyond escape from whoever this creep was, I skidded around the front of a bright orange stroller, its front wheel catching the edge of my foot. I almost fell, but my arms windmilled like a vaudeville comic's, and the sunglasses flew off my face. I forced myself to move forward, to run, the camera bouncing against my chest in a rhythm that mimicked my pace.

I looked back long enough to ease my conscience. Thankfully, the stroller hadn't fallen— its occupant was unaffected.

But the white-blond man was gaining on me.

I shot forward, heading for the blue-and-white tour bus kiosk. They had phones in there. They could call security. "Help," I screamed, banging flat-handed against the Plexiglas windows as I raced around the kiosk's left side. The woman inside the booth recoiled in alarm. "Call the police," I shouted. "There's a killer after me."

As the words escaped my lips, I realized they were true.

Naveen was dead.

I couldn't wait.

The world froze and narrowed. There was only me—my shouts ringing hollowly in my ears—and the man close behind. His face wore anger like a grotesque mask.

I read his expression—there was no doubt that he would catch me. And soon I would be just as dead as Naveen.

I concentrated on putting one foot in front of the other.

Weren't there people around? As though standing at the mouth of a bright tunnel, I couldn't see anything beyond ten feet in front of me. Colors meshed, shapeless forms surrounded me. I heard nothing but the *whoosh*ing blood in my brain and the echo of my gasps as I skipped the curb, vaguely aware that I was supposed to check for cars.

Let the damn car hit me. Then maybe the assassin behind me wouldn't.

Horns blared.

I didn't stop. Didn't turn.

Just across the street was the welcoming red brick of the Arts and Industries Building. A haven. There would be security inside. I tripped up the steps and yanked at the door.

It didn't budge.

Horns blared again.

Brakes screeched.

"Help me!" I screamed. My voice, raw with emotion, pierced my consciousness enough to let me read the sign: CLOSED FOR RENOVATIONS.

I spun.

The blond man was on the ground in the middle of the street. Rolling. A taxi had hit him. People called for help.

My breath caught. Thank God.

And then—unbelievably—he righted himself. Back on his feet, he slammed both hands on the hood of the taxi and started to push his way past the bystanders who'd stopped to stare.

Where were the gapers when I needed them?

I took off to my left. To the Castle. There had to be someone there.

"Help!"

But I'd hesitated too long. The blond man was almost on top of me. His footfalls echoed my own on the short run across the brick walkway that separated the two buildings.

He snatched the neckstrap of my camera, yanking me to a halt. The camera slammed into my face. I saw sparkles before my eyes. He seized my arm and turned me to face him.

All my self-defense practice with Tom paid off in that moment. Muscle memory, he'd called it. With an instinct borne of many hours of repetition, I slammed the heel of my hand against my attacker's temple. Then I sent a knee to his groin.

The man hadn't expected me to fight. His fingers loosened just enough for me to wiggle away.

I turned away, screaming again for help. Where was everyone? How could they just ignore me?

Still hampered by tunnel vision, I strove for focus. I ran past the flowered fountain. Purple flowers glowed in the sunlight.

Why on earth was I noticing flowers?

I heard scrambling behind me and I knew the killer had gotten up.

Three white-shirted security men came running around the front of the Castle, just as I was about to turn the corner. One grabbed me by the forearms.

I pointed behind me. "Get him!"

The black man holding me kept a tight grip. "Get who?"

I turned, still pointing.

The assassin was gone.

"He . . . he . . ." Safe now, in the presence of Smithsonian Security, I tried to pull away, looking for the white-blond man. But the guard held tight.

"You're not going anywhere, lady."

High-pitched wheezing shot out of me as I gasped for breath. "But he killed a man. He killed . . ." What was I supposed to say? That the guy who'd jumped the White House fence a couple days ago had been killed? And I didn't even know that it was true. Maybe Naveen had fainted.

I hoped.

But I knew better.

"Have you been drinking, miss?" one of the other guards asked.

I shook my head. "Follow me," I said, still trying to catch my breath. "I'll show you."

The black man holding me exchanged glances with the other two guards. They were all about my age, and their looks seemed to suggest that they were unwilling to humor me. "I think we better call for some help."

They started to walk me toward the Castle's front doors. "No," I said. "I have to get back to the bench."

For the first time I noticed I was shaking. Not chilly-outside-shaking, but whole-body trembling. All that had just happened, and my narrow escape from what I imagined could have happened was affecting me physically. I wanted to sit, but I couldn't. Not with Naveen lying alone by that bench. Please let someone have called for help.

An answering siren sounded nearby. "Thank God," I said, "maybe they can save him."

"Are you on medication?" my guard asked.

"Would you stop with the accusatory tone?" I'd been polite long enough. "There's a man over there who needs help. I saw him get . . . get . . ."

"Get what?"

"He slumped over. I think he's dead."

One of the other guards grabbed at his radio. "I'll call it in," he said, but the siren's wails were close now.

I shot my captor a look that said, "See?"

CHAPTER 13

THE PARAMEDICS ARRIVED ON THE SCENE JUST AS I MADE IT BACK
to the bench, double escort in tow.

Naveen had been flipped onto his back by someone trying to administer
CPR. The paramedics moved the Good Samaritan out of the way as other
Smithsonian Security personnel worked the inquisitive crowd backward. I
scanned their faces, searching for the white-blond man. But the gawkers, shifting as they watched, were just an average mix of curious tourists and nosy
locals. I recognized some from my ride on the carousel.

I steeled myself to look down.

There was no doubt. Naveen was dead.

I bit my lips tight. He'd wanted to talk with me. He'd poked me in the back
not ten minutes earlier. He'd claimed to have important information.

Most of all, however, he'd been alive.

Half his face was covered with dirt from where he'd fallen after the blond
man's visit. Whoever had turned him, I'm sure, had been surprised by the body
armor. Hard to do CPR on someone wearing Kevlar, I imagined. But even I
could tell from here that Naveen hadn't had a chance. The blond man's bullet
had done terrible damage. I couldn't believe the volume of blood. It mixed with
the dirt to create an enormous black puddle under his body that the paramedics couldn't help but track through.

The sight of sticky footprints as Naveen's lifeblood seeped into the ground
made me want to look away. But I couldn't turn my head.

The guys holding me hadn't let go the whole time it took to walk over here.
They weren't letting go now, either. They hadn't handcuffed me, but I found
myself the object of scrutiny as people around started to take notice.

The old lady in the red shorts pointed from across the circle of onlookers surrounding Naveen's prone form. "I saw that girl running." She turned to her husband. "We saw her running, didn't we, Egbert?" The man didn't have time to respond before the woman pointed again, and with old-lady vehemence called out. "You killed him!"

The black guy who'd first grabbed me tugged my arm, "Let's go," he said.

The elderly woman called after us, "Was he a terrorist?"

WHEN I FINALLY SAT, IT WAS IN A HARD PLASTIC CHAIR IN WHAT was undoubtedly an interrogation room. My face ached from the hit I'd taken with the camera. At my request, which had come out in little more than a bleat, someone had placed a paper cup of water on the table in front of me. I drank fast, my greedy throat parched from so much screaming.

My two guards had been replaced by two Metropolitan Police officers. One white, one black. Both standing, they looked at me with identical scorn. I'd shown them my White House ID, hoping that would buy me a little consideration.

I drained the paper cup. I guess that had been all the kindness I was going to get.

We'd gone over the events of the afternoon several times, and I'd begged to call the White House to let Henry know what was going on, but they hadn't let me near a phone, yet.

And just when I thought it couldn't get worse, a knock at the door admitted three Secret Service agents. Craig Sanderson, a woman I didn't know, and Tom, whose demeanor was just as professional as ever, but whose eyes bore into mine with an anger that sent white-hot fear racing across my chest.

"Thank you, gentlemen," Craig drawled to the two police officers. "We will take it from here."

They left, but I had no doubt the officers were simply shifting position to the other side of the room's one-way mirror.

"Ms. Paras," Craig said, taking a seat the moment the door closed. "I have a copy of your statement in front of me, but I have to ask: What were you doing on the Mall this afternoon?"

I tried hard not to look at Tom. I wanted, more than anything, for him to know that I hadn't broken my promise.

"Naveen," I began, focusing on Craig as I spoke, "called me." Now I did look at Tom, repeating. "*He* called *me*."

Unruffled, Craig said, "But that does not explain why you were out there with a dead man, a former operative, and why the witnesses believe you killed him."

"I didn't kill him. You've got to know that, don't you? It was a guy. A really blond guy."

Craig sat up. "You mean to tell me that you saw the killer?"

"Yes," I answered, surprised. "Didn't they tell you?" I'd gone over my statement with the Smithsonian Security guys and the Metropolitan Police at least five times. I'd made that point very clear. What now became clear to me was that the security staff and the police hadn't shared information with the Secret Service.

"Ms. Paras," the woman spoke up. She, too, had a drawl. Where on Craig it came across frighteningly passive, on her it sounded demure and inquisitive. "Why don't you tell us exactly what transpired here this afternoon?"

"Can I call Henry first?" I asked. "He's got to be worried. I should've been back hours ago."

Tom hadn't sat down. Now he pushed an unoccupied chair out of his way, making an angry scrape against the tile floor. "I'll call Henry," he said, without looking at me. Two heartbeats later, he was gone.

I felt my whole body react. He was furious. Once I explained, he'd understand. He had to.

My eyes stayed on the closed door for a long moment.

"Ms. Paras?" the woman prompted.

BY THE TIME I GOT BACK TO THE KITCHEN IT WAS AFTER SEVEN. With the president and First Lady out at a charity event at the Kennedy Center, it was very quiet. My shoes made soft noises as I made my way to the kitchen. Other than those standing guard at their posts, I didn't want to run into anyone else tonight. I wanted to gather my things and make my way home, hoping for a chance to connect with Tom along the way. I needed to explain myself.

Henry sat at the computer screen. He twisted his bulk around as the sound of my tiptoeing. "Ollie," he said, standing, "what happened?" He moved toward me. I let myself be enveloped by those big arms, and even though it hurt to press my bruised forehead against his chest, it felt so good to be held. "I was so worried."

"What did they tell you?" I asked into his chest.

I felt his grumble of relief. "Not much. Agent MacKenzie called here. At first I thought you'd been injured, but he said you were all right."

I broke away from him. "How did he sound?"

"How did he—? Ah . . . yes, I understand. Tom. He was . . . professional. Terse and to the point. Nothing more, nothing less. He told me that you would be late returning." Henry glanced up at the clock. "I didn't realize he meant this late. What on earth happened? We heard about the shooting at the Smithsonian. Did you see it? Are you a witness?"

I wanted to tell Henry everything. He had such a positive outlook on life and he seemed to see everything so clearly. I could've used a dash of his insight. "I'm not supposed to talk about it."

He nodded. "I understand." But his slight frown said just the opposite.

As he returned to his computer musings, I gathered a few things, added a couple of notes to my plans for tomorrow, and started to head out. "Henry," I said, suddenly remembering, "I didn't pick up your book."

He didn't turn. "It's okay."

His words were quiet, resigned. "It's okay." That bothered me more than if he'd made a joke or teased me about forgetting.

"See you tomorrow," I said, hoping for something more.

Henry nodded, but didn't say another word.

My shoes made their quiet squeaks across the floor, taking me through the dim hall toward the East entrance. I passed the wall of windows to my right, wondering who was out there in the night, and what they were planning. The sooner I got out of here and was able to call Tom, the happier I'd be.

"Ollie?"

I spun, gasping. I sucked saliva down into my lungs, which threw me into a coughing spasm. "My God," I spluttered. I hadn't heard Paul come up behind me. Bent in half, and supremely embarrassed, I held a hand up to cover my mouth.

He looked ready to slap my back. "I'm sorry, are you okay?"

I was already recovering, so I stepped just out of his reach. "Yeah, I just got scared is all."

"After this afternoon's excitement, I'm not surprised."

"What . . ." I coughed again. "What do you know?"

He looked off into the shadowed recesses of the long hallway as though considering what to say next. "You've had a tough day."

I thought of Naveen. I thought of how close I'd come to sharing his fate. "It could've been worse."

Paul nodded. "Which is why I waited for you tonight."

My stomach clenched—as though someone had reached in and squeezed. "You did?"

"About the executive chef position . . ." he began.

Here it comes. I'm out. My actions today killed my chances. I knew it.

When it took forever for Paul to finish his thought, I prompted him, holding my breath even as I said, "Yes?"

"The First Lady believes . . ."

The fist around my stomach tightened.

". . . it's imperative that you *are* present when Laurel Anne has her audition."

I let my breath out. All I could think of was that I wasn't being fired. As disappointed as I knew I should be by Paul's pronouncement, I was elated that they hadn't decided to toss me out on my butt. Yet. And, I seemed to still be in the running for the promotion. After all that had transpired today, I took this as a positive sign. "All right," I said. "That's good news, right?"

Paul gave me a pointed look. A "don't get your hopes up" look. "Mrs. Campbell said, and I quote: 'If I decide that Laurel Anne's talents are the right choice for the White House kitchen, Ollie will be reporting to her.'" He shrugged with the resignation of someone imparting bad news. "She thinks it's a good test to see if you work well together."

"Sure," I said in a small voice. "Of course."

"See you tomorrow, Ollie."

"Yeah."

The walk to the McPherson Square station gave me the opportunity to try Tom. I called him three times. It rang before it went to voice mail. That meant he had his phone turned on, but wasn't taking my calls. The first time that I got his voice mail, words failed me and I hung up. The second time, I started to explain, but was cut off by a disembodied voice letting me know my recording time was up. The last time I just apologized.

As I took the escalator down toward the rushing trains, I gripped my cell phone tight. "Please call," I whispered. The little display registered no service and I got on the first train to Crystal City, with the firm belief that there would be a message from Tom waiting for me by the time the train emerged into the night at Arlington.

I WALKED FROM THE METRO TO MY APARTMENT HOLDING THE cell phone in my right hand in case it rang. Just to be certain that I hadn't missed Tom's call, I checked the display every so often as I slowly closed the short distance from the station to the apartment complex. Too slowly. I weighed a thousand pounds.

But the night was clear. Despite the plethora of lights from the surrounding buildings and those from the nearby airport, I could make out stars. Hundreds. One of them, bright and winking, made me stop to make a wish.

I held my breath and waited.

But the phone still didn't ring.

Maybe it wasn't a star, I reasoned. Maybe that one had been Jupiter.

A quick cold breeze shot past as I trudged up the walkway. Chilly night. Matched the state of my mood right now.

I worked up a smile and said hello to James at the front desk. While my building wasn't posh enough to have a real doorman, James tried hard to fit the bill. He took his job seriously, manning the front desk and walking the corridors each evening in a sort of pseudosecurity endeavor. He and two other fellows traded hours, and for their trouble they got a hefty reduction in their rent. James's white hair caught glints from the recessed lighting above, and he nodded a greeting.

"Who were those two fellas who came to visit yesterday morning?" he asked.

That was just yesterday? It seemed like months ago. "Friends of mine," I said.

"We talking about the same two fellas?" James asked. He was ready for conversation, but all I wanted was to grab an elevator and get to my apartment. "They didn't want me to buzz you. They showed me Secret Service ID, so I let them by. They looked pretty upset. Is anything wrong?"

I punched the "up" button, and was rewarded with an immediate "ding." At this time of night, there wasn't a lot of activity up and down the shafts. "Everything's fine," I said and sighed with relief when the elevator doors closed, cutting off further commentary. I punched the button for thirteen. I didn't put much stock in superstition, but other people did. Which is why I'd chosen the floor. Rent was cheaper.

Mrs. Wentworth must have been waiting for me, because she popped out of her door the moment I stepped off at our floor. "Olivia," she called, waving a sheet of paper at me with her free hand—the one not gripping her cane. "Come here."

Rather than taking the right to my apartment, I veered left to hers. "I have to—" I began, but she cut me off.

"Is this you?" She thrust a computer-printed page at me and pointed an arthritic finger at its color picture. "I found this on the Internet. Did you really kill a terrorist today?"

I grabbed the sheet. "Does it say that?" I asked, scanning the article, looking for my name and hoping desperately not to find it.

"No, of course not," she said. "They don't say who killed the terrorist. But I figured it must be you. You had those two Secret Service men come visit you last night, and then you were there when this terrorist got shot."

I should have known Mrs. Wentworth would have found out that Craig and Tom were Secret Service—probably from James. Fatigue loosened my lips and I blurted, "He wasn't a terrorist."

"A-ha. Then this is you."

"Where?" I asked. "I don't see anyone in this picture that looks like me."

"Right there." She pointed to Naveen's prone form, dead center of the crowd. Her finger moved to the picture's very edge, where the side of a nose and a slice of cheek had made it into the shot. Barely. "That's you, isn't it?"

"No," I said. I looked closely. It could've been me. "I wasn't there," I lied.

Her pale eyes sparkled and a grin played at her pursed lips. "If you weren't there, honey, then that's the first thing you would've said."

Wily old lady. I should've been more careful, but my weariness was taking its toll.

"I should go."

"So, did you kill him?"

My stomach wrenched. In a way, I guess I had.

"I'm really not sure what happened there." That, at least, was the truth. "Good night, Mrs. Wentworth."

Her skeptical eyes watched till I shut the door. Leaning against it, I realized I still had the cell phone clamped in my hand. My knuckles ached.

A swift glance at my hall clock—Tom should've called by now. It had been a helluva day. "Come on," I pleaded with the little phone. "Give me a chance to explain."

It took all my effort to push myself off the door and get ready for bed. There were no messages on my home answering machine, not that I expected any. If Tom called, he would use my cell. I pulled on a pair of cotton pants and a T-shirt, brushed my teeth, and stared solemnly at my reflection in the mirror. I was different tonight, in a way I couldn't explain. But my eyes told the story.

Suddenly not tired at all, I grabbed my butterfly afghan—my nana had made it for me—and pulled it tight around my shoulders as I made my way out onto my balcony. No chairs, so I sat on the hard concrete. There wasn't much of a view down below, but high above was a wide swath of sky.

My cell phone sat next to me, silent as ever.

The breeze was cold. The night, very quiet.

I gazed up at the stars and thought about Naveen.

CHAPTER 14

BUCKY WAS KNEADING DOUGH WHEN I WALKED INTO THE kitchen the next day.

"Good morning, Ollie," he said.

Bucky's uncharacteristic good cheer, coupled with the bleak looks I got from of the rest of my colleagues, stopped me in my tracks.

Cyan met my eyes. "What are the bruises from?" she asked, pointing to her own forehead as she stared at mine.

"Altercation with a camera," I said. "Long story. What's going on?"

She then glanced over to Henry, who turned away. Marcel appeared to be muttering to himself as he worked at a floral sculpture made entirely of sugar. Bucky whistled. It was the happiest I'd ever seen him.

"What happened?" I asked.

Cyan broke the news. "Laurel Anne's coming tomorrow."

"What? She can't."

Bucky stopped whistling. "Oh, yes she can."

"But . . ." I protested. I'd been here late last night when Paul told me I was required to be present for her audition. He hadn't said anything about moving up her audition day. "But we have a state dinner next week."

"Yes," Henry said. "Due to unexpected circumstances, however"—he gave me a look that told me my actions yesterday had had more repercussions than I'd anticipated—"Peter Everett Sargeant III believes it is in the White House's best interest to get Laurel Anne in here as soon as possible." He turned away again.

Bucky added, "Sargeant says that her audition is merely a formality now."

I'd done it, all right. By agreeing to meet Naveen, I'd seen a man get murdered, nearly gotten killed myself, jeopardized my career, endured interrogation by the police, and alienated Tom. I swallowed hard. And I still didn't have the commemorative pan returned to me for Henry's retirement party.

Looking at my mentor's back right now, I realized that was the least of my worries. Henry was angry. He had chosen me to be named executive chef. And I'd blown my chances. I'd blown them spectacularly.

"Well then," I said with forced energy, "it looks like we'll have to work twice as hard today to get the state dinner arranged, doesn't it?"

Cyan and Marcel looked at me as if I'd gone stark-raving nuts. Bucky went back to his dough. But Henry's big head came up, and he turned. I thought I detected a glimmer of pride in his eyes. At least I hoped it was.

"Yes," he said, "that's exactly what it means."

BY SIX O'CLOCK, WE'D COME UP WITH THREE PRELIMINARY MENUS, all variations on a theme involving American cuisine with the two countries' unique flavors as accents. Bucky and Marcel had gone home an hour ago, Cyan was just finishing her preps for the next day, and Henry and I were hashing out the remaining state dinner details, including filling out orders from our vendors and contacting the sommelier to have him begin choosing suitable wines. Aware of the added complication of having to pass Sargeant's taste test, we'd decided to develop these three menus, with interchangeable courses. Sort of a mix-and-match plan.

We had a hunch that, if he remained true to form, Sargeant would toss aside at least one of our offerings. Probably more.

The intensity of our planning had taken my mind off my troubles with Tom, but now, as Cyan called good night, I thought about her going home to her boyfriend, and I pulled my cell phone from my pocket. I hardly ever kept my cell phone with me at work. But today I had.

No messages. Still.

The disappointment made my heart hurt.

"Ollie," Henry said, pulling me out of my reverie.

I tucked the phone away again. "Yes?"

He tapped at the computer screen. "Why did you remove the pine nut appetizer from our submission list?"

Work was the best panacea for a broken spirit. "The prince's wife," I said, reaching past Henry to dig through my notes. "We have a reminder here that she's allergic to nuts. The pine nut appetizer was the only item that might've caused an issue."

He stopped and looked at me. "You ready for tomorrow?"

Tomorrow.

The kitchen grew suddenly quiet, as though the entire White House was holding its breath, waiting for me to say her name out loud.

"Laurel Anne's big day," I acknowledged. I focused on a small spot near the ceiling so I wouldn't have to see the lie in Henry's eyes when I asked him, "This audition really is just a formality, isn't it? She's got the position wrapped up already, doesn't she?"

Henry didn't answer.

Eventually, I lowered my eyes to meet his.

"Ollie," he said in the paternal tone I'd come to know so well, "if that's what you believe, then that's exactly what will happen. If you give up, then she wins. With no effort." His mouth curled down on one side and he shook his head. "Seems to me an executive chef ought to earn her position, not have it handed to her on a silver platter."

Paul Vasquez knocked on the wall as he entered the kitchen. "I don't mean to interrupt, but Ollie has a visitor."

Could it be Tom?

"The Metropolitan Police need you to look at some mug shots," Paul said, dashing my hopes, "to see if you can identify the man from . . . from yesterday. They wanted you to come down to the station, but I convinced them you were needed here. I know how busy you are with everything you've got going this week."

I guess my face must have communicated my disappointment, because Paul was quick to jump in and ask if this was a bad time.

"No, it's fine," I said, just as Henry agreed and told me he'd wait for my return.

Before heading off with Paul, I gripped a handful of Henry's tunic and leaned close to his ear. "I am not giving up."

UNABLE TO RECOGNIZE ANYONE IN THE POLICE PHOTOS, I MADE my way back to the kitchen about a half hour later. Along the way, I passed our social secretary coaching her team through this foreshortened lead time. "Nothing's impossible with the right attitude," I heard Marguerite say.

The team had set up a large felt board where they tacked, removed, and retacked names to devise the dinner's seating arrangements. This was a tough one. I wasn't even sure all the invites had gone out yet. I couldn't imagine the logistical nightmare the social office faced for this event.

When I got back to the kitchen, I found Henry just outside the door, in conversation with Peter Everett Sargeant and a man I'd never met before.

Henry called me over. The new man, wearing a smartly cut suit, full beard, and blue patterned turban, turned slowly at my approach. His hooded eyes were expressionless, yet I was aware of his immediate and thorough inspection of me. I ran the dossier information I'd studied through my head and deduced he must be a representative of Prince Sameer.

"Ambassador Labeeb bin-Saleh, allow me to introduce my first assistant, Olivia Paras," Henry began.

Sargeant interrupted. "We're finished here." He started to guide the ambassador away.

Henry continued as though Sargeant hadn't spoken. "Olivia, you and I will be working closely with Ambassador bin-Saleh and his assistant, Kasim."

I smiled at bin-Saleh. I knew better than to shake hands. He bent forward, slightly, in acknowledgment.

Bin-Saleh's words were melodious as they rolled out of his mouth. "The prince and his wife very much anticipate sampling your talent for food making."

"And we are honored by your presence," I said. "I look forward to working with you and your assistant."

"Kasim," he said, "has not been well on our journey, and he has retired to his room at the house of Bah-lare for the evening."

I knew he meant to say Blair House, the expansive residence across the street where visiting dignitaries were usually accommodated.

"I'm sorry to hear that he's ill," Henry said. "I hope he recovers soon."

The ambassador bent forward again. "I will intend to convey your pleasant wishes."

"Yes, well," Sargeant interrupted as he insinuated himself between Henry and bin-Saleh in an effort to guide the man away. "The ambassador has had a long trip, and I'm certain he would prefer to retire for the evening." To us he added, "We will continue this tomorrow afternoon at two o'clock."

I blurted. "Tomorrow afternoon?"

Sargeant fixed me with a cool stare. "Yes, Ms. Paras," he said. "Two. That will give me time to prescreen the menu items you're proposing for the state dinner."

Did he mean that we were supposed to create our menus for him by tomorrow morning?

As he and bin-Saleh turned away, I called after them. "Wait."

Sargeant's eyes glittered. Ooh. He was not happy.

Bin-Saleh simply blinked, his expression mild.

We needed clarification—tonight—and I knew this was my best shot. I didn't like to air grievances before guests, so I tried to keep my voice neutral. "You do remember that Laurel Anne is coming tomorrow, right?" I asked. Then, with the hope that wishing made it so, I added, "Or has she been rescheduled?"

"Of course I remember that Ms. Braun is due here tomorrow. And thank goodness for that." Sargeant looked to bin-Saleh as though sharing a joke, but the ambassador said nothing. He blinked again, still without expression.

Henry's hand grazed my shoulder blade. I didn't know whether he was encouraging me to continue or warning me to stop. But I pushed. "She's taking over the kitchen for the day. The whole day."

Sargeant rolled his eyes. "Yes. That's why Mrs. Campbell and I are planning to conduct the taste test tomorrow morning—eight thirty sharp. With Laurel Anne here, the First Lady and I will have much to look forward to. Now," he added, "we have other staff members to meet. Good night."

Bin-Saleh bowed our direction. Henry nudged me. I was so flustered by Sargeant's pronouncement I almost forgot to respond.

"What are we going to do?" I asked, the moment they were out of earshot.

Back in the kitchen, Henry scowled. He was silent for a very long time. "How early can you get here tomorrow?" he asked.

"I can stay all night."

"No." He shook his head. "Go home. Sleep fast. You'll need every bit of energy and strength tomorrow. I'll call the others. We'll meet here at four and get as much done as we can before the 'star' arrives." He smiled down at me. "It's just been one thing after another lately, hasn't it?"

I pointed out the doorway, in Sargeant's direction. "And I can tell you exactly when it all started."

I TOOK HENRY'S ADVICE TO GET HOME QUICKLY. MY CELL PHONE was out of power—not that it mattered. As I rode the Metro to my stop, I realized that Tom wasn't going to call. Not now. Not until the whole Naveen situation was settled. Or maybe, I thought—with a sudden lurch to my gut—he might never call again.

Last night I'd felt the weight of the world pressing me down. Now, as I walked to my apartment building, I realized I'd never felt so low.

Tonight was much worse. I couldn't even summon enough hope to wish on a star.

The last twenty steps to the building's bright front doors were up a gentle incline, but it took all my energy to climb it. As I reached out to grasp the front door handle, I heard footsteps behind me.

"Ollie."

I turned.

Tom crossed the driveway, closing the distance between us in ten steps. His face was set, his expression unreadable. "You got a few minutes?"

CHAPTER 15

WE PASSED THE FRONT DESK WITHOUT JAMES SAYING A WORD beyond, "Good evening." He raised his eyebrows and gave me a look that asked a thousand questions. All of which I chose to ignore.

Tom and I started into the elevator, but a woman who lived several floors above me called out for us to hold it. The twentysomething blond shot in as though finishing a run and stood in the small area's center, effectively keeping us silent for the entire ride up to my place. Tom looked good. So good. I was sure the blond had to notice him—who wouldn't?—even as she studied the rising floor numbers. Tom was strong and trim and the sight of him, so near—with the way the ends of his hair twisted this damp evening—took my breath away.

He wore a pair of pressed khakis and a dark polo shirt open at the collar. I caught a whiff of aftershave. That was a good sign. At least I hoped it was. He never wore any scent at work—only when we went out. He claimed he only ever wore it to impress me because I liked the smell so much.

Then again, he might have come to break up, officially, with a plan to spend the rest of the evening looking spiffy and gorgeous, and smelling great for some other woman. But he wasn't eyeing the blond's obvious attributes. He was staring at the numbers, too.

The elevator's climb to the thirteenth floor was agonizing.

"Excuse me," we said in tandem, when we finally arrived. Tom followed me down the carpeted hall, his soft footfalls reassuring and terrifying at the same time. I begged the fates not to let Mrs. Wentworth waylay us tonight as I fumbled to let us in. I couldn't get my hand to work right—couldn't get the key into the lock.

Tom said nothing.

I let him step past me when I finally got the door open. As I shut it behind us, I remembered Henry's admonishment to "sleep fast." Glanced at the hall clock. Almost nine. I had to be up again by two. But Tom's face made me realize some things were more important than sleep.

"We need to talk," he said.

We were both still standing in the tiny hallway. "Are you hungry?" I brushed past him and caught wind of the soft spicy aftershave again. My heart beat faster and I swore I could hear it banging inside my breastbone. I cleared my throat. "Want something to drink?"

I ducked into the kitchen, partly to open the fridge and pull out a beer for Tom, and partly because I couldn't look at him right now. I needed to compose myself before I spoke one word of apology. I'd had all day to think about what I'd say to him, but right now my head was in knots, not to mention my tongue. I wanted to tell him how sorry I was that I'd tried to meet Naveen, but the truth was, given the circumstances, I didn't see how I could have handled it differently.

I'd been frightened yesterday. More than ever before in my life. I'd seen death and I knew what he looked like. He was short and white-haired, with pale blue eyes. And his hands had been on me.

I stared at the bright inside of the refrigerator, not seeing anything. When I blew out a breath, it trembled through my chest. I don't know how long I stood there, cool air rushing at me, but Tom reached around and pushed the door shut.

"Ollie."

I finally looked up at him.

"You lied to me."

"I didn't."

He flexed his jaw. "You told me that you were not going to try to contact Naveen again."

"*He* called *me*." I splayed my fingers across my chest, my voice betraying my anxiety. "I told you that. I must have said that a hundred times already. I didn't try to contact him."

"Oh, come on." Tom's expression hardened. "Give me just a little credit. The only way he could have called you is if you called him first."

"But I didn't . . ."

"You told us. You told us right here," he said, jamming his finger toward the floor, "that you weren't going to pursue this. How long did you wait till Craig and I left before you tried calling Naveen again?"

"I didn't call him." Shaking my head, I tried to continue, my voice rising in frustration. "After you left, I stopped. I swear I did. Remember, we talked about it the next day?"

"Uh-huh." He was biting the insides of his cheeks. He only did that when he was really angry. "One problem with your story, Ollie. If you never called him, then how did he get your number?"

I shook my head again. "I don't know. I can't figure it out. I was going to ask him, but . . ."

Tom's gaze shifted to the room's near corner. "It doesn't add up."

"But . . . you and Craig found my number—because I called the D.C. Jail," I said, trying to make sense of it all. "Maybe he did the same thing."

He fired me a look of disdain. "Unlikely. And even if he did. Even if I give you that. Even if I believe you—and God, Ollie, I want to—why didn't you tell me you were going to meet him?"

"He asked me not to."

Tom stared.

My words sounded small, lame. "He said there was a leak. High up. That he couldn't trust anyone."

"And you believed that? You trusted him more than you trust me?"

"No, of course not."

He asked me again, his words coming out measured and crisp. "Then why didn't you tell me you were meeting him?"

I had no answer. Everything seemed so clear all of a sudden. He was right, I should have told him. My voice was low as I tried to explain. "I couldn't tell you. I promised you . . . and if I would've said anything, you wouldn't have let me go."

"Damn right I wouldn't have let you go," he shouted. "You could've been killed out there!"

"Shhh."

"I will not be quiet. Damn it, do you have any idea the danger you're in?"

With a suddenness that took my breath away, I understood. Tom was worried for me. "But I'm okay now," I said. "I didn't get hurt."

The look in his eyes told me I didn't comprehend.

"Not yet," he said, turning away.

"What do you mean?"

He blew out a breath and faced me. "Ollie, you are the only person we know who's still alive who can identify the Chameleon."

My knees went weak. "That's who killed Naveen?"

"Yeah." He nodded. "You came face to face with the world-class assassin. And he came face to face with you. We've done our best to keep your description and name out of the news media. Just like we did with Naveen." He closed his eyes. "For all the good that did him."

"Oh." I sat hard on one of my kitchen chairs, trying to process it all. Finally, I asked, "But . . . where were the guys?"

"What guys?"

"Secret Service. I thought you told me that you had him under surveillance."

"Yeah." Tom paced the small area. "Naveen lost them. He must have known he was being watched. He shook the tail."

"I was so afraid of any agents recognizing me that I was hoping he would lose them," I said. "Now I wish they'd have been there. They might've saved his life. Tom," I began, to stave off the storm brewing in his expression. "Listen—"

"No, you listen. For once, okay? Just once, you listen to me."

I tightened my lips.

"Yes, there's more, and you'll be hearing more about precautions we're taking. Yes, Little Miss Nosybody, Naveen gave us information. Good information. But he was supposed to get us more. He didn't. Because he was killed trying to meet you."

I opened my mouth to ask a question, but thought better of it.

"Could this new information be what Naveen wanted to tell you?" Tom asked rhetorically. "I don't know."

Of course it was, I thought. But Tom paced again, talking more to himself than he was to me. He rubbed his face with both hands.

"Is there anything I can do?" I asked.

"We know the Chameleon is planning something big. We don't know what it is."

I nodded.

"At this point, all we can do is be alert. Keep watch for anyone who fits his description." Tom heaved a deep sigh. "We'd like you to talk to a sketch artist."

"Sure," I said. "Of course."

"Good. I'll arrange for you to meet with him tomorrow. Right now you're our key witness. We need that sketch as soon as possible."

My heart sank again. Was that the only reason he came here tonight? To smooth things between us enough so that I'd cooperate?

"As soon as possible—just in case he gets me, huh?"

Tom flashed a look of such anger, I leaned back. "Do not ever say anything like that again, Ollie. Do you understand?"

"Yes," I answered. There wasn't anything else I could say.

"What's your day look like tomorrow?"

I gave him a quick rundown about the taste-testing and Laurel Anne's audition. He rubbed his face again. I began to realize just how much frustration I had caused.

"What time are you going in?"

"Three thirty."

Tom looked stricken—then glanced at his watch as he moved toward my front door. "Damn it, Ollie," he said. "You're not going to get any sleep tonight."

I gave a helpless shrug.

"Didn't I just tell you we all have to be alert?"

He moved for the door.

I stood up. "But—" I couldn't help myself. "What about us?"

I wished his expression would soften. I wished he would take me in his arms and tell me everything was going to be okay. Instead he shook his head. "I can't do this, Ollie."

"Can't do . . . what?" I asked in a small voice.

He took a long breath and flexed his jaw. "I think we should take a step back."

His words hit me like a gut-punch. I wanted to say something—anything—to make him change his mind, but no words came.

"I'm sorry," he said. "Maybe this was a bad idea."

"No," I said. "It's a good idea. *We're* a good idea. I blew it. It's my fault. I'm sorry."

A trace of affection flitted through his eyes. He tried to smile. "Maybe, when all this is over," he said, "we'll talk."

CHAPTER 16

THERE WAS NO GOOD REASON TO WHISPER, BUT HENRY AND I kept our voices low just the same. It was almost as though we had a tacit agreement to tiptoe around the kitchen, lest we disturb the fates and bring Peter Sargeant charging down upon us, to tell us what we were doing wrong.

Cyan and Marcel showed up shortly after we did. Bucky followed and didn't grouse, not even a bit, about the early start. We'd all been through enough state dinners before to know the drill. Having to produce an amazing and flawless dinner for over a hundred people, including two heads of state in addition to our own president, took enormous effort. The fact that we had to create this event in less than a week demanded nothing short of a miracle.

But then again, we worked miracles in this kitchen every day.

"As soon as we receive approval from all parties and a guest count," Henry said, "Cyan, you organize the stock we'll need—get in touch with some of the vendors today to put them on alert. Does that work for you?"

Without waiting for Cyan's nod, he turned to Marcel. "I'll need samplings of your desserts—taste is paramount today, designs later—by eight. Is that enough time?" We all knew Henry's questions were simple courtesy. Eight was the deadline. No negotiation there. "Once your creations are approved, be sure to coordinate with Cyan for whatever you need to order."

While Henry continued his orchestrations—with Bucky and with additional directives for Cyan—I watched him. He had a safe, straightforward manner that inspired confidence even while he encouraged us to perform Herculinary tasks. I wanted to cultivate that talent in myself, whether I took over as executive chef or not.

Bucky would contact our temporary help—state dinners required that we bring on additional staff—and we had a queue of folks who waited for "the call." This time the call would go out to several of our Muslim chefs as well. In order to keep halal, butchered meats must be prepared and transported according to rigid standards. We were prepared for this, and we had many reputable chefs willing to work at the White House on a moment's notice.

Depending on availability, most would be professionals we worked with before—others would be delighted to get their first shot at working in the White House. All of them had undergone rigorous background and health checks, coming to our attention via trusted sources. Temporary pay was nothing special, but working for the White House held great prestige. Every temp hoped that his or her performance would lead to a permanent job offer next time the White House kitchen had an opening.

I made a face. After all that had happened recently, it could be my job they'd be vying for.

"Ollie," Henry said, winding up, "you're with me. We've got less than three hours before Laurel Anne is due to arrive."

Bucky huffed. "It's ridiculous, having her audition today," he said. "She deserves her own day, when everyone's attention isn't pulled elsewhere."

I opened my mouth to argue that she'd had two prior opportunities for her "own day," and that she'd been the one to cancel those. But Tom's visit last night had knocked me for a loop. I didn't feel like arguing.

We made a good team, the five of us. Although Marcel, as the pastry chef, tended to work independently, we all worked to pull together everything we needed for the taste-test offerings later this morning. We would still need to cook many of the items on the spot because we wanted to serve them to the First Lady while they were fresh.

Laurel Anne had sent along her ideas for the day's meals, both for the First Family and for official events. She'd created two menus, and had originally wanted to bring her own ingredients, but we shot that idea down in a hurry. We used only approved vendors, and incoming meats, produce, and other fresh items were checked for palatability as well as for safety. In today's world, you never knew.

With that in mind, we'd set aside several locations for Laurel Anne. She had one shelf in both the walk-in refrigerator and the freezer for her requested items. She also had one station in the kitchen itself that we tried not to encroach on, even before her arrival.

"Knock, knock," came a voice from the hallway.

We turned to see Peter Everett Sargeant enter the kitchen, two men close behind. Sargeant looked like he just rolled out of bed. Although dressed impeccably, as always, his face still had a long sleep-crease down one side and his eyes were tiny. The men behind him, by contrast, appeared wide awake. The first one I recognized as the ambassador Henry and I had met last night, Labeeb bin-Saleh. He was again dressed in a dark suit and again wearing the bright turban. The other man, taller than bin-Saleh by a good four inches, wore flowing robes and walked with a slight limp. He, too, had a full beard, but wore his differently than his boss did. Bin-Saleh was natty in an exotic sort of way; this new fellow—who I assumed was the formerly ill assistant—was swarthy. He looked unhappy to be here.

He murmured something to bin-Saleh, who then murmured to Sargeant.

Before beginning introductions, Sargeant excused himself and escorted the assistant down the hallway. We could guess where they were going even before bin-Saleh apologized for the interruption. "My assistant, Kasim, is still recovering from our long journey."

"Welcome, again, to our kitchen," Henry said. I could tell he was thrown by this early morning visit. It wasn't yet five thirty. And we had a whole lot to do before Laurel Anne arrived. Still, he made introductions all around.

"I requested of Mr. Sargeant to allow us visiting you early," bin-Saleh explained. "We are remained on a different time and we find it most difficult to maintain to sleep at unwelcome hour."

"Of course," Henry said.

Sargeant and Kasim returned shortly, the taller man looking somewhat more relieved. Again, Henry made introductions and before Sargeant could correct him, he informed bin-Saleh and Kasim that I would be their primary contact with regard to dietary requirements.

The room went quiet. "I've studied the dossiers," I began. I smiled and enunciated clearly. I knew I had a tendency to talk too fast and I didn't want to confuse them if their command of English was limited. "It is my understanding that the princess is allergic to nuts, is that correct?"

I expected them both to nod. Instead, bin-Saleh turned to Kasim for explanation. Kasim translated—I supposed *allergic* and *nuts* weren't in bin-Saleh's English vocabulary yet. Kasim spoke at length, then turned to us, vehemently shaking his head. "Where did you get that erroneous information?" he asked in accented English. He wasn't angry. He seemed confused. "The requirements we sent ahead of time were quite clear. Our prince and his wife have preferences, and there are several dishes we prefer you avoid, but what you have suggested is incorrect."

I knew what I'd read in the dossier. There had to be some mistake. I opened my mouth to ask for clarification, but Sargeant's glare kept me silent, even as my face reddened. The three men continued to discuss the upcoming event and I followed along, still stung.

Kasim's syntax was perfect. For the first time I felt a shred of relief. Working with him would be a lot easier than working with Sargeant, or even with the ultrapolite though laconic bin-Saleh.

Henry and I exchanged a glance. It looked like the pine nut appetizer was back on the menu, but it bothered me that I'd gotten bad information. I'd have to look into that.

"We will provide you with menus for approval later today," I said to Kasim. "In the meantime, is there anything we can prepare for you now?"

He closed his eyes briefly and I realized that offering food to a man who was unwell was probably not the smartest thing I'd done today.

Bin-Saleh chimed. "We have taken much time of you here. Now we must return to the house of Blair. Thank you. We will return this afternoon to discuss the menus." He bent forward again and turned away.

They were only out the door for a half a minute when Sargeant returned, glaring at me. "What were you talking about?" he asked.

I had no idea what he meant.

"The prince's wife allergic to nuts? Where did you get that?"

"It was in the dossier," I said.

"You aren't in the habit of confirming information?"

I was. I always confirmed everything. In fact, I wanted to say, my bringing it up in conversation could be considered a confirmation of sorts. An attempt at confirmation, at least. "Yes, I am."

"Then think before you open your mouth in front of dignitaries again," he said. A little bubble of spit formed in the corner of his mouth. "Did you ever stop to consider that the prince might have more than one wife?"

I swallowed a retort. I hadn't considered that.

"I didn't think you had," he said.

My cheeks pulsed hot with racing blood. But Sargeant was gone and I was glad he couldn't see me.

The kitchen phone rang moments later. I picked it up. Just as Paul Vasquez informed me that the Secret Service was escorting Laurel Anne to the kitchen—more than an hour ahead of schedule, I heard her bright voice call out, "We're here!"

CHAPTER 17

LAUREL ANNE MADE A BEELINE FOR BUCKY. "I HOPE YOU DON'T mind our coming early," she said, flashing her camera-ready smile. "But I wanted to be sure we had plenty of time to set up." She spun to face a technician who tramped in behind her, carrying equipment. "Carmen," she ordered, pointing, "that's where I want to work from." Great. *My* favorite workstation. I wanted to protest, but I didn't know how. "I told you it was tight in here," she went on. "I wasn't exaggerating, was I?"

The dark fellow shook his head and claimed a spot, where he began to set up. "Got it." Three other assistants followed him into the kitchen, all bearing clunky machinery. Carmen ordered them into position with quick, terse commands. In the space of two seconds, the place went from tight to claustrophobic. And it smelled of sweaty men.

Laurel Anne spun again. "How are you, Bucky? I miss working with you."

Bucky looked like a fourteen-year-old waiting to be kissed by a supermodel. He opened his mouth to speak, but no words came out.

I wished I could say the same for Laurel Anne, but she whirled, yet again, and raked her nails down Henry's sleeve. How the heck she could maintain such nice nails in this business was beyond me. They weren't overly long, but they were shaped and even. I guessed that things were just different for people on camera every day.

"It's so nice to be back here, Henry. How have you been? I bet you can't wait for retirement, can you? This is such a demanding job."

Henry shrugged. "I find it exhilarating."

"Well, of course you do," she said, in the kind of voice I used when I cooed at puppies, "and that's why it's time to make room for the younger generation."

She scrunched up her face in what was supposed to be a smile as she tapped the left side of his chest. "We don't want to get too exhilarated these days, do we?"

Henry's face blushed bright red, but it wasn't from embarrassment. Anger sparkled brightly from his eyes, but he kept his mouth shut. Henry never took guff from anyone, and I didn't understand why he was doing so now, until I spied Carmen behind me, filming it all. His trio of assistants spilled around us, setting up a spotlight with white umbrella reflector, positioning a boom microphone, running extension cords, and setting up a second, stationary camera.

"Get in closer," Carmen said in a quiet voice.

Laurel Anne pulled Henry's arm around her, and she bussed his cheek with a quick kiss.

"Say your line again, sweetheart," Carmen urged.

"It's been too long, Henry." She directed her attention to the camera. "I'm so glad to be back here. It's just like coming home."

Carmen lowered himself to a crouch, filming from the low angle. He mouthed the words along with Laurel Anne as she spoke. I stepped out of the camera's view and watched his lips work and his brow furrow.

A half-beat later, Laurel Anne sighed dramatically for the camera. She tilted her head, and delivered the remainder of her introduction. "Henry, you taught me all I know about *Cooking for the Best*. How perfect it is that I'm back here today, at the White House, where it all began." She turned and kissed Henry's cheek again, then blinked four or five times. I swore it was to conjure up wet eyes for the film. "You will be missed."

"Hey," I said, striding into the scene. "He's not going anywhere yet."

"Cut." Carmen glowered at me, stood up. "Who are you?"

I ignored him and addressed Laurel Anne instead. "It's nice to see you again," I lied.

"Olivia." With the camera turned off, the smile turned off, too. "What are you doing here?" She glared at Carmen, who came to stand next to her. "I thought we agreed that she wasn't to be here today."

Carmen took me in with new eyes. Down to my shoes, up again to my face. Then he turned to Laurel Anne. "This is your competition?"

Okay, so I was at least six inches shorter than Laurel Anne and I didn't usually wear makeup to work—there were far too many times I needed to brush flour off my face—and my fingers were those of a worker, not of a television star. I'm sure I didn't look like much to Carmen, here.

"Olivia Paras," I said, grabbing Carmen's hand and shaking it. "Pleased to meet you."

I must have taken him by surprise—to be honest, I was taking myself by surprise with my forwardness—because Carmen was suddenly struck silent.

He finally turned to Laurel Anne. "It was my understanding—"

"Good morning," Paul Vasquez said, as he entered the kitchen. The smile in his words died almost immediately when he found himself navigating around the equipment to join our little tête-à-tête. "What's all this?"

Laurel Anne's beaming smile flicked back to its "on" position. "Paul will sort all this out," she said to Carmen, then twisted back. "Won't you, Paul?"

He shook his head. If I were to characterize his expression, I'd have to say he was befuddled. And Paul Vasquez was rarely befuddled. "When we agreed to your filming here today, we also agreed that you were only to bring one cameraman."

Carmen said, "Well . . . yeah," stringing the word out. A fireplug of a guy, he placed his hands at his hips and addressed Paul. "One cameraman," he said indicating a tall fellow leaning on the counter near the door. "Jake."

"Then the rest of you need to get out of here. I'll arrange for an escort."

Thank God. There wasn't a day that went by that I wasn't delighted to have Paul as our chief usher.

"Uh-uh." Carmen punctuated his response with a shake of his head.

"Excuse me?" Paul said.

"You specified one cameraman. We agreed. One cameraman needs one sound man"—he pointed to a young guy near the boom—"Sid. One tech." He pointed to the last of the three. "Armand. And one director." His fingers splayed across his chest. "Me."

Paul's lips tightened and he rubbed his eyebrows with the fingers of his left hand. "You've got two cameras."

Carmen acknowledged his observation with a nod. "As director, it is my prerogative to capture my own view. I need the freedom a handheld camera provides. Your cramped conditions here," he gazed around the small area, grimacing, "require that we keep our main camera stationary. That's hardly conducive to creativity."

"Boss?" Jake the cameraman said. "Should I be filming this?"

"Yes, yes," Carmen said, throwing his arms out flamboyantly. "It's all flavor, and flavor is what we are all about, aren't we, Laurel Anne?"

If it were possible, she beamed even brighter.

Of course she did. The camera was back on.

Paul cocked an eyebrow and took a long look around the room.

I couldn't read him, but I could tell he was taking the whole enchilada into consideration. He always did.

"Three things," he said, finally, "and there will be no argument." He ticked off his fingers as he spoke. "One—Henry and Ollie's first priority today is to the First Lady's taste-testing for the upcoming state dinner. Cyan and Bucky can assist Laurel Anne. Ollie will join them once the taste-testing is complete."

Laurel Anne's pretty face fell. She shot me one of the nastiest looks I've ever received, her vehemence taking me aback. I felt myself blanch. Great, I thought. Jake over there caught my shocked expression on tape.

"Two—I will allow this . . . this . . ." Paul looked as flustered as I'd ever seen him, "intrusion," he said with emphasis, "only if the White House is provided a complete and uncut tape of the day's activities."

"No problem, man," Carmen said.

"Lastly—I get final say on what, if anything, from today's activities—is used for broadcast."

"No can do." Carmen shook his head. "As director, I get final say on what stays and what's cut. We worked all this out with Peter Sargeant already."

"Peter Sargeant does not have the authority to grant such requests," Paul said, his teeth tight.

Carmen raised a big hand over his head, as though to dispel further argument. "This is a creative endeavor. We let 'the man' in on our decisions and we lose the beauty. The flavor. It's all about the flavor."

Paul nodded, pensive. I held my breath.

"Laurel Anne," he said, "welcome back. Today the kitchen is yours." To Carmen, he said, "I will personally escort you—and your associates—out."

"But," Laurel Anne sputtered, "we have to film this." She shot frantic glances to Carmen, whose large eyes had gone wide. "We're going to broadcast this as my final episode of *Cooking for the Best* when I get the executive chef position here."

Henry cleared his throat. "*If* you get the position here."

At that, Laurel Anne almost lost it right in front of all of us. I held my breath as she worked her face back into a careful smile and rolled her eyes. "Of course. That's what I meant. *If* I get the position." With a quick tilt to her head, she faced me. "I'm up against a truly worthy opponent."

I bit my lip, hard, and forced a smile of my own. I wanted to retort, but no matter how I worded it, it could come out badly.

"Can't we please keep filming?" she asked Paul. "Carmen, I know Paul understands how important the creative process is. I'm sure he's just concerned about security. We can compromise on this one, can't we?"

Faced with his pleading starlet and an impending toss out the door, Carmen relented. "Sure, sure. You're the boss, man," he said, clapping Paul on the back.

Ooh. Huge breach of protocol.

Paul was, above all, a diplomat. "Well then," he said, clapping his hands together, "we're agreed." He gave the room another long look, and something behind his eyes made me sad. He didn't like this setup any more than I did, and yet his hands were virtually tied. I knew that he had to juggle Peter Sargeant's newness on the job, while keeping in mind that Laurel Anne and the First Lady shared the bond of having the same home state. He couldn't afford to offend any one of these people, and I knew he wouldn't. The sadness, I believed, was directed toward me and to Henry. He knew that if there was any fallout, Henry and I would be catching the brunt of it.

"One more thing," he said. "I need Ollie."

Carmen raised a dark eyebrow.

"Now?" I asked.

Paul nodded, turned, and strode out the door. I followed.

CHAPTER 18

"DON'T BE ALARMED," PAUL SAID AS WE MADE OUR WAY TO HIS office. "We just don't want to get into specifics in front of visitors."

I walked double-time to keep up with him, but I couldn't figure out how not to be alarmed. I'd been in way over my head these past several days. I'd been called in, talked to, scolded, reminded of being scolded, terrified, and virtually shut out by my boyfriend.

"Is it about the taste-testing?" I asked. I knew my tone was hopeful, but I couldn't help it. "Do we really need to clear menus through Peter Sargeant first?"

He hesitated. "It's not that the First Lady needs an additional taste-tester," he began. "As we all know, Mrs. Campbell has strong opinions on the subject of meal planning."

That was an understatement. Mrs. Campbell had trained in culinary school herself—the same school where Laurel Anne had apprenticed, of course—and the First Lady often suggested changes. To be honest, some of them were very good ideas. And the ones that were not, she was gracious enough not to argue. Mrs. Campbell, while strong-minded, was not difficult to work with.

I waited for him to continue.

"Sargeant was brought on board to keep a close eye on the White House where matters of political correctness are concerned." As we walked, Paul made a sort of so-so motion with his head. "The president's platform of unity means that he wants us to be attuned to the needs of everyone, regardless of race, creed, gender, sexual orientation, etcetera. Peter Sargeant's job is a lot less structured than most around here. He's to ingratiate himself into all White House areas to be our last line of defense. So that no one makes a mistake that costs us dearly in the press."

I nodded.

Paul turned apologetic. "He's keeping an eye on the menus to determine if anything being served could somehow offend a guest. Or put a guest off in some way. If a country has an embargo against a product from another country, we surely don't want to serve it at an official dinner, do we?"

I shook my head.

We turned the corner. "So, no," he said, finally answering my original question, "this isn't about the taste-testing."

I was about to ask what it was about, when I noticed a lanky young man in Paul's office. He stood.

"Olivia Paras," Paul said, "this is Darren Sorrell. He's a police sketch artist here to help put together a picture of the man you . . . saw . . . the other day."

The man I saw the other day. Of course I knew who he meant. I wondered if the vague wording was for Darren's benefit, or for that of the other folks in the office area who might not yet have heard about the skirmish at the merry-go-round. Though how anyone didn't know by now was beyond me.

"Sure," I said. I didn't know how much good this would do, and I worried about Henry getting things ready for Sargeant by himself. Without thinking, I glanced at my watch.

"This shouldn't take too long," Darren said. And then to Paul, "Is there someplace we can go where it's quiet?"

Twenty minutes later, the amazingly speedy Darren had produced, on his laptop, a likeness of the murderous blond man that matched my recollection. As he'd zipped me through choices of eyes, noses, and face shapes, I doubted my accuracy. Did I really remember, or did I think I remembered? "See him in your mind, Ollie," he coached. "Now tell me: Were his ears more like this," click-click, "or like these?"

Even now, barely two days since the altercation, I couldn't swear that this was what the man truly looked like. Darren printed out a copy of the finished product. I stared at it. It looked like the man I remembered, but had I remembered correctly? In all the excitement, had I really noticed all these details, or was my imagination filling in what I couldn't recall?

"You can keep that one."

I shot Darren a look. Why would I want it?

As if he'd read my mind, he continued. "Copies will be distributed to everyone on staff. The Secret Service and the Metropolitan Police are working together to keep this man from breaching security."

I studied the bland features. Even though the pale eyes that stared back at me were rendered in black and white, I could see their color in my mind's eye. That was probably the only feature I'd been confident about. I understood how this assassin could make himself invisible. He blended. He had no distinguishing facial characteristics. Aside from the fact that he was short in stature, he was blah. A combination of shapeless and personalityless features.

I sighed. "I don't know what good this will do."

Darren packed up his laptop. "Sometimes all we can do is our best, and we have to hope that's good enough."

I FOLDED THE PORTRAIT IN QUARTERS, TUCKED IT INTO THE pocket of my apron and headed back to the kitchen where Carmen was doing *his* best to soothe Laurel Anne's obvious distress. He stepped in front of her, begging her to be reasonable.

"I will not settle down. Not when my reputation is on the line." With her fists jammed into her pale pink apron, she glowered at Cyan. "You call yourself a chef and you don't know the difference between fresh and frozen?"

"Of course I do," Cyan answered, with an insolent lift to her chin. "I ordered fresh asparagus for today's delivery." She held the printout of Laurel Anne's e-mail request in her hand. Now, she pointed. "Right here. Asparagus. Five pounds."

Laurel Anne whipped the page out of Cyan's hand. "I wanted frozen."

"Frozen?"

I don't know who said it. Maybe we all did. Frozen? We rarely used frozen produce, and the word stopped us all in our tracks.

"Yes, frozen. I find it much easier to work with for this particular dish."

Cyan aghast, caught sight of me in the doorway, and shrugged.

"Where's Henry?" I asked.

Carmen shook his big head. "You're supposed to join him in the lower kitchen. Bucky is down there, now. Go on, we're handling this."

I ignored him. "Let me see the list."

Laurel Anne didn't want to relinquish the note, but as I stood there, hand extended, waiting, her good manners apparently won out.

Before Cyan had ordered anything, she and I had gone over the list together. If she'd ordered incorrectly, it was as much my fault as it was hers. "This does not specify frozen asparagus," I began.

"Well, it should have." Laurel Anne's face took on a look so heated it could have defrosted the asparagus, had the frozen stuff been here. She whisked the sheet out of my hand and stormed away, studying it. "Let's see what other screwups I have to deal with today."

Carmen trotted after her. "Sweetheart, I'll send Armand out for frozen. We got ya covered, baby. Don't sweat the small stuff."

"It's not that easy," I said.

He spun. Glared at me.

"We have certain vendors we work with," I explained. "We have specific protocols we have to follow. There is no compromise on that. Laurel Anne knows it."

Laurel Anne had taken a position ten steps away, perching her butt against the counter as she studied her list. Carmen kept his back to her and his voice low. "I'm not about to tell her she can't get her frozen asparagus," he said, holding both hands up.

I sighed again, worried that Henry needed me. I knew I should leave Laurel Anne to deal with this situation herself, but I couldn't allow the kitchen to continue in crisis. "Let me see what we can do, okay?"

Carmen gave an abbreviated nod and went to powwow with his team members, who were still exactly where they'd been when I left.

"Listen, Laurel Anne," I said, "I've got some pull with the vendors. Let me know what else you need and I'll see that it gets here fast. Okay?"

"Puh-lease," she said, dragging her eyes from the list. "Like *you're* going to help *me*." She laughed, but it came out more like a bark than an expression of amusement. "I'd rather use the damn fresh asparagus than have you in charge of getting me what I need. That'd give you the opportunity you need to sabotage my chances. You'd like that, wouldn't you?"

"No," I said, although right now I couldn't imagine anyone less deserving to take control of the White House kitchen than Laurel Anne. But sabotage? "No," I said again. "I would never do anything to hurt your chances."

She rolled her eyes, snapped her fingers at Cyan. "You," she said, pointing. "I'm sure you have just as much pull with the vendors as"—a venomous glance at me—"she does. Get on the phone and get the asparagus here by nine thirty."

Cyan looked to me for guidance, but Laurel Anne wasn't done. She turned to me. "You're supposed to be downstairs with Henry, aren't you? Send Bucky up when you get there."

I went.

* * *

DOWN IN THE LOWER KITCHEN, BUCKY AND HENRY WERE PUT-
ting the finishing touches on a sample I didn't recognize.

"What is it?" I asked, leaning closer to take a whiff. It smelled wonderful—
warm and garlicky.

Bucky grinned. "My latest creation. Brussels sprouts stuffed with goat
cheese, dill, walnuts, and garlic."

He offered me a sample, which I took, tasted, and pronounced fabulous.

"It is, isn't it?" he said, with contagious confidence.

Henry joined in the admiration. I reminded Bucky about Laurel Anne's
audition upstairs. "I hate to see you stop while you and Henry are really cookin'
here, but . . ."

Bucky, still reveling in his success, gave us both a wry smile as he took his
leave. "You'll include me when you present this to the First Lady?"

"Of course," Henry boomed. "You've contributed a new taste sensation.
You're in this now as much as we are."

The small room practically glowed with our combined good cheer.

Finally. Something had gone well.

When Bucky left, Henry asked me how things were going in the main
kitchen.

I told him.

His sigh spoke volumes. Rather than dwell on the negative, however, Henry
stole a look at the clock before reminding me: "Time's precious. Especially
today. Ollie, our First Lady awaits. Let us not disappoint her."

We got to work.

AT EIGHT TWENTY, WE WERE READY. THERE WERE TWO SIDE DISHES
in the oven just about ready to be pulled out—one of them was Bucky's Brussels Sprouts Extravaganza. Several ingredients for other dishes warmed on the
stove, others cooled in the refrigerator. We would put them together to create
appetizers, entrées, sides, and garnishes when the First Lady was ready to start
tasting. Three of our butlers stood nearby, prepared to serve the food once it
was plated.

Marcel e-mailed from upstairs to let us know that he, too, was prepared with three sample desserts for Mrs. Campbell's assessment. We waited for Sargeant's call, eager to get started.

He showed up at the lower kitchen's door at eight thirty on the nose. "Are we ready?" he asked.

"Absolutely," I said. I headed to the refrigerator for the salads.

Sargeant addressed the maître d', a handsome man named Jamal Walker. "You will serve in the library today."

What?

"The library?" Henry asked. "But the First Lady usually takes her taste tests—"

Sargeant silenced him with a glare. "Mrs. Campbell prefers the library today." His nose twisted as though it was unpleasant to have to explain. "We will conduct all taste tests there."

Jamal turned to Henry, who shrugged. "So be it," Henry said. "I've always liked the library."

"You do remember that you'll be preparing two portions of each course?" Sargeant asked. "I'm sampling, as well."

I forced a pleasant expression. "How could we forget?"

Within minutes, Henry and I had plated and garnished seven appetizers, two salads, and three soups. Of necessity, the portions were small, but the preparation still took time. We planned to return to the kitchen for the entrée courses when the first round of testing was nearly complete.

As we started out the lower kitchen's door, Sargeant stopped us, with an "Ah-ah-ah." Apparently his favorite refrain.

Henry and I waited for explanation.

"You are not to accompany me."

"What?" we said in unison.

We were *always* present at taste-testings. It was how we gauged the First Lady's opinion, how we knew what worked and to what extent it succeeded. Or failed. Getting Mrs. Campbell's opinion firsthand was invaluable in preparing future menus.

"Another change," Sargeant said with a prim shake of his head. "There is no need to clutter up the library with two chefs and three butlers."

I started to protest. Little did Sargeant know that Bucky planned to join us, which made three chefs. Even so, the butlers would be in and out, serving, not participating in the discussion. The sizable library would hardly be considered crowded.

Henry had finally hit his breaking point. "Is this your decision, or the First Lady's?"

"I don't see how that makes any—"

"Whose decision?"

Sargeant straightened. "My decision, and I stand by it."

Henry folded his arms. "No. I refuse."

Sargeant looked at him with something akin to shock. "But," he said, clearly thrown, "with the tables I've had set up in there . . . there just isn't enough room . . . Perhaps, I suppose, there would be enough room for you, Henry, but two are too many."

"Fine," Henry said, "a compromise then." He turned to me. "Ollie, will you conduct the taste-testing with the First Lady, please? I will remain here and prepare the entrées and sides." To Sargeant, he raised eyebrows and added, "Bucky will join Ollie for a portion of the taste-testing as well. Will that arrangement be suitable?"

He didn't wait for Sargeant's answer.

"Get going," Henry said to me.

I caught the sparkle in his eyes, even as fast panic rushed up my chest. I'd never conducted a taste test on my own. I'd done it plenty of times with Henry, but never had I sat in the position of executive chef for this important duty. I knew I could do it, and do it well, but high stakes—not to mention marinated steaks—were on the line.

I was thrilled.

I wished I could call Tom.

MRS. CAMPBELL STOOD WHEN WE WALKED INTO THE ROOM, WELcoming our little entourage. I almost felt like Laurel Anne but with butlers instead of cameramen to assist me. The thought made me grin. Mrs. Campbell caught my expression and smiled back.

"Let me begin by apologizing for the minimal forewarning you were given on this state dinner," she said. Her crisp apricot skirt-suit and pale print scarf at the neck complemented her trim frame. Gently coiffed dark hair. With hands clasped in front of her, and deep smile lines at her eyes and mouth, she looked more like a kindly librarian than the First Lady of the United States of America.

Sargeant made an exaggerated show of directing the waitstaff, even though

we'd all been through this procedure before and he hadn't. "No apology necessary," he said. He would have continued talking, but Mrs. Campbell interrupted.

"No," she said softly. "I am apologizing." She had one of those voices that
made people lean in to hear. Though born and bred in Idaho, her accent made
it clear that she'd spent many years in the Deep South of her husband's home.
Turning to me, she continued. "You and Henry have worked miracles in the
past. I know how much effort is required to come up with a creative menu. For
you to do it on such short notice is remarkable. I thank you for your patience
and your considerable effort."

"My pleasure." I was just a little bit flustered by her speech, but she wasn't
finished.

"My husband has a unique opportunity to bring two opposing nations to
the same table. It is up to us." She glanced about the room. "It is up to each and
every one of us to give this initiative the very best chance of success."

With that, she reclaimed her seat.

Showtime.

"I will be conducting today's taste test," I began, gesturing the first butler
forward. Mrs. Campbell seemed unsurprised by Henry's absence. "We've prepared two portions of each item."

Now she looked perplexed. "Two?"

Sargeant took a chair next to her. "I'm sampling as well."

She glanced at me. I kept my expression neutral. This was not the time
nor the place to air dirty laundry. Her face tightened, almost imperceptibly. A
beat later, she smiled. "Well, then, Mr. Sargeant, you and I are the lucky ones,
aren't we?"

He sniffed, looking over the first item the butler placed before them. "Yes,"
he said slowly. His expression said, "That remains to be seen."

I took a seat nearby, pulled out my notebook and pen and paid attention.

Four samples later, Mrs. Campbell had pronounced all but one extraordi-
nary. Sargeant had eliminated two, grudgingly complimented the others. He
claimed the first to be too bland, the third to have too strong of a garlic flavor.

I nodded for Jamal's first butler to serve number five. This next one was an
appetizer that included chocolate liquor as an ingredient. I expected commentary as soon as the First Lady and Sargeant read the ingredients list and I was
not disappointed.

"Can't serve this," Sargeant said, pushing the plate aside.

I knew what was coming.

Mrs. Campbell had already raised a forkful to her mouth and seemed to be enjoying the appetizer. "This is wonderful, Ollie." To Sargeant, she said, "You haven't even tried it."

He snapped a finger at the provided list. "Chocolate liquor." He shook his head, staring at me. "You should have done your homework. Muslims are not allowed any liquor of any kind."

"I did do my homework," I said quietly. Maybe if I spoke like Mrs. Campbell did, people would lean forward to hear me, too. "Chocolate liquor has no alcohol. It is considered halal by Muslims—which means that it's approved for consumption."

"I know what halal means," he said.

"You may be thinking of chocolate liqueur." I spelled the two words for him, emphasizing the difference. Mrs. Campbell was paying close attention to our interchange so I made sure to keep my voice upbeat—helpful. "That would be considered haram. And not allowed."

"I still think—"

The First Lady interrupted in her understated way. "Ollie, you are quite certain that all the ingredients in this appetizer are suitable for our guests?"

"I'm certain that all the ingredients in *all* our selections are suitable."

She graced me with a smile. "Well then, Mr. Sargeant. I would hate to pass up serving this delightful dish over a simple misunderstanding. Ms. Paras has made it clear that we will be quite safe serving this. Additionally, our guests' chefs will go over our choices and note any inadequacies based on their requirements. Now, why don't you take a taste and rate it on your sheet before we move forward? I'm sure you'll adore it as much as I do."

Sargeant looked ready to spit a mouthful of appetizer at my head. "You've kept detailed instructions on how to prepare each of these items on file, have you not?"

I nodded. "Yes."

"They've been added to the recipe system? All of them?"

"Yes. We've made that our standard procedure."

"Good." He took a moment to scribble a note on his taste-testing evaluation sheet. "I'm concerned. If Laurel Anne Braun takes over the kitchen sooner than expected, she'll need to access these files. I don't want any mishaps."

The First Lady's brow furrowed. "Mr. Sargeant, I have not yet made my decision regarding the appointment of the executive chef."

"Yes, of course," he said. "My mistake."

* * *

BUCKY ACCOMPANIED THE WAITSTAFF AS THEY WHEELED IN THE cart laden with our entrées and side selections. Sargeant's mouth tightened when Bucky sidled next to me. The moment the butlers stepped back, I stood up and began.

"The first accompaniment we have for you today is an invention from our assistant chef, Buckminster Reed."

The First Lady glanced over at Bucky, who beamed.

I took my seat.

As Mrs. Campbell and Sargeant started in on the first main course and the Brussels Sprouts Extravaganza, Bucky's foot shook with the rhythm of nervousness. We had a cloth-covered table before us; no one could see the furious movement except for me.

I watched the First Lady's reaction. I watched Sargeant's. Bucky bit his lip.

Mrs. Campbell seemed about to speak, when Sargeant interrupted. "The flavor is . . . good," he began. "But why on earth did you choose Brussels sprouts? Now that I'm overseeing the kitchen staff I've taken it upon myself to do some research on food, and Brussels sprouts are one of the most hated vegetables. In fact, I believe it's the number-one most hated vegetable in the nation—of all time." He gave a tiny head shake, his mouth pursed. "Yes, I do believe that's a fact."

Bucky's mouth gaped. He looked to me.

I might not like my colleague overmuch, but if I were ever to take the position of executive chef, I'd have to learn to stand up for my people.

I stood. "Mr. Sargeant, if you and Mrs. Campbell don't like the taste, the appearance, or the presentation of that particular dish, we have several other choices for you to sample."

Sargeant scratched his pen across his notepad, not looking up. "Good."

I wasn't done. "But, I suggest not dismissing this item just because of Brussels sprouts' reputation. As you tasted yourself, this is an excellent side dish. We would never serve anything we believe our guests would hate." I worked a smile, glanced over at the First Lady, whose expression was unreadable. "What do you think?" I asked.

She put down her fork. "I think the combination of dill and walnut with the goat cheese is unusual and quite wonderful. I would be proud to serve this to my guests."

I could almost hear Bucky's exhalation of relief.

"But," she continued, "I have not done the research that Mr. Sargeant apparently has taken upon himself to do. This upcoming state dinner is, perhaps, the most important one my husband will ever host. I'm afraid that, for this event at least, I must rely on Mr. Sargeant's expertise."

Expertise? The man had no expertise. He was a protocol guru and knew nothing about food preparation. He probably went online to look up the top-ten most-hated vegetables and used the tidbit he found there to position himself as an authority. I'd read the Brussels sprout report myself, when it came out. In my humble opinion, Sargeant was skewing the results. Something had to be the "most-hated"—that's what happens whenever there's a poll. But just because folks were judging based on the boiled, bitter, tight-packaged greens their mothers served them as kids, didn't mean that these tender, garlicky offerings from Bucky should be dismissed out of hand.

My mind raced. I didn't know how to react without my words being seen as a confrontation to the First Lady's decision—one with which I most heartily disagreed. A quick glance at Bucky confirmed he was deflated, angry, embarrassed.

What would Henry do?

I said, "The official dinner scheduled for August has a cauliflower side dish on the menu. Would you consider allowing us to replace it with Bucky's Brussels sprouts creation?"

Sargeant began to shake his head, but this time Mrs. Campbell interrupted.

"What a clever suggestion, Olivia. Yes, I believe that would be an excellent change. Thank you."

CHAPTER 19

BACK IN THE KITCHEN, CYAN'S HAND SLIPPED. A CABINET DOOR slammed shut with a bang.

"Cut!" Carmen yelled, and lowered his camera.

The crew relaxed.

Laurel Anne's million-dollar smile dropped like rotten tomatoes on hot cement.

Jamming his free fist against his hipbone, Carmen advanced on Cyan. "What the hell is wrong with you? I told you all—no unexpected noises." He turned to face the rest of us. "Control, people. We gotta maintain control." He wagged his wide head, the mop of black draping over the front of his face when he finished shaking. "I need a goddamn cigarette," he said, and stormed out the kitchen doorway.

I hoped he knew there was limited smoking on the White House grounds. And that he'd have to be escorted to the designated smoking area and escorted back. Each administration set its own policy regarding tobacco. President Campbell occasionally perched an unlit cigar in his mouth, but I'd never seen him smoke one here, or anywhere. Why the news media folks cared one way or another was beyond me. But these days, every tiny tidbit of a politician's life was fodder for commentary.

Carmen's departure notwithstanding, Jake continued to film.

Laurel Anne paced the small kitchen. Fury emanated from her like heat from a banana flambé. "I can't believe I'm doing this," she said. Grease splatters covered her pink apron. It was her third one, at least—she might've changed aprons again while I'd been out of the room. "They wouldn't let me bring in a wardrobe or makeup person, can you believe it?" she asked rhetorically.

I returned my attention to the computer to finish recording the results of our taste-testing. Henry stood over my shoulder as I noted which items had been approved, which rejected, and why. We had a comprehensive list of possibilities out there. Some we'd try again someday, others we knew better. But we kept them on file, just the same, for reference. No such thing as too much information where individuals' tastes were concerned.

Despite Sargeant's dark cloud of input, and Bucky's disappointment, I considered the taste test a success. We had the equivalent of three complete menus to submit to our guests' dietary consultants for final approval.

I typed while eavesdropping on Bucky's conversation with Henry. Poor Bucky. He chopped artichoke hearts even as he dissed Peter Sargeant. "Good thing I'm not an alcoholic," he said in a low voice. "I'd be tempted to break into the cooking sherry today."

"Will you be done soon?" Laurel Anne asked.

She repeated herself twice before I realized she was talking to me.

"I'm finished right . . ." I hit "Save" and "Exit" as I spoke. ". . . now."

"It's about time. Not only do I have to work with half a staff," she flung an arm toward the other end of the kitchen, "but I'm stuck trying to impress the First Family on a day when the president's wife is probably stuffed from your taste-testing."

She had a point. A good one. I'd questioned Sargeant's wisdom on the timing of this audition, but he'd made it clear that I just couldn't see "the big picture."

And as much as I didn't care for Laurel Anne personally, I could empathize with her plight. I wouldn't want to be auditioning today, either. At this point, however, there wasn't much to be done. I attempted to soft-pedal. "Mrs. Campbell didn't eat much," I said. "I'm sure the little bit she sampled this morning—"

Laurel Anne plunked her hands on the countertop and spoke through her teeth. "Listen, I don't need you to tell me what to do. What I need are bodies. I've been short-handed since early morning. I'll never make the lunch and dinner deadlines unless you get off that damn computer and start helping get things done."

I bit the insides of my cheeks to keep from lashing back. Next to me, Henry made an unintelligible noise, then brought his lips close to the back of my head. "It's her kitchen today, Ollie."

A reminder to go with the flow, which I knew all too well—even if Henry hadn't prompted me. Difficult as it was to take with a smile, I wasn't about to complain. But taking the high road didn't make Laurel Anne any easier to deal with.

She wiggled her fingers and turned. I followed.

As far as I could tell, Laurel Anne had done nothing in the past hour. Nothing of substance, in fact, since she'd arrived.

I stole a glance at Marcel. His head tilted, his aristocratic nose wrinkled, he studied a set of directions Laurel Anne had provided him. When left to his own devices, he was brilliant—unstoppable. I knew Marcel well enough to recognize that his expression, his stance, and his pursed lips were precursors to a major eruption.

Cyan chopped lettuce. Bucky still had a pile of artichokes to work through. Henry was stuck boning fish, the worst job of all.

Or so I thought, until Laurel Anne gave me my assignment. She stopped at the wide, piled-high-with-detritus sink, pivoted, and smiled. "Here's your station."

"Clean up?" I said, "But . . ."

She silenced me with a look, then leaned close so only I could hear.

"I'm not stupid," she said in a minty-breath hiss. "I'm not letting you *any-where* near the food." Righting herself, she spoke louder then, so that everyone understood. "If we keep one person dedicated to sink duty, we'll be that much more efficient."

No one grumbled, but I caught pity in my colleagues' eyes. I knew why. This wasn't just scut work: This was Laurel Anne sending me a clear message.

Carmen returned, looking no more relaxed from his cigarette break than he had before he left. Laurel Anne scurried over to talk with him.

I stared at the sink. Long-dissipated suds gave way to floaters—pieces of lettuce, onion, chicken, fish, grease. I plunged my hands into the tepid brew and fought the heaviness in my heart as I faced reality. Cooking for the White House had been my dream. A dream I'd achieved through hard work and determination. I loved it here. But Laurel Anne's shrill directives sounded my wake-up alarm. This dream was about to end.

I pulled the drain open, sighed, and took a moment to stare over my shoulder, watching Laurel Anne direct Carmen, who then directed everyone else. If this was how she behaved when the camera was running, I shuddered to think what this kitchen would be like when she thought no one was watching.

Water swirled around my submerged hands—a descending vortex of spinning waste—and I thought about my ultimate goal to become the executive chef at the White House. My chances of achieving the position were about the same as any of these churning foodstuffs showing up on the president's plate tonight. Worse, when Laurel Anne got the nod—and we all knew she would—I'd have to find a new home.

"Sorry," Cyan whispered, dropping off her cutting board and knife sink-side. "She wouldn't let us keep the mess under control. Said to leave it. I didn't know she meant it for you to clean up."

"No problem."

Cyan gave me a wry smile and started on her next task.

The five of us had always maintained a clean-up-as-you-go mentality. We handled our messes individually. There were waitstaff folks we could press into service when necessary, but we kept their participation to a minimum because of space issues. We just didn't have the room for extra people in this kitchen, so we made do ourselves as much as possible.

I pulled bowls, utensils, and hollowware from the drained basin, metal scraping against sink's stainless steel sides, clattering when a fork took a nose-dive from my fingers.

"Keep it down," Carmen shouted.

I twisted long enough to meet his glare. He must have read the expression on my face because his hands came up in a placating gesture. "I know I haven't called 'Action' yet, but quiet is a good habit to cultivate." The corners of his mouth curled up grotesquely. I guess it was supposed to be a smile.

I turned my back on him, rearranging the crusted baking pans as silently as I could, filling them with hot sudsy water and letting them soak while I attacked the remaining stack of dirties. Before I could wash, however, I needed to remove all the floppy, wet food lumped at the bottom drain.

Just as I plopped stringy chicken fat into my left palm and reached for a fish part with my right, Cyan was back.

"Ollie," she said, but this time her whisper held a note of urgency, "what does she mean by 'sauté over quince'?" She twisted around to ensure that Laurel Anne wasn't watching, as she pointed to the back side of a pale pink, plastic-encased index card.

I read the loopy script twice—why Laurel Anne handwrote her directions rather than printing them out was anyone's guess—but I still couldn't decide what was meant by sautéing over quince. "What are you making?" I asked, just as quietly.

Cyan flipped the card and I scanned the recipe.

"People!"

Carmen clapped for our attention.

We turned. I gave Cyan a little shove, propelling her toward her station with the hushed reassurance that I'd figure things out. Her grateful smile worried me. I had no idea what Laurel Anne wanted with the butter, onion, egg, artichoke, grape, and quince concoction she'd assigned to Cyan.

The area was small, but Carmen raised his voice anyway. We all stopped moving. "Everyone has a job, yes?"

We nodded.

"Wonderful," he said. He stroked Laurel Anne's left arm like one would a very tall dog. "You all keep doing your . . . thing, whatever it is. As we film, our star here will walk among you. What I want you each to do is to greet her with a smile, *but don't stop what you're doing.* She'll reach in, make some adjustment, and then you smile at her again, say 'Thank you,' and you're done. Got it?"

Marcel stepped forward, wagging an index finger. "No, no, no." In his other hand, he carried a pink note card. He slapped it onto the countertop next to Carmen. "I 'ave been very agreeable to your demands zis morning. But I do not allow the executive chef to dictate my methods." He cast a pointed glance at Laurel Anne. "And neither will I allow *her* to tell me how to prepare my masterpiece. I can not—how you say—compromise my integrity by preparing this . . . this . . . *ordures.*"

Carmen turned to Laurel Anne, who shrugged. The rest of us waited, wide-eyed. So Marcel wasn't the only one who considered today's menu garbage. I just hadn't realized how worked up he'd become.

Carmen tried to placate our pastry chef. "Let's take a look at what Laurel Anne assigned to you," he said. "I'm sure we can work things out."

"No!" Marcel said, thrusting his shoulders back. He jammed a finger against the small pink note. "Do you see what she has given me for direction? *Sacre bleu!* I will not accept assignment from one so clearly untrained."

"Untrained?" Laurel Anne asked, giving an angry wiggle. "Before I went to Media Chefs International I attended the prestigious California Culinary Academy, where I worked my butt off."

With a comedian's perfect timing, Marcel twisted his head, made a show of inspecting Laurel Anne's backside, and said, very clearly, "I think not."

She stamped her foot. Literally. "How dare you!"

Cyan giggled. My hand flew to my mouth.

I knew I shouldn't laugh, and I was about to suggest we all take a moment to settle down when Henry pushed his way into the little group, forcing all parties to take a step back. "Marcel is correct," he began. "I do not control his portion of the meal. We do, however, *confer*."

I knew Henry well enough to understand that his emphasis on the word *confer* was meant to impress upon Laurel Anne the importance of teamwork.

The subtlety was lost on her. Lost on Carmen, too. The two began arguing that the success of the final broadcast of *Cooking for the Best* required they take a little liberty with procedure.

As Henry strove for compromise and Marcel strove for calm, it became clear to me that Laurel Anne and Carmen were unwilling to budge on anything.

Bucky joined their little group but didn't say a word. I got the impression he wasn't quite sure whose side to take this time.

While they "conferred," I dried my hands and studied the recipe Cyan had given me. She tiptoed over. "I can't make sense of that," she said, with a cautious glance at the growing mêlée.

Laurel Anne was one of those people who didn't list ingredients first. She included each individual item and its quantity as it was utilized. Side one of the card gave directions for the eggs, butter, artichokes, and onion. It ended with "sauté over." Side two began with "quince" and continued with the tossing of grapes and the additions of sugar and heavy cream. "What's it supposed to be?"

"A quiche."

I wrinkled my nose. "Didn't she do her homework?" I asked. "We sent all sorts of information about the Campbells' likes and dislikes. President Campbell hates quiche."

We kept our backs to the agitated crowd of chefs and camera crew, but stole occasional glances to check on their progress. Things were growing more heated by the moment. Even Henry, who almost never got riled, was speaking more slowly than normal, his face red with the exertion of keeping his temper in check. As though by tacit agreement, the combatants all kept their voices low, out of respect for the White House protocols, I hoped, and not because Laurel Anne didn't care for noise.

"You know what I think?" I asked Cyan.

"What?"

Turning the card over, then back, then over again, I gave her the only explanation that made sense. "She's got two recipes here. She must have started one on the front, and finished the second one on the back. Quiche. Quince. Makes sense. It's alphabetical."

Cyan turned the card over a few more times. "Duh," she said. "You're right. But now what do I do?"

"Is this for lunch?"

"Yeah."

I thought about it. "Don't make the quiche. It's just a bad idea." I tilted my head toward the computer. "She probably meant to assign you the fruit recipe anyway. Check our database of recipes. See what you can come up with using the ingredients on the back. Make that. As long as it's a success, she'll never know you substituted."

"Thanks. You're a doll."

"Yeah, well," I said, "in about two seconds, you're going to be the only person in this kitchen who thinks so."

With that, I turned and strode toward the furious group, calling out for them to stop. This was getting ridiculous. We were in the White House kitchen, for crying out loud. And I refused to let it be treated this way. "Marcel," I called. He ignored me.

I tried again. "Henry!"

I couldn't believe this was happening in our kitchen. Conflagrations of this sort would not, and should not be tolerated in the home of the president of the United States. The only reason nearby Secret Service hadn't intervened, I knew, was because we had our doors closed, and the cleaning staff was running the floor buffers in the hallway, masking the rapidly escalating argument.

That was it. I clapped my hands together loudly, just like Carmen had done earlier. "People!" I shouted.

They stopped and stared.

I held up my left wrist. "It's almost noon. Back to work."

CHAPTER 20

"AND SO ENDS ANOTHER EXCITING DAY IN THE WHITE HOUSE kitchen."

My colleagues didn't react much to my pronouncement, other than to shoot me derisive stares. Henry, perched on the computer stool, rested his florid face in deep hands. "Thank God that's over." He raised his eyes to meet mine, and then scanned the room. "But . . ." I could hear his bright-side-tone returning, "I'm sure that if Laurel Anne is chosen to replace me, things will go much smoother than they did today." One shoulder lifted. "At least she won't have a camera crew following her every move."

Cyan leaned against the countertop, her arms folded, head down. She lifted it to say, "You wound up being the lucky one, Ollie."

"How so?"

"She shrieked at me," Cyan said, squinting for emphasis. "Shrieked. I thought the quince thing was supposed to be served in a compote glass. But noooo . . ." She strung the word out. "Laurel Anne wanted it served like a parfait instead." She returned to staring at the floor. "She could have just asked nicely. At least you weren't working with food today. That kept you safe from her attacks."

I sneaked a glance at Bucky, expecting him to rise to Laurel Anne's defense. He didn't. Just like the rest of us, he'd found a comfortable spot—leaning in the doorway—and stared at nothing. Even prim and proper Marcel reclined, sort of. He sat on a step stool, elbows on knees.

"Oh," he said, leaping to his feet. "I have forgotten."

Henry raised weary eyes. "What?"

Marcel checked his watch, then the wall clock, then his watch again—all in the space of two seconds. His eyes popped as he spoke. "The ambassador—oh, his name escapes—the Muslim ambassador—he is due here in fifteen minutes to discuss menu changes."

No one moved.

"Marcel?" I said quietly, "are you sure?" I knew it had been a trying day for all of us, Marcel in particular, but we always got more notice than this.

He collapsed back onto the step stool. "Oh, it is my fault. My grievous fault. It was I who answered the telephone during the . . . the . . ."

Bucky supplied: "The meltdown?"

Henry snorted a laugh. Elbows on the countertop, he covered his face with his hands as his shoulders shook.

Cyan started to laugh. I did, too. Even Bucky turned away, his grin belying his normally taciturn expression. Marcel looked confused but cheered by the room's sudden lightheartedness.

I tried to hold back, but bubbles of laughter accompanied my words. "We need to get ready for the ambassador."

Henry planted both feet on the floor. His face, red with mirth, was a welcome change from being red with fury as it had been earlier in the day. "And so we shall. Troops," he said, as we quieted, "we have yet another battle to face. If they are sending their ambassador here to discuss the menu selections, then we must rise to the challenge—fatigued though we are from Laurel Anne's incursion." He wiggled bushy eyebrows, narrowing his eyes as though preparing for attack. "Where are the ingredients we used for the taste test this morning?"

"I have them set aside," I told him.

"Good. We must be prepared in the event Ambassador bin-Saleh requests his own tasting."

Cyan groaned—stopped when she caught Henry's frown—and worked up a smile. "I'm rarin' to go," she said.

I spoke up. "I'll print up working copies of the menu items so we can take notes."

Marcel apologized again.

"Don't worry about it," I said, "we all had a lot on our minds this evening. I'm glad you remembered before they showed—"

My words died as Peter Everett Sargeant barged into the kitchen with Labeeb bin-Saleh and Kasim Gaffari close behind. "You will want to speak with our executive chef and executive pastry chef," Sargeant was saying over his shoulder. "They're both here tonight."

He carried a sheaf of papers, and despite the late hour, looked crisp and clean as though it were the start of a new day. He stopped the little parade short, just inside the door.

"Is *everyone* still here tonight?" he asked.

No longer lounging against countertops or doorjambs, we stood in a rough semicircle. I said, "Today was Laurel Anne's audition. It took a while."

Sargeant's face went through a two-second contortion. "So I heard." Sargeant turned his full attention to Henry and gestured Marcel forward. "Ambassador bin-Saleh and his assistant Kasim have just a few questions regarding the items you plan to serve at the state dinner." He stepped back like a well-trained emcee, passing the spotlight on to the next performer.

"It will be our pleasure to answer all your questions," Henry said, bringing me into the group. He called Marcel over, too. "What are your concerns?"

As it turned out, we were able to preserve all our first choices for the meal. Once the ambassador was assured that we knew how to keep halal, his worries were put to rest. He told us, through Kasim's translation, that he'd been worried that our kitchen would equate kosher with halal, when in fact the two were not identical. We knew that, and further assuaged his concern.

Kasim asked if we would be holding similar discussions with the prime minister and his entourage.

"Yes," Henry told him. "We will ensure that all parties agree."

"You will not adjust the menu beyond these parameters without consulting us?" Kasim asked.

Henry started to explain our procedures, when Sargeant piped in, "Certainly not."

Kasim bent toward us. "Then I am satisfied with the arrangements." He turned to Labeeb, spoke in their native tongue, then asked in English, "Ambassador, are you ready to return to our quarters?"

It had been a long day, and even Henry's jovial face showed strain. I could detect a bright glimmer of hope that Labeeb would depart with Kasim, allowing the rest of us to go home for the night. I held my breath.

"No," Labeeb said. "I am yet unready. I am . . . intrigued with the usage purpose of herewith item." He picked up a garlic press and turned the handles into an upside-down V while the press-part of the device dangled. "What is the need of such item?"

Always the perfect host, Henry demonstrated. He even allowed Labeeb to press several cloves of garlic till the ambassador had gotten the hang of it. The room was cramped, getting warm, and I inched away for breathing space.

Thoroughly enraptured by our gadgetry, Labeeb asked to see how another small item worked. He grinned, white teeth dazzling against his dark skin. "Very highly technical," he said. "For perhaps James Bond to cook, no?"

We laughed. It was funny.

Cyan, Bucky, and I exchanged glances as we huddled near the door. So near, yet so far. It would be the height of impropriety to leave at this point, but my feet ached and I wanted to be home.

I thought about Tom.

As Henry and Marcel regaled Labeeb with more gadget magic, Sargeant made his way to our little group. I already knew what was on his mind. "So," he began, addressing me, "how many assistant chefs does it take to destroy a competitor's chances?"

"We did nothing to Laurel Anne," I said. "She brought it on herself."

Cyan agreed. Bucky said nothing, but he didn't defend Laurel Anne, either. I took that as a good sign.

"You're very fortunate," Sargeant said, "that her food presentations to the president and Mrs. Campbell went as well as they did. I know that they were impressed with Ms. Braun's variety. The trout was superb, the side dishes imaginative. Mrs. Campbell particularly enjoyed the Asparagus Hollandaise."

I winced. Hardly what I'd call imaginative. The items she'd prepared were basics I'd mastered early in my career. And the fact that she'd used frozen vegetables for her White House audition was mind-boggling.

Sargeant, still extolling Laurel Anne's virtues, continued. "Oh, and the quince parfait . . ." He pressed his fingers to his lips and kissed them into the air. "Magnificent."

Cyan chimed in. "That's only because Ollie covered Laurel Anne's—"

"Ah-ah-ah," Sargeant said, stopping her midsentence. "The only reason everything worked is because Ms. Braun was able to pull it off. Despite your attempts to make her look foolish."

I opened my mouth to argue, but he cut me off. "She told me everything."

"I'll bet she did."

He fixed me with a stare. "She has no reason to lie. She knows she's as good as in."

My heart dropped. I looked away. Clenching my teeth to keep from an improper outburst, I avoided eye contact with Cyan. Seeing her sympathetic face would have put me over the edge. "Believe what you want," I said. "Are we excused?"

Sergeant rolled his eyes and turned to see Kasim headed our way. "Yes," he said. "Henry and Marcel seem to have matters in hand. You may go."

Kasim and Sergeant began a quiet discussion next to us, while I pulled on my coat and made small talk with Cyan and Bucky. "What do you have planned for tomorrow?" Cyan asked. "You're off, right?"

"Henry gave us both tomorrow off?" Bucky asked. "What, is he nuts?"

"No," I said. "You and I are off tomorrow. Henry and Cyan are off the following day. Marcel—I have no idea. Henry said since we're all prepared, all put together, it should be fine. You both know that it's the last-minute work that's a killer. He wants us all to be rested and refreshed before we tackle those eighteen-hour shifts."

Cyan nodded. Bucky shrugged.

"So, any big plans?" Cyan asked again.

Still in discussion with Kasim, Sergeant edged closer to our position. I started to move past them. "I might go to the gun range," I said. "I can use the practice."

"The one out in Frederick?" Bucky asked. While Tom had been eager to teach me the rudiments of shooting, Bucky was a firearms aficionado. The mere mention of a range outing was enough to make him salivate. I'd forgotten that.

"One and the same," I said. "I've been out there a couple of times."

"You like shooting?"

I did. "It's fun."

"What time you going to be there?"

I shrugged. Tom usually went in the afternoon. "Two, maybe."

"Well, hey, maybe I'll see you there."

Just what I needed. More Bucky on my day off. But then again, I reasoned that if by some wild coincidence Bucky and Tom and I all showed up at the same time, it would look a whole lot less suspicious than if I were there by myself. I could claim serendipity. And then it wouldn't be the least bit odd to invite Tom out for coffee afterward.

CHAPTER 21

ARLINGTON NATIONAL CEMETERY'S SERENE BEAUTY SPREAD before me, beckoning. I hadn't been here in a couple of weeks, but even if it had been years, I knew I'd never forget the way. Despite my late hours the past few nights, I hadn't been able to sleep, so I arrived early, getting here when the cemetery opened at eight. With my fingers wrapped around a colorful bunch of blooms—only fresh-cut flowers were allowed on graves here—I made the long trek past acres of white government-issue headstones. So many heroes. So much death.

And yet, it was the sameness of those headstones that provided quiet comfort. As though the souls of all those buried here whispered, "We served together under one flag, now we rest together, united."

Somewhere in the distance, a lawn mower hummed.

My footsteps *shush*ed against wet grass as the sun worked its way up the sky, burning off the dew and chasing the chill from the air.

Dad had wanted to be buried here. Mom had been aware enough of that to make Dad's final arrangements with a measure of objectivity, despite her crushing grief. I'd been young. Almost too young to remember him. Mom didn't like to talk about how he died. And I often wondered if the reason I chose to live and work in Washington, D.C., was to be close to the memory of the father I never really knew.

I slowed. Came to a stop. Pulled my sweatshirt tighter around me.

Anthony M. Paras. Silver Star.

I stood quietly for a long time.

"Hi, Dad."

With no one around at this early hour I gave in to my desire to talk to him even though I knew he wasn't really here. I knew that whatever lay beneath the soft, wet grass was just a shell of who my dad had been. And yet, my powerful need to connect won out.

"I might . . . I might be leaving the White House."

Half the conversation went on in my brain, as though my father's spirit could hear both my innermost thoughts as well as my spoken words. "I don't want to go, but . . ."

I mulled over everything—my first encounter with Naveen, his death at the merry-go-round, Tom's disappointment in me, Laurel Anne's audition, and my current failure to make any single facet of my life go right.

"What could I have done differently?"

The breeze wrapped the smell of fresh-cut grass and the sound of the lawn mower around me. My hair lifted and I raised my face to the burgeoning sun asking again, rhetorically: "What could I have done differently?"

I didn't have an answer. And despite the calm my visits to Arlington usually brought me, I wouldn't get an answer, either.

I bent to place the flowers on his grave. "Keep an eye on me, Dad."

AT THE RANGE THAT AFTERNOON, I REALIZED I'D PICKED A PERfect day to come shooting. The combination indoor/outdoor location was ideal no matter the weather. But today bright sun in clear skies warmed the otherwise cool day and brought out crowds of eager marksmen, everyone cheered to be outside enjoying the beautiful weather.

Tom would want to be here today, too. I knew it. So that made the day even more perfect for arranging an "accidental" meet.

I got there before one thirty. There was plenty to keep me busy, indoors and out, and I was determined not to give up on catching Tom till they closed the place at five. Of course, once I started target practice, I could keep shooting for hours. And while it was great fun, I never lost sight of safety issues. The range guides kept a close watch on everyone, too. As long as they made sure other patrons took the same care with firearms that I did, I knew I was safe.

The range had storage facilities, so I stopped at the front desk first to pick up my nine-millimeter Beretta and purchase some ammunition. I wore a fanny pack that I'd bought here on an earlier trip. It looked just like an ordinary, albeit large, waist-purse, but a second zippered compartment behind the purse was designed to hold a firearm.

I chose the closest open station, the third of five positions under a cement canopy that shielded us from the sun. I readjusted my ear plugs—snugging them in tighter to protect my hearing. With every spot active, the sound of popping gunfire could be deafening. Literally.

I loaded my magazine, slammed it into place in the Beretta's grip, released the slide, squared my safety goggles tight, and popped my Chicago Bears hat on my head. Ready to go.

My first several shots went wide as shell casings danced out of my gun. My target: a black and white bull's-eye, maybe twenty-four inches wide, fifty feet away. Even though this wasn't considered a difficult shot, I was out of practice. Whenever a bullet hit, it made a fluorescent green hole. No mistaking where my off-center shots went, or even when they missed entirely.

I wanted a bull's-eye.

No, I amended. I wanted them all to be bull's-eyes.

Which meant I needed a lot more practice.

As I reloaded, I took the opportunity to check out all the other patrons under the canopy. No Tom. But just about everyone wore round-necked, long-sleeve shirts and jeans, baseball caps, goggles, and ear protection, and it was a little difficult to be sure. The shirt I wore was bright yellow, not just for safety reasons, but because it was a shirt Tom had seen before. Maybe he'd recognize it—and say hello.

There were two other sets of stations on the far side of the main office. I gave myself a thirty-minute time limit at my current spot. After that, I'd take a walk and see what the rest of the range had to offer.

Head up, shoulders back. Arms outstretched, slightly bent. Hands around the grip. My trigger finger rode straight along the firearm's frame, not inside the trigger guard, not yet.

I concentrated. With the gun's sights set on the target's center, I gently eased my trigger finger into position within the guard. I took a long, slow, deep breath, let it out, and squeezed.

Off the mark. Damn. I'd pulled up. Just enough to leave a fluorescent green ding on the edge of the target's outer circle.

A half-hour later, my arms were sore, I smelled like cordite, and there were four people waiting their turn under the canopy. I collected my target via the overhead pulley, packed away my pistol, and headed down to the front office again, where I ducked into the restroom. I washed my hands thoroughly to get the lead off, and removed my goggles and ear plugs.

My face was dirty where the glasses hadn't covered it, and my hair had gone flat. I decided to keep the hat on—it looked better. A quick glance at my watch convinced me it was time to put the plan into action. This was Tom's favorite time of the day to come shooting.

The second set of stations was full, too. I stood well behind the yellow safety line and pretended to watch. My prior visits here convinced me that target shooting was largely a male-dominated sport. Today there were no females up front, and two of the older gents who worked the grounds smiled and waved me over.

They leaned on push brooms as they conversed. Whenever the range was declared "cold," as it was every hour or so, they'd move in, sweep the casings from the concrete floor and dump them into the nearby garbage drums. Bill was taller, Harold shorter, but both wore overalls and skin toughened from years of being outdoors. Bright white skin remained tucked deep inside cheerful wrinkles. "How've you been, honey?" Harold asked.

"Busy," I said, "how about you?"

Bill snorted a laugh. "Tell me about it. You see the crowd over there?" He snapped a thumb over his shoulder. "I'll be chasing brass all afternoon."

"I was over there before it got busy." Casually, so as not to arouse the male protect-our-brother mentality, I asked, "Have you seen Tom MacKenzie here today?"

Harold's eyes narrowed. "The guy who brought you here the first time? The Secret Service guy?"

I nodded.

Bill asked, "You didn't come together?"

"No."

They exchanged a look. Harold's eyebrows raised, and he thought about it for a couple of seconds. "Yeah, he's here."

Bill pointed to the range's far side. His look said he was reluctant to share the information and all of a sudden I realized why. "Is he with someone?"

The two men leaned back from their brooms, surprised. "No," they said in unison.

"He's practicing pretty hard today," Harold said. "Never seen him so focused." He shrugged and shared another glance with Bill. His eyes twinkled. "Maybe he's taking his frustrations out, or something. You should probably go over there and say hey."

"I think I will," I said.

By the time I reached the farthest set of stations, I'd convinced myself that this was a stupid move. I'd apologized to Tom. I'd been rebuffed. Appearing here now would only make him feel claustrophobic and I risked pushing him further away.

I was about to turn back when I caught sight of him.

I couldn't help myself. I drew closer, watching him as he nailed that target—*pop—pop—pop—pop—pop—pop*. Bull's-eyes, every one.

He didn't turn. Didn't seem to notice anything or anyone around him, save for the occasional glances side-to-side when shooters in his periphery moved or changed firearms. Harold was right. He was focused.

From my position behind a small shed, I could watch without looking too obvious to passersby, and if Tom should turn, I'd be able to duck behind the shed quickly and avoid any uncomfortable confrontations.

I felt like a high-school girl, gazing adoringly at my crush.

And I felt stupid being here, unwilling and afraid to approach him.

Tom switched the Sig Sauer to his left hand. Firing off-handed, he consistently hit within the second circle of the round target. When he stopped, he shook his head as if disappointed in his performance.

I thought he did great, but I couldn't bring myself to tell him so.

When he changed firearms again, and began practicing with his revolver, I realized he was winding up. He always finished with the Smith & Wesson six-shooter, and even if he had several speed-loaders on hand, he'd be finished soon.

What was I was doing here? This was silly. Again, I felt schoolgirl crush monsters devouring my usually solid self-esteem.

I fingered the brim of my Bears cap—and decided to punt.

Under bright blue canopies strategically placed around the range, the owners had set up vending machines and washroom facilities for the comfort and convenience of their patrons. The nearest oasis was about a hundred yards away. If Tom finished soon, he'd be thirsty, and he'd probably stop here before heading back to his car.

I trotted up to the vending machines, hoping at least one offered ice cold water. My lucky day. I dug two dollars out of the front pouch of my purse. Two bucks for water was highway robbery, but there wasn't much choice.

"You come here often?"

I turned. The man who spoke to me was just an inch or so taller than I was, with dark brown hair and even darker eyes. Tanned, but not leathery, he'd either spent yesterday in a tanning booth or an afternoon being sprayed that color. For being at a shooting range, he was oddly dressed. Short-sleeved gray button-down dress shirt, navy blue Dockers, and polished loafers. He smiled, inched closer. A little too close. I backed up. "Often enough," I said.

"Let me buy you a drink," he said. "What do you want?"

"I've got it." I stepped forward to insert the first of the dollars into the slot, jamming it in fast and following up with the second dollar so my new friend didn't get any ideas to help.

"Oh, is the lady taken?" He smirked and glanced back toward the shed where I'd been watching Tom shoot. Had this guy been watching me?

I hit the machine's wide blue button and heard my relief tumble to the bottom shelf. "She is now," I said.

Letting the cool water trickle down the back of my throat, I strode away. Fifteen steps later, I realized I'd been rude. I thought about the guy behind me—he was just being friendly.

Maybe I'd been too hasty. Not with this guy in particular, but in my attitude. I'd rejected him out of hand because he tried to pick me up. A pessimistic thought caught a beat in the background of my mind. I tried to ignore it, but it played there nonetheless: If Tom and I broke up for good, I'd be encountering these Vending Machine Romeos and their brethren everywhere. Worse, eventually I'd be seeking them out.

I wasn't interested in Mr. Tan Boy, but I shouldn't have been so discourteous brushing him off.

That little bit of remorse was enough to make me turn.

Romeo was following me.

He smiled. But not the kind of smile you use to pick up a girl.

I picked up the pace.

The shooting station was still about fifty feet away.

Behind me, Romeo's shoes chafed the asphalt. His pace picked up, too.

I had a sudden flashback to the merry-go-round. It couldn't be. Could it? I turned again.

"Just a minute," he said. "Wait. Please. I have to ask you something."

The "please" almost stopped me. But in a heartbeat I decided I'd rather be rude than take my chances. Something about this man was unpleasantly familiar. "No!" I dropped into a flat-out run. Up ahead I saw Tom packing up, getting ready to leave. "Tom!"

He turned, gave me the oddest look. "Ollie? What are you doing—"

I stumbled as I reached him. Tom grabbed me by my wrists—holding me at arm's length. My brain ticked off that "distancing maneuver" tidbit despite my panic. "That guy," I said, panting, pointing behind me. "He's following me. I think he's—"

"Hold on a minute," he said. "Who?"

And just like at the merry-go-round, he was gone.

"IT WAS THE SAME MAN," I SAID. "IT WAS THE CHAMELEON."

We sat in my car, Tom staring at me as if seeing me for the first time.

"How can you be sure?"

From my pocket, I pulled the picture that sketch artist Darren Sorrell printed for me and now I spread it out against my steering wheel. For some reason I carried it everywhere, thinking it might come in handy. Hoping it wouldn't.

But now it did. I shook my head. Could it have been the same guy? There were similarities in height and build, but the coloring was different. And I couldn't be sure about the face.

"Just . . ." I hated it when I faltered over words. "Just . . . I just feel it."

"But you're not sure."

I didn't know what to say, what the right answer was. I couldn't swear it was the same man I'd encountered at the merry-go-round, but it *felt* the same. "His hair was different. And this guy wasn't pale. And his eyes were a different color."

"But you're convinced it was the same man."

Skepticism in Tom's tone. His expression, too. I couldn't blame him, but I knew what I felt. "I am."

"Why did you come to the range today?"

Yikes. Good time for a fib. "I needed the practice."

"And you believe the Chameleon followed you here?" Tom's tone was half-disbelieving, half-coy, as though he saw all this as a manufactured stunt to get back together. I could understand why it looked suspicious. But I couldn't dismiss my very real fear.

"You said yourself I'm the only person who can identify him."

"Okay, calm down," he said. "It might have just been a guy who wanted your number. He just got overeager. Guys do that sometimes."

I usually hate when people tell me to calm down, but I had to face facts.

Tom could be right. I could be overreacting. I took a deep breath and gave it one last shot. "Listen, there was something about this guy that felt familiar. Felt wrong. And he followed me. He chased me. And he disappeared into the crowd, just like the other day."

"You get a good look at him?"

"I did."

"Do you think another visit from the sketch artist will do any good?"

"So we can have two versions of the Chameleon floating around?" I gave a laugh I didn't feel. "We already know he blends into the background. What good would it do?" Morosely, I added. "And I have to face it, you're right. I'm not even sure it was the same guy."

"Two minutes ago you swore it had to be."

I dropped my head into my hands. "I'm confused."

A long moment passed, both of us quiet.

Tom broke the silence. "For what it's worth, Ollie, I'm confused, too."

I waited, but he didn't say anything more.

"I guess I should get going," I said.

"Yeah."

I still waited. He finally said, "You going to be okay?"

"Yeah," I lied.

I watched him drive away before I started my car.

Some fun day off.

CHAPTER 22

FOR THE SECOND TIME IN LESS THAN A WEEK, I WAS AWAKENED by pounding at my door before the sun was up.

"Hang on," I called as I navigated through my dark apartment. What time was it? I squinted at the digital readout on my stove as I scurried past the kitchen. Three in the morning. The door cracked again. Sounded like someone banging against it with a stick.

It had to be Tom. Who else could it be at this hour?

I peered out the peephole.

Mrs. Wentworth had her cane in the air, ready to bring it down against my door again. Before she could, I swung it open.

"Mrs. Wentworth," I said with alarm. "Are you all right?"

"Of course I'm all right. Damn foolish question. Could I be standing here in the middle of the night talking to you if I weren't? Let me in."

When an elderly neighbor lady says "Let me in," you let her in.

I turned on a hallway lamp and ushered her into the living room, thanking heaven that the place was clean. "What's wrong?" I asked.

"Let me sit, first."

"Can I get you something?" I asked, thinking how ludicrous the question felt at three in the morning with both of us wearing nightclothes. But I didn't know what else to say.

Mrs. Wentworth was tiny in a formerly tall sort of way. She stooped as she toddled over to my leather sofa. Giving it a glance of distaste, she changed trajectory and headed into the kitchen. "Hard chairs are easier to get out of. I'll have tea, if you got it. No caffeine."

The bright overhead light gave the kitchen a surreal glow. I filled two mugs with water, placed them in the microwave, and sat. Mrs. Wentworth had hung her cane over the back of her chair and folded her gnarled hands atop the table.

"Don't you use a teapot?" she asked.

I bit my tongue. I normally would use a teapot, but I'd opted for the microwave in the hopes of moving this impromptu visit along a little faster.

"Would you like anything else?" I asked. "Cookies?" What I really wanted to know was why she was here at this crazy hour, but she seemed in no hurry, content to study my kitchen's décor.

"You make the cookies from scratch?"

"Yes."

"I'll have some."

She took one of my Crisp Triple Chocolate Chip cookies but didn't eat it. Instead she finally turned her shrewd stare in my direction. "Don't you want to know what I saw?"

What I wanted was to go back to bed. But I was raised to be polite. And now that I was awake, I sure as hell did want to know what was so important that had her banging on my door in the middle of the night. "What did you see, Mrs. Wentworth?"

She took a mouthful of cookie, and then took her sweet time chewing. "You did a nice job decorating the place. How come you don't have a boyfriend here?"

Taken aback, I stammered. Then lied. "He's working."

She nodded. Finished the cookie.

"I didn't think he was here. That's why I chased the guy away. Knew you didn't have anyone here to protect you except me."

"Chased? What guy?"

She jerked a thumb toward my door. "He was trying to get in here."

I stood. "Tonight?"

"Just now. I chased him away."

I opened my mouth, but the microwave dinged, cutting off further comment. I used the distraction of steeping tea to gather my thoughts before asking, "Why don't you tell me what happened—from the beginning?"

Mrs. Wentworth's eyes sparkled. She clawed another cookie from the plate. "I heard the stairway door open," she said. "You know nobody here ever uses the stairs."

She waited for me to nod before continuing.

"I happened to be near the door, so I peeked out the peephole."

"You happened to be near the door?" I couldn't keep the skepticism from my voice even as I placed the steaming mug in front of her. "It's three in the morning. Why weren't you in bed?"

She fixed me with that intelligent gaze again. "I'll be sleeping permanently one of these days, you know. I don't plan to waste my time doing it now."

With no idea how to respond to that, I took a sip of too-hot, pale tea.

"And you should be grateful I haven't keeled over yet. The guy I saw creeping around here was up to no good."

"Who was it?"

"How should I know?" she asked with asperity. "He was trying to break into your door, not mine. Maybe it's someone you know."

Suddenly weak at the knees, I sat. After today's encounter at the range, I felt vulnerable. Mrs. Wentworth's pronouncement fed into my newfound paranoia.

Determined to keep a firm grip on logic, I said, "Couldn't it have been James? Or one of the other doormen? Or maybe one of the custodians?"

"Would James be picking your lock?"

I gasped. "You're sure?"

"Honey, I may not be fast on my feet, but there's nothing wrong with my eyes."

I stood. "I'll call nine-one-one."

"Already done."

As if on cue, my buzzer rang, making me jump. "Yes," I said, pressing the intercom.

James tried to sound official, but his voice came through tinny. "Police here for you, Ms. Paras. Is there a problem?"

Mrs. Wentworth eyed me over the top of her tea mug.

"I need to report something, yes," I said. "You can let them come up."

"Should I come up there, too?" James asked.

"You better keep an eye on the door," I said to him. Mrs. Wentworth nodded her agreement. "By the way, James, was there anyone down there looking for me a little while ago?"

"You mean that one Secret Service guy? I haven't seen hide nor hair of him."

"No, someone else. Anyone else."

"No, Ms. Paras. No one's come through the door since before eleven. That's when I locked up. Anybody'd have to ring the doorbell after that."

"Thanks, James."

When the police arrived, Mrs. Wentworth gave them a surprisingly detailed description of the would-be intruder.

"Short," she said. "No taller than five-three, I'd say. He had a clean-shaven head, dark skin."

Two officers stood in my tiny kitchen. One male, one female. Both in their late twenties. Both buff but looking wide at the hips with all the equipment they wore. The female officer, Duffy, sat next to Mrs. Wentworth and took notes. "Black?" she asked.

Mrs. Wentworth shook her head, clearly enjoying the attention. "No, more like tan. Like somebody who lives at the beach."

At my sudden intake of breath, they all turned.

"You recognize this individual?" Rogers, the other officer, asked.

"Yes," I said. "No . . . well . . . maybe."

Twin stares of annoyance from the two cops. I could practically read their minds. They were thinking this was simply a case of boyfriend troubles—that I knew who the intruder was, but was trying to protect him.

Hurrying to dispel that thought, I explained. "Today . . . er, well, I guess I mean yesterday . . . a guy followed me. That's what he looked like. He was tan. Very tan, like he sprayed it on or something. Except the guy at the range had dark hair."

The annoyed looks were replaced by quick concern. "He followed you home?" Duffy asked.

"No." I went on to tell them about my experience at the shooting range.

Rogers asked, "Do you have a gun on the premises?"

"I do. He made me so nervous that I brought it home with me."

"You have a permit?"

"Yes," I said, "of course."

"May I see it?"

"The gun or the permit?"

"Both."

I wanted them to jump up and set off to find the guy who'd been at my door—to figure out how he'd gotten up here without James being aware of it—but instead I found myself questioned and my gun examined. They seemed impressed by the fact that I worked at the White House.

"What about the guy?" I asked, as they pronounced everything in order and admonished me to keep practicing.

Duffy said, "We'll talk with the doorman, run prints on your door—don't touch your outer doorknob until we—"

"He was wearing gloves," Mrs. Wentworth said around a mouthful of cookie.

The officers' eyebrows raised as though impressed. Duffy turned to Mrs. Wentworth. "Is there anything else you can think of that could help us identify the guy?"

She thought about it for a long moment, and I could see her replaying the scene at my door in her mind. "Yes," she said slowly, stringing the word out. "When I opened the door and yelled at him, he said something. Shouted it, in fact. Like I scared him."

We all leaned forward.

"I did frighten him, you know. I said that I'd already called nine-one-one."

"What did he say?" Rogers asked.

Mrs. Wentworth shook her head. "It was another language. I couldn't understand the words, but I most certainly understood the meaning. That's when he took off down the stairs."

And downstairs, James hadn't noticed anything amiss. How did the guy get out? How had he gotten in?

My building's lack of a security staff had never bothered me before. Now, goose bumps raced up the back of my neck.

Before they left, the officers inspected my locks and told me they were as good as I could get. Rogers said, "No signs of tampering . . . But if somebody really wants in . . ."

I must have blanched because he quickly added, "If you hear anything suspicious, call nine-one-one."

I thanked them, thanked Mrs. Wentworth.

She grabbed a handful of cookies and tottered back to her apartment, leaving me alone, unable to sleep, knowing that nightmares awaited me whether or not I closed my eyes.

CHAPTER 23

I DEBATED CALLING TOM. DECIDED AGAINST IT.

Our last conversation had left me feeling foolish. As though I'd manufactured the incident at the range as an excuse to see him. He had promised to report my sighting, but I'd gotten the distinct impression that he didn't really believe it was the Chameleon who'd approached me. Now, after last night's unpleasant happening, I wondered if my cover was totally blown. Did the Chameleon know who I was and where I lived?

It scared me. More than I cared to admit.

What would Tom say? Warn me to be more careful? Tell me to sleep with my gun under my pillow?

Would he come racing to my rescue to protect me from the Chameleon?

No.

I slid my Metro pass through the gate's reader on my way out at McPherson Square, shuffling with the crowd toward the exit—keeping alert for anything, anyone—out of place.

I needed to get used to the fact that Tom wasn't there for me anymore.

The thought depressed me. But I couldn't let the weight of disappointment slow me down. Reminding myself that a fast-moving target is a whole lot harder to hit than a static one, I practically shot from the station's maw to the White House's Northeast gate. I should tell someone here about the attempted break-in. But who? Tom told me that my involvement—from the very start when I whacked the pan against Naveen's head—to the incident at the merry-go-round, was considered confidential. I didn't know who, beyond Tom, Craig Sanderson, and unknown higher-ups were in on it.

By the time the White House front lawn came into view, I'd worked up a sweat, and my breaths came fast and shallow as I slid my ID through the card reader.

Freddie wasn't in the booth this morning to answer the shrill beep. "Hi, Gloria," I said as the woman came out of her building to double-check it was me.

"You okay?" she asked.

Now that I was inside the gate, I felt enormously better. With Secret Service at every turn, and snipers atop the roof, I knew I was safe from the Chameleon here, at least.

"I'm fine," I said, as I tucked my pass away and wiped my dotted brow. "Warm today, huh?"

"Supposed to be midseventies this afternoon."

She gave me a funny look as I walked, more sedately now, to the East entrance.

"WHAT ARE YOU DOING HERE?" I ASKED HENRY WHEN I GOT INTO the kitchen. "You're supposed to be off today."

He turned from his hunched position at the computer. "Change of plan," he said, his face making the transformation from furrowed-brow to bright. "You and I are going on a field trip. I thought about calling you last night, but I knew you'd be in early anyway . . ." He glanced up at the clock, "but this is really early, even for you."

I donned my tunic. "Couldn't sleep."

The kitchen was quiet for a long moment as Henry returned to his document. He hadn't turned on many lights, and I took a deep breath—the scent of disinfectant over the lingering smells of yeast and garlic—and was comforted by the closeness of it all. This was my haven. I could happily live here. I pictured the adjacent storage area, and wondered how easily I could convert it to a sleeping space until I felt safe in my apartment again.

I smiled at the absurdity of the plan. Not a chance I'd escape the Secret Service's notice. For one thing, my pass would alert them that I hadn't left for days. And showering each morning might prove problematic.

Still, a girl could dream.

"What's so funny?" Henry asked.

I wanted to tell him about my early morning visitor, about the range, but I couldn't start down that path without betraying confidential information. Or compromising the plan to keep me safe. Oh, yeah, that plan was working.

"Nothing, really," I said. "What kind of field trip?"

He hoisted himself off the stool, and clapped his hands. "We are going to Camp David."

"Today?"

"Yes, ma'am," he said, brushing past me to pull out his stash of favorite recipes. "On a helicopter."

Henry looked and sounded like a little kid who'd just been promised a pony ride. I couldn't help grinning—his excitement was contagious.

"What time?"

"They'll call for us after nine. We're in charge of dinner there tonight. The Camp David kitchen staff is already preparing some basics, and getting ready for our arrival. But! The president specifically requested our presence." He graced me with a look that said "Impressive, huh?" and then went back to rummaging through his file. "This trade agreement summit must be pretty important to insist that you and I oversee the meals. This time there is a real possibility for cooperation. The president realizes that, and he is doing all he can to make it a reality."

"I'd say. These two countries have been at war with one another for . . ." I blew out a breath. ". . . for as long as I can remember. If President Campbell is able to facilitate a trade agreement, it'll be an important first step toward achieving peace in the Middle East."

"Here." Henry handed me three recipes, having tuned me out in favor of planning meals. "Let's figure out what we need to make these."

WE WERE SHEPHERDED TO THE HELICOPTER JUST AFTER NINE, leaving Marcel in charge of the kitchen during our absence.

The presidential helicopter, *Marine One*, had already shuttled President Campbell and his guests to Camp David. The rest of the delegations attending the summit would arrive either by separate air arrangements or chauffeured motorcade.

The helicopter taking the two of us to Camp David was one of the ordinary, run-of-the mill designs. The Secret Service fellow who led us toward it seemed to view it as no big deal.

I found it incredibly exciting.

An earphone-wearing man in a flight jacket held up a gloved hand, motioning us to wait outside the marked perimeter while the enormous blades whirled overhead, their movement making loud *whup-whup* noises in the otherwise quiet morning. I held my arm up to shield my face from dust zipping into my eyes.

"Henry! Ollie!"

We turned. Craig Sanderson trotted toward us, papers in hand, his short hair flipping up from the copter's air current. "Did we forget something?" I asked Henry, shouting to be heard.

"No. I have everything here." He patted his laptop case.

Craig wasn't out of breath, but he had to raise his voice over the sound of the rotating blades. "This has just been released," he said, handing a flapping paper to Henry, and another to me. The look he gave me was anything but friendly, and as soon as I saw the face on the picture, I knew why.

Henry leaned in, firmly holding the paper by both ends. "Who is this?"

Craig explained that the White House, and indeed all of Washington, D.C., was on high alert for the assassin known as the Chameleon. He pointed to the face I'd described to Darren Sorrell, the face that stared up at us now. "This is the most recent composite we could come up with. We're notifying everyone at Camp David. This guy's slippery, and we want him caught."

"I've heard of this Chameleon," Henry said, nodding. "Someone has actually seen him?"

I felt myself blush.

Craig nodded, without looking at me. "We think so. Just keep a close eye out, all right? We believe he's targeted President Campbell. That's why these trade negotiations were moved. It will be more difficult for the Chameleon to attempt an attack in the new location; Camp David is much less problematic to secure than the White House—but until we tell you otherwise, anyone who looks like this, or who behaves in a suspicious manner, should be reported immediately."

I thought about my decision to not tell Tom about the attempted break-in.

Dumb move. I should've swallowed my pride and called him last night. I opened my mouth to tell Craig, but the pilot shouted for us to board and Craig jogged away.

Next chance I had to talk to either one of them, I decided, I would.

The seventy-mile trip from one landing strip to the next was the most exciting I'd ever experienced. I was part of something big. Henry had been to Camp David before, but this would be my first time. There was a separate cooking staff at the retreat, so we were rarely called in to participate. This business summit could become a turning point in world history, and I was proud and elated to be part of it.

We circled the camp once before landing. The 125-acre retreat in Maryland's Catoctin Mountains was just as breathtaking as Tom had proclaimed. He'd been here before, too, several times, and he couldn't get enough of it. I could see why. Below us, cottages, paths, and gorgeous mature trees covered the top and one side of a small mountain. Lots of rocky terrain. Lots of greenery. I caught sight of a small portion of the security fence, and the agents who guarded it.

I sighed deeply. I'd be safe here.

The place was bustling with arrivals when we set down. We were directed up a path to the camp commander's office. On the way, we watched limousines navigate the roads to the various cabins to drop off riders before setting off again to the staff parking and guest barracks farther north.

Neither Henry nor I would be staying the night, and as we walked the path I regretted that. An idyllic spot, there were tennis courts, a staff pool, and that deep green smell only a forest of cool trees can provide. I breathed in the springy newness. For the first time in days, I felt alive with comfort. I vowed to put aside my worries about Tom, my worries about being a target for the Chameleon, and concentrate on doing the best job I could while soaking up the sense of well-being that pervaded this place.

Henry must have sensed my contentment; he smiled and winked.

I could understand why Franklin Delano Roosevelt had originally named this USS Shangri La. It was, indeed, a haven. It had been called Camp David since before I was born, when Dwight Eisenhower renamed the retreat in honor of his grandson.

As I followed Henry and our guide, a kitchen staffer named Rosa Brelczyk, I found myself wishing the original name had endured. Jimmy Carter had chosen well when he staged his peace talks here.

Rosa kept us to the right on the long path. Round and short, she had the smile of a saint, and she maintained gentle chatter, welcoming us as we walked. All the cottages on the premises were named for trees: Chestnut, Hickory, Dogwood.

A limousine cleared the gatehouse and passed us on our left. The car stopped just outside the Birch guesthouse. As we approached I saw Ambassador bin-Saleh and his assistant, Kasim, alight. Accompanying them was a woman, dressed in a full *burqa*, her face and body completely obscured by her flowing blue garment.

Henry whispered. "That's the princess."

"How do you know?"

"Watch," he said.

As though he'd timed his comment, two women emerged from Birch, both also fully covered, but in fabrics far less opulent than the silk of the princess's. They flanked their mistress and all three kept their heads together as they disappeared back into the cabin.

"I see."

"Labeeb told me there were three women in their party: the princess and two handmaidens."

I raised an eyebrow. "Handmaiden? What is this, the Middle Ages?"

"Labeeb's word." He shrugged. "Seems to fit."

Rosa veered right at a large, beautiful building. "Aspen Lodge," she said brightly.

"We're working in the president's cabin?" I asked.

She nodded, still walking, passing the front entrance. "The north wing houses the kitchen. We've been anticipating your arrival, Henry. Yours, too," she said to me, but I could tell she didn't remember my name. "I hope you're used to working in tight quarters. We have a lot of . . . help . . . here today."

She wasn't kidding.

"There are so many people," I said to Rosa after being introduced to the entire Camp David kitchen staff and a couple of others—chefs from the two visiting dignitaries' countries.

She gave me a rueful smile. "The kitchen isn't the only place that's crowded. Not only do we have the summit leaders here, but each of them brought along several ambassadors, foreign ministers, legal advisors, defense ministers, public relations advisors . . ." She gave an extended sigh. "From what I understand, they've all had to cut back on the size of their entourage. As it is, we're stretching ourselves to make do."

The word *entourage* gave me a little start. It reminded me of Laurel Anne's audition, of the day we'd endured with her in control. If you could call it that. I swallowed hard as I thought about this glorious refuge and all it represented. And the fact that I might never come back.

Bringing myself back to the present, I nodded. "We met only a couple of the ambassadors at the White House when they stopped by for a visit. And I haven't even seen the prime minister yet. Mostly, the guests and their people stay offsite. This," I said, looking around, "is a whole lot more cozy."

She laughed. "That it is. And you'll interact with people you've only seen on TV up till now. Come on, let's get you set up."

Ten minutes later, aproned and toqued, I noticed Henry in deep discussion with the two other chefs. I deduced from their expressions that they weren't comprehending everything Henry was saying.

I edged closer to their huddle, and Henry waved me in.

"This is Olivia," he said, taking extra care to enunciate his words. "She works with me." He pointed to himself.

He then introduced the two men. The first, Avram, was an older fellow; he had at least five years on Henry. He was tiny, almost effeminate in his bearing, and because he had his toque in his hands instead of on his head, I could see straight over the top of his shiny pate. The second man, Gaspar, was taller than Henry—wider, too. His dark features and loud voice combined to produce an imposing presence.

They'd been arguing, in a Tower of Babel sort of way.

All three men smiled at me, and Henry took the opportunity to tell me that they had met before, several times, at chef summits, held every August, in places all over the world.

Avram and Gaspar had a decent command of the English language, and since I knew a little bit of French—in which they were both fluent—we were able to get by. Whenever stumped, we lapsed into hand motions and food-charades. By the time we'd settled on the upcoming dinner menu, we were proficient at deciphering each others' needs.

Avram held up a finger. He dug into his apron pocket and pulled out a folded paper. It was a copy of the list of foods the First Lady had taste-tested. "Here," he said, pointing to one of the items, "is good, not spiceful?"

I ran my finger down to see where he indicated. While everything we planned to serve at the upcoming state dinner had been approved by both camps and was both kosher and halal, we still understood that our guest chefs might have questions. They didn't disappoint. "Not spicy," I said, fanning my mouth and shaking my head. "No."

His face broke into a wide grin.

A separate section of the kitchen had been set aside for Avram's preparations to allow him to keep kosher. Separate utensils, kept on hand for this express purpose since the Camp David Accords, were pulled out and Avram pronounced the setup satisfactory.

Gaspar grabbed the note from Avram's grasp, lifted it up near his eyes, then pulled reading glasses from his pocket. He grunted twice as he followed the list with a fat finger.

Avram didn't seem to mind—he apparently didn't see Gaspar's snatch as anything but professional interest. In fact, he tilted his face upward to watch the taller man peruse the list and Avram asked a question in a language I didn't understand.

I glanced at Henry, who shrugged.

Gaspar answered Avram, again in a language unfamiliar to me and it surprised me to realize that these two were more alike than I would have expected. I said as much to Henry.

"That's why the chef summit is so special," he said. "There are no politics. We put aside our countries' differences to come together, to learn, to grow. Mostly, to cook. I'm glad you're seeing this Ollie. It's good experience for you before you go to your first summit."

"*If* I go," I corrected him. "I'm pretty sure Laurel Anne has already made her travel arrangements."

He waved a finger at me.

Avram, Gaspar, Henry, and I set to work together, surrounded by a bevy of helpers including our own Camp David staff and one assistant each from the two other countries.

While we worked, we talked. And despite the language difficulties, we got plenty done in a short period of time.

Until the room went suddenly quiet.

I looked up.

At the kitchen's doorway, a Marine, at attention.

A charge of fear ricocheted through our friendly atmosphere.

"What happened?" Henry asked.

The young man in uniform spoke clearly, but quietly. "Dinner plans have changed. President Campbell, Prince Sameer bin Khalifah, and Prime Minister Jaron Jaffe will take their meal in Hickory. They will be joined by . . ."

He rattled off more names of other political bigwigs.

Avram asked why the change. I didn't understand his exact words, but I knew what he meant. The Marine understood, too. "You will be contacted soon with regard to further details. In the meantime, the First Lady and Princess Hessa bint Muaath will take their dinner at Aspen cottage."

He pivoted and left.

The moment he was gone, our group began buzzing. What was that all about?

CHAPTER 24

ONE OF THE SOUS-CHEFS, JESSICA, CUT HER HAND BADLY ENOUGH to warrant medical attention. I volunteered to take her to the dispensary, and together we walked back up the same path Henry and I had taken from the helicopter pad. Jessica and I moved quickly, with me holding her hastily bandaged hand above her heart level to stem the bleeding.

The staff at the dispensary didn't waste time. They went to work on Jessica, throwing thanks to me over their shoulders—an effective dismissal.

As I passed Birch cabin on my return trip, the front door swung open and Kasim emerged. He called to me to wait. Again he wore the traditional full-length robes of his culture. Today they were brown. With a bright red turban atop his head, he towered over me by a foot and a half, at least. Back in D.C., with the temperatures warming up nicely, Kasim must have sweltered. Here, at the higher elevation and beneath the canopy of trees, I'm sure he was much more comfortable. He seemed less tense, although I noticed he moved slower than he had in the past. I asked him how he was feeling.

"I am much improved," he said.

"If I may say so, you look better."

He blinked acknowledgment, and I wondered if I'd breached protocol by commenting on his appearance. Henceforth I promised myself to watch my words.

He changed the subject. "I have several questions with regard to the final dinner and to preparations at this location. Your Mr. Sargeant is not present here?"

"No, he's not." When Rosa had explained how each of the delegates had cut back their staff, she hadn't mentioned Peter Everett Sargeant III. It wasn't until later, after we'd begun dinner preparations, that we found out he hadn't been included on the list of invitees. I was exceptionally happy to realize that when it came down to it, the sensitivity director wasn't as necessary as he thought he was.

"Shall I then speak with you about these matters?"

"Of course you can . . ." I hedged. I didn't want to sound like someone who passed the buck . . . "but Henry is executive chef," I said. "I'll be happy to help you any way I can. I'm on my way back to the kitchen now. Would you care to join me?"

He nodded. "The princess has asked me to see to it that dinner is halal."

"I can assure you, it is."

A gentle smile. "And I can assure you that my princess will not be content until I have overseen the preparation facility myself."

"I understand."

"Are you staying in that cabin?" He pointed to our right, a smaller structure adjacent to the president's cottage named Witch Hazel.

"Not me." I laughed. "I don't know who's in that one. Maybe one of the Cabinet members."

"I would expect the president's staff to be housed close by. Your accommodations are elsewhere?"

"The staff has its own section." I pointed far north and a little bit west of our position. "There are barracks out that way—I've never seen them, but they're supposed to be nice—and there are even recreational facilities for those off-duty." I sighed. "I wish we *were* staying here tonight."

"You are not?"

I shook my head. "No, Henry and I are heading back after the evening meal."

Emotion flashed in his eyes. Regret? Sympathy? I couldn't tell. "This is a most beautiful setting," he said. "And I am most fortunate to have been chosen for this assignment—I certainly understand your desire to remain here. I find myself very . . . content . . . to spend the next several nights on these premises in anticipation of the successful completion of our trade agreements."

We were silent for several footsteps. A golf cart whirred behind us and we stepped aside. Two Cabinet members sped by. They were both clad in Camp David windbreakers—and were both looking quite pleased. They acknowledged us with twin nods.

"Where is Ambassador bin-Saleh?" I asked, when Kasim and I continued walking.

"He will join the prince in . . ." He paused before pronouncing it. "Hickory . . . for dinner."

"Oh."

"You disagree?"

Embarrassed to come across as disapproving, which my "Oh," probably had, I quickly explained, "When we were in the kitchen earlier, they announced the guests who would be dining in Hickory. I noticed that your name and Ambassador bin-Saleh's were not among them."

"Ah," he said, "I understand your confusion. The ambassador originally was to remain in our cabin"—he pointed behind us toward a small structure near Birch—"with me. But after speaking with the prince, it is agreed that recent events in Europe have demanded the ambassador's presence at the discussion table."

Before I could stop myself, I asked, "We heard something was up, what happened?"

Another golf cart passed us, its riders so intent in their discussion that they didn't acknowledge us. They wore cool Camp David windbreakers, too. I wondered if there was a way to get one of those for myself.

"It is on your network television news, so there is no reason not to share the information with you," he said gravely. "It is a good day for peace. The French have announced the death of a well-known assassin."

"The Chameleon?"

"You know of this assassin?"

"Just a little," I said, suddenly confused. It couldn't be. He'd been after me. Just yesterday. This morning, in fact. Something didn't make sense. "Are you sure?"

"The French authorities, acting on word from an informant, discovered the assassin attempting to detonate a bomb in Paris." Kasim's mouth set in a grim line. "This was during very busy hours yesterday and could have easily devastated the entire city. The *gendarmes* were able to prevent him from setting off the explosion, but he could not escape this time. He was shot."

I stopped walking. "Wow." At the moment, it was all I could say. If the Chameleon had been killed in Paris yesterday, then it couldn't have been him running after me at the gun range, or trying to break into my apartment.

Instead of a world-class assassin after me, I was being stalked by your run-of-the-mill criminal. Or maybe I wasn't being stalked at all.

"This happened yesterday?" I said. With so much on my mind, I hadn't paid any attention to the news.

"Yes," Kasim said as we walked into the loud, busy, heavenly smelling kitchen. "The French authorities waited until they were certain of the assassin's identity. They made the announcement just hours ago and the wires have picked it up."

"Thanks," I said. "I didn't know."

"There is much to be grateful for in our world tonight."

WAITERS HUSTLED THE COMPLETED MEAL OVER TO HICKORY, where it would be plated and served to all our delegates and honored guests. We'd originally expected to serve dinner just outside Aspen Lodge, where an enormous table had been set up in view of the putting greens and pool, but plans changed. President Gerald Ford had once entertained an entire delegation outdoors. For myself, I preferred serving and dining indoors. No wind. No gnats.

Henry and I worked next to each other, putting the finishing touches on the meal we would serve to Mrs. Campbell and the princess. Because he didn't have a national representative dining with the women, Gaspar took the opportunity to rest; his assistant retreated to the barracks.

From his corner seat in the kitchen, Gaspar threw out occasional suggestions for arrangement or garnish, all of which Henry and Avram took in stride. I saw it as an opportunity to learn new techniques and was thrilled to be surrounded by three giants in the field.

Which reminded me of something that I didn't understand. When Avram set off to get ingredients out of the refrigerator, I moved closer to Henry.

"Why are we here?" I asked him in a whisper.

He shot me a quizzical glance as he twisted sprigs of parsley. "Because of the importance of these meetings." He pointed to the desserts. "More raspberry on that one."

"What I mean is . . ." I added more raspberry. "Camp David is obviously fully staffed, and the prince and the prime minister have their own chefs . . ."

He waited.

"Why fly us—you and me—out here? I think they could have handled everything perfectly with the staff on hand."

Henry graced me with one of his "here comes a lecture" smiles. "You and I are President Campbell's best. Today is the first day of important negotiations. It sets the right tone for him to bring us here, to show that he understands the magnitude of these talks. We are a symbol of the president doing his utmost, of offering the best he has."

I nodded. I hadn't thought of it that way.

"And when we leave tonight, to return to the vital job of preparing for the state dinner, we will have imposed ourselves on the Camp David staff and on these two visiting chefs. Imposed," he repeated, "in a very good, very powerful way. All remaining meals served during these negotiations will be seen as our progeny."

"That's heavy."

He winked. "Heavy as whipping cream."

IN AN UNUSUAL TURN OF EVENTS, WE CHEFS WERE CALLED UPON to serve courses in the Aspen dining room. Highly uncommon, but then again, the entire atmosphere at Camp David was different. Everyone was more relaxed here. It was as though serenity hung in the fragrant air, just waiting for us to take a deep breath and share it.

I tied on a fresh apron before meeting the First Lady and her guest. It wouldn't do to have raspberry splatters all over my chest as I served the women their first course.

When I voiced my concerns about taking on the added responsibility of actually serving a meal, Henry waved a hand in the air as if to say this would be no trouble at all. I had two assistants: one Camp David regular and one Muslim assistant, both female. That was the primary reason we'd been tagged for service. Our waitstaff tonight was predominantly male, and we'd been given explicit instructions by Kasim to have only females serve the princess.

Fair enough.

Just before we served, the three of us stopped to give the food-laden cart another inspection. We'd begin with soup: a light combination of vegetables, lemon, and coriander, accompanied by an assortment of breads prepared without lard or milk.

I was particularly proud of tonight's entrée, a roasted squab—boned by our Muslim assistant—stuffed with curry-coconut flavor–infused rice. I couldn't wait to see if our menu passed muster with the princess. Still clad in the sky-colored robes, she sat erect, hands in her lap. Behind, the handmaidens sat, dressed in pale beige gowns and scarves that covered only the lower portion of their faces. Across the table from the princess, the First Lady smiled. Dressed more casually, in linen slacks and a plaid gauze shirt, she licked her lips twice before saying, ". . . and walking trails. Do you enjoy walking outdoors?"

One of the handmaidens blinked, tilted her head, then stood to translate in the princess's ear.

The princess faced her handmaiden—or so I assumed, because it was impossible to tell through the fabric precisely which way her attention was turned—and whispered in return. The handmaiden said, "No. The princess does not," before returning to her seat.

Mrs. Campbell's smile didn't fade. I gave her credit. In her position, I'd be wishing for a face-scarf of my own.

I smoothed my apron, gave the cart one more check, then grasped its stainless steel handles. My assistants fell in behind me.

"Good evening, Olivia," Mrs. Campbell said with obvious relief.

The princess immediately leaned back, then lowered her head.

I made eye contact with the First Lady, then turned to our guest. "Good evening, Mrs. Campbell, Princess Hessa."

She didn't acknowledge me, and I worried that I'd made some gross faux pas by addressing her directly. The First Lady didn't miss a beat. "Thank you for preparing this lovely meal," she said, with a smile powerful enough to banish my princess-addressing doubts, "This soup looks deli—"

Before she could finish her sentence, the princess stood. Her handmaidens rushed to her side. The two girls chattered in high-pitched foreign voices, until the princess quieted them with a raised hand. She gestured, and one of the assistants rushed to the door, summoning Kasim from outside.

He brought his face close enough to hear the handmaiden whisper.

I stood, soup bowl still in hand, unsure of my next move.

"I am sorry," Kasim said a moment later. "The princess begs your indulgence to be excused."

Mrs. Campbell had already come to her feet. Concern tightened her gentle features. "Of course," she said. "Would the princess prefer to have dinner served in her own quarters?"

Kasim asked the handmaiden in their native tongue. Then he listened. The handmaiden spoke softly; I couldn't hear her.

Facing us once again, Kasim said, "We thank you for your kind hospitality, but the princess is overheated and does not care to eat at the moment."

Mrs. Campbell looked as puzzled as I felt. "I hope she's not ill," she said. "Please let us know if there's anything we can do."

Kasim thanked her. The two women left to escort the princess to her cabin. Kasim watched after them, looking confused. "I shall return to my cabin as well," he said. "Good night."

Mrs. Campbell said, "Good night," to Kasim and then looked at me.

"Did I do something wrong?" I asked as my assistants swept in to clear away the princess's place settings.

"No," the First Lady said, her forehead wrinkled. "I don't understand what just happened." She sat.

I placed the bowl of soup in front of her.

"Is there anything we can do for you?"

"No," she said again, drawing out the word. "I made certain to familiarize myself with their customs, and yet . . . I couldn't get her to talk with me. At all." Her expression relaxed, turned almost despondent. "I hope I haven't inadvertently done something to impede my husband's efforts."

"I'm sure you haven't," I said.

She smiled up at me with a mixture of gratitude and regret. "Thank you, Ollie." With a glance at her soup, she finished the sentiment she'd begun before the princess's peculiar departure. "This *does* look delicious. Thank you."

When I returned to the kitchen, enough of the waitstaff was back from Hickory, and I was spared further serving duties. I never minded pitching in. No one did. But the scene with the princess unnerved me. I didn't want Mrs. Campbell to associate my presence with such a negative moment. Not when she still had her executive chef decision to make.

We cleaned up as the waitstaff hustled, and before long Henry and I were ready to go. Right on schedule. I smiled. If there was one thing White House and First Family staff members were good at, it was punctuality. Avram and Gaspar were scheduled to remain at Camp David for the duration of the trade talks, a prospect that delighted them both. Henry and I thanked them for all we learned, and we wished them well over the coming days and in the future.

The path back to the helicopter pad was much darker now that dusk had settled. I breathed in the damp greenery, again, and wished I could stay just another day. "It's gorgeous here," I said, throwing my arms out to encompass the expansiveness. "It's so peaceful, so . . . calming. It almost makes me for-get . . ."

"Forget what?" Henry asked.

I dropped my hands to my sides, remembering all that had transpired before my trip to this Shangri-la. Although the Chameleon was dead, and my fear of him now gone, I still had the stalking-weirdo issue to deal with. Not to mention my concerns about my future with Tom. If I had a future with Tom. Too much to burden Henry with, so I shot him a rueful smile and said, "Boy troubles."

He laughed.

We were passing Birch, our footsteps making soft shuffling noises, when we heard it. Strange noises—coughing, crying, and gasped directives in a foreign tongue. The cabin's front door stood open, and one of the handmaidens who had been approaching from the opposite direction rushed in, accompanied by a man I hadn't seen before. The door slammed shut behind them.

We stood in the shadows, watching.

"What do you suppose that's all about?" I whispered to Henry.

His lips drew into a line. "I have no idea."

BACK AT MY APARTMENT THAT NIGHT, I COULDN'T WAIT TO TURN on the news, but I had one very important stop to make first.

Mrs. Wentworth answered almost before I finished knocking.

"There you are," she said. "I've been worried."

"Why, did anything happen while I was gone?"

She shook her snowy head. "Nope. All quiet. But you're late."

"I am," I said. "Busy day. But I wanted to stop by and thank you again for what you did last night. I don't know who the guy was, but I'm glad you were awake. I hate to think what would have happened if you weren't."

She wrinkled her nose and gave a sidewise glance, snorting. But I could tell she was pleased with herself. "Turns out there's been a rash of break-ins."

"There has? In our building?"

She shook her head. "Not just here. Nearby, too. Three in the complex across the street. All three in one night. Five more about half-mile away. They figure the fella who tried to break in here was expanding his territory." She licked her dry lips. "Police called me today. Wanted me to look at some pictures. But I didn't recognize the guy who was here."

"Wow," I said. I hadn't been specifically targeted after all. Relief washed over me like an unexpected sun shower.

"Your boyfriend coming to stay tonight?"

"No."

Feathery eyebrows tugged upward. "Why not? He should be here. To protect you."

"I'll do okay," I said, then thanked her again and said good night.

"Oh, I get it," she said as I made the short trek to my apartment door. I turned.

She waved her cane at me. "You two better make up pretty quick. You never know if that creep will try again."

"Good night, Mrs. Wentworth."

"POLICE IN PARIS TONIGHT CONFIRM THAT THE ELUSIVE ASSASSIN known as the Chameleon is dead." The handsome anchorman averted his gaze slightly off camera—as though to direct viewers' attention. On cue, the scene shifted and my television screen became the street just outside the Louvre. In the background, over the shoulder of the onsite female reporter, I could make out the familiar, I. M. Pei–designed glass pyramid, which served as the museum's entrance.

My tape was in, my VCR was set on "Record," and I sat forward, watching intently.

The American reporter fought to speak over the rain and winds that buffeted the Parisian avenue. She pushed damp hair off her face, and spoke with somber inflections. "It is here, at the world-famous Louvre, the largest museum in the world, that the Chameleon intended to wreak havoc on not only his target, French President Pierre La Place . . ."—the network cut to a stock photo of the smiling world leader, hand raised in greeting—". . . but on priceless history, art, and innocent bystanders as well.

"Other than the Chameleon, whose true identity is being withheld until further notice, no one was injured in yesterday's gunfire. Authorities from Interpol are not commenting on how they learned of the Chameleon's plans in time to protect the president, but there is much celebration tonight as a mysterious killer's long reign of terror comes to a bloody, and final, close."

The anchorman provided a few more details about the shooting, and explained why Interpol had delayed announcement of the Chameleon's death.

Apparently he'd been such a master of disguise that they hadn't been immediately certain that the man shot at the scene was truly the Chameleon. According to reports, and "respected sources," there was no doubt at all that the French *gendarmes* had rid the world of this terrible assassin, once and for all.

The scene shifted again, and there, big as my twenty-seven-inch screen would allow, was an artist's rendering of the Chameleon's face. Had they drawn this picture after he'd been killed? I didn't know. What I did know was that he didn't look at all like the man I'd seen at the merry-go-round. He was darker skinned, with dark hair and dark eyes. I waited till the segment came to a complete end, before stopping the tape, rewinding, and freezing the man's face to study it.

I pulled out the artist's rendering.

Not the same man. But then again, this was an individual who made his living occupying other identities. The broadcast hadn't said a word about his height or build. From the drawing onscreen, the face was slim enough to be right. The cheeks slightly concave, the shape of the face narrow, though not long.

I stared at the screen, then at the drawing in my hands. Then back at the screen.

Maybe. But it was a stretch.

I already knew that the prospective suitor at the range and the potential intruder at my door couldn't have been the Chameleon. Not possible for the assassin to have been here and in Paris at the same time. But the merry-go-round guy . . . that was another story. That man had *murdered* Naveen. I'd seen it happen—it was a scenario that would play before my eyes again and again for the rest of my life.

Tom and the rest of the Secret Service had assumed the killer was the Chameleon. I'd assumed so, too. Comparing these pictures made me second-guess that assumption.

With a sigh, I folded the paper and put it away again. I didn't know who killed Naveen. Maybe I never would.

IN THE WHITE HOUSE KITCHEN ALL THE NEXT DAY, WE WERE AT full staff and would remain so for the duration. Tomorrow a slew of temporary help would descend upon us to prepare for the dinner, just over forty-eight hours away.

The most important consideration in preparing a meal of this magnitude was the preparation. And not just food preparation: The timing of pre-work, the organization of manpower, the boiling point of both water and tempers, all had to be taken into account when preparing for such an event. Which meant that until this dinner was over, I needed to put my personal issues aside. Tom hadn't left any messages. Hadn't stopped by to visit, either.

I'd expected him to call last night, when word of the Chameleon's demise hit the news. But, nothing.

It was time for me to face facts. To put things into perspective. Right now, nothing was more important than our upcoming state dinner and the trade agreements in the Middle East it might represent. This state dinner, perhaps the most important one we would ever experience, was Henry's swan song, his crowning glory—the meal that would be talked about for years after his retirement.

I sighed. This might be my swan song, too. But for a whole different reason.

Jamal, the maître d', would be in charge of Wednesday night's event. He and I stood over the large gray bins that held different varieties of china that the White House possessed. We anticipated a full house, 140 guests, seated at tables of ten in the State Dining Room.

"I suggest the Reagan china and the Wilson china," Jamal said, as he scrutinized his records. The Campbells hadn't yet decided on their own style of dinnerware for their White House legacy and we were often required to combine settings when entertaining a large group of guests. "Both are elegant, yet understated. Or—"

"No, unfortunately," I said, interrupting him. "Both of those," I pointed, "have gold in the design. Since many of our guests are male Muslims, we have to take into account that they are not allowed to consume food served on silver or gold."

Jamal nodded. "Serving trays, too, then?"

"Yep."

We had several options open to us, but I knew we needed to make a decision quickly if we were to move forward. "Surely we aren't the first administration to welcome Muslim guests to our table," I said, "so let's take a look at what serving pieces were used last time the kitchen faced this situation."

Jamal said he would take care of it, and left.

Peter Sargeant took that moment to drop in. His eyes scanned the whole of the storage area, then focused on the china before me and announced that

I needed to be aware of our Muslim guests' requirements before making snap—and uninformed—decisions that could easily ruin the negotiations that President Campbell was so tirelessly working to facilitate. He then began a lecture, attempting to inform me of the Muslim rules.

"We know the protocols," I said crisply. "That's why Jamal and I were here. We've already dismissed these." I pointed to the bins. As I continued, my voice rose. "We were already coming up with alternatives before you arrived."

He blinked, evidently surprised by my "Back off, bucko," attitude. It took mere seconds for him to recover. "You're wasting your time, here," he said. "I've already seen to that."

"You have?" I was curious. "Which china did you choose?"

"Since when do I answer to you?"

Like I'd been slapped, I froze—speechless. Grasping for composure, I decided to face this bully once and for all. "Mr. Sargeant," I began, "we apparently got off on the wrong foot, somehow." I didn't add that our "wrong foot" was a direct result of him targeting me for harassment. "I'd like to rectify that."

If he'd been taller, he would have looked down his nose at me. "I see no need."

"You see no need?" I repeated his words, disbelievingly. "And why is that?"

"Ms. Paras, you may not want to hear this, but since the truth is always the best approach, I will tell you, for your own good, that I believe your days here are numbered. Specifically, I see your tenure at the White House coming to a close immediately after Laurel Anne is named executive chef. I see no need to cultivate a 'relationship' with you if you won't be here next week."

When he said Laurel Anne's name, he smiled. Like a teenager with a bad crush.

"Well then," I said, fighting the sting of his words. "I will leave you to your china choice." I brushed past him.

"Ah-ah-ah," he said.

I turned.

"I just came from informing Henry. You should know, too. The atmosphere at Camp David did not agree with the princess. She is back at Blair House with her assistants. Her chef remained at Camp David with the prince, so our kitchen may be called upon to assist with meals."

I nodded acknowledgment.

"Kasim will act as liaison between the White House and Blair House."

"He's back here, too?" The poor guy. He'd been so content at Camp David.

"Is there a reason he shouldn't be?"

I was in no mood to argue anymore. I said nothing. As long as I worked in the White House, I intended to maintain dignity in my position. "Thank you for letting me know," I said, and then left the room.

KASIM DID, INDEED, STOP BY THE KITCHEN TO INQUIRE ABOUT obtaining ingredients for Blair House. Peter Sargeant accompanied him. Cyan, Bucky, and I offered to make anything the princess required, but Kasim demurred. "If the items we discussed will please be delivered to Blair House," he said, "the princess's assistants will prepare her meals."

"Is she well?" I asked.

"Thank you for your concern, yes, the princess is much better now that she has returned to the apartments."

"Has the social secretary discussed dinner with you?" I asked. "Has she explained how the courses will be presented?"

Kasim nodded, addressing us all. "I am pleased to say that Ms. Schumacher has been very thorough. The prince and princess, as well as the rest of our delegation are aware of the finger bowls, if that is your concern."

It was. Guests at our official dinners often didn't know what to do when presented with a doily-covered plate, glass bowl of water, fork and spoon. Waiters placed these finger bowls before each guest after the main course. Once a guest was finished availing himself of its cleansing benefits, he was supposed to move the doily and bowl to the side and place the fork to the left and the spoon to the right. This indicated that the guest was ready to be served dessert. I couldn't count the number of times this tradition had resulted in confusion. I was glad Marguerite had taken time to explain the procedure to Kasim.

"Don't you have something to do?" Sargeant asked me.

I bit the insides of my cheeks. Hard. "Yes," I finally said. "I have a great deal to do."

"Then why aren't you doing it?"

I could take a hint.

Kasim held up a hand. "Your indulgence. Please. I have a question."

"Yes?" I said, happy to be doing anything that might irritate Sargeant.

"Are you"—his wide brown eyes made an encompassing gesture about the room—"the entire staff? I cannot see how so few of you will accomplish such a substantial endeavor."

"We have many more chefs arriving tomorrow," I said.

"I have not seen others." His gaze corralled the room again. "I have only seen those who are here, now."

Sargeant started to interrupt. Kasim waved him away, focusing his attention on me.

Pleased to be granted the limelight despite Sargeant's disapproval, I continued. "We have temporary staff members scheduled to arrive tomorrow. They'll be here at eight, and Cyan and Bucky," I gestured, "will take them through what needs to be done. Most of these chefs and assistants have worked with us before. That's nice because they know our procedures." I smiled. "I'll be here by ten or so, and I won't leave until everything is perfect for the next day's dinner."

Sargeant butted in. "You're not coming in until ten? Why not?"

"That's how we set up the schedule."

"That makes no sense. Come in earlier. This is an important dinner. We can't have the kitchen working at half staff."

Henry joined the conversation from across the room. "Peter, let me assure you. Everything is covered. We are all well aware of the importance of the state dinner and we are equally well-prepared. *I* scheduled Ollie to come in at ten tomorrow. I'm also coming in at ten. We are not needed here any earlier than that."

To me, he said, in a gentler tone, "You mentioned stopping at Arlington tomorrow morning, right?"

I nodded, not giving voice to my answer. I didn't want Sargeant asking why I visited Arlington. Henry knew that before big events I liked to take a few moments there. Even though my dad wasn't a part of my life—not really—he was all the family I had here. Spending a few minutes at his graveside gave me peace.

"Why on earth—" Sargeant began.

As though to protect my private rituals, Henry interrupted. "We will be here very late tomorrow evening. Cyan and Bucky will handle the early shift, Ollie and I will handle the later shift, which is when things have a tendency to go wrong. We will ensure that they don't." Henry glanced over to our pastry chef. "Marcel keeps his own hours as he sees fit."

Mollified, Sargeant stopped arguing.

Kasim thanked us for the insights into the workings of our kitchen.

"Watch it!" Bucky cried.

Sargeant stood to my right, Kasim to my left. As one, we pressed ourselves against the countertop avoiding Bucky's race to the sink, flaming skillet in hand. I felt the waft of heat as he rushed past us. He dropped the pan in the sink, clunking it loudly. Water on the hot surface sizzled and smoke billowed upward.

"Why didn't you use baking soda to put that out?" Henry asked.

Bucky spoke over his shoulder. "It was out of reach, this was faster."

Kasim blinked several times. "The smoke," he said. "It is affecting my contact lenses." He turned away, blinking more rapidly. Cyan, too, seemed to be struggling as the dark cloud spread through the room.

"Should have used a fire extinguisher," Sargeant complained, loud enough for Bucky to hear.

With his back to us, Bucky answered. "And have to fill out a dozen reports in triplicate to explain why it wasn't a breach of security that caused me to use it? No thanks."

"Geez," Sargeant said. "It's bothering my contacts, too." He coughed, blinked several times, and caught a lens in his palm. Keeping his head down, he tore out of the kitchen, anger radiating from him like the heat off Bucky's pan. Kasim followed Sargeant, and Cyan brought up the rear, her eyes streaming from the smoke's irritation.

Marcel, Henry, and I braved the haze, while Bucky—apparently unaffected—washed the burnt skillet. "Can I clear a room or what?" he asked merrily.

We flicked the exhaust fans to high, and soon Cyan returned. "Where's Sargeant?" I asked. "And Kasim?"

She shrugged. "Gone. Kasim said he was heading back to Blair House, and Sargeant said he had plans for tomorrow he needed to solidify today."

"Bucky," I said, slapping him on the shoulder, "how can we ever thank you?"

AT NINE O' CLOCK THE FOLLOWING MORNING, I GOT OFF THE Metro at the Arlington Cemetery stop. About twenty people got off at the same time. A family of four with a stroller, some couples, a group of tourists, and a couple of stragglers. We all followed the signs to the Arlington Visitor Center and a few of us branched off from the first-time visitors, clearly knowing where we were going. I was back for another visit sooner than my usual interval, but with everything that was going on I felt the need.

Another woman and two men headed in the same direction as me. The woman, in her sixties, grasped a bouquet of cut flowers as she headed toward the Tomb of the Unknown Soldier. A man with a briefcase and a rapid pace quickly outdistanced the rest of us. The other man carried a small potted plant. I knew that sort of arrangement wasn't allowed in Arlington. I wondered if I should say something, but I decided it was too late. He'd brought the thing, and if it gave him happiness to leave it there, so be it. The cemetery workers would remove it as soon as they saw it. And this guy would probably be none the wiser.

He walked the same direction I did, though far off to my left, like a wing man. I tried to figure out who he'd be here to visit. A parent? A sibling? I couldn't tell his age. He wore a baseball cap over long, red frizzy hair, a black T-shirt that read LINCOLN CITY, a blue short-sleeve dress shirt open over the T-shirt, and baggy blue jeans. He walked with a loping gait but he was short, so he didn't get far fast.

I was about to give into my helpful-Hannah instincts and mention the restrictions on grave decorations when he veered off far left and disappeared around one of the buildings.

An omen. I wasn't supposed to say anything.

Alone now, I made the quiet trek to my father's grave. Clear skies with a wind so harsh it nearly knocked me sideways, it was cool enough to need my hoodie, warm enough to promise a sparkling day ahead. I would miss most of it, sequestered in the kitchen until every possible last-minute issue had been covered, but I planned to enjoy this peaceful respite while I could.

Somewhere beyond my vision to the far right, a lawn mower did its job, the sound coming in spurts as the wind quieted and rushed up again. With 260 acres to manage here at Arlington, it always seemed a lawn mower, or four, hummed nearby. I crested a rise and noticed that the section next to my dad's was in the process of being mowed. I loved the smell of the fresh-cut grass, and the cool dew damp of the morning. The intermittent roar of the nearby machines didn't bother me. It was nice to have a reminder of life, of continuity, of normalcy as I visited those who'd died for the freedoms I took for granted every day.

My hair lifted, twisting as it escaped my hood. I sighed, enjoying the sensation.

"Hey Dad," I said aloud. Nobody near to hear.

As always, the only answers were the calls of birds, the push-pull *shush*ing

of the wind, and the ever present activity in my own mind. I sought to quiet
my thoughts, to take in the calm that surrounded me here. To let it take root
in me so that the next several days would go as smoothly as I wanted them to.

Whether or not I had a job at the White House when all this was through,
I could do no less than my best. Ever.

"You understand that, don't you, Dad?"

The whirr of the nearest lawn mower shifted from active cutting to soft
idle. I glanced up. A worker, just beyond a copse of trees, swung out of his
grass-cutting seat and waved over another worker in a white pickup truck,
towing a wood chipper. The pickup driver stopped, got out, and the two men
trotted a couple hundred feet behind the mower and dropped to their hands
and knees, searching the ground. I wondered what was lost.

Had the lawn mower not quieted just then, had the wind not taken that
moment to still, I might not have heard the out-of-place noise to my left.

I twisted my head to see the red-haired guy in the baseball cap walking
toward me. No potted plant in his hands. Evidently he'd found whoever he
was looking for. I smiled a hello. This was a big place; he must have gotten lost.
I figured he needed directions back to the Metro.

But as I took a step toward him, my skin zinged an early warning. The
man's expression wasn't right. His face, getting nearer by the step, was angry,
determined . . . and familiar.

CHAPTER 25

TUNNEL VISION SWALLOWED MY AWARENESS. FLASH FEAR HELD
me immobile. A rush like a giant wave crashed in my ears as my terrified brain
took forever to delineate options. Torn between running—to where? my mind
screamed—and fighting, indecision froze me to the spot.

One second, maybe two.

It felt like hours.

The killer from the merry-go-round reached behind his flapping shirt to
his waistband and I spun away, knowing he had a gun and a bullet meant for
my brain.

My feet pounded the grass. Silenced by fear, I zigged to my right between
headstones, wondering, absurdly, if ducking behind one might render me invisible. I knew I should scream, but irrationally decided it could slow me down.

Stupid, stupid.

I needed cover. I raced for the trees.

My screams finally came as I skip-stepped past more headstones. In perfect
alignment, so low to the ground, they offered nothing in terms of cover. I didn't
have my own gun with me—of course not—and I didn't know what else to do.
I ducked to my left this time, remembering Tom's admonishments about moving targets.

On the wind, I heard a pop, like a cap gun.

I didn't turn.

Fifty feet away, a hundred? I couldn't guess—I didn't care—the
groundskeeper and pickup driver still knelt on the grass far behind the riding
lawn mower, searching the ground. I called to them, but my voice whipped
away on the swift wind.

A horrifying thought occurred to me. What if the groundskeepers were in cahoots with the man chasing me? What if I was supposed to run to them, seeking safety, only to find myself trapped?

I shut my mouth, concentrating every muscle on moving forward, racing, running, putting distance between me and the killer.

Life didn't flash before my eyes. Ideas did.

My late-to-the-party brain finally kicked in with a suggestion, and I swerved left then right, then left again.

Another pop.

He was shooting at me.

Dear God, why?

Because I'd seen him at the merry-go-round.

Thirty more steps. Twenty.

I counted as I ran, leaping as my short legs strove for long strides, repeating: Don't fall.

Don't fall.

Don't.

Fall.

Ten more steps.

A noise, a shout.

To my far right, the groundskeeper got to his feet, gesticulating, hollering. Even if these workers weren't in league with the killer behind me, I knew I'd never outdistance the killer behind me in time to reach them. They were too far.

They continued to shout, but I couldn't make out anything over the hum of the motor, now three steps away.

Two.

One.

I bounded into the seat, taking precious seconds to shift the lawn mower into gear and jerk the front wheels far to the left, directly into the runner's path. The mower lurched forward, too slow, too slow. I leaped off the other side. The groundskeeper ran at me from behind. The killer ran at me from my left. The pickup truck driver must have known what I had in mind, because he came at me, too.

Too late. I made it into the white pickup, pulling the door shut out of habit and slamming the vehicle into gear.

I floored it. The equipment bed behind me bounced over the uneven ground and I prayed it wouldn't overturn.

Perspiration beaded down my face, puddling at my collarbone. Desperate sweat caused my shaking hands to slip on the steering wheel. I stole a quick glance in the side view mirror where I saw the two groundskeepers shaking their fists and shouting. I could see their mouths moving, but I couldn't hear a word.

The killer was gone.

Again.

Blowing out breaths, I fought to achieve enough calm to make sense of all this. I needed to drive to the entrance, or one of the maintenance locations. I needed to talk to people I could trust.

I drove the long aisle of grass between white headstones, apologizing to the dead upon whose graves the tires trampled. It felt wrong. Everything felt wrong.

At the first road, I took a left, my mind still not working the way it should. What had happened? If the Chameleon was dead, then who was this?

Only one option made sense. It *hadn't* been the Chameleon who'd killed Naveen. Someone else had killed him. And that someone wanted me out of the picture.

Still shaking, I pulled the truck to the side of the road, and stopped. By now the groundskeepers would have called in the theft of the pickup. I was sure to be arrested soon. I needed to know what I could or couldn't say about Naveen's killer to these local authorities. I needed to think. I needed to call Tom.

I eased off the brake and dug for my cell phone, heart pounding again. But this time for a completely different reason.

I heard sirens in the distance. Coming for me. I knew it and felt a combined sense of relief, fear, and agony knowing whatever happened next would prevent me from getting to work on time. Poor Henry.

With resolve, I increased pressure on the gas pedal. The visitor's center was far off, but I knew how to get there. But before I did, Tom had to know. I pulled up my cell phone, ready to dial.

The click to my right should have warned me.

I didn't react in time.

The passenger door flew open and the pale-eyed killer pointed his pistol right at my head.

Without thinking, I jerked the wheel to the left and slammed the gas pedal hard as I could, praying I wouldn't flood the thing.

I didn't.

The killer fell away; I heard his grunt as he hit the ground. He got a shot off. It hit the pickup's back window, making me scream, shattering the glass into an instant zillion-piece spiderweb.

Sirens grew louder.

My cell phone remained in my right hand as I gripped the steering wheel and drove for my life. I thought I heard another shot hit the truck, but when I heard it again and again, I realized it was the memory of the hit replaying in my mind.

I watched through my rear- and side-view mirrors, not looking where I was going.

Flashing lights directly ahead.

I hit the brake, held my hands up, shouting, "I'm not armed," as the pickup was swarmed by police.

I'd gotten away.

But for how long?

CHAPTER 26

I WAS LUCKY, IN MORE WAYS THAN ONE. BOTH GROUNDSKEEPERS—the man with the lawn mower and the one with the pickup truck—were bona fide cemetery workers. And both had seen the killer chasing me. Not well enough to offer a description, but well enough to support my claim of hijacking the pickup in order to save my life. The shot that took out the pickup's rear window helped, too.

Once the police officers who surrounded me understood that I wasn't a threat—the cell phone practically had to be pried from my petrified fingers—they were more than willing to allow me to call the White House to let Henry know, again, that I'd be late, although again, I couldn't tell him why.

I was beginning to believe that Laurel Anne might be the best choice for executive chef after all. It seemed that everywhere I turned, I was involved in trouble that prevented me from doing my job.

I sat in a small cemetery office with a paper cup of water in my hand, waiting for my ride. The police had generously offered to escort me back to the White House and I'd accepted. No way was I getting on the Metro again. Not a chance.

My cell phone wasn't receiving service, so I got up and walked the short hallway, until near the windows, I got a signal.

Tom answered on the second ring. "Hey," he said, without his customary joviality, "what's up?"

Words failed me. I opened my mouth, but nothing came out. It was too much. The weight of it all crushed my throat closed.

"Ollie," he said, tersely. "I got a busy day here. Can I call you later?"

Like a geyser, I burst forth all at once. "He tried to kill me. He's here in Arlington. He shot at me. I stole a truck."

"Say that again," he said. "Slow."

"The guy who killed Naveen. He's here."

"How do you know?"

"He tried again, Tom." I hated the desperation in my voice, hated the water shaking in the cup from my unsteady hand, but I couldn't help myself. "He tried to kill me. Today. Here. Just now."

"Where are you?"

"Arlington Cemetery." I enunciated carefully. Hadn't I just said that?

"Where?"

I looked around. I had no idea. When they'd bundled me into a car and driven me here, I'd blanked out. "In an office." I looked out the window and realized where I was. "In the administration building."

"I'll be there in fifteen."

"Wait," I said. "I've already given my statement. They're going to drive me back to the White House."

"No," he said, and there was something different in his voice this time. It scared me. "I will come get you. Do not leave there."

"But," I said, glad of his concern, but worried about him now, "you said you have a busy day. They're finding someone to drive me, right now. I'm not hurt."

"Ollie." The frightening tone was back. "Do not go anywhere with anyone. I will come get you now. Do you understand?"

I nodded and realized he couldn't see me. My voice was croaky. "Yeah."

"Promise me."

"I promise."

CHAPTER 27

TOM WAS SILENT FOR THE FIRST FULL MINUTE OF OUR RIDE TO the White House. Like a chastised child I sat near the passenger door staring out the window, unsure of his mood, unsure of mine, and utterly unable to explain what had happened out there by my dad's grave.

"We need to talk," he finally said.

"I need to get back to the kitchen."

"This is more important."

I couldn't believe that anything was more important than working on tomorrow night's state dinner, but I didn't argue.

We whipped past cars, well over the posted speed limit. I thought he'd drop me off at Pennsylvania, but he didn't. He continued to E Street, signaling to the guard who protected the closed avenue. In all, the trip had taken us half the time it should have.

"I never come in this way," I said.

Tom waited till we were within the White House grounds to stop the car. He pulled to the side and turned to me. "Ollie," he said. "There's been a development."

My stomach made a flip-flop and I knew what he was going to say. "What?" I asked.

"The Chameleon isn't dead."

Now my stomach twisted. "Oh my God."

"Yeah."

We were both silent a long moment.

I fought to keep calm, but my heart raced and I felt suddenly lightheaded. "It was him at Arlington," I said.

"I'm sure it was."

"He got away."

Tom stared at me. "We'll get him Ollie. I promise."

"Why is he after me?" I asked. "I saw him, sure, but I thought he was here for some big assassination plot. Isn't that what Naveen was trying to tell me?" I told Tom about the attempted break-in at my apartment and I reminded him that it was the same night the fellow at the range followed me. I thought they were all related and I said so, even though I didn't think it made any sense at all. "The Chameleon didn't come all this way to target an assistant chef."

Tom shrugged, draped an arm over the steering wheel, and stared out at the grounds. "You're a loose end. You're a liability. This guy hasn't had his successes—if you want to call them that—by leaving loose ends." He studied his hand. "Don't leave here tonight without me, okay? I'll make sure you get home safe."

I started to say, "I'll be fine," but thought better of it after what had just happened. "Thanks."

He put the car in gear. "I'll sleep on your couch."

HENRY AND I WALKED FIVE SOUS-CHEFS THROUGH THEIR INDIvidual responsibilities for tomorrow night's dinner. We'd worked with all of them—three men, two women—before, and they understood what we wanted, and took to their tasks with such confidence, it allowed Henry and me to take a breather to visit Marcel's corner of the kitchen.

Before we did, Henry pulled me aside. Over the sounds of pans clattering on stove burners, whisks against stainless steel pans, and cabinets opening and closing, we didn't worry about being overheard. "There's something else going on, isn't there?"

I wanted to say, "Yes, yes!" but instead, I asked, "Going on with what?"

He pulled a paper from his pocket. "This."

It was the picture of the man who'd killed Naveen. The picture the sketch artist had come up with based on my description. When I saw it, I assumed Henry had kept his copy folded in his pocket, just like I kept mine, until he said, "They say this Chameleon is dead, but yet this morning, we were handed these pictures a second time. We were instructed to be watchful. Extra careful with everyone we encounter."

He looked back toward where our sous-chefs were hard at work and where the additional temporary staff members kept busy under Bucky's and Cyan's sharp eyes. "I find myself scrutinizing every one of those young people. And yet, I know most of them. I don't know what is going on here. But I think you do."

I hesitated, but it was enough to let Henry know he'd hit the mark. "I can't talk about it," I began. "But—"

"I understand. Of course I do. But—"

"I'm sure I can tell you this much," I said, touching a corner of the drawing. "This man is very dangerous. Whether or not he's the Chameleon."

"Ollie, I'm afraid for you." Henry seemed suddenly old. "Every time there's been some altercation recently, on the White House lawn, at the National Mall, and even this morning, at Arlington . . ."

"You know about that?"

"I know that there was a shooting. Again. And coincidentally—again—you called to tell me you'd be late coming to work."

"I'm sorry."

He held up a hand. "I'm not looking for an apology, nor an explanation. I'm simply . . ." Henry ran his fingers through his sparse hair, closing his eyes for a couple of beats. "I'm simply asking you to be careful. Both for your safety"—he gazed out over the banging, clattering, bustling kitchen—"and for your chances at taking over my job." He stared at me, and it hurt to see the emotion there. "I don't want Laurel Anne to take over my home." He sighed. "Promise me you'll watch your step. In everything."

Just like when Tom had made me promise to call him when I needed to leave, I said, "I promise."

"Come on, then," he said. "We have much yet to do."

Marcel's desserts were always breathtaking in their beauty, but this time the master claimed to have bested himself. He held up his hand as Henry and I drew near. "One moment," he said. Then, to an unseen assistant around the corner, he called, "You are ready?"

A muffled, affirmative reply.

Marcel's bright smile gestured us forward and we followed him. Just inside the next room, a small table butted up against the countertop. The item in the middle was covered with wide white butcher paper, making it look like a sharply angular ghost. I knew from prior experience that Marcel preferred to keep his creations dust-free this way. Cloth had a tendency to catch on his desserts' delicate edges and break them off.

Now he asked us, "You are ready?"

Henry and I nodded.

Marcel and his assistant lifted the paper.

The beauty caught my breath.

Tomorrow night's dessert centerpiece—about twelve inches high—was, indeed, his most magnificent creation yet. Like a giant flame, three distinct tongues of fire twisted upward around a crystalline sphere.

Henry whistled.

I walked around it. "Sugar?"

"Mais évidemment."

If I hadn't been familiar with Marcel's methods, I would've assumed the centerpieces were created from glass. Each twist, representing the three countries in negotiations, was colored with each nation's national hues. I bent close to the American one, amazed at how Marcel had been able to spin sugar to such a vibrant red at the base, only to have the color melt away to white and then finish at the very tip with a curve of blue. The crystalline globe suspended in the center of these three twists was painted—if that was the right description—to represent the world. It was held, protected, embraced, by the three nations' "arms."

"Wow," I said. There was nothing else I could say. "Wow."

"Marcel," Henry said, smiling widely, "I bow to your brilliance."

Marcel nodded acknowledgment, beaming.

The sculpture's base was clear, almost colorless. Etched into it—how he'd accomplished such a feat, I'll never know—was the word *peace* in all three languages. On my best day, my handwriting didn't look this good. It was almost as though he'd taken his creations to an engraver to complete.

The thought—engraver!—made me realize that I still hadn't received Henry's commemorative skillet back from the Secret Service. I needed to do that. Even if it was the last thing I did here, I'd get that gift to Henry. I decided to ask Tom about it tonight when I called him for my escort home. I made a mental note.

With another admiring glance at Marcel's creation, I asked him, "How many do you have left to make?"

"I have completed all of them, of course."

Of course. Since the day I'd met him, Marcel had been the picture of professionalism—always working ahead. With dinner planned for 140 guests tomorrow night—at ten guests per table—Marcel would have made fourteen of these. He amazed me, constantly raising the bar. His pursuit of perfection encouraged me to push myself to be better, always. "They're wonderful," I said.

"They are, are they not?"

And I loved the way our pastry chef took compliments.

"My only concern," Marcel said, with a mournful expression, "is ensuring that each of these makes it safely to the State Dining Room. We cannot allow any breakage. I trust Miguel here," he nodded to the small man who'd helped him lift the cover, "but I do not know these new assistants well enough to trust them with my work."

We briefly discussed the matter, and then left Marcel to finish whatever he could on the rest of the dessert project—the smaller, individual items that would be placed around each sculpture and served to our guests for consumption. Not that they couldn't consume the globes or flames. But who would want to destroy such beauty?

Peter Everett Sargeant was standing in the center of the kitchen when we returned. "I've been waiting for you two."

He pulled out a list, and began reciting, starting with tasks to be done. He kept going despite Henry's assurances that we'd already accomplished all that, and more. Next, he launched into his version of what we needed to do, beginning tomorrow morning. I wanted to jam a dishrag into his mouth, to put an end to his babble. We'd been through the rigors of state dinners over and over again before he'd ever stepped foot in the White House. We didn't need this intervention.

"Although most of your support personnel have worked in the White House before," he continued, "I do not have all their resumes. I need a copy of each curriculum vitae so that we have that information on hand when we need to fill permanent positions here."

Henry said, "I make the hiring decisions for the kitchen."

Sargeant gave him a funny look. "Ms. Braun has made it clear that when she takes over the kitchen, she will require my assistance in these matters. Assistance I am most happy to provide, might I add."

"Ms. Braun is not the executive chef!" Henry's voice boomed. "And she won't ever be, if I have anything to say about it." Face red, he moved in close to Sargeant, towering over the little guy, pointing his finger. "I will thank you to remember that you are not responsible for making that decision. And, Mr. Sensitivity Director, I will also thank you to remember that Olivia Paras is in contention for the position. Your constant innuendo that Ms. Braun has the position wrapped up—over my trusted and capable assistant—shows a tremendous *lack* of sensitivity."

The room went suddenly silent except for Henry's heavy breathing and the slight backward shuffle of Sargeant's shoes against the floor.

Leaning back now, Henry worked a passive expression onto his face. In a most civilized voice, he asked, "Is there anything else before you leave?"

Sargeant hesitated, then said, "Yes. Yes, there is. Princess Hessa is due here shortly."

"Here?" I said. "Tonight?"

Sargeant said, "Yes, tonight," so matter-of-factly that we might have been discussing a network sitcom schedule. Henry and I exchanged looks.

"Why?" I asked. "It's late. Heads of state never come for visits this late at night. And, even if they did, there'd be ceremony, a big hoopla." Incredulity made my words race. "The president and Mrs. Campbell are still at Camp David until tomorrow afternoon. There's no one here to receive her."

"*I'm* here," he said with a sniff.

"But . . ."

Henry asked, "What's the purpose of the visit?"

"The princess is concerned about meal preparation for her husband. He has very specific likes and dislikes—"

In that instant, plans for the dinner crumbled like falling rocks. I blurted, "Our menus were approved days ago. It's too late to make changes."

Sargeant cast a withering glance at me, then glared at Henry. "This is your choice for successor?"

"Ollie is right," Henry said. "Everything has been approved."

Sargeant shook his head. "I'll be back shortly with Princess Hessa and Kasim, who will translate. I trust you'll have your issues under control by then."

Once he was safely out of earshot, I looked at Henry. "That man infuriates me."

He patted my shoulder and said, "You deserve the position of executive chef, Ollie." With a sad look, he added, "But if for some reason you aren't appointed," he sighed, "maybe it is for the best."

I braved a smile. "Maybe it is."

"THIS," PETER SARGEANT SAID AS HE STRODE INTO OUR WORK area, nearly bumping into four assistants in the process, "is the main White House kitchen."

As Sargeant waited for Kasim to translate, he stepped to his right. There were white-clad sous-chefs and assistants in every corner of the space, every-one busy. The clatter of pans, the brief barked questions and orders, and the sizzle as vegetables were dropped into searing olive oil made it difficult to hear over the din.

Kasim leaned close to the princess, who tonight wore a beaded orange *burqa*, again in full headdress. I couldn't make out her features beneath the chiffonlike fabric, but every so often the air current would press the material against her face, giving a sense of the shape of her features. Still, not enough for me to determine whether she'd be considered attractive or not. If a groom wasn't allowed to see his prospective wife before the wedding, it could make for an interesting honeymoon.

Kasim towered over the small woman, holding his beard to the side when-ever he leaned down to speak to her. I wondered if he did so because his beard wasn't allowed to graze the princess's coverings, even accidentally.

"Good evening," Kasim said to us. "I trust that our visit does not adversely impact your preparations for tomorrow."

"Not at all," I lied.

Henry whispered, "You handle this, I'll keep the troops busy."

Although we'd sent about half the temporary staff home for the night, with strict instructions not to be late tomorrow morning, we still had more people busy in the kitchen than the small area could comfortably handle. The presence of Kasim, the princess, and Sargeant limited our ability to access certain areas.

Kasim held his hands clasped together at his waist. "The princess appreci-ates you taking the time to show her around and share your plans for tomorrow."

The princess stood in front of Kasim, Sargeant behind. Now, the sensitiv-ity director was poking his head around Kasim's figure, giving me the evil eye.

Like I wouldn't know how to respond without his input. "I'm delighted to do so," I said. "What would the princess like to see first?"

Kasim didn't consult her. They must have discussed the matter before they arrived. "Princess Hessa is most pleased with your choices for tomorrow night's dinner. She would be very interested to sample the cucumber appetizer."

Lucky for us, we always made extra of everything. The item she wanted to taste, Cucumber Slices Stuffed with Feta and Pine Nuts, was being worked on by one of our Muslim assistants, so I led her, Kasim, and Sargeant around the busy assistants to where a tray of items was being prepared.

Just as I was about to pull a completed cucumber slice from the tray, xylo-phone music pierced the air.

"What's that?" I asked.

The princess reached into her *burqa* with her right hand, and pulled out a cell phone. She answered with a murmur, and held her left hand over her ear.

"Perhaps you should escort the princess to the hallway," I whispered to Sargeant.

To my surprise, he took the suggestion.

I turned to Kasim. "I didn't realize the princess carried a cell phone."

If eyebrows could shrug, his did. "Do you not have one?" he asked, as he pulled a cell phone from beneath his flowing robes. "I carry mine always. As a travel facilitator, it is imperative that I am always able to be reached."

"I do have one," I said, flustered. I realized my gaffe. Because Kasim and the princess came from a Middle Eastern country, I'd made the erroneous assumption that their access to technology was far behind ours. The phone Kasim tucked away, and the one the princess had used, both looked to be state-of-the-art. "What I mean to say is that I didn't realize they worked here. That is, mine doesn't work when I leave the country. Are these the same cell phones you use at home?"

"I understand your confusion. As diplomats, we are required to avail our-selves of technology that spans international borders." He lifted one shoulder. "These are special telephones. The princess insisted on acquiring one before we departed. She is concerned about her children's well-being while she is away. This is one of the reasons she did not prefer to stay at Camp David." He gave a regretful smile. "There was no signal there. And she is quite the devoted mother. She is often in contact with her family."

The devoted mother and Sargeant returned just then. Within minutes I'd walked her through the preparation of the filling for the appetizer without her saying a word. I offered her one to sample, but she waved me away, stepping backward as she did so. Her braceleted wrist jangled bright silver and gold.

Realizing that she might be uncomfortable consuming food in our pres-ence, I offered to package up some of the appetizers for her to enjoy back at Blair House. Kasim translated.

She shook her hands at me again.

There was no pleasing this woman. Nor a chance of getting her to speak aloud.

"What time will you be here tomorrow morning?" Sargeant asked me. "Not late again, I hope."

"Henry and I will be here before the sun comes up," I said.

"How long are you staying tonight?"

Henry joined us. "Is there a reason you need to know?"

Good old Henry, rushing to my rescue.

Flustered, Sargeant stammered. "I . . . I'm concerned about leaving temporary help here unsupervised."

Henry's wide face split into a grin. But it wasn't a happy one. "That will never happen."

"You understand," Sargeant said, "what with heightened security . . . we can't afford to take chances."

"As I said, you can put your mind at ease. But Ollie and I don't plan to stay past ten this evening. We don't want to be exhausted for the big event tomorrow."

Kasim interrupted to ask Sargeant a question. I gathered that the princess was ready to return to Blair House. I'd learned my lesson; I didn't offer her any food. As they spoke, Henry edged closer to me. "I'm worried about you getting home tonight. How about I take the Metro with you and make sure you get in safe? I can call a cab from there."

"Henry, my apartment is ridiculously out of your way," I said, "that's not a good idea."

"It's not that bad," he said. "I don't like the idea of you traveling alone at night, any night. With recent events, you shouldn't be left alone at all."

"I'm okay."

"Olivia," he said.

With a sidelong glance to Sargeant, who appeared to be oblivious to our conversation as he chatted with Kasim, I spoke in a low voice. "I've got someone taking me home tonight," I said.

Henry's eyebrows shot upward. "Who?"

I bit my lip, rolled my eyes, then whispered, "One of the . . . guys."

Henry said, "Ahh," and grinned at me. "I understand." He winked. "Your secret is safe with me."

I looked up to see Sargeant, Kasim, and the princess watching us. Oh great. So much for keeping secrets. Thank goodness I hadn't mentioned Tom by name.

Sargeant eyed me with distaste. But I was getting used to it. "The princess will be leaving now," he said. "Kasim and I will accompany her back to Blair House."

"Good night," we said as the trio left.

Kasim nodded. "And to you."

The princess and Sargeant kept walking without a word.

WHEN THE LAST POSSIBLE TASK THAT COULD BE DONE, WAS DONE, and all the temporary help had gone home, I called Tom. Past midnight, our quitting time was far later than Henry had estimated.

The phone rang twice, then went to voice mail. I left Tom a vague message about being ready to leave.

Henry shuffled in from the other room, yawning. He had his jacket on. "Problem?" he asked.

"No, just a delay."

He considered this, then started for the kitchen's stool. "I'll wait with you."

"That's okay," I said. "I'm sure he'll call back any minute now. He made me promise not to go home alone, so don't worry. He'll be here. Just a little bit tardy."

One eye narrowed. "You wouldn't be telling a fib just to let the old man go home early and grab some shut-eye, would you?"

"No," I said, "I swear."

"Okay then." Relief tugged a smile out of him, but weariness pulled harder. He was exhausted and tomorrow promised to be twice as busy as today had been. We both needed to get some sleep, and there was no sense in both of us waiting for me to be picked up. "You're sure?"

I'd been in this situation with Tom a hundred times before. If he was on duty he couldn't always answer his phone. But he remained aware and always called me back at his earliest opportunity. I forced a smile, knowing that it sometimes took him over an hour to get back to me. "I'm sure," I said.

Fifteen minutes after Henry left, I was still sitting in the too-quiet kitchen, waiting. Despite the fact that this place for all intents and purposes was my second home, I shivered. The hum of the refrigeration units, the occasional *whoosh* of machinery nearby, oddball sounds—they were just part of the background during the day. Now each sounded loud as a shout, and every time some device kicked on, or off, I jumped.

I dialed Tom again.

"Ollie," he answered.

"Did you get my message?"

"Just now. I was listening to it when you beeped in."

There was something weird in his voice.

"What's wrong?" I asked.

"I . . ." He swore. "It's a bad time right now."

"Oh," I said not knowing what to do with that information. "Do you want to call me back?"

He swore a second time. I heard a toilet flush.

"You're in the bathroom?" I asked.

"My only chance to check my phone. Listen, Ollie, I . . . I can't get away tonight."

"You can't?" I looked at the clock. Nearly one in the morning. The Metro stopped running at midnight.

"I'm so sorry. Is there anyone else you can call?"

I started to answer, but over the rushing water I heard a male voice call, "MacKenzie, let's go."

"I'll be okay," I said.

"Ollie—"

"Go," I said. "It'll be okay."

I hung up feeling lonelier than I ever had before.

Had I known this, I might've taken Henry up on his offer to see me home safely. But, no use crying over spilled sauerkraut. This wasn't the first time I'd worked past Metro hours. I zipped through my cell's phone book until I found the speed dial for the Red Top Cab company and requested a car be sent right away.

The dispatcher told me it would be just a few minutes. I set out for Fifteenth Street to wait.

Before I cleared the gates, I turned back to look at the White House. The heart of the nation, at night.

Beautiful.

And, right now, peaceful.

I thought about the negotiating country's delegates, still at Camp David tonight. Probably asleep right now. Had they reached an accord? Would the state dinner celebrate new trade agreements that could herald the dawn of peace? I stared up at the sky, wishing I could see more of the stars, but still comforted knowing they were there. Despite the fact that I wore soft-soled shoes, my footsteps brushed against the pavement so loudly. They rang out evidence of my passage, and it made me feel vulnerable.

The statue of General William Tecumseh Sherman atop his horse provided a place for me to park myself to wait for the taxi's arrival. All four of the horse's hooves rested on the ground. An urban legend had begun—I didn't know when or where—suggesting that the placement of a horse's hooves on a statue tells how the rider died. All four on the ground indicated that Sherman died a peaceful death, which was true—if dying of pneumonia could be considered peaceful.

Not all statues were "correct" as far as this legend was concerned, but as I sat on the cement steps I was glad of the thought. Concentrating on peace kept me from panicking.

Then I thought about Sherman's "scorched earth" initiatives.

Not so peaceful.

I stood.

A high-pitched squeal to my left made me jump. A homeless man, bearded and shuffling, pulled an overstuffed wheeled cart in his wake.

He didn't approach me and for that I was grateful. With the Chameleon known for his ability to alter his appearance and blend into the background, I might've decked the guy if he asked me for loose change.

Thirty seconds later, the cab pulled up. Right on schedule. I scooted in. The dark-skinned driver nodded when I gave him my address. Before I closed the door, I asked him how late Red Top provided service, even though I already knew they ran twenty-four hours a day.

I just wanted a look at the guy.

When he answered me, I stared, paying no attention to his words, but close attention to his features. Not the guy at the merry-go-round. Not the guy at Arlington. I was being paranoid, but if it kept me safe, so be it. Contented, I realized I'd been gawking when an extended pause and a peculiar expression on the guy's face brought me back to the present. He'd asked a question.

"I'm sorry, what?" I asked.

"Please close the door?" His accent was thick, Middle Eastern. Not the same as Ambassador bin-Saleh's or Kasim's, but I guessed it came from the same region.

"Sure," I said, and pulled it shut.

I sat back and watched out the window as the quiet city flew by and we made our way into Virginia. The chances of the Chameleon suddenly showing up as a taxi driver—*my* taxi driver—were about a zillion to one, but I knew the assassin had it in for me, and I knew he had resources. What had Naveen said?

That higher-ups in our system had been compromised? Was that it? Tom hadn't seemed overly troubled by that information, but I was. It explained a lot.

The worst of it was that with Naveen's death, we still were no closer to knowing what the Chameleon had in store. I was pleased to know that, due to the importance of the trade negotiations going on at Camp David, and the upcoming state dinner, the Secret Service had increased security measures not only around the White House, but in the surrounding areas as well. At least the president would be safe.

Now I just had to hope I was.

Again I stared at the cab driver. This guy wasn't the Chameleon. Of that I was certain. But could he be an accomplice?

The driver must have felt the weight of my gaze because his eyes kept flicking to the rearview mirror to stare back at me. I looked away. He looked away. When I checked again he was watching me. And I watched him.

"Something is a problem?"

"No," I said, lying again. I'd been doing a lot of that recently. "Have you lived here long?"

He shot me a look of utter contempt.

Great. Now I was the suspicious person.

"I have been in this country fifteen years," he said with no small degree of pride. "I have come here legally and I have made the United States of America my home. I passed all the tests," he said. "I am not a terrorist."

Oh, Lord, now I'd done it.

"I didn't think that you—"

"I see your look in your eyes." He pointed at his own eyes in emphasis. "You have suspicion. What, do you think every Muslim man is going to blow you up?" With that he threw his hands off the steering wheel and the car jerked hard to the left, crossing the yellow lines.

I screamed, but fortunately the absence of oncoming traffic prevented our instant death, and he righted the vehicle quickly.

"Sorry," I said.

He gave me a look that said, "You should be."

I wanted to correct him. Tell him that I wasn't feeling bad for partaking in my own brand of profiling, I was just sorry I'd screamed. I *didn't* assume every Muslim man I encountered was ready to blow me up, but I had an assassin after me. An assassin who made his living by committing murder and slinking away, disguised as . . . as anyone.

If I wanted to look at this guy suspiciously, then it was my prerogative to do so.

"Last time I checked, there were no limits on freedom of personal thoughts," I mumbled.

"What?" he asked. "What do you say?"

The moment of tension now past, I realized that if he'd been in cahoots with the Chameleon, I would've been dead ten minutes ago. "Nothing."

After an extended, awkward silence, I gave him a fair but unapologetic tip, slammed the car door, and thanked the stars above that I was finally home.

CHAPTER 28

FIRST THING THE NEXT MORNING, WHILE THE SKY WAS STILL dark, chief usher Paul Vasquez popped into the kitchen. "Henry, Ollie. Follow me."

The corridor was cool and quiet. Dark. In just a few short hours, the very same area would be filled with fervent reporters, eager politicians, and polite dignitaries. All hungry.

Paul held open the door of the China Room. I remembered the last time he'd called me in here, and I watched his face for some indication that I'd inadvertently stepped out of line again. The fact that Henry was with me ruled that out, thank goodness.

"There's been a change," Paul said as he closed the door.

"In the menu?" Henry asked.

"No." He stood close, the three of us making a tight triangle, tighter than would normally be considered comfortable for a casual discussion. His voice dropped and we edged closer still. "The information I'm about to share with you is being released on a strict 'need to know' basis." He looked at me for a long moment, then at Henry.

We both nodded.

"You understand that you are not to share a word of this with anyone, unless you clear it with me first."

We both said, "Yes."

The tension in his face relaxed, just a bit, and he looked about to smile. "I am extraordinarily pleased to report that negotiations at Camp David have resulted, not in a simple trade agreement, but in a peace treaty." Paul's careful expression gave way to a full-blown beam. "President Campbell has been successful in facilitating a peace agreement between the two warring countries. When this treaty is signed, it will be as big, or possibly bigger than the accords between Egypt and Israel."

Henry and I kept our exclamations of cheer in check, so as not to bring a batch of Secret Service agents bursting in on us. "That's wonderful," I said.

Paul looked as pleased as if he'd facilitated the treaty himself. "It is," he said. "And the reason I wanted you both to know ahead of time is because we're changing plans for tonight's dinner."

Uh-oh. Last-minute changes were never a good thing.

I held my breath.

"We're taking the celebration outdoors," he began.

Henry and I cut him off right there, both of us protesting. Henry was louder. "We can't serve the dinner outside," he said, "we've got everything set up for the State Dining Room. The places are set, the room is decorated, and . . . and . . . there are bugs outside." Vehement head shake. "It would be a disaster."

Paul waited for Henry to finish, holding up a placating hand. "Let me explain and perhaps we can find some common ground here. Because of the success of the accords and the ideal weather conditions, President Campbell prefers to make the announcement of the peace treaty outside the South Portico."

I pictured it. The South Lawn offered plenty of room for the dignitaries, their staffs, invited guests, and the press to spread out. The South Portico and the Truman balcony provided a beautiful backdrop for photos that would, no doubt, find a place in history books for all the ages. I waited for the rest of what Paul had to say.

"What we intend to do, is have the welcoming ceremony, introductory speeches, and official reception outdoors as usual. At that point, the honored guests and their entourages will be invited to partake in refreshments."

"Dear God!" Henry said, "We don't have enough food for the entire crowd."

Paul quickly interjected. "I know. We realize the difficulty. And we've come up with what we think is a workable option given the circumstances. We will have the cocktail hour outdoors at four o'clock in the Rose Garden," he held up both index fingers, "which will include appetizers and beverages. You are authorized to order prepared items from our approved contacts to augment the food you've prepared here. Once everyone is satiated, at precisely five o'clock, the president will announce the agreements. More speeches. Tables will have already been set up for the official signing. The signing will take place immediately, in front of the South Portico. More speeches, again. We anticipate a half-hour's worth of questions and photographs. Shortly thereafter, at precisely seven, dinner will be served in the State Dining Room."

Henry covered his eyes with his hands. This was no expression of frustration, I knew, nor of surrender. He was thinking, planning, figuring ways to make this work.

He dropped his hands. "Okay."

Paul, who expected nothing less, said, "Good. Let me know if there's anything you need."

I WALKED TO THE ROSE GARDEN TO SEE FOR MYSELF THAT EVERY-thing was in place the way Henry and I expected it to be. While I walked, I checked my cell phone. Tom had called and left me a message. I listened.

"Thanks for texting me that you got home safe. I was worried about you. I have to run—there's a lot going on. Call me when you get in. And, don't head home by yourself tonight. Give me a call when you guys are cleaning up. Talk to you later."

I berated myself for not checking messages sooner, but when I dialed his cell, it went immediately to voice mail. I told him I'd made it to the White House safely and I agreed to call him later. I purposely didn't add that I'd taken the Metro this morning. He would not have been amused. As I shut my phone I realized that this crisscross communication, while far from romantic, was promising. He was worried about me.

And I was worried for him. I knew that today's ceremonies and dinner—even if an agreement hadn't materialized—made for a tempting target. The Chameleon would be wise to stay away today, though. Despite the fact that all the guards knew me and I knew them, this morning I'd been subjected to the most thorough search I'd ever encountered. Freddie and Gloria were both on duty, and Gloria had patted me down. When I'd asked why the extra precaution, Freddie had mentioned Chameleon concerns.

Outside the front gates, in Lafayette Square, demonstrators from the prince's country chanted. Bearded men shouted. All wore traditional turbans and long flowing robes as they gesticulated and yelled. Their vituperative verbal assaults, some in English, others in what I assumed was their native tongue, made it clear that not everyone supported the newly crowned prince.

I turned to Gloria. "I thought camping out overnight in Lafayette Square was prohibited."

She stared through the gates at the angry crowd. "They didn't camp. They started arriving just a little while ago. Heard this is just the first wave, and we've got lots more coming our way. They're protesting in shifts, I guess."

The men screamed, occasionally in unison. Those without upraised fists carried signs. Hand-lettered, they were written in a language I couldn't read. They could have crossed the lines of vulgarity for all I knew. I watched the sweating, angry men and realized that they probably had.

I'd headed quickly to the entrance. Could the Chameleon be in that crowd? I doubted it. From everything I'd learned about the assassin, he had no political ties. No policy he supported. He was a mercenary who went in, got the job done, and raced out again without leaving a trace.

With security heightened to greater tension than I'd ever seen before, the assassin would have a tough time getting close enough to President Campbell today. That, however, didn't mean that Tom was safe.

Now at the Rose Garden, I blew out a breath as I inspected the tables. A centerpiece of yellow and white blooms on each of the seven tables stood taller than the four complementary arrangements accompanying it. Although the smaller bouquets were by no means tiny, they were dwarfed by the taller arrangements. The White House floral designer, Kendra, had pulled the original designs from their places in the State Dining Room and created these centerpieces last minute. Even now, I knew she was hard at work making replacements for the smaller items. Their exposure to the outdoors could make the blooms droop. Like the rest of us at the White House, she strove for perfection.

From across the expanse of the South Lawn I heard the Marine Band practicing. Everyone practiced until there was no chance of error. Even the aides who were assigned to move dignitaries to their proper positions practiced. I heard someone ask, "We've got Princess Hessa standing next to Mrs. Campbell at this point. Is that right?" and someone else answer in the affirmative.

Camera technicians and other media folk had gotten here early and were already setting up. Outside the South Portico, on the North Lawn, and in other strategic spots, high-beam lamps on tall black poles, augmented by light-reflecting umbrellas, waited for important people to arrive.

Two cameramen ran extension cords to their equipment. I wandered nearer to them on the pretext of examining another table. One was short, with a vague resemblance to Laurel Anne's buddy Carmen, and the other one lanky and blond. They ignored me, but I sidled closer, checking them out. Could I recognize the Chameleon if I saw him again? If he were disguised? I had my doubts, but I planned to study every single new face today. If my life was in jeopardy because I could recognize the guy, then I might as well do my best to use that information to pick him out.

"Could you believe security today?" the blond guy said.

Carmen's lookalike shook his head. "It's always bad, but geez. Did they make you take your camera apart, too?"

"Hell, yeah. I tried to tell them that this equipment is sensitive, but it was either take the thing apart in front of them or—"

"—you don't get in," the dark guy finished.

"What the hell do they think I could have in here anyway?" The blond guy held up his press pass, dangling from a lanyard around his neck. "And who the hell would try to look like me, anyway? The uniforms here know me. I've been doing this for months."

They muttered back and forth as I started past them. Nope, I decided. Neither one looked like the face burned into my memory from the merry-go-round. Or from the range. Or from Arlington.

Their talk of tight security made me glad. Maybe we'd be safe today after all.

"OVER HERE, OVER HERE," CYAN CALLED TO ONE OF THE TEMPS. "Yeah, that's it," she said as the girl brought the tray of appetizers to the kitchen's far side, narrowly avoiding collision with two other tray-bearing assistants. "Yikes," Cyan exclaimed at the near-miss. Then, waving her hand at the girl who'd deposited the food before her, she added, "Not you. It's just—"

The girl waited.

"Never mind. Thanks," Cyan said, "I think Bucky needs help over there."

"Stressed out yet?" I asked as I worked.

"Most of these kids have been trained in bigger facilities," she said. "They don't get the fact that we have to think about our activity. They can't just jump up and do something. They need to think first. Otherwise . . . disaster."

I smiled at her use of the word *kids*. Cyan was the youngest member of our team and more than half of the chefs she'd hired had mastered technique while Cyan was still learning the difference between a teaspoon and a tablespoon. The fact that she was a White House sous-chef at her tender age was testament to her talent. But we still needed to work on her ability to remain calm during tense situations.

"What color are the eyes today?" I asked, to change the subject.

She leaned toward me and blinked.

"Brown? I don't think I've ever seen you in that color."

"They're new," she said, smiling. "With all the brown-eyed folks traipsing through here these past few days, I thought I'd join the party."

I gave her a quizzical look. "You mean like Laurel Anne?" I asked, "Or Ambassador bin-Saleh? Or Kasim?" As I ran through the names of the brown-eyed people we'd encountered recently, I realized how many there were. "Or . . . Peter Everett Sargeant III?"

She stuck out her tongue. "No thanks."

"I bet the princess has brown eyes, too," I said. "Of course, we'll never see them."

"How is she supposed to eat in front of all the guests if she can't remove her veil?"

I shook my head. "No idea. Maybe I'll ask Kasim."

Just as she giggled, Henry returned from his inspection of the serving tables outside. "Troops," he said, his voice booming loud enough for everyone to hear. The kitchen silenced immediately. "I need my team to follow me," he said.

Cyan gave out some last-minute instructions to those nearby, and I handed cinnamon and powdered sugar to another assistant to mix. We made our way through the obstacle course of temporary help and headed for the door.

"This way," Henry said. Marcel and Bucky got there just as we did, and the five of us tramped to the nearest storage room, where it was blessedly quiet.

"As you know, since plans have been changed, we will be running tonight's dinner by the seats of our pants."

Okay, that was an exaggeration. We had everything planned—micromanaged to the very minute—and even though the outdoor cocktail reception threw our best-laid plans into chaos, we were managing the chaos. Pretty well, too.

Henry read from his list. "Cyan, you will coordinate the staff to ensure the hors d'oeuvres are placed outside at the proper time. The head waiter is assigning a team to you, and we will have less than ten minutes from the close of the welcoming ceremonies until the food needs to be out there. We have to stay on top of this."

She nodded.

"Bucky, you're in charge of dinner's first two courses."

His head snapped back like Henry had punched him. "Me?"

"Yes." Henry pointed. "I need you to oversee the final preparations just before the food is plated. I've prepared a list of those who will assist you, and you will work together with the indoor waitstaff to ensure the proper plating and prompt delivery of the first courses to the dining room." Rolling wide eyes, Henry continued, "Dennis, our sommelier, is beside himself. He'd planned vintages to complement tonight's menu—he had not arranged for a full assortment of aperitifs. But," he added with a rueful smile, "that's not currently our concern. He will be marvelous; he always is."

"What am I doing?" I asked.

"Before the first guest arrives, we are all gathering our troops to make as many more appetizers as we possibly can in the allotted time. All of us. While Cyan and Bucky direct their people, you and I, Ollie, with the help of some assistants, will be making more appetizers. Thank goodness we made as much as we did, and thank goodness you ordered those extra supplies, Cyan."

She blushed at the compliment.

"Once we have the situation under control—and I expect to arrive at that state shortly—Ollie and I will take charge of overseeing operations. This event tonight will require *orchestration*. We will probably all step out of our comfort zones." He took a moment to make eye contact with each of us. "And assist where we're needed, whether it's our job or not."

Henry was preaching to the choir. Not one of us approached our positions as a prima donna would—my mind lurched as I pictured Laurel Anne faced with this state of affairs—but Henry's coaching gave me reassurance. He huddled our team before every big event. This was standard. This was reassuring. Suddenly these last-minute changes didn't seem all that insurmountable.

If I ever ran my own kitchen, I'd do it exactly the same way.

AT THREE THIRTY, WITH HENRY'S BLESSING, I SNUCK OUTSIDE TO watch the ceremonies, keeping close to the South Portico doors. The prime minister and the prince and princess had arrived in limousines earlier and had been welcomed at the south doors and into the oval-shaped Diplomatic Reception Room with a flurry of pomp and circumstance. After that "official reception," the president and Mrs. Campbell, with the assistance of the well-practiced aides, guided the dignitaries outdoors, amid snapping camera shutters and microphones thrust forward from behind velvet ropes.

Each of the dignitaries found his or her place on a line of artificial green turf that had been rolled out several hundred yards south, where official ceremonies were usually held. Each dignitary's name was marked on the ground with white tape. Every movement of this entire day had been scrupulously choreographed; such preparations were necessary so that an event of this magnitude ran smoothly.

I winced at the loud pops of the twenty-one gun salute and watched as the cameras moved in to capture the president's official inspection of the troops.

The Marine Band, also known as "The President's Own," played several national favorites including "Yankee Doodle Dandy," and two songs I didn't recognize, but I knew must be the national songs of the prime minister's and prince's respective countries.

For a breathless instant, the music stilled.

And then, the Marine Band began the "Star Spangled Banner." When the familiar opening notes of our national anthem sounded, so clear and strong on this exceptional spring afternoon, shivers ran up my back. I blinked once . . . twice, and then again.

As I stood there watching, I marveled. The photographers stilled their cameras, the reporters lowered their microphones. We all stood at attention to salute the most beautiful flag, the most powerful symbol of freedom on Earth. Next to me, the waiters halted their work to place hands over hearts. Several mouthed the words to the song so many of us learned in grammar school.

As always happened, when the lyrics came to ". . . gave proof through the night, that our flag was still there . . ." goose bumps raced across my arms and chest, down my back. I took in a deep breath and thanked heaven that I'd been born here, that my parents' grandparents had come to this country for a new life so many years before. I had much to be thankful for.

I whispered along with the final line, ". . . and the home of the brave."

How true.

I knew I should hustle toward the West Wing, where the appetizers, beverages, and incidentals were being set up for the cocktail reception just moments away.

But I couldn't resist taking a quick moment to sidle near the dais that had been erected just outside the south doors. Atop a carpet of bright red, three tables were being set up, and I knew that the reason they were there—for a three-way discussion for the cameras on the nature of the Camp David trade agreement—was pretext. These were the tables where the president, prime minister, and prince would sit to sign the peace treaty that would change the fabric of life in this world forever. And our president had facilitated this.

Had the day been overcast and rainy, I would have felt just as ebullient. I was part of this moment. I was part of history. As workers placed chairs, tablecloths, and flags in place on and around the dais, I ran my finger along the edge of the signing table. A lineup of miniature flags, representing a myriad of countries, topped the tables with a festive, though profound touch.

Out of the corner of my eye, I thought I saw Tom near the West Wing. Even though I'd been on my way back to the kitchen, I couldn't resist delaying long enough to see him and say hello.

My short legs could only take short strides, and I certainly didn't want to call attention to myself by running, so I walked purposefully toward the West Wing and was disappointed to see Tom catch up with Craig and disappear inside before I had a chance to talk with him. At least I knew he was here. And that made me feel better. Within the White House gates, I felt so much safer than I did in the rest of the city. I glanced up at the black-clad snipers on the building's roof, pacing with their rifles, keeping a close eye on all of us below.

While at the Rose Garden, where chafing dishes had just been set up, I corralled Jamal. "As a last-minute addition, we've prepared extra fruit trays," I said, pointing to spots on the tables between the silver servingware, "which I think should go here, here, and," I stretched out both arms, "there."

Jamal nodded, asked a couple of questions about timing, and headed back in via the West Wing entrance.

I caught sight of Kasim working his way toward the food tables, dodging workers who carried chairs, tables, and other accoutrements. Kasim was in a robe of navy blue with a brown turban. Poor guy. Today was warming up and even in my white tunic and toque, I was hot. I could only imagine how he felt. He spent his entire life wearing dark clothing in a hot climate. How uncomfortable. And he'd been ill recently, too.

I also wondered how he felt, being left out of the ceremony taking place on the South Lawn. As one of the underlings, Kasim wasn't privy to the big events. Like Henry and I, he was there to make himself available, to facilitate and to assist. When it came to the formal procedures, he was left in the background to make sure things went smoothly for his people.

I was about to ask him if he needed assistance when I noticed Peter Everett Sargeant. He called out to Kasim, who turned. I ducked out of sight, then inched closer to hear.

"This came for you moments ago," Sargeant said, handing Kasim a large diplomatic pouch.

Kasim nodded his thanks. "I am most grateful. The princess was quite distressed to have left these things behind this morning. I will see to it that she receives this promptly." He turned his back to Sargeant, but the shorter man trailed behind the foreign assistant, talking animatedly. He, too, was relegated to the background to assure smooth transitions. The problem was that Sargeant didn't like to be left out.

The last thing I needed was another run-in with Sargeant. I stepped out of their line of vision, behind one of the colonnade's white pillars, and started to make my way back to the kitchen.

"If she prefers me to hold onto anything of hers, I can make a page available to assist."

"Thank you," Kasim said, "the princess will be most appreciative of your offer. But I believe one of her female assistants will be present later."

The words were polite but strained, and Kasim's long-legged, limping strides punctuated his obvious desire to distance himself from Sargeant.

I could relate.

Sargeant scurried double-time to catch up. Decked out in another smartly cut pinstripe suit, this one the same shade of navy blue as Kasim's robes, the two looked like a multicultural Mutt and Jeff. "I'm sorry you missed the opening ceremonies."

"It is my duty to serve my prince and his wife at their pleasure. If I am required here, then this is where I remain." Kasim spoke as he walked. I ducked deeper behind the pillar and hoped to get past them both without being seen. "Just as I am certain that you are more needed here to facilitate than you are out there." He gestured toward the crowd.

"I wanted to take special care of your delivery," he said with a degree of annoyance. "I will join the celebration as soon as I am certain that you and your colleagues are well taken care of."

Kasim wiped his brow and coughed. He stopped, turned, and looked down at our eager sensitivity director. "What I am in need of at the moment, my dear sir, are your lavatory facilities. I am feeling unwell."

"Of course," Sargeant said. "Let me show you the way. I'll take my leave then, and see you at the reception."

"Thank you," Kasim said. He wiped his face again and made a noise that underscored his discomfort. "I may be required to return to Blair House if I continue to feel this unwell."

"Is there anything I can do?" Sargeant said again. Now he started to look as though he'd like to get away from the other man.

"The lavatory."

"Yes, yes, of course."

Just then Sargeant spied me. "What are you doing out here?" he asked.

Kasim lurched toward the doors leading into the West Wing. Sargeant called a Secret Service agent over and asked him to escort Kasim to the washroom that I knew was just outside the Oval Office. The foreign diplomat nodded to me, briefly, looking relieved to be able to get indoors out of the heat.

I nodded back, then turned to Sargeant. "I'm here to make sure things are set up properly."

"And why wouldn't they be?"

I bit my tongue. Literally. Then said. "In the White House kitchen we leave nothing to chance."

"You will not be out here when the guests are."

"I don't intend to be."

He tugged at his suit jacket. "That's all," he said, dismissing me. "Do not let me see anyone from the kitchen out here again. You especially. Are we understood?"

"Yes, sir."

If he was taken aback by my crisp retort, I didn't know it. I executed a quick turn and had my back to him before he could respond. At this point I had nothing to lose. All I wanted right now was to make tonight's event a success— an amazing success—for Henry's sake. This would be our final hurrah together. Whether I stayed at the White House or not, I was determined that Henry would go out with a bang.

As luck would have it, however, I found myself outdoors again, just as President Campbell finished his welcoming speech. I glanced at my watch.

Right on time. Paul Vasquez stood near the presidential contingent, and I knew he kept a precise eye on every movement, maintaining an exact schedule.

When President Campbell closed, the crowd burst into eager applause. As it died down, White House personnel moved in to ensure the crowd followed the plan. The Marine Band began playing low background music, which they would maintain until it came time for more speeches.

Leading the way to the Rose Garden, President Campbell walked between the prince and prime minister. Behind them followed the First Lady and Princess Hessa. Although the prime minister was married, he'd come alone to the United States. This was the first I'd seen of him. While the prince and princess were settled at Blair House, the prime minister had been accommodated at a nearby hotel, the best Washington, D.C., had to offer. Despite Blair House's size and accommodations, it was not acceptable to house two delegates in the same abode at the same time. Since the prime minister and his group was smaller, and did not require the same level of privacy that the prince did, he'd agreed to the hotel.

From all accounts everyone was happy, although it seemed that everyone would have preferred to remain at Camp David.

All but the princess, that is.

I caught sight of Kasim as I made my way to the tables to give everything a last look and to ensure that the food we'd prepared was being displayed properly. Kasim pushed at his headdress, as he made his way back toward the West Wing. He looked sweaty and uncomfortable, eager to avoid the crowd, and I guessed he was again heading to the washroom.

"Were you able to get the diplomatic pouch to the princess?" I asked. He wasn't carrying it, but neither was the princess. If it was something she needed, I worried that Kasim's apparent illness would have a ripple effect on the rest of the day.

I must have startled him because he shot me a strange look, his brown eyes squinting even as he shook his head. "No," he said, "that is, yes. She has what she needs. Her assistant is taking charge."

Within minutes the crowd made its way to the appetizer tables. The important and the beautiful: senators, ambassadors, celebrities, media giants, and star-gazing assistants milled around the grassy area, all smiling. The crowd would thin down considerably before dinner began.

I knew I should head in, but then I saw Tom. He stood, looking smart and strong and brave, wearing a gray blazer, navy slacks, and sunglasses. A curly clear cord wound from his earpiece to inside his jacket. "Hey," I said as I passed.

"Hey, yourself," he whispered, eyes forward. His expression was all business. "You see anybody who looks familiar?"

"Nobody. I think you guys scared him off."

"Don't count on it," he said, never breaking his attention from the hundreds of people in the garden. "Keep your eyes open."

I started back inside, then stopped. "Say, Tom, do dignitaries go through security?"

His face twitched. Enough to know that I was taking too much of his attention.

"Sorry. Stupid question. Never mind," I said. I thought I knew the answer to that anyway. I mean, when the queen of England comes to visit, they don't ask her to put her tiara in a bin and step through a magnetometer. Dignitaries and heads of state were always who they said they were, and security was gently applied. "You going to be here all day?"

He gave an almost imperceptible shake of his head. "I'll be inside."

"It's cooler inside," I said.

He grimaced.

I took another look at the princess, who again, was keeping to herself. One of the two handmaidens stayed close—I assumed to translate. But every time anyone came near the princess to talk, or with a microphone, she turned her veiled head away.

I made my way around the business end of the food, and I noticed that one of the fruit trays was nearly empty. Already. The food was moving faster than we expected and I looked around for Jamal. He was nowhere to be found, so I took the tray and lifted it onto my shoulder, hoping to avoid running into Sargeant. He'd have something disparaging to say about me if he caught me doing the waitstaff's work. But that's how we did things at the White House. We didn't spend time worrying if picking up a scrap of paper or moving a table was someone else's job. If it needed to be done and one of us was there, we did it.

I carried the picked-over tray, making my way to the Family Dining Room on the first floor. We used that room as a staging area for big dinners, and even though it was a considerable walk from the Rose Garden outside, it was still the best place to keep everything we planned to serve.

Henry was on his way out when we crossed paths. "How is it out there? Do we need another tray of fruit?"

"We do," I said. "I figured I'd bring this one in and—"

One of the waiters lifted the tray from my hands and started for the kitchen downstairs. "I'll grab a new one," I said.

Another waiter turned the corner. "Let Brandon do it," Henry said, calling him over.

Brandon looked apologetic. "I'll be back as soon as I can. Mr. Sargeant sent me on an errand," he said. "The princess has requested a female serve her, so he sent me to get Tanya or Bethany."

"I'll do it then," I said. "We can't let the table sit empty for this long."

"Go," Henry said.

I went.

But first: "Let me take this off," I said removing my toque. If Sargeant saw that tall white chef's hat amid the bustling waitstaff, I'd hear it for sure. Without it, no one would pay me any attention.

Henry winked. "Good idea."

Timing-wise, we had only about another five minutes before the announcement. I wanted to be out there, have the tray in place, and make myself unobtrusive before President Campbell let the guests know the real reason for today's gathering.

Cyan was in the Family Dining Room, orchestrating staff. It would be another two hours before dinner was served, but this was the bewitching time, the time when everything had to be handled exactly right or our careful plans would fall apart. Henry had insisted that, once the food was completely prepared, I stay out of the kitchen. He knew me well enough to know that I'd be in there, doing all the last-minute jobs myself instead of delegating them. He used to say that when I took over as executive chef I'd need to learn the skill set that allowed me to let go, but today he said it differently, "When you're running your own kitchen . . ."

That hurt. He hadn't meant it to, but we both needed to face facts. This was it. By the time Henry retired next week, we were both pretty sure I'd be looking for a new position.

I worked hard to take on more of a management role. Of course, sometimes that meant grabbing a tray of fruit.

The round, crystal tray was piled high with strawberries, kiwi, cantaloupe, grapes, and some of the more unusual choices, such as star fruit. Our temporary staff had spent hours making each piece perfect, and the tray was arranged as though ready for a *Bon Appétit* photo shoot.

I lifted the heavy platter and made my way outside, enjoying the cool air-conditioning as long as I could.

The best way to avoid the hordes of people gathered outdoors was to take the corridor that led through the West Wing before I went outside.

As I passed several of the Secret Service agents along the corridor, I looked for Tom. Not there. I narrowly avoided bumping into a man coming out of the washroom outside the Oval Office. Since he and I were about the same height, I couldn't see his face over the tray, but I could see his slacks. Uh-oh. Sargeant's blue pinstripes. He went east, I went west, and I breathed a sigh of relief when he didn't take me to task about being out among the populace again.

As I traversed the corridor, I watched the activity outside. The White House chief of staff was at the microphone under the lights the two techs had set up earlier. He called for everyone's attention and, for about the fourth time this afternoon, introduced the president of the United States, Harrison R. Campbell.

The Marine Band began "Hail to the Chief," and President Campbell smilingly stepped up onto the raised platform to take the microphone.

The heat rolled over me when the page opened the door. I made my way to the table with the open spot and laid the tray down, making sure to uncover it. A waiter nearby took the cover from me and asked if there was anything he could do.

There wasn't, so I quickly rearranged the table to accommodate the new tray.

The princess, who I thought should have been up near the prince, made her way toward the table farthest from the dais. I didn't want to turn and give her my full attention—somehow I sensed that would make her recoil—but I noticed her slip her hand out and pull a slice of kiwi under her veil.

So the princess does eat after all, I thought.

She took another piece of fruit and then another. With everyone's attention on the president, no one paid her the slightest heed. From the quickness of her movements I had to figure the poor woman was starving. She picked at each of the hors d'oeuvres trays, devouring the small tidbits as quickly as she could get them under her veil. When her hand reached again, she picked up two pieces of Baklava Stuffed with Almonds, Pecans, and Pine Nuts.

Good thing she didn't have that nut allergy after all.

I smiled, and worked at cleaning up the garnishes that had fallen off trays and stained the pristine tablecloths. From the tiny sounds to my left, I knew she was busy eating, though I detected her inching farther away.

Just then, a young man in navy blue, pinstriped slacks stepped backward out of the crowd. The tables were set up in roughly a U shape and he was at the very end of the U's top, which put him directly to the left of the speakers at the dais. The prince and prime minister had joined President Campbell at his invitation, and the three of them stood together, looking chummy—freezing their movements and smiles for pictures.

With his back to the table the young man didn't seem to know I was there. He wore a white, long-sleeve shirt that looked crisp, but enormous sweat stains created dark moon shapes under his arms. It was hot, but not that hot.

I fussed with the table, making everything look good, and I gave the guy another glance. The side of his face, the shape of his head.

I jerked at the charge of familiarity.

No, I told myself. This guy was not the same guy from the merry-go-round. Not the guy from the range.

Was he?

Pale, yes, but this guy had brown hair.

He was the right height.

I scanned the area, looking for Tom.

Not there.

I froze, my hand poised over the fruit tray. What should I do? I couldn't say for sure that this man was the Chameleon. I couldn't see his face. Not yet.

What could I do?

What was he going to do?

The nearest Secret Service agent was thirty yards to my left. If I called out, I'd alert this guy, cause a disturbance, and he'd get away. He was inching forward, closer to the action. If I ran over to the agent, I could lose sight of him.

And I wasn't even sure this was the Chameleon. He could be a reporter. A cameraman on break. He wore a press ID on a lanyard around his neck and he shifted his weight, his back now completely toward me.

All I knew was that standing here frozen was not the way to go.

Freezing nearly got me killed at Arlington.

I had to move.

I grabbed the next tray of fruit. Almost empty.

Wanting to get a better look at him, I started to ask the guy if he wanted any fruit—when he jammed his right hand into his pocket and pulled out . . .

A cell phone.

Panic, then relief. I nearly laughed in spite of myself.

I looked at him again.

Inched closer.

He pulled another item out, this from his left pocket. It looked like an antenna. A sizeable one. Without dragging his gaze from the speeches in front of us, he connected the antenna to the top of the cell phone and twisted it into place. That was odd. Usually antennae stayed attached to phones. And then I remember Kasim telling me about the specialized models he was required to carry. This one looked a lot like the one he'd shown me that day. Maybe international phones had unique construction.

"Today," President Campbell said, beaming as cameras flashed and shutters snapped, "we are changing the face of the world as we know it. For we are not here today just to celebrate a trade agreement." He paused, waiting for the silence to ripple through the crowd. It didn't take long. "We are here today to celebrate peace. A true peace in the Middle East. Today we sign a treaty ending war between two great countries in that region."

A roar of applause. The president kept a hand on the shoulder of the prime minister to his right and the prince to his left. "Today's treaty promises our children a safer world."

More applause.

The crowd, breathless, waited for the president's next words.

And that's when she screamed.

The princess fell to the ground, gasping for air. Her veil fell askew and I saw a portion of her face for the first time. Her mouth hung open and she made noises humans don't usually make. I knew we needed Kasim, or one of the woman's handmaidens. Or even Peter Sargeant. Where were they? I was about to rush to her side when one of her handmaidens appeared at her side.

"She's having an allergic reaction!" someone yelled. I wasn't sure who.

The crowd rushed to the princess's side. Everyone in the immediate area reacted. Everyone, but the young man in the blue pinstripe pants. He didn't turn.

He didn't turn?

He pointed the elongated antenna of his cell phone at the prime minister. My mind skip-stepped. He's going to make a call now? From that position? And then I understood.

"Gun!" I screamed just as his finger grazed the dial buttons.

I threw the plate of food at his head, while rushing at him, prepared to tackle. The plate of food knocked him sideways, throwing off his aim.

Still I was too late.

I heard a *pop*. And another.

The prince jerked back, fell to the ground. The side of his head flowered red.

The young man in the navy slacks turned.

Pale blue eyes met mine.

In that instant, I knew.

The Chameleon.

His gaze flickered. I sensed a split-second of indecision. Kill me first? Or run?

Agents covered the president, the prime minister, the prince. The man with the cell phone gun shoved me to the ground and took off, running not away from the White House grounds, but into the building itself. In the mêlée that erupted, no one saw him go.

No one but me.

I scrambled to my feet and ran after him.

"The Chameleon," I shouted. No one heard. It was chaos outside. But now the Chameleon and I were inside. "Tom!" I called.

The corridors were empty. All the Secret Service agents had rushed out to protect the president.

I stood outside the Oval Office. I had no idea where the man went or what I could do.

"Tom," I called again.

I headed through the corridor to the east end where I knew a guard would be stationed. A guard who would not have moved from his post. But he wasn't there.

I heard a noise behind me.

The bathroom door opened and Kasim lunged out, grasping the walls as he tried to walk.

"Kasim," I said, rushing to his side.

He tried to wave me off, but he didn't look well. His turban was askew again and he headed for the doors.

"Wait," I said.

"Something has happened," he said, "I must be with the prince."

"No, don't go out there. A man—"

The words died on my lips as Kasim stumbled. He caught himself before he fell, but he made his mistake when he turned.

One eye was brown—the other blue. A pale blue.

The Chameleon's eyes.

I kicked at his shin and knocked him completely to the ground. On his feet were strange platform-like shoes, which gave him at least ten inches of height. No wonder the man always walked with an odd gait. And I thought he'd been sick. He'd played us all the whole time.

With surprising agility he threw off the shoes, got up, and came at me.

I ran.

But this time I didn't have a head start.

Kasim, or whoever he was, grabbed me. He smashed his left hand tight over my mouth and nose, cutting off my air. "Your lucky day, Ollie. I'm not going to kill you till I'm safely out of here. You be a good little chef and I'll consider doing it quickly." His voice was low and devoid of Kasim's usual crisp enunciations.

Running, he dragged me backward with him, but I didn't cooperate, making his passage difficult. I knew he needed to get me out of the corridor now. The place would be crawling with agents in about fifteen seconds.

I pulled my lips back, fighting the painful pressure of his hand till I could bare my teeth. I bit him, hard as I could. He bellowed, and I screamed for help again, raising my hands over my head to rake across his face. He shouted expletives at me.

I tore at his beard, my fingers digging into the matted mess, the gum-like adhesive stretching as the artificial hair came off in one clump.

"Freeze!"

I wriggled around. Tom stood at the far end of the corridor, his gun aimed at us.

"Let her go," he shouted.

Kasim pointed the barrel end of the cell phone to my head, his finger close to the number seven. Lucky number.

For someone else, maybe.

"Drop the weapon or she's dead," Kasim shouted back at Tom. He dodged behind me, keeping my head in front of his. It was an impossible shot. Even for Tom.

I didn't think. I reacted. Time to make my own luck. I jammed the heel of my shoe hard against Kasim's instep, scraping downward, using all my weight. It wasn't a lot, but it was enough to make him flinch. He winced and stepped to his right as I tried to break from his hold.

He grabbed me by the hair, yanking me backward, pointing the cell phone pistol at Tom. I heard that popping sound again, just like at Arlington, only much louder in these close quarters. As Kasim fired I fell backward, trying to knock the gun from his hands.

He held onto the gun, but not for long.

Tom had gotten him center mass and again in his forehead. Kasim slumped to the ground, pulling me with him. I yanked my hair free from his grip, my eyes tearing from the tender pain. The cell phone slipped from his fingers, clattering to the floor as his body seized up, trembled, then relaxed.

Blood poured over the back of my neck.

But it wasn't my blood.

The pale blue eye and the brown one were both fixed in a glassy death stare. Kasim, the Chameleon, had finally been killed. I knew it even without checking for a pulse.

For a very long moment, all I was aware of was my rapid breathing and the sound of my heartbeat in my ears. What a wonderful thing to hear.

Then—where did all the people come from? The room was suddenly filled. Secret Service agents, reporters, White House staff. How long had they been here? Had they seen what happened? I couldn't say.

Little by little, noises, sights, smells came back to me.

A tall agent I didn't know checked the fallen Kasim. Craig Sanderson was there, too. More agents. The tall agent picked up the cell phone pistol. He gave a low whistle and hefted the phone in his hastily gloved hand. "Look at this," he said to Craig. "I heard about these things coming out of Europe. Never seen one before."

Craig snapped at him. "Apparently neither did our security team. We will look into this."

My knees buckled and I sat.

Tom pulled me to my feet, wrapping me in a hug. "Oh, God," he whispered into my hair, "I thought I'd lost you. I thought I'd shot you myself."

I knew I should be worried about what the other agents were thinking, but I was just too shaken to do anything more than hold Tom tight. "I never doubted you for a second."

He murmured something I didn't catch.

Panic made me chatter. I couldn't stop talking. If I did, I thought I might collapse. "How did you know? Where did you come from? Did you see him outside? How's the princess? Was she in on it?"

Tom just shook his head. "All in good time."

I remembered to breathe, and someone shoved a glass of water into my hands. I think I thanked them, but I wasn't sure. All I could see right now was Tom. He'd been there when I needed him most. "You know what they say about saving a person's life, don't you?"

His grin was infectious. "No, I don't. Why don't you tell me?"

"You're responsible for them forever. You saved me. Now you're stuck with me," I said, giddy with relief. "You couldn't get rid of me even if you wore a Teflon suit."

"Ollie, I would never want to."

Now that, I heard.

CHAPTER 29

THE REST OF THE DAY WAS CHAOS, WHITE HOUSE-BRAND CHAOS. In any other public venue, the afternoon's pandemonium might have continued with hundreds of people running around, screaming. Here, chaos meant ordered disarray. The Secret Service took charge with swift efficiency. They put us under immediate lockdown. Invited guests were placed in the State Dining Room. Reporters, camera people, technicians, and their staff were sent to the East Room.

We all waited, enduring the systematic scrutiny of every person present, and we knew it would be hours—if we were lucky, only hours—before life returned to normal.

Good thing we had lots of food.

The president and First Lady had been whisked to safety. Prince Sameer and Princess Hessa were airlifted to hospitals; she recovering from her allergic reaction, he in surgery after being shot in the head. Prime Minister Jaffe had been hit, too. A bullet had grazed his shoulder, causing only a minor flesh wound, but he was being kept under medical observation as well. I'd gotten this information from the Secret Service detail that was currently guarding me. Basic information, but enough to keep me satisfied. For now.

I'd been sequestered right away. They told me it was for my protection, but I knew better. They wanted me for questioning, and they needed to ensure that no one talked to me before I spoke with them.

Kasim was dead, and for the first time since I'd smacked Naveen with the pan, I knew I was truly safe from the Chameleon. The four agents assigned to me, three men and one woman, kept me company in the China Room. Of all the places to be holed up. This is where it all began, just about ten days ago.

This time, however, I faced the door. I wanted to see what I was in for when it came.

Five other chairs had been placed in the room, along with several coatracks—the China Room often doubled as a coat-check during state dinners. Thinking about our comprehensive pre-dinner preparation made me feel sad. Tonight should have been a sparkling celebration. Henry's last official hurrah. Mine, too. Instead, I sat in this room of empty chairs and lonely coatracks, trying to calm myself.

All the agents remained standing, their faces impassive, their hands clasped in front of them. Outside the room I could hear muted crowd sounds: conversation, movement, the opening and closing of doors.

Eddie, the one closest to me, asked, "Do you need anything?"

"No," I said, "thanks." My voice quivered.

I wanted to see Tom, but I knew he'd be the last person I'd be allowed to talk with right now. It was imperative that our statements be taken separately, without any chance of one person's impressions contaminating the other's. I knew this.

And so I waited.

The White House filled to capacity—and then some, a reporter's dream. Five times in the space of ten minutes, eager journalists tried to sneak to the China Room and tried to talk their way into getting an exclusive interview with me. They were pointedly refused. I'd never felt so well-protected in my life. Seconds after terse orders were murmured into microphones, instant backup arrived to escort these wayward guests back to the East Room.

Eventually, three men in suits came in. No knock, they just barged in—the suddenly open door allowing a three-second blare of corridor noise. I didn't know these men, nor did I know precisely which branch of the government they worked for. Eddie encouraged me to be as thorough and as forthcoming as possible. They took turns. They asked me about the incident, which I answered as fully as I could. Their excruciating politeness made me more uncomfortable than anything else. I was too scared to quip. I licked constantly dry lips, and spoke into a handheld digital recorder that saved every trembling answer I gave, punctuated with many nervous "ums," and "uhs." One of the three took my picture—without forewarning—but what was I going to do if they told me it was coming? Smile for the camera?

Finally finished, they thanked me and left.

"Can I go now?"

"Not yet," Eddie said.

After about a half hour the door opened again. The two agents there stepped aside. Not knowing what to expect, I stood.

Special Agent in Charge Craig Sanderson came in with Paul Vasquez right behind him. Again I felt that flood of familiarity. Last time here, I'd been chastised. What now? Termination?

I swallowed, hard.

Our honored guest, Prince Sameer of Alkumstan, had been shot in the head. I'd knocked the Chameleon's aim off from his target, the prime minister, and the resulting shot might've cost the prince his life. If he died, would I be held responsible? Had I inadvertently saved one man only to cause the death of another? The countries in question had been warring for decades. These were nations with suspicious tendencies, short tempers, and long memories. Termination of employment might be the least of my worries right now.

"Sit," Craig said to me. He gestured for Paul to take the wing chair opposite mine and he pulled up a seat for himself.

I sat.

Paul spoke first. "You're being released."

"I am?" I asked, my façade of calm ready to crack. "I'm fired?"

"No, no," Paul said quickly. "I meant released from this room. You're not being fired."

"I'm not?" The quiver in my voice shifted from one of panic to delight, "You're not firing me?"

"We're here to talk with you, Ollie," Craig said in his soft Kentucky drawl. "We need to go over precisely what you can and cannot say to the media."

He called me Ollie.

All of a sudden, I felt a whole lot better.

Craig's directives came as no real surprise. The story, as provided to the American public, would be the absolute truth. I saw the cell phone gun. I called a warning. I threw a fruit plate that changed the shot's trajectory. What I was *not* to say was that I had an indication of the Chameleon's target.

"After all, you don't know for certain that he was trying to kill the prime minister," Craig said. "Keep it simple. You saw the gun. You reacted. That's all you need to say."

"He was targeting the prime minister, wasn't he?"

Craig's eyebrows rose. He repeated, very slowly, "You saw the gun. You reacted. That's all you need to say." His stern look softened. "Wait a few days, Ollie. We'll have more we can share with you then."

"Okay. By then no one's going to remember that I had anything to do with this."

Craig frowned. "Let's hope you're right."

Suddenly remembering to ask, I said, "How is the prince? Will he survive?"

"Too soon to tell," Paul said. "I'll let you know when we find out more."

They went over a few more protocol issues with me, and I practiced answering some of the more difficult questions that might be thrown at me in the coming days. I didn't think anyone actually saw me with the fruit tray. I didn't think anyone saw me being held by Kasim when Tom took his shot. But then again, I'd been focused on survival, not my surroundings. Time would tell.

"I think that about covers everything," Paul said. He stood.

Craig stood up, too. "Is there anything you need from us, Ollie?"

I started to shake my head, then said, "As a matter of fact, there is. Remember that silver skillet that started it all?"

BY THE TIME I GOT BACK TO THE KITCHEN, JAMAL AND HENRY had seen to the feeding of all our captive guests, and once that had been taken care of, the temporary staff had been efficiently questioned by the Secret Service and allowed to go home.

Dusk settled over the White House. As the last remaining "witnesses" were freed, the tension from the long day began to dissipate.

Cyan, Marcel, Henry, and even Bucky welcomed me back with obvious relief. Seems I wasn't the only one who thought my days here were over. After the heartfelt homecoming, the five of us settled in to work, almost silently, cleaning up the final reminders of the state dinner that wasn't. I thought again how this was supposed to have been Henry's final huzzah. His last big event as executive chef. Instead of a magnificent dinner for 140 dignitaries, we'd served a hasty supper to a queue of media folks.

"I'm sorry," I said very quietly when Henry came by.

"For what?" He seemed truly perplexed.

"For . . . everything. Nothing worked out the way it was supposed to—not the dinner, not my efforts to earn the executive chef position, not"—I'd been about to blurt my complaint that I didn't even have his retirement gift in my possession, but I caught myself in time—"not anything. I'm so sorry, Henry. This was supposed to be your big moment."

"Olivia," he said, and the fact that he used my real name made me look up. "Don't you realize all you've done?"

I blinked. I wasn't sure where he was going with this.

"You prevented a man from getting killed today. Your actions thwarted the Chameleon, the *foremost assassin* in the world. Do you think this is some small matter? The finest law enforcement departments in our country and in others—the FBI, the CIA, our Secret Service, Interpol—weren't able to do what you did."

"Well," I said, feeling more than a little embarrassed by his heaping praise, "we don't know that the prince will be okay . . ."

"He will."

"How can you be sure?"

"You don't serve as executive chef for this many years without developing some good contacts. Prince Sameer is out of surgery. The bullet only skimmed his skull and he is expected to make a full recovery. His wife is fine, and the prime minister is back at his hotel."

I let out an enormous sigh of relief.

"All because of you," Henry said.

I shook my head. "It was really Tom MacKenzie who—"

"Ollie." Henry's voice warned me not to argue.

This time, I didn't.

"And as far as the dinner . . . what can I say? Things happen. When your job is on the world's stage, you must be ready for anything. And so we are. How sad it would be, Ollie," he continued, "if my entire career at the White House was dependent on the success of one event." He shook his head, but his eyes sparkled. "I have so many wonderful memories, and so many successes." Glancing around the kitchen at the rest of the staff, finishing up for the night, he placed his hand on my shoulder. "And today I think I have achieved the best success of all."

I DIDN'T EXPECT REPORTERS TO BE WAITING FOR ME AT THE Northeast Gate. In fact, I didn't even see them at first. They must have been lying in wait across the street at Lafayette Square, because Pennsylvania Avenue was quiet when I slipped out the front to make my way to the Metro. It was dark out, and when a voice shouted, "There she is," I didn't have a clue that they meant me.

I detected a rushing movement from my left and I was suddenly swarmed by at least a dozen microphones, pushed so close that if they'd been ice cream cones, I could've taken twelve bites.

"Ms. Paras, is it true that . . ."

I didn't hear the rest of the question. The street lit up with sudden brightness as cameras honed in on me, white-hot and too close. I blinked, looked away. But I couldn't move. They had me surrounded.

A push from my left.

"The Chameleon. How did you recognize him?"

Nudges from my right. "Is this related to the terrorist's murder by the merry-go-round?"

"Who else was in on the assassination attempt? Was the Chameleon working alone?"

I tried moving forward. They jostled me back.

"Ms. Paras, over here."

I held up a hand to block the light. In the distance I saw trucks. With Pennsylvania Avenue closed to traffic, they'd parked in the distance and come to assault me by foot. Vans and trucks with antennae and satellite dishes protruding from their roofs sat at either end of the street. It looked like an alien invasion.

"I have no comment," I said.

"Come on, Ms. Paras, play fair."

I shot that reporter an angry look. How dare he?

From behind me, a woman asked, "Are you afraid that today's incident has destroyed your chance to be appointed executive chef?"

That hurt. I opened my mouth. Closed it again.

"Ms. Paras," another voice. Male, female, I couldn't tell. Whatever it was, it was testy. "Don't you think the American people deserve to hear the truth?"

I shouted. "The truth is . . ."

They all went immediately silent.

"The truth is . . ." Now I spoke quietly, amazed at the fleeting power I held. "That I have no comment."

They erupted. Yelling, berating, pushing.

"The lady says she has no comment."

I turned.

Tom and a group of Secret Service agents surrounded the group that was surrounding me. It was an impressive sight. I counted seven agents, all male, all tall, all very imposing. They wore no-nonsense expressions and the look of predators ready to pounce. Tom directed his attention to me, "Have you anything more to say to these reporters?"

"No."

"Then," he said, addressing them, "you will all leave the area. Now."

The stalwart agents stepped back enough to allow the media folks to scurry away. And scurry they did. Though not silently. They grumbled and complained that they deserved access to me. That they had every right to be on the public thoroughfare.

I didn't care how much they protested. At this point I was thrilled to be free from their claustrophobic clutches.

Once we were alone, Tom addressed his colleagues. "Thank you, gentlemen. I will see to it that Ms. Paras gets home safely." They nodded and melted away, disappearing through the White House gates like magic. Tom swung his arm toward New York Avenue. A car idled, waiting for us. He handed me into the passenger side and the driver stepped out, nodding to Tom. Tom nodded back, and the other man returned to the White House compound.

I leaned my head against the seat. "Thank you," I said.

Tom grinned at me. "Nothing but the best for our hero."

I smiled back. "You driving me home?"

"Yep."

"You coming up?"

He looked over to me and smiled. "That's the plan."

I felt wonderful again, for the first time in a very long while. "Good," I said, "but on one condition."

"What's that?"

"You are *not* sleeping on the couch."

CHAPTER 30

"OLLIE," HENRY WHISPERED, "TAKE A LOOK."

He pulled me in to the old Family Dining Room, where we'd staged all the food prepared for his retirement party. "You're supposed to be in there," I said, pointing toward the State Dining Room, where about fifty people milled, waiting for the party to begin.

"I know, but this is good. You have to see it."

A television stood on a wheeled cart in the far corner. Someone had plugged the TV in. Henry had a remote control in his hand and he perched his tongue between his teeth as he fiddled with the controls. "This'll just take a minute."

"You're not supposed to see this yet," I said, grabbing for the remote.

He avoided my hands. "This isn't my farewell tape," he said.

"You know about that?"

He shot me a look.

The staff had put together a montage of images from pictures taken over the years—from Henry's first day on the job through the last week's disaster. It was a ten-minute retrospective, which we'd planned to show right after lunch. I shouldn't have been surprised to discover Henry knew about that.

"Then what is this?"

The TV's blank blue screen switched to that of an unfamiliar logo.

I started to ask again, but Henry said, "Hang on."

"They're waiting for us in there," I reminded him.

"You think they'll start without us?"

I was spared answering when the logo morphed into action. Henry pressed the fast-forward button three times and the tape whirred into super-high speed.

"I should have cued this," he said. I caught a snippet of our kitchen. And people zipping around.

"Laurel Anne's audition tape?" I asked, aghast.

"Yeah," he said with such pleasure I was taken aback.

"But . . ."

"Here it is."

Henry hit "Play" and that horrible day came back to haunt in full glory.

"I was there, remember?"

He winked at me. "Patience."

The camera zoomed in on Laurel Anne's pretty features. She smiled. "And over here," she said as she moved to stand next to Bucky whose back was to the camera, "is one of the helpers I trained during my original tenure in the White House."

Bucky twisted to look at her, his entire body tense. I winced. She'd referred to him as a "helper." Bucky was an accomplished chef. Not always the most pleasant person to be around, but a sheer genius in the kitchen. I hadn't caught this part of the filming, and I leaned forward to hear better.

"Assistant chef," he said quietly.

"Huh?" she asked.

Bucky repeated himself, barely moving his lips. "I'm an assistant chef, not a 'helper,'" he said. "And *I* helped train *you*."

Laurel Anne's smile didn't fade. She patted him on the shoulder. "Whatever."

Turning her gaze toward the camera, she said, "I'm happy to be back here today to see the fruits of my labors." Affecting surprise, she laid a hand on Bucky's arm. "No," she said with affected clarity. "Not like that. Let me show you."

Bucky stepped back, hands on hips. "Excuse me, Miss Priss, but I'm chopping your asparagus. The goddamn frozen asparagus you insisted on. We don't use *frozen* asparagus in this kitchen, or have you forgotten everything I taught you when you were here for those," he held up his fingers in quote marks, "'two horrible years' that you always complain about?"

"Oh my God," I said. "I had no idea."

The interchange erupted into a shouting match. All perfectly recorded for posterity by Laurel Anne's camera team. As I watched, I felt a smile spread across my face—I didn't even try to tamp it down.

"Little bit more," Henry said.

I nodded. "This is where I came in."

This was "the meltdown," as I'd seen it. Laurel Anne, in a huff, had picked up Cyan's quince concoction. She held it up for the camera's benefit and began to systematically criticize the dish's preparation. As she poked fun at Cyan's work, Laurel Anne walked through the kitchen, keeping her face toward the camera, making rapid, disparaging remarks.

The kitchen is small. Too bad Laurel Anne didn't remember that.

She didn't see the stool.

Well, not until she fell over it.

The quince mixture went flying. Cyan's recipe had included a fairly generous helping of cherry juice. Combined with the honey, the quince, and all the other multicolored ingredients, it made for a really eye-catching mess. A mess that covered Laurel Anne's last clean apron, and—I laughed out loud—her face as well.

The star of *Cooking for the Best* bellowed as she fell. Fortunately, she wasn't hurt, but as she sat on the floor, she dissolved into tears. Not despondent tears. Tears of frustration, anger, and unadulterated fury.

I remembered that moment. I'd hurried from the kitchen to get some maintenance folks to help with the mess. I also grabbed a few rags from the storage room. The honey–cherry juice combination would be a bear to clean up. The more soaking cloths we brought to the party, the better.

While I was gone, the camera rolled.

And now I watched what had happened in my absence.

"How dare you put me in this position," she screamed. I think she was addressing Carmen. "I told you I hated this stupid kitchen. I told you I hate everyone who works here. Especially that nosy-face Olivia. She left this damn chair here on purpose." Still seated in a mass of muck, Laurel Anne threw a hand out and whacked the stool. It toppled. "She did this. I can beat her any day. Any goddamn day. I did work my butt off at the California Culinary Academy. Marcel is an idiot. He thinks he's so great because he's French. Well, la-di-da. You hear me?"

She wiped at her face.

"Damn it. Shut that damn camera off."

Someone finally did.

"Oh my God," I said again, when Henry hit the power button. "Why didn't you tell me?"

He shook his head. "There's been a lot going on, Ollie."

"You can say that again." I stared at the blank screen. "What do we do if she gets the executive chef position?"

"I borrowed this tape from Paul Vasquez," Henry said. He licked his lips and put an arm around my shoulders. "Let's get to this party, shall we?"

TOM SLID INTO THE ROOM AND PULLED UP A CHAIR NEXT TO mine. "How was lunch?" he asked just as the waiters brought dessert to our table. Much to Marcel's dismay, Henry had requested a simple treat: rainbow sherbet. His ultimate favorite.

"You missed a good one." I pointed up toward the dais where the screen for the montage was being taken down, in preparation for the speeches. "I'm up after the First Lady."

"You ready?"

I blew out a breath. "Hope so."

Henry sat at the head table with the First Lady, chief usher Vasquez, and a number of other department heads. I shared my table with Cyan, Bucky, Marcel, and some of our favorite waitstaffers.

Cyan tugged at Tom's sport coat. "Is there any more scoop on the shooting?"

He nodded, placing his elbows on the table. "You'll hear more on the news tonight. But . . ."

Everyone leaned forward.

"The Chameleon infiltrated the Alkumstan regime with help from the inside."

"The prince hired him?" I asked.

Tom shook his head. "The faction that supported Prince Sameer's brother hired him. That faction is still very strong. They oppose everything Sameer stands for, but they hope to eventually turn Sameer to their way of thinking. Despite the fact that Mohammed was overthrown, he issued an edict that his brother must not be harmed." Tom shrugged. "So the faction hired the Chameleon. They placed him with the delegates in an underling's position, figuring it would get him close enough to kill the prime minister. We think Labeeb bin-Saleh might've been in on it, too. We're almost sure of it."

"Why did he wait till the signing ceremony? Couldn't he have assassinated the prime minister in a much less public location?"

"It was bad luck and bad timing for the Chameleon. And we had an inkling of what he was up to because of Naveen." Tom addressed an aside to the rest of the table, "Naveen is the man who was caught running across the White House North Lawn a week and a half ago." Tom turned to me. "He knew about the Chameleon's mission, but he didn't know whether the prime minister or the president was the Chameleon's target. Plus, he believed there was a conspiracy in our ranks. He thought Deputy Jack Brewster had been turned. We have since checked him out. Thoroughly. He's clean. It's too bad Naveen didn't trust us. If he had, he'd be alive today."

Jack Brewster. I'd met the assistant deputy of the Secret Service. I sighed. Maybe if I'd had my chance to talk with Naveen, I could've prevented him from being killed.

As though he read my mind, Tom said, "Naveen had good intentions, and we could've used his help. But he brought his death on himself." His mouth tugged down at the corners. "You understand, Ollie, from the time you saw the killing at the merry-go-round, your presence changed all the pre-set plans. Once Kasim—the Chameleon—realized he wouldn't have the opportunity to get near the prime minister before the negotiations began, he decided to get you first. Tactically speaking, it was the perfect strategy. You were the only person alive who could identify him."

I shivered. "Why didn't he do anything at Camp David? That would've provided Kasim plenty of opportunity to get at the prime minister. To get at me, too." Yikes. I'd been alone with the guy. More than once.

"You've seen the place," Tom said. "He'd never have gotten away. And that's what he does best. Camp David is a fortress. It was too much, even for the Chameleon." He smiled. "As were you."

Henry made his way to the dais. I rose.

"Thanks for being such a crack shot," I said to Tom, and kissed him on the tip of his nose.

"AND SO, HENRY," I SAID, AS I WRAPPED UP MY FAREWELL SPEECH with a catch in my throat, "we're here to say—in Marcel's words—au revoir. Or maybe *á demain* would be more appropriate. Till tomorrow. Because when we all come back tomorrow, you'll be here in everything we do. In every menu we design. You will *always* be here. Your soul is in the White House kitchen and you're as essential as the pots, the pans, the spices. You are what brings this kitchen to life. I know your legacy will remain part of White House history forever, just as I know you will forever remain in my heart."

The crowd cheered and clapped. Henry stood up to hug me.

When the applause subsided, I reached into the bottom shelf of the lectern. "The staff and I have a little something to give you—something we hope you'll remember us by." I pulled up the heavy yellow gift bag and watched with pleasure as he removed the sparkling silver pan from within the tissue paper. Henry ran his fingers over the lettering: TO HENRY COOLEY, FOR THE JOY YOU BROUGHT TO THE WHITE HOUSE. YOUR COUNTRY THANKS YOU. YOU WILL BE MISSED.

His eyes glistened.

I leaned forward, pointing, as I whispered in his ear. "See that little dent? Remind me. I've got a story to tell you."

I was about to return to my seat when the First Lady asked me to remain on the small stage for just a moment. She took control of the microphone for a second time. I sidled next to Henry.

"Henry has assured me that my next bit of business would be most welcome, and that he would be delighted to have his retirement party end with an announcement about the future."

She smiled and paused.

My stomach dropped to my knees. I glanced out into the audience and stared wide-eyed at Tom. Next to me, Henry squeezed my elbow.

"Henry Cooley has been the life of the White House kitchen for five administrations. And, as he's often said, he's seen it all and he's done it all. Especially after last week." A titter of nervous laughter ran through the audience. The First Lady took a deep breath, and smiled. "Despite the fact that the White House has benefited from his experience for all these years, and despite the fact that he is retiring today, I have no intention of replacing Henry." She shook her head.

I noticed I was shaking, too. Not quite the same way.

"Today we begin anew. With recent international events happening, literally, on our doorstep, we know that we're at the dawn of a new era. Keeping that in mind, the White House is choosing to welcome a new era in the kitchen as well." She glanced at Henry. "I can never replace this man. Nor would I try. But, I can appoint a woman. It is with enormous pleasure that I announce to you today, the first female White House executive chef . . ." She turned to me and extended her hand. "Ms. Olivia Paras."

Henry wrapped me in a hug. I couldn't breathe, I couldn't move. But when he released me, I somehow managed to cross the stage and shake Mrs. Campbell's hand. "Thank you," I said.

"No one is more deserving than you."

The room, full of staffers, jumped to their feet, applauding. My eyes were on Tom, who grinned with pride and clapped harder than everyone else.

"Thank you," I said into the microphone. I sure hoped they could read lips.

As the applause continued, Henry pulled me aside. "I knew you'd get it."

"How did you know?"

"It's not every chef who can please the president's palate and also save his skin."

I touched Henry's cheek. "I'm going to miss you."

People rushed up to congratulate, tugging me into their midst, pulling me into a massive group hug.

Henry winked, and stepped aside.

A PRESIDENTIAL MENU

ONE OF THE STRANGEST CONUNDRUMS OF BEING A WHITE HOUSE chef is that, perhaps because they spend so much time eating fancy food at official functions, most First Families want simple fare or comfort food when they eat in their private quarters. What the White House chefs are expected to provide for official functions often has nothing to do with the kinds of food that the president likes to eat when he's away from the public eye. A White House chef might spend weeks organizing the hautest of haute cuisine for a single state menu, while in private the president's favorite foods might be cereal for breakfast, a bowl of soup and a sandwich for lunch, and barbeque and corn on the cob for dinner.

These kinds of extremes in the menu keep the White House kitchen on its toes. In addition to the wide range of cooking, there is also the issue of getting a new slate of "Deciders" in as primary customers every four or eight years. Each president is unique, and that includes what he likes to eat. Early in the presidency, the kitchen staff sits down with the First Family and gets copies of favorite family recipes from them, as well as lists of allergies, food likes and dislikes, and sample menus and wish lists. As time goes on, those menus are updated and refined until tuned to the liking of the primary customers.

Through the years, presidential appetites have varied widely. FDR insisted on serving hot dogs to the king and queen of England and wanted to serve chicken á la king for his inauguration luncheon only to be told that the White House chefs had no way to keep that much food hot. He settled on cold chicken salad instead. Given Washington, D.C.'s weather in January, there was no problem keeping that much food cold. Dwight D. Eisenhower liked to cook, he said he found it relaxing. His beef stew recipe was a staple for White House chefs during his administration. JFK and Jackie had a fondness for upscale Continental cuisine. President Johnson, not surprisingly, loved good Texas beefsteak. Both the Carters and the Clintons liked down-home Southern fare, though both also appreciated voyages into more stylish cuisines. President George W. Bush made simple homestyle food a staple during his White House years, while his father, the First President Bush, had more formal tastes—though, of course, no broccoli.

"Whatever the president wants": That's the ground rule for the job of White House chef. My first duty is to make the president happy. And the First Family, as well. Or, at least, their stomachs. So I listen when the commander in chief speaks about his food. What the inhabitants of the White House do with their political capital is somebody else's problem. I'm concerned with their taste buds—in public and in private.

The commander in chief I work for is a fan of simple meals, which makes my job both easier and harder. In private, he prefers peanut butter and honey sandwiches and chicken pot pies. In public, we both know it's important to fly the flag and impress the sophisticated visitors at state dinners and official functions—but he still wants to enjoy the food. So I get to design menus that work on both levels—impressing the guests, and not being too fancy for the current gourmand in chief.

Here are some representative foods I serve to the First Family in the current White House in a typical twenty-four-hour rotation. Given the president's taste, all are simple enough for any kitchen:

Breakfast

Honey-Almond Scones
Virginia Ham and Spinach Omelet
Henry's Famous Hash Browns
Broiled Grapefruit

Lunch

Peanut Butter and Banana Sandwich on Cinnamon Bread
Matchstick Vegetables with a Kick
Apple Tart

<u>DINNER</u>

Oven-Fried Chicken

Garlic Mashed Potatoes

Ollie's Green Beans

Chocolate Angel Food Cake with Fresh Berries

HONEY-ALMOND SCONES

SCONES

¼ cup buttermilk or plain yogurt

¾ cup honey

2 eggs

¼ tsp. almond extract

3 cups flour

4 tsp. baking powder

½ tsp. baking soda

½ tsp. salt

½ cup chilled butter

¼ cup sugar

½ cup finely chopped almonds

GLAZE

3 tbsp. butter, melted

1 tsp. vanilla extract

2 drops almond extract

1 tbsp. hot water

1 cup confectioner's sugar

Preheat oven to 375°F.

Grease scone pan or place parchment paper on a baking sheet, spray with cooking spray, and set aside. Add honey to buttermilk, stir, then beat in the eggs. Sift together flour, baking powder, soda, and salt. Cut in butter with a pastry cutter. Add sugar and almonds. Toss to coat.

Add the wet mixture to the flour mixture. Stir with a fork just until a ball forms. Turn out dough onto a floured board. Knead 5 to 6 times to make sure it is well mixed.

If using scone pan, spoon dough into the pan, spreading evenly among the indentations. If using baking sheet, roll dough into a ball and flatten it some. Cut into 8 wedges. Bake for 25 minutes or until medium golden brown. Cool on a wire rack.

In a medium bowl, mix melted butter, vanilla, almond extract, and hot water. Add confectioner's sugar. Stir. If glaze is too thick to pour, add more hot water, 1 teaspoonful at a time, until the glaze has the consistency of thick syrup. Spoon the glaze over the warm scones.

I usually wait at least an hour before serving for the scones to stabilize, absorb the glaze, and develop a fine crumb texture, but the First Family likes them hot from the oven.

VIRGINIA HAM AND SPINACH OMELET

2 tbsp. extra virgin olive oil

4 ounces good Virginia ham, diced

½ cup raw spinach leaves, well rinsed in water combined with 2 tbsp. vinegar in it, then rinsed again, drained, and dried (the vinegar rinse should take care of the threat of bacterial contamination)

1 tbsp. minced onion

3 eggs

2 tbsp. plain yogurt

½ tsp. tarragon

Couple of dashes Tabasco pepper sauce or other hot sauce

⅓ cup cheese of choice (Asiago, cheddar, Swiss, Monterey Jack, pepper jack, or any mixture of these), grated

Preheat oven to 350°F.

Place 8-inch seasoned cast-iron skillet or good-quality omelet pan on stovetop over medium heat. Add 1 tbsp. of olive oil to pan. Add ham, spinach, and onion to the hot oil.

Stir until ham warms through, spinach wilts, and onion turns translucent. Remove mixture from pan and set aside. In a small mixing bowl, whisk together eggs, yogurt, tarragon, and hot sauce. Place skillet back on stove. Add remaining 1 tbsp. olive oil to skillet and spread to cover entire surface. Pour egg mixture into oiled pan. Cook until bottom is set, then flip egg mixture in pan. (If this isn't something you do regularly and you don't want to destroy your kitchen attempting it, you can also pull the cooked egg to the center of the pan, and rotate the remaining liquid egg in the pan to cover the oiled surface. Either way, the eggs are cooked through, without leaving an overcooked and tough brown layer on the bottom of the omelet.) Top the cooking eggs with the warm ham mixture. Sprinkle grated cheese over top, reduce heat to low, cover, and cook just until the cheese melts. Take off cover. Fold omelet in half.

Serve immediately on warmed plate.

 ## HENRY'S FAMOUS HASH BROWNS

(WITH FRESH CHIVES AND FRESH THYME)

> *4 tbsp. extra virgin olive oil*
> *3 potatoes, peeled and grated*
> *6 sprigs fresh thyme, rinsed and stems removed (use ½ tsp. powdered*
>   *if fresh is not available)*
> *¼ cup finely chopped fresh chives (green onions will do in a pinch)*
> *⅓ tsp. salt, or to taste*
> *Fresh chive stalks and thyme sprigs for garnish (optional)*

Place olive oil in a large nonstick skillet over medium heat.

Mix remaining ingredients in a large bowl. Place grated potato mixture in a potato ricer and squeeze any excess water out of the potatoes. (This makes them crispy.) If you don't have a ricer, place the grated potatoes between sheets of paper towels and press to remove excess moisture.

When oil is heated to a simmer, pour potato mixture into skillet and mash it down to a thinnish pancake using a spatula. Cook until bottom layer is browned and crispy, about 4 minutes. Turn over and cook other side until browned and crispy, about 3 minutes. Place onto warmed plate or platter and serve garnished with sprigs of fresh thyme and chives tied together with a knotted chive leaf, if desired.

 ## BROILED GRAPEFRUIT

2 ruby red Texas grapefruit
2 drops almond extract
Scant ¼ cup brown sugar, loosely packed

Turn oven to Broil on high heat.

Cut grapefruit in half across the fruit, exposing halved sections. Place cut sides up in ovenproof pan or on baking sheet.

Mix almond extract into brown sugar. Sprinkle sugar mixture on halved grapefruits.

Place under broiler until sugar melts and turns bubbly, about 3 minutes. Since ovens differ greatly, watch carefully.

Serve immediately.

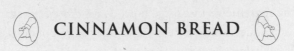

CINNAMON BREAD

1 package yeast

¼ cup warm water

2 cups milk (any kind will do nicely—the richness of the dough will
*   increase as you add fat)*

½ cup sugar

½ cup butter

2 tsp. salt

1½ tbsp. cinnamon

6–7 cups flour

2 eggs, beaten

Cinnamon sugar to garnish (optional)

Preheat oven to 375°. Grease two standard loaf pans and set aside.

Mix the yeast and water in a medium bowl.

Gently heat the milk, sugar, and butter in a saucepan over low to medium heat until the butter melts; do not boil. Remove from heat and set aside.

Sift salt, cinnamon, and 3 cups of flour together into a large bowl. Add the frothy yeast and milk mixtures and beaten eggs to the dry ingredients. Mix until a soft doughy ball forms. Turn dough out on floured board. Knead until dough is smooth and has the soft and rubbery texture of your earlobe. In the course of this process you may need to add up to 4 more cups of flour to get a nice, springy dough. Knead for 10 minutes.

Cover dough loosely with either a damp towel or greased plastic wrap and leave to rise for 1 hour. Punch down and then divide into two balls of dough. Form into loaves, place into loaf pans, cover, and then leave to rise about 30 minutes, or until doubled in size.

Dust the tops with the cinnamon sugar if desired and bake for 35–40 minutes. If the loaves start to brown too quickly, cover with foil for the remaining cooking time.

Excellent served buttered for breakfast, or as a base for peanut butter and jelly sandwiches.

PEANUT BUTTER AND BANANA SANDWICH ON CINNAMON BREAD

2 tbsp. peanut butter

2 tsp. honey

2 slices Cinnamon Bread (page 238), warmed

1 small banana, ripe, sliced into rounds

1 tsp. sunflower seeds (optional, but gives a nice crunch)

In a small bowl, mix together peanut butter and honey. Spread over slices of Cinnamon Bread. Scatter the peanut butter mixture with banana slices and sunflower seeds, if desired. Sandwich can be served open-faced, or the two slices can be merged into a traditional sandwich.

For a lovely fall option, when apples are at their peak, substitute thinly sliced apple for the bananas. Honeycrisp apples are fabulous this way.

MATCHSTICK VEGETABLES WITH A KICK

3 tbsp. olive oil

2 cloves garlic, peeled and crushed

2 tsp. finely grated fresh ginger

1 tsp. Chinese five-spice powder

¼ tsp. chili powder

3 large carrots, peeled and cut into matchstick strips

1 cup fresh green beans, ends removed and strung, sliced diagonally

3 large ribs celery, cut into matchstick strips

½ small head cabbage, roughly chopped as for slaw

1 tsp. salt, or to taste

Heat oil in a large pan.

Add garlic, ginger, five-spice powder, and chili powder, and stir for 1–2 minutes. Add carrots, green beans, and celery. Stir over medium heat until vegetables are half cooked, about 2–4 minutes. Add cabbage and continue to toss and cook for a further 5 minutes or until all the vegetables are tender but still crisp. Sprinkle with salt, mix well, cover and cook for 2 minutes.

Serve immediately.

APPLE TART

1 pie crust (Marcel makes it from scratch at the White House,
but when I make this at home, I cheat and buy the rolled,
refrigerated ones)

Roughly 2 pounds (generally about 5 or 6, depending on size) of tart,
sweet apples; Granny Smith or McIntosh, generally about 5 or 6,
depending on size

Juice of 1 lemon

½ cup sugar

2 tbsp. fresh lemon rind, grated

3 tbsp. unsalted sweet butter, cut into small pieces

1 tsp. cinnamon

½ cup clear apple jelly

Preheat the oven to 400°F.

Place pie crust in a 10-inch pie or tart shell with a removable bottom and set aside.

Peel the apples and cut them into quarters. Cut away and discard the cores. Slice thinly. Place apple slices in a bowl, add lemon juice and toss until the apple slices are coated (this will keep them from browning).

Arrange the apple slices on the tart pan in a tight pattern like fish scales, in overlapping layers. Continue until all apples are used. Sprinkle the apple slices with the sugar and lemon rind. Dot with butter. Sprinkle with cinnamon.

Place on a baking sheet in the preheated oven and bake for 15 minutes. Reduce the oven heat to 375"F. Bake 25 minutes longer. Keep an eye on the tart for the last 15 minutes of baking. If necessary, cover with foil to keep from browning too much.

While tart is finishing baking, melt the apple jelly over low heat, stirring until liquid. Gently brush the top of the hot tart with the melted jelly.

Serve hot or cold, as preferred.

 # OVEN-FRIED CHICKEN

½ cup butter

1 cup flour

2 tbsp. garlic powder

1 tbsp. onion powder

1 tbsp. salt, or to taste

1 tsp. freshly ground pepper, or to taste

1 tbsp. fresh lemon zest, finely diced

1 roasting chicken, rinsed and cut into pieces, giblets (if any)
*   removed (I make stock out of them, but it's perfectly acceptable*
*   to just toss them)*

Preheat oven to 350°F.

Place butter in ovenproof baking dish large enough to hold chicken pieces in a single layer, or a 9 × 13 cake pan. Put in oven to melt.

Place flour, garlic powder, onion powder, salt, pepper, and lemon zest in a large, sturdy resealable plastic bag. Shake until mixed.

Remove pan with melted butter from oven.

One piece at a time, place chicken pieces into bag with flour mixture, seal, and shake until chicken is coated. Remove from bag, and roll in melted butter in pan. Place in pan, skin side up.

Continue until all pieces are coated in flour and butter, arranged in pan.

Place pan in oven. Cook until chicken is brown and crispy on top and cooked through—about 40 minutes.

Remove chicken from pan. Plate and serve.

Should you desire it, pour off most of the liquid from the baking pan, deglaze the pan, and make gravy. It's fabulous. But the president, though blessed with a good metabolism and a fondness for running, is watching his waistline, so I generally don't serve him gravy with this dish.

 GARLIC MASHED POTATOES

2 lbs. peeled and diced potatoes (I like to use traditional Idaho
russets, but just about any variety of potato will do)
6 tbsp. butter
½–1 head garlic cloves, peeled and mashed

½–¾ cup milk, warmed

1 tbsp. salt, or to taste

½ tsp. freshly cracked pepper, or to taste

¼ cup fresh chives, chopped, for garnish (optional)

Place potatoes in a large, heavy-bottomed pan. Add water sufficient to cover them. Put lid on pan and bring to a boil over medium heat, watching to be sure pan doesn't boil over. Once the water is boiling, reduce heat slightly and simmer until potatoes are fork-tender. Approximately fifteen to twenty minutes.

Drain cooked potatoes and set aside. Return empty pan to heat and add butter. When butter melts, add garlic. Cook until tender. Return cooked potatoes to pan. Mash or whip with immersion blender until nearly smooth, gradually adding warm milk until potatoes are the desired consistency. Add salt and pepper. Place in warmed serving dish, top with chives if desired. Serve.

Some people salt the water the potatoes are boiling in, which raises the temperature of the boiling water and lets the potatoes cook faster. I prefer to add salt at the last stage, when I have more control over the amount the dish has—I think it leaves the potatoes more tender, too. But either method works.

 ## OLLIE'S GREEN BEANS

2 tbsp. olive oil

3 cloves garlic, peeled and thinly sliced

1 small onion, finely diced

2 lbs. fresh green beans, rinsed and strings removed

Salt, to taste

Place oil in large, heavy skillet over medium heat.

Add garlic and onion, stirring until softened and onion turns translucent. Add green beans. Stir to coat. Continue cooking until beans are still bright green and slightly crunchy but cooked through. Salt to taste.

Serve immediately.

CHOCOLATE ANGEL FOOD CAKE WITH FRESH BERRIES

¼ cup boiling water

2 tsp. vanilla extract

4 tbsp. Dutch processed cocoa powder

1 cup cake flour, well sifted or pulsed in a food processor

2 cups sugar

½ tsp. salt

12 jumbo egg whites, or egg whites equal to 2 cups (this can be
*   accomplished with 16 large eggs, or even meringue powder, if*
*   you don't want to deal with so many leftover egg yolks—but egg*
*   yolks make fabulous puddings, a nice Lord Baltimore cake, or*
*   custard sauce, so Marcel never minds having leftovers)*

2 tsp. cream of tartar

1 pint fresh berries, rinsed, drained, and chilled

Confectioner's sugar and cocoa powder, for garnish

Preheat oven to 350°F.

In a medium bowl, combine boiling water, vanilla, and cocoa powder. Stir until smooth and glossy. Set aside. In another medium bowl, or in food processor bowl, whisk or pulse together cake flour, 1 cup sugar, and salt. Set aside.

In a large, clean bowl (the slightest bit of fat will keep your egg whites from whipping properly), beat the egg whites until foamy. Add cream of tartar.

Continue beating until egg whites form soft peaks. Gradually add 1 cup sugar until stiff peaks form.

Remove 1 cup of egg mixture from large bowl and fold gently into cocoa mixture.

In large bowl, take remaining egg mixture and incorporate flour mixture into it by gently sifting ⅓ cup of the flour onto surface of beaten eggs, and folding them together. Don't overwork this batter or it will lose its incorporated air. Work gently but efficiently and quickly.

Gently fold cocoa mixture into egg batter.

Spoon or pour batter into an ungreased angel food cake pan. Run a knife through the batter in a circular motion to eliminate any large air pockets. Smooth the top of the batter with a spatula.

Place in oven and bake for 45 minutes. Do not open oven door during the first 30 minutes of baking. Top of cake will crack—this is part of its charm. Cake is done when surface springs back when gently touched or toothpick inserted into middle of cake comes out clean. Remove cake from oven and invert pan.

Let cool completely (at least 2 hours) at room temperature.

Remove cake from pan by running a sharp knife around sides and center of tube pan to release from sides, then remove cake from pan. If cake has removable tube, run knife around bottom of cake pan before removing.

Dust cake and berries with confectioner's sugar. To serve, place cake slice on individual plate dusted with cocoa powder and confectioner's sugar. Heap berries to side of cake. Dust with more confectioner's sugar. Serve.

As a special treat,
here are a few more of Olivia's White House favorites.

 # CRISP TRIPLE CHOCOLATE CHIP COOKIES

2 cups flour
1 tsp. baking powder
1 tsp. salt
1 cup (2 sticks) unsalted butter, room temperature
1 cup brown sugar (light or dark)
¾ cup white sugar
1 tsp. vanilla
1 egg, beaten until yellow
1 (6-oz.) package milk chocolate chips
1 (3-oz.) bar dark chocolate, diced into chunks
1 (6-oz.) package white chocolate chips
Parchment paper to cover cookie sheets

Preheat oven to 350° F.

In a medium bowl sift together dry ingredients and set aside.

In a large bowl, cream softened butter and sugars. Stir in vanilla until smooth. Stir in egg until smooth. Add dry ingredients 1 cup at a time, stirring to incorporate. Dough will be soft and uniform. Stir in chocolates.

Shape into quarter-sized balls. Place on parchment paper covered cookie sheets, in 3 widely spaced rows—this batter will spread during cooking! Bake until cookies are browned and flat, roughly 15 minutes. Cool on cookie sheets. Remove cooled cookies from parchment paper and store in a tin.

These are excellent crumbled and served over ice cream.

CUCUMBER SLICES STUFFED WITH FETA AND PINE NUTS

½ cup feta cheese, crumbled

2 tbsp. mayonnaise

3 drops Worcestershire sauce

¼ cup toasted pine nuts, chopped

1 clove garlic, crushed and finely chopped

½ tsp. dried dill weed

Salt and cracked pepper to taste

3 large chilled cucumbers, sliced thinly

¼ cup fresh parsley, chopped

Kosher salt, to taste

Combine cheese, mayo, Worcestershire sauce, pine nuts, garlic, dill, salt, and pepper. Spread 2 tablespoons of filling between two slices of cucumber. Place on platter. Repeat with remaining filling and cucumber slices. Garnish with chopped parsley and sprinkle with salt. Serve cold.

BAKLAVA STUFFED WITH ALMONDS, PECANS, AND PINE NUTS

1 package fillo dough (Even chefs buy it rather than making it by hand!)

1 lb. (4 sticks) butter, melted

8 ounces almonds, roughly chopped

4 ounces pecans, roughly chopped

3 ounces pine nuts, roughly chopped

3 cups sugar

1 cup water

¼ tsp. ground cloves

1 tsp. ground cinnamon
Ground cinnamon and powdered sugar, for garnish (optional)

Preheat oven to 350° F.

Mix the chopped nuts with 1 cup of sugar. Set aside.

Remove fillo sheets from package to work surface and unfold. When not handling, keep covered by a damp paper towel or cloth dish towel. Fillo dries out and becomes unworkable fast.

Cut the sheets in half to fit a 9 × 13 baking dish. Cover the fillo with damp towel again. Working quickly using a basting brush, paint the bottom of the 9 × 13 pan with melted butter. Remove a sheet of fillo, place it on the bottom of the buttered pan, brush the fillo sheet well with melted butter. Repeat 6 times. Sprinkle with a thin layer of chopped nut mixture.

Place six more sheets of buttered fillo in the pan and top with chopped nut mixture. Repeat these layers with remaining fillo and chopped nut mixture, ending with 6 layers of buttered fillo.

With the sharpest knife possible, cut the layers of fillo and nuts into four to six long rows. (Piece size is a personal preference.) Turn pan and slice the fillo into diamonds by cutting diagonally across the long rows.

Bake until golden brown and toasty, about 35 to 45 minutes.

Remove from oven, cool pan on a rack.

While the pan is cooling, place remaining 2 cups sugar, water, cloves, and cinnamon in a large, heavy saucepan over medium to medium-high heat. Bring to a boil. Turn heat down slightly and simmer for 20 minutes.

Pour boiling syrup gently over fillo and nuts in pan.

Cool completely. To serve, place a doily or paper cutout over a dessert plate. Dust with cinnamon. Move the pattern carefully a half inch to the right and lightly dust with powdered sugar. Remove the pattern. Serve the individual diamonds of baklava on cinnamon and sugar-dusted dessert plates.

HAIL
TO THE
CHEF

For Rene
and
For Karen

ACKNOWLEDGMENTS

I wish I could cook as well as Ollie does, because then I would invite everyone over for a lavish dinner to express my heartfelt gratitude.

Since I can't do that, my sincere thanks here will have to suffice:

To the wonderful people at Berkley Prime Crime, especially my editor, Natalee Rosenstein; Michelle Vega; Catherine Milne; and Erica Rose. I hope you know how much I appreciate your guidance, help, and support. And to the great folks at Tekno Books: Marty Greenberg, John Helfers, and Denise Little, without whom Ollie would never exist.

When I asked my brother, Paul, how to rig up an electrical charge strong enough to kill a person and possibly destroy the White House, he was delighted to help. He even created a mock-up and patiently explained how to make it work. In the book, Stanley does the same for Ollie. Any errors in that scene, or others, are mine alone.

I read and reread former White House chef Walter Scheib's book, *White House Chef*, but there's no substitute for talking with someone who's actually been there. I owe a special debt of gratitude to this kind and gracious man who answered my questions about room locations, staff meetings, and certain protocols. Again, any errors are mine.

Thanks to the Southland Scribes, Mystery Writers of America, Sisters in Crime, and Thriller Writers of America for camaraderie and support, and to readers who e-mail to tell me what they think about the newest book. Means a lot to me.

Special thanks to my writing partner, Michael A. Black, whose wise counsel keeps me going and who always has my back.

And, as always, to my family: Curt, Robyn, Sara, and Biz. You guys are the best.

CHAPTER 1

I STOPPED SHORT AT THE DOORWAY TO THE WHITE HOUSE SOLAR-ium. I knew better than to interrupt the First Lady when she was in such deep discussion with her social secretary and the assistant usher. Particularly today. But when Mrs. Campbell saw me, she beckoned me into the top-floor room.

"Ollie, thank goodness," she said, silencing her two staff members. "Talk to Sean, would you? Persuade him to come to Thanksgiving dinner."

Seated apart from Mrs. Campbell's conference, across the expansive room—I'd missed him at first glance—Sean Baxter sprang to his feet. With his sandy blonde hair and boy-next-door good looks, he could have passed for Matt Damon's younger brother. "Hey," he said. "It's good to see you again."

The two staffers had stopped talking long enough to acknowledge my presence with polite smiles. As soon as Sean stood, however, they resumed peppering the First Lady with their requests.

"Mrs. Campbell," the social secretary said, her voice strained, "if we don't confirm these last-minute updates today, the final batch of Christmas cards won't be sent until next week."

The assistant usher added, "The press will skewer us for slighting these folks."

Mrs. Campbell nodded. "Then let's not wait a moment longer. How many—"

Sudden, hard footfalls above us halted all conversation. One breathless instant later, a flash—like black lightning—streaked past the room's floor-to-ceiling windows. Though distorted by the sheer curtains, the silhouette was clear. A man. Carrying a high-powered rifle.

Sprinting along the adjacent promenade, the shadow moved at hyper-speed.

I barely had time to process his appearance when the gunman burst through the solarium's outside door, ordering us all into the central hall.

"Move!" he shouted, darting around us to take the point position at the doorway. "Come on!"

His all-black garb and bulletproof vest didn't scare me. Neither did the gun.

But the look on his face sent prickles of panic tingling down the back of my neck. This was Dennis, one of our rooftop snipers. His words were terse. "Follow me."

The First Lady stared at him. "But—"

"No time," he said. "Secret Service agents are on their way up. We have to get you out of here. Now."

We had been through drills before, so we knew what to do—but the peculiar energy wrapped around this situation made everything seem louder, brighter, scarier. Dennis tensed. He'd slung the rifle onto his back and now gripped a semiautomatic pistol in one hand, and another weaponlike object I didn't recognize in the other. His head twisted side to side as he walked, the picture of stealth. "Stay close," he whispered as he stopped to peer around the corner. "Stay low."

Two suited Secret Service agents joined us in the central hall, using hand signals to shepherd us toward the stairway nearest the music room. Secret Service agents didn't generally accompany the First Family into the residence. That must be why Dennis had been tagged for getting us out. As one of the many snipers on the rooftop, he was closer to the First Lady's position than an agent would be.

The moment we entered the stairway, Dennis ran back the way we'd come. The five of us from the solarium tried to be quiet, but our shoes clattered down the steps, just loud enough to mask the thunderous pounding of my heart. I watched our escorts, knowing better than to question, knowing better than to say a word. The two suited men spoke into their hands in low, brusque tones as we made our way to the bottom level of the East Wing. The First Lady, Sean, and I were herded by Agent Kevin Martin. The other two were taken by Agent Klein.

I knew where we were headed. The bunker.

This was no drill.

I started back toward the kitchen. "My staff," I said. As the White House executive chef, the safety of my people was of paramount importance to me.

Agent Martin shook his head. "We've got your people covered, Ollie," he said, tension making his blue eyes darken.

He hustled us down, deeper into the fortresslike bunker. The enormous tubelike structure, built back when Franklin Delano Roosevelt was president, was purportedly designed to withstand a nuclear blast. Officially known as the Presidential Emergency Operations Center, it had several meeting rooms and conference areas outfitted with televisions, telephones, and communications systems. Sleeping rooms, too. Agent Martin stopped us in front of the first one on the right.

"Get in there. We'll come back when it's clear."

I couldn't let it go. "Where's my staff now?"

Before he could answer, Mrs. Campbell interrupted. "Where's my husband? Is he safe?"

"He's been evacuated."

"Is he all right?"

Martin nodded. "Please remain here until you're given the all-clear."

"But what—"

"I'm not at liberty to—"

"Agent Martin," Mrs. Campbell said with more than a little snap. "You will tell me exactly where my husband is. And exactly what's going on."

He pursed his lips, shooting a derisive look at Sean. "Only staff members . . ."

"You can talk in front of Sean," Mrs. Campbell said. "He's family. Now, where's my husband?"

Agent Martin's jaw flexed. One of our more handsome Secret Service agents, the man was blessed with Irish good looks and rigid determination. With obvious reluctance, he said, "Marine One evacuated the president to Camp David." He started to move away, but Mrs. Campbell stepped forward, laying her hand on his arm.

"Tell me why."

"The president is safe for now," he said. "But we have reason to suspect an explosive device may be present in the White House."

I couldn't decide whether the loudest gasp came from me or Mrs. Campbell. She recovered immediately, however, and nodded, surprisingly cool. "Thank you."

I had to know. "Who went to Camp David with him?"

Martin fixed me with a meaningful look. "Everyone you would expect."

I sighed with relief. That meant Tom had been evacuated, too. At least he was safe. "What happens next?" I asked.

He ignored my question. "I'll be back when I can."

The armored door closed behind him with a *thunk* of frightening finality as the three of us turned inward, forming an uncertain triangle. "Where do you think they found a bomb?" I asked.

Mrs. Campbell paced. The room we occupied was small, with a curtained, fake window on its far wall. Lights behind the plastic panes strove for a sunny-day touch, but their cold, blue fluorescence fooled no one. Designed for safety rather than lavish entertaining, the room was nonetheless comfortable with a kitchenette, a set of bunk beds, chairs, recent magazines on the dining table, and cabinets that I assumed were stocked with shelf-stable foods and water. I took a quick peek behind the far door and found a full bathroom. Good. Just in case we were stuck here for a while.

"This may be just a precaution," the First Lady finally said. "I'm sure there's no bomb. Perhaps the Secret Service is running an unusual drill."

Sean asked, "This is an awful lot for just a precaution, isn't it?"

Neither Mrs. Campbell nor I answered. He was right. The White House and its inhabitants received threats on an almost daily basis. Precautions were taken as a matter of course, but rarely to this extent.

Something occurred to me. "Wasn't the president conducting meetings in the West Wing today?"

Mrs. Campbell nodded, the lines between her brows deep with worry. "I was originally scheduled to meet Sean in the dining room outside the Oval Office," she said. "We planned to lunch with Harrison. He hasn't seen Sean in such a long time."

"Did you say lunch?" I asked.

Mrs. Campbell waved away my concerns. "I didn't put it on the schedule, Ollie, because we planned to grab a bite from the White House Mess. But then the president needed to meet with his advisers about this new terrorist threat, and everything shifted. In fact, that's why I called you up to the solarium—to inquire about getting lunch." She smiled, but I could tell it was less for my benefit than for her own. "And here we are."

So they hadn't eaten yet. In an effort to inject normalcy into our bizarre circumstances, I started opening cabinets, assessing what ingredients I had at hand to play with. "If they evacuated the president to Camp David," I said, musing, "then the bomb must be located between the Oval Office and here. Otherwise he'd be in the bunker, too."

Sean pulled a box of cookies from the cabinet's very top shelf. "Thank God they found it. And that they got him out. You're right, Ollie. They wouldn't want to transfer him across the residence. Can you imagine the risk . . . ?" He let the thought linger. I wished he hadn't.

"I'm certain this is just a precaution," Mrs. Campbell said again with unnatural brightness. "Any minute now they'll give us the—"

A high-pitched siren cut off the rest of her words. Loud even through the bunker's thick walls, the danger signal rang clear. Jolts of fear speared my gut. Above the door, a Mars light undulated—its beacons of red shooting across the room, like an ON-AIR signal gone haywire.

When the siren silenced, the intercom crackled. "Do not leave your assigned room . . . I repeat . . . do not leave your room. Do not open your door. Wait for further instructions. This is not a drill."

Sean dropped the box of cookies. The shock in his face was no doubt a mirror of my own. Mrs. Campbell collapsed into one of the chairs, her head in prayerful hands. "Dear God," she said, "protect us all."

CHAPTER 2

"I KNOW THAT THIS ISN'T MUCH," I SAID, AS I PLACED A THROWN-together lunch on the small table, "but we don't know how long we'll be here. We need to keep our spirits up."

"Do you need any help?" Sean asked me.

I shook my head. We'd been sequestered for more than an hour. In that time, one of the Secret Service agents had stopped by long enough to let us know that the purported bomb had been located and disabled by the bomb squad. Before allowing any of us to resume our duties, however, the entire residence would be swept for additional explosives. The special agent requested our patience for the duration.

While we waited, I scrounged. In addition to the bottled water and Pow-erBars, I'd found a supply of interesting ingredients and freeze-dried packets. What used to be called C-rations were now more appealingly known as MRE—meals ready to eat. Augmenting these were canned foods and a few necessary staples. I went to work.

Less than fifteen minutes later I'd pulled together canned chicken chunks, added a bit of soy sauce, peanut butter, a splash of oil, and a dash of pepper flakes, then heated it all in the microwave, and served it on a bed of microwave-cooked rice.

I'd then drained a can of carrots and bamboo shoots. With a little maple syrup and more soy sauce, I had a serviceable side dish. Next up, three-bean salad—again from a can. Drained and tossed with Italian dressing, it wasn't half bad. We were ready to serve.

"This is amazing, Ollie," Mrs. Campbell said as she and Sean sat at the table to enjoy the meal I'd cobbled together. I was used to using fresh vegetables, herbs, and even flowers as garnish. Here I presented a no-frills meal on utilitarian plates. Still, the chicken smelled good. "I can't believe how wonderful this all looks. You are a miracle worker."

I thanked her and began cleaning up.

"Aren't you planning to join us?" she asked.

Just as I opened my mouth to demur, my stomach rumbled its displeasure at the thought of turning down a meal.

Mrs. Campbell laughed. "That settles it. Sit down, Ollie."

I took the chair to the First Lady's left, which set me across from Sean. He smiled at me as he popped a forkful of bean salad into his mouth and said, "This is really good."

Ravenous, I nonetheless managed restraint as I helped myself to some chicken and carrots. Two bites in, I knew I'd done well. In fact, I wished I would've written everything down as I'd put it together. White House chefs were always hounded to create cookbooks. I envisioned my future tome with a chapter titled: "Bounty from the Bunker."

"I wonder when they'll let us out," I said with a glance at the room's digital readout. The White House assistant usher had called a staff meeting for this afternoon. With Thanksgiving only two days away, and holiday decorations going up the day after that, we were already operating under tight deadlines. Every hour delay squeaked the schedule ever tighter. While we ate, I formulated alternative methods to get everything done on time.

As though reading my mind, Mrs. Campbell said, "How are plans for Thanksgiving dinner progressing?"

"Perfectly," I said. It was true—mostly. I'd taken over the position of executive chef in the spring, and since then I'd come to learn just how difficult it is to manage meals, staff, and administrative responsibilities at the same time. So far, however, plans for Thanksgiving were right on schedule. And they would continue to be, as long as we got out of our bunker prison soon. "Your guests are in for a treat. And Marcel has another spectacular dessert planned." Just to keep conversation going, I asked, "Are we still planning for six guests in addition to you and the president?"

Mrs. Campbell sighed. "Unfortunately, yes. The rest of my husband's family won't be attending this year, so we've invited my Washington, D.C., business partners—they're practically as close to me as cousins. But I have to admit, I was hoping to host a bigger event this year." She directed a pointed look at Sean. "Thanksgiving is a time for families to be together. Isn't that right?"

Sean considered the question. "It may be better for me to skip this one, Aunt Elaine." When he looked up, his eyes were clouded. "You know your partners wouldn't want me there."

She leaned toward him and placed a hand over his. "*I* want you there." Sitting up, she gave a bright smile. "And Ollie does, too. Don't you?"

Startled by the apparent non sequitur, I answered, "Of course."

Sean smiled at me from across the table. "Well, then, maybe I could reconsider."

My brain skip-stepped. Comprehension struck me—and I could only hope my instantaneous panic didn't show. If I was reading this interchange correctly—the First Lady was attempting to play Cupid. But she was obviously unaware of my relationship with Secret Service Agent Tom MacKenzie. Although the excitement from last spring might have led people to suspect there was more to our companionship than dodging bullets might warrant, Tom and I chose to keep information about our love life quiet. We leaked details of the relationship on a need-to-know-basis only. And until this moment, I'd decided Mrs. Campbell didn't need to know.

From the looks on Mrs. Campbell's and Sean's faces, however, it was clear the First Lady had designs to fix me up with her nephew. Here was a wrinkle I hadn't anticipated. At once I was honored that she thought so highly of me—because I knew the esteem she held for Sean—but at the same time I was quietly horrified.

How, I wondered, could I disentangle myself from this particular dilemma without ruining her image of me—and, just as important, without coming clean about my relationship with Tom?

For the moment I could do no better than deflect. I wracked my brain to come up with the Thanksgiving guest list. "The three couples attending are the Volkovs, the Blanchards, and the Hendricksons?"

Mrs. Campbell shook her head. "Helen Hendrickson isn't married. She's bringing a guest."

"Her attorney," Sean said to me. Shaking his head, he again addressed his aunt. "Don't you see? They're planning to surround you with their arguments to convince you to sell your stake in Zendy Industries. Why else would Helen bring Fitzgerald along? I'll bet he's already drawn up all the papers. They'll be pressuring you to sign before the gravy congeals."

She laughed. "Don't be silly. Thanksgiving is a time for being grateful for all our blessings this past year. No one will be talking business."

"I changed my mind," he said. "I'm coming to dinner after all."

"Good."

"Somebody needs to look out for your interests."

As they talked, I realized I was in a peculiar position—although I was most certainly present, I was not part of the conversation. Feeling like the eavesdropping elephant in the room, I desperately wanted to extricate myself.

Although I kept my seat, my right knee twitched with the beat of anxiety. I wanted to be busy in the kitchen. My *real* kitchen.

Questions raced through my brain. And although I tried to maintain a neutral, disinterested demeanor, an errant thought must have skittered across my face because Sean turned to me, explaining the one thing I'd wondered about—why Mrs. Campbell wouldn't have a champion in her husband. "Uncle Harrison—that is, President Campbell—makes it a point to stay as far from decisions like this as possible. At least publicly." Turning to the First Lady, he continued. "He's against you selling the business, Aunt Elaine. We both know that. I also realize that he can't make a big deal out of it. His influence on your decision—if made public—could cause economic repercussions. It's a tough position to be in."

"Which is why Sean is my personal financial consultant," she said with obvious pride. "Other than my husband, Sean is the most trustworthy person I know."

Sean's cheeks flushed pink. Though obviously pleased, he waved off her praise. "I'll be there for Thanksgiving dinner. You two talked me into it."

"Great," I said, and then with over-the-top peppiness, I asked, "Will you bring a guest?"

Their twin looks of incredulity cemented my earlier matchmaking assumptions. "No," Sean said, meaningfully. "I'm not seeing anyone right now."

"Well, then," I said, suddenly at a loss for words, "I'll let the staff know to set a place for you."

Whether it was the close quarters, the long wait for an all-clear signal, or the fact that I was being double-teamed in my love-life department, I didn't know. I just suddenly needed to break free. I stood. "Let me clean up," I said, reaching for Mrs. Campbell's plate.

Sean stood, too. "I'll help."

"No." I whisked his plate away before he could touch it. "You visit with your aunt. I've got this."

"But—"

"It sounds as though you have a lot to talk about," I said, effectively cutting off his path to the sink area. To my surprise, he sat back down. In an attempt to guide the conversation back to safe territory, I then turned to Mrs. Campbell. "I didn't realize you were part of Zendy Industries. They're huge."

"They are," she said. "My father started the company with three friends—years ago when I was young and his friends' children weren't even born yet. That's why Nick, Treyton, and Helen are invited for dinner Thursday. We grew up together. Now, they're all my business associates. I guess you could say I inherited the business and I inherited them, too."

The sudden sadness in her eyes reminded me of her recent loss. Mrs. Campbell's father, Joseph Sinclair, had been killed in a horrific car accident about two months earlier.

"You also inherited your father's good business sense," Sean said. "All I'm suggesting is that you rely on your own instincts now, and not defer to your colleagues' demands. No matter how convincing Volkov and the others might be."

"You're a good boy, Sean," Mrs. Campbell said, patting his arm.

By the time I had the bunker room's kitchen back in order, I'd overheard enough about the Zendy Industries situation to understand why Thursday's dinner had the potential to get ugly. I made a mental note to talk to Jackson, the new head butler, to keep his eye on the alcohol intake. Mrs. Campbell was a social drinker—limiting herself to an occasional glass of wine—but the Blanchards, the Volkovs, and Helen Hendrickson had been our guests only a couple of times in the recent past. I couldn't remember if they'd achieved status on our "Do not serve" list. I made another mental note to check.

While the White House is first and foremost a gracious host, it is also a wise one. Over time, certain guests have proved to be unable to handle liquor in a responsible manner. We would never deign to refuse anyone a drink—but one must not dance on White House tables, literally or figuratively. If someone does, he or she earns an immediate place on our "Do not invite" list. If, to our great disappointment, we find that this person *must* be invited in the future, our sophisticated staff manages to keep the inhibition-loosening beverages just out of the ersatz performer's reach.

With nine diners—including Sean—for dinner on Thursday, Jackson would have a relatively easy time of keeping tabs on the intake.

I continued to listen in, even as I puttered around, trying to tidy up an already Spartan room.

The First Lady stood up and walked over to the fake window. "All discussion about this Zendy situation should be tabled until after the holidays," she said. "How I wish we could get out of here. I have so much to do."

"The deadline for a decision is December fifteenth," Sean said. "That's why I think they'll be pressuring you to agree to the sale of the company."

She turned. "I thought we had until March fifteenth."

Sean shook his head. "The trust was very clear: Ninety days after the death of the final founder—your father—the four of you are required to file a decision as to whether you intend to sell the company or not."

"And if we don't, we have to wait ten years to decide again." Mrs. Campbell sighed. "Such a peculiar requirement."

Sean gave a wry shrug. "Not so peculiar when you think about what the founders intended. They envisioned this company as they would one of their kids. One that they all fathered. The four men who brought Zendy Industries to life were wealthy, successful businessmen in other ventures. They didn't need Zendy's income. They needed to believe they'd made a mark on this world."

The bunker door opened, cutting Sean off. Special Agent Martin gestured us out. "Follow me," he said.

CHAPTER 3

"ALL CLEAR?" MRS. CAMPBELL ASKED. "WHAT A RELIEF. WAS IT ACTU-
ally a bomb? Or was this all just precaution?"

Kevin Martin licked his lips. "We are confident that the White House is
currently safe from any explosive or incendiary device."

We'd made our way into the Center Hall. Mrs. Campbell turned to face
Martin. "But earlier you said that a bomb was located on the property," she
said. "Is that true? Was it really a bomb?"

He flicked a wary glance at Sean, who clearly understood his cue. "I have
to be going anyway," he said. "See you both on Thursday. Take care, Ollie."

Another agent stepped up to escort Sean out, but before I could make my
own hasty exit, Kevin Martin answered the First Lady's question. Incurable
snoop that I am, I stayed to listen.

"The device we found was not a bomb."

"Thank goodness," the First Lady said. She closed her eyes for a long
moment, and I felt as though I could almost read her mind. And, I could totally
empathize. The relief washing over me was as powerful as it was sudden. This
was Mrs. Campbell's home, and the president's. But in many ways, it was my
home, too. A bomb had threatened to destroy the world's symbol of freedom.
I'd compartmentalized my fear while we were sequestered—I'd pushed it aside
to deal with matters at hand. But now that we were back in the residence, and
safe, I felt the full weight of the ordeal we'd been through.

Kevin continued. "The fact that there was never an actual bomb on the
premises, coupled with the time crunch the staff is under to prepare for Thanksgiving and Christmas"—he acknowledged me with a look—"has convinced us
to allow everyone back into the residence for now. However," he added, arch-

ing his brows, "we are at a state of heightened alert. And we are asking the entire staff to be our eyes and ears wherever possible. We'll call a meeting later with further instructions."

"If it wasn't a bomb you found," I asked, "what was it?"

Kevin hated when I poked my nose where it didn't belong—a habit I'd gotten into quite often recently, and one he repeatedly tried to quash.

Before he could tell me to butt out this time, however, Mrs. Campbell chimed in. "Yes, what was it?"

"An apparent prank. We're investigating it now." He fixated on some middle distance with such laser intensity that I almost pitied today's prankster. Knowing Kevin and the rest of the Presidential Protection Detail (PPD) as I did, the guilty party would be found. Very soon. "An alert will be distributed to all departments describing what was discovered, and what to look for in the future. We're bringing in a team of experts to educate the staff."

When the First Lady turned the conversation to the happenings at Camp David, I made a polite excuse and hurried off to the safety of my kitchen.

Marcel met me as I walked in, his dark face tight with concern. "Where 'ave you been?" he asked. His French accent was ladled on heavier than normal. "We 'ave been very worried."

"Long story." I gave my staff a quick rundown of the past several hours.

Bucky frowned. "That's nice. They put you in a bunker with the First Lady, and they make us wait out on the South Lawn in the storm." He shook his head. "And now they tell us it's safe and we're supposed to believe them."

"Outside?" I said. Although we were still in the mid-fifties this late in November, it was pouring rain, and definitely too cold to remain outside for very long. "Kevin Martin told me you were safe."

Cyan, washing dishes, turned off the water and wiped her hands as she came toward me. "We *were* safe, Ollie," she said, glaring at Bucky. Although she was at least fifteen years younger, Cyan was almost as accomplished in the kitchen as our senior chef. And in the past couple of months, I'd watched her confidence grow even more. "We weren't out on the South Lawn; we walked down to E Street, where we sat on buses until they gave the all-clear."

"It was still storming," Bucky said. "And cold."

When I glanced at Marcel, he shrugged. "Eh, the temperature was tolerable. But the boredom was not. We have much to do and this incident has thrown a . . . *flanquer la pagaille* . . . into my plans for the day."

"If Henry was still here, he would've been out in the buses with us. Not cozying up with the First Lady in the bunker."

Arguing with Bucky over this matter served no purpose, so I changed the subject.

"There will be another guest at Thanksgiving dinner," I said. "Sean Baxter is coming after all."

Bucky snorted and headed back to his station, where I could see tonight's dinner preparations were already under way. "That SBA chef was due here over an hour ago. I'll bet she gave up when she couldn't get in."

"I'm sure the bomb scare changed a lot of plans," I said evenly. "But I do hope she shows up. We need another pair of hands here by tomorrow at the latest." The chef in question, Agda, was the first new recruit sent to join our staff. Service-by-Agreement chefs, or SBAs, worked in the White House on a temporary, contractual basis, until a hiring decision was made, or until the SBA chef found another job elsewhere. I'd been an SBA before I accepted a position here. In my opinion, there was no better opportunity anywhere. I hoped this particular chef agreed—after all, we needed the help.

"We're already behind schedule," Bucky said.

I bit back the urge to snarl. Hurling sarcastic retorts at those who reported to me was petty. Worse, it was unprofessional. I was beginning to see why Henry never stooped to fight meaningless battles. It wasn't worth the effort, and it only accomplished the lessening of oneself.

I forced a placid smile. "You're right, Bucky. That means that we need to work faster if we hope to get tonight's dinner together on time. Not to mention all the prep work we need to do for tomorrow and Thursday."

"And Friday," Cyan added.

I sucked in a deep breath. Friday promised to be a media circus day. Not only was it the last day the White House would be open to the public before the official holiday season began, it was the date of a long-awaited luncheon. Preparations for Thursday's intimate Thanksgiving meal paled in comparison to those for Friday's buffet.

On Friday, Mrs. Campbell would open the White House doors to mothers from all over the country. Her goal was to find commonality among all mothers, whether they be working, single, stay-at-home, or sharing child-care duties with a partner. Almost every state would be represented, and every mom was bringing kids, along with homemade decorations for Christmas, Hanukkah, and Kwanzaa. Each invited child had been sent a template of a gingerbread person on which to base his or her artwork. Continuing the theme of how we are all different, yet we celebrate together, the kids were encouraged to create masterpieces within the template's parameters. Each handcrafted gingerbread man—or *person*, in these politically correct times—brought to Friday's celebration would be added to the hundreds we received by mail per an open call for participation. I could only imagine how tough this security nightmare would be for our Secret Service personnel.

"And Friday," I finally echoed.

We weren't quite sure what to expect. We only knew it would be fun for the attendees, and that the news folks would be all over this one like ants on spilled sugar. Not that you would ever find ants in my kitchen.

"Ollie!"

I looked up. Gene Sculka, our chief electrician, stood in the kitchen's doorway.

"You heading down?" he asked.

I caught myself before asking, "Down where?" Darn. He was talking about today's staff meeting. In all the excitement, I'd lost track of time.

"Hang on," I said, grabbing my notebook and pen. "I'll go with you." To Bucky, I said, "If Agda shows up, put her to work."

"Henry would have insisted on a formal interview first."

I swallowed my frustration. If Bucky planned to challenge my every move, we were in for a long holiday season. "She's coming from the Greenbriar, so she's no slouch. She's been screened and cleared." Keeping my tone as nonthreatening as possible, I added, "I'll risk putting her to work right away. We'll worry about the interview later."

He turned his back to me. "Whatever you say."

"That's the spirit, Bucky." Without waiting for a reply, I hurried to catch up as Gene headed toward the elevator.

I would have preferred taking the stairs, but that wasn't an option for our master electrician any longer. Gray-haired and big-boned, he wore his double chin and spare tire with comfort—as though he'd been born with them. He'd joined the White House staff during the Carter administration, and had worked his way up to the top position with his know-how and can-do attitude. "Can't believe they're still holding this meeting, what with all the hullabaloo this morning."

"There's a lot to be coordinated, especially over the next couple of days. This meeting is probably just to make sure we're all on track. I'm sure it'll be quick."

"It better be," he said.

"How's the knee?" I asked, as we rode one floor down to the basement-mezzanine, often referred to as the BM level.

He slapped his right leg. "Good as new," he said. "I told those doctors they had to get me back to work here by Thanksgiving. And they did." With a nod to no one, he added, "Nothing was going to keep me from working on the Christmas decorations. I've been running the electric here for who knows how long and I'm not about to let anybody take over during my favorite time of the year. No way."

"We're all really glad you're back." It was true. During Gene's knee-replacement recuperation, I'd had the misfortune of having to deal with Curly, Gene's second-in-command. Although the two men were close in age, Curly was as unpleasant as Gene was friendly. I only hoped that when Gene retired, Surly Curly did, too.

We were the last two to arrive for the meeting of the dozen or so department heads. I couldn't help but think about how much time I was spending away from the kitchen today—in the bunker this morning, and now here in the lower-level cafeteria, where a few staff members were taking lunch breaks.

Our florist, Kendra, leaned forward to talk to me around Gene's massive form. "No samples for us today?"

I knew what she meant. Today's cafeteria offerings were pretty basic. For our standard staff meetings, I usually made sure to have a new creation available for my colleagues to sample. Not today. "Limited facilities in the bunker," I said as I took my seat. "Unless you'd be interested in a hermetically sealed brownie topped with freeze-dried ice cream." Not an entirely accurate description of MREs, but it garnered a laugh.

"What kind of floral arrangement do you think I should come up with for that little delicacy?" she asked. "Maybe we ought to consider installing silk flowers in the bunker, huh?"

When we both laughed, I started to relax. Sure, this was our busiest time of the year, but now that the morning's excitement was over, we could finally get to the work at hand.

Up at the front of the room, Bradley Clarke took a few minutes to get himself organized. I seized the opportunity to talk a bit more with Kendra. "Great theme this year," I said.

"Do you like it?" Kendra asked, clearly not expecting me to answer. "We've been working on this since early summer. I think it's a good one, given the nation's climate of fear these days." She shuddered, then went on. "And I like the way it dovetails with President Campbell's peace platform."

The First Lady was always credited with the concept, but the truth was, from start to finish, this was a team effort. It took months for the social secretary, the florist, and a myriad of designers to bring the project to life. Most of the decorations were chosen from a vast collection stored nearby in a Maryland warehouse. Our florist alone had a team of more than twenty-five designers who worked odd hours to assemble wreaths, arrange bouquets, and bring design elements from concept to reality.

"Together We Celebrate—Welcome Home," I recited. "Who came up with the title?"

Kendra blushed. "I did."

"I love it. And I love the way we've used the theme to pay tribute to diversity,"

She gave a little self-deprecating shrug, but I knew she was pleased. "My team has been working hard," she said. "They've put in a lot of time."

"It shows. I can't wait to see it all put together."

Bradley Clarke cleared his throat and called the meeting to order. Tall, and with a perpetually friendly smile, Bradley was the kind of man you worked hard to impress. After a few brief announcements, he said, "Let's start with the big-ticket items before we go over this morning's situation. Thanksgiving first. Ollie?"

I brought the staff up-to-date on our menu and made sure that the waitstaff as well as Marguerite, the social secretary, knew that Sean Baxter would be in attendance. Everyone who needed to scribbled notes, as did I when Marguerite informed me that Mrs. Blanchard had sent her regrets.

"Does the First Lady know?"

"I'm meeting with her right after this."

"Thanks for the heads-up." Mrs. Blanchard had been our only dietary-alert guest invited to dinner Thursday. "That opens up some possible last-minute additions to the menu," I said. As I wrote myself a note, I added, absentmindedly, "We're going to be heavy on male guests this time. Sean Baxter's coming alone, and now without Mrs. Blanchard . . ."

Marguerite interrupted. "Treyton Blanchard is bringing his assistant instead."

"Bindy?" I asked.

Marguerite nodded. "It will be nice to see her."

"Isn't that a little odd?" I asked. "Shouldn't he be with his wife on Thanksgiving?" I knew I'd blurted my thoughts before corralling them, but this was a staff meeting, after all. It was where we were supposed to air our questions.

"Senator Blanchard's family is hosting dinner at their home later that night for both sides of the family," she said with a sniff. "Mrs. Blanchard appreciates the invitation, but she knows the Thanksgiving luncheon at the White House will be mostly business. She'd rather stay home with the kids and keep their traditions alive." Turning down an invitation to the White House was considered sacrilege. "All of this according to Bindy, that is."

Bindy Gerhardt had been part of the White House staff until she'd accepted a position on Treyton Blanchard's team. She'd fast-tracked her way into his inner circle, and I started to hear Sean Baxter's refrain in my head. These people weren't coming to share a Thanksgiving meal, they *were* intending to conduct business.

As a former colleague and White House staffer, Bindy would be uniquely qualified to secure Mrs. Campbell's ear. I was suddenly glad Sean would be at dinner. And especially glad the president would be there to back up his wife.

Marguerite added, "And you know Helen Hendrickson is bringing Aloysius Fitzgerald, right?"

Her attorney. "Yeah," I said. "And who is Nick Volkov planning to bring? His financier?"

The other department heads looked at me in surprise. Marguerite's brow furrowed. "The last I heard, he's bringing his wife." She tilted her head. "Is there something I should know?"

I waved off her concern. "Sorry. Stressful morning. My mind took a tangent." Smiling brightly at the group, I continued my update before passing the floor to the next person.

We were just finishing the meeting when one of the assistants came in with a note for Bradley. "Gene," he said, after he'd read it. "I thought you said the power to the Map Room had been restored."

Gene rocked back in his chair. "Yep. Last week, just like you asked."

"Not according to the cleaning crew. They were just in there and couldn't get the lights to work."

Gene sat forward, the front chair legs landing with a *whump*. "Curly said he took care of it." Shaking his head, he stood. Like the rest of us in the White House, he knew better than to place blame. "I'll take care of it right now," he said, and started out as the rest of us got up to leave.

Bradley held up a finger. "We're almost done here. Before you go, I want to let everyone know that the Secret Service has arranged for"—he hesitated—"classes to educate the staff in threat assessment."

From the group: "Does this have to do with the thing they found this morning?"

Someone else asked, "What aren't they telling us?"

Bradley raised both hands. "You guys know the Secret Service. They'll tell us when and what they need to tell us. Just be aware that you'll be contacted soon, and that these classes are mandatory."

Above the disgruntled murmurs, Kendra voiced the concern we all had. "Don't they know we're gearing up for Christmas? Can't this wait till after New Year?"

"Terrorists don't care how much work we have," Bradley said. That reflection sobered us all. "Sorry," he said. "I know the deadlines we're all up against. If everyone cooperates, we'll get through this quickly. Okay?"

Gene had already bolted to the door, muttering something about not being able to depend on his people. Curly was in for an earful when Gene got down to the electrical office. Staff members were rarely caught falling down on the job, and Curly, for all his unpleasantness, was generally quite dependable. I wondered what was wrong.

CHAPTER 4

THE SBA CHEF, AGDA, WAS HARD AT WORK WHEN I RETURNED TO
the kitchen. Even though I felt I knew her on paper, this was the first time we'd
met in person. I didn't know what I'd expected, but it certainly wasn't a
six-foot-tall bombshell who chopped carrots faster than a food processor on
high speed. Wielding a knife so long she could have used it in battle, she halted
her *chunk-chunk-chunk* carrot-hacking and smiled hello.

From Agda's curriculum vitae I was able to determine how old she was—late
twenties—right between Cyan's age and mine. But heightwise, she had us both
by about a foot.

I was in for another surprise. Her command of English was limited.
Severely.

"It's nice to meet you, Agda," I said, reaching up to shake hands with her.

With a supermodel's smile, she nodded down to me. "Hallo," she said, then
hesitated. I could practically see her searching her brain before her next words
came out, enunciated with care. "You are born France?"

"I was born in the United States," I said, thinking that was a mighty peculiar question to ask the first moment on the job. From the sound of her last
name and the natural blond of her chignon, I'd already deduced her to be of
Swedish descent.

When she spoke again, haltingly, I smiled at the lilt in her words, even as
I worried about communication in an already stressed kitchen. "They tell me
you are . . . Paris."

"Oh." Realization dawned. "I get you," I said, knowing she was clearly *not*
getting me. Slowing down, I pointed to myself. "Olivia . . . Ollie . . . Paras." I
nodded encouragingly. "My name is Ollie Paras."

Her mouth turned downward. "I am to work for French chef."

"Marcel has an assistant," I said. "He's the pastry chef."

"No, no. No pastry," she said, shaking her head in emphasis. "I can be sous-chef. I work here for French chef."

"You speak French?" At least we could have Marcel translate when necessary.

She shook her head apologetically. "Ah . . ." she said as she put her fingers up to indicate, "*un peu.*"

"Well, now that that's cleared up," Bucky said from the far end of the kitchen. "Isn't this great? Even if she's capable, the best we can do is give her tasks we can pantomime." Using exaggerated hand motions, he pretended to stir an imaginary handheld bowl. "Like this. And you wonder why Henry always insisted on an interview first."

Agda's forehead crinkled. She may not have understood him completely, but his manner was distressing her.

"What a laugh," he continued. "We're working shorthanded, and instead of sending us someone we've used before, the service expects us to be the United Nations."

"Bucky, that's enough," I said.

He fixed me with a glare, but at least he shut up.

"Come here," I said to Agda, leading her to the side of the room farthest from Bucky. The White House kitchen is surprisingly small. For all the meals that come out of this place, everyone expects a larger area and state-of-the-art equipment. To be fair, some of our stuff is cutting-edge, but because all purchases must come out of a budget supported by the public, we learn to make do with what we have. "When you finish the carrots"—I pointed—"why don't you begin making the soup?" I pulled up the recipe from our online files.

Agda's eyes lit up. "I read," she said with some pride. "I know how"—she searched for the right phrase—"follow recipe."

"Great," I said. As I headed to the computer to update my notes from the staff meeting, she called out to me.

"Ollie," she said, making my name sound like *oily*. "You are kitchen assistant, yes?"

Bucky barked a laugh.

"No," I said, slowly, moving back toward her. "I'm the executive chef." Even now, months after my appointment, I still felt a little thrill anytime I said it. Pointing to myself yet again, I smiled. "I'm the boss."

"You? Boss?" She laughed, not mean-spiritedly. Her voice went up an octave as she hovered her hand, flat, just inches above my head. "You are little for boss, no?"

From the corner, Bucky guffawed. "I like this girl already."

NOT TEN MINUTES LATER, ONE OF THE SECRET SERVICE GUYS appeared in the kitchen. "Time for the meeting, Ollie," he said.

My hands and attention deep in the floured batter that would become soft biscuits, I looked up. "What meeting?"

"The Emergency Response Team. The ERT guys. They have that department-head meeting going in the East Room."

Bucky and Cyan grumbled. Marcel was out of the room at the moment, and Agda clearly didn't understand.

"Now?" I asked.

He tapped his watch. "Hurry up. The sooner we get in there, the sooner you'll get back."

"But—"

"I know, I know. I've heard it from everybody so far. Too much to do. No time. Today's bomb scare threw everyone off and believe me, we're hearing about it." Pointing upstairs he added, "It's mandatory."

I washed my hands and dried them hastily on my apron as he talked. For the second time that day, I grabbed my notebook and pen and put Bucky in charge of the kitchen. "Get as much done as you can," I said. "I'm sure I won't be long."

"Uh-huh," Bucky said.

Cyan rolled her eyes. Agda smiled and waved her knife.

Measuring about eighty by thirty-seven feet, the East Room is the largest room in the White House, and is generally used for social events, such as when singer Karina Pasian performed here, in celebration of Black Music Month during the George W. Bush administration, or in the 1980s for President Ronald Reagan's seventieth birthday bash. Although the room is also used for more down-to-business purposes, such as bill-signing ceremonies and award presentations, I liked to think of it as the party room. The White House's first architect, James Hoban, probably had a similar idea in mind, because he had dubbed it the "Public Audience Chamber."

Today, in addition to the stunning eagle-leg grand piano that sat beneath a protective dust cloth in the southern corner and the collection of chairs brought in for the staff, the room was lined on two walls by folding tables. Whatever they held was also covered by white cloth, but I didn't imagine their role was to keep away dust. The lumpiness beneath the white fabric led me to believe that whatever was under there was to be kept from the staff's prying eyes.

I took a folding chair toward the back, finding myself seated near Gene again. "How's it going?" I asked, not really expecting much of a reply.

"I can't find Manny or Vince," he said.

I wasn't quite sure what to do with that information. Manny and Vince were journeymen electricians who did a lot of the maintenance work around the grounds. "They're . . . missing?"

"Damned if I know," he said, leaning close enough for me to smell his stale coffee breath. "Curly told them to get the Map Room hot again, but now he's gone for the day and I can't find either of the two young guys."

Vince might be considered youthful. Manny, not so much. Of course, from Gene's point of view, twenty- and thirtysomethings probably did seem like youngsters.

"Curly's gone? With everything we have to do?"

Gene shook his big head. "His wife's in the hospital. They called him out there. What could I do?" he asked rhetorically. "I need to make sure they take care of things. With the Map Room out of juice, I start worrying about the Blue Room and the Red Room. Even though they're on the floor above, they're close, you know."

I knew where the Blue and Red rooms were, but I also knew Gene was just working off stress by explaining it to me. The Christmas tree, due here in just a few days, would be set up in the Blue Room for White House guests to see and admire. The Red Room would host the gingerbread house. Lack of electricity in either location was not an option.

Just then, three men dressed in black marched into the room. All had enormous rifles, solemn expressions, and baseball caps pulled low. Behind them four other men followed. These guys were dressed in camouflage gear. When the procession came to halt before our gathering of department heads, the men pivoted and came to attention. I didn't know whether I should stand, salute, or what.

"Welcome to the first round of educational seminars scheduled for White House personnel." I leaned to see around the people in front of me. A tall, fortyish man stood in front of us on a raised dais. Watching us, he ran both hands through his sandy hair before he leaned forward to grip the sides of a lectern. With a voice like his, he didn't really need the microphone, but that didn't stop him from using it. "I am Special Agent-in-Charge Leonard Gavin. I am in command of this endeavor." He worked his tongue around the inside of his mouth, and tugged his head sideways the way men do when their collars are too tight. "In the course of White House business, you will refer to me as Special Agent Gavin."

Now I really felt like saluting.

Still booming, he continued. "You will be given name tags and asked to sign in so we know you were here. I will attempt to learn all your names. We have a lot to accomplish, so we will begin by passing out a study guide. Nickerson?"

One of the camouflage men stepped forward to begin distributing booklets.

Gene muttered under his breath, "We're never going to get out of here."

"Don't say that." I took one of the handouts and passed the rest to Gene, whispering, "I've got two big events—"

Special Agent Gavin pointed to me, his voice loud and irritated. "Is there a question?"

Startled, I shook my head. "No."

As though I wouldn't be able to hear him, he came around the lectern, his voice still about fifty decibels higher than it needed to be. "What is your name?"

"Ollie," I said. "Ollie Paras."

"What is your position?"

I stood. "I am the White House executive chef." Wow, I got to say that twice in an hour. But would he view me as "too tiny" like Amazon Agda had?

"Come up here," he said.

I started to protest, then thought better of it and decided to comply. Wasn't this great? I'd inadvertently become today's troublemaker for talking in class. Just like in school. Years of not knowing when to keep my mouth shut taught me it was better to go along with the teacher's orders and take my lumps right away, than to suffer built-up wrath later. I scooted sideways from my chair and made my way forward. Going with the flow might help things move along faster here, too.

I skipped up the steps to the dais, presenting myself as willing and cooperative. Or at least I hoped that's how I came across.

"Now, Ms. Chef, look out there," Gavin said, pointing to the audience.

Department heads and assistants stared back at me from the safety of their folding chairs.

I followed Gavin's direction. "Okay."

Way back, next to where I'd been sitting, Gene squirmed. A half beat later he sat up and twisted, as though someone had called his name. Apparently someone had. Manny stood in the room's doorway, beckoning to Gene, who needed no further encouragement. Hefting his bulk, he was up and out the door within seconds. I was glad for Gene that Manny had found him. At least one of us was getting something accomplished.

I chanced a look at Special Agent Gavin, who stood next to me—imposingly—looking as unperturbed as I was discomfited by the heavy silence in the room. I opened my mouth to ask a question, but he silenced me with a look and pointed out to the audience again.

Was there something I was supposed to notice? Something amiss? I shifted from one foot to the other, thinking about my crew downstairs. About Bucky running things. About Agda's professed ability to follow recipe directions in English. That made *me* squirm.

The camouflage guys and the black-clad snipers were busy organizing the displays on two of the long tables at the far side of the room. They'd peeled away the white coverings to reveal an odd assortment of gadgets. No doubt Gav here was supposed to be the warm-up act, and I the unfortunate audience volunteer.

I wanted to be back in my kitchen. Now.

When I bit my lip in impatience, I noticed Peter Everett Sargeant III grinning viciously up at me from the front row. Sargeant, the head of cultural and faith-based etiquette affairs, and I had never been able to see eye-to-eye about anything. I smiled back at him, as evenly as I could manage.

Finally, Gavin asked, "What do you see?"

I had an answer ready. "My colleagues."

"No." He shook his head somberly, as though I'd given a bad answer to a very easy question.

"No?"

"You see safety."

I could feel this little demonstration stretching out ahead of us. If he'd chosen someone else—anyone else—I might have been able to sneak out of this meeting after signing the attendance sheet. Here, out in front of everyone, I had no choice but to go along.

"You operate in a state of bliss," he continued. "You have no worries, no cares."

I wanted to ask him how often he'd plated a dinner for more than a hundred guests. From the looks of his downturned mouth and icy-sharp gaze, I'd wager he didn't have enough friends to entertain often. Still, I didn't argue.

"One of these people here"—he pointed outward again—"could be a killer." He twisted to face me. "*You* could be a killer."

Was he joking? "I'm . . . not."

"We don't know that. None of us know that. Today you're a cook. . . ."

A *cook*? I bit the inside of my cheeks to keep from reacting.

"Tomorrow, who knows? You could . . . snap!" He flicked his fingers in emphasis. Right in front of my rapidly heating face. "I will ask you again: What do you see?"

Obediently, I offered, "Safety?"

"Yes!" he said, smiling and raising two fists in the air like a TV evangelist wannabe. Even louder, he asked, "And *who* here could be a killer?"

I knew I should give him the answer he wanted. I knew I should resist temptation. But I couldn't stop myself. With a smile as wide as Gavin's, I pointed directly at his chest. "You!" I shouted.

The audience exploded with laughter. But old Gav was not amused. "The cook has a sense of humor," he said without smiling.

Cook, again.

"How funny would it be if half the White House exploded on your watch?" he asked, pummeling the room's mood into the floor. "Then who would be laughing?"

I started moving toward the steps. "Are we done here?"

"We're only just beginning." His drill-sergeant demeanor grew stronger with every snarl. He tugged my elbow, forcing me back to center stage. "And when we're done with you—with all of you," he said, facing the crowd, "you will all know better than to just trust one another blindly. Do you understand?"

I held my breath, almost expecting everyone to yell, "Sir. Yes, sir!"

Instead, they fidgeted.

A camouflage guy smiled up at me sympathetically as he handed Gavin a weighty item. It looked like a dirty bottle one might find at the seashore, with a desperate message tucked inside its opaque shell. Gavin held it in both hands as he stared down at it, almost prayerfully, for half a minute.

Come on, I wanted to say. Let's get this show moving.

Keeping his head bent, Gavin's eyes flicked up, encompassing the shifting, murmuring crowd. "Do you all know what this is?" He waited. "Does anyone know?"

Silence.

"I didn't think you did." His grip tightened, as did his lips. I wondered how many times he'd practiced that meaningful stare in the mirror. "This, ladies and gentlemen, is an Improvised Explosive Device—an IED. A bomb."

With a collective gasp, and amid scraping chairs, staff members got to their feet. I jumped back.

"Sit down," Gavin ordered. "I wouldn't bring a hot IED into the White House."

When everyone resettled themselves, he continued, holding the bottlelike item high over his head. "This is the device we found in the West Wing this morning."

The West Wing. I'd been right.

"Although the exact location of the IED's placement is not being broadcast at this time, I can tell you that this is not now, nor has it ever been, a danger to the First Family—nor to any personnel. So, yes, you may all breathe a sigh of relief. Anyone can see that this was designed to mimic the workings of an IED." He hefted the bottle in front of himself now, frowning almost as though he were disappointed. "But it was never loaded with explosives. What that means, people, is that we have received a warning. Whoever placed it in the White House did so to test our diligence."

I started to back away, eyeing my seat at the far end of the room.

Sensing movement, Gavin half turned and directed his next question to me. "And what do you think this warning means?"

What else could it mean? "That we have to be more conscientious going forward."

The surprise in his eyes told me he hadn't expected my answer. He recovered quickly. "You are correct," he said, turning once again to face the audience and raising his voice. "What if this had been armed?"

No one answered.

"We don't even want to think about the devastation a weapon like this could cause, do we? But before today, how many of you had ever seen an IED before?"

No one raised a hand. Gavin cocked an eyebrow. "What would you have done had you encountered this? We are fortunate that one of our military-trained experts came across it. If any of you had found this where it had been secreted, you may have simply tossed it aside, thrown it away."

Watching him gesticulate as he paced the dais in front of me, I frowned. This guy didn't know our staff. We didn't take anything for granted. Perhaps none of us had ever seen something like this, but working in the White House taught us all not to take anything lightly. Finding a strange device in an unusual location would be enough to call for Secret Service support.

Gavin pointed to the camouflage-and-sniper contingent—the men were now standing at their tables, hands behind their backs, eyes staring straight ahead. Before them, they'd uncovered a display that resembled a collection of grammar school science projects.

"Today is the beginning of your training," Gavin said. "Over there, my men are waiting to demonstrate a variety of disarmed IEDs for you. We want you to acquaint yourselves with some of the known designs. But remember that terrorists are always improvising, dreaming up new models every single day. You must be on your guard, always. Take your time and learn all you can. We will keep the display available to you here for the remainder of the day. We will then move this exhibit across the building to the Family Dining Room, to continue your training tomorrow and throughout the week."

The crowd took their cue, getting up from their chairs. Some headed for the training tables. Others headed for the door.

I tapped Gavin's shoulder. "Thursday is Thanksgiving," I said.

Gavin twisted to stare at me. "So? Terrorists don't take days off."

"I realize that," I said equably. "But we're serving Thanksgiving dinner in the Family Dining Room this year." I pointed west. "You won't be able to set up there."

"This is the White House," Gavin said. "Don't tell me you have nowhere else to serve dinner."

"Mrs. Campbell requested—"

Before I could finish, Bradley stepped up to do what assistant ushers do best: He took control. "Let me handle this, Ollie," he said. When he faced Gavin, he shook his head. "Can't allow you to set up in the Family Dining Room. Sorry."

Grateful for the reprieve, I excused myself, hearing Gavin argue that safety was paramount, more important than a roast turkey's placement in a particular room. Although I knew old Gav would disapprove, I made only a cursory study of the bomb exhibit before heading back to the kitchen.

I'd just made my way to the ground floor, crossing the Center Hall, when I ran into Gene, muttering to himself. Wearing his tool belt and carrying a massive black drill, he looked like he'd just come in from a jog around the Ellipse. Streaming rivulets of sweat dripped down the sides of his face. His dark shirt was so wet that it could've used a good wringing out.

"You okay?" I asked.

He pointed to the Map Room. "Still no power. Manny says Vince bungled something up when he tried to fix it. Vince says it was Manny's fault. Damn idiots. Where did those two get their journeyman cards anyway? A cereal box?"

Since it was asked rhetorically, I let him vent.

Using the drill as a pointer, he indicated the rooms to my left. "Curly's out and the two screw-ups are nowhere to be found. So this repair, which should've been done already, is still waiting to be taken care of."

"So now you're stuck with the job?"

"You see anybody else stepping up to volunteer?" Shaking his head, he offered a wry smile. "Sorry, honey. I didn't mean to take it out on you."

"Don't worry about it," I said. "This time of year is always a little stressful."

"Yeah, and I shouldn't be standing here talking when there's work to be done." He pointed the drill skyward. "Wish me luck. I've got ten jobs that should've been done yesterday, and I'm working with this lousy equipment."

"What's wrong with it?"

He started toward the power closet behind the elevator, directly across the hall from the Map and Diplomatic Reception rooms. "This baby works just fine. But it's ancient. I keep these things around for emergencies"—his voice rose, almost as though he were hoping for the guilty parties to hear and respond—"like when people take my good equipment who knows where and don't bring it back when there's a job to be done. You know?"

"Same thing in the kitchen," I said. "My favorite mixer's a monster from way back. Maybe even Eisenhower's time." Laughing, I added, "It's huge and super noisy, but it handles heavy batter like nothing else. And I hate it when someone's using it when I need it."

Gene checked his watch. "I better get this done before Bradley calls me again."

"Stop by when you're finished. I have a couple of interesting dishes we're trying out. I think you deserve a treat after all this."

Gene swiped an arm across his sweaty brow. "Sounds great, Ollie. Count me in."

Back in the kitchen, Bucky and Cyan brought me up to speed. As she'd promised, Agda had indeed completed the soup without trouble. She was currently busy with the spiced pecans.

Cyan seemed impressed. "That girl is quick," she said. "Had everything put together in enough time to get started on the pecans for the appetizer tray. So I just handed her the next set of instructions and she was off."

"Wonderful," I said. "Things are finally going our way."

"How was the meeting?"

Before I could answer, the lights flashed off and on. A heartbeat later, like too-close lightning, a violent buzz seared the room.

Through it all, a scream so primal it froze all movement.

Except for the unmistakable *thud* of a body hitting the floor.

"What was that?" Cyan asked.

I was already running toward the sound. "Stay here," I ordered the wide-eyed staff. I had no idea what I would find, but if it were bomb-related, I didn't want all of us to be in danger.

With our kitchen so close to the Center Hall, I was the first on the scene. All the lights were out here; the passage was dim, but there was enough illumination to see the figure sprawled on his back, arms extended wide to his sides.

"Gene!" I cried, running to him.

Gene lay just outside the elevator power-closet door. His hands were empty, but one was blackened. A sudden stench of scorched flesh rose up, nearly causing me to retch. A metal stepstool had tumbled next to him, lying atop his right leg, while one of the stool's legs remained lodged against something inside the closet. I started looking around for a tool to free Gene's leg from beneath the metal trap. "Cyan! Bucky!" I called, enunciating to make my panicked shouts understood. "Bring me the wooden rack. Now!"

The rack kept our most-often-used spices handy. About eighteen inches wide and just a few inches tall, it was the only thing I could think of at the moment that was safe to use in the presence of high voltage.

When neither of them answered, I cried out again. Finally, I heard Cyan yell back that she was coming.

One of the laundry ladies, Beatta, came running, as I had. "My God!" she said.

She reached down to touch Gene's face.

"Don't!" I shouted. "He might have been electrocuted."

Just then, Bucky arrived with the rack, Cyan running behind, carrying all the spices in a bowl. "Did you want these, too?" she asked.

I grabbed the empty rack, ignoring the question.

Cyan stepped out of my way as I pushed the rack beneath one of the stepladder's footholds. I tried levering the contraption away from its contact with Gene, but the rack twisted, slipping out of my fingers. "Damn," I said aloud.

"Be careful," Bucky said.

I took precious seconds to wipe perspiration from my hands and I inched forward to try again. A buzz emanating from within the room underscored the danger. Whatever electrical charge had hit Gene was still live. I scooted closer, my left foot less than four inches from his prone form, but I had to get close enough to get the leverage I needed.

"Get me a flashlight," I said. "And get the doctor."

Someone said they would, and hurried away.

More people came. Secret Service agents swarmed, then worked hard to manage the gathering crowd. One of the agents stepped in to take over for me, but I was so close I couldn't stop now. Although Gene was a big guy, it was only his foot that maintained contact with the metal ladder. I could do this. The agent must have sensed my concentration because he stepped back when I shook my head.

Amid shouts and questions and frantic babbling, I hooked the corner of the rack—the little lip at one end—under the rim of the stepladder's top foothold. Crouching, and using two hands, I forced the ladder upward, knocking it farther into the room.

All of this took less than a minute, but I felt as though hours had passed. "I think I'm clear. But I can't see. There's not enough light."

One of the agents came up with a flashlight. He shined it into the dark space.

"All clear," he said.

I dropped to my knees beside Gene, pushing my ear close to his mouth and nose. "Quiet, everyone!"

The hall rippled to silence.

The pounding I heard was my own heart beating—frenzied with fear for Gene. My CPR training rules rushed through my brain even as I pushed my head closer, hoping, waiting, trying to—

Warm air crossed my cheek. A baby-soft hiss followed.

"He's alive!"

I pulled my kitchen jacket off and covered Gene, hoping to stave off shock. A voice from behind the first circle of onlookers called out for everyone to make room.

The group parted. An emergency medical team raced in, the White House doctor heading the charge. Our on-staff nurse-practitioner followed two assistants, who carried a stretcher.

I was already scurrying out of their way when the team fell in around Gene, starting immediate care. The nurse-practitioner turned to me. "We've got him now."

Slowly we all backed away, giving the team a wide berth. The sickening scent of cooked flesh hung in the air around us; I wondered if I'd ever be able to forget that smell. The Secret Service agents worked their crowd-dispersal magic, and I sent Cyan and Bucky back to the kitchen.

As the corridor cleared, I caught sight of Manny. His wide, lined face was pale gray, like the underbelly of a dead fish. "What happened?" he asked. Nobody answered him, so I made my way over.

"Where were you?"

He swallowed. "Me and Vince were outside." He pointed south. "We had to get some wiring set up."

"It's raining."

"Not anymore. Stopped about an hour ago. That's why we got out there. We were waiting all morning for the big storm to clear up." Behind us the medical personnel spoke in low tones as they ministered to Gene, preparing him for transport. Manny asked again, "What happened?"

"Gene had an accident."

Manny shoved a hand through his thick hair, holding it there for an extended period of time. The medical team raised the stretcher, taking a moment to be sure they had everything they needed. I thought Manny might be going into shock.

"Where's Vince?" I asked, just to snap him out of it.

Staring at Gene's unmoving form, Manny could only shake his head.

As though summoned, Vince came around the corner, moving at his customary loping pace. About twenty-eight years old, he had a chiseled look, from his solid muscularity to his narrow face, so perfectly structured it looked to be carved of pure ebony. His smile dropped the moment he caught sight of the corridor's activity.

"Make way, folks," one of the technicians said. We moved out of the way, allowing them a clear path out the White House's south entrance.

"Was that Gene?" Vince asked.

I nodded. Manny remained speechless.

In his haste to get out of the stretcher's way, Vince nearly tripped. "Is he going to be okay?"

That was the one question I was wondering myself.

CHAPTER 5

JUST AFTER SEVEN O'CLOCK THAT EVENING, THE ASSISTANT USHER showed up at the kitchen. I had already sent Agda home, but Cyan, Bucky, and I were still hard at work, trying our best to catch up.

The first thing out of my mouth was, "How's Gene?"

Bradley hesitated.

There's a sorrow people get in their eyes when news is very, very bad. I've seen it often enough to recognize the look even before I hear the words. Bradley's eyes held that look now.

"Gene didn't . . ." He shook his head. "I'm sorry."

I dropped the knife I was holding, and steadied myself against the stainless steel counter. Staring down, I was vaguely aware of Cyan's gasp—and of Bucky backing up to sit on a nearby stool.

Cyan snuffled, but I couldn't look at her just now. I forced myself to focus on Bradley. "Electrocuted?" I asked.

"The hospital said the damage was incredible. They were surprised he hadn't died on the scene . . . that he lasted as long as he did."

In unspeakable pain, no doubt. The little I knew about electrocution was enough to realize it was a ghastly way to go.

We were silent for a long moment, until I had to ask. "There's no connection between Gene's . . . death . . . and the bomb scare today, is there?"

Bradley grimaced, taking his time before answering. "We don't believe so. There will be a full investigation into the electrical system. In fact, that's going on right now. The Secret Service can't overlook any possibility of a correlation, of course, but preliminary findings suggest this is just a terrible coincidence."

I stared down at the diced mushrooms before me and as hard as I tried, I couldn't remember what I'd planned to do with them. I cleared my throat. "Thanks for letting us know, Bradley."

"We'll be sure to keep everyone informed about arrangements."

I nodded.

"Go home," I said to Bucky and Cyan as soon as Bradley was gone.

Cyan's eyes were red. "But . . ."

"We aren't going to get anything done tonight," I said. "Not after this. I'll clean up. It'll give me a chance to clear my head. You guys go home now. We'll just work harder tomorrow."

For once Bucky didn't fight me.

When they were gone, I stood in the silent kitchen, reliving Gene's final minutes in the White House. Could I have reached him sooner? Would it have mattered? Fragmented recollections raced through my brain, out of order and seemingly without purpose. Why had I noticed that the laundry lady's hairnet made her ears stick out? Why did it matter that the drill Gene had been holding cracked the marble floor when it fell? Why did I notice that salt was the top jar in the bowl that Cyan had erroneously carried out to us?

Instead of noticing these unrelated, irrelevant details, why hadn't I done more for Gene?

I closed my eyes, pressing fingers into my eye sockets, as though that could wipe the visions of his stricken body from my memory. Maybe, if I pressed hard enough, I could wake myself up and discover this terrible day had been a figment of my imagination. Maybe—

"Ollie?"

Startled, I jumped. Sparkles from the sudden release of eye pressure danced before me, but I recovered. "Mrs. Campbell," I said, ready to jump into action. "What can I do for you?"

Waving away my concerns, she made her way around the stainless steel worktable. "How are you doing?"

I opened my mouth, but no words came out. I bit my lip.

By then she'd reached my side and placed a warm hand over mine. "I wanted to see you because . . ."

Words didn't often fail the First Lady. She looked away.

When she faced me again, her eyes were shiny. She took several deep breaths before she spoke again. "I want to share something with you—something not a lot of people know." She took another deep breath and I got the impression she was steeling herself. "A very long time ago, when I was a teenager, a friend of mine drowned. We weren't twenty feet apart, Ollie, not twenty feet. We were in a public pool being watched over by lifeguards, and Donna was a good swimmer. But when I looked for her, she wasn't there." When she took a breath this time, it was labored. "She was at the bottom of the pool and . . ." Mrs. Campbell stared up at the ceiling, wrinkling her nose as though to dispel the emotion. "By the time we got her out, there was nothing any of us could do for her."

I didn't know what to say.

She gave me a wry smile. "Everyone told me that I wasn't to blame. But I didn't believe them. I was seventeen, you understand, and I *knew*, I just knew, that she'd died because I hadn't been more careful. It was my fault."

Politeness urged me to contradict her, but good sense warned me not to.

"I lived with the guilt for a long time." She sighed. "A very long time. It wasn't until years later that I found out Donna had suffered a heart seizure that afternoon. It didn't matter that we were in a pool; she would've died at home in bed that day." Swallowing, Mrs. Campbell gave a resigned shrug. "Her parents never told me because they didn't know the guilt I was carrying. They were carrying their own. They believed they should have seen it coming, and that they could have prevented her death." She shook her head. "I'm telling you this because you were the first person to reach Gene. I know you feel responsible." She squeezed my hand. "Take it from someone who's been there. I'm here to tell you that when it's truly a person's time to go, there's nothing any of us can do about it."

My throat raw, I managed to say, "Thank you."

WHEN I FINALLY REACHED MY APARTMENT BUILDING THAT NIGHT, I'd taken to heart what Mrs. Campbell had said, yet I felt strongly that it hadn't really been Gene's time. With the new knee, his determination to be part of the White House Christmas preparations, and the intensity with which I knew he approached safety issues, I couldn't shake the feeling that something was not right. With wonderment, I realized, too, that it had been just this morning that the First Lady and I had been sequestered with Sean in the bunker. It seemed like it had been weeks.

James sat in the front lobby. Although my building's owners hadn't hired James to sit at the front desk and screen visitors, they encouraged his continued cooperation by reducing his rent. A win-win situation. James, with his fixed income and empty apartment since Millie died, enjoyed the constant busyness. The building's owners liked the idea of the added, albeit limited, security James provided at the front door.

Though his build was slight, James had a deep voice. He greeted me with a gusty, "Hiya, Ollie! How's the president today?"

I answered as I usually did. "Great. He sends his best."

James laughed at our little joke. "You're home kinda late," he said. "I bet it's a lot of work to prepare for a White House Thanksgiving."

James loved any presidential tidbits I cared to share, and although I never gave him information that couldn't be found online or in the newspapers, he always felt as though he was getting the scoop from me. I started to answer, but a random thought stopped me. "Is Stanley around?"

"I saw him go up a little while ago. Why? You having power problems in your apartment?"

I shook my head. "I just want to ask him a couple questions." Realizing swiftly that Gene's death would make the early news tomorrow, I added, "We had an accident at the White House today and I just want to pick his brain a little."

"An electrical accident?"

"Yeah, but if Stanley's done for the night . . ." I let loose a sigh of frustration. Stanley was another of our building owner's priceless finds. He took care of building maintenance in return for a small stipend and free rent. I wondered if, when I retired, the mighty owners would consider putting in a restaurant on the main floor and give me free rent, too. "I'll try to catch up with him tomorrow."

But James was already dialing. "This may be a matter of national security," he said with mounting excitement.

"No, not at all—"

He waved me quiet when Stanley answered. "I've got Ollie down here at the desk," James said, his voice low, and heavy with importance. "She wants to talk with you about an electrical situation at . . ." He faltered a moment, looked at the receiver, then continued, very slowly, ". . . at the location where . . . she . . . works. You got that?"

He hung up. "Stanley will be right down."

"You didn't have to—"

His voice barely above a whisper, he asked, "So what happened? Are you allowed to talk about it?"

"You'll hear more tomorrow," I said. Before I could bring the words forward, my stomach dropped, silencing me. I didn't want to say it out loud. Gene was dead, but talking about it to someone who didn't even know the man made this afternoon's tragedy seem gossipy and trivial.

James's eyes were bright with anticipation. "Yeah?"

There was no question about it making the news tomorrow. Heck, I was sure it was racing across the Internet already.

"Our head electrician was . . . killed today."

James's mouth dropped. "Electrocuted?"

"Autopsy is scheduled for tomorrow, but that's what it looks like."

"Electrocution is a bad way to go."

I looked away. "I know."

"You didn't see him, did you?"

The elevator dinged its arrival, sparing me from having to tell James that I'd been the one to find Gene. I could already sense James's fatherly comfort welling up. In a minute he'd rise from his chair to pat me on the back. I didn't want that right now. All I wanted, really, were answers. Maybe I'd never get the ones I sought. But maybe Stanley . . .

He alighted from the first car on the right, his graying hair mussed on one side, his face creased, his pajama shirt tucked into blue jeans, and his feet in house slippers. "What happened?" he asked, bouncing alarmed glances between me and James. "What kind of emergency?" Stanley's words tumbled out fast, more slurred than usual. Probably owing to the fact that he'd been sound asleep up until a moment ago.

I reached him before he made it to the desk. "No emergency," I said, placing a restraining hand on his arm. "I just have a few things I wanted to ask you. But I didn't mean to wake you up. Really—this can wait till tomorrow."

James boosted himself from his seat, eager to join the discussion. "I told Ollie you'd want to help her right away."

Stanley blinked twice. "'Course. But I can't do much until you tell me what happened."

This was not going the way I'd planned. But there was no sense sending James back to the desk or Stanley back to bed at this point. Both were waiting for me to spill whatever revelation they thought I carried. Except for the three of us, the lobby was empty, the elevators quiet.

I wanted information. There seemed but one way to get it. I told them about Gene, about finding him outside the elevator closet, about the subsequent news of his death. The two men standing before me stood silent a long moment when I finished.

I got to the crux of my reason for being there. "I thought there were safeguards against electrocution," I said, addressing Stanley. "Gene wasn't working on power lines. He was inside the White House. A residence. Things like this shouldn't happen, right?"

We'd drifted back toward the entry desk and Stanley rested his hip against it. He scratched at his gray-stubbled chin. "Well," he said slowly, "the problem is, electrocutions do happen. Not too often these days, but still . . ." He ran his fingers across his chin again, staring just over my head. "What was he doing?"

"I'm not entirely sure," I said. "I know that one of the rooms was out of power, and I know he was drilling something."

"Go over it all again, real slow."

A phone call pulled James's attention away from our conversation. Still feeling guilty about waking Stanley up, I decided the best thing I could do was to make this interruption worth his time. I launched into a detailed play-by-play of the scene, starting when I found Gene on the floor.

"Back up," Stanley said. "How did you know he was restoring power to one of the rooms?"

"We'd talked about it earlier, and then right before he started the repairs. He had just complained that the power should've been fixed before and that he wasn't using his favorite tools. . . ."

"What was he using?"

I described the tool belt, the old-fashioned drill, the stepladder.

As Stanley pondered that, I continued, "Gene was always such a sweet guy, but he was in a bad mood today. With all the problems, though, I couldn't blame him."

This time, instead of rubbing his chin, Stanley ran his hand over his mouth. Talking between his fingers, he said, "Can you describe the drill?"

"It was old," I said. "Black, but shiny where the paint had worn off."

"Shiny?" he repeated. "He was using a drill that wasn't insulated?"

I had no answer for that.

"What was he drilling?" Stanley seemed agitated now. "Where was he standing when this happened? Describe it."

I desperately wished I had more details, but even scraping my brain to provide the best account of the incident I could wasn't working; I knew it came up short.

Stanley kept his hand over his mouth and his gaze on the floor. He was quiet so long I worried he'd fallen asleep. James finished his phone call and must have had the same impression because after a long, silent interval, he said, "Stanley? You got any ideas?"

His head came up and he pointed at me as he spoke. "A guy with that much experience knows not to take chances. If he was using a drill that wasn't insulated, he had to be pretty damn sure he wasn't puncturing anything hot. You with me?"

I nodded.

"Was he wet? Perspiring?"

I thought about it. "Yeah. A lot."

"I gotta tell you—he would have known better. Mind you, we all take risks, try for the shortcut. And I don't know this fellow, but if he was a master electrician—"

"He was."

"Then I have to think he knew exactly what he was doing. If he's been with the White House for all those years, then he knew that place inside and out. He wouldn't have taken that risk with the drill unless . . ."

Stanley's gaze dropped, and the hand came back to rub his chin.

"Unless?" I prompted.

He made a thoughtful sound. "We had a big storm today, didn't we?"

James and I nodded.

"Tell you what, Ollie. Let me think about this one. I'll get back to you."

CHAPTER 6

BY THE NEXT MORNING, A GREAT PALL HAD SETTLED ON THE White House. As I shredded sharp white Cheddar for our baked farfalle, I tried without success to fight the sadness. Today hardly felt like the day before a holiday. Although Cyan, Bucky, and I went through the motions of preparing this year's Thanksgiving meal, we did so with little of the joy that usually accompanied our planning. There was no banter, no chitchat. Conversations were brief, and even our more fun-loving assistants kept to themselves when stopping in to pick up or drop off necessary items. Agda, of course, remained unaffected by the situation's gravity, but as she kneaded dough that would later become tiny rolls, she must have sensed our collective sadness because she gave us sympathetic glances whenever she looked up from her work.

"We have another SBA chef coming in today," I told the group.

Bucky had been adding chunks of pork roast to an open pan on the stove. We always prepared the meat filling the day before assembling tamales. He turned. "Did you bother with an interview this time?" he asked with a pointed look at Agda.

"As a matter of fact, I didn't," I said. "We were able to get Rafe."

"Rafe!" Cyan said, exhibiting the first cheer this kitchen had seen all day. "That's perfect. He's a genius with sauces."

"Hmph," Bucky said, which I took as his version of support. Without an opening to badger me, he returned to his task, covering the pork with water and setting the flame below the pan to medium. Before long the kitchen would be filled with the succulent, roasty smell of the simmering meat. Keeping his back to me, Bucky asked, "Did you talk to Henry? About Gene, that is."

"I called him last night before I left here," I said. "Henry's planning to come to the wake."

"I figured he'd want to know." Despite Bucky's persistent crankiness and his singular ambition to prove himself right in all instances, he wasn't a bad fellow. His shoulders and arms moved around a lot as he worked—as though in an animated conversation with himself. The back of his bobbing head, freckled in the small patch where he'd begun to lose his hair, looked suddenly vulnerable and weak. He shrugged to no one, talking softly. "Hell of a way to go."

I was about to agree, when I thought about my conversation with Henry. He'd been shocked and saddened by the news of Gene's death, but then what he'd said next struck a chord with me. "I've had friends at the White House pass away before, but never like this. Never had to deal with an accident of that magnitude. I give you credit, Ollie. I don't know how I would cope."

I'd demurred, knowing full well that Henry always found ways to deal with new situations. He'd have certainly found a way to cope.

I stopped shredding the Cheddar to take a look around my kitchen. Agda kneaded her dough at one corner of the center workstation, humming softly. Cyan slumped before the computer, an open cookbook on her lap. Bucky moved as though by rote.

"Before Rafe gets here," I said, clearing my throat, "I think we all need to—"

"Talk?" Bucky asked. "Share our feelings? Should we stand around the countertop, hold hands, and sing 'Kumbaya'?" He blew out a breath, raspberry style. "This is a kitchen, not a grief support group."

Cyan looked taken aback. So did Agda, whether she understood or not.

But I'd caught the look in Bucky's eyes before he'd masked it with sarcasm. I realized our resident curmudgeon was afraid we'd see that he was hurting, too. If Henry had been here, male camaraderie might have allowed him to pat Bucky sympathetically on the back. Maybe that would've started the healing process. I didn't know. All I knew for certain was that I wasn't Henry. So I'd have to do what I felt was best, given the circumstances.

"I think we all need to recognize something." I wiped my hands and came around to his side of the kitchen. Cyan rounded in, too. Bucky took a step back, looking as though he expected bodily harm. I continued. "Gene was where he wanted to be when he died. He loved the White House more than he even loved his own home. Ever since his wife died, Gene's been more than a fixture here; he's been the embodiment of the White House itself." Cyan stared downward. Bucky's mouth twitched and he looked away. "If anyone else had just gone through knee surgery, they would've been slow coming back. But Gene wanted to be here for the Christmas preparations."

Cyan nodded. Bucky worked his jaw.

I lowered my voice. "And he *was* here. Doing what he loved most."

Arms folded, Bucky finally met my eyes. "I don't believe he was being careless."

For once he and I agreed. "Neither do I."

"That's what they're saying."

"Who?"

At that moment, Special Agent-in-Charge Gavin stepped into the kitchen, stopping just as he entered, holding his hands behind his back, surveying us. "Good morning," he said.

I started to make introductions, but he held up an index finger. His other hand swung around, holding a leather portfolio. "As you were," Gavin said. He eased over to where Agda was working, smiling as though engrossed in what she was doing. "Pretend I'm not here."

Oh, sure. Like that was possible. I focused my attention back on Bucky and spoke quietly. "Who's saying Gene was careless?"

Bucky lasered his gaze on Special Agent Gavin. "His guys."

Realizing our "Kumbaya" moment was over, I sent Cyan and Bucky back to their stations and returned to my shredding, my attention taken not by the hunk of cheese in my hand, but by the chunk of agent in my kitchen.

Agda offered Gavin a tentative smile. He smiled back. This happened several times while he stood next to her. She may not have known who he was, or what a man in a suit was doing in our kitchen, but she was clearly uncomfortable. She inched away. The two were close in height, and every time she looked at him, he nodded encouragingly. Whether he was trying to ingratiate himself here because he was on a get-to-know-the-staff mission, or because he wanted to ask my new assistant chef out on a date, I didn't know.

I was about to break up this little meeting of the eyes when he spoke. "That smells delicious. What is it you're making?"

Agda nodded, smiled, and continued to knead the dough.

Gavin's grip tightened on his portfolio. He used his index finger to point. "What is it?" he asked again. "It looks good."

Agda kneaded harder, nodded harder. Her cheeks pinkened and her brows shot up.

Bucky exhaled loudly. "She's Swedish," he said. "She might not understand."

"Sweden?" Gavin asked. "I visited Göteborg last year."

"Göteborg!" Agda brightened. She exploded at once, chattering, speaking in lilting, excited, rapid Swedish, making me wonder if the famous Muppet might not have a human cousin counterpart after all.

"Sorry," Gavin said, backing away. Then to me: "She doesn't understand English?"

"Not much," Bucky and I said in unison.

Perplexed, Gavin asked, "Then how does she—"

I'd had enough of Gavin's kitchen inspection, and I was still more than a little annoyed with his belittling me onstage yesterday. This was my territory and unless he was ready to start sniffing for bombs himself, I wanted him out of here. "Was there something you needed?"

Realizing she didn't have anyone to talk with after all, Agda's shoulders slumped and she moved back into her kneading rhythm.

Gavin licked his lips. "Your department was inadvertently left off the schedule for today's classes. I'm here to ensure you take the necessary steps to get all your employees to training." He shot a thumb toward Agda. "I don't know what to do about her. Don't you see her lack of communication as a security threat?"

"My job is to bring the best food to the table every time the president, his family, and his guests sit down to dine. Isn't it *your* job to ensure our safety?"

He waited a beat before answering. When he did, his words were clipped. "I'm glad you realize that. Makes things easier for me." His chin came up, surveying us once again. "We will call you out one at a time so as not to unduly burden your staff. Since there are four of you—"

"Seven."

Our man here didn't like being interrupted. Maybe that was why I enjoyed doing it. I explained: "Our pastry chef and his assistant are elsewhere at the moment. And we have another chef joining us later today. But the new chef and Agda"—I pointed—"are SBA chefs, which means they are not permanent employees of the White House. I don't know if they should be counted. Does that make a difference?"

"How long will they be in service here?"

"As long as we need them. Given that we have Thanksgiving tomorrow, the Mothers' Luncheon on Friday, and a couple of other events over the next week, I see them both staying until at least next Thursday. If the social calendar changes, I may keep them on longer."

Gavin shook his head. "Neither will be required to participate in our training sessions. Just send your permanent employees down. Here's the schedule." He pulled a copy from his portfolio and wiped the already sparkling countertop clean before he put it down. "All personnel are required to attend three sessions, designated A, B, and C. We will commence this afternoon and we expect to have everyone sufficiently trained by the weekend."

"This weekend?"

Gavin spread his hands and gave me a look that said, "Duh."

"Is there a problem?" he asked.

I bit back a retort. "No," I answered, deciding right then that I'd wait until Saturday to send any of us in for training. I'd consult with Marcel, of course, but I knew he'd agree. We faced an already hindered, overpacked schedule, and the next two days would be backbreakers. There was no way I could spare even one person. "How long are the classes?" I asked.

"Depends on class participation. Could be as short as an hour, could be as long as three. If people catch on quickly, we'll move quickly." Holding up a finger, he said, "But we can only move as fast as the slowest man. Er . . . woman." He smiled, like he expected me to laugh.

I picked up the schedule, glanced at it, and placed it with the rest of my important papers in the already overflowing computer area. "Got it," I said. "Thanks."

He tugged at his collar. He hadn't expected to be dismissed.

Recovering, he nodded. "As you were," he said, then left.

I WAS HEADING TOWARD THE FLORAL DEPARTMENT, JUST PASSING the basement bowling alley, when Curly Sheridan emerged from the long hall that led west to the carpenter shop. Manny shuffled behind him. They both wore workpants and chambray shirts with rolled-up sleeves. Manny was only a few years older than I was, but he seemed to have aged in the past couple of days. He grunted hello and turned away, but I stopped Curly. "How's your wife?" I asked.

He squinted at me. "How do you know about my wife?"

"Gene . . ." I started to say. My voice faltered. For the briefest moment I'd forgotten all of yesterday's horror. "Gene . . . He told me you'd been called to the hospital. Is she all right?" I'd met Mrs. Sheridan a couple times. Sweet woman. Tiny and dark-haired, she didn't talk much. I attributed that to her being foreign-born and the fact that she was married to truculent Curly.

He grimaced. "She's having a rough time."

I didn't know quite what to say to that. "I'm sorry."

"Yeah."

Not for the first time did I question Curly's nickname. The man was mostly bald, with a long scar like a *J* around his left ear, stretching up and across his shiny pate. It dawned on me suddenly that with Gene gone, Curly was next in command. Manny mumbled, letting Curly know that he'd be upstairs in the Blue Room. Curly started to leave, too, but I stopped him with a hand to his bare forearm. He reacted as if burned.

"What do you want?"

"What really happened yesterday?" I asked. "I mean, Gene was always so careful. . . ."

The squint came back. "Why you asking me?"

"You know these things. You understand them better than I do."

His perpetual scowl deepened and he shook his head, blowing out an angry breath. "Why does everybody think I know what happened there? I wasn't with him. I wasn't there. You were there."

I felt suddenly small, and the words came out before I could stop myself from asking, "Could I have done something more? Could I have saved him if I'd done something differently?"

The scowl moved, fractionally. Enough for me to wonder if he harbored any sympathy at all, or if he was just trying to decide if I was a crackpot.

"Listen, I'll tell you what I've been telling everybody, including those explosives guys. What are they, anyway? Secret Service? Or military?"

I shook my head. "Not sure."

"Whatever." He took a plaid handkerchief out of his back pocket and wiped around the scar. "Gene hit something hot, that's for sure. I'm working on figuring out exactly what happened. That's my job today. That, and getting a million other things done." He grabbed at his empty shirt pocket, as though reaching for phantom cigarettes. Another grimace. "Gene was a big guy, and if you want to know what I think, I'm guessing he leaned up against something metal when he hit the power. He knew better, yeah, and there shouldn't've been enough juice to kill him, but he was using a bad drill. And Gene was always sweating. I think it just all added up to him being careless."

"You really think so?"

Taking offense to my skeptical tone, he said, "As a matter of fact I do, missy. You asked your question. You got my answer. Now go take care of the food handling and let me do the job they pay me for."

CHAPTER 7

WHEN I GOT BACK TO THE KITCHEN, RAFE HAD ARRIVED. BUT WE had other company as well. I stopped short. "Sean," I said in surprise. "I didn't expect to see you today."

Sean Baxter was wearing a white apron over his charcoal pants and pale gray shirt, standing at the center workstation, slicing red peppers. "Hey, I was wondering when you'd show up. Look," he said, "they put me to work."

Cyan gave a one-shoulder shrug. "He wanted something to do," she said with a grin. "I figured you wouldn't mind."

Just wait till security-crazed Gavin sees this, I thought. But then again, Sean was cleared for much more classified stuff than tomorrow's Thanksgiving dinner. If we couldn't trust the president's own nephew, who could we trust?

Rafe called out, "Hey, Ollie, how's it going?"

I waved a hello. "Welcome to the team," I said to both of them. Still trying to understand Sean's presence, I turned to him. "What brings you down here?"

He fixed his attention on a pepper, giving it a good slice even as his cheeks rivaled the vegetable for redness. "Aunt Elaine and I were going over some of her decisions. You know, that financial stuff we talked about in the bunker yesterday."

He didn't elaborate, but behind him, Bucky raised his eyebrows and shot me a look that underscored his earlier comment about "cozying up to the First Lady."

I ignored him.

Sean continued. "She was called away and will probably be busy for about an hour. I had some time to kill, so . . ."

All I could think about was the time crunch we were under. "Are you sure you want to be down here?" I hoped to talk him out of helping. The last thing I needed was an unskilled amateur gumming up our plans for the day. It was one thing to have too many chefs spoiling the broth. It was another to have one who didn't speak the language. Add an assistant who didn't know his way around the kitchen and we'd be lucky if we managed to create any broth to spoil.

"Yeah," he said, concentrating on the peppers again. "I'm just about done here—so if you've got anything else . . ."

I thought about it. One of the surprises I'd discovered when I took over the position of executive chef was that I did less actual cooking than I had in the past. While I was certainly involved in the preparation of every meal, my duties were to create menus both for the family and for events. I also had a number of administrative issues to juggle, not unlike those of the director of a small company. In addition to managing each staff member's vacation time and sick days, I had to sign off on purchases, attend meetings, coordinate with other departments, and nurture my subordinates' growth as professional chefs. The administrative stuff took a lot more time than I'd expected, and I began to see why Henry had come in early and stayed late most days. That was what I'd been doing myself since he'd left.

Part of making this kitchen work was learning how to delegate. Why not put Sean to work? I didn't want to appear ungrateful. I reasoned that another pair of hands was another pair of hands. And we needed a lot of help if we were to get both big events plated on time with the panache to which Mrs. Campbell had become accustomed.

"Cyan," I said, "have you cleaned the shrimp?"

She gave me a mischievous look. "Not yet."

"Why don't you show Sean how that's done?"

"Sure," Cyan said, amused. I wanted to explain to her that I wasn't punishing him for helping out—shrimp cleaning was a job I abhorred—but rather it was a task that gave Sean a wide berth for error. No matter how hard he tried, he couldn't ruin things too badly. Once he got the hang of it, we'd have plenty of shrimp for our cocktail display. If any were messed up, we could chop those and use them for other purposes. This was a safe bet.

"Shrimp, huh?" Sean asked. "Is this for tomorrow?"

"Sure is. I hope you like it."

"One of my favorites." When he smiled at me, I felt my breath catch. There was that sparkle in his eyes that I usually saw only in Tom's. "Of course, I'm happy with anything you make, Ollie."

I didn't know what to say. Sean was a sweet guy. I liked him, even though I didn't know him particularly well. But he wasn't Tom. "Thanks," I said, moving in the opposite direction.

Bucky and Rafe were conversing near the stove as I inched toward my computer station. Between the two men sat a large pan of cranberries, fresh from the oven. All the cranberries had popped and the tangy, sweet smell permeated the area, making me feel for the first time that Thanksgiving really was just one day away.

Agda had proven to be the quickest knife in the kitchen, and she was now chopping vegetables at the center island, full speed.

By the time Sean had followed Cyan around to the refrigerators, Agda had scooped up what was left of his peppers and had all of them chopped before Sean and Cyan returned with two huge bowls of raw shrimp. Sean caught my eye as he settled in to work. "I'm really glad to help out," he said.

"And we're glad to have you." Okay, so it wasn't exactly the truth, but Sean seemed so . . . sincere . . . that I couldn't have said anything else.

I sat on the stool at the computer station with my back to the bustling staff, Gavin's paperwork on my lap. Logging in, I immediately accessed the training schedule. He wasn't kidding when he said we'd been left out. There were enough training spots still open for all of us, but most of them were at times that conflicted with meal preparations. That figured. What was considered prime time for us was prime time for the rest of the staff, too.

The soft sounds of a busy kitchen—muted clatters, bumping, stirring—served to soothe my frazzled nerves. For as much as I'd tried to put the accident, the bomb scare, and the next two days' events in perspective, I realized how impossible a task that was. There was no perspective on situations like these.

A warm, yeasty scent rose up and I turned long enough to watch Agda pull a perfect tray of rolls from the nearby oven, her cheeks red from the heat. She caught my glance and smiled, her pride evident.

Back to the computer. Marcel would take care of his own training, I knew, and that of his assistant. I just had to worry about my own staff. When I'd finished placing Cyan and Bucky in A, B, and C classes that minimized impact on the kitchen, I set to the unenviable task of assigning myself.

Unfortunately, there weren't a whole lot of choices left.

As much as it pained me to do so, I took one of the open slots set up Thanksgiving night. I reasoned that dinner would be complete, Cyan and

Bucky would have gone home to rest up for the next day's hoopla, and I would probably be staying late after dinner to clean up and prepare for the next day's luncheon. Tom had plans to go home for the holiday, so that left me free. We hadn't yet made the leap of meeting each other's family. I glanced toward Sean and wondered, idly, if by this time next year Tom and I would be willing to come forward with our relationship.

Regardless, I was destined to be by myself this year, so I might as well sign up for the security class. Let Cyan and Bucky enjoy the holiday with their families. And maybe, if I was lucky, old Gav would be sitting at the head of his own dinner table and I'd get someone else teaching the training this time.

Sean interrupted. "Ollie?"

I half turned. He'd made little progress on the shrimp-shelling, but he didn't seem overwhelmed. Yet.

"Hang on," I said. Returning to my task, I reserved two more open spots, one each on Friday and Saturday. There. Done.

With a flourish, I clicked the file closed.

"What's that?" Sean asked.

I told him.

He scratched the side of his face. "Would you mind me borrowing your computer for a minute? I didn't check my e-mail yet today."

"Sure," I said, thinking it an odd request. "Let me get you to the Internet."

Within seconds I had him set up and gave him some privacy. "Let me know when you're done."

Although we all shared the same computer in the kitchen, it felt strange to allow an outsider—even if that outsider was the president's nephew—access. But what harm could he do? Change the ingredients in one of our recipes? Unlikely.

I kept myself busy for about a quarter hour, until Sean raised his head. "Hey, Ollie," he said.

"What's up?" I asked, coming over to him.

"I just got an e-mail from Aunt Elaine. Treyton Blanchard is bringing his assistant instead of his wife to Thanksgiving."

"That's right."

He closed out of the Internet connection and headed back to his prior task. "You knew about that?"

"Sure. We're always informed about guest changes."

Sean pulled a shrimp from the pile and worked it. As he started up again,

I could tell that he'd begun to develop a feel for the job—but the guy still had a long way to go. "Any idea why?"

Helping him, I grabbed a shrimp, removing the legs, shell, and tail with swift movements. I zipped the vein out and grabbed a second shrimp. "Mrs. Blanchard begged off," I said. "Something to do with keeping traditions at home."

He snorted.

I deveined the second shrimp and tossed it into a large bowl of ice. "You think there's another reason?"

He frowned down at the crustacean in his hand. "Maybe."

I tugged a new shrimp out of the bucket, disentangling its legs from the rest of them. "You think there's something between Blanchard and Bindy?" The words popped out before I could stop myself.

"No," he said with a headshake. "It's not that. It's just . . ." He glanced about the room. We were talking in low enough tones, and there was enough busy noise that the rest of the staff couldn't hear what we were saying. "You know about Nick Volkov's problems, don't you?"

I didn't.

"Well . . ." Another furtive glance around the room as he fought the little shrimp in his hand. "Do a Google search online. He's been having problems. He could use a windfall right about now to pay his legal bills. And I think he's convinced Senator Blanchard and Helen Hendrickson that it's in their best interests to sell Zendy Industries." Sean finally finished cleaning his shrimp and picked up another. I'd managed three in the interim.

"And you think tomorrow will be some sort of ambush?"

"That's what I was trying to tell Aunt Elaine," he said. "But she just sees the good in everyone."

I tossed another shrimp in the completed pile. "It's a nice quality to have."

"Unless people are out to screw you."

"You don't really believe that?"

Sean stopped working. "The problem is, I do. I'm just glad Uncle Harrison will be there. They can try to sway her, but if she holds her ground, I know he'll back her up."

"And you'll be there."

He smiled at me again in a way I wish he hadn't. "I will be. And so will you."

"My food will be there," I said, looking away. "The butlers will be there. I won't."

"Hmm," Sean said, beginning to work the shrimp again. "Maybe you could put a drug in the food that makes everybody tired. Then we'd all just have a great meal and go home and sleep. No business talk."

He laughed. I didn't think it was funny. Above all, the food that came out of my kitchen had to be safe. That wasn't something I ever joked about.

Sean must have sensed my displeasure because he sobered at once. "Listen, Ollie, I just have to tell you, I have a bad feeling about all this. The stakes are high. Aunt Elaine doesn't realize how desperate Volkov may be. I'd hate to see her get taken."

I put my hand on his, belatedly realizing that was probably a mistake. "Mrs. Campbell's a smart lady. She's strong. I'm sure she won't give in if she really doesn't want to."

Sean had just begun to answer when Peter Everett Sargeant III strode in, one eyebrow cocked at us. "Well, well," he said. "I see we've got a whole slew of new recruits."

Leave it to Sargeant to pop in at the exact wrong time. I sighed, reconsidering. Lately, with all the trouble and with two major events still behind schedule, was there ever a good time?

"Hello, Mr. Baxter," Sargeant said. Sean was the only person in the room he directly acknowledged. "It's a pleasure to see you again."

"Same here." Sean glanced from Sargeant to me. "Guess I ought to be going, huh?" He shot his last shrimp a distasteful look and gave me a sideways smile. "I think I'll stick to the turkey tomorrow," he said. "See you then, Ollie."

When he left I washed my hands and wiped them dry. "Peter," I said. Ever since taking on the role of executive chef, I had the privilege—if one could call it that—of addressing our sensitivity director by his first name. "What can I do for you?"

"What was Sean Baxter doing down here?"

I no longer had to answer to Sargeant. Gave me a good feeling, deep down. "Something you need, Peter?" I asked again.

He pulled out a notebook from his jacket pocket. "Friday's luncheon," he began. "I took the liberty of reviewing the guest list and I want to ensure you've provided for all the different religious and dietary issues we'll be facing."

I refrained from rolling my eyes. "We've got it covered."

"But I haven't had a chance to oversee the actual food preparation—"

"And you won't," I said, guiding him back toward the doorway. "I sent a copy of our complete menu to your office. If you chanced to read it, you'd see that everything has been handled with our usual aplomb."

I couldn't resist a tiny bit of bravado. We'd worked hard to come up with the perfect menu, with choices that would not only please a multitude of palates, but offer varieties to keep kosher, vegan, halal, low-fat, low-carb, and nondairy, among other things. To say this buffet had been one of my greatest challenges yet would be understatement. But everyone in the kitchen knew our guests would talk to the press afterward. We wanted—and expected—nothing short of a glowing account.

Sargeant was shaking his head. "I didn't read it yet. I would much prefer it if you walk me through—"

"And I much prefer to maximize the little time we have to get our meals together. So, Peter," I said, relishing the use of his first name again, "I have to ask you to allow us to do our jobs and to come back some other time. Preferably after the new year."

Blinking, he squared his shoulders and left without another word.

Bucky slapped his hands together in slow-motion applause. "Good job, kid. I didn't think you had it in you."

CHAPTER 8

ON THURSDAY, WITH LESS THAN AN HOUR TO GO BEFORE THANKS-
giving guests were due, food was flying. Not literally, of course. But we were
all moving so fast that everything seemed a tiny bit blurred. Though there were
only nine for dinner today, there were still dozens of last-minute details to
attend to. We concentrated hard and talked very little.

I glanced at the clock. Just past noon. Mingled scents of roasting meat—the
turkey breasts in the far oven, and the Virginia ham resting on the counter
behind me—gave me enormous comfort. We were on time. Despite the fact
that we left nothing to chance, I always panicked about the turkey; in my
opinion, there was nothing worse than dried-out fowl. As I poured onion gravy
from a pan into a temporary tureenlike container, I shot a glance at the oven
door. "Bucky," I called over my shoulder, "can you—"

"I just checked on them," he answered, reading my mind. "They're perfect.
Nicely brown. Right on schedule."

"Thanks."

Agda was in charge of putting the finishing touches on each course. Every
plate was arranged with exquisite precision just before it left our kitchen. At
the White House, food did not simply sit on a dish—our meals required presentation. With her speed and accuracy, Agda was a natural to handle that job.
Even though today's dinner would be served in a traditional, family-style manner, the trays and platters required her full attention before they were sent to
the table.

Bent over the first tray of hors d'oeuvres, Agda was carefully placing fruits
and cheeses in meticulous formation, interspersing crackers and spiced nuts
to make for a beautifully appetizing display.

I glanced up when our head butler, Jackson, came in. He'd recently taken over the position, though he'd been on staff for many years. A tall black man with curly salt-and-pepper hair, he smiled often and could always be counted on for White House scoop. Right now, however, he wasn't smiling.

"The president is not returning to the White House until this evening," he said.

All activity stopped. "What?" I asked.

Jackson shook his head. "A change in plans."

Before inquiring as to what great world event prevented the president from attending his family's Thanksgiving dinner, I needed to know the truly crucial information. "Are we still serving?"

"We are," Jackson said, still not looking happy. "Sad day for the missus. She was counting on her husband's support with these guests." He met my gaze. "You have heard some stories?"

I had, and I remembered Sean Baxter's warnings. "This isn't going to be a friendly social dinner after all, is it?"

Jackson shook his head again. "I am concerned. But there is nothing we can do."

"Except feed them well and keep them happy," I said, "and hope that they're all so impressed with dinner that they forget about business."

The corner of Jackson's mouth curled up. "We can try. I will return when the guests arrive." Looking around the area, he asked, "Have you seen Yi-im?"

One of the newer butlers, a tiny gentleman of an Asian descent I couldn't deduce, Yi-im never seemed to be available when there was work to be done. It had taken me a while to get the hang of pronouncing his name: Yee-eem. I pointed downward. "He said something about heading to the cafeteria."

Anger sparked Jackson's eyes. "Lazy man."

"WE ARE READY," MARCEL SAID, AS HE CAME AROUND THE CORNER, wheeling a cart. The top shelf held a tall pumpkin trifle and a selection of four different varieties of minitartlets: pecan, orange chiffon, lemon cheese, and Boston cream. The cart's second shelf held Marcel's famous apple cobbler with oatmeal crumble.

"Do you need me to heat that up when the time comes?" I asked.

His dark face folded into worry lines—he hadn't even heard my question. "I hope I 'ave made enough."

I started to assure him that there was enough dessert to satisfy twenty hungry guests when he turned and beckoned someone behind. The missing Yi-im stepped into the kitchen carrying a large silver tray almost as big as he was. Just over forty, the junior butler was slim and so short that in his tuxedo he might have passed for a ring-bearer in a wedding. Except for his bald head, which he kept shaved and shiny enough to reflect lights.

"Just in case they are very hungry, I 'ave created another option," Marcel said, with a hint of superiority. "Chocolate truffles. Do you think they are a good choice?"

Again, as I was about to answer, Marcel's attention shifted. He ordered Yi-im to begin sending the desserts to the staging area: the Butler's Pantry just outside the first-floor Family Dining Room. I recognized in Marcel the same controlled panic I felt right before an important meal. He wasn't interested in my opinion—he simply wanted to bring me up to speed. And probably show off a little. The chocolate truffles would be a huge hit. Of that, I was certain.

When Yi-im left the area, I told Marcel that Jackson had been looking for the diminutive butler.

Marcel's hands came up in a gesture of supplication. "But he told me he had been assigned to help out here today."

I didn't have time to quibble. "At least we know he isn't shirking his duties," I said in a low voice. "And heaven knows we can use all the help we can get."

Marcel wiped his hands on his apron, looking thoughtful. "Yi-im has worked very hard today. As a butler, he is perhaps in the wrong department, no?"

I followed his logic. Marcel was always on the lookout for pastry assistants. With the number of dazzling and delicious desserts his department produced, he was usually understaffed. At the moment, however, I didn't have time to discuss personnel with him. "Let's talk about this next week," I said. "Monday morning staff meeting?"

"Excellent plan," he said. "Now I shall go upstairs to be certain my creations arrive safely."

Thirty seconds after his departure, Jackson returned, making me think about one of those old movies where people chase one another and keep missing their quarry by moments. "Mr. and Mrs. Volkov have arrived, as has Senator Blanchard with Ms. Gerhardt. She has requested a few moments of your time."

I was surprised. "Bindy wants to talk to me?"

He nodded.

"Sure," I said. "You can let her come down after dinner."

"She would prefer to visit with you now."

Great. Another interruption. "Go ahead, Ollie," Bucky said. "We've got you covered."

He was right. One of the things Henry had told me before passing the potholders was that in order to succeed, I needed to be able to rely on the efforts of others. "You can't do everything yourself anymore," he'd said, chiding me. He knew how much I liked to feel in control. "You have to be able to let go. Let your staff show you how good they are." With a wink and a smile, he'd added, "That's how I recognized talent in you."

"Thanks, Bucky." I took a deep breath. "Okay," I said to Jackson. "Send her down."

Bindy Gerhardt had been a staffer in the West Wing during her tenure at the White House, and I liked her well enough. But she and I weren't the kind of girlfriends who sought one another out. Although she looked like central casting's answer to the nerdy girl with the heart of gold, she'd always struck me as a power groupie—doing her best only when people in authority were apt to notice. In fact, immediately after she'd accepted the position on Blanchard's staff, she'd stopped visiting the White House altogether. Probably to stave off any impression of impropriety. This was the nature of Washington, D.C.—rumor and innuendo ruled. We all knew that perception was often more important than reality. Especially where the news media was concerned.

Cyan sidled next to me. "That's weird," she said. "I hope she isn't looking for a special menu at this late date."

"I don't remember her having dietary restrictions." I was pretty good at remembering unusual requests. Plus, Bindy would have known to send her preferences early. I couldn't imagine why she'd asked to come down here, so I shrugged. I'd find out soon enough. "Maybe she wants to swap recipes."

Cyan laughed. I washed and dried my hands, taking a long look around my kitchen. It hummed. Without a doubt, this would be the best Thanksgiving dinner any of our guests had ever experienced. I savored the moment—the instance of absolute certainty that we'd achieved greatness. I couldn't wait for our guests' reactions.

Deciding it would be best to keep Bindy out of the kitchen proper—and hence out of the staff's way—I came into the Center Hall just as she made it to the bottom of the stairs. "Ollie!" she said when she saw me.

I almost didn't recognize her. Bindy had lost at least twenty pounds, and although I knew it was impossible, it seemed she'd grown taller, too. "Wow!" I couldn't stop my reaction. "You're . . . so . . ." I almost said, "slick," but caught myself before the word escaped. "So . . . chic. I mean . . . not that you weren't before, I just . . ." I'd fallen so far into the open-mouth-insert-foot trap that I couldn't escape without a massive recovery effort. "What I mean to say is that you look wonderful. The new job must be going great."

Sunny smile. "It is. And believe me, everyone has the same reaction. Quite the change, isn't it?"

Understatement, I thought.

She spun on a navy blue heel. Her dress was navy, too, a perfect contrast to her pearly skin. "What do you think?"

"You look fabulous." She did. Although she hadn't been exactly overweight before, the new, slimmer look suited her. The last time she'd been here, she preferred easy-comfort clothes and ballet flats. Back then she'd had loose, curly hair that she wore to her shoulders. No makeup. Now her hair was cropped short and slicked back, framing her carefully made-up face and exposing a pair of pert diamond earrings. The nose was still wide, the chin still weak, but she'd evidently been schooled in how to play up her better features because her eyes drew my attention first. Bindy would never be considered beautiful, but the change in her appearance certainly made her more attractive.

She tapped one of the earrings. "Fake," she said, "but aren't they great?"

At the moment, I would have much preferred to be discussing turkey dressing with Bucky than fake baubles with Bindy. "So, you're here in Mrs. Blanchard's place today?" I asked. I knew my voice held just enough curiosity to prompt her to get to the point.

"Yes, yes," she said. "There are some personal business items Senator Blanchard needs to discuss with the First Lady." Bindy wrinkled her nose, giving a little giggle. "Mrs. Blanchard didn't want to be in the way. I've done a lot of research for the senator. . . ." She waved both her hands at me. "That sounds so stilted. I do a lot for Treyton and his wife, and they both thought it would be smarter, strategically, for me to be here today when the partnership is discussed."

So Sean's fears had been warranted. Again, I was thankful he was due to arrive soon. "I thought this was supposed to be a Thanksgiving celebration."

"That, too. There's never any downtime in D.C., is there?" She licked her lips. "But that's not what I wanted to talk with you about. I wanted to ask you about the gingerbread men."

"The ones Marcel is creating?"

"No, the ones being sent in from across the country." She giggled again. I'd forgotten that she had the tendency to do that when nervous. "Treyton knows that you're choosing the best ones from the thousands you've received to display in the Red Room next to the gingerbread house. Is that right?"

"It's not just me; Marcel has the final—"

"Yes, but you're in on it, right?"

"Sure."

"Treyton's kids are submitting gingerbread men they've been working on. It would mean a lot to them to have their work displayed in the Red Room during the holiday opening ceremonies."

I raised an eyebrow. "Where all the cameras will be?"

"Well, yes. . . ." She punctuated her words with another little laugh. "You know those pictures will be seen everywhere as soon as the celebration is complete. . . ."

She let the thought hang and I finally understood why she was uncomfortable talking with me. Treyton Blanchard wanted his kids' handiwork plastered all over every newspaper, White House–related website, and on TV. Rumor had it that the man was considering a run for the presidency. Getting his kids' artwork prominently displayed must feel a little like squatter's rights. A thought occurred to me. "Aren't his kids kind of young for this?" Blanchard had three little ones, and the oldest was eight or nine.

With a bouncy little so-so motion of her head, Bindy said, "They've had help with the project. The gingerbread men are really beautiful, Ollie. I wouldn't ask you to do this if they weren't worthy of presentation."

Sure, she wouldn't. Treyton Blanchard probably thought his kids' scribbles with a blue crayon were genius. And I knew that if the powerful senator asked Bindy to do something, she'd do it.

I shuddered inwardly at the thought of what these homemade gingerbread ornaments looked like until Bindy said, "If the kids had actually done all this on their own, they'd be snapped up as protégés." She laughed. "The family chef did some of the work. He's amazing." The spirit with which she added that last remark made me wonder if she and Blanchard's chef were the new hot item in D.C. I knew the guy. But I couldn't see them together.

"And the kids think they did it all themselves?"

She bit her lip, nodding.

"I'll look into it." I held up my hands, staving off further pressure. "But there's no guarantee the photographers will snap the right angle to get these in print, you know."

Tiny shrug. "I realize that. But I just wanted to ask you to do your best. The kids will be so thrilled. They've been invited to the ceremony, too. Their mom's bringing them. Can you imagine how excited they'll be to see their artwork in the Red Room of the White House?"

Realizing I wasn't going to get back into the kitchen until I gave her something to take back to Blanchard, I said, "I'll talk with Marcel and the decorating staff. That's the best I can do."

When Bindy smiled, relaxed now, I was taken aback again by the change in her. She'd morphed from ordinary to fabulous in just a few short months. And she seemed to have acquired a new confidence, too. "Thanks," she said. "It'll mean a lot to us."

She turned and headed for the stairs before I could ask whether "us" meant her and the kids, or her and Treyton Blanchard.

I STEPPED OUT OF THE KITCHEN FOR THE DOZENTH TIME IN THE last hour. As Jackson passed me in the Center Hall, I grabbed his arm. "Any updates?"

Headshake. "No word. Nothing."

Five minutes before one o'clock and Sean Baxter hadn't arrived yet. We should have begun staging already.

"When do you think we'll be able to serve?" Visions of wilted lettuce, dried-out turkey, and soggy rolls raced through my mind.

"The First Lady suggested we wait until half past one. If Mr. Baxter still has not arrived, then we will begin without him."

A half-hour delay. Not great, but it could be worse. "Okay," I said, heading back in to deliver the news to my group. "Let me know if anything changes."

Over the next twenty minutes, I divided my time between overseeing progress in the kitchen and the Butler's Pantry upstairs. We staged our offerings in the pantry, waiting impatiently for the signal to serve our guests in the next room. The Family Dining Room occupies a space on the north side of the White House, with the pantry directly west. The State Dining Room—where most of our larger seated dining events are held—is a large area immediately adjacent to both rooms. In fact, we often used the Family Dining Room for staging when serving in the State Dining Room. The three-room setup is perfect whether we're serving a hundred guests, or fewer than a dozen.

I maintained a position in the empty State Dining Room, close enough to the gathering to listen and watch without being seen. Although I had every excuse to be there—to gauge how the hors d'oeuvres were going and to determine if I needed to make any last-minute changes to dinner—the real reason I parked myself at the door was pure nosiness. I knew Mrs. Campbell was a strong-minded and resilient woman, but I didn't know many of our guests. If they were planning on ambushing her, as Sean expected they might, I wanted to help him with information-gathering. I caught Jackson's eye. He stood nearby, facing the cross hall. I could tell he and I were on the same page.

I hadn't met Nick Volkov before, but I recognized him from the recent news items I'd checked online at Sean's suggestion. Volkov and his wife had had some trouble lately—involving allegedly bogus land deals, kickbacks, payoffs, and property liens. Volkov was a man—whether guilty or innocent—for whom a windfall would be salvation. No wonder he was pressuring Mrs. Campbell for a quick sale.

As they chatted and mingled with the other guests, the couple never seemed to lose physical contact with each other—his arm grazed hers, his fingers skimmed her back. Younger than the First Lady by about ten years, Nick was stout and fair, with youthful Eastern European features and a prominent brow. Mrs. Volkov, by contrast, wore her age like a road map. She looked considerably older than her husband and was a little bit hunched. Maybe all the jewelry she wore weighed her down. I hadn't seen this much sparkle since I passed Tiffany's in New York City.

"I don't understand your reluctance, Elaine," Nick Volkov said to the First Lady. His voice was even bigger than he was. "The sooner we put your uneasiness behind us, the sooner we can enjoy this blessed Thanksgiving day. Don't you agree?"

Mrs. Campbell held her hands together, clasped low. She was the only diner in the room not carrying a glass of wine. "Oh, Nick," she said, with a touch of reproof, "I'm certainly not reluctant to talk, nor uneasy about my position with the company. I just don't want to discuss things twice. Why don't we wait for another opportunity, when both my husband and Sean can be here?"

I glanced at Jackson again. He shook his head. Sean still hadn't arrived.

Volkov lowered his voice. I almost didn't hear his next words. "If we wait too long, Elaine, we will miss our opportunity. Ten years from now the market may not be as good as it is now."

"And in ten years the market may be better," Mrs. Campbell said smoothly. "In fact, my father counted on that. He didn't want me to—"

"Your father didn't understand how things have changed."

"I believe he did." The First Lady's lips twitched. "And I certainly do."

Volkov's voice rose. "It comes down to this: We need to act and we need to do so right now."

"Nick," she said, and I caught the impatience in her tone, "once we sell, everything our fathers worked for will be gone. Zendy Industries will belong to others—to people who might take it in a direction we can't control."

"What difference does it make after we've been adequately compensated? Our fathers worked hard to provide us with security for our futures. Isn't this exactly what we're taking advantage of? Don't you think they would approve?"

"I don't think they would approve, no," Mrs. Campbell answered. She unclasped her hands and gestured around the room. "I don't think any of us is financially insecure right now. None of us needs the money—not for any legitimate reason."

Nick Volkov's face reddened.

He looked ready to say something unpleasant when his wife interrupted. "Where is Sean, anyway?" she asked. "I believe I've only met him once before. Such a nice young man."

Volkov sniffed. "Too young to understand the subtleties of business."

I backed away as Mrs. Campbell glanced toward the open door. "I don't know. I'm sure he said he was coming."

Nick Volkov cleared his throat. "He's irresponsible, if you ask me."

I slid around fast enough to catch Mrs. Campbell's tight smile. "Well, it's a good thing I didn't ask you, then, isn't it?" she said. With a pleasant nod to Mrs. Volkov, Mrs. Campbell excused herself to mingle with the other guests.

Call me Nosy Rosie, but I couldn't let it go. I continued to watch the interactions in the next room, listening closely to as many conversations as I could. The only people I knew who had the First Lady's interests at heart were the president and Sean. I hoped to overhear some tidbits of information that I could pass along to Sean later. Again, I wondered where he was. After our conversation yesterday in the kitchen, I couldn't imagine he would have forgotten the time. But things happen, and I decided that until he showed up, I was on spy duty.

Nick Volkov muttered under his breath. I didn't catch his words, but I couldn't miss the grimace he made behind the First Lady's back. Helen Hendrickson didn't miss it, either. Practically sprinting away from Treyton Blanchard's side, she hurried over to join the Volkovs. Helen Hendrickson was not a small woman, nor a young one. The quick movement left her breathless. "Did she say she'll sign?" she asked.

"Hardly," Nick answered. "She's unwilling to even entertain conversation until that damn Baxter arrives." Turning to his wife, he said something else I couldn't catch. She broke away from him to intercept Fitzgerald, who'd been heading toward them. Mrs. Volkov looped an arm through his and led him away toward the room's fireplace.

Helen Hendrickson chewed her thumbnail before addressing Volkov. "What can we do?"

Cyan came around the corner from the pantry. I walked over to meet her. "Still no news on Sean," I said, keeping my voice low. Looking at my watch, I added, "Not too much longer before we serve."

"I hate this tension," she said. "Can't do anything but wait and be nervous. Everything's ready now."

"I know, but we've been through worse," I said.

She glanced at the open door where I'd been standing. "Anything interesting?"

"So-so."

By the time Cyan returned to the pantry and I made it back to my unobtrusive position at the doorway, Treyton Blanchard had joined Nick Volkov and Helen Hendrickson. It was neat to be part of the wallpaper—seen but not noticed.

"What good gossip am I missing here?" Blanchard asked. The junior senator from Maryland had a pleasant face, but his natural charisma and wide smile made him seem even more handsome in person than he appeared on camera. "I hope you two haven't been talking about me."

Volkov made a noise. Frustration, it seemed. "We've been talking about our . . . partner." The way he said it made my skin crawl.

"Give it time," Blanchard said.

"Time?" Again, Volkov grew red-faced. "We don't have that luxury."

Blanchard took a small sip of his wine. "We have time enough," he said.

"Elaine can't be forced to make a decision without consulting her trusted advisers, can she?"

Volkov sputtered, "Some trusted adviser. That Baxter fellow can't even make it to dinner on time. How can we expect him to help her make the right decisions?"

"I'll talk with Elaine one-on-one when I get the chance," Blanchard said. "I think she's just overwhelmed right now. She's still grieving for her father. . . ."

"Her father's death is what precipitated this decision."

Blanchard held his wineglass to almost eye level, gesturing with it for emphasis. "Don't tell me things I already know, Nick. I understand what's at stake here. But today is Thanksgiving." He tempered his admonishment with a smile. "Or have you forgotten that?"

From the ping-pong movement of her head as the conversation went back and forth, Helen Hendrickson seemed unwilling—or too mousy—to join in. I was surprised when she focused her attention on Blanchard. "Easy for you," she said. "Nick and I don't have the benefit of political donations to help us make *our* dreams come true."

Blanchard replied, but I missed it because Jackson was on the move. As he passed me, he whispered, "Showtime."

I followed. "Sean Baxter?" I asked.

He spoke over his shoulder. "Not yet."

Within minutes, the guests were seated and we were ready to serve. I had Cyan in the narrow pantry with me and we scrutinized every dish to make certain it was absolutely perfect before one of our tuxedoed butlers carried it into the next room. I heard exclamations of delight as the platters reached the table, and I blew out a breath of relief.

When the door connecting the pantry to the Family Dining Room was open, I snuck a glance. With the president unavailable, the First Lady had taken her seat at the head of the table. Treyton Blanchard sat to her right, Bindy Gerhardt across from him. The Volkovs sat across from each other, too, with Nick next to Bindy. The male-female pattern continued with Helen Hendrickson next to Nick. Helen's guest, the elderly Mr. Fitzgerald, had settled himself across from her. Only the seat across from the First Lady was unoccupied.

As he passed me on his way back into the pantry, Jackson said, "We will seat Mr. Baxter when he arrives." A shrug. "If he arrives at all."

Cyan came close, whispering, "Do you think maybe Sean is with the president? I mean, that's his uncle. Maybe whatever's keeping President Campbell is—"

I shushed her. The other room had silenced. No conversation. No movement. Rather than push the connecting door open to peek, I hurried around into the State Dining Room where I could peer in unnoticed. I wondered if something was wrong with the meal. What could possibly have happened to stop everything so completely? I strained to hear, and was rewarded only by the flat-toned words from a voice I didn't recognize.

In a moment, I understood. Two Secret Service agents had positioned themselves inside the Family Dining Room. One of them had apparently requested Mrs. Campbell's presence away from her guests. I slowed to a stroll as I made my way across the expansive room, hoping I appeared nonchalant. Pretending I was heading into the hall.

Mrs. Campbell emerged just as I crossed her path. She'd been about to address the taller of the two agents, but stopped me with a hand to my arm. "Ollie," she said, "dinner is wonderful. I—"

"Mrs. Campbell," the agent said. He touched her elbow in an effort to guide her toward the doorway to the Red Room. "Please."

She didn't move. "What happened?"

Both agents glared at me, making me want to shrink and run, but the First Lady gripped my arm, effectively freezing me in place.

She blinked rapidly, then took a steadying breath. "Is it my husband?"

"No," the shorter agent said quickly. "The president is safe."

"Thank God." Her grasp loosened, but she didn't completely let go. "Then what is it?" she asked the agents.

The taller one cleared his throat. "Ma'am, perhaps it would be better for you to come with us to the residence."

"No." Mrs. Campbell's jaw flexed. "Just . . . tell . . . me."

The agents exchanged glances.

She gripped me again. "Agent Teska, if you don't tell me what's going on—"

The thought hung there a long moment.

"With the president tied up in negotiations . . . we thought it best to talk to you first." The urgency in his face settled into the dispassionate expression that always heralds bad news. We waited. I barely breathed.

"There's been an incident," Teska finally said. "Please, ma'am. If you'll come with me . . ."

Her face was tight. Her voice even tighter. "Just tell me."

"It's Sean Baxter, ma'am. He's dead."

CHAPTER 9

THE FIRST LADY MANAGED TO FIND HER WAY BACK TO HER CHAIR in the dining room, waving away those of us trying to help her. She sat for a long time, eyes covered, head down.

There was no recovering from news like this—not surrounded by colleagues who had planned to enjoy Thanksgiving dinner and who all now sat, staring. Doing the best they could, Secret Service agents quietly ushered the guests out to waiting limousines. Helen Hendrickson broke away from the group long enough to press Mrs. Campbell's hands between her own and hug the First Lady, blinking back tears and murmuring condolences. All the guests were gone in minutes. Their sudden departure left us in suffocating silence.

Inexplicably, the First Lady asked me to stay with her after the guests were gone. I had a tremendous desire to beg off, but one look at the sadness in her eyes convinced me otherwise. "Of course," I said. My staff would handle whatever cleanup and storage needed to be done, and though they'd wonder at my absence, they'd certainly manage without me.

Jackson brought Mrs. Campbell a glass of water, which she took but didn't sip. She held it in both hands, almost prayerfully, still staring downward. "Thank you," she said to the butler, and when he inquired what else he could get her, she said, "Nothing. Nothing now."

The two Secret Service agents remained: Teska and a female agent, Patricia Berland. They seemed perplexed by my presence. I couldn't blame them. I'd taken the seat vacated by Blanchard, my mind racing a hundred thoughts at once: how badly I felt about Sean, what I could do for Mrs. Campbell right at the moment, why she had asked me to stay, how soon I could get back to the kitchen, and why this had to happen today. Of all days.

Sean, who had been working in my kitchen just twenty-four hours ago—was dead. I couldn't get my mind around that. I couldn't grasp how he could have been here, so alive, so much fun, and now no longer exist. But I also knew I couldn't dwell on that right now. My first duty was to Mrs. Campbell.

She finally raised her head to face Teska. "You said, 'incident.' What do you mean?"

The two agents exchanged a glance. Teska squinted, as though he were fighting a hard internal argument. "His death is under investigation."

"What are you not telling me?"

Teska's face twitched. He spoke slowly. "Sean Baxter may have taken his own life."

"No!" Mrs. Campbell said, starting to stand. "I don't believe that." Berland's gentle touch on the First Lady's shoulder was enough to keep her seated. "What happened? Where is he?"

At this point the two agents seemed to forget I was there. But the First Lady hadn't forgotten—she reached out and clasped my hand with hers. It was very cold.

Berland spoke. "Preliminary reports suggest that Mr. Baxter shot himself."

"No," Mrs. Campbell said again. This time, however, it was not an exclamation of disbelief, it was a flat refusal. "Sean didn't like guns. He never would have done that."

"Let me assure you, ma'am, the Metropolitan Police will fully investigate this as a homicide until the evidence proves otherwise. But . . ."

"But?"

"He left a note, ma'am."

Mrs. Campbell crumpled in on herself, her silent crying more poignant than if she'd wailed and screamed. I reacted instinctively, forgetting this was our nation's First Lady and seeing only a woman who'd suffered immeasurable loss. I stood next to her, putting my arm around her shaking shoulders, murmuring how sorry I was.

Berland's eyes met mine. "Let's get her upstairs," she mouthed.

I leaned in to whisper to Mrs. Campbell that it might be best to return to her own rooms. She nodded and stood, keeping her face covered with one hand, grabbing my arm with the other.

"We'll help you," Berland said, stepping between me and the First Lady.

She didn't release her hold. Instead, she tugged me close so that her whispered words were almost inaudible. "He cared about you, Ollie. He told me he saw a future with you." Though tears raced down her face, she managed a wobbly smile. "He asked me to fix you two up."

I opened my mouth, but no words came out.

"He would have wanted you to know," she added, and she finally let go of my arm. Turning to face Berland, she gave a quick nod. "I'm ready now."

For the second time that week, I fought scalding pain in my throat, my eyes, and my heart.

CHAPTER 10

I WOKE UP CRAMPED AND ACHY FROM SPENDING THE NIGHT ON the small bed in my third-floor office. The mattress was comfortable enough, but I suffered from the dual distractions of not being in my own apartment and anxiety as I replayed the prior day's events.

Throwing on spare clothes I kept in my office for emergencies such as this, I made it downstairs to the kitchen while it was still dark. I usually loved the morning's solitary quiet—moving about at my own pace, transforming this cool stainless steel room into a warm, bustling nest of activity. I always felt as though I held the power to wake up the world.

Today, however, that simple pleasure eluded me. Despair weighed me down because again, one of our White House "family" had died—and again, under horrific circumstances.

I pulled biscuits out of the freezer, set them on the counter, and fired up one of the ovens. Sean hadn't struck me as despondent or suicidal. And yet the Secret Service had mentioned a note. That made no sense.

So acute was my concentration on Sean, and on preparing breakfast for what would be a long, grueling day for the First Family, that I didn't notice one of the butlers come in until he was almost next to me.

My head jerked up. "Red!"

His pale eyes widened in alarm. "I'm sorry," he said, taking a step back.

Red had been here forever, and though the man was spry, he'd crossed the line to elderly at least a decade ago. Along the way he'd lost the hair color that had given him his nickname. I hadn't meant to shake him. Waving off his apology, I pointed up, toward the residence. "How is she?"

"Bad times here," he said, with a sad shake of his head. "And no one is stopping long enough to grieve."

My puzzled expression encouraged him to explain.

"The president returned last night. He'll be taking breakfast early with his wife," he said. "Then he will depart for a meeting in New York."

I hoped that didn't mean the First Lady would be left alone at a time like this. "Is Mrs. Campbell going with him?"

Lines bracketing Red's eyes deepened. "The First Lady will remain in the residence to host the Mothers' Luncheon this afternoon."

"What?"

"The luncheon will proceed as scheduled."

This couldn't be right. "But, after the news. After what happened to Sean . . ."

He stopped me with a sigh. "Yes," he said, "the family has much to deal with today. And on top of everything else, Gene Sculka's family is holding his wake tonight."

Dear God, I'd almost forgotten about that. I was about to ask if the president and First Lady were planning to attend, but Red anticipated my question.

"The president will not return to the White House until Saturday. The First Lady has called the Sculka family to pay respects."

I made a mental note to make an appearance myself this evening. But right now only one thing was on my mind. "I thought they would cancel the luncheon."

Red sighed. "Mrs. Campbell doesn't want to disappoint all the women and kids who have flown from all over the country—at their own expense—to be here today."

"But surely people would understand—"

"You know our First Lady."

I did. Selfless to a fault, she was notoriously stubborn but always looking out for the greater good. I admired her—and I hoped to achieve that serenity someday myself. "Well, then, I suppose I'd better move a bit faster here."

Cyan arrived moments later, followed by Bucky, Rafe, Agda, and a few more SBA chefs we'd hired for the day. I was glad I hadn't canceled the extra staff. Even if today's luncheon had been scrapped, we had a great deal of work ahead of us. The holiday season officially began Sunday afternoon—two days from now—when the president and First Lady would attend a presentation at the Kennedy Center. Extra hands in the kitchen were never a waste.

While managing breakfast and cleaning up, we got to work on the afternoon's event. Buffets were so much less stressful than plated dinners—for us, and for the waitstaff. We'd prepared as much as possible ahead of time, but there was still a lot to be done before the guests arrived.

More than two hundred moms and tots were expected, and we'd been careful to include plenty of kid-friendly fare in our offerings. One of the president's favorite sandwiches, peanut butter and banana, was on the menu today. We would offer a choice: served on plain white or on cinnamon bread. In fact, the staff had taken bets on which would be more popular with the kids.

Rafe expertly sliced away the crusts from a peanut-butter-on-white sandwich. "Kids will go for plain, every time."

"Cinnamon tastes better," Cyan said, sing-song.

Rafe raised his own voice up an octave, continuing the sing-song cadence. "Won't matter if they refuse to try it."

Shaking her head so her ponytail wagged, Cyan slathered peanut butter on yet another slice of cinnamon bread. "They'll try these."

I was happy to hear their chitchat. Although normalcy was not to be expected—not so soon after the two unexpected deaths—any little bit of happiness was worth grabbing.

Just as we started in on our next project, Special Agent Gavin strode into the kitchen. He stopped short a half breath before running into one of our SBA chefs who carried a massive bowl of salad on his shoulder.

"Watch where you're going," Gavin said, flattening himself against the wall just in time.

The assistant turned fully, in order to see the man who'd almost tossed our salad. "Sorry," he mumbled, then set off again for the refrigerator. Gavin's presence here just as time was getting tricky was enormously unwelcome. There was nothing this man could say or do to help today's event, and the sooner he got out of my kitchen the happier we would all be.

As he righted himself, he tugged at his suit coat and adjusted his tie. Before he could seek me out, I'd positioned myself in front of him. "What can I do for you?" My words were polite, my demeanor dismissive.

"You're scheduled for emergency response training."

So why was he in my kitchen now? I'd set the staff up myself; we were already on the hook for Gavin's classes. "We haven't forgotten," I said. "We'll be there. As scheduled."

"You're scheduled right now."

"No, we're not."

"Not them," he said, pointing. "You."

"No," I said, straining to process this. "Not possible."

He spoke solemnly. "It is my personal responsibility to see that department heads are fully trained. You missed your class last night."

"Do you have any idea what went on here last night?"

Gavin gave me one of those looks meant to make people wither. I didn't. "Ms. Paras," he said. "When someone's faced with a life-or-death situation, do you think it's more important that they've learned how to react swiftly, decisively, and accurately, thereby saving lives? Or do you believe it's more important that they've mastered the preparation of white roux?"

My eyebrows shot up.

Half of his mouth curled. "I am not so ignorant in matters of haute cuisine as you might imagine."

I didn't care if he was the next Paul Bocuse; I wasn't about to let him drag me away from the kitchen right before a major event. I tried again. "The reason I missed—"

He interrupted. "I know you believe your work here is important, but I'm sure you agree that the safety of the White House trumps all other concerns."

"I'm not saying—"

"Is your staff incapable of handling the situation on their own?"

"Of course not."

"Then come with me."

He turned, fully expecting me to follow. I stood my ground. "Special Agent Gavin," I said to his retreating form. "Just a minute."

He turned and his expression told me he wasn't entirely surprised that I hadn't complied.

"Today is a major event for the First Lady," I said. "She's depending on us. If you haven't already heard, and what I've been trying to tell you is, she suffered a devastating loss last night."

Gavin nodded. "Yes."

I continued. "If Mrs. Campbell is prepared to move forward with her luncheon today, then I'm damned certain going to stay here to make sure it's perfect."

I got the feeling I was amusing him. In a snarly sort of way.

"So you're telling me you refuse to attend training?"

"I refuse to attend *now*."

He made a show of looking at his watch. "And when, exactly, will you be finished here?"

I blew out a breath. "The luncheon is scheduled for one o'clock. . . ."

"One o'clock," he said, before I could finish my sentence. "I'll be back for you then."

When he left, I massaged my eyes. "There's always one, isn't there?" I said to nobody in particular.

Cyan patted me on the back. "Don't worry. We've got you covered."

CYAN WAS RIGHT. OUR LUNCHEON PREPARATIONS MOVED WITH balletlike precision. We'd sent up trays of garlic–green bean bundles, blue-cheese straws, and other savory side dishes to stock the buffet, with replacement trays on hand, ready for replenishing as the mothers helped themselves and attended to their children.

Jackson and Red made frequent trips to the kitchen, and I asked them how Mrs. Campbell was holding up. "She's a true lady," Red said cryptically. "Tough and soft at the same time."

My heart went out to her. I knew how terrible I felt, and I'd only just gotten to know Sean over the past few months. How hard it must be to lose someone you'd known since his birth.

The two men helped load the next batch of trays. Both rolled their eyes when I asked how the festivities were progressing. "Lotta whining going on up there," Jackson said.

Red shook his head. "In my day, children were seen and not heard."

For the first time since I'd come to work here, I was relieved not to be interacting with White House guests. "It can't be that bad," I said.

Jackson arched an eyebrow toward Red. "How many kids you figure are jamming themselves into that bathroom at one time?"

"Too many."

"What about the food?" I asked. "How do people like the cheese straws? What about the mint brownie bites?"

Red gave me a sad smile. "Those poor moms are having a devil of a time getting a chance to eat. The minute any of them tries to take a bite, their kid spills something."

"It really isn't that bad, is it?"

Jackson gave me a so-so. "They're well-behaved for the most part," he said. "They just take a lot more fussing than what we're used to."

"Not *more* fussing," Red corrected. "Just different fussing."

Jackson laughed. "Yeah. Different."

I was about to ask what he meant when Gavin returned. Without even a perfunctory greeting, he pointed at me. "It's after one o'clock," he said. "Let's go."

Realizing that it was not only useless to argue, but it was unnecessary because aside from cleanup, our work was done—I followed Gavin out of the kitchen and into the Palm Room.

"We're going into the West Wing?" I asked.

He didn't answer.

I rarely crossed into this section of the White House. The Palm Room connected the residence's ground floor—our floor—to the West Wing's first floor because of the lay of the land. The residence itself sat on a small slope. A casual area, with white latticed walls and a gardenlike feel, the Palm Room boasted two gorgeous pieces of art: *Union* and *Liberty*, both painted by the Italian American artist Constantino Brumidi.

Gavin walked with purpose, not looking back, and evidently not noticing how often I was required to scurry to catch up to his long-legged strides. He rushed me through the obstacle course of press corps offices, where eager reporters glanced up as we passed—each one startling into a hopeful, then disappointed expression when they realized it was only the chef coming through.

The air was different here. Too many bodies to avoid, too many wires to step over, too much electronic equipment to dodge, and the atmosphere of constant urgency gave the area a cramped, stuffy feel. I could hear the whir of a motor and I guessed air-conditioning ran in this section year-round. How else to cool off all the power equipment and panic?

"Where are we going?" I asked again.

Gavin didn't answer, but he stepped to the side to open the next door for me. And there we were: the Brady Press Briefing Room. I'd been in this room only a couple of times; it had been renovated a few years before I began working here.

Gavin took a few more strides to the center of the room, then stopped.

"What is here?" he asked. "What do you observe?"

I was sick and tired of Gavin's bizarre questioning methods. "I don't see a training class, if that's what you mean."

He graced my smart-aleck answer with a lips-only smile. "Due to your absence at last night's class, I have the dubious honor of bringing you up to speed by myself."

"It's not like I played hooky," I said. "Can't I just take one of the other classes?"

"When?" he asked. "All you've been talking about is how shorthanded you are. You have your staff scheduled tomorrow and Sunday. I highly doubt you'll find time to attend and shortchange your kitchen further."

He had me there.

"Listen," I said. "I'm a quick learner, and I don't want to waste your time. Can't you just give me some handouts and I'll catch up?"

"The next round of classes builds upon knowledge you glean from the first round. You can't expect to get anything out of further instruction without learning the basics first."

As he said this, he made his way up to the president's large, bullet-resistant lectern, also known as the "blue goose." When he positioned himself behind it and placed both hands on the lectern's sides, he seemed to forget I was there. His palpable craving for power washed over me like a wave. This was one intense guy.

Blinking himself back to awareness, he noticed me still near the door where we'd entered. "What do you observe?" he asked again.

The sooner I played along, the faster I'd get back to work. I took a deep breath. "Okay, give me a minute."

A picture of elegant efficiency, the bright room with the presidential motif boasted blue leather seats, state-of-the-art electronics, and a small raised dais at the far end of the room, where a door connected it to the heart and brains of the West Wing.

I didn't have a clue of what to look for. A quick glance at Gavin warned me not to ask.

Okay, fine. I was on my own here. Something out of place. Something that didn't belong.

Palladian windows adorned the north wall. I checked each one to ensure it was secure. I checked the doors, even the ones across the room that led south out onto the west colonnade. Everything clear.

But that would be too obvious. Special Agent-in-Charge Leonard Gavin was not the type to let me off easy. Whatever he'd set up in here would be designed to be difficult to find. I tried to think like old Gav. More precisely, I tried to think like an assassin.

Gav probably didn't realize I had a bit of experience in that arena. And I'd learned a few things.

What would an assassin do? He'd have to be better than clever. He'd have to be brilliant. Anything out of place would be noticed by our eagle-eyed Secret Service personnel. So if, say, a terrorist wanted to plant a bomb in the room, he'd have to ensure that it looked like something that belonged here. Up-front and obvious. Something so plain-as-day that every eye in the place would glaze over it without a second glance.

I stood in the fourth row of seats and I made a slow circle—a complete 360-degree turn—taking everything in at a pace that would make slugs weep.

"We're not here for the tourist show," he said. "You're supposed to be finding a security breach, not studying the symmetry."

I ignored him. Closed my eyes. Silently reasoned with myself.

Let's assume Gav planted one of those IEDs in here. He'd warned us that shapes and configurations of the deadly devices changed almost daily. So the one thing I knew I *wasn't* looking for was an opaque, bottlelike item.

Where would it do the most damage?

I opened my eyes. Right here, in the middle of the room, during a crowded press conference, a bomb would guarantee the greatest loss of life. But would that be an assassin's goal? Take out the innocent media folks, just like terrorists took out civilians on 9/11? Maybe, but if a fanatic killer was able to get this far—past White House security—then he'd be aiming for a bigger target.

I scooched out of the row and made my way up to the dais. "Excuse me," I said to Gavin.

With reluctance, he stepped away from the lectern, and I took a moment to stand behind it myself. The "blue goose" was tall, as speaking stands go, but I could still see over it with ease.

Running my hands along the sides, I felt the power, too. Twisting around, I cast a glance at the large medallion hanging on a curtained wall behind me. This wide blue oval, with an image of the White House at its center, was seen behind the president whenever he addressed the press from this room.

Gavin was watching me, his face expressionless.

I turned back toward the empty seats. Gav was setting me up to fail, I was sure of that. Maybe I should just give up and let him have his fun.

No. My personal pride rebelled. Not without a fight. Or at least, in this case, my best effort. But after the past few days, I didn't know how much effort I really had in me for Gavin's games.

I blew out a breath.

He sidled up. "Are you expecting the answer via ESP?" he asked. "When we held this exercise in the cafeteria yesterday, your colleagues at least searched the room before they gave up." He made a show of looking at his watch. "I'm giving you another minute. Then I'll explain what you should have been doing."

I could practically hear the clock tick as I gripped the lectern with both hands. Closing my eyes again, I thought about how *I* would wreak havoc on the White House if I had to do it in this room.

"Thirty seconds."

"Yeah, thanks," I said, wasting another two ticks to answer him.

This room was new. Why was that popping to the forefront of my thoughts just now? What was significant about its relative newness? Everything here had been changed. The place was practically sterile—and the housekeeping staff worked to keep it that way.

New. *Changed.*

A thought tickled my brain, just a breath out of reach.

"Fifteen seconds."

I opened my eyes. Turned to face the wall behind me. Stared at it

"Ten."

The curtains were . . . wrong. This wasn't the right backdrop.

As I argued with myself—realizing that nothing prevented the president from switching backdrops from time to time—my hands searched the royal blue curtains. Last time I'd seen President Campbell speak, the background had been flat—as though made of drywall—and the medallion's suspension wires were visible.

This time, the medallion's method of suspension was *in*visible—a means of support I couldn't detect.

"What are you doing, Ms. Paras?"

I didn't bother answering. My fingers groped the medallion's edge—looking for what, I didn't know.

"Three . . . two . . ."

"Got it!" I shouted. I yanked at a fist-sized piece of plastic that had been duct-taped to the back of the medallion. Pulling it forward, I held it up for Gav to see.

"What exactly do you think you have?" he asked.

"This!" I said, feeling my face flush with pride.

He arched an eyebrow.

"This is what I was supposed to find, isn't it?"

Gav tilted his head, approaching me slowly. Taking the device from my hands, he said, "First of all, let me congratulate you, Ms. Paras. You're the first person to find one of our planted IEDs." He fingered two wires that reached out from the bottom of the plastic, playing with them so they bounced at his touch. "And guess what else you did that no one else did."

I shrugged.

"You just set off the bomb," he said.

"But—"

He stopped me with a withering gaze. How could anyone stay as cold and detached as this guy? He played with the two wires, pointing them at me.

"Know what this means, Ms. Paras?"

I shook my head.

"*Kaboom!*" he shouted into my face.

My shoulders dropped.

"It isn't enough that you're able to spot things out of place," he said, stepping back, again the picture of calm. "You need to learn what to do when faced with an emergency."

I opened my mouth to argue. I'd been in my fair share of emergency situations and I'd handled things nicely, thank you very much—but I realized he was right. When it came to explosive devices, I had no idea what to do. I closed my mouth without saying a word.

"Very good," he said with a tone that made me want to *kaboom* him myself. "Now that we've tested your powers of observation, let's work on reaction protocols."

Forty-five minutes later, he finally released me for the day. "Not a bad start," he said. From him, I supposed that rated as high praise.

"Thanks a lot," I said, pushing bangs off my damp forehead. He'd really kept me moving—in the hour we'd worked together, we hadn't had two minutes of downtime. Truth was, though, I'd learned more than I'd expected to and certainly more than I ever hoped to need to know. Throughout my tutorial, Gavin constantly prefaced his demonstrations with, "We didn't get a chance to do this with the big group . . ." so I got the definite impression that I'd received more in-depth instruction than had my colleagues. He really warmed to the subject matter when he taught one-on-one. Maybe I could even skip the next class.

We walked back toward the residence, through the Palm Room, in silence.

When he and I were about to part company at the kitchen, I stopped him. "Special Agent Gavin?"

He turned. "Call me Gav."

Little did he know I'd already been doing that under my breath.

With a shrug, he added, "That is, use the nickname when we're working together. If we're out here, then use Special Agent Gavin."

"Sure," I said. But I sincerely hoped we wouldn't be working one-on-one again, ever.

"What were you going to say," he asked, "when you stopped me?"

Despite the fact that he was an arrogant jerk, and dismissive of my role as executive chef, I realized I was better prepared for emergencies even after today's short session. "Just wanted to say thanks," I said. "I learned a lot."

He frowned. "I'll be tougher on you next time." With a quick turn on his heel, he walked away.

Peculiar man.

I'd just about gotten into the kitchen when I ran into Bindy coming out. What was she doing here?

"Ollie!" she said, startling us both. "Where have you been?"

I didn't feel like explaining, so I pointed west. "Busy."

"The senator's wife, Maryann Blanchard, is upstairs," she said. "She wants to meet you."

"Me?" My hand instinctively brushed hair out of my eyes, and I was disappointed to discover I was still perspiring. "Why?"

Cheeks flushed, Bindy appeared a good deal more frazzled than she had yesterday. Although she was again super-snazzily dressed, she lacked the polish from the day before. "I was supposed to introduce you hours ago. Treyton insisted on it." Her eyes were restless—as though she were afraid that he would suddenly swoop down and scold her for taking too long. She giggled, which I recognized as Bindy's unusual expression of nervousness. We were all put in uncomfortable situations all too often. Her method of release didn't speak well of her professionalism. "Mrs. Blanchard wants you to meet the children."

"Now?" I glanced at my watch. The Mothers' Luncheon should be over. Guides should be taking groups of moms and tots on tours of the open rooms of the White House, and then everyone would gather in the East Room for a final discussion of the day's events. "Where's the First Lady?"

Bindy tilted her head, as though the question surprised her. "Upstairs with Mrs. Blanchard and a few others."

"How's she holding up?"

Finally, the light dawned. "Oh, of course. Yes. That's right. She lost her nephew yesterday."

My God, how could she have forgotten?

Bindy glanced away again. Maybe this job was too much for her. "I mean, we feel terrible about the First Family's loss," she said.

Too little, too late.

"But, Ollie, if you could just come upstairs for a little bit . . ."

"Does this have to do with the placement of her kids' gingerbread men in the Red Room?" I asked.

Bindy blushed more deeply. "Just five minutes, okay?"

I shook my head. "I can't. I haven't been back to the kitchen in over an hour and there are a million things to be done. Sorry." I started to move away, but she cut me off.

"Please," she said. "I promised her she'd get the chance to meet you."

"I told you I'd take a look at the gingerbread men the kids made. Isn't that enough? Tell her I'm busy. It's the truth."

"You have to do this, Ollie," Bindy said. Her voice had changed. "You don't understand what it's like."

I stared at her but she averted her eyes. "I don't understand what *what's* like?"

She bit her lip, wrinkling her nose. When she looked at me again, I thought she might cry. "Look at you. You've made it. You're at the top. You've gotten there."

I had an idea of where she was going, and though I didn't really want to travel down this track, I couldn't think of a way to stop the train.

"This is *my* chance," she said. "This is a dream job. This is what *I've* been working for all my life." She jabbed a finger into her own chest so hard it had to hurt. "But I'm still new. And I'm still trying to prove myself. What's it going to look like if I can't do something simple like make an introduction that Mrs. Blanchard requested?"

"You shouldn't have promised—"

"I know. You're right. I shouldn't have." Bindy looked as miserable as a person could, despite the trim suit and snazzy shoes, and she held out her hands, abdicating all power.

I had to ask. "Why are you so keen on keeping a job that makes you unhappy?"

For the first time since we started talking, Bindy smiled. "I love my job."

"I never would've guessed."

"It's just the pressure," she said. "I'm not used to it yet. But I'm getting better. And Treyton has plans. Big plans. If I'm good at what I do, he'll keep me around. That's all I want."

Big plans. Like a run for the presidency? He was the same party as President Campbell. I doubted he'd make a primary bid against an incumbent, but I didn't doubt he fantasized about it.

I felt for Bindy, but I was sticky, tired, and not in the mood to meet anyone—especially one with a "choose my kids' artwork" agenda on her mind.

"Please," she said again.

I rubbed my eyesockets. "I'm a mess."

"Nobody will care."

And that was how I came to meet Mrs. Blanchard upstairs in the Entrance Hall. She was a dark-haired, petite beauty. Bindy introduced me. "Call me Maryann," Mrs. Blanchard said.

I knew I could never do that, but I smiled and said hello to the three young children hanging on her. "And what's your name?" I asked the oldest.

He squirmed and smiled. "Trey," he said. "Are you the cook?"

"I sure am," I said.

"The food was good," he said, ever so politely. "Except Leah didn't like the banana pudding. She smashed it on the floor."

His mother shushed him, and shrugged. "Sorry."

"It's okay," I said as I turned to the other two little ones. Leah was about three and John was five. They all looked like they couldn't wait to get home and out of their dressy clothes. Leah wrapped herself around her mother's leg and whimpered.

Behind us, small groups wandered in and out of the Green Room, Blue Room, Red Room, and State Dining Room. Tour guides kept them moving. I was amazed at how well—relatively speaking—all the children behaved. I heard an occasional outburst and an accompanying reprimand, but the groups were more sedate than I'd expected, especially after Jackson's and Red's descriptions. I really wished Mrs. Blanchard had taken the tour.

Mrs. Campbell stood a few feet away, watching us. She maintained a serene smile, but from the look in her eyes, I knew she wanted to be away from all these people—to be alone to grieve for Sean. I marveled at the woman's strength in light of all that had happened.

"Are they touring the West Wing, too?" I asked at a lull in the conversation.

"They're almost everywhere," Bindy answered. "But we wanted a chance to talk with Mrs. Campbell alone. It's probably our only opportunity, isn't it?" she asked.

Mrs. Campbell nodded, without expression.

Couldn't they leave the poor woman alone?

Above the soft conversation and sounds of people moving around, we heard a speedy *click-clack* of two sets of high heels on the hard floor. A moment later, the social secretary, Marguerite, and her assistant joined us. Marguerite apologized for interrupting. "Mrs. Campbell," she said quietly, "you're needed upstairs."

The First Lady offered regrets for being called away. She thanked Mrs. Blanchard for attending the day's festivities and then procured a promise from the assistant secretary that everyone on the tours would be looked after properly.

Once the First Lady and Marguerite departed, I started to move away myself. "It was nice to meet you," I said. To the children, I added, "I hope you enjoyed your gingerbread man project."

Little Trey gave me a solemn look. "I didn't have fun making those," he said.

Bindy piped in. "This is the lady who will put your gingerbread men up for everybody to see. Right, Ollie?"

I didn't have any idea how to answer. "I'll do my best," I said.

Trey's mother gave his arm a tug. "Say thank you."

"Thank you."

Mrs. Blanchard smiled at me. An embarrassed smile. "We didn't turn them in with the rest. Bindy didn't want them to get lost in the confusion. She knows where they are."

"I'll make sure to get them into your hands directly," Bindy said.

"The tours are winding down now," the assistant secretary interjected, effectively ending this uncomfortable line of conversation. "Is there anything else you wanted to see before we return you to your car?"

What a nice way to shoo people out.

"No, we're done here," Maryann Blanchard said. She settled a high-wattage smile on Bindy, who winked at me.

"I'll call you tomorrow," she said.

I didn't answer. I couldn't wait for them to be gone.

CHAPTER 11

FROM THE FRYING PAN STRAIGHT INTO THE FIRE.

That's how I felt at Gene's wake. I'd been here for about fifteen minutes, but couldn't help but believe I'd inadvertently thrown myself into the flames just by showing up. I hadn't anticipated the enormous impact my presence might have. Standing next to the casket, I hadn't expected to be surrounded by Gene's well-meaning relatives, all asking me what really happened, what I'd seen, what I'd done, and did I think Gene had suffered? With everyone asking at once, it was difficult to know exactly what to say to give each of them the most comfort. Above all, I wanted to be helpful.

Try as I might, I couldn't keep the family straight. A tall woman rested her hand on my right shoulder, turning me to meet yet another relative. An elderly, suited gentleman. "This is the girl who found Gene," she said by way of introduction.

She was about to continue when a man to my right tapped my arm. He, too, wore a suit—and the look of a successful businessman. "What was done for him?" he asked. "I mean, on the scene. Did you administer CPR?"

The woman to my right tugged me again, trying to pull my attention back to the elderly fellow, who I now learned was Gene's older brother. "I'm very sorry," I said, taking his hand in both of mine.

His eyes sagged under the weight of unshed tears. "Thank you."

"Excuse me," a familiar voice said. A big hand clamped my left shoulder with solid authority. "Ollie," he said, "I need to talk with you."

I turned to see a very welcome and familiar face. His hair had gone almost completely gray, but his customary cheer sparkled from those blue eyes. I started to smile, but remembered where I was and immediately tamped down my reaction. "Henry!" I reached to give him a big hug. Relieved to have an out, I turned back to the family. Again I offered my condolences—and then apologized for having to leave so soon.

"Thank you," I said as we moved to the lobby. "I didn't know how to answer them." I shot a look back into the room as the group clustered together again. Circling the wagons, as it were. "It's so difficult to know what to say. And what not to say."

"It's always hard," he said, his eyes scanning the large vestibule. "And a situation like this one makes it worse." He winked at me. "I've been waiting for you. I knew that unless there was some emergency, you'd be here tonight."

Henry had lost some of the weight he'd put on in his last few months as executive chef, and his face looked less flushed. Although his waistline would never be characterized as trim, it was certainly under control. In fact, the suit he wore gave the impression of being almost saggy. "You look good," I said.

He blushed. "How's your kitchen?"

"*Our* kitchen?" I asked.

That made him smile.

"I'll tell you all about it, if you want to go for coffee."

Henry's eyebrows lifted. "Such a beautiful young lady asking an old man like me out for coffee? I would be a fool to refuse."

I placed a hand on his arm. "With an attitude like yours, Henry, you will *never* be old."

There was a Starbucks half a block away, and though it was cold outside, we walked. I knew it wouldn't be long before Henry started peppering me with questions. He didn't disappoint. As soon as we'd settled at a small table, him with a cup of coffee, me with a caramel apple cider, he asked, "So, how are the holiday preparations progressing?"

I told him, then said, "You heard about Sean Baxter?"

His eyes, which had crinkled up at the corners when I'd talked about the menu, now drooped. "How could I not? It's been on every news station." He shook his big head. "I've often wondered why anyone would choose to be president. You lose all privacy." Waving a hand in the direction of the funeral home, he said, "Gene Sculka's family has had to deal with some reporters asking questions, but for the most part, they're allowed to grieve privately. They can be *family* to one another. They're able to hold one another up without worrying about the world staring in on them."

When he sighed, I picked up his train of thought. "I know. I've seen the papers. Any move the president or Mrs. Campbell makes is scrutinized and analyzed ten times over."

His eyes didn't hold the twinkle they usually did. "Sometimes the news needs to step back and let people just *be*."

We were silent for a long moment. I took a sip of my frothy concoction, and enjoyed the sweet, hot trickle down the back of my throat. "You've heard about the bomb scare, too?" I said, knowing he had. In this day and age, one would have to be as hermitlike as the Unabomber to avoid the deluge of news that constantly sluiced over us.

"Were you evacuated?"

I told him about being sequestered in the bunker with the First Lady and Sean. I watched emotion tighten Henry's eyes, and I shared with him my impression that Mrs. Campbell had intended to set me up with Sean.

Henry patted my hand. "This has been hard on you, too."

I swallowed, finding it a bit more difficult this time. "Yeah."

We talked about Bucky's constant temper tantrums, Cyan's burgeoning talents, and Marcel's quiet genius. When I told Henry about Agda, he laughed.

"Bucky was quick to remind me that you would never have hired her with such a language barrier."

Henry stared up toward the ceiling, as though imagining the kitchen. "He's wrong about that. We aren't there to talk. We're there to create superb food. To make the president of our United States forget his troubles long enough to enjoy a wonderful meal." He launched into one of his patriotic speeches. I smiled as he waxed poetic on the virtues of a good meal and how national leaders made better decisions when they were well cared for. I'd missed Henry's pontifications. "We're there to contribute to our country's success. We aren't there to make friends."

Now I rested my hand on his. "But sometimes we make lifelong friends anyway, don't we?"

He grabbed my fingers and held them. The twinkle was back in his eyes. "That we do."

Walking to my car after saying good night, I blew out a long breath, watching the wispy air curl in front of me on this cold night. Partly a reminder that I was alive, partly a sigh of frustration, I realized that, despite being able to visit with Henry, I was happy to be on my way home.

Back at my apartment building I wasn't terribly surprised to find James napping at the front desk. I tried sneaking past without disturbing him, but he woke up when the elevator dinged.

"Ollie," he said, getting up.

Politeness thrust my hand forward to hold the elevator doors open. "Hi, James," I said. "How are things?"

Making his way over, he waved his hand at the open car. "Let that one go. I've got some information for you."

Reluctantly, I let the doors slide shut. "Information?"

"Yeah, yeah," he said quickly. Still blinking himself awake, he amended, "Well, I guess I mean Stanley has information for you. He told me to let him know when you got in."

"Did he say—"

James raised his hand, and looked both ways up and down the elevator corridor. "It's about that incident the other day. You know, the one where you work?"

"The electrocution?"

James nodded, shooting me a look of mortified annoyance.

My curiosity piqued, I thanked him and pushed the "up" button again. "I'll stop by his place. He's on eight, right?"

The same elevator opened.

"Ah . . . you might try him at your neighbor's . . . Mrs. Wentworth's."

"Okay, thanks." I got into the car and wondered what electrical issues were plaguing my neighbor's apartment that required attention this late at night.

James blushed scarlet as the elevator door closed and it wasn't until Mrs. Wentworth opened her door, dressed in only a bathrobe—with Stanley behind her similarly attired—that I understood.

"Oh," I said. "I . . . I heard Stanley was here. Hi, Stanley."

"For crying out loud, Ollie, don't stand there gaping like a grouper," Mrs. Wentworth said. "Come in here. Stanley has lots to tell you."

They settled themselves together on Mrs. Wentworth's flowered couch and I suddenly realized I didn't know her first name. Stanley was always Stanley to me. She was always Mrs. Wentworth. Not knowing how to address them together added to the discomfort I was feeling right now, facing these two sleep-clad seniors, both wearing a contented sort of glow. . . .

"I had a thought, Ollie," Stanley said, breaking into my thoughts. Thank goodness. "Remember the day of the accident? It stormed that day, right?"

It had. I remembered Stanley commenting on it. "Yeah . . ."

"Well, I got to thinking that your electrician there—what was his name?"

"Gene." My voice caught as I relived the past few hours and Gene's wake.

"That's it." As Stanley talked, Mrs. Wentworth smiled up at him in the way lovestruck teenagers do. All of a sudden, my discomfort vanished. They weren't bothered by my interruption, so why should I be? These two were adorable. "Yeah, I wager he didn't get to be the top electrician at the White House by being stupid. If he knew he was going anywhere near high voltage, he would've taken precautions."

"Gene knew the layout of the electricity better than anyone."

"Exactly my point," Stanley said. "Which is why I'm betting Gene was killed by a floating neutral."

"A what?"

"A floating neutral," he repeated. "Dangerous, and unpredictable."

Mrs. Wentworth patted Stanley's knee. "Show her the thing you made."

Stanley blushed. "I put together a mock-up to explain it better." He padded out to the kitchen, with Mrs. Wentworth watching him until he was out of earshot.

"He's been at this all day making the mock-up to show you. And he's really proud of himself. Even I understand these neutral thingies now."

When Stanley returned, he carried a board, about eighteen by twenty-four inches. On it, he'd mounted five sockets. Two held forty-watt bulbs, three held fuses. In the center was an on/off switch. All of the parts were connected to one another with wires and the entire contraption was attached to a scary-looking triple-thick gray cord that sported a round plug as big as my palm. On it were three very long, odd-shaped metal prongs.

"This is a 240 plug," he said, holding it up. "You don't see too many of these around the house. But I bet you got one on your dryer." He waited for me to shrug—I had no idea. "No matter. Some appliances need 240 instead of the regular 120 volts. Like dryers. Check it out when you get back, you'll see."

"I will."

"I'm going to keep it short and simple, but you stop me if you got questions, okay?"

I promised I would.

"Storms can knock out your neutral—your ground. And that's a bad thing, because your ground is what keeps your house from catching on fire from too much voltage." He licked his lips. "You got a curling iron?"

"A couple of them," I said, even though lately I'd been foregoing using them in favor of a quick ponytail.

"Curling irons don't produce enough heat to catch your house on fire. So if you ever get worried you forgot to shut it off, don't sweat it."

"I have one of those auto-shut-off ones—"

"Even better." He waved that away. "But you most likely don't ever have to worry. Because your appliances are using 120 volts, and most of the time, if everything's working right, that ain't going to give you any headaches. But," he said, warming to his subject, "your house has to have 240 volts coming in so you can run your clothes dryer. It's too dangerous to send in 240 at once, so you got two wires coming in sending 120 each. Follow?"

"So far."

"The neutral acts like a buffer between them. I could get really technical here, but there's no need. All that's important to know is that if your neutral is broken, then the two 120s don't have anything keeping them apart. Your curling iron or your heating pad or your toaster can go crazy and heat up hot enough to catch fire."

He gestured to me to follow him. Mrs. Wentworth got up and came along, too. Stanley led us into the small closet that housed the furnace, washer, dryer, and slop sink. I was amazed at how pristinely clean the tiny room was. I sincerely hoped Mrs. Wentworth would never see the need to visit mine. She'd see delicates hung from cabinet handles, and to-be-washed items lying in piles on the floor.

The Lysol-smelling room was tight with the three of us, but Stanley urged me to lean over the back of the dryer. "See that?" He pulled the plug from a special outlet on the wall. The plug was a near duplicate of the one he'd attached to the board-contraption. "Now, I'm going to fire up my mock-up and I can show you what probably happened to your friend."

I stepped back, fearful of some explosion or something. Mrs. Wentworth hovered close, blocking the doorway.

When he plugged it in, the two lightbulbs went on. "Looks normal, right?" He flicked the switch, which I now noticed was labeled ON—NORMAL, OFF—OPEN. Nothing happened.

"These two lightbulbs take the same voltage," he said. "They keep things balanced. Even when the neutral is missing, you're not going to notice anything wrong." He unplugged the cord. "Now, watch what happens when we have an imbalance."

He replaced one of the forty-watt bulbs with a big spotlight version, turned the switch to "on"—meaning normal—and plugged it back in.

Both lights lit—the spotlight was, of course, brighter than the little forty-watt bulb in the accompanying socket, but I couldn't see anything amiss.

"Ready?" he asked.

Mrs. Wentworth stepped back. I said, "Ready."

"I'm now eliminating the neutral," he said, and flipped the switch.

"Whoa!" I said, raising my hand to protect my eyes.

Stanley pointed to the spotlight. "Big difference, huh?"

There was. The spotlight glowed so brightly I couldn't look at it. The light was so intense, the beam so strong, I felt as though the bulb was barely hanging on. At any moment I expected it to explode.

"Now, y'see, this here is an imbalance," Stanley continued in his unflappable manner. Mrs. Wentworth had backed out of the tiny room completely. I didn't want to be rude, but the bulb in the socket was unnervingly bright.

"Is it safe?" I asked.

Stanley made a so-so motion with his head. "You don't want to keep this on for long," he said. "Playing with neutrals is never a good idea. That's why this is all mounted on a wooden board. You see how I'm being careful not to touch anything metal? I'm sure it's not dangerous at the moment, but I like to take extra precautions just the same."

He must have noticed me squinting, because he reached into the center of the board and flipped the switch to "on." Immediately, the two bulbs resumed their normal brightness.

"Does that mean that all 240 volts were in this bulb?" I asked.

"Not quite. Can't say for sure how much was feeding into here. Maybe 220, maybe a little less. But that's the thing with neutrals. You gotta have 'em. Things are too unpredictable if you don't."

"So you think Gene was killed because of a floating neutral?"

Much to my relief, Stanley unplugged the contraption before answering. "Again, I can't say for sure. Something got him—and I'd be willing to bet it was something he didn't expect. If there were 240 volts flying through those lines, the man didn't stand a chance." He gave me a wistful look. "I'd know it if I got a look-see, but that isn't going to happen, is it?"

"Doubtful." I smiled. "The electricians on staff probably thought of this, right? I mean, this is something you'd look for in an electrocution."

Stanley cocked a white eyebrow. "Might be worth talking with them just to be sure. Floating neutrals aren't real common. People don't think to look for them. And I could be wrong about this—could be something else entirely that shot all that voltage into your friend. But storms are notorious for wreaking havoc with your wiring, including unpredictable damage—grounds, neutrals—you get the idea. I think it's worth a mention."

CHAPTER 12

MANNY JOGGED ACROSS THE CENTER HALL, HIS TOOL BELT JAN-
gling to the beat of his pace. I called out to him, but he didn't hear me. Even
though it was still before eight in the morning, the White House was bustling
with activity. No matter how much time we allowed to get the residence ready
for the official opening, it never seemed to be enough.

"Manny," I said again, this time loud enough to be carried across the hall.

He turned, his eyes narrowing when he realized it was me. I could practically read his mind. No matter what the executive chef was going to ask, he
knew it wouldn't be good.

Without closing the distance between us, he said, "I'm working on the
setup," jerking a thumb to the south. I knew he had a hundred tasks ahead of
him, not the least of which was setting up the holiday lights for the massive
tree that would be erected outside, but I needed only a couple minutes of his
time.

I made my way toward him, wiping my hands on my apron. "I have a quick
question."

His attention was at once caught by something behind me. I turned to see
Vince loping toward us. "It's about time," Manny said. "Where have you been?"

"Curly's looking for you," Vince said, half turning as though he expected
the acting chief electrician to materialize behind him.

"Again? That guy has been on my case all morning." Manny made a face,
muttering in such a way that I knew if I hadn't been present, he would've let
loose with a string of expletives. "What's with him anyway? He's been—"

I was about to interrupt, to ask Manny and Vince about the floating neutrals, when who should turn the corner but the man himself. "Hey, Curly,"

Vince said, hurrying away from our minigathering. "I'm heading out now." He pointed. "Found Manny for you."

Curly harrumphed. "What the hell are you doing still inside? I thought we were supposed to have the power up and running out there an hour ago."

Manny opened his mouth, but I interrupted. "I stopped him to ask a question."

"Go," he said to Manny, who took off like a shot. When Curly turned to stare at me with furious contempt, I nearly took a step back. He practically snarled. "What do you want?"

"It's about Gene."

"He's dead."

I bit the insides of my cheeks. "I have a question about how he died."

Curly's jaw worked. I jumped in before he could dismiss me.

"Listen," I said. "I just want to ask if you've considered the possibility that Gene was killed by a floating neutral?"

For the first time in my life, I could tell I caught Curly by surprise. He was dumbfounded. "What?"

"I said, I was wondering—"

"I heard that. How the hell do you know about floating neutrals?" His flabbergasted expression was replaced by the surly look I was used to. "Why are you pushing your nose into my business? Don't you have a kitchen to run?"

Though not entirely surprised by his reaction, I was still taken aback by his vehemence. I forced myself to hold my ground. "Have you considered the possibility?"

"I don't know what you've been reading, or think you know, missy, but floating neutrals don't just pop up out of thin air."

"But the storm—"

He snorted. "What, you think you're some sort of expert on our system now? Here, tell you what." With a flourish, he unfastened his tool belt. Removing it from his waist, he held it out to me. "Juncture number sixty-four is out. And we have a low-voltage issue at K-thirty-five. You take care of those while I go bake cookies, how's that sound?"

I fixed him with my most pointed, angry glare. "I'm just trying to help."

"Gene's dead," he said again. "Nothing you can do can change that."

"But I thought if we found out why—"

"Tell you what, missy," he said as he replaced his tool belt around his waist. "You get yourself a journeyman electrician's card—then I'll talk to you. But for now, I've got a White House to keep hot." He started down the same path Manny and Vince had taken. Two steps away, he turned and spoke to me over his shoulder, not breaking stride. "Don't bug me with this crap again."

RAFE TOOK UP A POSITION NEXT TO ME AT THE KITCHEN'S CENTER counter. "What did those chicken breasts ever do to you?"

I looked up, realizing I'd taken out my aggression by pounding the meat so thin, the breasts could've been served as high-protein pancakes. "Geez," I said, embarrassed, "I didn't realize."

"It's your first holiday season in the executive chef position," he said. "You're bound to be a little stressed."

If he only knew. I glanced at the clock. "I think there should be a law against aggravation before nine in the morning."

Rafe laughed. "Not going to happen. Not around here at least." He flicked a fleeting look across the kitchen, where Bucky was preparing a new salad dressing of his own concoction, and separately, stirring beef stock we would need later in the day. My second-in-command was murmuring, apparently having an argument with himself.

I took in the rest of the kitchen. Cyan was uncharacteristically silent, and even as Agda rolled dough out, I noticed veins in her arms standing out, and a crease on her forehead.

"How come you're so chipper?" I asked Rafe.

He shrugged. "Stress manifests itself differently in each of us."

I thought about Bindy's tendency to giggle. "Too true."

The phone rang. I was closest, so I wiped my hands with one of the anti-septic towels we kept just for that purpose, and answered it.

Jackson informed me that the First Lady would be out all day, meeting with relatives to make arrangements for Sean's funeral. His parents lived nearby in Virginia, and Mrs. Campbell was not expected to return to the residence until after dinner.

"The president is returning this evening as well," he said.

"For dinner?"

"No. He'll be joining Mrs. Campbell at his sister's home first, and the president and his wife are expected back here after eight o'clock."

"Thanks," I said, and hung up. Not having to prepare lunch and dinner today made things easier on us, but I couldn't imagine how hard the day would be for the First Couple. It was a wonder that Mrs. Campbell had made it through yesterday at all, but having to prepare for the funeral of someone so close and so young had to be devastating.

I announced the change in plan to the rest of the kitchen staff, and I watched tension seep out of them—by the change in their stances, the position of their shoulders, their very breathing. "We still have a lot to get done," I added, unnecessarily. "Let's hope that . . ."

Before I could finish my wish that the rest of the day proceed uneventfully, Marcel stormed in, with Yi-im trotting faithfully behind him. Without greeting any of us, Marcel began ranting. "I 'ave no method to make use of these . . . these . . . childish efforts." He held out a tray displaying some of the gingerbread men that had been turned in yesterday. "These do not complement the gingerbread house I am slaving over. The house that is my crowning achievement this year. No. These are . . . *le pire.*"

I stepped closer to look.

"Do you see?" he asked. "How can I use such a terrible mess as these? No one will look at the exquisite structure. No. Their eyes will all be drawn to this mishmash."

Although Marcel and I generally worked independently of each other, we had a friendly, symbiotic relationship. He needed to vent and I was happy to oblige him. But maybe there were options he hadn't considered. "Have you spoken with Kendra?" I asked.

"She is the one who presented these to me! She wants me to *fix* them. I have no time for such nonsense."

While I had to agree that the workmanship on the eight-inch cookies left a great deal to be desired, I thought they were kind of cute. "The idea is to showcase the country's kids," I said quietly.

"Are we raising a nation of imbeciles?" he asked, his big eyes bulging. "Look at this." He pointed to one of the corner pieces. The cookie man was missing one eye and half of one foot. The squiggled icing that decorated the cutout's perimeter had been squeezed off the edge repeatedly, but it was the smudgy unevenness of it all that made it look like it was put together by a bored kindergartner. Marcel practically sputtered as he spoke. "This was made by a boy of seven. By the time I was his age, I was creating three-layer cakes with handmade candies. Each one I produced was perfect."

I didn't doubt that. "Kendra is in charge of the overall design," I said soothingly. "And you know what a perfectionist she is. I'm sure she's hoping to use most of the submitted cookies." I took another pointed look. "Did you ever consider that these are the best she received?"

The horror on Marcel's face would have been laughable if I didn't know how much pressure we were under to get the residence together and ready for presentation in the next two days.

"I cannot work with this," he said. He dropped the tray in the center of the countertop and backed away from it, with an unconcealed look of contempt. "I will not use these. You may crumble them up and feed them to the dog."

Marcel left the kitchen. I blew out a breath as I stared after him. Although he occasionally had his prima donna moments, he didn't usually draw such a hard line. Bucky, Cyan, and Agda shared a glance of wariness before returning to their tasks. I locked eyes with Rafe, and it was as if we both shared the unspoken sentiment about stress manifesting itself differently in each of us.

"Ho, ho, ho!"

I turned at the exclamation to see chief usher Paul Vasquez come in, carrying a diplomatic parcel and wearing a wide grin.

"You're back," I said, stating the obvious.

"And the tree is beautiful," he said. "This year we have a magnificent Fraser fir. Breathtaking. I can't wait until we get it set up." His jovial expression dropped. "That's the good news. Unfortunately we've had our share of bad, haven't we?" He made eye contact with each of us in turn. Paul had a way of making every staff member feel important. "I've been in contact with the White House over the days I was gone," he said, "so I am aware of what has transpired. We will discuss everything at the next staff meeting. In the meantime," he handed me the diplomatic pouch, "this came for you."

"Me?" I said, surprised. Belatedly, I realized I knew exactly what this was. As I opened the parcel, Cyan edged up. I held my breath.

"More gingerbread men?" she asked.

I nodded. "These must be the ones created by the Blanchard children." And they were. A letter from Bindy accompanied them. I pulled the three men out, one at a time. They'd been boxed separately, and wrapped in tissue paper surrounded by bubble wrap.

"Somebody isn't taking chances on these getting damaged," she said. Then, "Wow. His kids made these?"

We stared at the first cookie I'd removed from its container. "This is amazing."

Paul whistled. "Kendra must be thrilled. If this is the caliber of submissions she's receiving—"

"Eet ees not," Marcel interrupted, coming up behind us. "*Sacre bleu.*" He held out both hands and I placed the little decorated man into them. "Where did this come from?"

Paul excused himself to return to his office and I took the opportunity to explain Bindy's request to Marcel.

"This is wonderful. *Marveilleux,*" he said, placing the cookie back into its box with great reverence. "Let me see the others."

The three cookies were whimsical and perfect. So perfect that not even Marcel could find fault with them. They were, of course, the right size, browned to perfection, and each of the three men sported a combination of patriotic red, white, and blue icing piped along their edges so perfect it looked fake. I commented on that.

"I don't care if it is plastic." Marcel said, beaming. "No one is to eat these. They are for display only."

The piped edge was the only requirement the White House had made for consistency's sake. I never would have thought to give them little sugar flags to hold, nor would I have come up with the idea of carving into the cookies themselves for a textured background. These were not cookie-gingerbread men; they were works of art.

"I promised Bindy we'd find a prominent place for these in the Red Room. I'm glad I did," I said, winking. "I had no idea the kids were so talented."

Missing my sarcasm, Marcel said, "Children did not make these." He pronounced the word, "shildren." He shook his head. "These are the work of a master."

"Bindy did hint that Treyton Blanchard's chef might have helped a bit."

Marcel barked a laugh. "I would say he created these single-handedly. And the project took several days, at least. I will have no problem including these with my own masterpiece."

I grinned, pleased to have one less thing to deal with, and handed him the three boxes. "All yours."

Marcel gave a little bow. "I accept with pleasure."

THE LAST THING I NEEDED WAS TO INCUR THE WRATH OF CURLY again, but when I saw Manny later, still wearing the clanking tool belt, I couldn't help myself. In a repeat of the morning's move, I called out to him.

He turned, and this time when he saw me, he shook his head and backed away.

"I just have a question for you," I said.

"What did you do to get Curly all fired up?" he asked. "The guy's been on my case all day. Vince's, too. He said you ticked him off."

"I asked him about floating neutrals, and he—"

Manny looked just as surprised as Curly had this morning. "What?"

I explained about Stanley's mock-up.

"No wonder Curly's so pissed. He wouldn't tell us what was going on, just that you keep bullying him about Gene getting electrocuted."

"*I* keep picking on *him*? Since when does asking a question constitute bullying?"

"Hey, I'm just saying. Vince has gotten his head bitten off about five times today, and whenever we ask Curly why he's so ornery, he just gives us more work to do. He keeps checking on us, too. Like every fifteen minutes, he's there again. You shouldn't have started all this. You have no idea what you're doing. And now he's worse than usual. But at least now I know what's behind it."

"What's so bad about me asking?"

In even more of a hurry to get away now, Manny shrugged one shoulder and shifted toward the door. "I dunno. Maybe Curly thinks you're trying to show him up. Maybe he's worried you'll cost him the chief electrician position."

"Don't be silly." I could tell Manny was ready to bolt, so I pressed my point, explaining again what Stanley had explained to me. "Is there any way you can check to see if Gene's accident was due to a floating neutral?"

He shook his head even before I finished making my request. "Let it go."

"But I don't believe Gene would've made an electrical mistake."

"I wouldn't be so sure," he said.

"Just check, please?"

"No way. It's not a neutral. I guarantee it. And even if I could check on it, I wouldn't want to mess with this one. Not with Curly around. If it were up to me," Manny said, lowering his voice to a conspiratorial whisper, "I'd kick his sorry butt out of here. The guy's got too much on his mind with the sick wife and all. And now he's so worried I'm going to make a mistake, or that Vince is, that he's not letting us do our jobs. That guy should get canned before he does more damage. Seriously."

CHAPTER 13

WHEN THE KITCHEN PHONE RANG AT SEVEN FIFTEEN THAT EVE-
ning, I was surprised to see the in-house ID indicate it was the First Lady
calling.

"Hello, Ollie," she said. "I'm glad it's you who answered. Are you very busy?"

A visit from Gavin—who pilfered Bucky and Cyan for half the afternoon—
had set us even farther behind than we'd been. We had all hoped to leave
by eight tonight, but from the looks of things now, we wouldn't get out until
after ten.

"Not at all," I said. "What can I do for you?"

"My husband and I are expecting a guest this evening. I inquired and found
that he hasn't eaten yet. In fact, neither have we."

That surprised me. I said so.

"Yes, I know," the First Lady continued, her voice just above a sigh. "We
had planned to, but I don't find myself with much appetite today."

With everything that was swirling around in their lives—the president's
high-level meetings, Sean's death, Gene's death—I couldn't imagine eating,
either. "I understand."

"I knew you would, Ollie. That's why I have a particular favor to ask. Would
you be willing to prepare something for us and for our guest this evening?"

"Of course," I said. I was about to ask a question when she interrupted.

"There's one other thing. Could you take care of all this up here? In the
family kitchen? I'd prefer to keep it informal. I don't want any other . . . anyone
else . . . present. Would you be willing to do that?"

"I'd be glad to," I said. "Can you tell me who the guest is, so I can look up
his dietary requirements?"

"Yes, of course. Senator Blanchard will be joining us this evening. He and I have much to discuss." She paused for a moment and I sensed it best to give her time to collect her thoughts rather than rush off the phone. "We have a lot to talk about that"—she hesitated before saying his name—"that matter Sean advised me on. You have been privy to information of which the rest of the staff is unaware. I would prefer to keep it that way. Just a limited contingent tonight. Dinner doesn't need to be elaborate. Do we have any leftovers you can use?"

In my mind, I'd already begun pulling together a menu. "How soon would you like to sit down?"

"Whatever works best for you. Just come up as soon as you can; the kitchen will be yours alone. After a day like today, I'd like to relax and not stand on ceremony for once."

WE KEPT SO MUCH ON HAND IN THE WHITE HOUSE KITCHEN that the First Lady's request made for no difficulty whatsoever. After assigning Bucky to take over holiday preparations—and it seemed there was no end to them in sight—I gathered ingredients, utensils, and assorted necessities onto one of our butler's carts and made my way up to the second floor.

The kitchen here was cozy—flowered wallpaper and warm-wood cabinets similar to those found in middle-class homes across the country. Although there would have been enough room for two of us to work comfortably together, I was content to handle this dinner for three myself. More important, that's what the First Lady had requested.

Dinner was to be served in the adjacent dining room. Occasionally referred to as the family's private dining room, it was often confused by non–White House personnel with the Family Dining Room on the first floor, or with the President's Dining Room in the West Wing. But we staffers knew the difference. This room, formerly known as the Prince of Wales Room, due to the fact that the Prince of Wales slept there during James Buchanan's presidency—before it was outfitted as a kitchen—became the First Family's private dining room under Jacqueline Kennedy's direction.

I'd just started breading the chicken breasts I'd pounded the heck out of earlier when Mrs. Campbell knocked at the doorjamb.

"I hope I'm not disturbing you," she said.

"Not at all. I'm hoping to be ready to serve at eight thirty. Will that be all right?"

She nodded, and wandered into the kitchen. "I asked the butlers to set places for three, but now I understand that Treyton may bring Bindy along. Would it be too much inconvenience to prepare dinner for four, in the event she does show up?"

I'd brought extras up with me. One doesn't get to be a top chef without preparing for such exigencies. "Not a problem," I said.

Mrs. Campbell began opening cabinets. "Can you believe I haven't yet figured out where everything is in here?" She gave a sad laugh. "I'm getting too used to having people wait on me all the time. I don't think I like that."

"Enjoy it," I said. "We're happy to be here."

She had her back to me, two side-by-side cabinets open. "I'm glad you're here, Ollie. I trust you."

I didn't know what to say to that, but Mrs. Campbell wasn't finished.

"My husband and I don't believe Sean took his own life. His mother doesn't believe it, either."

I hadn't expected her to talk about Sean, but I covered my surprise as best I could. She turned to me, tears swimming in her eyes. "You knew him, too. Maybe you saw something we didn't see? Do you think it's possible that . . . that he—"

"No," I said quickly. "I don't."

She graced me with a sad smile. "Thank you."

Although I was often sorry for speaking out of turn, this time I really couldn't help myself. "If I may say so . . ."

Mrs. Campbell inclined her head. "What's on your mind?"

"I just want to tell you how much I admire your composure." I groaned inwardly. Composure? There had to be a better word. That wasn't what I meant and it was coming out all wrong. "Dignity, I mean. I admire the way you handle everything. What I mean to say is, Sean's death has been so hard on you. On everyone . . ."

She flinched at Sean's name, but her eyes urged me to continue.

"I can't imagine how hard it must have been to entertain all those women yesterday. And yet you're still always . . ." I was trying hard to get my point across without babbling. Failing miserably. Summing up, I said, "You truly are the epitome of grace under pressure."

Another sad smile. "When my husband agreed to serve our country by taking on the presidency, we knew we would be held to a higher standard than we had been as civilians. As First Lady, my actions have a ripple effect across the country." She seemed to be speaking to herself. "It's frightening in some ways, empowering in others. I realize the effect my actions have, and try to comport myself in a way that deserves emulation, no matter how hard the circumstances." She squinted at me. "I see a lot of that trait in you, too, Ollie. We have a core"—she pulled both fists in, toward the center of her body—"that holds us steady even when the rest of the world is falling apart. You have the same strength you claim to admire in me. I just pray you never have reason to call upon it the same way I've found myself doing these past few days."

I felt my face grow hot. Worse, I was speechless.

Mrs. Campbell must have sensed my surprised amazement. Without waiting for me to reply, she turned her back to me again and grabbed a stack of white bowls in the cabinets. "You can use these," she said setting them on the table between us. "Like I said, I had dining places set out earlier. We can serve ourselves family style. After all, we are practically family. I've known Treyton since before he was born."

One of her assistants peeked around the door to let Mrs. Campbell know that Blanchard had arrived. I secretly hoped Bindy wasn't with him. If Mrs. Campbell was looking to share memories with an old friend, the last thing she needed at the table tonight was an ambitious political emissary who giggled whenever she got nervous.

IN FAIRLY SHORT ORDER I GOT ONE OF THE CAMPBELL'S FAVORITE dinners started. Nothing fancy, a simple breaded lemon chicken served over angel hair pasta, with capers. The pre-course salad would be served with Bucky's newest dressing. I'd pre-tested it myself and pronounced it wonderful. Dessert would be simple, too. Fresh sorbet, in hollowed-out oranges, waited in the freezer for a whipped cream and peppermint leaf garnish. The preparation took some effort, but I wanted to bring a touch of cheer to what promised to be a difficult evening.

I was so immersed in preparation that I didn't notice Bindy until she called my name.

Startled, I glanced up, hoping as I reacted that my disappointment didn't show.

"This is nice," she said, walking into the kitchen. "I've never been in this room before." She carried a plate, silverware, napkin, and crystal water glass. In addition, she held a diplomatic pouch under her arm.

"What's going on?"

The disappointment on her face told the story before she could. "Treyton asked if I minded excusing myself." She flushed. "How embarrassing. We thought this was supposed to be a real dinner, downstairs, with a few other people. I guess I should've . . ." She shook her head. "Doesn't matter now, does it? I'm here. I'm stuck till it's time to leave. Do you mind if I sit in here with you?"

She arranged her place settings on the table, as though preparing to be served. With care, she placed the package on the chair next to hers. "That's for later," she said cryptically.

I'd planned to clean up as soon as dinner was served, and then beat a path back downstairs. My estimated ten o'clock departure was looking ever more unlikely. "Sure," I lied. "Have you eaten?"

She shook her head.

"Well, I've prepared plenty," I said. "Let me just take care of them first, okay?"

If I'd expected an offer of help, I was mistaken. But in truth, I was glad. Preparing a dinner for this small group wouldn't be difficult, and I'd rather do it myself than have to coach an amateur. Bindy sat at the table, watching me work, occasionally asking a question about preparation or presentation.

She had the good sense to speak in a whisper. Since we could hear most of the conversation going on in the next room, it stood to reason they would be able to hear us, too.

I wheeled out the salad, dressing, and bread, feeling more like I was serving my mother and nana at home than the president of the United States, his wife, and their guest. Meals in this home were usually served by tuxedoed butlers, amid much pomp and circumstance. Right now, in my tunic and apron, I felt positively slovenly.

"Good evening, Mr. President, Senator Blanchard," I said, nodding to each of them and to Mrs. Campbell. The president greeted me by name and Blanchard smiled. I saw in him what most voters must have seen. He exuded charm and confidence—so much so that it almost seemed as if he had the power to dispel the house's sad pall.

I set the food items on the table. "I'll be in the next room, if you need anything."

Having gone silent when I entered, they started conversation right up again as I crossed the threshold into the adjacent kitchen.

"I know the timing is terrible," Senator Blanchard said, "but this is the situation we're faced with. This was brought on by our fathers. It's unfortunate that we're required to deal with their shortsightedness. Especially at a time like this."

Bindy made a face that let me know she was as uncomfortable as I. "Salad?" I whispered.

She nodded, so I set one in front of her and used the remaining time to finish preparing the entrée. As she ate, I couldn't help listening to the terse conversation in the next room.

"My wife has shown me the corporation's financials," President Campbell said. "Based on the company's projected growth, I don't understand why any of you want to sell right now."

"I beg your pardon, sir," Blanchard said, "but I believe my analysts have a better grip on the company's financials than either you or I could hope to have. We are, after all, in the business of serving our country rather than wizards in the financial world."

"Still," President Campbell said, "when Sean took a look at the books—"

"Your nephew would have advised you to sell, too."

"No," Mrs. Campbell said. "He advised me *against* selling."

I heard a chair scrape backward and I could picture Blanchard's reaction. As I poured sauce over the chicken breasts, I fought to tune out Bindy's mouth sounds and listen in to Blanchard's reply.

"You must be mistaken."

"I am not." A *clink* of silverware. I could imagine Mrs. Campbell sitting up straighter. "Don't you remember? I told you on Thursday." Her voice faltered. "Before we learned . . . before . . ."

"I truly am sorry to bring up such a difficult subject at a time like this," Blanchard said again. "But I can't imagine such a fine young man giving you bad advice."

Whispered: "Ollie?"

I turned. Bindy held up her glass. "Do you have anything stronger than water?"

I pulled open the refrigerator door, wondering why she didn't get it herself. Then again, she might not feel comfortable puttering around in someone else's kitchen, especially one in the White House. "Orange juice, milk, iced tea . . ."

"Iced tea, thanks."

As I served her, I listened again to the conversation in the other room. Bindy's body language suggested she was eager to keep me from hearing what was going on, so I strove for nonchalance, moving with care, trying to make as little noise as possible. Not that it mattered. The adjacent room's conversation came through loud and clear.

"No, I don't believe this is our fathers' fault," Mrs. Campbell was saying. "I believe they wanted to ensure their children's security. And my father would not have wanted me to sell out at the first opportunity after his death."

Blanchard spoke so quietly I almost couldn't make out his words. "But you must understand that my father, Nick's father, and Helen's all died years ago. We couldn't move on this business venture until . . . well, until you inherited your share. This can hardly be considered too quick of a decision."

"It is for me."

"But don't you see? That's the problem. Our fathers believed—erroneously, I might add—that the four of us needed to reach a decision unanimously. If they hadn't put that codicil in their agreement, I can guarantee Helen would have sold out within a year of her father's death. She's been waiting ten years for her portion of the proceeds."

The president chimed in. "What I don't understand is why the need to sell? None of you is destitute; you don't need the funds to survive. Why the rush?"

I carried a platter of succulent chicken breasts and steaming pasta into the dining room. As I set the dish down, I wanted to ask if there was anything else the diners required, but Blanchard was talking, so I held my tongue.

"It's Volkov," he said. Then, with a pointed look at me, he stopped talking and took a drink of water.

I grabbed my chance. "Will there be anything else for now?"

"No, thank you," Mrs. Campbell said. "Is Ms. Gerhardt faring well in the kitchen?"

"Just fine."

"Thank you, Ollie."

The moment I left, one of the president's aides, Ben, met me in the kitchen, coming in from the hallway. He gestured to me. "Where's everyone else?"

"Informal tonight," I said.

The assistant didn't hesitate. "He's needed downstairs."

"Now?"

Without answering, Ben strode into the private dining room and spoke quietly to the president. I watched from the doorway. Sighing deeply, President Campbell wiped his mouth with his napkin, then dropped it on the table. "If you'll excuse me," he said.

I ducked out of sight.

As soon as the president left, Blanchard spoke again, now more animatedly. "Volkov is going to bring us all down. This scandal he's involved in is not going away anytime soon. In fact, I see it getting worse. Every day that we keep Zendy Industries alive with his name as one of our co-owners is a day that we risk losing everything."

I heard the sounds of passing plates, and then Mrs. Campbell said, "Surely, Treyton, you exaggerate."

"Not at all. In fact, he's the one spearheading this sell effort. At first I dismissed the idea, just as you're dismissing it now. But think about it. He may be desperate for funds to cover his legal bills, but he's right. We need to sell now, while Zendy's at the top of its game. Not later, when Volkov's troubles expand to include us all." Blanchard made a sound, like a *tsk*. "It's just a terrible shame that our fathers insisted on that unanimous vote."

There was silence for a long moment, with only scraping sounds of silverware on china and bodies shifting in seats.

"My father would not have wanted me to sell Zendy. Not this soon after his passing."

"Elaine," Blanchard said. "I know you're suffering still from the loss of your father. I offer you my sincere condolences on his passing and on Sean's, but we have very little time to make this decision."

"I disagree. We have ten years."

Blanchard took in a sharp breath. I assumed it was Blanchard, because he then said, "Perhaps you misunderstand. We have to wait ten years only if we decide *not* to sell at this time."

"And that's what Sean advised me to do."

The silence was so heavy I felt it in the kitchen. Bindy watched me with wide eyes. The chicken on her plate remained untouched.

"I hate to say this, Elaine, but if that's what Sean advised you, he was wrong. In fact, as distasteful as it sounds, I'm now beginning to wonder . . . if that's why he shot himself."

I heard Mrs. Campbell gasp. "No. No. Of course not."

"Can't you see it, Elaine? He might have believed he disappointed you by giving bad advice. He might not have seen any way out but to take his own life."

"Treyton, that's the most ridiculous thing I've ever heard. And I will thank you to not discuss Sean's death anymore. That subject is closed."

I heard him sigh. "I'm sorry."

"Yes, well, I would also like to table the Zendy discussion as well. We can talk about it another time."

A long moment of silence. "Just remember one thing, Elaine," Blanchard said. "Our window of opportunity won't stay open for long. And once it's closed, we won't have another chance to sell for ten years. There are buyers out there now. The time to sell is now."

"Actually, now is the time for two old friends to enjoy dinner together. No more business discussion tonight. Are we agreed?"

I couldn't see Blanchard's face, but I could imagine it as he said, "Whatever's best for you."

When they moved on to other topics, including the exploits of Blanchard's kids, I pulled the sorbet-filled oranges from the freezer and began to prepare them for serving. I liked to allow the sorbet to soften slightly for easier eating. Bindy broke the silence in the kitchen by asking, "How much do you know about this Zendy situation?"

I shrugged, shooting a look toward the other room. Even though she spoke quietly, I worried about being overheard. "Not much." I didn't want to tell her what Sean had shared with me. For some reason it seemed to be a betrayal of trust. I had no doubt that if Bindy perceived any value in my musings, she'd scurry to share them with Blanchard at her first opportunity.

The girl watched me work. Halfway between anxiety and expectation, the expression on her face told me she was hungry for any specifics I could give her. Little did she know that when it came to the First Family's business, I was as mute as a mime.

"Why all the fuss?" I asked, lowering myself into a chair opposite Bindy's so we could talk like girlfriends sharing a common concern. "I mean, really. Why can't the three other people sell and leave Mrs. Campbell to hold on to her share?"

"That's the thing," Bindy said. She seemed to fight back her natural reluctance to talk about her boss's business. Maybe she believed she'd glean some vital information from me. Bringing her head closer to mine, she whispered, "According to the company history, the four men who founded the company never wanted their children to sell. Zendy was set up as a research company with the mission of bettering the world. It's done that. In fact, the company has done it so well that it's made billions on research. Most of that money goes to philanthropic causes."

"Oh." I was beginning to understand. Although I trusted Sean's instincts, it had made no sense to me to put an investment on hold for ten years with no promise that the current successes would continue. I knew there had to be more to the story. "And Mrs. Campbell is reluctant to sell, because . . . ?"

Bindy glanced toward the doorway leading into the dining room. "They can't hear me, can they?"

I shook my head.

"The company looking to acquire Zendy intends to change its mission."

"How so?"

"Zendy is worth more in pieces than it is as a whole." She licked her lips. "If they sell now, Zendy will be split up into smaller units and sold off one at a time."

"What will happen to the philanthropic agenda?"

She shrugged, then gave a slight giggle. "That's one of the downsides. But that's a small price to pay for all the good the four partners can do with the proceeds."

"I understand now why Mrs. Campbell is opposed to the sale." I remembered her comment on Thursday, arguing that the new owners might not respect the same goals.

"That's it," she said.

"Sounds like Senator Blanchard is tired of giving away the money to the needy and wants to collect the proceeds of the sale for himself."

Put that way, my reflections made Bindy squirm. "It isn't Treyton," she said. "It's that Nick Volkov. You heard about all the trouble he's in."

"There's no way he's hurting for money to pay for legal counsel," I said. "I don't buy it."

"You have no idea how deep he's in debt."

"But you do."

She looked away. "I know stuff," she admitted.

I had a sudden thought. "Is Senator Blanchard planning to run for president?"

When her eyes met mine in that immediate, panicked way, I knew I'd struck a nerve.

"No," she said unconvincingly. "He's the same party as President Campbell. That would be silly."

"True."

I stood and finished setting up the serving trays, arranging the sorbet so it would look pretty as well as appetizing. I peered into the dining room and saw that both Mrs. Campbell and Senator Blanchard had pushed their empty plates just a little forward. They were done. Moments later, I had their places cleared and dessert served.

Back in the kitchen, I asked Bindy, "And so why are you here?"

"I told you. We thought that this dinner was involving more people."

For some reason I doubted her. But I couldn't think of any other plausible reason for her presence, so I let it go.

When the First Lady and the senator were finished eating, I cleared the table one final time, but since they were deep in conversation, I didn't interrupt. As I washed the remaining dishes and put everything away, Bindy and I discussed the gingerbread men. "They're incredible," I said.

"Thanks. We worked hard on them," she said.

"You and the Blanchards' chef?" I asked with a tilt to my head and a tone in my voice that asked if she and the chef were romantically involved. She turned away without answering and tried to listen in to the dining room conversation again. Mrs. Campbell and the senator had gone so quiet that there was no hearing them at this point.

"Oh, I almost forgot," she said, pulling her package onto the tabletop. She gave the top of the diplomatic pouch a little pat. "This is for you."

I was confused.

Bindy explained. "Treyton is so grateful you agreed to handle the gingerbread men that he asked me to give you this." She pushed it toward me. "Just to say thank you."

"I can't accept . . ."

"I know, but it really isn't for you exactly. It's for the kitchen. He figured that'd be okay."

As I opened the weighty bundle, Bindy bit her lip. I wondered if she'd picked it out.

"Thank you," I said, as the object came free of its packaging. "It's lovely."

It was a clock. A bit large for a desk clock—about the size of a hardcover novel—it would have looked more at home in a French Provincial sitting room than in the White House kitchen. The clock face was small, but it was surrounded by a wide border of gold-colored heavy metal. Had it been real gold, I probably could have retired. As it was, the garish thing looked as though someone had picked it out as a joke, or for a white elephant gift exchange. "Thank you," I said.

Bindy breathed a sigh of relief. "You like it?"

"Sure!" I said. "I'll keep it in the kitchen right where we all can see it." To myself, I added that we'd keep it there long enough for Bindy to see it a couple of times. Then off to the warehouse with this clunker. "You really shouldn't have," I said, wishing she hadn't, "but thank you."

I offered coffee on my last foray into the dining room, but Blanchard declined. He stood. "Has Bindy been good company?" he asked me. "I'm so sorry we had a misunderstanding, but she said she hoped she might be of help back there."

She must have heard her name because before he finished asking, she was at my side. "I enjoyed reconnecting with Ollie," she said, with a little lilt to her voice that belied her words.

"That's great," Blanchard said. To Mrs. Campbell, he smiled and nodded. "It's been a pleasure, as always, Elaine. I hope you'll give some serious thought to the matters we discussed."

"Of course," she said.

"The clock's ticking," he said, tapping his watch. "I don't want you to forget."

With a smile that took the sting out of her words, Mrs. Campbell said, "How can I, when you're so eager to remind me?"

BY THE TIME I GOT BACK TO THE KITCHEN—MY KITCHEN ON THE ground floor, that is—everyone had left for the day with the exception of Cyan and Bucky. They looked as exhausted as I felt. "Go home," I said.

Cyan tried to argue, but I shook my head.

"We'll start fresh in the morning," I said. "It's been a tough few days, but I think we made good headway. Tomorrow we'll turn the corner."

The relief in their eyes made me glad I'd insisted. "What time tomorrow?" Cyan asked.

With the president in residence, we'd be preparing full meals all day. As Cyan and Bucky traded information and agreed on plans for the next morning, I had a happy thought: The president back in town meant that Tom was back in town, too. Our schedules had kept us apart for too many days in a row. I needed to talk with him. Heck, I just needed to *be* with him.

Fifteen minutes after Cyan and Bucky left, I was headed to the McPherson Square Metro station for my ride home.

A train pulled into the station just as I made it to the platform. Perfect timing. I claimed a seat near the door and rested my head against the side window, allowing myself to relax just a little bit. I decided to wait to try calling Tom until I was walking to my apartment building. Less chance of losing our connection than if I tried to call while racing underground.

When I emerged outside again, it seemed the temperature had dropped ten degrees. We'd been in the mid-fifties lately, but tonight's raw air and sharp wind caused my eyes to tear. I shivered, pulling my jacket close, trying to fight the trembling chill.

I loved my jacket. Filled with down, I'd brought it with me from Chicago, where it very effectively blocked the wicked wind. January in Chicago always meant bundling up with a hat, a sweatshirt hood covering that, and big, insulated mittens. Today, here in D.C., I took no such precautions. It was just me and my jacket against this peculiarly icy wind.

With my head ducked deep into my turned-up collar and wisps of hair dancing around my face, I couldn't see much more than my feet beating a quick pace to my apartment building. I gave up the idea of calling Tom. My right hand pressed deep into my pocket, hiding from the cold, while my brave left hand pulled the collar close to my face so only my eyes and nose poked above it.

When the clouds above me opened and the rain came, I squinted against the sharp prickles of ice that stung my face. My quick walk became a hurried trot. It was then I noticed the accompanying trot behind me. Someone else was hurrying to get wherever he needed to go. Despite the fact that I was moving pretty fast, the person behind me was moving faster.

I glanced back. A man in a black Windbreaker was closing. With it being so dark, and with the icy rain blurring the street and my vision, I couldn't tell the guy's age, but he had to be fairly young—or in very good shape—to be moving at such a quick clip. Wearing blue jeans and shoes that made a unique double-clicking sound as he walked—almost as though he wore tap shoes—the man kept his head down. He wore a baseball cap with a dark hooded sweatshirt pulled tight around his face. Both hands were stuffed in his pockets.

Maintaining my own hurried pace, I eased to the right of the sidewalk to let the runner go by, peering over the edge of my collar as he got close enough to pass. He was tall—maybe six foot—and if the tight jacket was any indication, he weighed more than two hundred pounds.

There was a tree in my path. I could scoot left and possibly bump this guy, or go way off to the right, near the curb.

I veered right, hoping to reclaim my wide sidewalk berth once the guy passed me.

But he didn't.

Coming around the tree, I was forced to either speed up or slow down. He'd slowed his own pace and was now blocking my way. This was like a bad merge on an expressway.

I wrinkled my nose against the cold and eased in behind him. My apartment was just another couple of blocks away, and I rationalized that this big, bulky guy would block the wind for me.

But when I got behind him, he slowed down again. The trot lessened to a brisk walk, then lessened again to what could only generously be called a stroll.

Was this guy playing games with me? Did he not know I was behind him?

Whatever was going on, it was giving me the creeps. My building wasn't much farther, and I'd planned to cross the street at the light, but common sense told me to change my course right now.

I shot over to the curb and waited for a pair of shiny headlights to pass before racing across the street. My heart pounded as I skipped up the far curb. I chastised myself for my anxiety. Just my imagination working overtime again. I knew I had a paranoid streak, but the truth was, that paranoia had come in handy more times than I cared to count.

I pulled my collar close again, and tried to make out where the guy across the street had gone. The sleet was heavier and the cold seemed to worsen with every slash of rain against the dark cement. I couldn't wait to climb into my flannels and pull a cover over my chilled limbs. I couldn't see the opposite side of the street, but I took comfort in the fact that it meant he couldn't see me, either.

Just the same, I resumed my trot. A moving target is harder to hit, as Tom always tells me. I smiled again at the thought of calling him. With any luck, he'd brave the elements and we could snuggle under those covers together.

My smile vanished when I heard the double-clicks again. Behind me. No way.

I was about to turn to see what I already knew—that the bulky guy was back—but by the time my head twisted over my shoulder, it was too late.

In a searingly hot second, he kicked me in the left knee. I shouted, both in pain and surprise. Unprepared for the attack, I flew facefirst to the sidewalk, my arms coming up just in time to break my fall. Even as I went down screaming, I prayed my hands and fingers wouldn't be hurt. They were my life, my livelihood.

The bulky guy didn't break stride, didn't turn.

Once I was down, he broke into a full-out run and was gone.

"Hey!" I yelled, noticing belatedly that my purse was gone. "Hey!" I said again, but by then I knew it was futile. I tried sitting up, but in the cold my knees felt as brittle as glass. At the same time, my palms burned from where I'd skimmed the sidewalk.

I shouted after him. "You big jerk!"

A soft voice next to me. "Are you okay?"

I felt a tug at my elbow. A small man hovered over me. Even from my seat on the wet sidewalk, I could tell he was shorter than I was. He pulled at my elbow again, trying to help me stand up. When I tried to get my footing, I slipped and sat down hard in wet dirt.

"Ick," I said, wincing as I struggled to my feet. "I'm okay."

"You are sure?" The man's voice held the touch of an accent and now that I stood up, I got a better look at my would-be rescuer. He was of Asian descent with hair so short as to be almost invisible. Although I couldn't peg his age, I guessed him to be on the far side of fifty. "What did that man do to you?" Using just his eyes, he gestured toward an idling car. "I was driving past and I saw him push you down."

I wiped my face with the back of my hand, trying to compose myself. The past several days had crushed the very energy out of everyone at the White House. But this was too much. After everything we'd been through, I shouldn't have to deal with this. Not today. I stared after the jerk who'd grabbed my purse, fighting overwhelming despair. All my ID was in there. Everything. I'd have to jump through a hundred hoops tomorrow just to get into work. I shook my head, then realized the little guy was waiting for me to say something. "I'm okay. He kicked me. Stole my purse."

"I am so sorry."

"Yeah," I said, blinking against the rain. "Me, too."

"I am Shan-Yu," he said, stepping forward.

"I'm Ollie," I said, responding automatically, thinking that I'd prefer to limp home in a hurry rather than stand in the sleet and chat. My mind was furiously trying to process everything that had just happened, but ingrained politeness kept me steady.

Shan-Yu gestured again with his eyes, keeping his hands together low at his waist. "May I offer you a ride?"

"No, thank you," I said, slapping my backside to release the dirt that crusted there. It hurt my hands, so I stopped immediately. "I live on the next block."

"As do I," he said, then mentioned his address.

"That's my building, too," I said.

He smiled. "Please, it would be my pleasure to help you after your encounter."

The biting rain had turned into a full-out downpour. I looked at the little guy standing next to me, his smile the only brightness in the dark enveloping rain.

"Thanks," I said. "That would be nice."

The Toyota Celica's windshield wipers were flapping as we made our way over. "Allow me," he said, and he glided ahead to open the passenger door.

We were directly under a streetlight, and as I started around him, I turned once more to take a look at my backside. "Oh," I said, "I can't get in your car like this. I'll get mud all over your seats."

"Not a problem," he said, just a little bit too quickly.

I turned, ready to explain again about the dirt on my backside, but the little guy's eyes suddenly shifted. Too close to me now, he said, "Get in."

"No, really, I—"

Before I could react, he hit me, hard, in the abdomen. I doubled over and he shoved me into the open door, pushing me down onto the seat. Neither of us counted on the ground being wet, however, and to his dismay and my delight, I slipped and fell to the ground, out of his immediate reach. Scrambling toward the back of the car on all fours, I screamed, both in terror and from the pain. "Help me!"

Every ounce of me surged out in my screams. I tried to get my footing, but he kicked me in the side. The darkness impaired his aim and it hit me only as a glancing blow. Still, it was enough to throw off my balance. "Help!" My voice carried along the wet street and I thought I heard an answer. My voice strained with effort. "Please!"

The little guy had begun to pull at the back of my jacket, and though I already knew I was no match for him, I remembered what Tom had told me about the knees—a lesson recently reviewed with the passing tap-shoe guy. With Shan-Yu's hands gripping the fabric on my back, I wrenched sideways and lashed out at him with my foot. I connected with his knee, just as Mr. Tap Shoes had connected with mine. The little guy went down.

Fighting sparkles of pain that danced before my eyes, I made myself stand—just in time. Although he'd gone down, he didn't stay there. In one smooth roll, he'd bounced himself back to his feet and come at me again.

I dodged him, spinning around the back of the car and racing to the open driver's-side door. I'd thought to jump in and drive away, but Shan-Yu was too fast, too close. Just as I got near the door, I whirled to face him. He hadn't expected that. When I ducked, he toppled over me. Scratching, biting, and screaming, I fought my way out from under him, hearing footsteps—loud ones—and knowing I had almost nothing left with which to fight.

"Hey!" someone yelled.

Shan-Yu turned long enough for me to get another good look at his face. I scrambled out of the way of the back tires as he leaped into the car and tore off down the street.

A big guy wearing jogging pants and a do-rag leaned down to me, rain pouring down his bewildered face. "Are you okay?"

CHAPTER 14

I SPENT MOST OF THE NIGHT IN THE EMERGENCY ROOM, GIVING the Metropolitan Police a statement, descriptions of both Mr. Tap Shoes and the man who identified himself as Shan-Yu, and a description of the car. Two things I learned from the cops—one: The bad guy hurts you, Good Samaritan helps you game is one of the oldest in the book. Two, the tap shoes were probably special steel-toed shoes designed to inflict maximum damage on kicked opponents.

Once I'd been identified, the Secret Service was called in to find out what sensitive items I might have lost in the theft. Agents Kevin Martin and Patricia Berland showed up while my knee was being examined. I was moved to a room with a door so they could interrogate me in private.

"We need a comprehensive list of everything in your purse," Agent Martin said. "I do mean everything. Even personal items you believe may have no significance."

I came up with the best recollection I could. In addition to my ID, I had keys: for my apartment, my car, and a number of them for the White House. The two agents were not happy. "I have some notes, a few recipes. . . ." Oh, God, what a mess. "My Metro pass . . ." I named everything else I could think of, including personal female items that made me blush when I listed them.

They asked me if I thought I'd been targeted specifically. "No," I said, then stopped. "Wait. . . ."

"What?"

"The guy in the car," I said, thinking aloud. "He told me he lived in my building."

The two agents exchanged a look. "Was this before you told him where you lived?"

"Yes," I said, warming to the subject now. "He rattled off the address of my building, so that's why I believed him—but he came up with the address first. He must have known where I lived."

We talked a bit longer, both agents peppering me with questions designed to jog my memory.

"Keep all this information to yourself when you're back at the White House," Agent Martin said when the interview was over. "When do you plan to return?"

"Tomorrow," I said. Glancing at the clock on the wall over his head, I amended. "I mean, today."

Although they attempted to talk me out of returning in the morning, they didn't forbid me to do so. Their grudging acceptance might have been due to my spirited explanation of the difficulties of getting the residence together for the holiday opening. Or, it might have been my nonstop pleading. Mostly I think they just wanted to shut me up.

From the doorway, I heard a familiar voice asking for me.

"Tom!" I called.

Tall and muscular, Tom looked even more handsome tonight than he usually did. He wore his customary Secret Service apparel—a business suit—but his hair was tousled as though he'd raced the whole way from the president's side to come see me. He edged around Agents Martin and Berland, acknowledging them with a nod. "I'll see Ms. Paras home," he said to them.

Kevin Martin's mouth twitched. "Yes, sir." He turned to me. "Are you comfortable with Agent MacKenzie escorting you home?"

At this point, despite my aches, I was all smiles. "I'm perfectly comfortable," I said.

Agent Berland was either in the dark about my relationship with Tom, or she pretended very well.

"Good night, then," Martin said. "We'll be in touch."

As soon as they were gone, Tom came close. He started to put his arms around me, stopped himself, and gently gripped my shoulders with both hands. "Are you okay?"

"Better now," I said. "God, you look so good." I started to reach around to hug him, but he held me at arm's length.

"I'm afraid I'll hurt you."

"I'm willing to risk it," I said, and pulled him close.

Yeah, it stung, but the hug was worth it.

I brought him up-to-date on the altercation that landed me in the emergency room, with him shaking his head the whole while. "Ollie," he said, "you've got to be more careful."

He was right, but I hated being told things I already knew. "I thought I was."

"Remember last time."

I shuddered when I thought about the terrifying incident right before I'd been promoted to executive chef. Tom took my reaction as an invitation to lecture me a bit more. Not that I blamed him.

"Those of us associated with the White House have to be extra vigilant."

"I know. I just can't imagine why anyone would target me."

"And that's why the criminals have the upper hand. Because no one expects to be attacked." With a pensive expression, he skimmed his fingers along the side of my face. "I wish I wasn't on duty tomorrow."

"I wish you weren't, either."

Once all the hospital paperwork was complete, Tom helped me to his car. He had keys to my apartment, which allowed us to get in, and he'd arranged for a locksmith to meet us there. Amidst a lot of drilling and scraping—annoying my neighbor till two in the morning—my apartment was outfitted with spanking-new locks.

"Here you go, miss," Lou, the weary locksmith, said as he dangled the keys in front of me. "Good, solid brand I put in. You'll really enjoy these."

Enjoying locks was not something I anticipated, but I thanked Lou and tumbled into bed the minute he was gone. Tom insisted on staying with me, and I finally relaxed with him stroking my cheeks and forehead. Thank God for kindness in this world, I thought, and drifted safely off to dreamland.

"OH, MY GOD," CYAN SAID WHEN SHE SAW MY HANDS THE NEXT morning. "You can't work like that."

"I know," I said. "What horrible timing, huh?"

She cocked an eyebrow. "Like there's a good time?"

She had a point.

"One positive thing," she said, as we got started. "Turns out the president and Mrs. Campbell are out all day, after all. That'll take some pressure off."

I hated delegating every task, but I was faced with little choice. Although I had no open cuts—that would have banished me from the kitchen completely for the duration of my healing—I wore an Ace bandage on my left hand and a splint on my right ring finger. The doctors told me I'd bruised my left ulna and jammed the finger on my right. Nothing debilitating, but bandages were hardly sterile when it came to working with food, so I found myself more the executive and less the chef for most of the morning.

Just as we started to hum, Gavin strode into the kitchen and came straight to me. "What happened last night?"

I'd taken to keeping my fingers clasped behind my back except when working at the computer. The move prevented me from inadvertently "helping" my colleagues.

"You mean this?" I asked, bringing my hands forward. "How did you find out?"

"It is my business to know about everything involving the security of the White House."

I figured as much.

Gavin fixed me with a piercing look. "I understand you fought off your attacker."

As much as I hated to admit it, I was still shaken by the experience, and I didn't appreciate the fact that Gav here wore an expression that told me he expected a blow-by-blow rehashing.

"'Fought off' is a bit of an exaggeration," I said. "I screamed like an idiot. If that jogger hadn't come along . . ." I shivered, remembering. "The two guys who got me really knew what they were doing. They set me up perfectly. I'm embarrassed to have fallen for their scheme." Though it was hard for me to say so, I admitted my gullibility. "I trusted the little guy who pretended to help me."

"I was told he used martial arts moves against you."

My hand came up of its own volition, and I touched the tender place under my ribs where he'd struck me. "Whatever it was, it hurt."

Gavin seemed about to say something else, but remained silent, staring at me. He finally said, "You aren't able to work?"

Bucky made eye contact from across the room. He arched an eyebrow and shook his head fractionally.

Message received. "I'm getting a lot done here, actually," I said, sounding more upbeat than I felt. "My predecessor, Henry, always told me I needed to learn to delegate more. Today I'm getting a perfect opportunity."

"I was hoping to continue your training."

Did this guy think I was planning to enlist in the military? How much more training did I need? My hands came up in response. I said, "I'm sorry," even though I wasn't.

I was, however, very glad when he left us again. "Tell you what," I said to the group. "Let me go get some of our holiday décor. While you guys work on the food, I'll start bringing a bunch of the fun stuff here."

They all looked up at me as though I was nuts. Rafe spoke. "With two damaged hands?"

I frowned. "I'll be careful. This really isn't that big of a deal."

Cyan shook her head. "You always get in such trouble, Ollie."

"How much trouble can I get into in the storage room?"

I MADE MY WAY THROUGH CONNECTING HALLWAYS, PAST THE carpenter's, electrical, and flower shops. I fiddled with my replacement keys to unlock one of the storage rooms the kitchen controlled. My White House ID and other important items had been replaced much more quickly than I'd expected. Thank goodness.

The storage room was large, about ten feet by fifteen, and it was packed. There was limited floor space and the shelves overflowed with stuff I knew I should inventory. For about the hundredth time, I promised I'd get to it just as soon as things calmed down.

Large gray storage containers lined one wall. About four foot square and just over two feet tall, each wheeled container held presidential china. We kept the most popular patterns closer to the kitchen, and since this particular room was the farthest from our work center, it held the china patterns we used least. I pushed at the closest of the gray monsters—this one held Lyndon Johnson's pattern—to access the boxes I intended to scavenge.

Every year, grinning with holiday spirit, Henry made the trek down here to pull out fun things for the kitchen staff to use during the holiday season. He loved decorating the kitchen himself. Kendra and her staff didn't mind because none of what we used was ever seen by the public. Henry usually waited until the entire White House was completely finished before exercising his decorating muscle. He called the final kitchen embellishment his pièce de résistance.

I liked Henry's tradition, and I intended to continue it. With all that we'd gone through recently, however, I believed our festive mood needed a boost sooner rather than later.

I pushed another of the big bins out of the way, but realized, in doing so, I'd blocked my path out. There was only one solution: I pushed the two out into the hallway, and pulled out the boxes of tchotchkes I planned to make use of.

There was not, unfortunately, any type of cart I could use to transport my treasures to the kitchen. With my tender arm and splinted finger, I wasn't in the best position to carry the boxes myself.

Heading out again, I started for the electrical shop with two purposes in mind: getting a cart, and talking with Manny again, if I could pin him down. Based on our prior conversation, there was little reason to believe he would have checked out my floating neutral question. But I'm nothing if not tenacious.

Manny was nowhere to be found, but Vince sat on a stool at a small workbench, eating. "Do you have a minute?" I asked.

Startled, he just about fell off the seat. "You scared me," he said around one stuffed cheek. His gaze took in my bandaged arm and splinted finger.

"Sorry." I wandered in. "What do you have there?"

He held up half a sandwich. "Chicken."

Unsurprised, I nodded. Tradesmen generally didn't eat in the lower-level cafeteria. They went out, or brought their own food in. This was a throwback tradition from the White House's early days, when the household staff was mostly black, and the tradesmen white. Because nineteenth-century black employees couldn't find establishments to serve them in the nearby D.C. area, the White House provided meals. White tradesmen, having no such difficulty, went out for lunch or dinner each day. Over time the White House staff became infinitely more diverse. Of course, now blacks and whites occupied all staff levels, but the tradesman tradition—if you could call it that—continued. To this day, regardless of their race or ethnicity, tradesmen rarely ate in the White House cafeteria.

He stared at me as I moved closer. I got the distinct impression he didn't like the idea of the chef entering the electrician's lair. His constant jumpy glances toward the doorway behind me led me to believe he was expecting someone. Probably Curly. I'd have to make this quick. "Did Manny say anything to you about floating neutrals?"

Vince moved the wad of food from his cheek and chewed it before answering. I'd expected him to nod or shake his head, but he waited till he swallowed to say. "Uh . . . yeah."

"And?"

Vince glanced past me toward the doorway again. "And what?"

"Did you guys check? Was there something wrong with the ground when Gene got electrocuted?"

A voice boomed behind me. "What the hell are you doing here?"

I turned and there he was. Surly Curly, in the flesh. Knowing I could no longer press my question, I changed direction and offered him the friendliest smile I could. "I have to carry a few boxes to the kitchen, but . . ." I held up my injured hands. "No way to get them over there. I was wondering if you had a wheeled cart I could borrow?"

His mouth worked, as though pushing his angry grimace to one side. "Yeah, I got one." Shuffling to a nook just out of view, he came back with a gray dolly. "Boxes, you say?"

When I nodded, he switched the handle of the dolly, converting it from vertical to horizontal. "Here," he said, "easier to manage. You bring this back, you understand? I don't want to go hunting for it when I need it next."

"I'll bring it right back."

Vince hunched his shoulders as though to render himself invisible. I thanked Curly and headed back to the storage area, wondering if I'd ever get anyone to give me a straight answer to the floating neutral question.

FOUR HOURS LATER, AFTER HAVING DECORATED THE KITCHEN TO the best of my holiday abilities given the collection of cute pot holders, trivets, and dish towels I'd pulled out, I headed back to the storage area to put the empty boxes away and to return Curly's precious dolly.

I wheeled it into the storeroom and had intended to replace the first box in its nook, when I realized that the china storage containers were not the way I'd left them. The Johnson china was pushed far to the right, completely out of place. That was odd. No one usually used this storage room except kitchen staff, and I couldn't recall anyone else mentioning a visit here in the past few hours.

Curious, I tugged the big gray bin, wondering what else might have been rearranged. Most of the time it wouldn't matter, but on the rare occasion we needed supplies from this area, I liked to be confident they were here. The idea that items had been shifted peeved me just a bit. Storage space was at a premium at the White House, and this area was designated for kitchen items only.

Another department must have tried to encroach on our space, hoping no one would notice a stray item or two.

I pushed the wheeled bin of Johnson china out of the way and found an unfamiliar square brown box, crudely marked STORAGE on one side and along the sealed top. This did not belong to the kitchen. Worse, it hadn't been here this morning. Someone had snuck it in here, very recently.

I did a quick, cursory examination of the room to locate any other stray boxes, but within a few minutes I realized this was the only unexpected addition to our stash.

There were no other markings on the box, and no way to tell which department had tucked it in here. I sighed with exasperation. I could just leave it here—it didn't take up an enormous amount of space—but doing so invited further incursions. Although this seemed like a trivial matter, and unworthy of the analysis I was affording it, I still suffered from the newness of my executive chef position. Sure, I'd earned the title, but I also needed to command respect. Were Henry here, I imagined he would nip this little nuisance in the bud.

I lifted the box onto the gray bin. I didn't have a knife to slice open the seal, but the dolly had metal clasps that Curly had used to readjust the handle. I pulled one of the silver clips from its anchoring hole, and pushed the metal end against the paper, ripping it. Within seconds I'd scored both ends and the center seam. I dropped the clip into my pocket and repositioned the box on the floor for leverage before attempting to open the flaps.

Whoever had sealed this thing had done a masterful job. I yanked three times before the first flap ripped free. The second flap snapped up with a quick pull and I pulled away excelsior to find out what was so important that had to be stored in my department's area.

More excelsior.

Finally, my fingers hit something hard. Metal or glass, I couldn't tell. I was on my knees, wrapping my fingers around the item's cylindrical shape, tugging upward. Stuck. Stray stuffing obscured my view of the article, but my fingers traced along its sides. Bottle-shaped, it seemed light enough, but as I pulled more shredded paper from around it with my left hand, my right discovered that both ends of the bottle were connected by wire to a flat board at the box's bottom.

I yanked my hand away. Heart racing, I felt my jaw go limp. I removed the remaining packaging material and stifled a scream of surprise when I saw the explosives.

This was an IED.

"Help," I said too softly, too weakly. I stood, calling out again, knowing no one would hear me. I ran out the door, intent on getting in touch with the Secret Service. But . . . I couldn't just run away. There were others in this area—in the carpenter's area, the florist's office, the laundry. I couldn't let innocent people there wait until something exploded.

I ran to the laundry room. "Get out," I screamed. "Hurry! A bomb. A bomb!"

I heard movement, and one of the laundry ladies came around the corner, looking confused.

"Get everybody out," I said, already running toward the florist's area. "Get out now, and get help!"

After warning as many people as I could, I ran into the nearest work area—the electrical shop. No one there.

Their phone was near the workbench. I picked it up and connected with the emergency operator. She told me to leave immediately and that help was on the way. I ran.

More than a dozen people were making their way quickly to the Center Hall, heading into the Diplomatic Reception Room, where they could evacuate via the south doors.

I skidded around the corner and rushed to the kitchen. My team stared up at me with wide eyes. "Everybody out," I said.

Bucky started to say something.

I waved them forward, toward me and the door. "Now."

They took one look at my face and filed out. Mentally, I tallied them, making sure that everyone was accounted for.

Secret Service agents moved in fast. Before I could even think about what to do next, they'd covered every inch of the White House, urging people out the doors, barking orders, and taking firm control.

By the time I made it outside myself, I estimated we'd evacuated the residence in under three minutes. Not bad for a staff of more than ninety. I stared at the building, waiting. Wondering what would happen next.

I made my way over to my group. Bucky was talking with Rafe and Agda, and Cyan was listening in. They shifted their small circle to let me in.

"It's freezing out here," Cyan said, hugging herself. "I hope we don't get stuck outside for very long. What happened?"

I rubbed my own arms but as I tried to explain, the wind whipped my words away. I had to raise my voice as I repeated myself.

"You found a bomb?" Cyan said, with incredulity in her voice. "Are you sure?"

I opened my mouth to answer, realizing I wasn't sure at all. Maybe I'd overreacted. "It was . . ." My words faltered. I turned, taking a look at my colleagues—the rest of the White House staff—all of us huddled in small groups against the bitter chill. We were all out here, freezing, rather than inside doing our work. Just because I'd sounded an alarm.

"I think it was a bomb," I said finally.

"You *think*?" Bucky said. "You don't know?"

My stomach dropped. With the benefit of hindsight, I realized I didn't really know what a bomb looked like. Just because this one had some of the same features as the one Gavin had shown us didn't mean that it posed any real threat.

Bucky wasn't happy. Breath-clouds poured out of his mouth as he asked, "Was it ticking?"

"No."

He exhaled sharply and walked over to join another group.

Maybe I should have simply called the Secret Service and let them handle it. Maybe if I'd done that, we'd all still be safely inside, and warm. The small groups of staffers snuck glances in my direction. I was sure they were discussing my "sky is falling" cries. The group around me chatted, keeping an eye on the activity just outside the south doors where a team of helmeted, black-cad individuals ran in.

"Bomb team," Rafe said.

We all nodded, silent now. Far enough away to feel safe, we could see the action but there was no way to make out faces from this distance. Secret Service personnel were maintaining a perimeter a distance away from the south doors, but I couldn't see who was on duty. I didn't expect any of them to be Tom, though. As part of the elite Presidential Protection Detail, he would be with President Campbell, wherever that may be.

Bucky wandered back with a swagger. "It's a fake."

"What?" we all asked at once.

Clearly pleased to be the source of insider information, Bucky took his time answering. "I was talking to Angela," he said. "She got a call from her brother, who has a friend on the bomb squad."

He continued. My stomach dropped.

"Nothing there. The thing Ollie found was probably just some junk. Not a bomb."

He kept talking about what a mess this was, and what a hassle we were all dealing with because of my too-quick-on-the-trigger response.

Feeling my face grow hot, I was about to argue that it's better to be safe than sorry, when Gavin stepped into our little group. Despite the bracing wind, he looked unruffled, though not pleased.

"Ms. Paras," he said. "Come with me."

Cyan gave me a pitying look.

"Is there some way we can get the staff inside?" I asked.

Gavin kept looking straight ahead. "It is being taken care of."

"What will they—"

"Ms. Paras, the comfort of your colleagues is not my immediate concern, but if it eases your mind, buses have been dispatched to pick everyone up and to keep them together."

I remembered how much time that took when I was sequestered with Mrs. Campbell and Sean in the bunker. I remembered Bucky's complaints. Had that been only a couple of days ago? So much had happened since then.

As we walked, I relived my adventure in the bunker and thought about Sean. My heart gave a little wobble. What had happened there? And how could I be missing someone I hadn't really known all that well?

A moment later it dawned on me that we weren't walking back to the White House. Gavin was leading me away, toward an idling black car. A Secret Service agent I didn't recognize opened the back door for me.

This was like something out of a spy movie.

"What—?"

"Just get in," Gavin said.

The car's warmth and smell of new leather helped lessen the goose bumps I bore from the cold. The ones from fear were still popping, mightily. "What's going on?" I asked when he sidled in beside me.

There was a driver and another man in the front seat. They both turned.

Gavin spoke, his enunciation so crisp, new goose bumps zoomed up the back of my arms and traipsed across my shoulders. "Tell me exactly what happened."

I did. They recorded my description of finding the box and opening it.

"Why didn't you call security the moment you saw the box?" Gavin asked.

I looked at him as though he was nuts. "It was a brown box in a storage room," I said with a little sharpness to my tone. "And it was marked for storage. Why would I ever be suspicious of something like that?"

The three men exchanged looks. I felt like the new kid at school, missing all the inside jokes because I wasn't considered "cool" yet.

"I already heard that I blew it," I said. "So why am I being questioned?"

Gavin gave me a puzzled look, but he answered. "In due course, Ms. Paras. Right now we need to go over your story again."

I sighed. "Okay." Again I recited the chain of events as best I could.

Gavin worked his lips as I spoke, his gaze never wavering from mine. I occasionally shifted my attention to the other two men, as though to include them in my narration, but Gavin grew more agitated by the moment. When noise outside the car drew the men's attention away from me, I had a moment of relief.

A man dressed all in black and wearing body armor rapped at the window. Gavin got out.

"You stay here," he said to me before slamming the door.

I turned to the other two. "Did I do something wrong?"

They were both about thirty years old. The shorter one had dark hair and a pale complexion. The taller one was broad-shouldered, with sandy hair. Since he was in the passenger seat and I was directly behind him, I could only see his face in profile when he turned to me. The two men exchanged another look.

"You guys are making me nervous," I said. "Can't you tell me what's happening?"

The driver stared out his side window. The passenger said, "No, ma'am," and shifted his attention away.

I watched buses pull up and I could imagine Bucky complaining about the fact that I sat in a warm black sedan while he and the others were relegated to school bus–quality accommodations.

Silence in the car dragged me down. Gavin had gone off with the black-clad man and I attempted to put the time to good use. I began prioritizing tasks, working backward from our next target: the reception after the White House official ceremonies. Although I'd pressed Marguerite for an answer, she still didn't know whether the Campbells would participate this year or not. Sean's death had changed everything. The White House would still open on Tuesday to the public; but in the meantime, everything else was up for grabs.

"How much longer, do you think?" I asked my escorts.

The bigger guy replied. "Don't know, ma'am."

I watched minutes tick by on the dashboard clock. More than forty-five minutes later, Gavin finally returned. He opened the door and gestured me out. "Thank you, gentlemen," he said to the two men up front. "You may return."

He didn't say where they were returning to, and they apparently didn't need to ask. As soon as I alighted and Gavin closed the door, they took off.

I felt like those little dogs who hustle their tiny paws to keep pace with their masters. Gavin didn't watch to make sure I was keeping up, he just made his way across the south lawn to the doors we'd exited from. "Special Agent Gavin," I called to his back.

He didn't stop moving, but his head tilted.

"What's going on?" I asked, a bit breathless from the wind and the running. He didn't answer, but it looked as though he shook his head.

As we reentered the White House, I stole a look backward to see what was going on with the rest of the staff. The buses were filled, but stationary. I hoped everyone had warmed up. Reporters were everywhere. They surrounded the grounds like a pack of eager hyenas waiting to pounce. News vans, with high-perched satellite dishes and camera crews, were everywhere. Pointing their lenses at us.

Inside, I wiped away tears that had formed from the wind beating against my face. Gavin caught me and something in his expression softened. "Everything will be all right, Ollie. This is just procedure."

Ollie? That was the first time he called me by my given name.

I was about to explain that I wasn't crying, but he started off again, expecting me to follow. His shiny black shoes made snappy clicks against the floor and I followed him back into the corridor, past all the now-quiet shops, to the storage area where I'd found the box.

CHAPTER 15

GAVIN MADE ME GO OVER MY STEPS, AS PRECISELY AS I COULD recall them. Very slowly. As I remembered and recited—again—another black-clad man took notes. Wearing body armor, a sniper rifle slung around his back and, a heated expression, he neither spoke nor made eye contact with me. I was sure everyone involved in this fracas was furious with me for having caused a major evacuation over nothing. Agents, snipers, and other assorted military folk were everywhere—the halls were filled with people speaking to one another and into radios.

The press would have a field day with this one, I was sure, and I only hoped I wouldn't be served up like a holiday turkey for them all to feast on.

After ten minutes of tracing my movements, we were still only about five feet inside the storage room. Gavin was insistent on stopping at each step so that the intense note-taker could get down every detail. Problem was, there was not much to tell. And I couldn't imagine why anyone cared about any of this. Unless they had reason to doubt my story.

I caught a quiver in my voice. God, I hated that. "This is where I noticed that the Johnson china had been moved."

Gavin nodded.

I took that as encouragement to continue. "So I pushed the bin aside, and found the"—I hesitated—"the box." I described it, even though I knew they both must have seen it.

"What then?"

"Well," I said, trying to be as precise as possible, "I knew it didn't belong here, so I decided to see what was inside." Shrugging, I added, "I planned to return it to whatever department had left it here."

"You said it was sealed."

Nodding, I remembered the clip from the dolly, still in my pocket. I pulled it out. "I used this to slice through the tape."

Gavin grimaced.

"Better than using my teeth," I said, in an effort to lighten the mood. Neither man smiled.

"It opened easily?"

I considered that. "Not really. I had to pull hard a few times in order to rip past the tape."

This time Gavin winced. "Dear God, Ollie. You ripped it open?"

"Yeah," I said, a little defensively. "It's not like I suspected anything when I first saw it. And it was sealed pretty tightly." I glanced at the two of them. Even the note-taker had looked up, and they were staring at me as though I'd done the stupidest thing in the world. "Geez, I understand we're supposed to be careful when we see things out of place, but you have to admit it really did look like normal storage stuff. There was no way I knew it was a fake bomb."

Gavin's eyes snapped to mine. "Fake bomb?" he asked. "What are you telling me? You found something else?"

"No . . ." Again I hesitated. "I'm talking about the thing I believed was an IED. The reason I called for help." My hands spread as though to encompass the entire White House grounds. "The reason I started screaming for everyone to evacuate. It was a fake, right?"

Gavin licked his lips and I could tell it was taking every measure of patience he had to slow himself down. "Ollie," he began, surprising me again with familiarity, "the thing you found was live."

My knees trembled. "It was?"

"Yes," he said, with high-strung tolerance. "You found a bomb. A real one." He ran a hand over his face. "Let's get through the rest of this and I'll tell you what I can."

We finished the how-I-found-a-bomb-and-learned-to-start-worrying exercise and the tall man with the notepad finally left us. The minute he was gone, I sat on the floor. It was cold.

"You okay?" Gavin asked.

"I suppose it would be a stupid question to ask if the bomb has been safely removed."

He took a seat on the floor next to me. "It's been defused and it's gone. We've done a sweep of the area and it looks clean."

Looks?

I rested my forehead against my upturned knees. "Why me?" I asked. "Why am I always the one who gets involved in this stuff?"

Gavin took a deep breath and I lifted my head to watch him. For the first time since I'd met him, he didn't seem furious with me. He seemed to be contemplating.

Commotion in the hallways continued, but no one poked a head in. All things considered, it was pretty quiet.

"I've been around these sorts of situations a lot, Ollie," he said, staring away. "Been on the job for over twenty-five years."

I waited.

"There are people who things happen to. And whether you consider it a blessing or a curse, you appear to be one of them." He turned to face me. "I read your dossier."

I winced.

"Don't be embarrassed," he said. "It's not that you have a black cloud over your head—it's that you have the ability to see and to sense things better than most." He wagged his head from side to side. "I'm not talking about ESP or clairvoyance, although maybe describing it as a sixth sense is apt. You have a great deal of intelligence and an acute awareness—more than most people— which allows you to notice things out of place. And you have the curiosity to find out why."

"It's a curse, all right."

"I disagree. We hire people with your talents every day."

I realized he was giving me a compliment. Fear, adrenaline, and now self-consciousness combined to render me speechless. I cleared my throat. "Thanks."

Back to staring away, he said, "With that in mind, I'm going to tell you something that isn't for public knowledge. But I want you to know so that we have another set of eyes out there." Gavin worked his tongue around the inside of his mouth. "The bomb was on a timer."

"When was it supposed to go off?"

Squinting, he said, "Sunday, during the White House opening ceremony."

My stomach lurched as I tried to digest that. At the same time, I was thinking how odd it was to be sitting here on the floor with Special Agent-in-Charge Gavin discussing bombs.

"If there's any consolation," Gavin went on, "and it isn't much, the IED was small. Personal size, if you want to call it that." He was so calm, it gave me a measure of comfort. "We get the impression this was meant to target one person."

"Me?"

He shrugged. "I doubt it, but after your altercation on the street, we're not overlooking the possibility."

"If it wasn't intended for me," I said, glancing around the storeroom, and hoping to God it hadn't been meant for me, "why put it here? If the intention is to do damage, there are much better places. This area is usually empty."

Gavin smiled. "You're right. We suspect the would-be terrorist wanted to get the IED inside first. He probably intended to move it later, to somewhere closer to the action."

"Makes sense," I said, still thrown by the relaxed attitude of our conversation. "I take it you're looking at everyone, right? Staff included."

"Every single person who's been inside the White House over the past twenty-four hours, cross-checked against everyone who was here the day the original prank bomb was found."

"I can't imagine anyone on staff being guilty."

"Remember what I told you at the introductory safety meeting," he said, looking at me again. "Don't see safety around you. Don't trust anyone."

"Aren't you trusting me by telling me all this?"

"I told you, I've been on the job for a long time." He stood and offered me a hand up. "I can see and sense things, too. You're okay, Ollie. You did the right thing."

"HE'S GOT THE HOTS FOR YOU," TOM SAID THAT NIGHT, BACK AT my apartment.

"Give me a break," I said, "Gav is probably fifteen years older than I am. . . ."

"Gav?"

Putting dinner leftovers away in the refrigerator while Tom rinsed the dishes, I gave a half shrug and turned away. "Yeah, he told me to call him that when we weren't around other staff members." All of a sudden I realized how that sounded. I spun. "It doesn't mean anything."

"He *definitely* has the hots for you."

Laughing now, I shut the fridge door. "Hardly. But I did catch something today that I didn't ever see before. I think he's actually beginning to respect me."

Tom wiped his hands on a dish towel. "He should. You single-handedly saved his backside."

"How so?"

"Gavin's the agent-in-charge, right?"

I nodded.

"You prevented a bombing. How would it look if it had gone off under his watch? If it weren't for you—"

"Just dumb luck," I said, waving away the accolades.

"Not just luck, Ollie. Gavin was right when he said you're one of those observant ones. Which is why I decided on the subject for tonight's lesson."

Over the past year and a half, Tom had taught me much—self-defense, gun handling, and target shooting, to name a few things. Many of these lessons had come in handy in the past and I was always eager for him to let me in on things that most people neither ever learn nor care about.

"Let me guess," I said. "Explosives?"

"Right."

I interrupted him before he could begin. "You do know that we've all had to take a class on this already, right?"

"Gavin taught it?"

"Yeah."

He made an unpleasant noise. "How is it that the executive chef can uncover an explosive device that the security forces missed?"

"Like I said, just dumb luck."

"No, Ollie. They should have found this one. And I hope to God they kept searching."

"They said they swept the place."

The look on Tom's face let me know what he thought of the team's competence. "*Now* they're pulling out all the stops. *Now* they're interviewing staff members. They should have done that when the prank bomb was found. They should have found the guy who planted that and found out why. The fact that they're taking so long to move on this is ludicrous."

"But how could anyone have known? Gav said—"

Tom silenced me with a look, and I realized I'd risen to Gavin's defense. "I'm not going to feel comfortable with the president—or you—in the White House until we get to the bottom of this bombing threat."

"Where is the president now?"

He frowned. "With family," he said. "I'll be headed to meet him in the morning. Then he's heading to Berlin. This is my only night off until Wednesday."

"Gotcha."

For the next hour, Tom walked me through Explosives 101. He was certainly more detailed than Gavin had been in class, but Tom suffered from not having examples on hand to share. He'd printed photos from declassified files and diagrams from Internet searches. By the time he finished, my head was chock-full of device strategies and configurations, all for methods of mass demolition. Fun stuff.

"The one thing you have to remember is this," he said, as he wound up. "There is almost always a secondary device."

"I'd heard that."

"It bears repeating. People in the business of destruction don't want to fall short. They set up fail-safes to ensure their plans move forward. To ensure their target is destroyed. Do you understand?"

A prickly feeling had come over me. "I do."

CHAPTER 16

SUNDAY MORNING, I RETURNED TO THE WHITE HOUSE KITCHEN, knowing I wouldn't hear from Tom again until Wednesday at the earliest. My mind was still reeling from all the bomb stuff he'd tried to teach me last night. I worked hard to assimilate information I hoped to never actually need.

To say I was jittery was an understatement. We'd gotten word that today's decorator tour at the White House was still on. Although Mrs. Campbell would forgo the Kennedy celebration, she would be here to greet guests afterward. With President Campbell out of the residence until Wednesday, the First Lady would be required to handle the event solo.

I still wore the splint on my right hand, which kept me relegated to working at the computer rather than putting meals together. Angry at the two men who'd put me in this position, I knew I needed to push through my harsh disappointment. Working on food was so much more fun than tapping away on a keyboard. Still, I forced myself to focus. While not as much fun as creating an entrée, updating files was a necessary chore, and I'd fallen way behind.

I took my seat in front of the monitor and glanced around the kitchen. My crew was preparing hors d'oeuvres for the afternoon's event—and they were doing so with terrific efficiency. Although I'd designed today's menu months ago—prepared samples and overseen the First Lady's tasting tests—today I felt utterly left out. My body still ached from the assault two nights ago, and my ego smarted from having to keep the bomb information secret. Not only could I not tell anyone else that yesterday's bomb had been real, I couldn't warn them that it had been scheduled to go off this very afternoon.

Bucky opened one of the cabinets. "Oh, my God!" We all turned to see him staring into the shelves with exaggerated, wide-eyed panic. He reached in and pulled out a bottle of cooking sherry. "Call security," he said, lifting the bottle over his head. "It might be a bomb."

I couldn't blame the kitchen crew for laughing. I pretended to, but I felt the heated rush of embarrassment fly from my chest to my face. Pointedly, I turned away to study the file open on my monitor. Nothing about it looked familiar, and yet it had been listed as one of my recent documents—which is why I'd opened it in the first place.

Bucky was now pretending the bottle of sherry was a machine gun. I ignored him for a long moment because we'd always bantered among ourselves and I didn't want to shut down our team's lighthearted teasing. But this time, mortification pounded in my ears. Suddenly too warm, I wiped the back of my hand across my brow. At least the rest of the kitchen staff was no longer laughing.

Changing tactics again, Bucky pranced around the center island, saying, "Get out before the cooking sherry explodes!"

I turned. "Enough."

"Can't take a little ribbing?" he asked.

If he only knew. "What I can't take is being behind schedule." I directed a look at the clock on the wall, then pointed to the eyesore Senator Blanchard had given us. "We've had plenty of interruptions this past week. Don't you think it's time we focused on our work instead of goofing around?"

Total silence in the kitchen while Cyan, Rafe, and Agda waited, wide-eyed, to see what would happen next.

Bucky strode over to the cabinet where he put the cooking sherry back and slammed the door.

I stifled an impatient response. Escalating the incident would only make things worse. I'd gotten what I wanted—what decorum demanded—but in doing so had I just quashed the easygoing cheer that characterized our kitchen? I bit my lip. Was it too much to ask that he comport himself like a professional rather than a troublesome fifth-grader? But that was Bucky, and such was the nature of temperamental geniuses. The man could nuance a dish in surprising and delightful ways, but put him in a social setting and all subtlety vanished like powdered sugar on hot pastry.

A voice behind me. "Ms. Paras. What are you doing here?"

I'd recognize Peter Everett Sargeant III's precise elocution anywhere. "Good morning," I said, turning. "What brings you to my kitchen today?"

He was perfectly pressed, as always. But today his characteristic etiquette was augmented by a nasty gleam in his eye. "I was under the impression you were scheduled for another emergency training session," he said. "After all, considering yesterday's . . . er . . . confusion it appears you're in need of remedial attention regarding proper protocols where security is concerned."

Did everyone intend to take a shot at me today? I wanted to scream the truth. But, to what end? To allow me to save face and possibly set up a panic situation? Yesterday, as we walked back to the kitchen, Gav had instructed me to keep quiet about what I knew. The Secret Service believed that the president's absence from the residence would prevent any future explosive attempts on the White House. At least until President Campbell returned. But by then, he assured me, they'd be ready.

"Thanks for checking with me, Peter," I said, minimizing the peculiar document I'd been studying. I slid off the seat. "But I think I'll be okay now. I was fortunate to be able to confer with Special Agent-in-Charge Gavin. He told me I did the right thing."

Sargeant had a squirrel-like way about him. He held his hands in front of his chest and tilted his head. "Wasn't that kind of him."

He looked ready to say more, but I interrupted. "Was there anything else?"

Nonplussed, he gave the kitchen a once-over. "Will everything be ready on time for today's reception?"

"Of course."

He sniffed. "I will return later."

As he left, I caught Cyan mouthing, "Much later."

I was beginning to think the entire place had turned negative. We were all stressed—this time of the year had that effect on us all—but Bucky and Sargeant were pushing it. If it hadn't been for Gav's pep talk and Tom's tutorial yesterday, I'd wonder if I were turning negative, too.

Back to the computer. I restored the minimized document and reread the first line. "Shrimp processing for the uninitiated."

What the heck?

Below that were crudely described directions for cleaning shrimp. I shook my head. I hadn't recorded this, and I doubted anyone else on my team had.

"What's up, Ollie?" Cyan asked.

I pointed to the screen. "There's a document here I've never seen before."

"That's weird," she said as she began to read.

"Yeah . . ." Then I remembered. I snapped my fingers.

"What?"

"Sean used this computer the other day," I said. "Remember?"

"To check his e-mail, right?"

I read the strangely worded preparations out loud: "Shrimp in a big bowl. Take them out one at a time. They can be slippery little buggers. Really hard to cut that vein thing out. See below for important safety warnings." Mystified, I turned to Cyan. "Sean must have recorded this, but why?"

"In case he ever came here to help again?" she said, but I could tell she was as unconvinced as I. "So he didn't forget how to do it?"

"No," I said, scrolling down the page. "I think he recorded this for us to find."

"For you to find, maybe." Cyan said. "I think he liked you."

Heaviness dropped in my heart like a lump of cold dough. Sean had indeed "liked" me, or so the First Lady had led me to believe. As I tripped past his crazy notes, I wondered why on earth he'd taken the time to write any of this up when he said he was checking e-mail.

I stopped scrolling when I saw my name.

A letter. Directed to me.

Ollie,

Hey. I don't know how soon you'll see this. Those shrimp are a pain to work with—did you give me that job because you think I'm a pain in your kitchen? Bucky seems annoyed that I'm on your computer. I'd swear he's baring his teeth at me. LOL. I hope you don't think I'm a pain. In fact I hope to pop in here more often in the coming weeks.

My heart jolted again. I bit my lip and continued to read:

Forget that for now. I've only got a second here before Bucky the wonder dog gets suspicious. I wanted to talk with you alone, but the more I spend time here, the more I realize that isn't going to happen. Not today. And tomorrow's going to be a tough one, too. I'll be here because Aunt Elaine asked me to, and because you did. Aunt Elaine doesn't know the people she's dealing with as well as she thinks she does. They've been trying to muscle me out. But their threats are meaningless. There's nothing to hold over my head.

But that makes me a pretty good catch, don't you think? LOL.

Ah . . . I've said too much.

Let me know when you get this. If I'm not already dead of embarrassment, we'll talk.

Yours,
Sean

I felt my shoulders slump.

"What's wrong?" Cyan asked.

I scrolled back up the page, unwilling to share this with anyone else just
yet. "I . . . I'm not sure," I said. Pressing my fingers into my eye sockets, I rooted
in my brain for ideas. What this note meant, I had no idea, but I knew with
certainty this could help prove that Sean hadn't committed suicide. I needed
to get this to someone in authority—someone with the ability to prove that
Sean hadn't taken his own life.

I clicked the print command and stood up. Easing the paper out of the
machine as soon as it was done, I folded it and tucked it in my pocket, then
closed out the file. My stomach jostled. If Sean hadn't taken his own life, who
had taken it from him?

"You okay, Ollie?" Cyan asked. "You're awfully pale."

"I'm . . ." I swallowed. "I'm okay."

Marcel's arrival in the kitchen prevented me from having to explain further.
In a tizzy, he stood in the doorway and begged for help.

"What's wrong?" I asked.

"The house. I cannot get it into the elevator," he said.

Bucky made a disparaging noise. "If we all run over to help him, who's
going to get the hors d'oeuvres done on time?"

The clock was ticking. "Rafe," I said, "can you get Agda to help put the
appetizers together?" He nodded. Agda, having heard her name, stood up
straight, apparently ready for whatever task I would assign. "Bucky," I continued, "you're doing fine there. Cyan will stay here, too." I held up my splinted
hand. "I'm off kitchen prep, so I'll work with Marcel."

More often than not, Marcel reacted first and thought things through later.
I hoped that was the case now.

When I followed him into the hallway, I understood the problem. The
gingerbread house was enormous. "Marcel," I said, in awe, "this is incredible."

Larger than last year's gingerbread house by half, this year's version was a meticulously perfect model of the current White House. We'd had a hard time getting the house in the elevator last year. I couldn't imagine why Marcel had decided to up the scale. A quick glance at his distraught face convinced me not to ask.

The annual gingerbread house creation always fell under the purview of our executive pastry chef. The rest of us in the kitchen helped out where needed, of course, but Marcel enjoyed this project more than any other all year.

The house itself took more than two weeks to create. Last year's version had weighed more than three hundred pounds, and this one was most definitely bigger. Marcel had designed this tiny mansion with staggering accuracy, creating individual baked gingerbread pieces in varying shapes and sizes and bringing them together with architectural precision.

This was no half-baked endeavor. Marcel had, in fact, made several duplicates of each section in anticipation of breakage. Every single piece was handcrafted in proportion to the whole. The gingerbread, though edible—and delicious—was never consumed. Marcel carefully shaped individual pieces, then baked and set them aside until needed for the final construction in the China Room. I'd walked in on Marcel and his team a few times over the past couple weeks. They worked with the quiet intensity of adults, but maintained the wide-eyed optimism of schoolchildren. Every little detail, from side walls to windowsills, was identified, numbered, and set aside for placement at exactly the right time.

Marcel had five assistants for this project. Three were SBA chefs, and two were permanent. Marcel usually made do with only one assistant, but Yi-im had proven so adept at the pastry tasks, Marcel had seized him for his own. Cross-training happened now and again in the White House, but it wasn't the norm. Yi-im's change of status from butler to assistant chef had caused a few raised eyebrows—particularly from the waitstaff. They weren't happy at the prospect of having to fill another empty position.

When I finished my slow-circuit inspection of the house, I had to say it again. "This is incredible."

"*Merci,*" he said, absentmindedly, his gaze flipping back and forth between the cookie house and the elevator doors. The giant structure sat on a massive piece of covered plywood, which itself sat atop one of our wheeled serving carts. The design took my breath away so completely that I nearly forgot the problem at hand—getting it up to the main floor.

Yi-im appeared from around the back of the gingerbread house. "I didn't see you," I said.

His cheekbones moved upward in a polite smile, but it came across more as an affectation than his being happy to see me. The dilemma of how to get this beautiful monstrosity to the Red Room was obviously weighing heavily on everyone.

"What are these?" I asked Marcel, pointing to the mansion's edges. Small postlike structures were attached to the miniature—and I use the term loosely—White House's corners. Like flagpoles, but without flying any banner, each inner and outer corner of the building had one of these, painted white with icing to make it less noticeable.

Marcel heaved a big sigh in front of the elevator. "I do not wish to disassemble my masterpiece," he said with a forlorn expression. "I have just now put it together. It is exactly right. If I were to take it apart once again, it will never be so perfect."

"Can't we just carry it up?"

"Are you insane?" he asked. "Do you know how much this must weigh?" He rolled his eyes and shook his head. "It would take the strength of six men to carry this up the stairs, and my assistants are not capable of such heavy lifting. Not only that, but if they were to tilt it to any extreme, the walls would crack and my masterpiece would be ruined." He looked ready to cry. "Do you hear me? Ruined!"

I blew out a breath. Marcel had been executive pastry chef for a long time. I couldn't imagine how he'd forgotten the limitations there were on transportation. Of course, when one is in the throes of creativity, sound reasoning often flies out the window. That's probably what happened in this case. Scope creep. A little flourish here, a little detail there, and pretty soon you've created a big monster.

I took another look at the grand cookie White House. I had to admit again it was gorgeous. Every window had icy corners, as though Jack Frost had decorated the panes himself. The Truman Balcony was not only perfectly represented, but it was dressed with snow, miniature evergreen roping, and wreaths decked with red bows. I couldn't see inside, but I knew Marcel had outfitted the piece with inner lights. I couldn't wait to see it lit.

Marcel paced as Yi-im fiddled with different sections of the structure. I asked him about the poles at each of the corners. He shrugged and did that nonsmile thing again but said nothing.

There was no way this creation would fit in any of the elevators. Not even close. I shook my head as I pondered our next move.

"You agree it is hopeless, no?"

"Nothing is hopeless," I said, walking slowly around it. Six men, Marcel had said. Personally, I thought it could be handled by four. "Who's available to help us?"

Marcel gave me a wary look. "What do you have in mind?"

"If we can get four sturdy men to each take one corner of the plywood, and if they go up those stairs"—I pointed—"very, very carefully, I think there's a good chance of moving this in one piece."

Skeptical, Marcel pressed me for reasons why I believed a bunch of burly men wouldn't be clumsy with his masterpiece. After a ten-minute discussion, he agreed to give it a try. "But if the men cannot lift this easily—immediately— we will call off the experiment," he said, the corners of his mouth curling downward. "And I will return to my kitchen to take my beautiful building apart."

"Don't get defeated. We haven't even attempted this yet," I said.

Marcel nodded and spoke to Yi-im. "Can you find us several men to help?" With a nod, he was off.

"What about the gingerbread men?" I asked, looking around the wheeled cart. "I don't see them here."

"They will come later," Marcel answered, still a bit more distracted than he usually was. "Yi-im will arrange those when the house itself is in place."

I glanced at my watch. Marcel noticed.

"I know. I know." He paced the corridor. "What was I thinking? Why did I not ensure the house was in place yesterday?" Turning to face me, he continued his one-sided conversation. "I will tell you why. Because I have had nothing but trouble with my assistants. Do they not know how important it is that we have our work of art in place when it is to be unveiled? Does that not follow? Do they have no sense?"

I glanced in the direction his assistant had gone and I gestured for Marcel to lower his voice. "I thought you said Yi-im was working out very well."

Marcel rolled bugged-out eyes. "He is, what you say . . . the harbor during the hurricane."

"Any port in a storm?"

He waved a hand dismissively. "Yes, yes. That. While he is willing to put in many hours, he is not trained in methods nor in kitchen procedure. He has much to learn."

Conversation from behind caused me to turn. Yi-im had drawn out the electrical staff. Curly, Manny, and Vince were following the small man; Curly looking ever unpleasant, and Manny and Vince sharing a joke.

Yi-im nodded, gesturing the other men forward. He'd snagged only three. We clearly needed four. Marcel, I knew, had no intention of helping carry the house, and Yi-im was just too small. I chewed the inside of my lip. I was strong for my size, but I had doubts about my ability to hold up my end of the structure. The last thing we needed was for the house to crash to the ground. And the very last thing I wanted was for it to be my fault.

Before I could step forward to lend assistance, however, Yi-im grabbed the corner nearest me. He grunted some imperative and the three other men took corresponding positions at each end. Marcel covered his eyes. "I cannot bear to watch."

The four men, with set expressions, wrapped their fingers around the curved ends of the platform, and as one, lifted the board into the air.

Marcel moaned, turning his back now. "Ollie, you must oversee this. Tell me when I may look." Hands covering his eyes like horse blinders, he started back to the kitchen.

"Marcel," I called.

He turned, but only enough to face me. "Take the cart in the elevator," I said. "We'll need this as soon as we get up there."

With pain twisting his aristocratic features into a horrified frown, Marcel quickly stepped forward, grabbed both handles, and maneuvered the cart out from beneath the men's pole positions.

Within moments, Manny and Vince were four steps up the staircase, Curly and Yi-im still on the floor, raising their end high to keep the house level. Marcel chanced a look back, let loose another groan of total despair, and practically ran the cart to the nearest elevator.

I hated accompanying the four men on their painstaking crawl up the stairs, but I sensed they hated my presence even more. They had all obviously carried cumbersome, heavy items up staircases before, because they used minimal conversation to guide the collective group effort. Although I had faith in the strength of these men, I sweated out my position, low on the steps as they climbed up. If, heaven forbid, the house did topple, I could just see myself now, crushed below it, my feet sticking out like those of the Wicked Witch of the East.

I scampered up past them and breathed a little easier.

Curly, Manny, and Vince labored against the project's weight, grunting as they inched up each individual step. Yi-im's face showed no such strain. All four were careful to keep the board level. Too late, I thought about borrowing an actual level from the carpenter's department; I could have monitored the progress up the stairs.

One look at the contorted expressions on these guys' faces, however, and I realized my coaching and calling out levelness might have tempted them to dump the house smack on top of my head.

Marcel met me at the top of the stairs, cart ready.

Several long, sweaty minutes later, Manny and Vince cleared the top landing, holding their ends low until Curly and Yi-im were able to join them. Relief washed over every one of their faces when the board was settled softly atop the cart. We wheeled the house into the center of the Entrance Hall.

"*Merci*, er, thank you," Marcel said to the men, but he clearly didn't care whether anyone heard him. Walking around the giant confection, Marcel slowly examined his masterpiece, inspecting every inch. If I would have had a magnifying glass on me, I would have offered it to him.

Curly was just starting back toward the steps when Paul Vasquez called out to him to wait. Our chief usher hurried across the hall, his shiny black shoes clipping in sharp measure. "I just left a message for you. I didn't realize you'd be up here."

Curly scowled, looking at me with contempt. The fact that he was helping us out instead of doing his own work needled him and I could tell he blamed me. I smiled innocently.

"We're having problems in the Red Room again," Paul continued. "Did you cut the power there?"

Manny and Vince were about to head downstairs, but Curly stopped them with an unintelligible command. "What did you two do to the Red Room's power?" he asked.

Manny looked at Vince, who shrugged. "Don't know what you're talking about," Vince said.

Manny lifted his hands. "No idea. But we've got a lot to do, so . . ."

They were almost to the steps. "Hang on, there," Curly said, his voice raised. He swore under his breath. The scar that stretched across his head reddened and a vein throbbed at his temple. "Listen," he said to Paul, "I've been at this all day. I checked the Red Room, everything's hot. You tell me something's wrong. I check it again, and there's still nothing wrong. You think maybe your staff don't know the difference between the on and off switch?"

Ever unflappable, Paul shook his head. "I checked it myself, Curly. In fact, I just came from there. We have no power in the Red Room."

Curly raised a hand to his two assistants, then pointed down. "You go see what's what. And I want a complete report."

"Hold off on that a minute," Paul said, preventing the two men from leaving yet again. "I'm also here to inform you about a change in plan. I've just gotten word that the First Lady will *not* be entertaining here this afternoon. We will not have the traditional decorator tour after all."

I breathed a sigh of relief. Not just for my team's sake, but for that of the First Lady. She needed a break, and it seemed that finally she'd be able to get one. "We aren't serving, then?" I asked.

Paul shook his head. "Today is off. Completely."

Pulled from his mesmerizing study, Marcel straightened. "The house is not needed for today?" he asked. With an indignant tug of his tunic, he shot blazing eyes at Paul. "Why was I not told sooner?"

Paul raised his hand in a placating gesture. "I just found out. There have been . . . developments . . . in Mr. Baxter's funeral arrangements."

My hand immediately flew to my pocket, where I'd stowed the letter from Sean. "Developments?"

I knew Paul was reluctant to share any information he didn't deem necessary. "Mrs. Campbell has opted to spend more time with the president's family. She's needed there."

"Did they say anything more about whether they're investigating this as a homicide?"

Paul looked away. "We'll let you know more when we can, Ollie."

Curly had lowered his chin and now sent us piercing looks as he rolled his head back and forth between us, his eyes wide with boredom. "And this affects the electricity how?"

Marcel muttered to himself about being left out of important decisions, but he'd gone back to studying the gingerbread house and was mostly quiet. Yi-im stood away from us, his hands clasped at his waist.

Tiredness settled around Paul's expressive eyes as he addressed Curly's concerns. "I'm bringing you all up to date right now. A memo will go out shortly. Please plan to have everything ready for display on Tuesday."

I piped up, "The day we reopen to the public?"

Marcel muttered. Paul nodded. "We plan to tie the opening ceremony for the holiday season with the decorator tour. The only difference between the two events is size. And once we put both together, don't be surprised if Tuesday turns out to be a wild media event." He relaxed his features. "Curly, you'll see to the Red Room?"

"These two will see to it right now. And I guarantee I'm going to check it myself when they're done."

Only too happy to get the heck out of there, Manny said, "Okay, thanks." He looked to Curly. "We good to go?"

Curly jerked a thumb. "Get."

Vince started toward the Red Room, but Manny tugged his arm. "We got to check it from downstairs, first."

"Oh, yeah."

Paul clapped his hands together, thanked us all, and left.

Curly looked like he was ready to depart, but I stopped him. "I think Marcel needs help getting this into the Red Room. Don't you, Marcel?"

Our pastry chef seemed to become suddenly aware of the recent departures. "I cannot do this alone. Where are the other two?" he asked.

If laser-eyed stares could kill, I would have been dead on the floor. Curly worked his jaw. "Let's get this over with," he said, taking a position at one end of the house. He ordered Yi-im to the opposite side and told Marcel to push the cart.

"But there are so few of us," Marcel said. "How can we—"

"Just push the damn thing," Curly said.

Marcel closed his mouth, fixing the other man with a glare of condescension. "But of course, you have no appreciation for art."

Curly ignored him.

We all quickly realized that Marcel had neither the upper body strength nor the inclination to push the heavy load across the massive hall. I was about to suggest that we ask a couple of other staffers to help when Yi-im took over for Marcel, and I took Yi-im's position. As though the huge structure weighed nothing, he pushed it smoothly and quickly into the Red Room, where we left it in the room's center. Kendra had given us strict instructions not to place it on its display table yet. That would come later, after she'd ensured that everything was exactly where she wanted it.

As we left Marcel to coo over his creation a bit longer, and Yi-im to continue to assist in his quiet, capable way, I tried one of the room's lights. It went on, nice and bright. "Looks like your guys got the power going in here again."

"Couple of idiots," Curly said.

We were in the cross hall now. "Hey," I said, turning. "The Red Room is right above the Map Room."

Curly didn't stop walking.

"Curly."

Impatiently, he turned.

I took that as an invitation to continue. "The Map Room is the room Gene was working on when he got that power surge."

"So?"

"Remember? The day of the electrocution, the Map Room had gone powerless."

"I don't remember," he said.

"That's right," I said, recollection dawning on me. That was the day Curly's wife had been taken to the hospital. "You weren't here. The Map Room didn't have power. Gene thought it had been taken care of, but when it wasn't, he set out to fix it himself."

Curly's calloused fingers skimmed his scar. "I don't know what this has to do with anything."

"Don't you see? Whatever killed Gene may be happening again. Remember those floating neutrals I asked you about?"

Curly scowled, throwing his hands violently sideways—as though swatting a giant fly. "You don't know what you're talking about. You learn one little thing, you think you're an expert. I told you once: You show me your electrician's card, and only then I'll start listening to what you have to say."

"But—"

"Just . . ." He shook his head, and held up his hands, swatting the air again. This time when he turned and left, I didn't call after him.

CHAPTER 17

BACK IN THE KITCHEN, I GAVE MY TEAM THE NEWS. "SLOW DOWN, everyone. Today's reception has been canceled."

Relief brightened their faces as they all stood back from their tasks and took a breath. Agda stared a long moment. "I stop now?" she asked.

"We all stop now," I said.

"What are we supposed to do with all the extra?" Bucky asked. "Look at how much we've already done."

He had a point. There were hundreds of appetizers lined up on enormous baking sheets, waiting to be served. "Let's freeze what we can," I said, letting them know that the event had been rescheduled for Tuesday. "And we'll take the rest down to the cafeteria to share."

"Tuesday?" Bucky said. "Won't that be a madhouse?"

The general public— those who had the foresight to prearrange a visit—and congressional leaders and their families were all due here to vie for photo-ops at the opening ceremony. The event today was supposed to have been for the local press and other highfalutin magazines. Dubbed the Decorator Tour, the Sunday event traditionally gave the world a sneak peek at the year's White House extravaganza.

"I can't even begin to worry about it," I said. "Since the decorators are coming Tuesday now, too, we'll just have to add what we can from today's menu to what we have planned. We'll be fine."

I kept my tone light, but I was concerned nonetheless. Today had been the day I agonized over because of food preparations, but I was also preoccupied with safety concerns. Last night Tom and I had discussed how today, Sunday, had been the bomb's target day. We agreed that if the Secret Service believed a threat still remained, they would have canceled today's event.

Now suddenly it *was* canceled.

I swallowed before continuing, rationalizing that if there were any real threat, we would have been evacuated by now. With the president out of town and the White House closed to outsiders, the likelihood of an attempt was cheerfully slim. The same held for Tuesday, when the First Lady would open the White House to the public—the president was scheduled for a trip to Berlin. No president meant no bomb.

That gave me comfort. And to be honest, I was happy for the recent change of plan. In fact, I was feeling better than I had in a very long time. President Campbell was safe for now. And the next possible chaotic situation—Tuesday's opening—would happen without him in town. That should buy us some safety.

Fingering the note in my pocket, I realized that things were not completely perfect. The note from Sean convinced me that those in authority needed to look more closely into the manner of his death. But who could I talk to? Tom would have been my first choice, but he was away and wholly incommunicado until Wednesday.

As if reading my mind, Cyan wandered over and spoke in a low voice. "That document Sean left you," she said. "Are you going to do anything about it?"

"Did you read it?"

When she flushed, I had my answer. "It doesn't sound like it was written by someone about to commit suicide," she said.

"I didn't think so, either."

Inching closer, she whispered. "You always seem to get in the middle of things, Ollie." When I reacted, she was quick to add, "That is, things seem to happen to you—around you. All the time."

She was starting to sound a lot like Gav.

"I can't help that," I said.

Keeping her voice low, she said, "I don't mean to hurt your feelings. It's just that I know you well enough to know that you're probably trying to figure out what happened to Sean all by yourself."

I shook my head, but Cyan wasn't finished.

"All I'm saying is to be careful."

"I am being careful."

She gave me a wry frown. "I know you don't believe Sean killed himself, but if he didn't . . . well, that means somebody else killed him. If you're trying to investigate this, and you've got a note like that"—she nodded toward my pocket—"you could be asking for trouble."

"I'm not trying to investigate."

Her look said she didn't believe me. "You're always poking around, Ollie. We both know that." Her wide-swept glance took in the rest of the kitchen. "We all know that."

Bucky, Rafe, and Agda were beginning to shoot curious looks our way. It wasn't often two people held a private, whispered conversation in front of the giant mixer. I grabbed Cyan's elbow. "I swear, I'm not touching this one." I gave a helpless shrug. "I don't even know where Sean lived. And so far, there hasn't been anything I can do to help anyone in this investigation, even if I wanted to." My hand curled around the note in my pocket and I pulled it up high enough for Cyan to see a corner of it. "Well, at least not until now, that is."

She gave a resigned nod. "Just be careful, okay?"

I WOULD HAVE PREFERRED TO TALK TO AGENTS TESKA OR BER-land, who'd been with Mrs. Campbell when she first received news of Sean's death, but they were again with the First Lady—wherever she was right now. I could have talked with any of the other agents assigned to the White House, but that would have involved explaining the whole story to them. No, I needed to talk with a person in the know, with the authority to get things done.

I found him downstairs in the cafeteria, alone, reading papers out of a manila folder, arms resting on the tabletop, fingers wrapped around the handle of a steaming mug. He wore gold half-moon reading glasses perched at the very end of his nose. The place was quiet, but at this time of day, and at this time of year, it wasn't surprising. No one had time for coffee breaks. Well, hardly anyone.

"Do you have a minute, Gav?"

His gaze and eyebrows arched over the tops of his glasses, and his mouth tugged down. Dressed as always in a suit and tie, he looked totally at ease, which is more than I was at the moment.

"What can I do for you, Ollie?" he asked, holding a palm out toward the chair next to his.

I sat. Then pushed a hard breath out.

"Feeling the effects of yesterday's scare?" he asked.

"Yes," I said, rubbing my upper arms. "But that's not what's bothering me this time."

He sat back, removed the glasses, and placed them on the table next to the mug. "Talk to me."

I dragged the note out and spread it before him on the small table. He was fully versed in the Sean situation, so there wasn't much to explain before he read it. "I found this on my kitchen computer," I said. "Sean Baxter left it for me."

Gav leaned both arms on the table and held the paper far from his face. One second later, he pulled the glasses back on and started skimming.

I added, "He wrote this the day before he died."

Gav looked up. For the first time, I noticed his eyes. Pale gray. "And you're bringing this to me because . . . ?"

"Isn't it obvious?"

Gav continued to read. I waited.

"You believe this is proof he didn't commit suicide?"

I nodded.

"I'd have to agree the wording doesn't sound like it came from someone depressed enough to take his own life."

"Can you show that to someone? Would you be able to get that into the proper hands?"

Gav sucked on his lower lip for a moment before answering. He stared at the page, rereading. "This is on your computer in the kitchen?"

I nodded again. "I almost didn't notice it. He'd opened it under an obscure heading."

"Obscure," Gav repeated. "But you found it."

"It seemed out of place."

One corner of his mouth turned up. "Just like I told you. You have an eye for things."

That was all nice and complimentary, but I wanted to be sure this paper did some good. "Can you get it into the proper hands?" I repeated.

He folded it into fourths and placed it into his shirt pocket. "Can anyone else access this letter?"

"Sure," I said. "But no one else will." I thought about Cyan and amended, "Hardly anyone. The kitchen staff only accesses recipes and other necessary documents. I handle the administrative issues. This is under my set of documents."

"Is it password-protected?"

"No, but there's no reason—"

"Ollie, what did I tell you about trusting people?"

"No one in the kitchen—"

He held a hand up. "Even if you're right and no one in the kitchen means anyone any harm, how do you know that individuals from other departments aren't accessing your files?"

I opened my mouth to argue, but realized I had nothing to say. Although I was savvy enough to manipulate recipes, files, and spreadsheets, I knew nothing about firewalls or security stuff like that. That wasn't my area of expertise. Now that I thought about it, however, I supposed it could be possible for others to access my files when I wasn't looking—either in person, or through the quirks of cyberspace.

He jumped into my awkward silence. "Has anyone else seen this?"

"Cyan."

"She's the little redhead?"

"Yeah."

"Anyone else?"

"No."

Gav seemed to weigh that information. "Probably best if you keep this to yourself. Can you trust Cyan?"

"Absolutely."

"Then tell her to keep mum, too."

"What will you do with the note?" I asked.

"Make copies. Show them to the officers in charge. I'll get one to the First Lady as well."

Any uneasiness I'd felt about sharing the letter with Gav had dissipated. My mood lightened. "Thanks," I said.

"When I say to keep this to yourself, I really mean that."

"I know."

He stole a look to the right and then to the left. The only other humans in the room were two maintenance men, who were wiping down the far countertop. "Ollie," he said, leaning forward, "if Sean was murdered—and I'm not saying he was . . ."

"I know."

"Then whoever killed him won't want this information out there."

I thought about how similar Gav's warnings were to Cyan's. "I understand."

He tapped his breast pocket. "But this gives us a place to start looking for suspects."

CHAPTER 18

I MADE MY WAY TO THE FIRST FLOOR TO TAKE A LOOK AT THE decorating in progress. Most days of the year we had crowds wandering through the White House to tour the public rooms. But today and tomorrow would be quiet now that the Decorator Tour had been canceled. I wanted to steal a selfish minute to breathe in the beauty of the holiday before things got crazy again tomorrow. I wandered through the Entrance Hall and, as always, appreciated its grandeur. While the White House was permanently a showplace and forever gorgeous, this time of year the mansion sparkled with holiday spirit.

I crossed the plaque in the floor that commemorated the White House's original construction and all the renovations that had taken place since—1792, 1817, 1902, 1952—and found it curious that most of the construction occurred in years ending in two. The building's most recent renovation, during Truman's tenure, had been so comprehensive that I couldn't imagine another one occurring in my lifetime.

Just ahead, Mrs. Campbell stood in the Blue Room, her back to me. She watched as one of Kendra's teams put the finishing touches on the tree. Hundreds of gingerbread men decorated the branches, peeking out from behind the white poinsettia blooms that sharpened the Fraser fir's intense green.

All the president's gingerbread men, I thought.

I wondered what the First Lady was thinking about right this minute. With all the beauty and cheer going on around her, it had to be difficult to face this happy time of year knowing Sean would not be here to celebrate. Not wishing to disturb her, I walked very softly to the adjacent Red Room.

One of the White House state reception rooms, the Red Room was always impressive, but decorated as it was today, with lighted garland surrounding the fireplace, handmade gingerbread men in every possible corner, and wreaths hanging in the tall windows, it was breathtaking. In prior years, the gingerbread house was showcased in the State Dining Room, but Mrs. Campbell had requested the change. This year, we had originally intended to use the State Dining Room for the very large, very busy reception following the Decorator Tour this afternoon. Now those plans had changed, too.

I scratched my forehead, assessing this last-minute rearrangement. The reception, rescheduled for Tuesday, including both days' invitees, would be larger in scale than anyone had anticipated. Maybe it was a good thing the house was set up in the Red Room after all. But I did find myself curious about all the power outages. Could it be that the Red Room wasn't electrically equipped to handle everything? Was that why we were having so much trouble?

The gingerbread house sat between the room's windows. Their swooping gold draperies, topped with fringed red swags, framed Marcel's creation to perfection. I sighed. Despite all the crazed goings-on these past few days, the comfort of this room filled me with a warm sense of contentment.

Opposite the wall with the fireplace, the waitstaff had set up a champagne fountain. Dry now, it would be primed and ready to go before the reception on Tuesday. Two of our butlers would flank it, serving directly from the cascading fountain, so that none of our guests would get his or her fingers sticky.

Everything sparkled, looking warm and wonderful. Standing by the fireplace, I ran a finger along the edges of some of the gingerbread men turned in by our nation's kids. These simple, homemade decorations added just the right touch.

I wandered into the State Dining Room. Decorated trees in the room's corners were heavy with dazzling white and silver decorations. Matching ribboned arrangements hung from the wall sconces and draped the fireplace. A long table ran down the middle of the room, topped with complementary centerpieces. And everywhere I looked—on the trees, the walls, hanging from sconces—were more gingerbread men. Kendra was on her knees in the room's far corner, strategically arranging two more little men on the lowest branches of a tree.

"This is gorgeous," I said.

She turned, her flushed face breaking out into a huge smile. "It does look good, doesn't it?"

"That's an understatement." Standing near her, I turned, slowly, in order to take in the whole display. To just appreciate the beauty of it all.

"I'm relieved to have the extra time," Kendra said, wiping her forehead with the back of her hand. "We would have had everything done by noon if we needed to." She glanced at her watch, then grimaced. "But I'm happy for the breather. Gives me the chance to do a little extra."

"This theme is fabulous," I said, stepping close to the east wall and touching one of the gingerbread men's arms. "It gives the White House such a cozy feeling."

"This is a first for me. I didn't know how hard it would be to sort through submissions from all over the country." Her eyes widened and her voice lowered. "It was a nightmare," she said. "Which is why we're running later this year than I expected. There's so much more involved with accepting decorations for the White House from people. Everybody has to be checked out thoroughly before we even think about using their pieces." She took a slow look around the room, a satisfied smile on her face. "But it was sure worth it."

"Did you turn anyone down?"

She wrinkled her nose. "A few. Some arrived broken, some didn't follow directions and sent gingerbread men that were the wrong size, or the wrong shape. Part of what makes an overall design work is consistency in the right places." She shot me a conspiratorial grin. "Of course, we don't tell people that their kids' artwork has been relegated to the basement cafeteria. We just send them the official thank-you letter and let them know their efforts are appreciated. They'll never know."

"Speaking of gingerbread men," I said, "I gave Marcel some from the Blanchard kids. I didn't see them in the Red Room like Senator Blanchard requested."

Kendra's eyebrows raised. "Preferential treatment?"

"You know it." I ticked my fingers. "One, he's a senator. Two, he's a special friend of the First Lady's, and three . . . the decorations are really well-done."

A skeptical look. "From Blanchard's kids?"

I winked as I started back to the Red Room. "Rumor has it the Blanchard chef put them together."

She shook her head. "Why am I not surprised?"

Back in the Red Room, I happened upon Yi-im, who was touching up the house with a cup of powdered sugar and a tiny paintbrush. "Did the house survive the move all right?" I asked.

He canted his head, nodded, then went back to work.

After a few minutes of checking the room, I approached him again. "Where are the gingerbread men from Senator Blanchard?"

Yi-im's jaw moved sideways, as though he were considering my question. Finally, he shook his head and shrugged. Did this man never talk?

Just as I was about to ask him again where they might be, Marcel came in, his face shiny from exertion, but his demeanor high and cheerful. "She looks marvelous, no?" he asked us.

Yi-im straightened and I told Marcel how fabulously things were coming together.

He beamed. "It is time to ensure that my masterpiece is fully functional," he said, moving to the rear of the platform upon which the house sat. He plugged it into the wall. "We must see." Turning to Yi-im, he waved his hand, one finger aloft, encompassing the room's illumination. "Please lower the lights."

Yi-im obliged. The moment the room was darkened—not terribly dark since daylight still brightened the windows—Marcel stepped back and rested his hand on the switch located behind the gingerbread building. "We are ready, yes?"

I nodded.

When Marcel flicked the switch, the gingerbread White House lit up from the inside. A warm, golden glow emanated from each frosty window and suffused the creation with a curious joy.

"Oh," I said, unable to conjure up anything else.

"But wait," Marcel said. "As they say on the television—there is more." He fiddled behind the structure for a moment. "Yi-im is seeing to it that the First Lady will be able to light this with a single control, aren't you, Yi-im?"

The smaller man nodded.

Marcel flicked a second switch and the corner poles I'd asked about before came alive with sudden brightness. "Sparklers?" I asked.

He shook his head. "No, but they mimic the illusion, do they not?" He drew me closer. "They are able to continue sparkling for hours by using a method of constant feed." He pointed to the bottom of one of the corner poles. "I have added these—they are spring-loaded to provide . . . what is the best word? Fuel? To each little flame."

"Aren't these a fire hazard?"

Marcel fixed me with a frown. "Do you not think that I have made certain to clear this with our Secret Service?" He shook a finger at me. "This is very low-grade. And not hot. Try touching it."

I waved my finger over the top of the bouncing brightness. "It's cool," I said, surprised.

"But of course."

"I'm impressed, Marcel. As always."

He smiled, the feathers I'd unintentionally ruffled back in place. Clicking the house "off" again, he asked Yi-im to restore the lights. When he did, Marcel explained, "I have more of this fuel in my kitchen to replace as necessary."

"Sounds like you have everything covered."

"Again I say: But of course." Big grin this time.

"By the way," I said, when Yi-im resumed his sugar painting, and Marcel started his own personal inspection, "have you seen the gingerbread men the Blanchard children made?"

"The children?" he said, with a snort. "Certainly not. But I do have the gingerbread men sent to us from the Blanchard household, if that is what you are asking."

I smiled at his clarification. "It is."

"We will incorporate those with the house." He pointed to a position on the wall just above the gingerbread building. "They will be placed there," he said. "I wanted to fully test my house first and then we shall add in finishes as necessary."

A soft voice from behind us. "Oh, Marcel."

We turned. The First Lady had come in from the Blue Room, her hands clasped high to her chest. "How exquisite."

Marcel's dark face blushed and I noticed a drip of perspiration wend its way down near his ear. For all his bravado and bluster, Marcel was just as nervous as the rest of us to make sure everything went perfectly well. "Thank you, madame."

Yi-im scampered out of the way as Mrs. Campbell made a slow show of inspecting the gingerbread house. "I am in awe," she said.

Not wanting to disturb her while she talked with our pastry chef, I began to back out of the room.

"Just a moment, Ollie," she said, holding up a finger. "If you don't mind."

What could I do? I mumbled acknowledgment and stood near the door to the cross hall, watching.

Mrs. Campbell took a few long moments to study the frivolous yet inspiring details worked into the piece. She smiled, but I thought it a sad smile. "At a time like this, it is good to be reminded of beauty. I am humbled by your talent, Marcel."

Marcel gave a little bow. "You honor me, madame."

"Thank you," she said, in a near-breathless voice. Nodding to Yi-im, she made her way to me and guided us both into the cross hall. She didn't stop there, however, instead waiting until we were in the center of the Entrance Hall to talk.

"Would it be too much trouble to arrange for a dinner tomorrow evening?" she asked.

"Of course not," I said quickly. When the First Lady asks for anything, the answer is always an enthusiastic yes. "For how many?"

"Four," she said. "My colleagues Nick Volkov, Senator Blanchard, and Helen Hendrickson will be joining me here."

I opened my mouth to say something, thought better of it, and clammed up again.

Mrs. Campbell blinked moist eyes. "You have been privy to a great deal of information lately," she said. "I apologize for that. I sense your apprehension."

"It's not my place. . . ."

"Perhaps not, Ollie, but I plan to get this matter settled once and for all."

I couldn't stop myself this time. "Have you decided to sell?" Horrified that the question popped out, I raised my hand to my mouth. "Sorry."

She didn't appear to get angry. Rather she smiled, then sighed, deeply, looking away, as though speaking to herself—convincing herself of what she planned to say to her three friends. "No matter what they tell me, I can't believe Sean took his own life. I also cannot believe that he gave me bad advice. I trusted Sean." She met my eyes again. "I can't make such a monumental decision with so much that hasn't been explained."

I hesitated, but knew that if I didn't speak up now, I'd be sorry later. "I have a letter," I said, "from Sean."

My words puzzled her. "What are you talking about?" she asked. "He sent you something? When?"

"He left it for me, on my computer," I said, explaining how I'd found it, and what the letter had said. I finished by adding that I was also convinced that the letter's tone was such that I couldn't imagine Sean taking his life, either.

"Where is it?" she asked.

"I still have it on my computer," I said, pointing down toward the kitchen. "But I gave a copy of it to Special Agent-In-Charge Gavin."

She considered that. "Would you please make a copy for me?"

"Of course," I said, starting for the stairs. "I'll do that right now."

"I'll come with you."

Everyone in the kitchen stopped what they were doing to welcome the First Lady. Her visit wasn't completely without precedent, but it wasn't the norm. "Thank you," she said, with her characteristic grace. "I won't be in your way for very long. Ollie has something of importance to share with me, and then I'll be out of your hair."

When her back was turned, Bucky's eyes rolled so far up into his head I thought he might be on the verge of collapse. I warned him with a glare.

Mrs. Campbell took time to speak with Cyan, Rafe, and Agda while I pulled up my files. Bucky whispered close: "Always nice to cozy up to the First Family, isn't it? Lots of perks can come your way when you're buddy-buddy with the boss."

"Back off," I said.

He did, but took a long moment to stare at me. I couldn't tell what crazy thoughts danced behind those murky eyes. I could tell he'd been surprised by my sharp retort, but I wasn't sure if the added emotion was amusement or fury. And I didn't have time to bother.

As I clicked at my keyboard, my stomach jittered. What if it had been deleted? Or what if someone else had come across Sean's letter and modified it? I eyed Bucky, who I discovered was eyeing me back. It would be just like him to think he was funny by messing with my stuff—and I remembered Sean's concerns about Bucky being annoyed with him for accessing my computer.

My head pounded with worry and potential embarrassment as I pulled up a list of recent documents. Even as I rationalized that a true copy still existed— with Gav—I worried that this one would be gone and I'd be the laughingstock once again. After the bomb incident—the bomb that everyone believed was fake, but I knew to be real—even *I* thought I was starting to sound like Chicken Little.

"Come on," I whispered, urging the computer to move faster. I double-clicked on the file, exasperated when I was rewarded by the little hourglass that warned me to wait.

The computer made that unwelcome and not-very-nice sound when it can't find what it's looking for.

"No," I said, softly.

Cyan broke away from the First Lady. "Are you looking for what I think you're looking for?"

Her eyes today were amber brown. I stared into them. "It's not here."

"Hang on." She leaned in to where I was working and commandeered the mouse. She double-clicked on a file titled "YEO" and then typed in a password when prompted. Winking at me, she whispered, "Buckminster." Bucky's full name. Good choice, I thought.

A split second later, Sean's document was on the screen.

"There," she said.

Amazed by her foresight, I thanked her. "YEO?" I asked.

"Stands for 'Your Eyes Only.' In my culinary school, students were always trying to steal one another's ideas. I learned to password-protect early." With a shrug, she started back toward the counter, but leaned forward to add, "I thought this one was worth protecting."

"You're good," I said, clicking the command to print.

"Just watching your back."

Mrs. Campbell continued talking with the other chefs as I pulled Sean's letter from the printer. When I had it in hand, she turned to me. "A moment, Ollie?"

We walked out across the Center Hall into the Map Room, where Mrs. Campbell read the letter. I would have preferred to allow her to read it by herself, but she asked me to stay when I offered to give her privacy.

When she looked up, her eyes were shining. "Thank you," she said. "I know just what to do with this."

"You know that Gav has a copy, too?"

She smiled. "I'm certain he's doing the best he can. But one of the benefits of my position is that it allows me to cut through red tape when I need to. You have done me a great favor, Ollie. And you've done the president a great favor as well."

I felt myself blush.

"I know you have a lot to do, so I won't keep you longer, but I want you to know that my husband and I appreciate all you do for us." She looked down at the letter, then up at me. "Today . . . and every day."

ON MY RIDE HOME, I STAYED HYPER-ALERT FOR ANY SIGN THAT I was being followed—any hint that people were out to get me. Today's stand-down on the reception, however, meant that our workload lessened and my commute home was at a more busy time than when I'd been attacked. It was getting dark, but it wasn't terribly late. There were people everywhere—and so many on the Metro that I had to stand for part of the trip. I didn't mind. Oblivious humanity provided a degree of comfort.

I reached into my replacement purse and smiled. How appropriate, I thought—the chef carrying pepper spray to defend herself. After my last altercation, I realized I needed to take a more proactive approach to guarding my safety.

I had to admit that I didn't expect to be attacked again, but what I really didn't expect was a reporter outside my apartment building. I didn't realize at first that the woman sitting alone in an idling Honda Civic was waiting for me.

"Olivia Paras?" the woman asked too eagerly as she alighted.

My stomach squeezed. What now? There were so many things going on—the two recent deaths, the fake bomb, the real bomb, the cancelation of today's event at the White House—that I couldn't begin to guess what this lady wanted to talk with me about.

I tried getting past her but she stepped in front of me. She spoke into a handheld microphone that appeared to be connected to a recorder on the hip of her fur coat. "Olivia Paras, you're the White House executive chef. . . ."

Tell me something I don't know.

"What can you tell us about tomorrow's dinner?"

She shoved the microphone at me. I blanked. "Dinner?"

"We understand that the First Lady is meeting with Nicholas Volkov."

As she said Volkov's name, she widened her eyes and slowed her speech, giving the name additional weight.

The microphone popped in front of me again. "I'm sorry. I'm going in now." I pointed up toward my floor. "And I'm cold."

"But don't you think the American public deserves to know if the First Lady is planning to meet with an accused murderer?"

My jaw dropped. I started to say, "What?" then thought better of it. Although I wanted to ask a million questions, I said, "I have nothing to say."

The reporter's shoulders drooped. "Ms. Paras, please," she said, her voice quietly entreating. "My name is Kirsten Zarzycki. I'm with Channel Seven News. May I call you Livvie?"

Livvie? My reaction must have shown, because she started to apologize. "Channel Seven?" I said, my eyes raking the Honda behind her. "I—"

"You've never seen me. I'm new," she said. "But I've been looking into all this for a while now and I think I'm onto something." She lifted one shoulder. "I can't get clearance to talk to any of the big shots involved, but I thought that maybe, since you're planning the dinner, you might have some insight into what's going on there."

I rubbed my forehead and stared at this girl. Kirsten Zarzycki was younger than I was, by at least five years, and taller than me by at least five inches. Blonde, eager, and looking as though the high-rise pumps she wore were squeezing her feet, she pleaded, with both her eyes and her words.

"Listen, I'm trying to make a name for myself here," she said. "You've got to be able to share something with me." Now both shoulders shrugged and I wondered how many innocent foxes gave their lives for her protection against the night's chill.

"I don't have anything, and even if I did . . ." My mind raced. Volkov accused of murder? Could he have been the one who—

"That's it," she said, the excitement in her voice pushing it up an octave. "I see it in your face. You do know something. I know you do. You just might not realize how much you know. Come on," she said, blinking rapidly. "You're where you want to be in this world. Can't you give a hand up?"

Plying me with almost the same argument Bindy had, she blinked again. I wondered if this tactic worked to better effect on men. I hoped not.

"Sorry," I said, starting for my front door. My woolen coat was no match for the cold air, although little Miss High Heels seemed toasty in her fur.

"What about Zendy Industries?" she asked, desperation shooting her voice even higher. "I hear that Mrs. Campbell refuses to sell out. But does she realize how much Volkov's involvement will hurt her investment?"

"Mrs. Campbell's investments are none of my business." I smiled. "Nor are they yours."

She called after me. "Don't you think this makes Mrs. Campbell a target now?"

I turned to face her. Anticipation sparked Kirsten's eyes.

"What do you mean?" I asked.

"I've been doing some research into Zendy," she said. "I'm trying hard to make this into a story. But nobody seems to care."

I shivered and wanted her to get on with it. "What did you mean when you said that the First Lady was a target?"

"It all revolves around Zendy." She bit the insides of her cheeks and I could tell she was weighing how much to share. "Volkov needs the money from the sale of the company, right?"

I shrugged.

"It's in the news. No secret there. His legal troubles are no secret, either. The other thing that's only slightly more confidential is that the company can't be sold unless all four of the heirs vote unanimously to sell it."

I knew that much. This girl wasn't going to make it big in the media unless she could come up with something hotter than that.

"Who did Nick Volkov supposedly kill?" I asked.

"You don't know?"

I saw my capital dropping fast in her estimation. I shook my head.

"Mrs. Campbell's father."

That took me aback.

She frowned. "You really don't have any information, do you?"

"And you think Mrs. Campbell is a target because . . ."

"With her father dead, she's the only person standing in the way of the sale of Zendy Industries," Kirsten said with exasperation. "I'm connecting the dots here. I think when Volkov killed Mrs. Campbell's father, he assumed she'd be ready to just sign everything away."

I decided not to remind her that in America people are innocent till proven guilty. That wouldn't have stopped this girl's cascade of information. By the way her breaths spun out into the night in short, agitated spurts, I could tell she was so tightly wound up with this story that the truth wouldn't stop her now. "But if you're right," I said, "and Volkov is arrested, then the danger's gone, isn't it?"

"Maybe," she said. "But I have to convince someone he's guilty."

"What else do you know?" I asked.

She twisted her mouth. "You're getting more out of me than I'm getting out of you."

"Maybe that's because there's no story here." I started for my front door again, not acknowledging any of the questions she shouted to my back. I waved without turning, and called, "Good night!"

CHAPTER 19

"WHAT'S GOING ON OUT THERE, OLLIE?" JAMES ASKED WHEN I made it through the building's front doors. Tonight Stanley was with him. The two of them wore nearly identical looks of concern.

I waved away James's inquiry. "Just more of the same. Everyone wants secrets spilled, but why they think I have them is beyond me."

Stanley had been resting his hip against the desk. Now he shifted his weight. "You ask anybody about those neutrals?" he asked.

James perked up immediately. "What are you talking about?"

Again I tried to dismiss his concerns. "Just a theory we discussed. About the . . . you know . . . electrocution." I addressed Stanley. "I asked three people already. The acting chief electrician and two of his assistants. None of them is interested in what I have to say."

Stanley fisted the desk, making James jump. "Damn it, they should. The more I think about it, the more I believe that's what got your friend. And if I'm right, it could still cause trouble. You got to get somebody to listen before another person gets fried."

His words shook me more than I cared to admit. What if something else did happen . . . if Curly, Vince, or Manny were electrocuted and I could have prevented it? How would I feel then?

I knew the answer. I couldn't live with myself. Despite the fact that I'd done my best to warn them, I realized I needed to push harder. And pushing was something I was good at.

"I'll tell you what," I said. "The guys I talked to think I'm just butting my nose in where it doesn't belong. I'll be sure to let the fellow in charge know that

I talked with you." I smiled at Stanley. "I'll let him know that a real electrician is behind my questions."

Mollified, Stanley eased back to leaning. "I don't need no credit, y'understand, but if you think it'll make them listen, you do that, Ollie."

IN MY APARTMENT, AND COMFORTABLY READY TO RELAX, I TURNED on the television, hoping for some mention of Volkov, especially after Kirsten Zarzycki's claims. My first choice was, naturally, her station, WJLA. Nothing. Nothing at all. I switched to CNN, then switched away again when no mention of Volkov, nor of Mrs. Campbell, hit the airwaves. If indeed this Kirsten was right, then news of this nature would have been splattered everywhere. Hers was an explosive allegation, and definitely too hot to let simmer.

After a half hour of channel surfing, I realized the rookie reporter had apparently gotten her signals crossed somewhere along the line. I tried searching the Internet, but found nothing there, either.

As I got myself together for the next day and prioritized my tasks, I removed my splint and flexed my fingers. Felt good to have the freedom of movement. Better yet, I'd be able to really dive into food tasks in the kitchen tomorrow. I sorely missed the hands-on work I was used to.

Tomorrow was Monday, the last day the White House would be closed to the public before the big holiday unveiling on Tuesday. I set my alarm for a little earlier than usual, snuggled under my covers, and wished I could talk to Tom.

MOST MORNINGS, I WOKE TO MUSIC, BUT THE FIFTEEN-MINUTE lead time I'd built in the night before set my wake-up to smack in the middle of a news report. A voice like dark chocolate roused me from deep slumber. I missed the first few words, but twisted my head toward the voice when I heard him intone: "It is not known whether Ms. Zarzycki knew her attacker. Police are canvassing the area, looking for clues to this shocking murder. They have no suspects in custody but are asking witnesses in the area to step forward if they have any information to help find her killer." The announcer continued with a hotline number to call.

I shook my head. This couldn't be right. I must have misunderstood the name.

Staring at my clock radio, I waited for the story to repeat. But all I got was weather and traffic.

Heading into the living room, I tried to convince myself that this was all a dream. That all the events from recent days were conspiring to play with my mind. But my bedroom floor was cold to my bare feet. The apartment was chilly, and I could see the dawn of a new day outside my balcony window. Dreams were not usually so rich with such sensory stimuli. As my TV came alive I searched the room, hoping for some out-of-place vision, some signal that this was not real.

Instead, the two on-air personalities at WJLA were speaking disconsolately into the camera. One male, one female. I didn't know these commentators well enough to know their names, but the elegant black woman spoke for both. "Our hopes and prayers go out to Kirsten's family tonight. Although she'd just joined us here at WJLA, she was part of our family, and she will be missed." The woman's lips tight, she glanced to her co-anchor.

He took the cue. "Anyone with any information should call the number you see on your screen."

I dropped back into my sofa, curling my knees up, wrapping my arms around them. I continued to stare at the TV, even after they shifted away and cut to commercial. What the hell was going on?

With a beseeching glance at my clock, I willed the hours to speed by so that I could talk with Tom. But he wouldn't be here till Wednesday. Two long days away.

I changed the channel repeatedly until I caught the story again elsewhere. I got a few more details each time. I kept trying, looking for more, but soon I realized I had as much as I could get. There just wasn't much information out there. Not yet.

Dropping my knees, I held my head in my hands and tried to make sense of it all.

Kirsten was dead. Attacked at home, in her apartment, she'd been shot in the head. This could be a random act of violence, I told myself. But I didn't believe that for a minute. She'd talked about Nick Volkov being responsible for Mrs. Campbell's father's death. Kirsten was dead, and yet the information she claimed to have was nowhere to be found on the news.

Murder has a way of adding deadly credence to unproven conspiracies. Could Kirsten have been onto something after all?

* * *

LATER THAT AFTERNOON, RAFE JOSTLED MY SHOULDER. "WHAT'S wrong, Ollie?" he asked. "You're usually in your element when your hands are deep in dough."

Cyan didn't wait for me to answer. "Maybe you forgot what it was like to do the real work around here," she said, winking.

"That's it. You found me out." I forced a grin. As much as I wanted to be able to join in their cheer, I couldn't shake the news report on Kirsten's murder.

Rafe had been working with Agda a lot over the past week and now she joined in the good-natured teasing. While she divvied up parsley, she eyed the ball of dough before me. "I do that with eyes closed," she said, blinking hard. I expect she'd meant to wink at me. "And I do in half of the time."

"You're right," I said, soberly, then smiled to take the despondency out of my words. Agda had proven herself to be a huge asset to our kitchen. In recent days, with all our setbacks, and with me being sidelined with the splint, she'd more than taken up the slack. And she'd started to join in on conversation as well. She'd even impressed Bucky. Now that he was coming around, I knew the girl was starting to be considered part of the team. It did my heart good to see how well everyone was working together. And I needed that boost right now.

I eyed the forlorn ball of dough before me. I should have had these icebox rolls done fifteen minutes ago. I was falling behind. Too much weight on my brain seemed to cause a drag on everything else. Twice today I'd tried calling the Kirsten hotline number to let them know I'd talked with her last night, but I'd gotten a busy signal each time. Maybe that was for the best. I slammed the dough onto the countertop and kneaded it hard. I'd talk with our Secret Service personnel, or with Gav. They'd know what to do.

"How soon before the guests arrive?" I asked.

Bucky shot me a weird look.

"What?" I asked.

"That's the third time you've asked."

Was it? Geez, I really needed to get my head back in the game. "Well, you know how fast things change around here," I said to soothe my own ruffles. "And so far, we're still serving just four people tonight, right?"

"Last I heard, no change."

Agda perked up. "Change. Yes."

"A change in the guest list?" My heart raced. I'd been playing one of those if/then games with myself all day: If Volkov shows up tonight, then he's *not* guilty of killing Mrs. Campbell's father, and also not involved in Kirsten Zarzycki's murder. I could breathe easier if that were the case. But if we found out he wasn't coming . . . it could mean . . . "What is it?" I asked. "What's the change?"

Cyan put a hand on my arm. "Ollie, what's wrong? You're the one who just said we're always dealing with changes here. What are you worried about? You're pale again."

Waving a floured hand, I worked up a cheery demeanor. "Nothing, nothing at all," I said, keeping my voice light. I turned to Agda again. "What change did you hear about?"

Her hands came up to either side of her head, fingers spread, and she shook them—excited, it seemed, to be able to contribute her piece of knowledge. She spoke slowly but clearly. "Not dinner in residence. Now serving in Family Dining Room."

That *was* a change. We'd been instructed to send everything upstairs, where the First Lady intended to meet privately with her colleagues. "Who told you?" I asked.

Agda smiled and nodded. Then, belatedly understanding my question, her eyebrows lifted and she nodded again. "Paul."

I rubbed the back of my wrist against my forehead. "Why the change?" I asked, rhetorically. "I didn't think the First Lady wanted to have anyone see the first floor until the official opening ceremony tomorrow."

Cyan shrugged. "No idea. But with all she's been through lately, maybe she just wants to keep her private rooms private again."

"You're probably right," I said. Addressing Agda, I asked her if there were any other changes.

She shook her head. "No."

"What are you expecting, Ollie?" Cyan asked again.

"Just wondering if the guests are still the same."

"Why wouldn't they be?"

Now I shrugged. "Just a hunch."

Rafe had been right about one thing: Keeping my hands busy in the kitchen had been the perfect panacea for my uneasy mind. We were serving chicken-fried beef tenderloin tonight. Topped with more of the white onion gravy we'd made earlier and served with my late-to-the-party icebox rolls, we rounded out dinner with a basic salad, some in-season vegetables, and homemade peppermint ice cream for dessert. About an hour before dinner was to be prepared, I had my first chance to steal out of the kitchen and find Gav.

I'd seen him earlier when I passed the China Room. Now that the gingerbread house was complete, Marcel had given up squatter's rights and Gav had been using it as a lecture hall. When I walked past, he'd been in the midst of talking to some of the staff, so I hadn't interrupted. But I definitely needed a few minutes of his time.

He was still there.

"Got a minute?" I asked.

They'd brought a folding table into the room, and he sat at it, staring down, elbow propped, holding his head. The rest of the room was empty.

When he looked up, he didn't seem very happy to see me. "What is it?"

I'd intended to ask his opinion of the Kirsten Zarzycki situation, but I faltered. "Is something wrong?"

When people's eyes crinkle, it's usually because they're smiling. In this case, Gavin looked as though he'd suffered a quick pain. He took a long moment to speak. "Why did you give a copy of Sean's letter to the First Lady?"

I started to answer, but he cut me off.

"She's involved a lot of . . . others." He shook his head, and it looked as though his phantom pain intensified.

"We were talking," I said. "She and I . . ." I stopped myself from the apology that nearly tumbled off my tongue. "Why shouldn't I tell her? The situation involves a family member."

I watched Gavin force himself to be patient. He came close to losing the battle.

Another hard pain-squint. "When you first presented the information to me, I had a unique opportunity to make discreet inquiries. Now," he said, bitterness creeping into his voice, "I have been shut out of the investigation by the agencies involved."

I didn't know what to say to that. All I could think of was that if other agencies were investigating, then at least some good was coming of my bringing it to Mrs. Campbell's attention. "Who's handling it now?"

His mouth set into a thin line. "What is it you needed from me?"

I felt stupid bringing up the Kirsten Zarzycki issue after being scolded. "Forget it," I said. "It's nothing."

He rubbed his temples and spoke with clipped consonants. "You came in here intending to tell me something. What was it?"

I really didn't want to get into it, but I also didn't want to bear the burden of this information myself. "Did you hear about that reporter who was murdered late last night?"

"Shot in the head?"

"That's her," I said, dejectedly. "She came to visit me yesterday evening."

"Here?"

I shook my head, then gave him a quick rundown of our discussion.

When I was finished talking, Gav's anger had all but dissipated. "Where did she get the idea that Nick Volkov was responsible for Mrs. Campbell's father's death?"

"She didn't tell me."

He stared upward, toward the ceiling, before meeting my eyes again. "Mrs. Campbell's father died in a car accident."

"I know."

He stood. "Who did you talk to about this?" he asked. "Besides me?"

I shook my head. "No one."

"This time, keep it that way," he said. Without another word, he bundled up his papers and left the room.

CHAPTER 20

IT WASN'T LONG BEFORE MRS. CAMPBELL'S DINNER GUESTS BEGAN
to arrive. With a sad sense of déjà vu, we staged dinner in the Family Dining
Room's adjacent pantry, just as we had on Thanksgiving—when these
same guests were present and we received the terrible news that Sean was
dead. I couldn't help but question Mrs. Campbell's decision to choose this
particular venue for tonight's meal. In addition to the recent sadness associated
with the room, it wouldn't be very private. Staffers in adjacent rooms were
working around the clock tonight to complete everything before tomorrow's
opening.

Cyan and I intended to handle tonight's dinner ourselves. With three
guests—possibly only two if Volkov didn't show—there was no need to clutter
up the pantry with extra bodies.

I warmed the onion gravy on the stove, about to ask Cyan a question, when
I heard Treyton Blanchard's voice in the next room. "Elaine, thank you for
having us. A shame about Volkov, isn't it?"

Turning down the heat, I inched toward the wall, hoping to hear more. A
shame? That hardly seemed an appropriate reaction to Volkov being responsible
for her father's death.

"I hope Nick is all right," Mrs. Campbell answered. "And I hope we hear
more soon."

"Let's hope we hear from him directly."

I pressed my fingers to my forehead. This conversation made no sense.

Jackson came in, letting us know that dinner would be served a half hour
later than we'd planned. When I asked why, he shook his head. He didn't know,

he just wanted to relay Mrs. Campbell's request. I thanked him and kept listening in.

Mrs. Campbell and Senator Blanchard moved into discussion about other things, family and such. I heard him murmur his repeated condolences about Sean, and Mrs. Campbell said something in return I couldn't catch.

"Hey, Nancy Drew," Cyan whispered. "What's so important in there?"

I moved away from my eavesdropping perch. "They're talking about Volkov."

"So?"

"He's still coming, right?"

Cyan twisted her mouth. "What's with you today? I think they're all coming." She glanced at her watch. "And no one is officially late, yet. But Helen Hendrickson hasn't arrived, either. . . ."

"Helen," Mrs. Campbell exclaimed in the other room. "I'm so glad you could make it."

I lifted my eyebrows. "She's here now."

Cyan and I arranged stuffed cherry tomatoes on one plate and set out another platter for the bacon-and-cornbread muffins while I waited for some word as to whether Volkov was coming or not. At the same time, I kept my ears open for any further mention of his name.

The silly bet I'd played with myself now rose up to mock me. I tried reasoning with myself. Even if the man didn't show up, it wasn't as though I could take that fact to the nearest police station and claim that he was guilty. But as the minutes ticked by and Volkov became officially late, I became ever more convinced that Kirsten Zarzycki's allegations had more going for them than just ravings of an eager-to-be-promoted reporter. The fact that she was dead sealed it for me. I wondered who else she may have talked to.

Then a thought hit me so hard it made me stagger.

"Ollie? What's wrong?" Cyan asked.

I held on to the edge of countertop, forcing my brain to slow down instead of making the terrible conclusions it preferred to leap into.

If Kirsten indeed had access to information that incriminated Volkov—and she had been killed to maintain silence—then I had to worry about who else she might have talked to. Because whoever was responsible for her death might have known she talked to me.

My fingers formed a vise around the counter edge.

"Ollie?"

"I'm okay," I whispered to Cyan, though I was anything but. The horrible thought bounced around in my brain—what if Kirsten had mentioned me? What if whoever killed her was looking to tie up other loose ends?

I'd had an assassin after me before—and although I'd survived, it had been close. Too close. The recent incident on the street took on new meaning. What if these were the same people who'd killed Kirsten? What if they'd planned to get me first? Would they stop now, or had I made myself an even bigger target by talking with the reporter?

"I think you ought to sit down," Cyan insisted.

"No." I wiped the back of my hand against my eyes. "I just had a moment there. I don't know what's wrong."

"Maybe you're coming down with something."

"I'll be okay."

Her look told me she didn't believe me. I wouldn't have believed me, either.

I made my way to a stool near the door to the Family Dining Room. "You know what? Maybe I'll just sit for a minute." I gathered some of the baby greens we intended to use for the salad, and four plates. "I'll get the salad started here."

While Cyan worked at the far end of the room, she cast occasional glances my way. For my part, I listened for mention of Volkov, for mention of Mrs. Campbell's father. Instead, the three old friends seemed intent on keeping the conversation light.

"There he is," Treyton Blanchard boomed.

I nearly stood up to see, but didn't need to. Within moments I heard the greetings indicating Nick Volkov had arrived—and in apparent high spirits.

"He came?" I asked aloud.

"Why shouldn't he?" Cyan asked. "We set a place for him."

As much as I knew my little he's-guilty-if-he-doesn't-show reasoning meant nothing, I felt relief begin to seep into my consciousness. Last night, Kirsten had made it sound as though an arrest were imminent. Volkov showing up here today suggested that the late reporter's musings could have been just that—musings. Solid logic was rapidly extinguishing the irrational fear that had gripped me. Perhaps Kirsten met her untimely end in a strictly coincidental fashion.

That didn't feel quite right to me, but the fact that Nick Volkov had shown up gave me enough release to let go and enjoy the rest of the dinner preparation.

Jackson came into the pantry, all smiles. "We are ready to serve at any time."

"Any idea why the delay?"

"Mr. Volkov was apparently in a fender-bender on his way over. His driver is still at the scene, and Mr. Volkov needed to remain until the police arrived."

"Is he okay?"

Jackson nodded and began mixing a drink using sweet vermouth, Tennessee whiskey, and bitters. "Both Mr. Volkov and the driver were uninjured."

"What about the other guy?"

He shrugged. "Hit-and-run."

"Poor Volkov. Is he shaken up?"

Jackson strained his mixture into a lowball glass and added a maraschino cherry. "First thing he asked for was a perfect Manhattan," he said, holding up the concoction, "And told me to keep them coming."

"Yikes," I said. "Think he'll be in any mood to discuss business with that much in his system?"

Jackson backed into the doorway, lifting his shoulders in silent response. He mouthed, "We'll see."

Plating and serving dinner took my full concentration. The little snatches of conversation I caught between tasks weren't much. It seemed as though, by tacit agreement, all four diners had agreed to table contentious discussion until after the meal.

Before the empty dishes were brought back to the kitchen, Cyan and I began to prepare for dessert. She had her back to me, one hand on the coffeepot, when she turned to ask me a question.

Instead of Cyan's voice, however, Volkov's rang out. "Why can't you see reason, woman?"

We both froze.

Mrs. Campbell's voice came next. "Nicholas—"

"Goddamn this stupid arrangement. Where the hell did our fathers come up with this ridiculous idea?" Then, a *whump*, sounding a lot like a fist, slammed onto a tabletop.

"How many did he have?" I asked Jackson in a whisper.

He held up four fingers.

Another one for our "Do not serve" list.

Helen Hendrickson attempted to say something, but Senator Blanchard interrupted. "Nick, this isn't helping. Elaine, you know as well as I do that if we don't move forward now—quickly and decisively—we won't be able to sell for another ten years."

Mrs. Campbell spoke up. "We have until December fifteenth."

"You think that's a lot of time?" Volkov shouted.

"I think it's plenty of time to wait to discuss this."

Volkov kept at it. "That's why this arrangement is such idiocy. You may very well have inherited your share of the company, but you have certainly not inherited any business sense."

A chair scraped. I imagined Mrs. Campbell standing up. "Excuse me?"

Volkov's words slurred. "We have a buyer interested, which means this is the time to strike. You may have all the time in the world to make up your mind on other matters, but for now, this is the most important item on my agenda. If you don't agree to sell, then I can't be responsible for my actions." Another *whump*. Louder this time.

I peeked around the corner. Secret Service agents had moved into the room, close enough to act, should the need arise. Mrs. Campbell, however, held them off with a raised hand. "I thought it would be a good idea to talk tonight," she said. "I see I was wrong."

From my vantage point, I watched her make eye contact with each of her colleagues, one at a time. She spoke softly. "Despite the range of our ages, we practically grew up together. Have you forgotten? Our fathers were friends, close friends. As I believed we were." She clasped her hands in front of her. "Time and distance and circumstances have caused the four of us to lose the closeness we once had, but I'd hoped we'd be able to reach an agreement." She sighed.

Helen Hendrickson remained seated, and Volkov, his energy spent, dropped back into his chair. Blanchard, standing to Mrs. Campbell's left, leaned forward, fisted hands on the table. "We can still reach an agreement, Elaine."

She shook her head. "I no longer believe that."

"If you'd only listen to reason."

She held up a hand. Blanchard stopped talking. "Our fathers were wealthy men." Again she stopped long enough to make eye contact with her guests. "They envisioned something bigger than themselves, something that would live on after they were no longer here. It was their dream to use their knowledge, their wealth, and their contacts for philanthropic purposes. And you all know what a great success they achieved."

Helen Hendrickson finally got her word in. "But that's the thing, Elaine.

Zendy Industries is bigger and more successful than our fathers ever imagined. It's got holdings in every major market in the world. Just think about the good that can be done if we were to sell it."

Mrs. Campbell shook her head. "The good can only continue if Zendy remains under the charter upon which it was founded. Our fathers entrusted us to carry on their vision. If we sell now, what will we be doing to future generations?"

Volkov growled, "My children *are* the future generation. Seems to me our parents would want us to ensure their security."

"My dad told me that Zendy Industries was the best investment he ever made," she said softly. "He believed in its mission. And he made me promise never to sell."

The three others gasped.

Mrs. Campbell licked her lips. "I invited you all here tonight to tell you once and for all that I will *not* sell. Not before December fifteenth. Not ever."

Volkov bolted upward, upsetting his chair. For a moment I thought one of the agents would grab him, but he strode away from the First Lady. "Idiocy!" He threw his hands upward, gesturing to the ceiling as he paced.

"I had hoped to . . . wait," Mrs. Campbell continued. "To discuss this more fully at a later point in time, when everything settled down. Sean's death . . ." She bit her lip.

Cyan nudged me. "Getting an earful?"

I nodded.

Blanchard flexed his jaw, in an obvious attempt to keep himself in check. "Did you discuss this decision with your own children?" he asked.

"This is not their concern," she said. "Not now. Someday when it becomes their decision, I hope they'll see the wisdom of keeping Zendy Industries under family control."

Volkov, at the far end of the room, shouted, "Then buy us out. We can sell it and you can control it all."

Mrs. Campbell returned to her seat. "You know I don't have the means to do that, Nick," she said.

I glanced up at Jackson and tilted my head toward the door, asking if he was ready to serve dessert. Maybe a little sweetness would bring these people around.

While Jackson placed the peppermint ice cream at each diner's place, Volkov returned to his seat, grumbling. He stopped Jackson. Holding up his lowball glass, he swirled it briefly before lifting it to his lips and draining the last few drops. "Get me another one of these, would you?"

Jackson nodded wordlessly, but when he returned to the bar area of the pantry, I watched him prepare the drink differently.

"Won't he know the difference?" I asked when Jackson added a liberal dose of tonic water.

"He's lucky to know the difference between his hands and his feet at this point."

When Mrs. Campbell excused herself to take a phone call, the three others talked among themselves. I hoped for a tasty piece of information—for some discussion of the recently deceased Kirsten Zarzycki—but they spoke in hushed tones, and all I could make out was their intense disappointment at Mrs. Campbell's decision.

Helen heaved a great sigh. "I guess there's nothing left for us to do."

I peeked around the corner long enough to see Treyton Blanchard pat her hand. "Let me talk with her one more time," he said.

"Fat lot of good it will do," Volkov groused. He knocked his dessert plate away with a look of disgust and staggered to his feet. "There's got to be another way around this. And I'm going to find it."

By the time Mrs. Campbell returned, he'd left. The Secret Service agents on hand were only too happy to guide the blitzed Mr. Volkov out of the White House. Helen made her apologies. "I can't tell you how disappointed I am with your choice, Elaine," she said. "We have a couple more weeks before a solid decision must be made. Just promise me you'll think about it."

"Helen," Mrs. Campbell said, warning in her voice.

"I know how much Sean's death has affected you. Perhaps it was wrong of us to push you so soon after he died. Just take your time. I believe you'll see our point if you just give it a little time."

"It isn't just Sean—"

"Please," Helen said. "Just promise me you'll think on this again."

I could tell Mrs. Campbell was torn. Stick to her convictions, or give her old friend some comfort? "I won't change my mind," she finally said.

Helen reacted as though given a great gift. "I know. I know. But as long as you give it more thought, I believe we have a chance to find agreement."

Helen said good-bye and was escorted out. Senator Blanchard remained. "A moment of your time, Elaine?"

They returned to their seats. A moment later, Jackson refilled both coffee cups and stood just outside the dining room. I was cleaning some of our utensils, and listening hard above the clatter from Cyan's dish washing.

"Volkov is a loose cannon," Blanchard said. "You need to be careful."

From what I could tell, Mrs. Campbell's voice sounded weary. "If I didn't believe I was following our fathers' wishes, I wouldn't be holding on so tight."

"You were the first child born to any of them and you're like the big sister to us all. It's only natural you feel a stronger bond to the company. You were there when Zendy was created."

She gave a light laugh. "Zendy was conceived when I was about five. Then Helen was born, then Nick, and then years later, you." A long pause. "Can't you see how wrong it is to give her up? Zendy Industries is like our sister. We can't just sell her to the highest bidder."

"Some of us have plans, Elaine."

"Like a run for the presidency?"

I couldn't hear Blanchard's answer, but I detected sarcasm in Mrs. Campbell's tone when she said, "Isn't that comforting?"

Cyan turned off the water and dried her hands. Thank goodness. Now I could hear.

Blanchard's next words were clear, and no longer held their customary friendly charm. "Let me be clear on this," he said. "You may believe that selling Zendy Industries is akin to cutting off a sibling. But by not selling, you will cut *us* off. You know as well as I do that Nick is about to blow. Helen is quiet, but she's unhappy with your decision. As for me, I cannot condone your decision. If you choose to keep Zendy, you thereby choose to dispose of my friendship."

Mrs. Campbell's sharp intake of breath preceded her question. "What are you saying, Treyton?"

I couldn't help myself; I had to peer in.

He stood, hands up. "You leave me no choice. Unless you change your mind. Unless you choose your flesh-and-blood friends over the pie-in-the-sky aspirations of our fathers' company, I will no longer support you." He licked his lips. "And I will no longer support your husband."

"That's blackmail."

"No, Elaine. That's how important this sale is to me."

When he glanced in my direction, I ducked away. But I'd heard enough. What pressure they were putting on the First Lady and at such a difficult time in her life. Had they no sense of honor, of decency?

Treyton Blanchard left, informing Mrs. Campbell that he would no longer consider himself a regular guest at the White House.

She pressed him, and I heard his parting words. "It has become apparent that my own aspirations conflict with your agenda. It no longer behooves me to keep company with you or with your husband."

He added: "With that in mind, my family and I will not be present at the opening ceremonies tomorrow."

"Treyton," Mrs. Campbell said.

"Good night, Elaine. I hope you sleep well believing your goals and dreams are superior to those of the rest of us."

Whispering, Cyan made a face. "Well, I guess we know what the next primary race will look like."

In a rush I could see it play out: Treyton Blanchard would indeed make a run for the presidency. And if I were any judge of character, I believed he'd start the process sooner rather than later.

The jerk. Whether he cared or not, Senator Blanchard had just lost my vote. Permanently.

THE RED ROOM WAS NOT DIRECTLY ON OUR WAY BACK DOWN-stairs, but I pulled Cyan with me to see how great the gingerbread house looked in its setting.

Kendra and her assistants were there, adding liquid to the champagne fountain.

Cyan stepped closer to the tall device, which sloshed when two assistants inched it closer to the wall. "Is that champagne in it now?"

Kendra laughed. "No, just water. I added a couple of gallons for testing. The reception starts at noon sharp and we don't want anything to go wrong."

Cyan and I were about to leave when Kendra called us to wait. "This is the first time I'm using this fountain," she said. "We just took delivery on this one. Want to see it in motion?"

Since we were done for the night, I said, "Sure."

Kendra looked like a little kid ready to blow out birthday candles.

The two assistants had pushed the fountain into place and one stood aside, ready to turn it on. "Should we lower the lights?" I asked.

Before she could answer, the assistant plugged in the fountain and Kendra leaned forward, fingering the switch. "I'm excited," she said. "This one is bigger than the one we had before."

She turned it on.

A loud rumble heralded the upsurge.

With a screeching rush, water shot high toward the ceiling, like an erupting volcano.

"Aaaack!" we all cried at once, lifting our arms above our heads. Water fell down on us all, a hard and fast rain.

The assistants ducked. Cyan cried out and turned away. Mouth open, Kendra was aghast. And dripping wet.

"Turn it off," I said, reaching for the switch.

Kendra beat me to it. One second later, the rain ceased.

"What the hell was that?" she asked.

"Look at the drapes," I said. "Can we get someone in here to clean these up?"

Cyan's red hair looked like a shiny helmet. "I'll get housekeeping," she said. And she was off.

Kendra held a hand to her mouth, surveying the sad scene.

My next worry was for Marcel's gingerbread house. Fortunately, however, it was far enough away that it missed the sudden rain shower. "Thank goodness the fountain only had a couple of gallons in it," I said.

"What's wrong with this thing?" she asked.

I had no answer. "Good thing you tested it tonight."

With a forlorn look around the room, she nodded. "This could have been a whole lot worse tomorrow." She closed her eyes. "Champagne can get sticky."

"This really isn't too bad," I said. "I think we bore the brunt of it. Look, the furniture didn't even get winged."

"You're trying to make me feel better," she said. "But what am I going to do for a fountain? It's too late to get a new one at this juncture."

Manny showed up just then. "What's going on?" he asked.

Kendra explained and he seemed to take it all in stride. As I left them, I heard him say, "I'll get this fixed in no time."

CHAPTER 21

"TODAY'S THE BIG DAY," BUCKY SAID UNNECESSARILY WHEN HE arrived the next morning at six. "What time did you get in?"

"Four," I said.

He whistled. "I thought you said we were all caught up."

I gave a so-so motion with my head. "We are. In fact we're in great shape. I just . . ." I shrugged, unwilling to share my feelings with Bucky. Give him an inch and he'd probably take the opportunity to ask if I'd come in early to sniff for bombs. I wasn't in the mood for his special brand of humor today. "I just like mornings here."

"Me, too," he said, surprising me with the sudden faraway expression on his face. "There's something impossible to describe about this place, isn't there?" As he tied an apron around his waist, he granted me one of his rare smiles. "Like knowing there's endless potential here. Like knowing we can make a difference."

Bucky never ceased to baffle me. One minute he would crab at nothing, the next he'd echo the very same protectiveness I felt about the White House.

"Exactly," I said.

He walked over to the computer and wiggled the mouse, bringing the monitor back to life. "What's the final count for today?"

I told him.

He whistled again. "What were they thinking when they invited so many?"

"Remember, this is a combined event. Everyone from Sunday's cancellation and all of today's invited guests as well."

"Still," he said, annoyance edging back into his voice. "We're going to be working our tails off to keep the food going with that many hungry people."

"Thank goodness it's just finger food today."

"But you'll be upstairs for the photo-op, won't you?"

I'd almost forgotten about that. "Yeah. Marcel, too."

"Great," he said. "Just what we need—to be shorthanded down here when we're expecting a full house."

Ah . . . cranky Bucky. We were back to normal.

I didn't bother to respond, and minutes later the rest of the crew trooped in. In short order, we were going full force, producing attractive and delicious hors d'oeuvres for today's crowd to enjoy. There was almost no sound in the room as the clock struck the next hour . . . and the next.

After we sent Mrs. Campbell's breakfast to the residence, I stole up to the first floor with Marcel to get another look at where the press conference would be held. "I do not appreciate the way they have been moving my house around," he said as we headed up the steps. "They can easily break it, and then where would we be?"

"They moved it?" I asked.

"Yes," he said. "They tell me this is a better location for crowd control." He sniffed.

"Maybe it would be better to display it in the State Dining Room after all," I said, trying to sound encouraging. "The photographers would have more room to maneuver and get better pictures."

"This, unfortunately, is not my decision."

"No matter where it's displayed, your gingerbread house will undoubtedly be the center of attention."

He acknowledged the compliment in his customary way. "Very true," he said, "but I still believe that the house should not be moved as often as it has been. We placed it properly and that is where it should remain."

When we made it to the Red Room, we were both surprised to find the gingerbread house against the east wall. "Where's the fountain?" I asked, turning in a circle to look for it.

Marcel wasn't paying me much attention. "Look at what they have done," he said, pointing to the house's back corner. "The clumsy fools!"

I rose to tiptoes to peer where he was pointing. "I don't see anything wrong."

"I took great care to cover the wiring with special décor," he said, huffing. Tugging his tunic, he straightened and informed me that he would see to repairs at once.

The moment he was gone, I looked again. A small green wire winding around the back of the structure had poked out from the white, snowy ground-cover. Unless you were looking for it, it could easily go unnoticed. But Marcel was a perfectionist. As were we all around here.

I poked into the Blue Room and into the State Dining Room, but saw no sign of yesterday's gusher. I knew that was not my concern; I needed to worry about providing food for our guests, making sure whatever we served was properly hot or cold, and ready to go precisely when the guests were shown to the State Dining Room. Marcel would accept accolades for his gingerbread creation and I would be expected to discuss the items we planned to serve today and for all other events throughout the holidays.

This would be my first Christmas talk to the media. Henry had always handled these and he'd told me they were a piece of cake—sometimes literally. Just as sweet and easy to enjoy. But nervous flutters danced in my stomach and I doubted I could handle any sort of cake right now. Having it or eating it.

I hadn't noticed the gingerbread men when Marcel and I were in the Red Room, because I'd been first taken aback by the fact that the house had been moved, and then my attention had been further drawn by Marcel's concerns about the visible wire.

Yi-im was back, evidently having been dispatched to make Marcel's repairs. He nodded to me as I came in. "See?" he said, pointing to the three Blanchard gingerbread men. They were positioned on the wall just above the gingerbread house, each of them connected to the house by means of a stick that resembled the little poles on the structure's corners. I was amazed yet again by the quality of the workmanship.

"This looks great," I said. "Thank you."

Even though I'd asked Yi-im to make sure the kids' creations were placed properly, I was no longer sure it mattered that they sat in such a place of honor. With Blanchard's pronouncement that he would no longer visit the White House, the pretty little decorations weren't doing that much good now.

As I inched to take a closer look at the piece, Yi-im moved me away. "Marcel say no one come close. Only me."

Annoyed, I stepped back, although I understood the mind-set. Fewer people messing with Marcel's handiwork meant fewer chances for things to go wrong. I stepped back, hands up. "You're the boss."

He grinned, showing teeth. "Yeah. I boss today."

Kendra's heels clipped at a brisk pace, and I heard her call out instructions to her staff even before she walked in from the adjacent Blue Room. "Ollie," she said. "Ready for the cameras?" A quick look at her watch. "Just a couple of hours away from the big unveiling."

"Ready as I can be," I said.

She pulled a tight breath in between her teeth and gave a mock shiver. "I always get so nervous right before a big event. Really, you'd think this was my first time doing this, wouldn't you? But what a feat we've pulled off, huh?"

"What happened to the fountain?" I asked.

"That electrician said he couldn't fix it where it was, so he took it downstairs to the shop. Last I heard there was nothing they could do to get it in place on time. I ordered a replacement, but that's not here yet, either." Her smile wilted. "Looks like we're going fountainless, after all."

"What a shame," I said.

She leaned in toward me, "To be honest, I was having nightmares about splashing and spillage. This may be a blessing in disguise."

About an hour later, I was checking on early lunch preparation down in the staff cafeteria when I happened upon Curly working on the very fountain Kendra and I had discussed.

He was on his hands and knees looking up into the underside of the contraption, scowling, as usual. I thought he looked like a little boy sent to sit under a table for punishment.

"What are you doing?" I asked.

He didn't acknowledge me.

I crouched next to him. "I thought Manny was fixing this."

"You are a nosy thing, aren't you?" he asked, his voice breathless as he rearranged himself to sit. I saw why in a moment. The new position allowed him freedom to lift his hands over his head and access the fountain's inner workings.

Nonplussed, I scooted forward until I could see underneath as well. "I didn't realize this was all one piece," I said.

He brought his hands down. "What the hell do you want with me?"

"You really want to know?"

"You've been dancing around, pointing your finger at me since Gene got himself killed," he said. "You trying to get me to say it was my fault?"

"No, I—"

"Because it wasn't my fault."

"I never thought it was."

"You don't know a socket from a volt ohmmeter," he said. "How the hell can you come to me and start asking me about electrical problems? You think I'm glad Gene got killed? You think I wanted his job? You think I arranged that?" Spittle formed at the corners of his mouth and, despite being in a confined space, he gestured wildly.

"No, of course not," I said.

He mumbled to himself, looked away, and began working over his head again. Then as though he just thought of something, he tapped the fountain's underside. "You were there when this thing broke down, weren't you?"

"Yes," I said slowly.

"And you swear you saw this thing shoot water to the ceiling."

"Just short of the ceiling."

"But you swear you saw it."

"Yes, I saw it."

"Well, there ain't nothing wrong with this here fountain," he said. "What kind of game are you playing, anyway?" he asked. "What do you want from me?"

"All I ever wanted from you," I said in a clear voice, "was to answer one question. And before you shut me up again, here it is: A friend I trust has been an electrician for more than fifty years. He told me that more than one expert has been killed by floating neutrals. We had that storm the day of Gene's accident, remember? My friend just suggested I ask you to check to make sure the White House is safe. All I ever wanted from you was to make sure the house was safe. Okay?"

Angry now, I stood and didn't intend to look back before I left him sitting under the fountain. But I did look back and was immediately sorry. Though not directed at me, the intensity of his furious gaze nearly made me miss a step.

CHAPTER 22

BINDY WAS WAITING FOR ME IN THE KITCHEN WHEN I ARRIVED.

"Are they there?" she asked me.

I didn't understand. "Are who where?"

Behind her, Bucky rolled his eyes. "We have a lot of work to do here," he admonished. "I hope you're not planning to stay long."

Bindy's face reddened. "I'm sorry to bother you. I just felt as though I needed to make sure. They've closed off the upstairs to everyone until noon." She looked at her watch. "But I promised Treyton I'd double-check on the placement of his kids' gingerbread men."

Senator Blanchard had very clearly washed his hands of the White House— at least until he himself could call the place home. There was no mistaking that, after last night's arguments. Bindy was apparently far out of the loop. "Maybe there's something you ought to know," I said. "Give me a minute here and we'll talk, okay?"

I went around to the computer where I checked my schedule, to ensure we weren't running behind.

Bindy watched as I took turns to speak with each of the chefs. My first duty was to make sure that the kitchen produced the quality edibles we were known for, so I didn't skimp on any of my questions. Nor did I harbor any fondness for Bindy's boss. Let her wait.

"I'll be out in the hall," she said when Cyan pulled me back toward the storage area.

"Thank goodness," I said under my breath.

Agda smiled and asked us to move out of her way as she slid a tray of petit-fours into the large stainless steel refrigerator.

I kept my voice low. "Can you believe she's still bugging me about those gingerbread men?"

"Give it a rest, girl," Cyan said. "Did you tell her they're safe and sound in their place of honor?" She shook her head, then turned the subject back to our current concerns. "Whatever. I've got a slight change to the design we decided on for the lobster cake appetizer."

She was about to reach into the same refrigerator Agda was using when the taller woman tilted her head and closed the door. "Pretty men?" she asked us.

We both looked at her, not understanding.

The blonde bombshell pulled her lips in as though trying to decide how to word what she wanted to convey. She held up three fingers. "Gingerbread from box?" she asked.

I remembered that Agda had been there when we received the three additions from the Blanchard family. I nodded. "Yes."

"Very pretty," she said again.

With Bindy waiting for me out in the hall and several thousand appetizers waiting for my approval in the next room, I was eager to put an end to this not-so-scintillating conversation. "They truly are," I said, eager to see the change Cyan wanted to show me.

Agda put her hand on my arm. "They are broken?"

"No," I said. "Last I looked, they were upstairs."

She shook her head. "Yi-im," she said, pronouncing his name Yim instead of Yee-eem. "He is fixing them, no?"

Now I was totally confused. "No. No one is fixing them. They're upstairs." I asked Cyan, "When did you last see them?"

She thought about it. "This morning. Yeah. All three were there. They looked fine to me."

"And I saw them about an hour ago," I said. I'd hate to think that one of them fell off their little posts. I turned to Agda. "Did one of them fall?"

She held up her hands in the universal language of "I don't know." Biting her lip before she spoke again, she said, "Yi-im tell me to shh." She placed a finger over her lips. "He say he break it, he fix it."

"When was this?" I asked.

Her big eyes moved up and to the left. "Eight o'clock, at night."

"Yesterday?"

She nodded.

"Wow, that's pretty specific," I said.

She may not have understood my surprised reaction, but she must have understood my meaning. "I have couple minutes before I go home last night," she said. "I want to see White House upstairs. Yi-im say, 'Shhh.'"

"You asked him about it?"

"Yah. He say he fixing." She tilted her head. "Fixing all three."

With Agda and Yi-im and their combined broken English, I couldn't begin to guess what either of them really meant. I rubbed my eyes. The last thing we needed was another loose end. "Maybe I should go check," I said.

Cyan gave me a look. "And what will you tell Bindy if one of her precious decorations is broken?"

I was already moving back into the main part of the kitchen with a plan to keep Bindy at bay. "Maybe she doesn't have to know."

She was pacing the Center Hall when I returned. "Took you long enough," she said.

I swallowed my annoyance at her snippy remark, deciding instead to go on the offensive. "I don't know why you even care about these gingerbread men anymore."

"I told you that Senator Blanchard was very eager to have his children's—"

"What difference does it make if he and his family aren't coming today?"

When her jaw dropped just a little, I realized she really hadn't been brought up to speed.

"Bindy," I said. "I am not one to tell stories out of school, but I have the distinct impression that Senator Blanchard is intent on severing his ties with the White House. And I have it on good authority that he is boycotting today's event. Or didn't you get the memo?"

That one struck a nerve. She pulled her shoulders back. "I spoke with Senator Blanchard just before I came here. And he told me to make sure everything was still in place for the photo-op. That's why I came. To make sure the kids' men are where they can be seen."

Blanchard must have had a change of heart, I thought. But he'd made things perfectly clear to Mrs. Campbell yesterday. I wondered what had changed, why his bitterness had suddenly made the leap to good sense.

I sighed. "I'll be the first to admit that plans change here faster than a collapsing soufflé. But I can't take you upstairs."

"Can you just go check and report back to me?"

Did she think I had nothing better to do than to double-check her boss's whims? I bit the sides of my cheeks to keep from a snappy retort. I knew the relationship between Mrs. Campbell and Senator Blanchard was on shaky ground today. Perhaps it wouldn't hurt for me to just take a peek and give her an update.

"Wait here."

I took the steps two at a time and turned left when I made it to the top. Crossing the Entrance Hall, I hurried past the tall pillars toward the Red Room, my soft-soled shoes making tiny squeaks on the shiny floor. There were photographers in all the public rooms. They'd been granted early access in order to set up. Big, shiny, white flash umbrellas decorated each corner, and bright spotlights were clicked on and off, as light meters were tested.

Despite the fact that I couldn't wait for Bindy to be gone and out of my hair, I stole a quick peek into the Blue Room where the Fraser fir stood, decked out in all its glory. Just like the rest of the house, the lights that decorated it were unlit. Everything had been tested as it had been installed. But the holiday season wouldn't begin until noon when the First Lady threw the switch.

In the Red Room, Marcel had an icing bag in his right hand, a tiny trowel in his left, and a panicked look on his face. "They have ruined it," he said.

"What?" I asked. "Where?"

"*Ici*," he said, pointing. "Again, I have found a piece that should not be open to the eye. This should have been covered earlier."

The flaw Marcel spoke of was another wire appearance. This time the wire was gray, and attached to the back of the structure. "Maybe when Yi-im was fixing the gingerbread men," I said, "he bumped it and the icing fell off?"

"Fixing what gingerbread men?"

The fear on Marcel's face made me sorry I'd said anything.

"Oh," I stammered. "Maybe I'm wrong. One of my chefs said . . ."

I purposely let the thought hang as I moved closer to inspect the three gingerbread men perched just above the cookie White House. Not one of them looked marred in any way. Perhaps Agda had been mistaken. Perhaps Yi-im had been working on other gingerbread men. They were all certainly fragile.

"I guess Agda meant different gingerbread men," I said. "She told me some were broken."

"And thank heaven for that," Marcel said with spirit. "Some of them were . . . *exécrable*, and I would be ashamed to show them to the public. Even if they are made by children in America, we must always strive for the best display we can manage."

Personally, I thought Marcel was missing the point of the exercise, but I kept quiet. Scrutinizing the decorations, I tried to see if I could find any evidence of them having been repaired.

Marcel was so intent on his own repairs that he no longer paid me any mind.

Each of the three men sat perched atop a pole. None of the poles had cracks or anything visibly wrong with them. I remembered being impressed with the gingerbread men because each held a tiny flag made out of sugar. Even these delicate details looked to be perfect.

"These are supposed to light up, too?" I asked, pointing to the three men.

Marcel gave me a brief glance. "No," he said. "Only the house is to light. And these poles." He pointed vaguely in the direction of a corner of the building. "You remember? The sparklers. We have added more for effect."

They certainly had. In addition to the three poles attached to the Blanchard gingerbread men, there were several additional ones along the side and back of the White House itself. I could only imagine what a beautiful background it would make for the house when the creation was officially lit this afternoon. I selfishly wished they'd had them in place when we'd tested it earlier.

But I would see it later. One of the nicest things about being executive chef was the fact that I was not only welcome, but featured, at many of these official events.

"Okay, thanks," I said. "Good luck with your repairs."

Marcel grunted.

WITH BINDY FINALLY GONE—PLEASED WITH THE KNOWLEDGE that her boss's kids' artwork was in place—and the last of the hors d'oeuvres complete, all we had to do now was wait. In twenty minutes, one of the assistants would come down to escort me upstairs for the media event.

I checked my watch for the fifteenth time in the space of twelve seconds.

"Nervous, Ollie?" Cyan asked.

I pretended not to hear her. The last thing I needed was to endure the well-intentioned jibes of my coworkers while I was fighting off butterflies in my gut.

"Agda," I said, trying to divert everyone's attention. "I checked those gingerbread men upstairs. None of them were broken."

Her brows came together in a puzzled look. "Yah," she said. "All three broken."

"Not the ones from the Blanchard family," I said patiently.

Her perplexed frown grew tighter. "Yah," she said again, with feeling. "Three from box."

As luck would have it, Marcel walked in just then. "Ask him," I said to Agda. "He and I both checked the gingerbread men. There's nothing wrong with any of them."

She seemed so miserable to be wrong, that I added, brightly, "It must have been some of the others," I said.

"No." She gave me the most direct look she had since she'd begun working here. "I see him fix *två*." She stabbed three fingers into the air for emphasis.

"What is wrong?" Marcel asked, glancing from one of us to the other. "Something is amiss?"

I explained, but even as I began, Marcel shook his head. "Once we installed the three gingerbread men above the house, they were not to be moved," he said. "Yi-im knew this. He would not move them."

Agda's lips were tight and her entire being seemed to reverberate with tense frustration. I rested the tips of my fingers against her forearm. "I believe you saw him fixing gingerbread men," I said. "But the three from the Blanchard family—from the box—are looking great." I didn't reiterate that they'd never been broken. I just wanted to put this matter to rest. In the large scheme of things—with an event the size of which we would be working today—this was nothing. "What's important now is that there are only about ten minutes to go before the ceremonies begin, and everything is perfect."

The words hadn't left my mouth before one of the assistants, Faber, appeared in the doorway. "Five minutes."

Marcel and I didn't waste another moment. "Bucky, come on," I said, inviting him to join us. "I'd like you to be part of this, too."

Pleased, he hurried along with us to don clean jackets—crisp, white, recently pressed—and our tall toques. While we kept them here in the kitchen for occasional use, we *always* wore them for media events. I liked the fact that wearing one made me seem taller.

Marcel was repeating things to himself in a low voice.

"What are you doing?" I asked.

With an abashed look, he whispered, "I am trying to remember key words to respond when the First Lady asks me the questions."

He and I had been provided with scripts, ahead of time. Nothing in them was difficult or unusual, but I understood his discomposure. We were supposed to recite from our prepared scripts, but make it look conversational. Sure. Get in front of the cameras and all memorization, all practice, goes out the window.

I'd surprised Bucky by inviting him to participate with me. My intention was not to make him eat his words about being left shorthanded in the kitchen but to foster a sense of inclusion. Henry was my idol where that talent was concerned, and I was eager to prove myself a worthy pupil. As my second-in-command, Bucky wasn't likely to be called upon to answer any questions on camera. But you never could completely predict these things.

Bucky's eyes were wild as he straightened and restraightened his white jacket. "Do I look okay?" he asked.

"You look great," I said. And it was true. Though he and I occasionally bumped heads and ideas in the kitchen, we had a mutual respect and I was, if not glad, then resigned to the fact that he would always be part of our crew. No doubt about it: In the kitchen, he was an asset. Unfortunately, he was also a pain in mine.

"Where's Yi-im?" I asked Marcel. "Didn't he want to be part of this? He's done so much lately."

Marcel wagged his head sadly. "He has taken ill."

I'd seen him this morning, and he'd looked fine to me. I said so.

Marcel gave a very French shrug. "What can I say? He tells me he is sick; I have to believe him. We do not want germs on our precious creations."

"That's true."

Faber led the three of us up, using the stairs closest to the usher's office. I felt the nervous jitters myself and I, too, started to rehearse my lines for when the First Lady would ask about menu preparations.

On our way up, we met Curly coming down. Looking a lot like an angry bulldog, he seemed not to even notice us until we passed him. But then he grabbed my arm and looked directly into my face. "You seen Manny?" he asked.

"No," I said wiggling my arm to dislodge his hand. But he held fast.

Faber cleared his throat. "We are on our way to the official opening—"

"I know where the hell you're headed," he said, his voice a growl that matched the bulldog visage to perfection. The long, pinched scar throbbed red. "But since you're always chasing after Manny and Vince, I figured you'd know where they are. It's the last minute before everything goes hot and they ain't anywhere."

Although he let go of my arm, he stood right in front of me, blocking my passage.

"So I'll ask you again," Curly said. "Where are they?"

Faber stood two steps higher than I did. "Ms. Paras," he said, meekly. "It's almost time."

"I don't know what your problem is, Curly," I said. "But I have a commitment and I believe in doing my job. Maybe it's time you started doing yours."

His face whitened even as his scar burned crimson. I stepped around him, shaken by the altercation. With Gene around all these years, I'd never had to deal with Curly directly before—at least, not so often. I sincerely hoped Paul would not see fit to promote him from "acting" to "permanent" chief electrician.

When we finally got upstairs, I was blown away by the number of people. Sure, we'd been given a list and a headcount, but it's one thing to expect a specific number of guests, and another to see them up close. On paper, and during planning, it's abstract. Here, it was very real. Warm, close, sweaty real. Hundreds of milling folks. Mostly Capitol Hill types, media moguls, and their families.

The holiday opening was, indeed, one of the more family-friendly events the White House threw each year and I was pleased to see so many little ones in attendance.

Camera crews behaved themselves, maintaining the decorum prescribed to them by social secretary, Marguerite Schumacher. She was on hand, of course, overseeing every minute detail. This was her moment, as well as Kendra's. The two had worked side-by-side with the First Lady to create the rich, warm, welcoming festival that was the official beginning of the White House holiday season.

Faber led us through a cordoned-off walkway where Marcel, Bucky, and I were directed to stand. He waited with us, one hand low, keeping us behind the ropes, until one of the other ushers nodded. Continuing along the cordoned-off path, we smiled at the reporters, who lobbed questions at us as we passed.

All three of us nodded, looking as happy and content as possible. We knew that we were not to answer any questions directly. The only time we were to speak to the reporters was in the Red Room, and only when we were addressed by the First Lady.

Marcel stood to the right of the gingerbread house. I stood to its left, with Bucky next to me. Had Yi-im been here, he would have taken my position, and Bucky and I would have stood a bit farther away. Photo-op-wise, however, it looked better to have the house flanked by two chefs. Symmetry and all that.

The crowd was currently enraptured by the show in the Blue Room behind us, while we waited, practically standing at attention. I twisted to peer into the next room, to watch the delight wash over the faces of the kids and the adults when the marvelous White House tree was lit.

I stifled a sigh. Marcel shifted his weight and adjusted his neckline.

We waited.

In the next room, the First Lady was answering questions. I could just make out her words, high and clear over the crowd sounds. The tree hadn't yet been lit, and she was explaining the logic behind this year's theme, and how she, Marguerite, and Kendra had worked together for nearly half a year, planning the celebration. Mrs. Campbell was effusive with praise for her social secretary and florist.

I let my gaze wander toward the First Lady.

In the doorway that connected the Red Room to the Blue Room, I spied a familiar face. Little Treyton Blanchard, the senator's oldest son, peeked around the corner. He smiled when he saw me, and gave a quick wave. I waved back. His mother, with her back to us, didn't notice.

Bindy was right, after all. I guess the temptation of seeing her children's creations up close and personal when the world got its first look was too much for Mrs. Blanchard to pass up.

Little Trey broke away from his mother and made his way over, all smiles. He pointed. "Those are ours," he said, with more than a little pride.

"They sure are," I said in a soft voice as I bent down to talk with him. "I bet you're glad now that you made them."

He gave me a face that looked out of place in someone so young. Cynical and amused. "We didn't really make those," he said, inching closer. "But we helped a little bit. I helped the most."

"I had a feeling you did."

Mrs. Blanchard had turned around to look for her son. When she saw him talking with me, she came over, carrying the youngest Blanchard on her hip, the middle one toddling behind. "I'm so sorry," she said in a stage whisper. "I hope he hasn't been bothering you."

Her eyes raked the gingerbread house and her gaze settled on the three gingerbread men just above it.

"Not at all," I said.

The murmurs in the other room grew, perhaps in response to one of the First Lady's comments. Maryann Blanchard shot a nervous glance back to the

Blue Room. "My husband didn't want us to come today," she said, with a guilty smile, "but I couldn't bear to miss this opportunity." She shifted little Leah in her arms and spoke to the children. "Do you see?" she asked them. "Look!"

Pointing with her free hand, she indicated the three gingerbread men. "You made those, and now the president of the United States is using them to decorate his house for Christmas." The woman positively glowed. "Isn't that great?"

John, the middle child, stepped back to see better. "Can't we take them home to our house?"

Maryann Blanchard shook her head. "We made these as gifts. It's like giving your country a Christmas present."

John looked unimpressed. Leah sucked her thumb and rested her head on her mother's shoulder. Only the oldest, Trey, had anything to say. "I wish I would've worked harder on it."

She patted him on the head. "You did a wonderful job."

From the sounds of things, the tree in the Blue Room was about to be lit. "Come on," Maryann Blanchard said to her brood, "we don't want to miss this."

I smiled after them. The three kids were nowhere near as impressed with the White House as their mother was, but I supposed someday they could tell their own kids about being featured. Of course, if their father had any say in the matter, after the next election, they'd be living here themselves.

I would have loved to watch the tree-lighting ceremony, but it was my duty to stay put, to be ready for my turn to talk to the country about the small part I played in bringing the holidays to the president's home.

The next room quieted, and someone lowered the room's lights. A hush settled over the onlookers and even the reporters assigned to this room craned their necks to see.

I tried peering over the tops of the guests' heads but had no luck.

After a prolonged silence, the room next door lit up, and everyone broke into spontaneous applause.

My heart pounded. Both because it was our turn next and because I was so proud of all we'd accomplished. Not just Marcel and I, not just the crew in the kitchen, but all of us. The country had been under siege—both from terrorists and economically—for an extended period of time. Those on the right side of the Senate aisle and their counterparts on the left could not agree on even the simplest matters, and pundits were having a field day.

These few weeks in the White House gave us all a respite. A time when we could just be together as citizens of this great country. A time for all of us to take a moment and reflect on the goodness that we all share. Whether we celebrated Christmas, Hanukkah, Kwanzaa—all of them, or none of them—we were doing so together.

Bindy appeared at the doorway to the Red Room, her hair blown back from her face, and her cheeks bright red, looking as though she'd run all the way from the East Appointment Gate. She scanned the room, one hand gripping the door frame, as though it was difficult to hold herself up. When she saw me, her expression changed. I would have characterized it as panicked. "Ollie, where are they?"

I had no doubt who she meant. I pointed. "In the Blue—"

She didn't wait for me to finish. Bolting away, she spied little John Blanchard and grabbed him by the arm. He protested loudly.

Maryann Blanchard turned, as though to admonish her son, then saw Bindy standing there. "What are you—?"

"We have to go," Bindy said.

I'd left my position next to the gingerbread house to follow. "What's going on?"

Bindy ignored me.

Mrs. Blanchard shook her head and answered the assistant. "The tour isn't over yet." She tugged John closer.

"Your husband wants you home," Bindy said. "Now."

That got Maryann Blanchard's back up. I watched fire light her eyes. "Oh really? Well, you can tell him that no matter what his quarrel is with the White House, I am not giving up the chance to have my children photographed at this event."

Bindy shook her head, and pulled Mrs. Blanchard's elbow. She spoke softly. "You don't understand," she said, her nervous giggle making its appearance. This time it sounded almost like a hiccup. "It's an emergency."

Mrs. Blanchard's eyes clouded. "What happened?"

"Come with me. Please."

"Mommy, I don't want to go," Trey said. "We haven't got our pictures taken yet."

Bindy's gaze floated toward the three gingerbread men, then back to Mrs. Blanchard. "We have to go. Now." She squeezed John's arm and he cried out. "I'm not kidding. You've got to listen to me."

The crowd around Mrs. Blanchard had begun to notice the minor fracas, and Mrs. Blanchard noticed them. Reluctantly gathering her children and shushing their complaints, she followed Bindy out the door. As soon as they were gone, the onlookers returned their attention to the question-and-answer session going on under the Blue Room's spotlights.

I returned to my post, and tried to process what just happened.

"What was that all about?" Bucky asked.

Marcel snorted. "Who can understand such females as these? You remember how Bindy behaved when she worked here. Always too impressionable."

Marcel was right. She'd been an unpredictable and often unstable staffer. I'd harbored hope that this new position, working for the senator, would have settled her down.

Senator Blanchard was apparently still angry enough at Mrs. Campbell that the very idea of his family being here appalled him. I didn't for one minute buy Bindy's excuse of an emergency. I'd seen the lie flit across her face as she grasped for a reason to persuade Mrs. Blanchard to leave the premises.

Bindy had been manic in her demeanor. Frantic, actually.

I looked up when Gav appeared in the doorway. Keeping one eye on the festivities next door, he sauntered over and spoke softly, close to my ear.

"This is not for public distribution," he said.

He waited till I leaned back and met his eyes. "Okay."

Bucky was close enough to listen in. At Gav's glare, he stepped a few feet away.

Gav whispered, "Sean Baxter didn't commit suicide."

I jerked away from him, looking again into his face. Although in my gut I'd known that to be true, it was far different to hear someone in authority say the words. "Who killed him?" I asked.

He shook his head. "We don't know yet."

"But they know for sure it wasn't suicide?"

He nodded. "And I checked that other rumor you asked me about."

"About Nick Volkov?"

"He didn't kill Mr. Sinclair," he said. "But someone has gone to a lot of trouble to make it look like he did."

"What does that mean?"

Gav gave a slight headshake. "Tell you more later. For now, just be aware."

Like a ghost, he slid away.

Be aware? Of what? I wondered.

Bucky moved to stand next to me again just as the group began to filter into the Red Room. This was it: my time to shine. But I couldn't feel the joy. Something was holding me back. A tight, annoying prickle told me something wasn't quite right.

Cameras were set up and the First Lady was led to her spot just in front of the gingerbread house. It was then I realized that I was standing next to the switch. Mrs. Campbell would have to get in close to me in order to turn it on. Which meant I would have to move when the time came. A perfect photo opportunity, with the pastry chef on one side and the First Lady on the other. Whoever had plotted this out had vision.

Too bad poor Yi-im had gone home sick. If he'd been standing right here, he'd have been in the picture, too.

A feeling prickled the back of my arms and creeped across my shoulder blades.

I stole a look at the three gingerbread men the Blanchard family had insisted we place prominently in this room. The three men that, according to Agda, Yi-im had supposedly been "fixing" late last night.

I'd convinced myself she'd been mistaken in her observation. But . . . why had I made that assumption? Agda had been the personification of precision since we'd hired her. And for some reason, I'd chosen to doubt her when it came to Yi-im.

Yi-im, a "lazy man" by Jackson's standards, who'd maneuvered his way into the pastry kitchen, even though he'd been hired as a butler.

I shook my head and paid attention to the ceremony.

Mrs. Campbell was wearing a black skirt suit, with no festive adornment whatsoever. Although she smiled as she took up her position next to Marcel, I knew from the look in her eyes that she couldn't wait for this tour to be over. But we'd all worked so hard, and I knew she wouldn't want to disappoint our nation's citizens.

I thought about the dysfunctional champagne fountain. I wondered if anyone even missed it.

My mind flashed—a quick recollection—Curly sitting under the fountain, proclaiming nothing wrong with the device.

And yet it had blown water to the ceiling when activated in this room.

Here.

I swallowed.

The gingerbread house was exactly where the champagne fountain once stood.

Marcel nodded in answer to a question Mrs. Campbell posed. I hadn't paid attention, but forced myself to refocus.

"And this only took you two weeks?" Mrs. Campbell said. "I don't think I could create something this beautiful in a year."

A titter of polite laughter from the audience. Marcel nodded again. "Thank you."

I leaned back and peeked behind the skirted table, hoping no one would notice me. In order to get the gingerbread house to light up at just the perfect time, it had been plugged in—into two separate outlets that would work together, to light up both the inside and the outside of the structure.

These were the same two outlets the fountain had been plugged into before. Two outlets. Just like the two sockets that Stanley had shown me.

Blood rushed from my face to my feet. Bucky sidled closer. "Hang in there."

I caught sight of Gav, watching everything from a far corner of the room, and thought about the real bomb that only he and I knew about. He gave me a funny look and I remembered, suddenly, Tom's one-on-one lesson. He'd told me that explosives could take almost any shape. He'd shown me pictures. I thought about Gav's training session with the simulated bomb in the presidential seal. I'd screwed that up because I hadn't noticed the wires. If only I'd seen . . .

The wires.

I twisted my head. The Blanchard gingerbread men.

"My God," I said, finally piecing everything together.

Mrs. Campbell started toward me—toward the switch.

Frozen by wild terror, I couldn't move. Bucky tugged at my elbow, urging me to step away.

"No," I said to him. "I think . . ."

It couldn't be. Could it? I stared at the gingerbread men again.

Bucky's teeth were clenched. "Ollie, come on."

Mrs. Campbell gave me an uncomfortable smile as she shoehorned her way between me and the house.

"And our theme this year wouldn't be complete without Marcel's masterpiece, an absolutely magnificent reproduction of the White House." Mrs. Campbell smiled, shooting me a look of confusion. I still hadn't moved. "I give you our holiday theme and invite you all to enjoy . . . 'Together we celebrate—Welcome Home.'" Her finger skimmed the switch.

"No!" I shouted, pushing her away from the table. I dove beneath the skirting and grabbed at the cords—one in each hand. They pulled free from the outlet with more ease than I expected, which sent me tumbling backward, dragging the tabletop with me.

Its base upset, the gingerbread house tilted for a crazed, breathless moment, then slid away, crashing onto the floor behind me, into a million tiny crumbles.

"*Sacre bleu!*" Marcel screamed. "Olivia, what have you done?" I peered out from under the skirting, flipping the fabric up to see him holding his head in his hands, a disbelieving, furious expression on his face.

I sat on the floor, looking up at Mrs. Campbell, who stared down at me for a long moment, her hands over her mouth.

I was vaguely aware of incessant clicking, of hundreds of flashes, as the photographers captured my moment of shame for all posterity.

Gav had moved in, as had a crew of Secret Service personnel. "That's enough. Everyone out."

As reporters and others plied them with questions, I heard the repeated refrain: "We will issue a statement later. No questions now."

I hung my head and sat under the table, with Marcel sobbing behind me, and Bucky shuffling through the broken pieces of house that littered the floor. "You sure did it this time, Ace," he said.

I looked up. "Thanks."

Mrs. Campbell had been whisked away by her protection detail, and I was surrounded by Secret Service who didn't wear happy-to-see-me looks.

Gav broke through their perimeter. "What happened?"

Now that I needed to put it into words, I hesitated. What if I was wrong?

I pointed to the gingerbread men that had tumbled to the ground along with the house. Not one of them had broken. "I think there might be plastic explosives in those," I said.

One of the agents behind Gav rolled his eyes, but Gav picked one up.

I bit my bottom lip. "And I think those two outlets have a floating neutral."

"A what?"

I explained, realizing how ridiculous everything sounded when spoken aloud. "If there is a floating neutral, then the gingerbread house would have gotten too much voltage," I said. "There are sparklers—little pyrotechnic things that Marcel added—but I think his assistant added more." I licked my lips, my voice cracking under the pressure. "If the voltage would have hit . . . Well, I don't know what would have happened."

Before I'd finished my explanation, Gav had picked up one of the three

Blanchard gingerbread men. His brow furrowed as he examined the back of the decoration. "I don't see anything—"

My heart dropped. I'd be sacked for sure this time.

"Wait," he said, turning the design around to the front. To one of the other agents, he said, "Get Morton up here."

"What is it?" I asked.

The agents around me had relaxed their positions a little. They'd taken the weeping Marcel away. Bucky had asked to stay but had been sent back downstairs.

Gav shook his head. Within moments a burly man wearing body armor arrived. Morton. Gav handed him all three gingerbread men to examine.

"Don't feel like standing up yet, do you?" Gav asked me.

I knew my legs wouldn't handle it. "No."

He sat on the floor next to me, and released the collection of agents whose very presence crowded the room more than all the reporters, visitors, and photographers had, combined.

"You're going to get crumbs all over your suit pants," I said.

"Hazard of the job."

"What did I do?" I asked.

"One of two things," he said. "You either gave the media a whopper of a story to ruin you with . . ."

I moaned and put my head down.

"Or you saved a lot of lives, including the First Lady's."

Morton spoke. "Special Agent-in-Charge?"

Gavin looked up. "Yes?"

"Clear the building."

CHAPTER 23

"WHERE'S THE FIRST LADY?" I ASKED AS GAV RUSHED ME FROM THE room.

Two Secret Service agents accompanied us, Patricia Berland and Kevin Martin. Agent Martin shook his head, refusing to answer.

I'd expected to be led outside, as we had when I'd shouted the alarm Saturday, but to my surprise, I was herded into the East Wing and down the now-familiar set of stairs. "The bunker?" I asked.

Gav kept his lips tight and never broke stride. When the agents ushered us into the first door on the right, I was visited with a peculiar sense of déjà vu. This is where it all had begun, just days ago, when the fake bomb had been found . . . when Sean was still alive.

My sense of repeating past events was heightened when I walked in to see the First Lady sitting at the table where the three of us had shared our lunch. She stood. "Ollie, I just heard what you did."

The enormity of the experience was making my legs heavy, my head tight. I made it to one of the chairs and didn't even think twice about etiquette. I sat down and blew out a shaky breath.

Gav and the two agents sat with us while we went over details. I explained again why I suspected an explosive, and a misfire in the electrical system that would trigger it. When I told them that this unusual phenomena could be purposely engineered, Agent Martin said, "Then they had to have had help from the inside."

"Curly!" I sat up, startled by my own realization. "The electrician who took over when Gene was killed. He's been fighting me the whole way. I tried to get him to look at the problem, but he refused." I spoke very quickly, gauging the three agents watching me, trying hard not to be stalled by their solemn expressions. "I think he might have set all this up. He was impossible to deal with. And . . ." I was grasping at straws, but I couldn't stop myself. "He might have even been the one who had me attacked."

Mrs. Campbell had been silent for most of this. When she spoke, she did so very quietly. "I can't believe that anyone would want to harm me," she said. "I know the gingerbread men were contributed by the Blanchard family. But how can you be sure that Treyton Blanchard is behind this? Couldn't it have been someone else?"

I looked to Gav. He answered, "We're rounding up a number of people for questioning right now. We'd been operating under the assumption that the president was the bomber's target, but with the information we have now, we believe that you may have been the target all along."

Mrs. Campbell looked away.

Agent Martin held a hand up. He held tight to his earpiece and listened closely. "We're needed back upstairs," he said, and started for the door. Agent Berland followed him.

Gav started to leave, too. "Will you be all right for a little while?" he asked.

The prickle at my shoulders was back. I was missing something.

He was just about out the door, when I said, "Wait."

Motioning for the two agents to go on ahead without him, Gav stopped. "What is it?"

When Tom had taken me through his version of Explosives 101, he'd been adamant on one point. In fact, he'd pounded the concept into my brain by making me repeat a mantra, over and over. "Always assume there's a secondary device."

"I think," I said, standing, pulling my thoughts together and attempting to make sense of them. "I think we need to go back to the kitchen."

GAV WANTED TO SEQUESTER ME IN THE BUNKER WITH MRS. CAMP-bell while he called the bomb squad back for a look, but I balked. "I could be wrong," I said.

He shot me an intense look. "You haven't been wrong yet."

I opened my mouth, but he interrupted.

"You cannot go traipsing around the White House when there might be a second bomb ready to go off," he said.

"You'll never find it without me."

"Wanna bet?"

The idea of going bomb-hunting was not high on my list of healthy activities, but the truth was, if I was right, they wouldn't find the second bomb for a long time. And by then it could be too late. I swallowed, unable to find the words to convey my need to protect the White House, but I saw that need reflected in all the agents' eyes. I knew they saw it in mine.

After a brief discussion on the possibility of setting up a camera for me to direct Gav and his agents from a safe distance, they decided there just wasn't enough time to arrange for that. "Putting your life in danger is not an option," Gav said. "We'll just have to do our best without you."

"Nobody knows the kitchen like I do," I said. "And the clock is ticking."

They knew it. I knew it.

I grabbed Gav's arm. "Literally."

The bomb squad took over our area of the bunker and outfitted me in protective gear. Just as they hustled me out, Mrs. Campbell asked, "Are you sure you know what you're doing?"

Covered by a helmet and a clear plastic face guard, I couldn't be certain she heard me assure her I did. Not that it mattered. I wasn't quite sure myself.

Walking with body armor was harder than I anticipated. Covered from head to toe, I felt as though I weighed six hundred pounds. Within moments of leaving the bunker, I was wet around my waist and collar, and rivulets of sweat dripped around my ears.

Gav, similarly outfitted, remained silent as we made our way through the hall and into the kitchen. Like I'd told them, I knew my kitchen like I would know my own children, if I had any. But to explain where to find something to a person unfamiliar with the area would be an exercise in futility. And the last thing I needed was for an army of military bomb experts to toss my pristine kitchen in an attempt to find an explosive device that I could put my hand on in moments.

Yeah, I was nervous. But more than that, I was determined.

Once in the kitchen, though, I faltered. My heart slammed so hard in my chest I could almost hear it clang against the body armor. If I was right, this entire room—the place I considered home even more so than my apartment— could be vaporized. Me with it.

I bit my lips, but it was hard to do since they were slippery with perspiration. My voice was hoarse. "Okay, here," I said, even though I wasn't sure they could hear me. I made my way to the far end of the room, bomb squad in tow. With the sinks to my left, I yanked up the drop-side of the center stainless steel countertop. "This is why you'd never find it." Once the side was secure, I crouched and reached beneath it to reveal a hidden cabinet door. Because of its inaccessibility, we rarely used this storage space except to shove junk we hoped never to see again.

I thought I heard them all gasp as I lost my footing, but it was just a quick stumble, and within seconds I'd righted myself, ready to root through the collection of useless items we'd retired here. I'd tucked this thing deep, hoping to forget about it until the time came for a seasonal clean-up.

Gav placed a hand on my padded shoulder. "I'll take over from here." His voice sounded far away. Blunted.

"But it's right—"

He silenced me with a look. "Think back to the Briefing Room, Ollie."

He was right. I remembered my mistake snatching the fake IED from its perch, risking setting off a bomb. Finding this device was one thing. Handling it was something else.

Gav pointed to the door. "And get out."

I scooted backward, but panic gripped when I realized I'd have to cross the kitchen again to escape. As brave as I'd been coming down here, the terror I felt now, knowing that any movement in Gav's peripheral vision could affect the outcome, froze me in place. His focus right now was inside that cabinet door and he couldn't see me huddled in a corner behind him. All *my* focus was on him as he took a breath and steeled himself.

Twisting, Gav pushed his arm deep into the cabinet's recesses, his fingers working along objects I could picture even though I couldn't see. "Careful," I breathed, clouding my face mask.

"Hang on," he said to himself.

Very slowly, Gav eased backward, his hands cradling the familiar, ugly clock.

"That's it!" I said.

Other bomb squad technicians rushed forward and gently removed the clock from Gav's hands, placing it into a thick, insulated box. With a nod of acknowledgment, they hurried out.

The moment they were gone, I pulled the helmet off. So did Gav.

"What now?" I asked.

He shot me a skeptical look. "Haven't you had enough?"

* * *

WITH THE GINGERBREAD HOUSE DESTROYED, THE OFFICIAL OPEN-
ing celebration abandoned, the First Lady relocated from the bunker to the
residence, and reporters trampling over one another to try to get the scoop, it
was a wild day, even by White House standards.

Not for the first time did I find myself the center of attention of a bunch of
serious-faced males. This time we were back in the Red Room, and I was walking five men—all agents and security personnel—through my thought pro-
cesses when I'd been waiting for Mrs. Campbell to throw the switch.

Though Gav was present, he didn't participate. He stood back as I fielded
questions from the group, explaining what I could about floating neutrals. "I
don't know how to test for them," I began, "and I don't even know if one was
present. . . ."

"There was." The voice came from the back of the room, and I was surprised
to see Curly Sheridan escorted in by two more agents. He looked as grumpy
as ever, but to my surprise, he wasn't handcuffed, or in any way restrained.

I took an instinctive step back.

"It's okay," one of the agents said. "This is the guy who disabled the voltage
problem."

I didn't understand.

"Damn Manny," Curly said. When he looked at me, his eyes narrowed.
"When you found me working on the fountain, I thought you were talking out
your a—your backside. But what you said made sense." He rubbed a finger
along his scar, which made me feel guilty even though I hadn't done anything
wrong. "I started looking into what you were talking about."

"The floating neutral?"

"Yeah," he said. "Looks like Manny, or Vince—or both of them—rigged
one up to set those outlets to blow 240." He nodded toward the wall.

He didn't admit that he should have listened to me earlier, but regret radiated off him like waves of heat. And that was good enough for me.

"They took off," said Gav from the back of the room. "We're picking them
up now for questioning."

"Yi-im," I said suddenly.

"We're after him, too."

CHAPTER 24

MARCEL WAS STILL MOURNING HIS LOST GINGERBREAD HOUSE the next day. "There are not even photos of it other than those I took myself," he said. "All the photographers waited until the lighting ceremony." He heaved a great sigh. "So much work. All lost."

We stood in the kitchen, having just finished preparing breakfast for the president and First Lady. Other than the fact that the upstairs was still being processed as a crime scene, life was back to normal. After the excitement yesterday, the president had come home to be with his wife. Tom had come back last night, too—in fact he'd picked me up inside the grounds, sparing me having to run the gauntlet of reporters that swarmed the place. Thank goodness. I'd needed to vent and he was only too willing to listen.

"There are plenty of pictures of Ollie in today's paper," Cyan said, pushing the front page across the countertop.

I'd seen them. Crisp color pictures of me sitting under a table amid gingerbread detritus graced the first page, under the headline "That's the Way the Cookie Crumbles." I turned away, groaning. "Can't we just forget yesterday ever happened?"

"The ace executive chef does it again," Bucky said, with more than a hint of sarcasm. "Olivia Paras, always in the middle of everything."

"Back off, Buckaroo," Cyan said. "She saved your life. All of ours, probably."

His mouth puckered and he glanced at Cyan, before turning to me. "I guess I never thanked you, did I?" He lifted his chin. "Thanks."

"No problem," I said, wanting to keep the mood light. "All in a day's work."

"You sound like James Bond," Cyan said. "Or . . . Jane Bond!"

Agda's eyes lit up, as she joined in on the banter. "Maybe she spy!"

Rafe nodded. "A Russian spy!"

"Russians are out," I said, laughing. "They're not the bad guys anymore."

Bucky wasn't being particularly unpleasant, but his words had more of a bite than anyone else's when he asked, "I still don't get it. How do you always get in the middle of all the intrigue around here?"

"Bad luck, I guess."

Gav leaned in the doorway. "Or good luck, depending on how you want to look at it." He greeted the staff and reminded them that even though recent events had thrown the schedule off, security classes would resume the next day. To me, he said, "Do you have a minute?"

I followed him to the China Room, thinking sadly about Marcel's weeks of planning and preparation and of all the time he'd spent in here creating his now-trashed masterpiece.

Gav closed the door and motioned for me to sit in one of the upholstered chairs. "There will be a press conference later this morning."

"I'm not going to have to say anything, am I?"

He sat across from me, shaking his head, elbows on his knees as he studied the floor. The stress of the job obviously took its toll. He seemed to have aged since I'd met him. "No. In fact we'd prefer that you say nothing."

"Can you tell me what's going on?"

He sat back. "You probably know it all anyway."

"I don't. Really. I've just been guessing. Trying to fill in the blanks."

One eye narrowed. "I told you I believed in your instincts. And I'm glad you trusted your gut." Leaning forward again, but this time staring at me, he continued. "I'll tell you what I can. Fair enough?"

I nodded.

"The Blanchard gingerbread men were outfitted with a sophisticated type of explosive," he said slowly. "We haven't seen much of this stuff because it's so new. It's very malleable." He pantomimed, rubbing his thumbs and forefingers together. "Just like C-4, but this stuff is so advanced, they were able to use it as decoration on the cookies and not have anyone notice. Plus, it's stable enough for transport. Powerful stuff. Had it been ignited by a straight 120 volt, it would've been bad." He stared at me. "Very bad. It probably would have taken out everyone within ten feet of the explosion."

I didn't know if he was exaggerating to make me feel better, but I actually felt a little bit worse. Shivering, I tried hard not to imagine what might have happened if Mrs. Campbell had flipped that switch.

Gav must have read my mind because he added, "With the additional surge from the floating neutral, those three gingerbread men would have taken out the back half of the White House."

"Oh, God."

"Yeah," he said.

"And Blanchard arranged everything? But how and why? And what about Sean?"

Gav held up a hand. "Slow down. We've got Blanchard in custody. Your electrician Manny Fortunato, too. He rigged everything from the inside."

"But it was Blanchard behind it all?"

"Not according to Blanchard. He's trying to point the finger at his over-zealous assistant."

"Bindy?"

Gav nodded. "Said she came up with all this on her own."

"No way."

With a shrug, Gav continued. "Blanchard claims he knew nothing about any of this. He's running real hard, trying to distance himself from the girl. Maintains he's completely innocent and seems just a little too eager to dump all the blame on her."

"What about her?"

For the first time all day, Gav smiled. "She's giving her statement now. Blanchard doesn't know, but she rolled right over now that he's pointing the finger at her. Oldest story in the book. Young, impressionable woman taken in by a powerful man. She was in it for love. He was in it for power." Gav added, "She's giving up every little detail in the hopes of getting off easy."

"Will she?"

"She was involved in trying to blow up the White House. What do you think?"

I grimaced. "What about Sean?"

Gav sobered again. "Blanchard again."

I sucked in a breath.

"Your friend Kirsten . . ." Gav began.

"I only met her once."

He dismissed my correction. "She was heading down the wrong path, but she was close. Turns out Sean was killed using Volkov's gun."

"What?"

"Crime scene investigators were able to prove that Sean didn't pull the trigger. That the note was planted, making the death a homicide. But." He bit the corner of his mouth. "The gun's serial number was mutilated. Not completely. Just enough to slow down its identification. When we figured it out, we realized the gun belonged to Volkov. He was brought in for questioning."

"That's probably what Kirsten heard about."

"Could be," he said. "Volkov admitted to it being his, but was as surprised as we were to discover how it had been used. He couldn't imagine how it could have gotten out of his house—until yesterday. He called the Metropolitan Police because he remembered that the last time he'd seen it, he'd been showing it to Blanchard." Gav placed a finger over his lips. "We asked him to keep that to himself, and told him that we'd be in touch."

"So it looks like Blanchard killed Sean and was trying to frame Volkov for it?"

"That's the premise we're working under." Gav licked his lips. "But he didn't do the messy work himself. According to Bindy there were a couple of other people involved."

I thought about the two guys who'd accosted me. "Who are they?"

He shook his head. "She didn't know their names. Just knew that Blanchard handled parts of the plan himself. He, or one of his operatives, may have fed the information to Kirsten. In fact, we believe they killed her, too."

My heart broke for the poor kid. She'd been trying so hard to make a name for herself and had instead been used and discarded by a powerful senator who was bent on a run at the White House. "How did Blanchard get to Manny, or to Yi-im?"

"His girl Bindy. She had all the connections from her days working here. In Manny's case, it was pure greed. Yi-im and Blanchard go way back to the senator's days as an army intelligence officer in Seoul." He gave me a look. "Yi-im was in the Korean CIA, although under a different name, of course."

"How did he pass the background check here?"

"Blanchard sponsored Yi-im into the United States. If he's who we think he is, your friend Yi-im and his brother were Korean operatives who may have been involved in the assassination of Park Chung-hee back in 1979."

My mind was having a hard time assimilating all this. "Then he's a dangerous guy."

"You think?"

"Have you arrested him yet?"

"We're working on it, but he's slippery."

This was too much for me. "And all this was so that Blanchard could sell Zendy Industries?"

"That's only part of it. The senator is an ambitious man. For a successful run at the presidency he needed the money from Zendy and spies inside the White House. And he wanted all that enough to kill. He might have had a hand in killing Mr. Sinclair; we're looking into that now."

I gasped.

"There are bad people in this world, Ollie," he said.

"I know. I just can't imagine. . . ."

"There's something else," he said.

By the look on his face, I knew it wasn't good news. "Go ahead," I said.

"When your chief electrician was killed . . ."

"Gene."

"Yes, Gene. When he was killed, he was felled by that phenomena you talked about—the floating neutral. But it looks as though it occurred naturally."

My stomach clenched. I knew what Gav was about to say, so I beat him to it. Maybe it would hurt less that way. "And I brought the idea to their attention?"

"You did," he said. "Blanchard's team had placed a bomb in the White House, in an effort to target the First Lady, but their attempts were crude and unsuccessful. Bindy kept in regular contact with Manny. He tossed out the idea of rigging a floating neutral after you kept badgering him about it. He said he thought he could make the blast look like a natural occurrence."

My head was spinning. "So I played a part in almost getting the White House destroyed."

"No almost about it. The White House is gone." Gav smiled. "The *gingerbread* White House, that is. Completely decimated, thanks to you." His eyebrows rose and the gray eyes sparkled. "But also thanks to you, the real White House is still standing."

MARCEL'S GINGERBREAD MASTERPIECE WOULD BE THE FIRST ONE to go down in history as a casualty of political warfare. But some good had come of it. In the First Lady's press conference later that night, she'd chosen not to dwell on what was lost, but on what remained. She'd reminded everyone in the televised event that all the gingerbread men sent in by the nation's children had survived intact.

She said: "That our children's contributions are still with us—that each one is still just as beautiful as it was when we received it—is really what's important. Thanks to our fine staff and American gutsiness, our White House is still standing, and we are still together to enjoy it. Our holiday theme has special meaning for us tonight because . . . together we do celebrate. Welcome home." At that she'd opened her arms, inviting the cameras into the residence for their much-belated Decorator Tour.

As I watched her, I realized that for the first time since she'd received the news of Sean's death, Mrs. Campbell was at peace.

CHAPTER 25

A WEEK LATER THERE WERE STILL A HUNDRED QUESTIONS I HADN'T gotten answers to, but knowing the tight-lipped nature of the White House security personnel, I counted my blessings for having gotten as much as I had out of Gav.

I thought about this as I sat in the kitchen, today's *Washington Post* on the countertop in front of me. It was quiet and I appreciated the solitude. I'd sent everyone home early tonight. Dinner was done, and with no big events scheduled till next week, I decided we all needed some time off. Agda smiled and promised to be in early the next day. Bucky actually thanked me again, and I was surprised to notice Rafe helping Cyan into her coat as the two of them made plans for spending the evening together.

The front page of the *Post* caught me up on the latest in the Blanchard Blowup, as they were calling it. There was yet another picture of Bindy, who, in every shot, seemed to be running past cameras, face covered, hopping into a waiting car or being hustled into the police station. Charges against her were still pending. Next to her photo was one of a smiling Senator Blanchard, who'd been indicted along with Manny and Yi-im.

Blanchard held his head high and gripped a microphone with both hands. The caption below the picture quoted: "I am innocent of these ridiculous allegations." His wife stood behind him, looking stricken and gaunt. The kids were nowhere to be seen.

I scanned for updates, but it was mostly just rehash. I turned to page five to finish the article.

The Blowup was hot stuff—real news—and I was thankful for the shift in attention away from me. Even though all the articles still made mention of my leap under the table to prevent the explosion—after all, that's where the Blanchard Blowup story started—my name was being mentioned less often. For that, I was grateful.

Secret Service personnel had been my constant companions. Two agents shuttled me back and forth to work since the big holiday commotion to keep me out of reach of the mob of reporters. Hordes of them camped outside the White House gates, every one of them eager to get an exclusive interview with the chef who had literally brought down the house—the gingerbread house. I didn't complain about my escort service—instead of taking the Metro, I'd been riding in the back of a luxury sedan, with door-to-door attention. Tom had at first offered to take over bodyguarding duties, but his schedule kept him busy until late in the evening almost every night. After all, his first duty was to the president. At least in the daytime. But he was always happy to do some extra undercover work with me.

Tonight, exactly one week after the fracas, I was on my own again. My personal Secret Service detail had informed me they deemed it safe for me to resume my normal commute. Thank goodness. As much as I'd miss the cushy comfort of the chauffeured car, I was happy to be free of constant surveillance. I wondered how the president and his family tolerated the never-ending attention.

I was about to close the newspaper when a related sidebar headline caught my eye: "Zendy Industries Sold." The sidebar directed me to the business section—E, which I turned to as quickly as I could.

It can't be true, I thought, as I pulled out the section to search for the article. Mrs. Campbell was adamant. What could have caused her to change her mind?

I didn't have to search far. On the first page of the section, the Zendy headline was repeated and a lengthy update appeared below. I scanned, then realized I wasn't comprehending. Starting from the top, I began again, trying to absorb this late-breaking news update.

Mrs. Campbell had, indeed, announced an agreement to sell Zendy Industries. But she'd done so in a spectacularly intriguing way. She was quoted: "With the recent developments of which we're all aware, I have decided not to continue my association with my former colleagues. While Treyton Blanchard and Nick Volkov are occupied with their own personal issues, I have come to understand that they have neither the time nor the inclination to see to the best interests of Zendy. With that in mind, I have taken Nick Volkov's offhand advice. He may have been joking, but I am quite serious.

"Although I am unable to finance an entire buyout, I do have sufficient resources to allow me a 51 percent share. The remaining 49 percent will be acquired by other investors."

When pressed to name these other investors, Mrs. Campbell was further quoted as saying, "I don't care to divulge that to the press, at this time. But I can tell you that it is refreshing to work with investors I can trust."

Good for her. I smiled as I pulled the newspaper back together, and dropped it into the recycle bin. After taking a moment to disinfect the countertop, I headed home.

CHAPTER 26

NO REPORTERS WAITED FOR ME AT THE GATE. NO CAMERA CREWS stalked me on my short walk to the MacPherson Square station. And yet . . .

That prickling feeling was back.

The evening was dark, as it usually is after eight at night in early December, but the cold, snappy air held a hint of electricity I couldn't put my finger on. I turned to see if anyone followed, but the street was mostly quiet. A male-female couple walked a prancing Pekinese, which wore little leather boots on each paw.

Across the street a few other pedestrians ambled, scurried, and strode, but no one paid me any attention.

Once at the station, I slid my new Metro pass into the machine, and picked it up when it popped out of the slot on the top of the turnstile. Over the past week I'd been able to replace almost everything that had been stolen, including credit cards. Replacement cards showed up in my apartment's mailbox with blazing speed. I guess they didn't want me to miss even one day of holiday shopping. I always kept my cell phone in my back pocket, so that was one headache I didn't have to deal with. My personal stuff, like the few pictures I carried, a little cash, and some recent receipts, were gone for good.

As I returned the Metro pass to my purse, my fingers sought and found the pepper spray. Just wrapping my hand around the little canister made me feel more secure. Still, the uncomfortable feeling of being watched stayed with me until the train arrived. I paid careful attention to those who boarded the same time I did, but saw no one suspicious.

Once settled in my seat, the feeling disappeared, and I attributed my paranoia to having gotten used to being followed by Secret Service agents every day for the past week. I'd get over it.

At my stop, I took care to take note of the folks who got off with me. A woman with a baby, an elderly gentleman, and two young men with Mohawks. So far, so good.

When I made it outside, however, the oppressive sense of being watched was back. I twisted, making a complete 360, but I saw no one of interest.

Keeping my head down to fight off the wind, I hurried to make the quick trek from the station to my apartment building. I'd just gotten past the very spot I'd been accosted when I heard it.

Double-tap footsteps behind me.

I spun. My hand dug straight for my pepper spray.

Nobody there.

The footsteps stopped.

I stole a quick glance in the direction of my building, gauging how fast I could get there, and how best to outpace the big guy, for I had no doubt he was back. In that instant I knew with certainty that the little Asian guy and his bulky cohort had been in league with Yi-im, and, it followed, with Blanchard.

I scanned the area, knowing they would be bent on revenge.

A rustle to my left.

Shan-Yu, my would-be abductor, stepped from the shadows.

I jumped backward as my heart thudded—crazed, like a gong in my chest.

"You not smart woman," he said. Behind him, Mr. Tap Shoes emerged, arms at his sides, his stance telling me he was ready to tackle me if I tried to move. I inched backward, my cold-sweaty hands fighting for a better grip on my pepper spray.

"I'm not?" I asked, buying myself precious seconds. My hand still tucked inside my purse, I needed to get my index finger and thumb into position. There. I released the safety catch.

Shan-Yu's eyes caught the streetlight's beam, glittering as he stepped closer.

"You think you so smart," he said, again. "But you not."

"Oh yeah?" I said, knowing I needed a distraction. "Then how come you didn't notice the Secret Service agents following me?"

Instinctively, they both looked up. I leaped forward, dragging out the spray, holding my breath as I shot them both in the face. I held down the plunger as long as I could before backing up fast and averting my eyes.

The two yelped, coughing and waving their hands as I bolted away from them, squinting to keep the chemical from burning my own eyes.

I'd gone only two steps when I slammed into something hard. My first thought was that I'd hit a wall, or a tree, but when the limbs reached out to grab me, I knew better. I screamed, scratched, and tried to bite.

"Ollie!"

At the familiarity I stopped fighting. I looked up. "Gav?"

He pushed me behind him and moved toward Shan-Yu and Mr. Tap Shoes, who were already being cuffed by two other agents. Seconds later, an unmarked car eased around the corner and the agents hustled the coughing creeps inside.

"What's going on?" I asked. "How did you know?"

Gav conferred with the men before turning to answer me. "We didn't."

Realization was beginning to dawn. "You suspected these guys were part of Blanchard's army."

He made a so-so motion. "We assumed."

"But you couldn't find them."

"No."

"So you hung me out as bait?"

Gav winced. "Something like that."

The two agents who'd corralled my attackers were finished loading them into the car. A second later they pulled away from the curb, and the agent in the passenger seat waved. I watched them for a long moment before I could speak again. "Well, thanks for letting me know."

"When you shouted about being protected by the Secret Service, I actually thought our cover had been blown," he said. His mouth twitched—an almost smile. "Did you *know* we were tailing you?"

"No."

"Well, you seemed to be doing just fine on your own. I don't think you even needed us."

I tried to smile, but I was shaking too much. Gav noticed.

He walked me to my door, one hand on my elbow. "We're packing it in, you know. We completed the staff training. Time to take the explosive show on the road."

"You're not coming back?"

"Not until we're needed again."

I was surprised to realize I was sorry to see him go. I said as much, then added, "But for the president's sake, I hope your team isn't called back for a long time."

He held open the building's front door. "Until then, Ollie," he said, "I'm counting on you being our eyes and ears."

I scooted inside, then turned back. But I didn't know what to say.

Gav gave a quick two-fingered salute, and was gone.

AN ADORABLE
ASSEMBLY OF APPETIZERS

FORGIVE THE TITLE—I CAN'T RESIST A GOOD ALLITERATION, BUT it's true that there's nothing better to have in your cooking repertoire than a bunch of appetizer recipes. Most appetizers are fabulously tasty, and many are good for you, too (though not all; the cheese straws, brownies, and cookies below are pure sin). When you want to throw a fancy reception or a party and you don't want to drag in waiters and bartenders to lend a hand, whipping together a big bunch of appetizers is a surefire way to feed a crowd and keep them happy without having to go through the trauma of a big sit-down dinner. Even at the White House, the number of affairs where we field a wide assortment of appetizers for guests to nibble on far exceeds the number of big State dinners we host each year. One real advantage of this kind of spread is that it makes it so much easier for people to mingle and talk. Washington really is a fairly small town, so the guests at most White House receptions are likely to have met one another before. But even when they haven't, conversations always start at the appetizer tables. Usually it's just advice not to miss a particularly succulent item in the array; but from such simple beginnings, real conversations grow.

And if you put out the right kind of appetizer spread, people can truly make a meal out of it. The recipes below, some of which Mrs. Campbell chose for her receptions this year, are easy to make, easy to eat, and work well together as a display. With a wide variety of colors, textures, and tastes, these items create a wonderful appetizer party. All are made with ingredients easily available at any supermarket. (Though I have to say, it's nice to grow your own herbs. If you have a sunny window, a few pots overflowing with chives, basil, sage, and parsley can really punch up your cooking. And they're very easy to grow.)

Most of these recipes can be prepared ahead of time, so you can enjoy your own party. Even the ones that need to be prepared right before the party are fast. Each recipe also stands well on its own, so you can also add them to your regular meal rotations if they strike your fancy.

Enjoy the party—and happy noshing!

Ollie

APPETIZER PARTY MENU

Blue-Cheese Straws

Stuffed Cherry Tomatoes

Asparagus Spears and Lemon Butter

Garlic–Green Bean Bundles

Mini Red Potatoes with Sour Cream, Cheddar, and Chives

Bacon-and-Cornbread Muffins

Little White Rolls

Sugar-Cured Ham with White-Wine Honey Mustard

Chicken-Fried Beef Tenderloin with White Onion Gravy

Brownie Bites

Gingerbread Men

BLUE-CHEESE STRAWS

½ pound blue cheese, softened
½ cup (1 stick) butter, softened
3 ounces cream cheese, softened
2 tablespoons heavy cream
¼ teaspoon red pepper flakes
¼ teaspoon kosher salt
3 cups flour, sifted
½ cup finely chopped smoked almonds (optional)

Preheat oven to 400°F.

Place blue cheese, butter, and cream cheese in bowl or mixer. Cream them together. Mixing by hand, add the rest of the ingredients, one at a time, until fully incorporated.

Turn the dough out on a floured board. Roll out to a medium-thin dough (about ¼-inch thick). With a sharp knife, cut the dough into ½-inch-wide strips. Twist each strip until it is a loose spiral from top to bottom and lay the spirals on an ungreased cookie sheet, not touching their neighbors.

Bake until strips are golden brown, 5–10 minutes. Remove to wire racks and let cool.

Store in tightly covered tins lined with wax paper until ready to serve.

STUFFED CHERRY TOMATOES

1 8-ounce block cream cheese, softened
¼ cup sour cream
1 small bunch chives, washed and chopped, about 3–4
  tablespoons (Reserve 1 tablespoon for garnish.)
2 cloves garlic, cleaned and minced
20 fresh basil leaves, washed and cut into thin strips
Pinch kosher or sea salt, to taste
1 pint cherry tomatoes, washed and dried

Make the filling by combining the first six ingredients in a bowl and stirring well. Place in a pastry bag fitted with a large star point, if desired. Otherwise, the filling can be spooned into the tomatoes. Set filling aside.

Using a sharp paring knife, cut a small slice off the bottom of a cherry tomato so that it will sit firmly on its tray without rolling around. Cut an X into the top of the cherry tomato with the same knife. Either use a watermelon baller to remove the pulp from the tomato, or squeeze it gently over a waste bowl to get the pulp out. Repeat with all the cherry tomatoes, laying them out in rows on the serving tray, ready to be filled.

Pipe the cream-cheese mixture into the prepared tomatoes, or spoon it, for a more rustic look.

Sprinkle finished dish with reserved chopped chives. Serve chilled.

ASPARAGUS SPEARS AND LEMON BUTTER

1 pound fresh asparagus stalks, washed, tough stems cut away
¼ pound butter (if unsalted, add ¼ teaspoon salt)
Fresh cracked pepper, to taste
1 tablespoon fresh chopped parsley
Juice of one medium lemon

Place asparagus in a steamer basket. Place steamer basket into a large pot with about a half inch of boiling water in the bottom, and cover. Steam asparagus until bright green, but still a bit crisp, about 3–7 minutes, depending on the size of the asparagus.

While asparagus is steaming, melt butter in a small saucepan. Add salt, pepper, parsley, and lemon juice and whisk well. Pour into serving bowl.

Remove steamed asparagus. Place on oblong platter. Place the bowl of butter on one end of the platter with a small ladle for guests to pour it over their asparagus as they serve themselves.

Serve warm.

 # GARLIC-GREEN BEAN BUNDLES

Two pounds fresh green beans, washed, ends and strings removed
1 pound good-quality smoked bacon, sliced
½ cup olive oil
3 cloves garlic, cleaned and minced

Preheat oven to 350° F.

On a sheet pan, cookie sheet, or jelly-roll pan (a large, flat pan with an edge sufficient to prevent the grease you're about to make from running all over your nice, clean oven), divide the green beans in bundles of roughly 10–12 beans, with beans bundles laid out in parallel formation.

Wrap each bundle loosely with a slice of bacon, tying it on top with a simple knot and arranging the loose ends artistically.

In a bowl, whisk the olive oil and the garlic. Brush oil liberally over the green-bean bundles.

Bake until the bacon is cooked to taste and the green beans are warmed through, approximately 15 minutes.

Remove bundles to a serving platter, using a spatula. Serve warm.

MINI RED POTATOES WITH SOUR CREAM, CHEDDAR, AND CHIVES

2 pounds small red new potatoes, scrubbed, peels still on
1 cup sour cream
1 small bundle fresh chives, washed and chopped (about
*   4 tablespoons)*
6 slices precooked bacon, crumbled
Kosher salt, to taste
Fresh ground black pepper, to taste
3 ounces good sharp Cheddar cheese, finely grated

Boil the red potatoes in enough water to cover until they are fork-tender, about 15–20 minutes. Drain the potatoes, and let cool enough that they are easy to handle.

Cut each potato in half. On the uncut end of each half, slice away a small amount of peel and flesh so the potato half will sit flat and securely on a platter. Using a melon baller or a spoon, scoop out the middle of the potato. Arrange the prepared halves on a broiler-safe serving tray.

Make the filling by mixing the sour cream, chives, bacon, and salt and pepper to taste. If the bacon is very salty, I often don't add additional salt. Spoon filling into potato halves. Sprinkle with grated Cheddar cheese. At this point the tray can be set aside, or even refrigerated, until ready to cook.

Place under broiler until cheese begins to melt and filling begins to bubble, about 3–5 minutes.

Serve warm.

BACON-AND-CORNBREAD MUFFINS

½ cup canola oil
¾ cup cornmeal (preferably stone-ground, but regular will work if
    you can't find the good stuff)
1 cup flour
1 teaspoon baking soda
1 tablespoon baking powder
½ teaspoon salt
1 tablespoon sugar
3 tablespoons cold butter
1 cup buttermilk
2 large eggs, beaten
½ cup grated Cheddar cheese (Sharp is what I prefer, but use a
    cheese you like eating.)
1 bunch chives, washed and chopped (about 4 tablespoons)
8 slices precooked smoked bacon, chopped into ¼-inch strips

Preheat oven to 400° F.

Put 1 tablespoon of canola oil into each well of a standard 12-cup muffin pan, and place muffin pan into oven to heat the oil.

Meanwhile, working quickly, sift flour, baking soda, baking powder, salt, and sugar together into a large mixing bowl. Cut in the butter until the butter is blended in. Add buttermilk and eggs all at once, and stir just until ingredients are barely blended. A few lumps are fine; this batter gets tough if you overwork it. Add the cheese, chives, and bacon, stirring only until the ingredients are roughly mixed in.

Pull hot muffin tin from oven. Drop batter into the muffin cups, filling each roughly three-quarters full. The hot oil should make the batter bubble and brown on the sides. Place pan into oven and cook until muffins are done and golden, roughly 20–25 minutes.

I like to serve them hot, but they're great at room temperature, too.

LITTLE WHITE ROLLS

I have to make an admission here: When it comes to bread making, I cheat. The pastry chefs at the White House do most of the baking, so it isn't a problem at work. But at home, I use a bread machine. I set it on the dough setting and let the machine handle the kneading. Then I shape the dough by hand and let it do a final rise in the pan or pans of my choice. I actually like kneading bread by hand, but I'm busy, so I sacrifice the fun of kneading for the time I save by letting the machine handle it. The instructions here are for any standard bread machine.

> *2½ tablespoons (1 standard packet) granulated dry yeast*
> *4–4½ cups bread flour*
> *2 tablespoons sugar*

> 1 teaspoon salt
> ¼ cup nonfat dried milk
> 1 egg, beaten
> 1–1½ cups lukewarm water
> ⅓ cup olive oil

Set your bread machine to the dough setting. Add the yeast, 4 cups flour, sugar, salt, milk, egg, 1 cup water, and the oil to the bread machine vessel. Turn on bread machine. After 4 minutes, look at the dough. If it's too floury, add water a few drops at a time, until the dough looks right. If it's too runny, add flour 1 tablespoon at a time, until the dough looks right. The dough should look smooth and have a texture that feels roughly like the lobe of your ear when you pinch it—yielding but resilient. Balance the flour and water additions until you reach that middle point where the dough comes together nicely in a ball without being too watery or too stiff. Then walk away and let the machine do its thing. Most machines take around 1 hour and 20 minutes to 1½ hours to run the dough cycle. The machine will usually beep when it's finished.

When the dough is done, unplug the machine. Grease the wells of two standard muffin tins with a spray-on like Pam or Baker's Choice, or rub with shortening. Pinch off balls of dough roughly the size of golf balls, and place a ball in each muffin-tin well. When manipulating the dough, it makes the resulting bread prettier if you stretch the pinched dough ends to the back of the ball, and put that side bottom down in the tin, leaving a smooth, rounded surface at the top of each roll.

Cover the tins with a damp dish towel and set aside to let rise until doubled in size. This time can vary enormously, depending on the temperature of the site where you are resting the dough. The warmer it is, the faster the dough will rise. In a busy commercial kitchen, where the temperature often hovers around the 100° mark, it generally takes about 30 minutes—but if it gets much hotter than that, the yeast will start to die and the bread will start to cook, so don't let the air temperature get over 100°. In a 70° home kitchen, it can take as long as two hours. A long, slow rise time often imparts more flavor to the bread. I find that putting the tins in a cool oven over a pan filled with hot water is just about perfect. The heat from the water warms the space, and the steam keeps the dough from drying out.

Preheat oven to 350° F.

Place the muffin tins in oven. Bake until rolls are golden, roughly 15–20 minutes.

Remove from oven. Let stand until rolls are cool enough to handle—usually about 5 minutes—then pluck them out of the muffin tins.

Serve warm.

For all you purists, if you prefer working this dough by hand, feel free to do it. The only thing that's different is that you'll need to proof the yeast—that is, dissolve it in the warm water along with the sugar, and let it get bubbly—before you mix the ingredients. Then knead until smooth, let it rise, punch it down, let it rise again, punch it down again, put it in the pans, and continue as the recipe indicates.

SUGAR-CURED HAM WITH WHITE-WINE HONEY MUSTARD

Ham is the ultimate convenience food when you're feeding a large group. It arrives in the kitchen fully cooked, seasoned, and sometimes even spiral sliced—though I much prefer slicing my own. All a cook has to do is warm it through and cut it up to serve it. Naturally, most chefs feel the need to put a more personal stamp on a ham, so there are thousands of recipes for glazes, garnishes, and rubs to augment the flavor of a purchased ham. Any of these will work, but I tend to go with pure simplicity: I like the flavor of a sugar-cured ham. And I find that a thin coating of plain old molasses augments the flavor perfectly. But if you don't like molasses, feel free to glaze your ham any way you see fit. (I've got a friend who swears by dumping a can of ginger ale on the ham when he puts it in the oven. I've tried it. Surprisingly, it's good.) The most important thing when serving this dish is to pick a good ham to begin with.

1 good-quality sugar-cured ham, sized to fit the crowd of people
   you're feeding (I generally go with 3–5 pounds for home use, but
   any size will do.)
1 cup molasses

Preheat oven to 300° F. (Ham needs a slow cooking process to keep it from drying out and the sugar glaze from burning.)

Wash ham well in cold water. Place ham, fat side up, in a roasting pan on a rack, and place in oven. Cook 15–20 minutes per pound. Pull ham out of oven and carve off any excess fat, leaving about ¼-inch fat layer on the meat. Carve into the remaining fat with any decorative pattern desired—I usually go with 1-inch crosshatches. Brush ham with molasses. Put back into oven for 20 minutes, until glaze begins to bubble and brown.

Remove from oven. Place on serving platter. Slice into serving-sized portions. Serve warm with White-Wine Honey Mustard on the side, and rolls and corn muffins handy, in case any guest feels like making a sandwich. Most of them will—you can trust me on this.

WHITE-WINE HONEY MUSTARD

1 cup good Dijon mustard
2 tablespoons white wine
2 tablespoons honey

Mix ingredients and chill. Serve with ham.

CHICKEN-FRIED BEEF TENDERLOIN WITH WHITE ONION GRAVY

This is an old-fashioned Texas crowd pleaser. In Texas, this is traditionally done with round steak, but here at the White House we upgrade to tenderloin. Feel free to use round steak, if you prefer.

> *Canola oil, for frying*
> *2 pounds (roughly) beef tenderloin, cut crosswise into ½-inch steaks*
> *1½ cups flour*
> *1 tablespoon garlic powder*
> *1 teaspoon onion powder*
> *1 teaspoon salt*
> *Fresh cracked pepper, to taste (I use about ½ teaspoon.)*
> *2 cups buttermilk*

WHITE ONION GRAVY

> *3 small onions, cleaned and sliced into thin rings, rings teased apart*
> *2 tablespoons flour*
> *2 cups milk*
> *Salt and fresh cracked pepper, to taste*

Preheat oven to 200° F.

This is a stovetop recipe, and you'll need a big, sturdy skillet, preferably cast iron, though any heavy-bottomed metal pan will do. Place about ½ inch canola oil in the pan, and set over medium heat. The oil should be at about 300°, or hot enough to make a drop of water dropped in it dance and sizzle, to fry the steaks.

While the oil is heating, place each steak between two sheets of good plastic wrap. Pound the steaks with a meat mallet to tenderize and to make them thinner. This ensures that the beef will cook through fully when it's put in the skillet.

In a large resealable bag, pour in the flour, garlic powder, onion powder, salt, and pepper. Close the bag and shake to mix.

Put the buttermilk in a bowl.

Place a steak in the bag of seasoned flour and shake to coat. Remove the steak and dip it in the buttermilk, then put it back in the seasoned flour and shake to coat again. Once all the steaks are coated, it's time to fry them.

Place a few of the steaks in the hot oil—you want the steaks to fit easily, with room to move around and not touch. I find frying 3 at a time works well for me. Fry until golden brown, about 3 minutes, then turn over and fry until golden brown on the other side. Remove cooked steaks to a warmed plate, and continue frying the rest of the coated steaks until done. Place the steaks in the oven to keep them warm while you make the gravy.

To make the gravy, pour off some of the oil in the frying pan. Leave a layer of oil sufficient to cover the bottom of the pan lightly. Add onions, and fry until brown and tender, stirring occasionally, 6–8 minutes. Gently scatter the flour over the cooked onions, stirring constantly until flour begins to brown and turns into a thick paste, about 3 minutes. Slowly add milk, stirring constantly. Gravy will thicken. Taste, and add salt and pepper to taste. Serve the steaks on the warmed platter, with a big bowl of gravy next to them, or plate the steaks individually, ladling a nice scoop of gravy over each.

BROWNIE BITES

¾ cup good-quality cocoa
¾ cup canola oil
2 cups sugar
4 eggs, beaten
1 tablespoon vanilla extract
1½ cups flour

1 teaspoon baking powder
½ teaspoon salt
24 pecan halves, for garnish (optional)

FROSTING

¼ cup butter, softened
½ cup cocoa
1½ cups confectioner's sugar
1 teaspoon vanilla extract
⅓ cup milk

Preheat oven to 350°F.

Place the cocoa, oil, sugar, eggs, and vanilla into a large mixing bowl and stir until the cocoa is fully incorporated, and the mixture is smooth and glossy. Add dry ingredients all at once and gently fold the wet and dry ingredients together. Stir just until the ingredients are mixed. Too much stirring makes the brownies tough.

Place foil (paper cups will shred, so using foil is important) baking cups into 2 12-cup muffin tins. Spray with cooking spray or grease with shortening. Fill the cups two-thirds full with the brownie mixture.

Place in oven and bake until the mixture is just set, and lovely cracks appear on the surface of the brownie bites, about 15–20 minutes. Remove cups from tins and let brownie bites cool.

To prepare the frosting, place the softened butter in a large mixing bowl. Add cocoa, confectioner's sugar, and vanilla, and blend until the mixture is fully mixed. Add the milk, 1 tablespoonful at a time, and continue beating the frosting. When the frosting looks glossy and forms soft peaks, it's ready to use.

Frost the brownies in their foil cups. Garnish with pecan halves, or the garnish of your choice. Serve.

Other options for garnishes include everything from mini–chocolate chips to a sprinkle of coconut to a fan of candy corn—cute in the fall—to white chocolate curls to chocolate-covered coffee beans to peanut butter cups to peppermint patties to other chocolates. Tailor your garnish to your anticipated diners. If you're feeding mostly adults, go for sophistication. If you're feeding lots of kids, raid the candy store. The pecan halves are a compromise—both adults and kids like them, and the people who don't like nuts can easily remove them. But the sky's the limit as far as garnishing these goes.

GINGERBREAD MEN

3 cups flour

2 teaspoons ground ginger

2 teaspoons ground cinnamon

½ teaspoon ground cloves

¼ teaspoon fresh ground nutmeg

½ teaspoon salt

1 pinch ground pepper (optional, but it gives the cookies a little bite)

Scant 1 teaspoon baking soda

¾ cup butter, softened

½ cup brown sugar, well packed

¼ cup white sugar

1 large egg

½ cup molasses

Raisins (optional)

ROYAL ICING

2 tablespoons meringue powder

Fresh lemon juice from 1 lemon

Roughly 2 cups sifted powdered (confectioner's) sugar

In a large bowl, sift together flour, baking soda, salt, and spices. Set aside.

In the bowl of an electric mixer, blend the softened butter, then add the sugars, and cream at medium speed until smooth and fluffy. Add in egg and molasses. Reduce speed to low. Gradually add in flour. Batter will be stiff. Divide batter into workable batches (I usually divide it in thirds), wrap each batch tightly in plastic wrap, and refrigerate overnight.

Preheat oven to 350° F.

Pull the first batch of dough from the refrigerator. Roll out on a floured board until dough ¼- to ⅛-inch thick. I aim for a roll of dough about 8 inches wide. That makes cutting out 8-inch gingerbread men really easy. I then cut out gingerbread men freehand from the dough using a very sharp paring knife. Luckily, a gingerbread man is easy to draw, even for the artistically challenged. You can also use cookie cutters, if you have them. Remove the dough that isn't part of the cookies, then gently lift the gingerbread men with a long spatula, and place them on ungreased cookie sheets. If desired, add raisins for eyes and mouth. Otherwise, these can be piped on after baking. Continue rolling out gingerbread men until all cookies are shaped. The unused dough can be kneaded together and rolled out at the end. If you plan to hang these cookies as decorations, be sure to cut a large hole where you want to insert the hanging ribbon. I find a sturdy drinking straw is the perfect tool to get a nice-sized hole, but canapé cutters or a toothpick can function equally well.

Bake cookies until gently browned on bottom, about 8–12 minutes. Remove from oven. Let cool for 5 minutes. (This makes the cookie stronger and less prone to breakage.) Remove gently from cookie sheets with a long spatula, and set on a wire rack to cool.

To prepare royal icing, mix the meringue powder with the lemon juice in the bowl of an electric mixer. Gradually add the powdered sugar. Stop adding sugar when the mixture holds stiff peaks and is of good piping consistency.

Load icing into large piping bag fitted with a small circular tip. Pipe clothes and features on the finished cookies. Lay the cookies out flat for the icing to dry. Once they are very, very dry, serve them, or store the finished cookies packed in a tin in layers separated by waxed or parchment paper.

The better the spices, the better the cookies. I get my spices online at The Spice House, which has outlets in Milwaukee and Chicago, as well as an excellent mail-order site at www.thespicehouse.com. I've found the spices I get there are simply the best available.

Piped royal icing makes for beautiful cookies. But kids much prefer these iced with buttercream icing and decorated with chocolate chips for the eyes, nose, mouth, and buttons. That's also faster. But since these cookies are wearing their party clothes, I'm giving the royal icing version here.

EGGSECUTIVE ORDERS

For my daughters, and in memory of my mom

ACKNOWLEDGMENTS

Sincere thanks to the great people at The Berkley Publishing Group, especially Natalee Rosenstein and Michelle Vega. And to copyeditor Erica Rose. And to the folks at Tekno, especially Marty Greenberg, John Helfers, and Denise Little.

A big and special thank-you to my daughter Sara, who always reads first.

It's great to have experts to turn to—and my sincere gratitude to Diane Springer who—between VJA marching band competitions—helped me come up with an efficient way to kill a character. Any and all errors with regard to this method, and its subsequent discovery, are mine.

Thanks to reader Barbara Czachowski for her catch in *State of the Onion*. Ollie greatly appreciated Barbara's kind correction and made note of it in this adventure while she and her family toured the National Mall.

Thanks to Mystery Writers of America, Sisters in Crime, and Thriller Writers of America for camaraderie and support, and thanks especially to wonderful readers who take the time to let me know what they think of Ollie's adventures.

CHAPTER 1

THE PHONE RANG WHILE I WAS BRUSHING MY TEETH. PHONE calls at four in the morning usually mean one thing: bad news.

I quickly swished water in my mouth to clear away residual foam, and hurried to my bedroom to stop the unnerving jangle.

As executive chef at the White House, I make it a point to get to work every morning before the sun comes up, so I reasoned that this might be one of my staff catching me at home to call in sick. Either that, or my mom and nana were having trouble getting to the airport. Despite the fact that our kitchen had a lot to do before the Easter Egg Roll next week, I sorely hoped this was, indeed, a staffer calling in. I didn't want to think that my mother and nana might cancel their plans to visit me.

I reached for the handset. A split second before I answered, I glanced at the Caller ID.

Not my mom. Not a staffer.

The display read simply: "202."

The White House was calling *me*.

"Olivia Paras here," I said as I picked it up.

"Ollie, it's Paul." Paul Vasquez, the White House chief usher, wouldn't call me at home unless it was a dire emergency.

"What happened?" I asked.

"There's a car waiting for you downstairs."

"Downstairs, here?" I asked. Although I'd been awake for nearly an hour, my brain was slow to comprehend. "Downstairs where I live?"

"That's right," he said slowly. "Two agents will escort you to the residence today."

"Why? What happened?"

"You'll be briefed when you get here. Just hurry. They're waiting for you now. Follow their lead."

"But—"

"Ollie." His tone forced me to focus.

"Yes?"

"For God's sake, don't say *anything* to *anybody*."

He hung up before I could ask what he meant.

TWO SECRET SERVICE AGENTS WERE WAITING FOR ME IN THE lobby when I came out of the elevator. Both male, both large, they were clad in nearly identical outfits of navy pants and gray sport coats, and wore similar buzz-cut hair. In a more chipper situation, I may have asked them if they were Tweedledee and Tweedledum, but I didn't recognize either of these guys, and neither wore an expression that encouraged levity.

The one closest to me nodded solemnly. "Ms. Paras?"

I nodded back.

"This way," he said. He started for the front doors, gesturing for me to walk directly behind him. I couldn't see around his broad back, and was about to step aside when his twin came in close behind, effectively making an Ollie sandwich.

I started to ask, "Why all the—"

But shouts from outside drowned out my question. "There she is!"

I still couldn't see much, but just as the damp morning air hit my skin, the sound of agitated scuffles reached my ears. A crowd rushed up, encircling us. Stark bright lights silhouetted the agent in front of me. I winced at the intensity and at the sharp shouts: "Ms. Paras, Ms. Paras!"

In an effort to see better, I started to move around Agent Number One, but Number Two placed a restraining hand on my shoulder. "Keep moving."

Half-turning, I started to ask what was going on, but the agent gripped harder, urging me forward.

Someone thrust a microphone into my face—and kept up with our brisk pace until the agent behind me strong-armed him away.

A woman's voice, shrill and plaintive: "Ms. Paras! What went wrong at dinner last night?"

Instinctively I turned. The agent tightened his grip on my shoulder, but that didn't stop me from hearing another voice boom: "What was in Carl Minkus's food?"

My right foot bumped the agent in front of me and I stumbled. Tweedle-dum's hold prevented me from falling on my face.

"She fainted!" someone yelled.

"No I didn't!" I shot back.

"You didn't?" someone shouted. "You're saying this wasn't your fault?"

A female voice this time: "Then what killed Carl Minkus?"

That stopped me. "What?" Carl Minkus was dead?

The two agents trundled me forward into the waiting car. A third agent held open the big black car's rear door as Tweedledee stepped to one side. The enormous men formed a wall on either side of me, with only one path open for me to go. I scrambled to safety.

Media mongrels clambered around the open door until the agents bull-dozed them back. Amid all the shouting, I heard one high voice ring out: "What was in his food? And who prepared it?"

One of the Tweedles lowered himself next to me. I scooched to the other side, where reporters peered in the side windows. Armed with microphones and manic inquisitiveness, they banged on the glass, straining to be heard.

The agent next to me pulled his door closed, effectively hitting the mute button on the craziness outside. I was bewildered by the sudden realization that we were in one of the agency's bulletproof vehicles. We pulled away slowly, then picked up speed as the gaping pack of news guerillas fell away.

I resisted the temptation to sink into the vehicle's soft leather seats and make myself small. Instead, I perched forward, facing the agent next to me. "Carl Minkus is dead?"

His twin was driving, the third agent next to him in the passenger seat.

Agent Number Three was a little younger than his counterparts—smaller, too. And while the Tweedles remained stone-faced, Number Three blinked at my question.

I focused on him. "What is going on?"

With his defined jawline and classic profile, Number Three reminded me a little of Tom. Younger though. He had the look of a newbie Secret Service agent.

When he blinked again, and started to turn, the agent next to me spoke up. "You will be briefed when we arrive," he said.

The agent in the passenger seat licked his lips and shifted his eyes front.

I sat back, trying to piece things together. Carl Minkus was a big shot with the National Security Agency. I didn't remember his exact title with the NSA, but I knew he was as much admired as he was feared. He'd been a bulldog fighting terrorism. Alone, he'd been responsible for the prosecution of more than a thousand suspected terrorists. Lately he'd turned his sights inward, accusing American citizens of terrible deeds. He'd gone after several high-profile celebrities, and had ruined more than one career. Some people called him the Joseph McCarthy of terrorism. Last night he'd been among the president's guests at dinner, but I didn't know whether the president had invited him to chastise or to congratulate.

Minkus, in his mid-fifties, was a vibrant, outspoken defender of the republic. My shoulders jerked in an involuntary shiver and I tried to suppress the wave of panic shooting up my chest. Good thing it was dark in the car—I felt the heat in my face and knew it was as red as a beefsteak tomato. Minkus had been at dinner last night, now he was dead, and the press was already blaming me and my kitchen.

But . . . it wasn't our fault. Was it?

Rubbing my temples, I reviewed last night's menu. Except for Minkus being a recent convert to vegetarianism, he had no other dietary restrictions. No allergies. Minkus wasn't vegan. Which meant that dairy and eggs were allowed.

Did we serve him an item we shouldn't have? I stopped myself. How ridiculous! The White House kitchen was freakishly conscientious about our guests' dining preferences. Minkus would not have been served anything that conflicted with his needs. And, even if he had accidentally ingested a meat product, it certainly wouldn't have killed him.

No, I reasoned, even as my knee bounced a panicked tempo, he must have had an aneurysm or something. That had to be it. Or maybe an undiagnosed heart condition. Something unpredictable. Maybe his recent switch to vegetarianism was to help combat high cholesterol. Maybe he was on doctors' orders to lose weight. It couldn't have been anything he ate. At least, not something we had prepared.

I looked at the three men accompanying me on our race to the residence. Not one of them returned my gaze. "I'll be briefed, you said?"

One of the guys in front nodded.

My voice kicked up an octave, despite my attempts to keep calm. "And they think Mr. Minkus died because of something we served last night?"

No reaction this time.

"Well." I folded my arms and sat back, striving for control. "As soon as I'm done being briefed, I'll be sure to run a complete investigation of my kitchen."

The agent driving the car met my eyes in the rearview mirror. "Already underway."

I should have guessed, I thought. With a frown, I leaned back in the very comfortable seat, although at the moment I was anything but.

CHAPTER 2

I WISHED WE WOULD JUST GET TO THE WHITE HOUSE ALREADY.
Despite the car's speed, I felt like we were moving in slow motion. I wanted to
get there—and get everything settled. Now. But no matter how hard I willed
it, I couldn't make the limo move faster.

Still dark at this hour, the streets were wet from heavy overnight rains.
Our tires sliced through deep roadside puddles, hammering dirty water against
the side of the sedan every time we took a turn. I touched the thick window
and hoped the storms hadn't delayed incoming flights. My mother and nana
were coming to visit me—for the first time. I'd been begging them to make the
trip, almost since my first day at the White House, but they'd come up with
excuse after excuse. I knew my mother was a reluctant flyer, and my nana
had never been on a plane. Fear of the unknown kept them in Chicago, and
now that I'd finally convinced them to come visit me, I should have been
ecstatic.

I wasn't. I was panicked. Today was now in turmoil. I had planned to get
breakfast finished and lunch started before heading to the airport to pick up
my family. Instead, I was racing along the streets of D.C. in a specially armored
limo because one of the guests I'd fed last night was dead.

I leaned toward the bulletproof glass and tried to see the sky. God, I hoped
their plane wasn't delayed. It might be all the reason they needed to cancel the
trip.

"My cell phone!"

The agent next to me startled at my exclamation.

I grabbed at my purse. Even as I pawed through its cavernous pockets, my heart dropped. The early morning call from Paul had thrown me off and I'd left the cell phone charging at home.

How would my mother get in touch with me?

I gripped my hands into fists and shut my eyes against the frustration of it all. Now she wouldn't be able to reach me.

"We have to go back," I said.

The agent next to me shook his head.

"My cell phone," I said again, in case he'd missed my distress. "I forgot it."

"You'll have to do without."

"But my mother is—"

"Sorry, Ms. Paras. Our orders are to bring you in as quickly as possible."

Oblivious to my concerns, the agent in the passenger seat spoke into a microphone. I couldn't make out what he said, but I wasn't focused on him as much as I was on my own irritation. Great. Of all days to leave my cell at home, I'd picked the absolute worst. Not only did I not know what was in store for me, I wouldn't know how Mom and Nana were progressing on their trip. I would be incommunicado until these agents saw fit to set me free. I would have to make other arrangements for my family, but at this moment, I couldn't quite figure out how.

Lost in my ruminations, I didn't catch what the driver said, but the next thing I knew bright lights surrounded us and a crowd of news media swarmed the car. They glowed like ethereal monsters clawing and reaching, shoving cameras and microphones at the bulletproof glass. I shrunk down in my seat as spotlights swept the car's interior. For the first time, I wished it was still storming. Then maybe these vultures would disappear. Dissolve on the ground like a hundred Wicked Witches of the West. But instead of stealing their brooms and handing them off to the Wizard of Oz, I'd be content to grab their microphones and crush them beneath my heel.

I hadn't had the happiest relationship with the press since my promotion to executive chef. They liked to portray me as a lucky bumbler. It didn't matter that I'd won awards, or that my menus were respected by prestigious culinary experts. What mattered was that I'd gotten myself in the middle of an assassination plot, and followed that up with a disastrous—though ultimately laudable— holiday spectacle. In order to sell newspapers and magazines, they'd portrayed me as either a good-luck charm for this administration, or as a fumbling cook who fed the First Family and, between courses, fought off assassins.

The press didn't know the real me. But the First Family did. What I wanted, more than anything, was for my mom to see me in my element. To understand that I was not just a cook, but a respected member of the White House staff.

I rubbed my forehead as we pulled through the security gates. This wasn't what I'd hoped for when my mom came to visit. For a chef, this situation—a dead dinner guest—couldn't be worse.

CHAPTER 3

TWO AGENTS ACCOMPANIED ME TO A UTILITARIAN OFFICE ON the second floor of the East Wing. Although it was no larger than ten by twelve, the area felt cavernous with its high ceilings and spartan furnishings. Blue-draped windows, white walls, and a man at a desk, scribbling. Two other agents flanked him.

I was hoping to see Tom there. No Tom. Not a single other Secret Service agent I could call a friend.

My escorts left me there, and the large man behind the desk gestured me forward. He glanced at his notes. "Ms. Paras?" He didn't smile. "Sit," he said, pointing. "Please."

I sat.

Jack Brewster kept his gaze on the papers before him, as he massaged his wide-set nose. "You know who I am?"

"Yes." I had met the assistant deputy of the Secret Service a long time ago, but he probably didn't remember.

He frowned. "Your name comes up in my files with increasing regularity." Still without looking up, his scowl deepened and he shook his head, as though he'd just smelled fish left out overnight. "You know why you're here?"

"Is Carl Minkus . . ." I stumbled over the words, "really dead?"

Bulging eyes finally met mine. His were bloodshot and yellowed—from lack of sleep, or lack of happiness, I couldn't tell. Maybe a combination of both. Brewster cleared his throat, but it came out like a growl.

"That is correct. Agent Minkus is dead. His body was taken from the White House last night."

"But I was here last night. Why didn't anyone tell—"

"Why should anyone tell you?"

I blinked. "Because . . . I mean . . ."

"Ms. Paras, contrary to your apparent belief, you are not the hub of information here in Washington."

That stung. I bit my lip as he continued.

"You obviously came to that conclusion due to the press's interest in your antics here at the White House." Under his breath he murmured, "If it were my decision you'd be out on your—"

"Mr. Brewster," I said sharply.

He looked up.

"I don't think of myself as a 'hub of information' as you put it," I began, anger bubbling up. "I'm only suggesting that if I'd been notified last night that Mr. Minkus had collapsed, maybe I could have started looking into things *last night*." I emphasized the words. "And by now we would have determined the kitchen's role—or lack thereof—in Mr. Minkus's demise."

He leaned toward me, thumping meaty forearms on the desk. "They told me you were a handful."

I bit the insides of my mouth. "I prefer to think of myself as proactive."

"Call it what you like." He massaged his nose again. No wonder it was so wide. "I've assigned a group of agents to determine your staff's culpability in this situation. You are to cooperate with them. Fully. Do you understand?"

"Of course," I said, bristling. "But I can guarantee that Mr. Minkus did not die as a result of anything that came out of my kitchen."

"That remains to be seen."

Brewster asked me a few questions about my employment at the White House—information he could have easily gleaned from my personnel file. Then he asked me about the meal we had prepared for Agent Minkus at last night's dinner. Whenever I tried to add commentary, he held up a hand and reminded me to "just answer the question."

When he finally finished, I wiped fingers along my hairline, and grimaced at the perspiration there. Brewster had that effect on me—he probably had that effect on everyone he met.

As though silently summoned, one of the matching-bookend agents came in.

"Agent Guzy," Brewster said. "Ms. Paras is ready for her interrogation with the Metropolitan Police. Take her downstairs."

My interrogation? What had *this* been?

I had turned when Agent Guzy arrived. Now I twisted back to face Brewster. "I don't have time to be questioned right now," I said, pointing to my watch. "I have to get breakfast ready for the president and the First Lady."

Brewster blinked. Like a bored cow.

"And my staff," I continued. "They won't realize why I'm not there. I need to talk with them." I was perched at the edge of my chair, leaning in toward the desk, as though the proximity of my speech would make my words more meaningful to Brewster. "You don't understand—"

"No, Ms. Paras," Brewster said slowly. "It is you who does not understand. Until we know what caused Agent Minkus's unexpected death, there will be no food coming out of the White House kitchen. Especially not to be served to the president or his family."

I sat back. "You can't actually believe that—"

Still speaking slowly, he licked fat lips. "You will cooperate fully with the team assigned to you."

I wanted to argue, but I couldn't decide what to say.

Brewster fixed me with an impatient glare. "Now, I will ask you again. Do you understand?"

I rubbed my forehead. "I'm beginning to."

Brewster turned to Guzy. "Have your brother bring in Buckminster Reed from the other room."

Bucky. My second-in-command. One by one, they would bring in everyone from the kitchen. Probably the sommelier and the butlers, too.

Suddenly I felt the weight of it all. Someone had died on our watch. This had never happened before. Although I understood the need to find out why— and how—I knew no one on my staff would have made such a tragic mistake with food. Minkus could not have died as a result of our preparations. He must have died naturally, or in some non-food-related way.

Brewster brought his face close to mine, interrupting my chain of reasoning. "You're dismissed."

As Guzy and I headed out the door, I remembered something.

I rushed back to Brewster's desk. "We had guests yesterday."

The way Brewster raised his eyes made it seem as though his lids weighed a thousand pounds. Each. "Yes," he said. "And one of them died. We have established that."

"No, I mean in the kitchen." The man's bored expression urged me to talk faster. "I can *prove* that no one in the kitchen did anything wrong. We had cameras rolling yesterday. All day. We had guest chefs in the—"

He held up his hand. "Guest chefs?"

"A TV special," I said. "Suzie and Steve." I wanted to make the point that I could prove that nothing had been handled improperly. We could get this whole thing cleared up if only someone would take the time to review yesterday's recordings.

"Suzie," he repeated without interest. "And Steve."

"You know, the SizzleMasters."

He rubbed his nose, then scribbled a few notes on the pages before him. With another impatient look at me, he turned to Guzy. "Get me everything you can on this Suzie and Steve. And round them up, too."

"Round them up?" I asked in horror.

Guzy tugged my elbow.

"You misunderstand," I said. "I'm not saying they did anything wrong. I'm saying I have proof that—"

"Lot of that misunderstanding going around here today, wouldn't you say, Ms. Paras?" Brewster pointed to the door. "Thanks for the tip. You think of anyone else who might be suspicious, you let us know."

CHAPTER 4

LOOKING SMALL AND SCARED, CYAN WAS SEATED ON A WHITE plastic folding chair when Agent Guzy brought me into the next room. "Cyan!" I said, rushing toward her.

She jumped to her feet. "Ollie."

"No talking."

We stopped, startled—feeling like criminals. Did they really believe we killed Minkus?

Taking a seat next to Cyan, I realized, belatedly, that that's exactly what we were up against.

Agent Guzy walked to the far end where his twin stood, staring straight ahead. Brewster had mentioned they were brothers, so I hadn't been too far off when I assigned them the monikers of Tweedledee and Tweedledum. Guzy One spoke in low tones to Guzy Two, and the second man left the room.

My chair wobbled. I tried to sit very still to prevent it from making noise in the silence. *Hard to do in such a chilly place,* I thought, suppressing a shiver. White unadorned walls prevented me from finding anything of interest to focus on. The only thing in the room I could watch was the agent, who stood unmoving, except for the occasional blink.

Cyan and I shared a look. She shrugged. Since we were forbidden to speak, there wasn't much else to do except try to put together what I knew. Carl Minkus's death was unfortunate, and I felt bad—the way you feel bad whenever you hear that anyone has died—but I didn't have any particular affection for the man. In fact, I don't think I'd actually ever met him. The closest I'd gotten was when he'd been a guest at the White House. And that had only been maybe twice before.

Third time's the charm.

Ooh. Bad thought.

"How long are we going to be here?" I asked.

Guzy One directed his gaze to me, but didn't speak.

Cyan whispered, "Isn't your mom arriving today? And your grandmother?"

I nodded. "I sure hope we're out of here by—"

"No talking."

Just as Guzy One said that, the door opened again and Bucky was ushered in, accompanied by Guzy Two. Brewster must not have had very many questions for my assistant chef. "That was quick," I said to Bucky.

He yanked himself out of the agent's grasp. "What the hell is going on here?" Bucky asked.

Guzy Two pointed. "No talking."

Bucky, Cyan, and I shared a look that spoke of our disbelief at the way we were being treated. I'd never met either of these Guzy brothers. They clearly hadn't been on the Presidential Protective Detail for very long. Then again, they might have just been brought in for the day. After all, it wasn't every day that a White House soiree ended with a dead guest.

The third agent from this morning's car ride came in. The weak link. I fixed him with a smile before he had a chance to join his comrades. "Hi," I said. "What's your name?"

He looked perplexed by the question, but answered. "Snyabar."

The Guzy brothers exchanged a look as I stood up. "Agent Snyabar," I began, "I think we've gotten off to a bad start here."

Snyabar moved closer to the Guzy brothers, who stepped apart to allow him into their midst. I advanced, noting that the little chef was causing the big Secret Service agents to circle their wagons.

"Please return to your seat, Ms. Paras," the first Guzy said. "You will be summoned by the investigators soon."

"Really, is all this necessary?" I asked.

The way the three men stared straight ahead, without even acknowledging that I'd spoken, scared me most of all. We were trusted White House staff members. At least, we had been yesterday. Right now I felt vulnerable—and guilty. I even started to doubt myself. Could there have been some combination of spices, foods, or beverages that was toxic to Carl Minkus? Was there some way I could have known this?

I was about to try breaking the Secret Service barrier again, when the door opened, and Peter Everett Sargeant III strode in. "Ah," he said. "Here you are."

I found it unlikely that he'd been looking for me for any valid reason. Peter Everett Sargeant and I had never gotten along. I'd say that we didn't see eye to eye, but I believed the fact that we were almost the same height was exactly the problem. Peter was an incredibly short fellow, obsequious and ingratiating to everyone in power, but condescending and obnoxious to those below him, and especially staffers who were shorter than he was. Which was . . . me.

"Is there something you need, Peter?"

Our Secret Service guards, surprisingly, didn't scold me. Apparently talking among ourselves was verboten, but conversing with the angry chief of cultural and faith-based etiquette affairs was not.

Sargeant paced in front of Cyan and Bucky, his hands clasped in front of him. "Well, well, well," he said. "How the mighty have fallen."

I folded my arms. "Care to explain?"

The agents shifted their weight, in sequence. Guzy One stretched his neck, then glanced at the door.

Sargeant's little eyes narrowed as he came close. "Do you have any idea the trouble we're dealing with out there?" He gestured vaguely toward the residence. "The trouble you've caused?"

That got my back up. "I don't believe it's been proven that the kitchen had anything to do with Carl Minkus's death. And until that time, I'll thank you to stop pointing fingers."

One corner of his mouth curled up. "Just wait, Ms. Paras. I've heard things."

I must have reacted, because Sargeant's smile got a little bigger. "Yes, it seems Agent Minkus commented about his meal, right before he collapsed."

We were talking about a person's death here, and yet Sargeant seemed almost gleeful in his explanation as he continued. "Something was most definitely wrong with the meal and it won't be long before every finger points at you." He sniffed, glancing as he did at Cyan and Bucky. "At all of you."

I couldn't stop myself. "What did Minkus say?"

At the far end of the room, the door opened and someone called for me.

Sargeant didn't reply, but before I could ask him again, Guzy One stepped between us. "Ms. Paras, you've been summoned."

"But . . ." I sputtered.

"Now," Guzy said. He nipped my elbow between his thumb and forefinger and guided me toward the door.

I wasn't done with Sargeant. Even though I was sure he was baiting me, I couldn't stop myself from asking again. "Minkus said something about the food?"

"He most certainly did." Sargeant's eyes glittered.

What kind of person found enjoyment only when someone else was suffering?

He raised a hand and gave me a little finger wave. "I'll fill you in later. I'll be here," he said. "And with any luck, *you* won't."

CHAPTER 5

GUZY ONE SHUTTLED ME OUT OF THE EAST WING INTO THE MAIN residence and up to the first floor. The walk through the majestic entrance and cross hall—which I'd done hundreds of times—should have felt comforting and familiar. But all I could concentrate on were the echoing squishes of my shoes against the marble floor and Agent Guzy's brisk *clip-clip-clip* beside me.

I'd assumed we were headed to Paul Vasquez's office, but instead wound up in the State Dining Room, where it appeared the authorities had set up a command post. The prior evening's dinner had been served in the adjacent Family Dining Room. That, to me, was a misnomer because when the First Family dined together, they tended to congregate upstairs in the private quarters. This Family Dining Room was on the main floor and the Campbells often used it for intimate business dinners, like last night's had been.

There were dozens of Secret Service agents in the State Dining Room. Several folding tables had been brought in and computers set up. There were uniformed agents as well as PPD agents, and I quickly scanned the room, looking for Tom.

Being short is a major disadvantage because I was lost in a sea of broad shoulders and hurrying clerks. Tom is tall, and I aimed my gaze upward, but Guzy tugged me toward the northwest corner of the room, near the pantry.

"Paul!" I said when I saw our chief usher.

Urgency must have been apparent in my voice because he left a group of agents, and hurried over to me. "Ollie, how are you holding up?"

I managed to squirm out of Guzy's grip. "I don't know."

Paul winced. "This is a bad one." He turned to Guzy and nodded. "Thank you."

Guzy seemed perplexed by the dismissal, as though not quite sure how to take the directive from Paul. As chief usher, Paul didn't control the PPD, but there was an understanding between him and veteran agents. Paul controlled the residence, and if he was taking responsibility for the executive chef, then Agent Guzy needed to find something else to do.

"Sir, I—"

"You're free to go."

Raising his voice to be heard above the din, Guzy tried harder. "But, sir—" He reached out a hand, as though to ensnare my elbow again. I sidestepped him.

From behind us, a familiar voice. "It's okay. I got it."

We both turned.

"Tom!" I said. Paul Vasquez rolled his eyes. Although Tom and I had tried to keep our relationship quiet amongst the White House staff, it was getting to be a joke that the only people truly unaware of the situation were the president and the First Lady themselves. And apparently Agent Guzy, too.

He looked dumbfounded. Which was quite a sight from this expressionless behemoth. "Agent MacKenzie," he said, his tone deferential.

Tom stepped between us. "I'll take it from here."

I leaned up to whisper: "Bucky and Cyan."

Tom smiled down at me, then addressed Guzy again. "Would you please see that Ms. Paras's assistants are escorted to the Library?"

Guzy nodded. "Right away."

When he left, Tom turned to me, asking the same thing Paul had. "How are you holding up?"

I started with my topmost concern. "My mom," I said. "I forgot my cell phone at home. In all the excitement—"

Paul looked confused.

Tom ran a hand through his hair. "They're arriving today?"

"They're supposed to touch down at eight fifty this morning."

He looked at his watch. It was just after five our time, which made it four in Chicago. "Early. Are they at the airport now?"

"They should be." I shrugged. "But I have no idea."

Paul cleared his throat. "The investigators need to talk with Ollie."

Tom shepherded us toward the pantry, where I'd expected it to be quiet. Instead, there were paper-booted, latex-gloved technicians taking apart every inch of my workspace. They were covered, head to toe, in Tyvek jumpsuits and wore masks over their faces and shower caps over their heads. I could only imagine that the scene downstairs in my kitchen was worse. I groaned.

"It's standard operating procedure, Ollie," Tom said. "They have to examine everything."

We both knew that before this episode was over, my kitchens would be turned inside out and upside down. Which was exactly the state of my stomach at the moment.

The door between the pantry and the Family Dining Room had been propped open and I could see more technicians in full protective gear. President Campbell stood at the doorway leading to the stairway and Usher's Room. He was having an intense conversation with Agent Craig Sanderson.

At that moment, the president looked up and made eye contact with me. His mouth was set in a grim line and I thought I could detect disappointment, even across the crowded room. I was sorry to see it there, even if I had done nothing to cause it. He nodded in acknowledgment, then turned slightly away from me, to continue his conversation.

"What is going on?" I asked.

Paul urged me back into the center of the pantry, then called for quiet. The busy technicians stopped what they were doing and turned to face us. I was glad to have Tom behind me.

"This is Executive Chef Olivia Paras," Paul said in a clear voice. "If you have any questions, she will be available in the Library."

From behind their obscuring getups, I could make out that three of the technicians were male, two female. One of the men wore glasses behind his safety goggles. Why were they dressed so protectively? Did they think Minkus died as a result of an airborne contaminant? If so, then wouldn't the other guests have been affected? Wouldn't we all be at risk? I wanted to get out of this room with its suddenly close quarters and heavy, stale air.

"You'll be happy to cooperate, right, Ollie?" Paul said, nudging me forward.

"Yes," I said. I caught his hint and spoke assertively to the group. "I know you have a job to do and I'm here to help in any way I can. My staff and I are at your service."

Paul nodded, then moved us back out the door, through the State Dining Room, where activity had grown to fever pitch. I wanted to stop, but Tom and Paul kept moving me forward.

"We've got to get you out of here," Tom said under his breath. "They've got Metropolitan Police here and we can't be sure of leaks."

"Leaks?" I asked, as the two men escorted me to the stairs adjacent to the East Room. "But what could be leaked?"

"That's the thing you learn in the world of politics," Paul said. "You never want to give out information you don't need to share. Anything that *can* be misconstrued, usually is."

I'd expected our path to take us to the Library, where Tom had told Guzy to take Cyan and Bucky, but as we reached the bottom of the stairs we walked across the hall to the China Room.

The door opened as we approached. The third agent from this morning, Agent Snyabar, was there, as were two Metropolitan Police detectives who proffered their badges for my inspection. A male/female team, their names were Fielding and Wallerton. Tom and Paul escorted me in and led me to one of the wing chairs. I declined, not wanting to be the only seated person.

Just then, the door opened and Craig Sanderson came in. Craig was a tall agent, handsome and crisp. As Tom's supervisor, he was aware of our relationship, but had enough regard for Tom that he preferred to remain "officially" uninformed.

Craig and I were cordial to one another. There were times his Appalachian drawl sent shivers up my spine. This was one of them. "Ms. Paras," he said slowly. "Why am I not surprised to discover your involvement in this terrible tragedy?"

"Hi Craig," I said, striving for informal. The less formal, the less intense our conversation would be. At least, that was what I hoped.

"Please, have a seat, Ms. Paras."

This time, I sat.

Craig took the wing chair opposite mine and the two detectives came around to flank him. They both held open small notebooks—a lot like the one Craig now held poised, waiting for me to speak. But what could I possibly say?

Tom and Paul stood on either side of my wing chair, and I twitched against the nubby fabric. I didn't want to stain the armrests, so I wiped both hands on the front of my slacks. I'd thrown on white canvas pants, a white T-shirt, and a light gray hoodie this morning. Although the day was cool, I was itching to remove my sweatshirt. The fireplace next to me wasn't burning, but I felt what it was like to sit in the hot seat.

"Agent Brewster talked with me this morning," I said to break the silence. Too late, I remembered the old adage "He who speaks first, loses."

Craig arched his brows. "And what did Agent Brewster have to say?"

"Not much," I said, wondering why I'd even brought it up. "He seems to think my kitchen—or I—had something to do with Agent Minkus's death."

"Did you?"

I blinked. "Of course not."

Craig's mouth twisted sideways. He wrote nothing, but the two detectives scribbled furiously. The forty-something woman—Wallerton—was tall and thin to the point of emaciation. I'd characterize her features as skeletal, and her wispy blonde hair did nothing to contradict that observation. The other detective, Fielding, was older. He had the look of a man who'd seen a lot in his day, but rather than fit the stereotype of paunchy veteran detective, he was trim and good-looking, with dark hair that was just beginning to go gray at the temples. Neither of them smiled.

Craig eased back in his seat, slightly. "We have a preliminary report from the medical examiner," he said.

I held my breath. "Already?"

Dumb question. This was the White House. Everything was done expeditiously. When something was needed, all stops were pulled out until it was accomplished.

"What did they say?" I asked, inching forward. "Do they think it was a heart attack?"

Craig's mouth turned down in a way that made my own heart drop. "It was not a myocardial infarction."

I swallowed.

The two detectives glanced up at me, then continued to write.

"What was it?" I asked.

"We expect to have more information within a day or two."

I wanted to scream, "Just tell me!" but I pulled my hands together on my lap and clasped my fingers, hard. "My kitchen is clear, right?"

Craig did that thing with his mouth again. When he fixed me with a stare, I felt my insides turn to jelly. Hot, slippery jelly. Like the kind Polish bakers fill their *paczki* with every Fat Tuesday. "No," he said.

My voice came out in a whisper. "What do you mean, 'no'?" I felt a hand on my shoulder. I didn't know if it was Paul's or Tom's. My vision telescoped, focusing solely on Craig's angry stare, and after the whoosh in my head silenced, all I could hear were pens scraping against notepaper.

"The medical examiner believes that Carl Minkus ingested something at dinner that killed him."

I sucked in a gasp. "'Ingested something that killed him'?" I repeated the words, but my brain couldn't accept the meaning.

Craig continued. "The medical examiner is doing very in-depth toxicology screenings today. They're waiting on results, but we won't have answers for a while."

I shook my head. This wasn't happening. "But that doesn't mean it was something he ate . . . something we served. Couldn't he have eaten something at lunch that did this?"

Craig wasn't budging. "Doctor Michael Isham is one of the finest pathologists in the country. We will have to wait and see what he says."

"But . . ."

"Until we can prove that food served at last night's dinner was not responsible for Carl Minkus's death, you and your staff are banned from the White House kitchen."

"But the Easter Egg Roll," I said. "It's a week from today."

"The Easter Egg Roll is not my concern."

"We have a lot of work to do. I mean . . . this is a big deal. Surely the president and First Lady understand that. How can we prepare for the Egg Roll if we aren't allowed in the kitchen?"

Craig licked his lips, but I interrupted before he could answer.

"And what about preparing regular meals!" I was growing indignant. I knew we could probably keep the house running by utilizing the family kitchen on the second floor, but that would certainly not give us enough space to prepare for the entire Egg Roll extravaganza. "We need the kitchen," I said pertly. The cafeteria on the basement-mezzanine level was an option, too, but I much preferred working in the kitchen I called home—the main kitchen on the ground floor.

"Until you are cleared, you won't be preparing any food at all."

"But the other kitchens . . ."

"You don't understand," he said. "It isn't just the kitchens we're investigating. We're investigating all of *you*."

My mouth dropped open. Again I felt a hand on my shoulder. I was pretty sure it was Paul. "You can't be serious," I said.

"When the safety of the president of the United States is at stake, I'm dead serious."

I pulled my lips shut—tightly, to prevent an outburst. Then: "What about the other guests?"

My question seemed to take Craig aback; the two detectives, too. They stopped writing long enough to send me quizzical looks.

"So far, the other guests are unaffected," he said. "But I understand you prepared a separate entrée for Carl Minkus. He was served food that the other guests did not touch."

"That's true," I said. "Mr. Minkus is vegetarian, and we made sure to follow his dietary guidelines exactly." I raised a finger and shook it for emphasis. "I made certain to personally oversee everything that went out that night." I knew such a statement put me at higher risk for investigation, but it was true. Nothing went out without my approval. "But if he had an allergy that we were unaware of—"

"His medical records indicate no such allergy."

"Maybe he recently developed one."

"Maybe you're grasping at straws." Craig consulted notes for a brief moment, then met my eyes. "You told Jack Brewster that you had two guest chefs in the kitchen yesterday."

"Suzie and Steve," I said. "The SizzleMasters."

The female detective shot a questioning look at the handsome older detective. He supplied the answer, and I heard his voice for the first time. "It's on the Food Channel," he said. "Suzie and Steve are big into steaks and barbecue. They have their own show." He shrugged. "It's pretty good."

Craig didn't look at him. "Why were they in the White House kitchen?"

"This is what I was trying to tell Agent Brewster," I said. "We were filming a segment for the *SizzleMasters* show. It's kind of like one of those challenge cooking shows where the TV personality shows up and challenges the competitor. We were working on the filets for last night's dinner and the network planned to air the segment about three weeks from now."

Paul interjected. "I approved this because Mrs. Campbell was very much in favor of giving viewers an intimate look inside the White House kitchen."

Craig looked confused, so I said, "We were not only being challenged by the SizzleMasters, we were serving the food prepared during the challenge." I waved both hands in front of me to ward off an anticipated argument. "But we weren't filming the guests actually enjoying what we'd prepared. We made extra for our judges."

"Judges?"

"We enlisted a couple of the butlers to sample the steaks. It's part of the schtick for the TV show."

Craig held up a hand. "I do not care about 'schtick.' What I do care about is the fact that we have a dead guest on our hands. A very prominent, very dead, guest. And I believe we are trying to find out what he may have ingested that took his life. Carl Minkus was a vegetarian, correct?"

"Yes, but—"

"Then I do not see the relevance in discussing this television challenge. I do not see what bearing any of this has on our investigation."

Exasperated by the slow deliberation of his cadence, I rushed to get my words out. "We had cameras rolling the entire time. They were supposed to send me a copy. I'm sure if you contact the production company, you'll be able to get one, too."

Craig glanced up to the female detective. She nodded, and Paul accompanied her out of the room.

Chalk one up for me.

"Did anybody else have a vegetarian meal at dinner yesterday?" Detective Fielding asked.

"No," I said. "We made Mr. Minkus's dinner especially for him."

My stomach dropped when I realized what I'd said. Why not just take out a full-page ad, announcing that the White House kitchen killed Carl Minkus?

Fielding flipped a page in his notebook. "What about side dishes? Salads? Desserts? Was there anything that all the guests ate?"

"Sure," I said. I rattled off the prior evening's menu, and told him that in addition to Carl Minkus's sesame eggplant entrée, he'd been served a lemon-broccoli side dish, a salad with homemade dressing, and he'd shared in one of Marcel's spectacular desserts. "That you'll have to get from Marcel. I know it involved spun sugar and ice cream, but beyond that—"

Craig interrupted. "He is being questioned as well."

"But no one else has gotten sick, right?" I asked hopefully.

"As of this moment," Craig said, "that is correct."

"You have the entire guest list?" I was pushing it, I knew, but I wanted to be sure they knew I was willing to help in any way I could. "We added Philip and Francine Cooper at the last minute yesterday."

"We have the entire list," Craig said.

Fielding grimaced, but dutifully wrote it down. "I didn't have that."

Craig didn't like to be one-upped. He went through the entire guest list with Fielding, ticking off names as he spoke. "Ruth Minkus was in attendance with her husband. Additionally, we had Philip Cooper; his wife, Francine; and Alicia and Quincy Parker," he said.

At the mention of Alicia Parker's name, Craig winced. Everyone knew our fiery defense secretary.

"Don't forget the president and First Lady," I said. "They were there, too."

Craig gave me a lips-only smile. "Yes, we are aware of that."

Detective Wallerton returned, and together with Detective Fielding and Craig they questioned me about everything that went on in the kitchen yesterday. I remembered almost every detail, but told them I needed to consult my files for a few of the ingredients used to prepare Mr. Minkus's meal. After listening to my exhaustive recitation and taking plenty of notes, the detectives seemed satisfied with my answers.

Craig surprised us all by turning his attention to Tom. "Agent MacKenzie, how long have you been on duty?" Before Tom could answer, Craig continued, "You have been here for over twenty-four hours. More than thirty, in fact. Am I correct?"

Tom nodded. "Yes, sir."

"Go home, Agent."

Tom started to argue that as a ranking Secret Service agent during a crisis, his place was at the White House, but Craig cut him off. "You are relieved. Get some sleep. And don't come back until you do."

Tom left without further comment, but I knew how disappointed he must be. I was disappointed as well. His silent presence had been a comfort.

By the time they were done asking me everything fourteen times each, I was sticky and clammy and wished I could race home and shower. Then I remembered Mom and Nana.

I glanced at my watch. Eight thirty. I'd never make it to Dulles in twenty minutes. Even if I were cleared to leave right now.

"Are we keeping you from something?" Craig asked.

Drained from the nonstop queries, I didn't even bother to explain. "No," I said, hoping that when I wasn't there to meet them, my mother didn't hustle Nana on the next flight back to Chicago.

Finally dismissed, I was led to the door. "So who will take care of the First Family's meals?" I asked.

Craig sniffed. "Several of our agents have agreed to take on that responsibility. They are working out of the second floor kitchen and the Mess."

My face must have telegraphed my disbelief, because he added, "Some of our agents are quite talented in the culinary arts. One of them was a full-time cook in college. He knows what he's doing."

I closed my eyes. This was worse than I thought. "What about us?" I asked. "Should I just stay home and twiddle my thumbs until you guys give me the all-clear?"

Craig's face remained impassive. "Do whatever you like, Ms. Paras," he said. "But plan on doing it here. You aren't going home anytime soon."

CHAPTER 6

WHEN I GOT TO THE LIBRARY, BUCKY AND CYAN WERE WAITING for me. Bucky stood up. "How long do we have to stay here? We've got work to do."

"No," I said, "we don't."

Cyan opened her mouth to question, but I held up a hand. "We're out of the kitchen until further notice."

"What?"

"Here's where we stand," I said, lowering myself into the wooden armchair Bucky had just vacated. "Until it can be absolutely proven that Carl Minkus didn't die as a result of our kitchen's negligence, we are forbidden to prepare food in the White House."

Bucky paced. "We couldn't have done anything. I mean . . . there's no way. We read his dietary requirements." He dragged the back of his hand against his forehead. When he turned to me, his face was pale and his voice cracked. "This has never happened before."

I stood and placed a hand on his shoulder. Surprisingly, he didn't move away. "We did nothing wrong."

Bucky shook his head. "This is terrible."

For the first time, I actually let the truth sink in. A man was dead, possibly as a result of something we'd fed him. Although we'd followed every protocol, the fact remained that our kitchen could be guilty of negligence. I'd been adamant about our innocence, but what if we *had* been negligent? Then Carl Minkus was dead prematurely. And, as executive chef, blame fell squarely on me.

Bucky practically choked his next words out. "Did you think about botulism?"

I was about to answer when he pushed me aside. He covered his mouth and hurtled himself through the adjacent door.

Cyan jumped to her feet. Disregarding the fact that he had disappeared into the men's lounge, the two of us followed Bucky in. He'd made it to the lavatory and into one of the stalls just in time. The sound of retching carried through the door. I tapped on the wood paneling. "You okay?"

We heard him cough and spit. "Yeah."

"Bucky," I said, "this wasn't your fault."

He sniffed, noisily. "I know."

I held up my hands in a helpless gesture. Cyan shrugged. "Then come out."

There was a long moment of silence, where we heard nothing but the faint rushing of water through nearby pipes.

Finally, Bucky said, "This is my life."

I leaned toward the stall door, not knowing how to answer that.

"We're always so careful," he said, his voice plaintive. "I've never worked anywhere with such stringent guidelines. And I like it that way. I want to stay here."

"Nobody's kicking us out, Bucky," I said, trying for levity. "Yet."

When he spoke again, his voice was a whisper. "What if they let us all go? What if they say we were negligent—even if we weren't? Then I'll never get a job anywhere. My entire career will be down the tubes."

To punctuate his words, he flushed the toilet. Cyan and I exchanged a glance, and stepped a little farther away from the door when we heard the lock turn.

Bucky emerged, looking less sweaty and pale. He wiped a handful of bathroom tissue across his forehead and offered a wobbly smile. "I've worked my whole life to get here," he said. "When I think of how easily it can all be lost . . ."

Bucky's eyes glistened and he turned away from us toward the sinks, where he turned on the tap and avoided looking into the mirror.

"Listen," I started to say.

He shook his head. "The two of you don't understand. You can't. I worked hard to get here. I put in the best years of my life—before either of you came to the White House. And I thought I would be named executive chef someday."

I stood behind him to his right, and in the mirror I could see the weak smile turning sour. He gave me a quick glance. "Instead, they gave it to you."

There wasn't much for me to say. This position wasn't a "gift." I knew I had earned it and I knew exactly why Henry had chosen me as his successor over Bucky. But I couldn't say that. Not now.

"Being the first female White House chef is a coup," he continued. "I get that. I understand that the First Lady had a point to make. But now I see the writing on the wall." This time his glance was for Cyan. "Ollie is grooming you to take over when she gets rid of me, isn't she?"

Cyan looked to me for answers. I had none. It was true that Cyan had really come into her own over the past year, but Bucky was a valuable member of my team. I said so.

"I'm not planning to let you go, Bucky. We're a team."

"After this fiasco, maybe we're all gone."

His face went pale and damp again and he looked like he wanted to make another mad dash for the stalls. Squeezing his eyes shut, he held tight to the countertop for a moment before splashing cold water onto his face. He turned off the water, then patted himself dry with one of the nearby linen hand towels.

Once he calmed himself, I asked Cyan to excuse us. She left the men's lounge and I waited until I heard the door close.

"Bucky, I have no intention of 'getting rid' of you. None whatsoever."

He stared down at the draining water. "Henry favored you from your first day on the job. And now you favor Cyan." I watched his hands flex. "I'm a middle-aged white guy. Nobody wants me. Maybe I should resign. But . . . where could I go?"

With Bucky's talent, and his White House résumé, he could go almost anywhere he chose. Instead of saying that, however, I assured him, "You're not going anywhere."

"You just keep me on because you haven't figured out my replacement yet."

"Not true," I said. "Bucky, damn it, look at me."

When he did, my heart broke for him. Bucky, my acerbic, temperamental, yet brilliant assistant was terrified of losing his life's work. I'd never seen him this vulnerable, and for possibly the first time, I understood that Bucky wasn't ornery because he wanted to be. He made things difficult because he felt he didn't fit in with the rest of us. And it was true. His personality kept us distant. But for him to think that he didn't belong in our White House family was anathema. He was as much a part of the team as anyone, and more so than most.

In that split-second I realized I hadn't been as effective a leader as I'd hoped to be. Henry had tolerated Bucky's occasional tantrums and quick criticisms, and I'd been trying to emulate Henry since I'd been promoted. But maybe this was an opportunity to do even better.

"What?" he said when several seconds passed and I hadn't said anything. "Feeling good about yourself now that you made me admit my failings?"

I kept my voice low, but strong. "You want a guarantee that you're not going to be fired? I can't do that."

If he had expected me to speak soothingly and to bolster his ego, he was mistaken. I read the surprise on his face. Bucky knew my need to keep people happy as well as he knew that his prickly nature kept most people on guard. But I decided the best way to get through to my first assistant was by speaking the language he knew best.

I continued. "Every four, sometimes eight, years all of us have to be prepared to be released by a new administration. That's the way this particular job works. And that's what we all signed on for. And if that happens, it happens. It isn't because we aren't the best chefs in the world—it's because the new family has different preferences. And if we tender our resignations to a new First Lady and she accepts them—there's no shame in that."

Taking a breath, I plunged on. "There *would* be shame in our being fired because a guest died. Huge shame. But we would all be in the same boat. We would all be faced with such a damaging mark on our records that we couldn't go anywhere and hold our heads high. It would be like starting over."

"But you're younger—"

"Not by all that much." That was a stretch. Bucky was at least fifteen years my senior. But aging—like seasoning—was often a good thing. "And if we go down, we go down together. You know that none of us would ever endanger one of our guests."

He nodded.

"And I believe the First Family knows that as well. I'm convinced that no matter what the medical examiner finds out, we will not be held up for ridicule on our own. I do not believe that the president or the First Lady will throw us under the bus."

He grimaced.

"Listen. You are my second-in-command. If you try to sneak out of here before all this gets settled—"

"Sneak?"

"The way you're talking, you're planning to put your résumé out on the market as soon as they let us out today."

"I'm being practical. If somebody's head is going to roll, I know it'll be mine."

"Bucky," I said, and waited for him to look at me again. He was afraid that *I* would throw him under the bus. But telling him that he was the most valuable chef I had on staff would be pointless now. He wouldn't believe me. He'd think I was just trying to be nice. "Pick yourself up. Nobody is going to be fired today."

He gave a snort. "Until they decide we poisoned Carl Minkus."

"And if they do, then you know exactly whose head will roll. Mine."

He said nothing, but I could tell by the look in his eyes that I was finally getting through.

"I'm the one on the chopping block here," I said. "I'm the executive chef and, by definition, everything that is served is done so with my approval. Until they find evidence that we had nothing to do with Carl Minkus's untimely demise, I can't even access the kitchen to help prove that we're innocent. But I'll be depending on you and Cyan to remember every single detail from the dinner preparations last night."

"Can't you figure out some way to get insider information from the Secret Service?" he asked. "I mean, can't Tom help you out a little bit here?"

I shrugged. "He was ordered to go home. I have no idea what's coming next from them."

Bucky wasn't his normal self again yet, but he did seem to be mulling over the problem. "I'll write down some notes."

"Careful," I said. "Make sure nobody has access to them except you. You never know what can happen when things are taken out of context."

He rubbed the corners of his mouth downward, kept his hand there as he asked, "What about Suzie and Steve?"

"They're already on the list to be investigated."

"You think there's any chance one of them did something wrong?"

"I certainly doubt it." My hand covered my mouth as a thought occurred to me. "You don't think someone did this on purpose?"

"Oh, hell. I never thought of that."

The door banged open and the two Guzy brothers came in, taking up more than their fair share of space in the small room. Their jaws dropped as they took in Bucky's startled glance, both our hands over our mouths, and the fact that we were standing in the men's lounge.

Guzy One looked a little confused, but his voice was brusque as ever. "When you two are finished being sick, we need you out here."

The two agents pivoted and left the bathroom.

If the situation hadn't been so miserable, I might have found it funny.

AFTER ANOTHER INTERMINABLE WAIT, FOLLOWED BY QUESTIONS from every possible branch of law enforcement, Cyan, Bucky, and I were released. I glanced at my watch and my stomach bubbled. Two fifteen. My mom and nana's plane had touched down hours earlier. I berated myself again for forgetting my cell phone at home. I could just picture them sitting on hard airport seats, dialing me at home, dialing me on my cell, and getting frustrated by the unending shifts to voicemail. They would have given me the benefit of the doubt until about ten in the morning. By now, they would have just felt sad and forgotten.

As we started for the East doors, the Guzy brothers swarmed us. Even though there were only two of them and three of us, their size and authority made us feel small and surrounded.

Guzy One held up a hand. "Not so fast."

The day's frustrations had taken a toll and my tone was less than accommodating. I was, in fact, snippy. "They told us we could go."

"Too many reporters outside."

"What, you expect us to hang around here all night?"

Guzy Two shook his head. "We're driving you back."

"What about Cyan and Bucky?" I asked.

"We're taking all of you."

I turned to my crew. Bucky shrugged. Cyan forced a smile. "At least we won't have to wait for a train."

As we made our way to the black limousine, we heard shouts from beyond the White House fence. I wanted to shroud my head so that the cameras couldn't exploit my face on the evening news, but I didn't. Neither did Cyan or Bucky. The three of us followed one Guzy agent, and his brother brought up the rear.

Cyan had been keeping tabs on my family issues and now she addressed Guzy Two. "You should drop Ollie off first," she said. "She needs to get home."

"No ma'am," one of them said. "We have orders."

"Orders to take us all home," Cyan persisted. "But not what order to drop us off, right?"

"No ma'am," he said again. "We have a specified route. Ms. Paras is our last dropoff because we have another stop to make in her vicinity after that."

So much for that idea. "Thanks for trying, Cyan," I whispered.

As Cyan and Bucky loaded into the limousine's cushy backseat, I realized that was the most either of the Guzy brothers had said to us. I was beginning to see the brothers' differences rather than just their similarities. Number Two had slightly darker hair, a slight lisp, and, apparently, more willingness to converse.

"What's your name?" I asked before I got in. "Your first name, I mean."

"Jeffrey."

"And your brother?"

Jeffrey looked to his sibling for approval, but Guzy One had already slid into the driver's seat and didn't acknowledge my question. "Raymond."

For some reason I expected them to be named Mark and Michael, or Dan and Don, or John and Joe.

"Is there any way at all you can get me back to my apartment quickly?" I asked. "My family is in town. That is, I hope they still are. I haven't heard from them and I need to grab my cell phone."

When Raymond half turned and cocked an eyebrow over his recently donned sunglasses, Jeffrey gestured me into the car. "No."

They'd confiscated Cyan's and Bucky's cell phones during the interrogation. Now, using Cyan's recently returned cell, I dialed my mom's phone about a hundred times on the ride back. No luck. I wanted to ask Raymond Guzy what his affection for the brake pedal was all about. The drive this morning had been at lightning speed. The trip back this afternoon was so slow, I swore I could watch roadside cherry blossoms blooming.

I'd never been to Cyan's or Bucky's homes and I was surprised and dismayed that Cyan lived so far outside of D.C. proper. To save time, I was half tempted to invite them both back to my apartment and then worry about getting them to their respective homes later. Tempting as it was, that wouldn't have been fair to them.

When it was finally just me in the backseat of the limo, I tried once again, this time in vain, to get Jeffrey to talk.

I sat in silence for the long ride back toward Crystal City, watching the world pass me by—slowly—unable to find beauty in the burgeoning spring just outside my window. Of course, poor Carl Minkus wasn't appreciating the fresh greenery, either.

I thought back to my conversation with Bucky and wondered if someone had done Mr. Minkus deliberate harm. I had to believe the Secret Service and the Metropolitan Police were asking the same question.

I should let it go.

I had enough on my plate figuring out how Carl Minkus died. I had to worry about the Easter Egg Roll on Monday, the welcoming event afterward, and about my mom's and grandmother's welfare. Where were they? The fear of not knowing overwhelmed me.

The morning's weather had shifted and the storms had moved out of the area. Skies were clear without a cloud. Clear enough for takeoffs.

I watched a southbound plane traverse the solid blueness above and gave silent thanks. At least I knew they weren't on that one. With the direction this one was going, it was probably headed for Atlanta, or Orlando. I allowed myself a small smile. *Find blessings where you can,* I reminded myself.

And then the plane turned. Headed west.

I stared at the back of the driver's head and tried not to think about missed opportunities.

CHAPTER 7

MRS. WENTWORTH WAS COMING OUT OF HER APARTMENT JUST as I made it to my door. One of her hands was wrapped, claw-like, around her cane; the other held a covered plate. "Ollie!" she said. "I'm so glad you're home."

As neighbors went, Mrs. Wentworth was pretty great. She paid close enough attention to my comings and goings to know when something was wrong, but was shrewd enough not to poke her nose in when it wasn't needed. Well, not too often.

"Sorry," I said, holding up my keys. "Can't talk today, I—"

My door was open. Just a crack. But enough to startle me speechless. I knew I'd pulled it closed behind me this morning. I remembered working the deadbolt, thinking that I'd yanked the door too loudly and that I might wake Mrs. Wentworth up. Although from what I could tell, the woman never slept. Had someone broken in?

I took a step back, putting my hand up to silence whatever Mrs. Wentworth might say next. But she didn't take the hint. "Ollie," she began.

"Shh," I said, then crept forward.

There were voices coming from inside my apartment. A quick laugh. Familiar voices.

Mrs. Wentworth tapped me with the foot of her cane. "They're here. Your mother and your grandmother." Still behind me, she called out loudly, "Ollie's home!"

A thousand questions flew through my mind at once. I knew I'd never given Mrs. Wentworth my key—although that was an oversight I'd meant to correct for years. I also knew that James, the doorman who knew me best, was out of town this week. I couldn't imagine anyone contacting the building supervisor to allow my family in. They didn't know my mom and nana, but they all knew I worked for the White House. Nobody would have been allowed in without my approval.

I didn't have any time to think because just then the door swung completely open and my mother stepped out, wrapping me in a bear hug. I hugged back, surprised, relieved, and completely joyful, all at once. Heat threatened to close my throat, but I managed to croak, "Mom."

She squeezed tighter, then let me go long enough to hold me at arm's length. "You look wonderful," she said, her wide eyes taking me in. "You are even more beautiful than you were last time I saw you."

I opened my mouth and told her that she looked beautiful, too. And she did. But she was shorter, and older than I remembered. Her hair was cut differently, and she'd let it go gray. The contrast between it and her olive skin gave her an overall wizened appearance. There was still the quiet strength that I remembered in her bearing—for all her disdain of flying, she was one of the most fearless women I knew—but today she looked more vulnerable than she ever had in my life. I'd joined the White House as a Service by Agreement—SBA—chef during the prior administration, and I hadn't been home in all that time. Sure, it had been a while. But to me, it looked like my mother had aged.

"Ollie?"

The second most fearless woman I knew grabbed me with both hands, pulling me away from Mom. "Nana," I said, bending down to give her a hug. A tiny woman, Nana was always wiry, always gray-haired. She hadn't changed so much. Her bright eyes sparkled and her face blossomed with wrinkled glee. "You didn't tell us," she said, shaking a finger at me.

"Didn't tell you what?"

Mrs. Wentworth knocked me with her cane again. "Move over, honey," she said. "I'm bringing my biscotti. Your family's never tried it."

My confusion was profound. "How did you get in?"

Instead of answering, my mother took me by the arm. "You must be hungry."

I was, but until that moment hadn't noticed. "I tried calling you," I said. "Over and over."

Nobody seemed to pay me much mind.

I stopped walking and placed a hand on my mother's arm. "Why didn't you answer your phone?"

"I turned it off."

That took me aback. "Why did you do that?"

"We knew you were busy," she said with a perplexed look, "and we were already here."

Mrs. Wentworth had tottered over to my kitchen table and was uncovering the dish while Nana looked on. They were two elderly women, separated in age by only a few years, and they seemed to be entirely too comfortable with one another to have only just met.

"How did you get here?"

Nana held a chair out for me, which seemed ridiculous. I was by far the youngest person in the room, I should be holding out a chair for her. But she pointed with authority. "We ate. You make yourself comfortable and we'll warm something up."

Mrs. Wentworth settled herself across from me and sampled one of her biscotti. She smiled as the dry cookie snapped between her teeth. "My favorite," she said.

"More tea?" Nana asked her.

"Please."

"Somebody please tell me what's happening here," I said, exasperated. "I've been worried sick about you all day and I'm thrilled to see you here, but . . . how?" I looked to Mrs. Wentworth, who had taken another dainty bite. "Did the super let them in?"

My mom half turned from reaching into the refrigerator. She locked eyes with Mrs. Wentworth and then with Nana. Like a shared joke.

Mrs. Wentworth chewed, then swallowed, as Nana poured hot water over a new teabag. "Why don't I let your mother tell you?"

"Mom?"

With her back to me, my mom shook her head. Her voice was a playful scold. "Why didn't you tell us?"

How *could* I have told them? I'd been debriefed in meetings all morning. But that didn't mean they hadn't seen it on the news. "Tell you?" I asked. "You mean about the dead guest?"

The three of them stopped. My mom turned. "What dead guest?"

"The one at the—" I stopped myself. Living with my mom and nana as I had for years before striking out on my own had prepared me for such disjointed conversations. But it had been a long time and I was out of practice. With my fist against my forehead and the other hand raised to halt further talk until my brain could catch up, I grabbed the floor before anyone else could beat me to it. "First things first. Tell me how you got here, and how you got in."

The alarm in their eyes at my "dead guest" comment hovered a moment, but they read my anxiety and decided to let the matter drop, for now. Their faces relaxed into tiny, conspiratorial smiles.

My mom set a plate of food in front of me, but I didn't even notice what she'd prepared because her eyes met mine and held tight. "Tom," she said.

"Tom?" I felt slow and stupid. My mother and nana had never met Tom. I'd mentioned him a few times, sure, but I'd held back on waxing too poetic on our relationship. I'd had serious boyfriends before and sometimes I thought Mom took the breakups harder than I did. I wasn't about to put her through another one, although I held out hope that this particular relationship would continue to evolve. "Tom let you in?"

Nana settled herself in the chair to my left. She reached over and clasped my forearm. "Why didn't you tell us he was so tall? And so handsome?" She laughed. "Tommy is a serious beau, isn't he?"

Heat shot up my face. "Tommy?"

My mom laughed. "Nana started calling him that on the ride over here. I think he likes it."

"The ride over here?" Again, I tried to stop my mind from reeling. "Start at the beginning," I asked again. "Please."

Nana pointed. "Eat."

I dug my fork into the heaping food on my plate. Homemade meat loaf. Whipped potatoes with a pat of butter swimming in the crater's center. I used to pretend my mashed potatoes were a volcano and the butter its lava. Green beans. Standard fare in homes around the world, this meal offered a savory taste of memory in every bite. My mom watched me from across my kitchen, beaming.

I forked off another small portion of meat loaf and watched the tender ooze before I took a bite. "Okay," I said, almost unable to contain my joy at eating favorite homemade foods that I hadn't prepared myself, "I'm eating. Now, all of you, tell me what's been happening here."

Mom set a glass of Pepsi in front of me, and the chilled can next to it. I was usually a water fanatic, but today I needed the treat. I took a long swallow and thanked her.

"Can I get you anything else?"

"Just sit down, please," I asked. "And talk to me."

As my mom took the chair to my right, I again noticed the group's conspiratorial air. It was disconcerting to sit in one's own kitchen and to be the only one not in on the whole story. I waited, firmly committed to staying mum until I got the answers that, despite their attempts to be coy, the three of them were clearly bursting to tell me.

"Our plane touched down right on time," my mom began.

Nana added, "You know we were scheduled for eight fifty."

I nodded.

Mom took up the story again. "We tried to call you while we were waiting for the plane to unload, but there was no answer. We tried again—quite a few times."

"My fault," I said. "I got called in early and forgot my cell phone at home." Putting my hand up to forestall further conversation, I ran over to my bedroom and rescued the little gadget, noting on my way back that I had seven missed calls and two messages. Undoubtedly all from Mom.

Back in my seat, I dug into my meal again. "Go on."

She exchanged a glance with Nana before continuing. "We were making our way to the baggage claim when we saw this really handsome young man— "

"In a suit," Nana added.

"Tom?" I asked.

Mom nodded. "Tom."

My heart swelled. When I told him my dilemma, he'd gone down to Dulles himself to meet my family. And after being on duty for so long. He must have been exhausted, and yet he still did this for me. What a sweetheart. I bit my lip. What a guy.

"In a suit," Mom continued, "holding a big white card that read 'Paras Family.' As soon as we saw it, we headed his way. It was funny, because even though we saw the sign, it seemed like he'd picked us out of the crowd and he was headed right for us."

"I must have described you both very well."

"Or we were the only two women 'of a certain age' disembarking together," Nana said with a wink. "Looking lost."

"Tom brought you here?"

"He did. Drove us the whole way in a big black car that had a phone and a TV in the backseat."

Almost finished eating, I sighed, feeling relief settle over me. "I'm so glad."

Nana tapped my forearm. "I noticed he had keys to your apartment."

I chanced a look at Mrs. Wentworth, who had grabbed another biscotti and seemed to be in her own little world.

My face flushed again. Having my mother and grandmother know that my boyfriend had keys to my apartment was a small price to pay when that little fact had saved them from being stuck at the airport for several long, boring hours. Mom and Nana had always been go-to-church-every-Sunday-and-sometimes-more-often Catholics. They attended rosary meetings, baked for fund-raisers, and brought casseroles to grieving families. The church—and in particular, our parish—fed their need to be needed. I expected them to chastise me—sharply—for what those shared keys represented. "As a matter of fact . . ." I began.

Nana stopped tapping and now gripped my forearm, hard. "Good," she said. "I worry about you alone out here. It's a big city and there are dangers everywhere. I'm glad you have Tom to keep an eye on you."

I turned to Mom, who gave me "the look." "Yes," she said. "I'm sure he keeps a very close eye on you."

Blood flushed upward into my face, again. "He and I are—"

I couldn't say we were just friends, because that was patently false. But we were more than just lovers. We'd reached a level of comfort and intimacy that I wasn't quite ready to share, but felt compelled to defend.

"Ollie," my mom said, mercifully stopping me, "he's a very nice young man."

"You think so?"

Mrs. Wentworth saw fit to chime in. "He knocked on my door and asked if I would mind spending a little bit of time here. He said something about having to get back because of a situation." She glared at me. "He wouldn't tell me what it was."

I rose to his defense. "You know he's really not supposed to talk about anything that goes on at the White House."

Nana hadn't let go of my arm. "Is he really in the Secret Service?"

I nodded.

"Are they all as handsome as he is?"

I grinned. "Just about. And they're all really, really nice." I remembered my recent interrogation with Craig, then I thought about the recalcitrant Guzy brothers before amending, "Well, most of them, at least."

"Any of them my age?"

"I want to know about the dead guest," Mrs. Wentworth said, interrupting. "I haven't had the TV on today, and I haven't been online, either."

All eyes were on me. I took a deep breath. "He was one of our dinner guests at the White House last night. Carl Minkus."

Mrs. Wentworth slammed her hand on the table. Biscotti crumbs went flying. "I don't have the TV on for one day and I miss all the good stuff. What happened? Somebody shoot him on the way home?"

Since the news of Carl Minkus's death had brought thousands of reporters to swarm the White House, I had no reservations discussing what I knew. I'd just started explaining how we all had to undergo questioning, when the doorbell rang.

"That'll be Stan," Mrs. Wentworth said. "I told him to come around when he was done working."

I went to the door. "Hi Stan," I said, letting him in and wondering exactly when I'd lost control of my apartment. Probably just about the time Tom brought my family in and put Mrs. Wentworth in charge.

I followed the elderly electrician into my kitchen, where I offered him my seat. "No, no," he said, backing up to lean against the counter. "Ladies, sit. I've been on my back all day fixing a problem in the basement and I could use a chance to stretch."

As he passed behind Mrs. Wentworth, he grabbed her shoulders and gave them an affectionate squeeze. The two of them had been an item for a while now, and seeing them together never failed to make me smile. He greeted my mom and nana in a way that let me know they were not strangers, either.

"We had lunch together," Mom told me. "Tom stayed long enough to grab a bite to eat."

Nana added, "He said he could see where you got your cooking talent."

"We had a wonderful time," Mom said. "He really cares about you."

Were we talking about the same Tom? While I never doubted his affection for me, he'd been Mr. Let's-keep-our-relationship-low-key from the outset. I was speechless.

Mrs. Wentworth didn't want to let go of the day's scoop. "He told us you were tied up today and that you'd be late. Why were they questioning you, Ollie? Did you know Minkus?"

Before I could answer, she boosted herself from the table and grabbed for her cane. Stan was at her side immediately. "What do you need, honey?" he asked.

She pointed a gnarled finger toward my living room. "Turn on the TV. We'll get the story there and Ollie can fill us in during the commercials."

Within moments we were tuned into the all-news station and sure enough, beautiful anchor people were providing updates. The White House served as backdrop for their solemn expressions and somber tones.

I settled myself cross-legged on the floor, allowing the elderly folks to take the couch and chairs.

"As we've been reporting, Special Agent Carl Minkus died earlier today, of undetermined causes. We are keeping a close watch on the White House, where he was a dinner guest last night and where the investigation into his unexpected and untimely death is being conducted."

The screen changed to a photo of Minkus and his wife, Ruth. Minkus had been a ruddy-faced, overweight man, fifty-three years old. The picture showed the couple at a recent government sponsored event—Minkus in a tux, with his petite, strawberry-blonde wife next to him. Minkus had his arm around her waist and she smiled up at her husband, apparently unaware of the camera, into which Minkus beamed.

The news anchor continued. "The couple has one child, Maryland State Representative Joel Minkus."

Stan gave a low whistle. "Look at them. That there's what's known as a trophy wife."

Next to him on the couch, Mrs. Wentworth arched an eyebrow. "They've been married for years. She doesn't count. Anyway, trophy wives are tall. She's tiny."

"Trophy is trophy," Stan said with a shrug. He waggled his eyebrows. "But I'd rather have you on my shelf than her, any day."

Mrs. Wentworth slapped him playfully.

I focused on the television, where the scene changed again. Ruth Minkus stood behind a gaggle of microphones. I couldn't figure out where she was until the cameras pulled back enough for me to see the hotel logo on the lectern. She was talking, but we couldn't hear her. The news anchors were giving updates as a lead-in. "Ruth Minkus has agreed to make a statement and to bring us up-to-date on her husband's death. She's speaking to us from a local hotel to keep camera crews and reporters away from the family home."

Ruth's voice now joined with her image. "Joel and I . . ." She paused to compose herself. A couple of people behind her placed comforting hands on her shoulders. "We wish to thank everyone who has been so supportive at this difficult time."

Reporters shouted questions at the weeping widow.

My mom made an unladylike noise. "Vultures."

Joel Minkus leaned sideways, toward the microphone. The man was about my age and tall, but otherwise took after his mother. From what I'd heard of him, he was a strong proponent of environmental issues, and despite his relatively young age, he inspired cooperation between opposing factions. He was a golden boy, and apparently deservedly so. "Please," he said. "Can't you see how hard this is for us?"

My mom shook her head. "They should leave the poor woman alone."

"My husband," Ruth continued, "would have been overwhelmed by all this attention. He was a determined man who loved this country very much. If there was one thing he always told me, it was that he hoped to die in the service of the United States." Tears streamed down her face. "I . . . I suppose he got his wish."

The tension in my living room was tight. No one spoke.

An off-camera voice shouted: "Do you think he was a target because of his investigations?"

Ruth's eyes widened as she turned to her son. "Target?" she asked.

Joel stepped up to the microphone again. "Please. Let's wait until the medical examiner gives his report." He licked his lips and made pointed eye contact with audience members. "Have some compassion. My father just died. He was the finest man I've ever known. He was strong, well-loved, and most of all, patriotic. Let's not make assumptions until all the facts are in."

The news anchor interrupted to resume commentary. "The White House has prepared a statement." With that, the scene whisked away from the grieving family to a press conference in the Brady Briefing Room. White House Press Secretary Jodi Baines stepped up to the microphone. I felt for her. There wasn't a rule book for this situation. As she expressed the White House's condolences for Special Agent Minkus's demise, the elderly people in my living room fidgeted. Caught up in the story, myself, I'd almost forgotten they were there.

Jodi said: "Medical Examiner Dr. Michael Isham just finished briefing President Campbell and will now take questions."

Slim, though not particularly tall, Isham had a long, pleasant face, and dimples so deep they looked like implanted studs. The dimples stayed prominent even though he didn't smile. Another somber face in a day of sad solemnity. He blinked several times, canting his head slightly to avoid the bright lights' glare.

"He *looks* like a morgue doctor," Mrs. Wentworth said.

I turned, wanting to ask what she meant, but thought better of it. Stan patted her on the knee. "Shh."

"Good afternoon," Dr. Isham said, with a deadpan gaze into the audience. "As you all know, Special Agent Carl Minkus was declared dead at approximately one fifteen this morning. His body arrived at the morgue shortly thereafter and we immediately initiated an autopsy. The cause of death is undetermined at this time. We are waiting for test results."

"What kind of tests?" a dozen reporters shouted.

Isham held up his hands and both rooms fell silent—the briefing room and my living room.

"At this time," Isham continued, "we cannot share that information."

An explosion of questions: "Could Agent Minkus have been a victim of bioterrorism?"

"What do you expect to find?"

"Is the president at risk?"

Jodi leaned toward the microphone. "Ladies and gentleman, please. One at a time." She pointed. "Charles, go ahead."

The reporter stood. "We've heard conflicting rumors about Carl Minkus's behavior just before medics were summoned. Do you believe he might have suffered a heart attack?"

Isham licked his lips. "Again, we have not determined cause of death at this time."

A voice piped up: "Didn't Minkus complain that something was wrong with his food?"

I sat forward.

Isham answered, "I can't answer that."

Jodi sidestepped toward the microphone. "Mr. Minkus did not say anything specific about food," she said. She raised her hands when the group began to protest. "Witnesses did report that Mr. Minkus's speech became slurred. Before he collapsed, he said that his lips were stinging and that his tongue was numb."

As she stepped away, the shouts rang out again for Dr. Isham: "Could a poison have done this?" And following up: "Is there a danger to the president?" "Is there danger to the general population?"

Isham held up both hands. "The problem with certain poisonous substances is that they are very difficult to identify. While we test for several known toxins, there are many we can't identify unless we know what to look for. At this time we've done preliminary tests, but we can't even speculate until the specimens we've sent out to special labs have come back."

"How soon can we expect results?" a reporter in the front asked.

"It may be a couple weeks."

After another eruption of questions, Isham held up his hands again. "This isn't *CSI*," he said. "We work in the real world. This is a painstaking process and we need to be patient."

The man in the front stood up. "Was it something Agent Minkus was served at dinner last night?"

Isham licked his lips. I held my breath. "As I said, we cannot speculate until we receive certain test results."

The front-seat reporter stared at the medical examiner, still pushing. "Did the White House kitchen staff kill Special Agent Carl Minkus?" He tilted his head for the follow-up. "Inadvertently, or on purpose?"

Isham shook his head. "It is much too early to make that determination. We will be looking into . . ."

The television screen changed and again we were treated to the grave face of the news reporter. "The White House has only commented to express its sorrow at the passing of one of its most dedicated citizens. When questioned regarding the kitchen staff's responsibility in this terrible tragedy, the White House had no comment." The news anchor raised an eyebrow. I hated him for it.

"We have footage of Executive Chef Olivia Paras, who was brought in to the White House for questioning in this matter." His gaze shot off-screen and the scene shifted.

"Ollie, that's right outside our building," Mrs. Wentworth said.

"Yeah." I knew what was coming.

The handheld camera lent an air of panic and immediacy to the dark, early morning scene. Guzy One—Raymond—emerged from the front of my apartment building, his right hand raised in a way clearly meant to stave off reporters. Instead, the microphone- and camera-wielding crowd clamored around his side where I had a hand up to block the bright glare. The garish lighting made it look like they were bringing out Public Enemy Number One. Our little threesome moved in relative silence—the network didn't broadcast the angry shouts from the piranha-like reporters who dogged our every step—and the television news anchor, in a voiceover, said, "When asked by our news crew if she'd inadvertently served a toxin to Special Agent Minkus, the current executive chef had this to say." His voice faded and they brought up the sound on the scene outside my building's front door.

My face was an angry glare. "No, I didn't!" I heard myself shout.

In my living room, I winced. Taken out of context, my indignant exclamation made me look like the bad guy.

"Ms. Paras refused to answer any of our questions," the news anchor said, "before being taken away in the custody of government security agents."

"Taken away in custody? They made it sound like I was arrested!"

Everyone in my living room said, "*Shh*."

The anchor was finishing up. "There you have it, the latest update in the shocking death of Special Agent Carl Minkus. Please stay tuned for updates as we find out more about the White House kitchen's role in the unexpected death of one of our most revered public servants."

"Oh, Ollie," my mom said.

I got up. "Turn it off."

Someone did.

The news anchor had referred to me as the "current" executive chef. As though there was another chef waiting in the wings for my head to roll. But I knew I couldn't have been responsible. I knew no one on my team could have been responsible. We were too careful, too determined for that.

My home phone rang. I started for it, but stopped myself when I didn't recognize the number.

"Maybe it's Tom calling you," my mom said.

I shook my head. "He would use my cell phone."

As though wakened by my words, the little phone buzzed. I checked the display. Another number I didn't recognize.

"Are you going to answer that?" Mom asked, then amended, "I mean, either one of them?"

"I have a feeling . . ."

The house phone silenced, waited a few beats, then rang again.

This time the display read "202."

I shoved the vibrating cell into my pocket and picked up the home phone. "Olivia Paras."

"Ollie, it's Paul."

I nodded. I'd figured as much.

"How are things going over there?" he asked.

"As well as can be expected," I said, glancing around the room at the four sets of concerned eyes staring back at me. "My family is here and that's helping take my mind off things." That was a lie, but I was determined to sound strong. The sadness in my mom's face almost made me falter. "What's up, what can I do for you?"

"Don't answer your phone if you don't know who's calling."

"Got that," I said. "The calls have already started coming in."

"You may still be hounded in the morning, so try to stay home as much as possible."

"What about coming in to work? Can I take the Metro?"

Paul's tiny delay in responding caused my stomach to flop. "Ah," he said slowly—too slowly, "let's hold off on that for now. We'll let you know when the time is right to come back."

That hurt. "Understood," I said as bravely as I could muster.

His voice was tight. "This is a bad one, Ollie. But, believe me, it will be over soon. And you and your staff will be back in the kitchen before you know it."

"I hope so," I said. But for the first time, I detected insincerity in Paul's tone.

The minute I hung up, the phone rang again. Another unfamiliar number. I waited, but the caller didn't leave a message. Two seconds later the phone rang again. As did my cell. Again.

I hit "ignore" on my cell, and unplugged my house phone. My mother, Nana, Mrs. Wentworth, and Stanley stood looking as helpless as I felt. "It's okay," I said. "We're still not allowed in the kitchen for now, but the chief usher says that we'll be back to normal in no time."

The looks in their eyes told me they didn't believe my halfhearted cheer. That was okay; I wasn't sure I believed it, either.

"What about Easter dinner at the White House?" Mom asked. "Don't you have to prepare for that?"

"And that big Egg Roll the day after," Nana added. "How are you going to boil all those eggs in time if you can't get back into the kitchen?"

Good question, I thought. Too bad I didn't have an answer.

CHAPTER 8

I GUESS I SHOULDN'T HAVE BEEN SURPRISED BY THE HEADLINES the next morning: MINKUS DEAD AT WHITE HOUSE, followed by an in-depth examination of his life from his boyhood home in rural Maryland to his exalted position as a special agent with the NSA, where he excoriated terrorists like St. George slew dragons.

As I read, I wondered how they gathered all this information so quickly. It occurred to me that newspapers and television networks must keep fat dossiers on every public figure in anticipation of the day that figure's obituary comes due. There was a lot here about Minkus. More than any normal person would care to know. His whole life, starting on page one and continuing on pages eight and nine. Complete with pictures.

My mom came in from her shower, poured herself a cup of coffee, and helped herself to one of my still-warm honey-almond scones. "Why are you putting yourself through all that?" she asked, gesturing toward the newspaper.

"Can't help myself, I guess." I pointed to the picture of Carl Minkus as a prodigious ten-year-old. "He was kind of cute as a little kid." I looked at the most recent shot they published. "I wonder what happened."

"Good morning," Nana said, then looking at us, asked, "What's with all the glum faces? I figure that we should look at Ollie's mandatory time off as a vacation. Maybe we can do something today."

Leave it to Nana to find the silver lining.

She came over to stand behind me, reading the newspaper over my shoulder. "He was an angry man," she said. "You can see it here." She pointed to the small space between his eyes. "He made a lot of people angry, too." As she took a seat at the table, she made a *tsk*ing noise. "They compared him to Joe McCarthy. He died young, too." She fixed me with a look that said he deserved it. While I appreciated the support, I didn't feel as though that was an appropriate outlook, particularly today.

"He was trying to combat terrorism," Mom said as she poured a mug of coffee for Nana. "Minkus, that is. I don't really remember McCarthy."

"*Pffft*. A poor excuse to invade a person's privacy if you ask me."

Mom and I made eye contact. I wondered what had caused this outburst. As though I'd asked the question aloud, Nana licked her lips and leaned toward me. "Look, I'm sorry this Minkus guy is dead. Not for his sake, mind you, but because of how it's affecting you. I saw what Joe McCarthy did to this country, and this Minkus guy was doing the same thing—all in the name of national security. He was making a name for himself by making other people's lives miserable. That's a hell of a thing." She reached out to grab another section of the newspaper as she gestured to mine. "I'll take that when you're done."

"Gladly." I started to close the paper when I caught sight of another article on page two. This one by Howard Liss in his *Liss Is More* daily column. "Uh-oh."

"What?" Mom asked.

To me, Howard Liss always looked like an aging hippie. His picture stared up at me, his salt-and-pepper hair pulled tight into a ponytail, which draped forward over his right shoulder. Whatever that signified. He wore one hoop earring, and a cocksure grin. "Liss," the caption read, "is always more."

"This guy." I snapped my finger against his face. "He's covering the Minkus story. And if I'm right, he's going to blame it on some right-wing conspiracy group."

I was wrong. He blamed it on me.

I'm not suggesting the president hire a professional taster, as monarchs did in the olden days to prevent assassination by poisoning, but I am asking the question: How safe is the food we serve to our administration? What real safeguards are in place? Who watches the chefs? Is our president's security really left up to the woman who has made a name for herself by allegedly saving the president's bacon, not once, but twice? Could our current executive chef, Ms. Olivia Paras (whose name you will recognize from prior action-packed features), be getting bored with her day-to-day cooking responsibilities? Could her taste for excitement have pushed her over the edge to take unnecessary chances with Sunday night's dinner?

How dare he!

"What's wrong?" Mom asked.

"This . . . this . . ." I couldn't find the words to express my fury. "He thinks I did this. He thinks I did this on purpose!"

Carl Minkus's untimely demise may serve as a valuable wakeup call. If we act now, we have a chance to save others from preventable disasters. Let's not be so quick to assume that Minkus was targeted by someone he was planning to investigate. Let's take a closer look at our own house first—the president's house. Maybe a little negligence? Maybe a strong need for attention? Maybe things just got out of hand? Perhaps someone added more than an extra teaspoon of salt to the soup.

"This is ridiculous!" I said, standing up. "What is he thinking? I'll sue him for libel. Or slander. Or whatever it is you sue for when people make up lies."

My mom read where I pointed. "He puts it all in question format," she said. "He isn't saying you're guilty. He's asking, 'What if?'"

I headed to the phone to call Paul, then belatedly realized I'd unplugged it. "Aaah!" I said when I picked up the dead receiver. Mom and Nana stared at me with twin looks of pained confusion. They didn't know what to do. Neither did I.

"How do I fight something like this?" I asked.

Nana picked up the paper. "This guy is a nutcase."

"That doesn't make it any easier for me."

Mom shrugged. "No one will pay his article any attention."

"I thought this guy was a liberal," Nana said.

"I thought so, too. Why do you ask?"

She pointed. "Here, farther down he talks about what a great guy Minkus was and what a blow this is to the country. He says Minkus was respected by heroes and criminals alike."

I came to stand behind her. "What an odd thing to say. I would have thought someone like Liss would never support someone like Minkus."

"I'm telling you, honey, that's why nobody will even remember this come tomorrow."

My cell phone vibrated and I looked at the number. Tom. "Hello?" I said. I caught myself smiling. Mom and Nana exchanged knowing glances.

"How are things?" he asked.

"I've been better."

"Did you read today's paper?" he asked.

"How could I miss it?"

"I'm sorry you have to go through this, Ollie." After a moment he asked, "How's the family settling in?"

I walked into the living room. "Pretty well. Things aren't going quite the way I'd hoped. Did you get my message?" I'd left him an effusive voicemail the night before, thanking him for taking care of my mom and nana and bringing them safely to my apartment. "I really appreciate all you did for me yesterday. If you hadn't picked them up . . ."

"Ah," he said, deflecting. "I was happy to do it. Hey, what do you have planned today?"

"My mom and nana want to go to Arlington."

"Visit your dad's grave?"

"They haven't been here since he died, and now that I happen to have so much free time on my hands—"

"Do you have any time this morning?"

"What did you have in mind?"

I could almost see him shrug. "I don't have to be back until noon, so I figured maybe, if you wanted to go for coffee or something . . ."

"You want to come up here?"

"No," he said, almost too quickly. "I think you and I need to talk."

I swallowed. "That sounds ominous."

He gave a half-hearted laugh. "Sorry. I just meant it would be better if we could meet one-on-one." He quickly added, "Not that I don't want to see your family. They're great. I just would rather we have a chance to meet alone."

When I got off the phone and returned to the kitchen, Mom and Nana were waiting expectantly.

"We're meeting for coffee," I said.

"He doesn't want to come up here?"

"Busy day. He's got to get to work," I explained. Being part of the Presidential Protective Detail—the elite of the Secret Service—meant that more often than not, our relationship came second to his schedule. I was used to it. Often, my responsibilities took precedence over our relationship, too. That might change over time; it might not. "He only has an hour or so."

"As long as we're not holding you back," Mom said.

I put my arm around her and gave her a kiss on the cheek. "You could never hold me back."

TOM WAS ALREADY AT THE RESTAURANT WHEN I ARRIVED. WE'D been coming to this out-of-the way place almost since we'd started seeing one another. Although it came up short in romantic inspiration, Froggie's offered all-day breakfast and endless cups of coffee, served by a staff that still hand-wrote receipts and called customers "hon."

We settled ourselves in an aqua vinyl booth, a framed photo of artfully arranged scrambled eggs on the wall next to us. "You hungry?" I asked.

Tom pushed the laminated menu away with a grimace. "Nah."

"Just coffee," I said to the waitress who appeared at our table.

"You got it." She turned both our mugs upright, poured, and collected our menus.

"So, what's up?" I asked when she was gone.

Tom stared down at the dark brew in his mug, like the coffee had said something nasty to him.

Uh-oh, I thought. I didn't like the feel of this. The look on his face made my heart pound faster, and my neck sweat. I thought if I came up with a witty comment I might relieve the tension, change the subject. But I couldn't come up with anything.

In the three heartbeats it took him to raise his eyes again, I thought how odd it was that I'd been singing his praises yesterday, so confident that his helping my mom and nana was proof he was willing to take our relationship to a new level. I was so sure we were moving forward. And now it felt more like he was about to break up with me.

"This is going to be hard, Ollie."

I didn't think my heart could stand it another moment. It banged so relentlessly I put a hand to my chest to keep Tom from hearing it thud. What had happened? What had changed since yesterday? His eyes provided no clue.

"What's going to be hard?" I managed to ask. My voice cracked. I hoped he didn't notice.

He opened a little creamer and poured its contents into the mug. I kept mine black because I didn't trust my hand not to shake when I grabbed a creamer for myself. I swallowed, my throat starchy-dry. "What are you trying to tell me?"

His brow furrowed and he stared down at the coffee again. Neither of us had taken a sip yet, and when the waitress breezed by with pot in hand, she didn't even slow at our table.

"Craig," he said.

"Craig?" My heart skipped. Had I misheard him? "Craig Sanderson?"

He nodded.

"What does Craig have to do with us?"

"Us?" Tom looked up. "Nothing."

Now I was confused. "Explain."

"Craig put me on this Minkus death investigation."

"That's a bad thing?"

"We've all been assigned a specific angle."

I waited.

"He's assigned me to you."

I didn't understand why Tom was so upset. "You know I didn't do it, right?"

That got the first smile of the day. "Of course."

"Well then, your job is done. Whatever you need from me, you've got. I'm going to be the most cooperative subject you've ever known."

As I spoke, my smile grew. Tom's didn't. "You don't see the problem, do you?"

I shook my head.

"Craig has made me responsible for keeping you *out* of the investigation."

"That doesn't make sense. If they think Minkus died because of something I served him, then I'm part of this investigation already. How can he keep me out of it?"

"Okay, maybe I misspoke. You can't exactly be kept out of it, but he wants your efforts controlled. That's my job. I'm supposed to make sure you don't get involved in this investigation yourself."

"Now, why would I do that?"

Tom shot me a look of exasperation. "Ollie, look at your track record."

"I never intended—"

"Uh-huh," Tom said, interrupting my lame attempt at defense. "That's exactly the point. You make us believe you're all innocent and out of the loop and then—*bam*—you're at the very center of a major conspiracy."

"That was an accident."

"Both times?"

We were silent a moment. Tom took a breath. "We will be asking for your help. There's no way we can proceed without your cooperation."

I made a "Duh," face, but didn't say anything.

"Craig's exact directive is that I'm to act as liaison between the Secret Service and the kitchen. I need to be aware of every single thing you do."

I started to speak, but Tom held up a hand.

"The reason he picked me," he said, reading my thoughts, "is because he thinks that if I'm in charge of you, you'll actually cooperate this time."

The waitress came by, pot in hand, again. She eyed our untouched cups. "You two positive you don't want something else?"

We assured her we didn't and as soon as she turned away, I added cream to my coffee and took a sip. It was something to do. And it gave me a moment to think.

Tom drank his, too. Bolstered, either by the interruption in what had become a tense conversation, or by the coffee, he sat up straighter. "Craig knows you had nothing to do with Minkus. We all know that. But that doesn't mean we can skate when it comes to your investigation. We have to follow every lead, have to take every step—just as if you were a true suspect. If we don't, we'll get raked over the coals." He held the mug in both hands and stared at me. "But the real reason Craig is doing this is because he doesn't want you involved."

I nodded.

"I mean, not at all."

"Okay," I said. "Done."

He waited a moment, then took another sip of coffee. "You promise?"

"Of course," I said.

"Do you have any idea what this means to my career if you don't stay out of it?"

I didn't understand why Tom was getting so worked up. He and Craig were friends. "I'm sure he wouldn't—"

"Craig has made it clear that if you get involved in this—like you have in the past—I will be dropped from the PPD."

"He can't do that."

"The hell he can't. He's my immediate supervisor."

"I mean, he can't make you responsible for someone else's actions."

Tom slowly shook his head. "Yeah, well, tell him that."

My fists were bunched and I saw Tom's gaze stray past them, before he met my eyes. "I know you don't *mean* to get into trouble . . ."

"I haven't gotten in trouble," I said, my voice rising. "In fact, I'd say I've helped when no one else could. And I've even saved a few lives along the way, too."

His hands came up, but my anger refused to be abated. "Just how, exactly, does Craig think to keep me out of this? For crying out loud, Tom, I work in the kitchen at the White House. And when a guest dies after eating one of my meals, you bet I'm involved."

Tom grimaced. *"Shh!"*

I lowered my voice. Too late, people around us had perked up. An avid eavesdropper myself, I recognized the body language. "All I'm saying is that Craig would be an idiot to refuse to use me as a resource."

"I told you. He intends to do just that."

"Now I'm confused."

"It gets complicated."

"Because officially"—I raised my hands to make quotation marks in the air—"I'm a suspect?"

"That's right."

"That's a crock."

We both took long sips of coffee. The waitress waited across the room, pot in hand, eyebrows raised. When I looked at her, she turned away and set about filling mugs at another table.

After a few tense moments of silence, I asked, "What about Suzie and Steve?"

Tom blinked. "Who?"

"The SizzleMasters. Remember, they were in the kitchen that day."

"You suspect them?"

I thought about it. "Not really. But my point is that we had a camera rolling most of the day. It would be enormously helpful if I could review it."

"Not gonna happen."

I waited for him to say more, but he didn't. "This is so wrong," I finally said.

"It's only temporary."

"It's still . . . wrong."

When he looked at me, I was taken aback by the alarm in his eyes. "Ollie, don't get involved. Unless the directive comes from me. Or Craig. Please. I know how you are. I know how you want to fix things. You think you're help-ing, but—"

With an almost palpable snap, hot anger shot furiously into my chest and spouted out my mouth. I couldn't stop myself. "I have helped. I *do* help."

Tom looked around the room and raised his hands. "Ollie, please."

"Please what? Please let the Secret Service do its job by itself? Is Craig so insecure that help from the chef unnerves him?"

Tom glanced around. "I think it's time we leave." He motioned for the waitress. Mistaking his call for more coffee, she poured eagerly.

When he asked her for the check, she pursed her lips. "Okay," she said. "Be right back."

I bit the insides of my cheeks tight, trying hard to hold on to my temper. As much as I wanted to help this investigation—both to clear my kitchen and to satisfy my curiosity—the fact that I'd been banished from doing so wasn't what was getting under my skin. It was Tom. He wouldn't admit that I'd been key to preventing some major disasters in the White House. Disasters that, for one reason or another, the Secret Service could not have anticipated. Naturally, the media continued to speculate about what a busybody, amateur-sleuth wan-nabe I was.

I expected more from Tom.

The lines on his face were deeper than they had been. He seemed to hold himself too tightly—too wound up. A small part of me softened when I looked at him. This had to be hard for him, too. Craig issuing the edict that Tom was responsible for me was mean-spirited. Not to mention unnecessary.

Tom didn't even look at the waitress when she dropped off the check. He mumbled a "Thank you," and stood next to the booth, waiting for me.

Tom hadn't asked for this assignment and I knew, clearly, that he wasn't happy with it. If we were to get through this, I needed to keep our lines of communication open. I got up and touched his arm. "By the way," I said, "thanks again."

He looked at me with total confusion.

"For picking up my mom and nana from the airport," I said. "For getting them safely to my place."

His cheeks reddened and he looked away. "They're nice ladies. I was glad to help."

"It means a lot to me."

Still not moving toward the cash register, Tom looked at me. "I don't want to fight about this."

"Neither do I."

He shook his head. "But I know how your mind works."

I nodded slightly. I had to give him that.

"I'm afraid that you *will* get involved, Ollie," he said. "You'll think that you're just asking a simple question—just checking the veracity of a small fact—but before you know it, you'll be in the center of everything." He shook his head. "Again."

"No one complains except Craig and the newspapers," I said. "Doesn't that tell you something?"

He seemed to consider that, but a moment later shook it off. "Let's go."

Outside he walked me to my car. "Do me one favor," he said. "If something, anything, comes your way that's even remotely related to this investigation—tell me."

"I would always—" The sentence died on my lips. There had been a few instances—more than a few, if I were totally honest—I hadn't remembered to alert Tom to my plans. I forced a smile. "I will."

The pain was in his face again. "I've worked hard to become part of the PPD. This is it—this is all I've ever wanted. You know that, don't you? There's nothing more prestigious than being part of the Presidential Protective Detail. Not for me, anyway. I don't know what I would do if Craig dropped me from his team—"

I ran my hand along his shoulder. "I promise," I said. "Anything comes my way—anything at all—I will tell you."

"And if I ask you to back off of something?"

"I'll back off."

"Thanks."

We shared a moment of quiet camaraderie, but then I had to ask, "Do you think there's any chance of my team getting back into the kitchen soon?"

His shoulders slumped. "Didn't you hear anything I said?"

I hadn't wanted to hurt him, but he didn't seem to understand. "This isn't about the investigation. This is about our commitments. We have Easter on Sunday, and then the big Egg Roll on Monday. I need to get back."

"A man died at the White House after eating there. You think they're not canceling everything as we speak?"

Exasperated, I stared at the sky. "Something needs to be done."

He waited until I looked at him. "But not by you. Right?"

I wanted to argue, but that would only cause him more anxiety. "No worries. I promise."

He leaned forward and kissed me on the forehead. Like an uncle or kindly grandfather might do. Not exactly a clear signal of how things would be between us, going forward.

"I'll be in touch," he said.

Yeah. Sure.

CHAPTER 9

"BACK SO SOON?" MOM ASKED WHEN I RETURNED TO MY APART-ment. She must have read the expression on my face, because when she turned away from the sink, her smile withered. "What's wrong?"

"Nothing." That didn't appease her, and I knew it wouldn't. So I came up with a white lie. "With this investigation, Tom is under a lot of stress. He and I can only meet if it's official business."

"The impression of impropriety?"

I nodded. "Something like that."

The way Mom studied my face I could tell she wasn't buying my story. Of course she wasn't. She knew me too well. "And I hate being banished from the White House," I said, dropping into one of my kitchen chairs. "The whole point of you coming out here was so that I could show you around the president's mansion. Now I'm not even allowed in myself."

She made reassuring noises, the kind she always made when I was disappointed or frustrated and there was nothing we could do about it.

I smiled across the table. "I bet you wish you had stayed home."

She patted my hand. "Of course not. Nana and I flew out here to see *you*. That's the whole reason we came. And you know that this problem will get worked out. In the meantime, it's nice having you all to ourselves."

"But the tour I promised you—"

"There will be plenty of time for that. If not this trip, then next time."

My mom always had a way of looking at the positive side of everything. Even when I didn't feel like it. I couldn't shake the sadness, but I wanted to let her know her efforts were appreciated. I traced a finger around on my table top. "Thanks."

"I *would* like to take that trip to Arlington, though."

I glanced up. "Of course."

"Now you have plenty of time to show us around Washington." Her eyes were bright and her smile just a little too fixed. She knew how much their trip meant to me. She sensed my disappointment and felt sorry for me. And that made me feel even worse.

Taking care of others always worked for getting my mind off my troubles. If I couldn't control the White House kitchen, I could at least take steps to improve my mood. "You got it," I said, standing. "Let's grab Nana and go."

Nana took that moment to come into the kitchen. Wearing blue jeans with turned-up cuffs, a black fanny pack, and a sweatshirt that read I ♥ WASHINGTON, D.C., she looked from my mom to me. "I'm ready. Where are we going?"

WE TOOK THE METRO TO THE ARLINGTON NATIONAL CEMETERY stop and made our way to the bright visitor's center. Sunlight poured in through the skylights, spilling onto the floor around us, and dappling the potted ficus trees. I was willing to bet they designed this place with extra cheer to help dispel sadness. It worked—to an extent.

"Let's take the Tourmobile," I said, grabbing an information brochure. "It's pretty reasonable, and we can get off and reboard wherever we like."

My mom placed a hand on my arm. "Will it take us near . . . ?"

I nodded. "I know just where Dad's grave is. We could probably walk to it," I said, "but I'm sure you'll want to visit some of these other sites as well."

"Don't think I can manage it, do you?" Nana asked. She smiled, but I sensed a tiny bit of hurt in the question.

I pointed in the direction of Arlington House. "I know you want to visit President Kennedy's grave, but that's an uphill walk," I said. "That, and the fact that there are more than six hundred acres to explore are just too much for me. But if you really want to walk it . . ."

Telling her I had a hard time making the trek up to Arlington House was stretching the truth a bit, but I knew we had a lot of ground to cover. Literally. The Tourmobile would allow us to enjoy the journey and maybe even learn a little bit from the narration as we traveled.

About fifteen steps away from us, a young man stood, staring out the windows by the front door. He worked his jaw. Handsome guy, from what I could see. Something about his profile seemed familiar, but I couldn't quite place it.

I was very good with faces, but I knew that until I got a direct look at him, I wouldn't be able to make the connection. I wondered if he was here to visit a grave, or just to sightsee. I bit my lip. I sensed a familiarity, but at the same time, a vague negativity. Whoever he was, he reminded me of something unpleasant. I turned away.

Nana spoke. "No, we'll take that bus of yours," she said with a grin. "I wouldn't want you to overexert yourself."

My mother studied the pamphlet I'd given her and eyed the information desk in the center of the room. "Do you think they're having any funerals?"

"Arlington averages twenty-eight funerals per day," I said.

They both gasped. "That many?" my mom asked. "Will we be in the way if we take the tour? I don't want to intrude on anyone's grief."

"We'll be fine," I said. "Let's just not take any pictures of people visiting graves." I turned toward the east wing. "How about we hit the washroom before boarding?" I asked, moving that way. "There won't be any others on the tour except—"

I stopped short when a woman emerged from the washroom. She was instantly recognizable: Ruth Minkus. She made eye contact with me as she skirted past and I couldn't help but notice the hot, red rims makeup couldn't hide. Ruth gripped a paper tissue in one hand, holding it close to her heart, and I held my breath, hoping she didn't know who I was. Instinctively I turned to watch the young man who had been staring out the window walk up to her. He took her arm. "You okay, Mom?" he asked.

Joel Minkus and his mother looked exactly as they had on television last night—except yesterday they'd seemed smaller, and somehow less real, less flesh-and-blood. And as much as I had been worried about Carl Minkus's death, and felt for his family, I had been insulated—at home, away from the immediacy, the fierce reality of their grief.

My mom touched my shoulder. "Ollie," she said in a whisper, "isn't that—?"

"Yes," I said, turning away from the twosome. "Let's move over there by the trees. We'll be out of the way."

Nana had bypassed us to disappear into the ladies' room. "Damn," I said, then addressed my mom. "You wait here for her, and I'll meet you . . ." I looked around, trying to decide whether I should say something to Mrs. Minkus. I didn't want to apologize, because I knew I wasn't responsible for her husband's demise, but as one of the players in this drama, I felt almost compelled to offer my condolences.

But what, exactly, should a person in my situation say?

My mom hadn't left my side. She whispered again, "I think she recognizes you."

I turned. Ruth Minkus was staring. The red-rimmed eyes now blazed with anger.

"Oh, God," I breathed, turning back. I gripped my mom's arm and guided her toward the washroom. "Go on," I said. "Take care of Nana. I'll find you."

I attempted to slink out the side doors, keeping my face averted, but an exclamation behind me caused me to stutter-step. "You!" Ruth Minkus shouted. "You're the chef!"

Her voice echoed loudly, and I wasn't the only person who turned to see her pointing at me. I closed the space between us, hoping she would lower her voice—hoping the horde of tourists milling about the visitor's center wouldn't recognize us. Hoping they would turn their attention away from our imminent and, undoubtedly uncomfortable, conversation.

"Mrs. Minkus," I said, offering my hand. "I'm so sorry for your loss."

She backed away from me, horror-stricken. "You killed my husband."

I don't know whether I was more shocked by her accusation or more relieved that she'd at least spoken quietly. I answered fast. "No," I said. "That's not true. I didn't."

"Mom," Joel said, stepping between us and keeping his voice low, "Please." Ruth whirled toward him. "She killed your father."

"Nothing's been proven yet." He shot an apologetic glance toward me, then placed his hands on her shoulders and made her look up at him. "Let's not make a scene. Please? Dad wouldn't want that."

Her posture slumped as her gaze dropped to the floor.

Joel stole a look at me. "I'm sorry," he said, shifting to stand next to his mother. He kept one arm protectively around her. "We've just come from visiting the site where my father . . . my father . . ." He faltered, then cleared his throat. "Where my father will be buried. My mother wanted to see it. To make sure . . ." He cleared his throat again, then shook his head slightly, as though berating himself for providing explanation. He turned to Ruth. "Come on, Kap is waiting for us outside."

Ruth grimaced, still looking at the ground. I couldn't tell whether she was reacting to Joel's mention of the grave site, or of "Kap." To me it seemed the latter. I was about to make a hasty exit, expressing condolences once again, when my mom and nana appeared, flanking me.

At almost the same moment, an older gentleman stepped up to take Ruth's free arm. He was tall and fit, with deep crow's-feet at his eyes, and a full head of white hair that picked up glints of light from above. While he was clean-shaven, he had the look of a man who probably needed to use the razor more than once per day. I put him at sixty-five, but good-looking enough to turn the heads of women of all ages. "You were in here so long, I was worried."

She recoiled from him, but he seemed not to notice.

"Hello," he said to us, a quizzical expression on his deeply tanned face. "Are you friends of the family?"

"No," I began, but Joel took charge.

"Kap," he said, relief in his voice. "Mom could probably use a little air. And I think it would be good if she sat down." At first I thought Joel was asking Kap to take charge of Ruth so that he could say something to me in private, but he surprised me by leading his mother away. "We'll be in the car," he said.

Kap nodded as they left. He turned back to us and flashed a smile.

"Well, it was nice to meet you," I said, even though we hadn't officially been introduced. I just wanted to get the heck out of there.

But Kap seemed unwilling to let us go. He raised an eyebrow. "You look familiar."

My face went hot. "I'm the executive chef at the White House."

"Ah," he said. I felt the weight of his comprehension. In the space of two seconds, his expression shifted from anxious to genial. "Today has been very difficult for Ruth, as you can imagine. We spent most of the morning at the funeral home, making arrangements. Carl, having been a decorated veteran, always wanted to be buried at Arlington, so we made those arrangements as well."

My mom had moved closer. I couldn't understand why. The last thing I wanted was to prolong this unexpected meeting. I desperately searched for a polite way to extricate ourselves, but Mom interjected.

"My husband is buried here, too."

Kap's awareness shifted. Where he'd been paying attention to me as though I were the only other living human being in the cemetery, he now turned his gaze toward my mother. "I'm very sorry to hear that," he said. "Has it been a long time?"

"Yes," she said. "Very long." And then she surprised me by adding, "Too long."

My jaw nearly dropped. What the heck was this? My mom was flirting with a complete stranger in the middle of Arlington National Cemetery. While it had been more than twenty years since my dad died, and my mother had had a gentleman friend or two since then, it seemed odd to see her so flushed and eager. Like a teenager.

"I'm here from Chicago visiting my daughter." Mom cocked her head at me like I was a little kid.

I felt like one—left out of the adult conversation. Who was this guy, anyway? A brother? Brother-in-law? This Kap didn't look like either Carl or Ruth Minkus. He was older than both of them and looked to be Middle Eastern, or Greek, whereas the Minkuses likely came from Western European roots.

Kap smiled broadly. This was one handsome senior citizen and I understood my mother's instant attraction to him. Still . . .

Holding out his hand, he said, "Zenobios Kapostoulos. But everyone calls me Kap."

My mother placed her hand in his and smiled back. "Corinne Paras."

"I am delighted," he said. "And were we in different circumstances, I would very much enjoy continuing our conversation. But, as it is, I must tend to Ruth and Joel."

My curiosity got the better of me. "You're part of the family?"

His smile still in place, he shook his head. "Carl and I worked together. He and I are—were—good friends. Business required my presence out of the country for many years and I've only recently moved back to the area. Of course, I had hopes of rekindling our friendship." His eyes tightened. "But, unfortunately, it was not to be. Carl and I had only a short time to catch up. And now this." He shook his head again. "It is very sad."

"Kap?" Joel called from the doorway. "We're ready to go."

Kap gave a little bow to us all, and held my mother's gaze for an extra few heartbeats. "It has been my pleasure, ladies."

Nana sniffed when he turned away. "How come nobody introduced me?" She fanned herself as she watched Kap leave. "My, my," she said approvingly.

Had my family gone nuts in the head?

"What was that all about?" I asked them. "I thought we were here to visit Dad's grave."

Mom still wore the remnants of a smile as she pinned me with a meaningful stare. "Don't chastise, honey. Opportunities to interact with charming men don't come around very often these days." She chanced a look out the window, but the Minkuses were gone. She shrugged. "Just a little distraction."

I would have said more, but it seemed pointless. "We'll probably never see him again anyway."

"Probably not," Mom said. She sounded wistful.

WE GOT OFF THE TOURMOBILE AT THE STOP FOR THE TOMB OF the Unknowns, but diverted from the rest of the group to follow the road that led toward my dad's grave site. I had been here plenty of times before. But not with my mom—at least, not when I was old enough to remember. I took Nana's arm as we stepped off the pavement onto the grass. "You okay?" I asked them.

Nana said, "Sure, sure," but she glanced nervously at my mom.

"Mom?"

She took in the expanse of green, all the identical white headstones. "I haven't been back here since . . ." Her voice caught. "I can't even remember exactly . . ."

I reached out and grabbed her hand, squeezing lightly. "I know where he is," I said.

We walked silently past rows and rows of headstones, our feet making soft shushing sounds in the almost-green grass. I came to visit my dad's grave from time to time because it gave me peace to do so. I thought about how I sometimes talked to my dad, but after noticing how tight my mom's face had grown, I decided not to mention that. This was going to be tough for her.

"Here," I said.

Nana stepped away from me to stand next to Mom. The three of us gazed at the white headstone, which read ANTHONY M. PARAS. SILVER STAR.

Mom looked around us. "The trees are a lot bigger now."

I nodded.

Nana patted Mom on her shoulder. "He was a good man, Corinne. And he loved you very much."

Mom covered her eyes and cleared her throat. She spoke, but I couldn't make out what she said. Not that it mattered. I got the feeling whatever she'd said wasn't meant for me or for Nana.

The three of us spent a long quiet moment there together. Finally, Mom looked up. "Thank you," she said throatily. "This was important to me."

I put my arm around her and hugged. "For me, too," I said.

From there we made our way back to the Tomb of the Unknowns.

"Oh," Nana whispered when we positioned ourselves behind the brass railing at the top of the rise. "Look at that."

I'd been here many times but I understood my grandmother's awe. Stretching out eastward beyond the tomb was a green vista that overlooked hundreds of other graves. But it was here, at the tomb itself, under the sharp blue spring sky, that her attention was captured.

The sentinel walked twenty-one measured steps. He then turned and faced the simple, white monument for twenty-one seconds. Whenever he switched positions, he first kicked out one leg in a taut, well-practiced move, then smacked the active foot against the stationary one with an audible clack. Turning, he faced back down the mat upon which he'd walked, shifting his weapon to his outside shoulder, with another tight, structured move. He then took twenty-one more steps back the way he'd come. A brisk breeze made the three of us shiver, but the sentinel never flinched. When he turned to face the tomb again, Nana asked, "He does this all day?"

"They operate in shifts," I whispered. I gestured for us to leave and we made our way up the marble steps into the adjacent museum. There were no words to describe the solemnity I always felt in the presence of deceased veterans. Keeping my voice down seemed the only respectful way to talk. And I knew from prior visits that any loud conversation would result in the sentinel's chastisement of the crowd. "They change every hour."

"Handsome man," Nana said, glancing behind us. "Tall."

"They all have to be between five-foot-ten and six-foot-four."

"Really? There's a height requirement?"

We were inside the small museum now, and although we spoke freely, we still kept our voices low. "There are a lot of requirements," I said. "You should look it up. They're a very dedicated group. And only about one-fifth of those who apply are accepted into their ranks."

"Look it up on the Internet, you mean?" Mom asked.

"You mastered e-mail. There's nothing scary about surfing the Net. Unless you're downloading from a questionable source, you really can't hurt your computer."

"Oh, she isn't afraid of that," Nana said. "She's afraid of becoming addicted to the thing."

I turned to my mom. "Seriously?"

"One of my girlfriends joined something called 'chatrooms' and now she never wants to come over for coffee or go out to movies."

"Who?"

I laughed when she told me. "You don't even like her."

"That's beside the point."

After strolling along the outer rim of the breathtaking Memorial Amphitheater and finishing our Tourmobile trek, we took the Metro back to my apartment, where Nana decided to nap for a little while. When she was out of the room and the place was quiet, I realized that I would usually have a phone call or an e-mail to look forward to from Tom. Not so today. My cell phone had been extraordinarily silent and when I checked my inbox, I had only two new non-spam messages. One from Bucky and the other from Cyan. Both were looking for updates. I wrote back, but confessed I had no news.

Speaking of news, I called Mom over to the computer in the spare bedroom—the room where I was staying while she and Nana used my queen-sized accommodations. "Here," I said. "Let's give you a quick tutorial."

She shook her head, but at least she took a seat on the daybed behind me. "I don't see why it's so important for me to learn this," she said, pointing at the headline that described a double-assassination in China. "I can get this from watching the news."

"True," I said. "But the news simply projects the day's biggest stories—or what they deem most important. If you're interested in something that doesn't have to do with China"—I motioned toward the monitor—"you can search for whatever it is you need."

"What happened there, anyway?" she asked.

I scrolled down the article to find out that two upper-level Chinese government officials had been shot, execution style, in a restaurant in Beijing. According to "unconfirmed reports," the two Chinese officials had been buying United States secrets from an "unnamed insider." It appeared that the Chinese government, believing their conduit had been compromised, had sanctioned the double-assassination.

Their killer had been immediately apprehended and offered no resistance when taken into custody. He had, however, been killed himself shortly thereafter. Details were sketchy, but the Chinese police were claiming that he had grabbed for one of their officers' weapons in a futile attempt to escape. Political pundits were speculating that the police were covering up the fact that the gunman had been shot in cold blood after carrying out his allegedly government-sanctioned hit.

"Just like Lee Harvey Oswald," Mom said.

"If you believe the conspiracy theories."

Her gaze was glued to the screen. "I don't believe our government killed President Kennedy. But Jack Ruby's oh-so-convenient shooting makes me wonder who did." She made a clucking sound. "And I'll bet there are people all over China tonight wondering who was behind this one."

Still at the helm, I clicked the browser bar and said, "I love the Internet. It's like having the most comprehensive library available to me twenty-four hours a day." I typed in the name of an author I knew my mother liked. "Look. Lots of information. Biography, book descriptions, reviews. This is great stuff." I gave her a meaningful look. "But don't believe everything you read."

She moved closer and I let her have my seat. I showed her how to search. It took a few tries before she was willing to take control of the mouse and keyboard, but eventually I stepped away. "Have at it," I said. "Look up whatever you like. Just keep it clean, okay?"

She looked up long enough to catch my wink.

"You're going to be sorry if I spend my whole vacation sitting in front of this computer," she said.

"Don't worry. I won't let that happen."

She was already typing. "You'd better not."

CHAPTER 10

MY BREATH CAUGHT THE NEXT MORNING WHEN I OPENED THE paper. With all the excitement yesterday running into Ruth Minkus at Arlington, I had almost forgotten about Howard Liss's accusations. Almost. But not completely.

The newspaper's headlines dealt with the Chinese assassinations, but I didn't stop to read the coverage. All my focus was on getting to page two to see what new mischief Howard Liss was up to.

Whatever Happened to Mean Minkus?

The media (and dare I say it—the government) is persisting with society's tendency to confer sainthood on an individual just because that person is dead. Have we so quickly forgotten the "Mean Minkus" appellation bestowed on our recently departed compatriot? I'm sure others aren't so forgiving. In fact, I would be willing to bet that several high-profile celebrities are sleeping a little easier tonight now that the bulldog has bitten the dust. Whether they deserve the respite, or whether they've just dodged a bullet remains to be seen. It will be up to Minkus's capable second-in-command, Phil Cooper, to determine what terrorist cells our favorite film stars belong to. If any.

My focus today is not on these superstars, but on the dead man. Let us stop singing his praises. Let us stop eulogizing him as though he were infallible and a loveable teddy bear just because he no longer walks in our midst. Let us admit he was a canker to many, and a hero to some. But if, indeed, he met his maker before his time, then I want to know who did it.

You should want to know, too. You should demand to know. Perhaps then
we will have ourselves a genuine terrorist to persecute. Who did it? I don't
know. Joel Minkus, the golden boy congressman—and soon to be senator
if Ruth has anything to do with it—has not yet seen fit to make time for
my questions. I hope he will reconsider soon. Time is our enemy. If anyone
knows who Mean Minkus was targeting, we may have our best clue to our
killer.

"You're not actually reading that garbage, are you?" Mom asked from
behind me.

Nana peered over my shoulder. "What does that crazy man have to say
today?"

I let out the breath I'd been holding. "At least Liss isn't attacking me again."

"Good," Mom said. "How anyone can subscribe to that man's rantings, I
can't understand."

"Rantings," I said. "Good choice of word. This *Liss Is More* column might
sell a lot of papers, but he sure seemed to be all over the place in terms of
accusations. Today he's on a whole new rampage. 'Who was Minkus's next
target?'" I frowned as I turned the page. "Maybe that's who the police should
be investigating instead of me."

"He's a lunatic," Nana said as Mom poured her a cup of coffee.

"What does that say about me?" I asked rhetorically. "I read him every
day now."

Mom patted me on the shoulder. "Well, of course you do," she said in that
soothing voice she used to use when I woke up during a nightmare. "He pulled
you into this situation."

I didn't want to argue that I was already part of this situation before Liss
ever got a hold of it, but the phone rang. I'd turned it back on this morning,
hoping the onslaught from the press had subsided.

Nana looked up. "Do you think that's your handsome hunk, Tommy?"

Mom and I exchanged a look. "No," I said, with more than a little disappointment. "Ollie Paras," I said into the receiver, forgetting this was my home
phone. "I mean . . . Hello."

"Oh my God, Ollie, there are people out on our front lawn. With cameras!"

In my effort to process the woman's panicked words, I couldn't place her
voice.

"Why does anyone think we had anything to do with Minkus? You know we didn't. Can't you tell them? Steve is ready to go out there with a baseball bat."

"Suzie," I said, relieved to know who I was talking to. "Please, don't let him do that, okay? It will just make it worse."

"I know," she said. "He knows it, too. But we can't even leave the house to get the newspaper on the driveway without a hundred people shoving microphones at us and asking a million questions."

"A hundred?"

"Well, at least a dozen. Hang on." I heard her counting. "Well, there are five on the lawn and two by the street."

"Have they been there since Monday?"

"No, just today. This morning. Why are they targeting us?"

I thought about that. Except for the camera crew and the White House staff, no one knew that Suzie and Steve had been part of Sunday night's dinner preparations until I'd mentioned it to Jack Brewster, and then to the two detectives when Craig interrogated me. I couldn't imagine who might have leaked that information to the press, but it was obvious someone had.

"I don't have an answer for you," I said, but my brain was trying to piece it together. "Did anyone come over to question you about Sunday's filming?"

"Yeah," Suzie said uncertainly. "Last night a detective stopped by and asked us a few questions, but he said it was just routine. Now this." I could practically picture her gesturing out her front window.

"Try to keep a low profile," I suggested.

"Do you have any idea what our schedule is like today?" Suzie asked, her hysteria returning. "We have two segments to film at the studio this afternoon. How can we get there if there are news vans blocking our driveway? What do they want from us?"

"Let's take it easy," I said, trying to work the same soothing magic on Suzie that my mom had been able to work on me. "First of all, they can't be on your private property."

"Hang on, let me peek out the window." I heard the soft shift of metallic blinds. "No, they seem to be mostly on the street. Some are under the tree at the parkway."

"Where do you live?"

She told me. I recognized the name as a posh Virginia suburb. "Okay," I said. "As long as they—"

Suzie screamed.

"What?" I asked into the receiver. "What? What happened?"

When she answered, her breath came in short gasps. "One of them jumped up at my front window and took my picture."

In the background I heard Steve swearing and threatening to grab a gun.

"Stop him," I said.

My mom touched my arm. "What's going on?"

I held up my palm to her. "Suzie," I said, concentrating. "Stop him. Call the police. They can make the media back off. Trust me on this one."

She dropped the receiver and I heard snippets of conversation as she pleaded with Steve to calm down. I turned to my mother. "The news folks are camped out at Suzie and Steve's house."

I'd already explained the SizzleMasters' role in the current White House drama, so my mom didn't need clarification. "Can they do that?"

I shook my head as Steve snatched up the phone on the other end. "God-damn media!" he shouted.

I held the receiver away from my ear. Steve bellowed expletives, complaining about the lack of privacy they were suffering. "And now they go and scare my wife. Ollie, can't the Secret Service do something about this?"

This didn't seem like a good time to tell him that this didn't exactly fall within the Secret Service's jurisdiction. In the background, I heard Suzie ask, "What do we do?"

"That's a good question, Ollie," Steve said into the phone. "What *do* we do?"

"I'd suggest you wait them out—"

"You mean cancel our filming for today? That's just wrong and you know it. We shouldn't be prisoners in our own—"

"You're right," I said, interrupting him. "You shouldn't. But can you think of any way to keep your commitments and avoid being run down by the news-hounds?"

He was silent for a long moment. "Do you think they'll give up by the end of the day?"

I doubted it. "Let me see if I can help," I said, thinking that this conversation was exactly the sort of thing Tom wanted me to avoid. "Give me your number." I had it on Caller ID, but giving Steve something rote to do might help calm him.

"Let me give you my cell and Suzie's, too."

I dutifully wrote down all the numbers he provided. "I'll get back to you as soon as I can."

"I think we ought to sit down with you and talk about all this," Steve said.

In the background I heard Suzie agree. "That's a great idea. When can she come over?"

Come over? No way. "I don't think that's a good idea," I said to Steve, effectively cutting off Suzie's train of thought. "Can you imagine what the press would do to us if I showed up at your house?"

"I still think we need to talk with you," he said gruffly. Then, away from the receiver he addressed Suzie: "We can't have her come here. Those vultures out there would skewer us."

Suzie's reply was inaudible.

"Let me call you back," I said. "We can talk after I get more information."

"Do you think they have our phones tapped?"

"Who?"

"The press. The Secret Service. The police. The NSA. Homeland Security." With each tick of his list Steve's voice rose until he reached fever pitch. "Do you think this is part of keeping us under surveillance? Do you know why they suspect us?"

"I don't believe anyone really does, Steve," I said. "I just think this is today's news . . ."

"They suspect us all right," he said cryptically. "But I'm not saying anything further on the phone."

When we hung up, I ran my hands through my hair.

"What's wrong?" Mom asked.

"I need to call Tom."

I wondered how this would sound to him. Less than a day after he'd warned me to stay out of the investigation, I was essentially dragged back into it. He had to realize this was no fault of mine. These were just friends who were asking for my help. But I couldn't do anything for them—nothing at all—without risking Tom's career.

Although I had no desire to keep secrets from my mom and nana, I stepped out onto my balcony when Tom answered, shutting the sliding door behind me. The morning was brisk but the bright sunlight that had kept us cheered during our trip to Arlington yesterday was nowhere to be seen.

"How are you?" I asked him.

His voice was wary. "What's going on? You sound like there's a problem."

"No," I said, trying to inject a tone of "pshaw" in my voice. "No problems. I just was thinking about what we talked about and I figured I should bring you up to date."

He expelled a breath. "What happened?"

I talked fast, explaining about Suzie and Steve and how they wanted to meet with me. I expected him to get angry about this turn of events, but after a long, thoughtful pause he spoke. "Some interesting facts have come to light," he said slowly. Then, as though anticipating my question, he said, "I can't tell you what they are, but we may need to talk with you again soon."

"Like an interrogation?"

He didn't laugh. That made me squirm. "I'll tell you what. I'll see what I can do to get the media to back off Suzie and Steve. And if you want to talk with them, go ahead. We're not suggesting you can't maintain your friendships."

The words were pleasant enough, but the effect was ominous. "You're going to be watching me?"

"Not necessarily."

"You're going to be watching *them*?"

"I never said that."

I pursed my lips, frustrated. I wondered what these "new interesting facts" were that he wasn't sharing. "There's something else you should know."

"Uh-oh."

I hesitated. There was no easy way to say this, so I just blurted. "I ran into Ruth Minkus yesterday and she accused me of killing her husband."

Tom was quiet for so long I thought he'd hung up.

"You there?" I asked.

"My God, Ollie. I can't keep up with you." I heard scratchy noises, as though he were rubbing his face. I shivered and it wasn't just because it had started to drizzle. I stared up at the overcast sky.

"We went to Arlington," I said, trying to explain. "And she was just . . . there. It wasn't as though I sought her out."

"Why didn't you call me about this yesterday?"

Why hadn't I? Truth was I'd been nervous about letting him know I'd had a run-in with the deceased's wife and son. "I called you today. Besides," I added, my own anger starting to return, "it's not as though I'm ingratiating myself into the investigation. For crying out loud, I had a conversation with Mrs. Minkus. There's no law against that, is there?"

I could practically see him shaking his head. "No, Ollie," he said with such resignation in his voice that I was sorry I'd raised mine. "There's no law against you talking with people you run into—or people you have a relationship with. I just . . ."

"You just . . . what?"

"I hope Craig is able to see things the same way I do."

"Does he have to know about any of this?"

"Suzie and Steve—yes. I'll want to suggest that you're present when we take a look at the DVD of that day's filming. For whatever good that will do. And if you do talk with them, he'll want to know if they said or did anything you consider unusual."

"So they are suspects!"

"I'm not saying that."

"Okay. Sorry," I said. But my mind was racing.

"I have a few other things I want you to take a look at."

"Like what?"

"It'll wait. I'll call you."

Effectively dismissed, I hung up, but I stood outside, leaning on the balcony's rail, even though it was wet and the chill seeped up through my forearms, making me shiver. When we'd first started our relationship, Tom and I both knew that our jobs—no, our careers—could cause strain. Emotional relationships were always fraught with peril, but his being a Secret Service agent, sworn to protect the president and his family above all else, made this one so much harder. I understood that there were things he couldn't tell me. I had no problem with that. I also understood the pressures he was under. Craig and I had been friends before the first time I'd inadvertently gotten involved in Secret Service matters. Since then he had cooled toward me, and avoided me when he could. I suppose he didn't believe I was worth his time, and I further supposed that Jack Brewster's antagonistic bent during my intake questioning had more to do with Craig's influence than with Jack's personal impressions.

The street below was quiet except for the occasional car slicing through puddles, causing a sad sound that made me want to retreat into the warmth of my apartment—to where my mom was probably making something for us to eat, and where Nana was devouring the newspaper in my absence, pretending that she wasn't hunting for mention of my role in this White House drama.

At least Tom had said he'd take care of Suzie and Steve. Still on the balcony, now ducking closer to the building to avoid the heavier rainfall, I dialed them back and let them know that the Secret Service had been alerted. "They better do something," Steve said with uncharacteristic roughness. "They got us into this mess."

I wanted to argue that it hadn't been the Secret Service's fault—but to what end?

"Where do you want to meet?" Steve asked as I was about to say good-bye.

"Excuse me?"

"We need to talk," he said. In the background, I heard Suzie reiterate his statement.

"I don't know if that's such a good idea."

Suzie must have been listening in, because she grabbed the phone and started in on me. "Please, Ollie. You know we only agreed to come film at the White House because you wanted us to. We did this as a favor to you."

That wasn't how I remembered it. "I thought your production team wanted to use this for ratings week."

"No," she said, chastising now. "We did this because we knew it was important to you."

It hadn't been important to me in the least. I'd done it as a favor to them. Correction: The White House had agreed to the favor. I'd been left out of this decision entirely. Although they were indeed friends of mine, I'd been against them being in the kitchen while we were preparing a dinner for actual White House guests. I would have preferred to stage a fake dinner and treat the staff to whatever delicacies we came up with. "Actually, Suzie," I began, but I was interrupted by a beep on the line. I took a look at the number. Tom. "I better let you go," I said in a hurry to hang up.

"Please," she said. "We really do need to talk."

"Later," I said. "I'll call you back."

"Please," she said again. "But we have to meet in person. Just in case others are listening in."

"I highly doubt anyone is tapping your line."

"I'm sure you're right," she said, sounding unconvinced. "But Steve and I will be more comfortable in person."

I heard another beep. I wanted to switch over to talk with Tom. Now.

"Okay, fine. But I really need to get going."

"Hang on."

Steve took the phone. "We can't get into this over open lines."

"Got it," I said, my exasperation evident. "But I can't . . ." I took a look at my handset and realized Tom was no longer waiting for me to pick up. I bit my lip in anger and hoped he would leave a message.

"Let's meet later," Steve said.

Tom had said that there was no law keeping me from talking with friends. And right now there was no longer any need to get off the phone quickly. I sighed. "Sure. Where and when? I know my mom and nana will be excited to meet real television personalities."

After a beat of silence, he said, "Just you, Ollie. Okay? Maybe we can meet your family another time."

This was starting to feel a little bit strange. Steve persisted. "How about tonight? Do you think these camera crews will be gone by then?"

I heard Suzie in the background. "A police car just pulled up."

"What do they want?" Steve asked her.

"How should I know?"

"Are they coming for us?"

"Steve," I said, "you sound busy. How about I let you go?"

The balcony door opened behind me. "Are you okay out there?" Mom asked. She held the receiver of my apartment phone.

"I'm fine," I said.

"Tom's on the line." She held out the receiver and looked at me with hopeful eyes. "Maybe you should take this one."

Steve was pleading in my ear. "Ollie, no. Don't hang up."

"I really have to—"

"The police are making them leave!" I heard Suzie say.

"But are the police coming for us?" Steve's obvious tension made me wonder what he was so worried about.

My mom gave me one of those looks only moms can give and shook the phone at me. "He's waiting."

I tried again. "Steve, let me give you a call back in—"

"This is great," he said. "They're all taking off." He breathed heavily into the phone. "The cops are gone, too. Good. We'll be able to make it to the studio after all. Thanks so much, Ollie."

"I really didn't—"

"Let's make her dinner tonight," Suzie said in the background. "Have her come to the studio."

"Yeah," Steve agreed. "The studio will be better than here." Sounding a bit distracted, he added, "Tonight, you're our guest. We'll have a chance to chat in real privacy."

"Okay, fine," I answered hastily, trying to pantomime my frustration to my mom. "You have my e-mail, right? Just send me the address and a time. I really have to go now."

"Sure thing, Ollie. And thanks again for all your help."

I said good-bye quickly and grabbed the apartment phone while snapping my cell shut. "Sorry," I mouthed.

My mom smiled and headed back in, leaving me on the cold balcony once again. "Tom?" I asked. "You still there? I was on another call with Suzie and Steve."

"That was quick. You sure didn't waste time getting in touch with them."

And just like that, his tone annoyed me. I faced the glass doors that looked into my living room. My mom and nana were watching me, turning away when I caught them. I scratched at my head and was surprised when my hand came away wet. I'd been out here in the damp morning longer than I thought.

"Like you said," I answered my tone sing-song, "there's no law stopping me from having conversations with my friends."

He made a noise—acknowledging the jab. "Are you going to be home later? Say, around eight thirty, nine tonight?"

I thought about Suzie and Steve's offer to make me dinner. I should be home by eight-ish. "I'll be here."

"Craig wants you to look at a few things." The dismissive tone was back. "I'll stop by then."

"You remember my mom and nana are still here?"

He blew out a breath. "I forgot."

I started to appreciate how much pressure he was under. "They'll give us privacy if we need it."

"Fair enough." He sounded all-too-eager to get me off the phone. "See you then."

When I reentered the apartment Nana shook her head. "You look like a drowned rat."

"Thanks."

Mom wore one of her worried looks. "What's up with Tom?"

"He's stopping by later."

At that they both brightened. I held up my hands. "Just official business," I said, and just like that, their cheer dissipated. "Sorry."

"Oh, Ollie," Mom said. "We just want you to be happy."

"Then let's get out today," I said, longing for something—anything—to get my mind off this mess. "I'd like to take you to the National Mall." Turning, I cast a glance outside at the rain. "Of course, it's not a very good day for that, is it?"

"It's going to clear up by noon," Mom said.

"It said that in the newspaper?"

"Nope," she said with a grin. "I checked the forecast online."

I TOUCHED BASE WITH CYAN, THEN BUCKY. NEITHER HAD HEARD anything more than I had, but my second-in-command was greatly agitated.

I searched for something calming to say. "It's just a matter of time before our staff is vindicated."

Through the phone's receiver I heard a rhythmic *click-clack* and I realized that Bucky was pacing across what sounded like a tile floor. At the same moment, I realized I'd been pacing as well. Weren't we a nervous bunch?

Click-clack, *click-clack*. "How can you stay so calm?" he asked.

I couldn't tell him that I wasn't calm. That every moment of every day was agony until the word came down that we'd be allowed back into the kitchen. I couldn't tell him that having my mom and nana here was both a blessing and a burden. If they weren't here, maybe there would be something I could do to hasten the process along.

I thought about my promise to Tom and reconsidered that. Maybe having my family close by right now was the best thing I could ask for. They kept me out of trouble.

"I'm calm because I believe in our team," I finally said.

"Do you? Or are you just saying that to make me feel better?"

"When have I ever said anything just to make you feel better?"

That got a laugh out of him, and I pounced on the break in the tension.

"Bucky, you know what a tight ship we run."

"But what if someone set us up? What if this is a conspiracy?" He sucked in an audible breath. "We all know what the press can do to us. Won't matter whether it's really our fault. People are just too happy to watch other people fail." There was validity in his words. "Every day people are uncovering dirt about each other. Even if none of it is true."

He had a point. How many times had I received forwarded e-mails bashing a political figure, only to find out that the so-called "breaking story" held no truth whatsoever? Occasionally these stories were rescinded, but after the damage was done. As I gripped the phone, I vowed never to forward another negative-spirited e-mail again.

I needed to convince Bucky that everything would be better soon. If I could make him believe that we'd come out on top, maybe through cosmic energy and all-is-right-with-the-world equality, it would become so.

"I can't stand all this waiting," he said. The rhythmic pacing started again.

"Neither can I, but there isn't a lot we can do right now. It's not like they're giving us access to the kitchen."

"Oh my God," he said, his voice panicked again. "Minkus's dossier."

"What about it?"

"You know we had it—we had all the guests' dietary dossiers on file before the dinner."

"So?"

"I—" He hesitated. "Remember that salad dressing we used?"

I started to get a crawling feeling in my stomach. "The one you came up with the day before the dinner?"

I heard Bucky swallow. "I created that one at home. I thought it would be a good idea to put a little extra effort . . ." He began to hyperventilate.

"I'm not understanding the problem," I said. "Bucky. Talk to me. Was there something in the food that—"

"I have his dossier," he said. "Minkus's dossier. I sent the file to myself at home so I would have all his dietary needs on hand. Here."

"You kept a list of his dietary preferences," I said slowly, to clarify.

"Yes, but—"

"I don't see anything wrong with that. Unless he had an allergy and you didn't—"

"Don't you understand? The fact that I sent this information to *my home computer* will be suspect. They're going to ask me why."

I did understand. But I couldn't react to the alarm I felt. "And you have a perfectly valid answer." I took a deep breath and tried again. "We all take information home. I've done that myself."

"But have you ever had a guest die before?"

I knew better than to answer. Bucky's voice had notched up a few octaves and he sounded on the brink of a breakdown.

He made an incoherent sound. "They're going to investigate and find this.

They're going to put me in a room and interrogate me. What's going to happen? My career is ruined."

"Bucky." I said his name sharply. "Is it just Minkus's dietary restrictions, or do you have the whole file?"

Misery wrung out every word. "The whole file."

While we were never granted access to classified information, we occasionally were given guests' entire files, rather than just a list of their dietary needs. It came in handy to know, for instance, if a guest spent years in South America, or Russia, or Japan. Little tidbits helped us design creative and enjoyable menus.

The first thing that came to mind was that Bucky was right. Pretty soon someone would notice that Minkus's information had been sent from our kitchen to Bucky's home. The second thing that came to mind was that I wanted a look at that file. Although we worked hard to never make even the slightest mistake, I wanted a closer look at the information we'd been provided. Having it on Bucky's computer was too tempting to pass up. I was sure we hadn't missed anything, but it would feel very good to reassure ourselves.

"Tell you what, Bucky, sit tight. Make a copy of the file, okay?"

I heard him *click-clacking* across his floor. "Don't you think I'll get in trouble if I do that?"

"Why should you?" I asked. "You're a member of the White House kitchen staff. You have every right to information about the guests you plan to feed. Make a copy—or two—and I'll come by later. We'll go over it together."

"When can you be here?" he asked. "How soon?"

I opened my mouth to say that I'd be right there, but I caught sight of Mom and Nana sitting in front of the television, with their spring jackets folded neatly on their laps, ready to shut off the TV just as soon as I hung up the phone. I couldn't disappoint them. "I've got a few things I have to do."

"Huh?" His voice squeaked. "I need help on this."

Subscribing to his growing hysteria would only make things worse. "As do we all right now," I said calmly. "Now sit tight and I'll be over later."

Bucky grumbled but we agreed on a time to meet. As I hung up I wondered if Tom would think this was "getting involved" in the case where I shouldn't. But I would argue that this dossier was given to me and to my staff. We had every right to examine it again now, especially if doing so would help prove our innocence. Though Tom might disagree, he would be wrong.

No, I decided. This foray with Bucky couldn't possibly come back to bite me.

CHAPTER 11

THE AFTERNOON DID CLEAR UP, AND WHEN THE SUN CAME OUT,
so did some unseasonable warmth. My mom tied her pale blue jacket around
her waist and pulled out her sunglasses as we strolled along the National Mall.
Nana kept her pastel pink–striped jacket on, but she'd unzipped it, not just
because the day was warming up nicely, but because it gave her easier access
to her fanny pack. She, too, wore sunglasses—the wraparound kind to protect
her recently repaired cataracts. Trailing behind my mom by a couple of steps,
she studied the pamphlet we'd picked up at one of the Smithsonian buildings.

"There's a lot we're missing," I said, as we walked west from the Capitol
building. "Don't you want to see the National Air and Space Museum?"

My mom shook her head. "It sounds a lot like the Museum of Science and
Industry at home," she said. "We can do that on a rainy day. Today I want to
be outside and enjoy this beautiful scenery."

Nana, shuffling behind us, said, "I want to see the Washington Memorial."

"That's *Monument*," I said gently. "It's the Washington *Monument* and the
Lincoln Memorial. I made that same mistake when I first got here," I said. "But
a kind woman named Barbara set me straight."

My mom turned around. "Do you and Tom come out here very often?"

I took a look at the blossoming trees, the clear blue of the sky, and the
crowds milling around out enjoying the gorgeous day. When was the last time
he and I had spent a day together just enjoying the beauty that surrounded us
in our nation's capital? I shook my head. "Not often enough." There was so
much here to be thankful for—so much to appreciate, and yet he and I were
constantly pulled apart by our conflicting schedules. The last few times I'd
been out here, I'd been on my own.

"Is that a carousel?" Nana asked, pointing behind us.

"Yeah," I said, hoping she wouldn't want to go for a ride.

"I bet the little kids love that."

I thought about my own experiences with that carousel—and witnessing a murder—as I made a noncommittal reply. "It's a long walk to see all the memorial exhibits. You sure you're up for it?"

We stopped a moment to stare out toward the Washington Monument. "Says here it's over 555 feet tall," Mom said, taking her turn with the pamphlet. "Guess how much it weighs?"

"Weighs?" Nana asked. "Why? You planning to pick it up?"

"Take a look," I said, pointing. "See that line? Where the color changes? They started building it in 1848 but ran out of money. It sat here for twenty years before they started work on it again."

The three of us stared at the tall white obelisk. With the sun almost directly overhead, we all had to squint. Tall, spare, stark, and circled by snapping American flags, it was a breathtaking sight.

"Hello again, ladies."

We turned. My mom made a funny noise, halfway between a teenage squeak and a gasp of surprise. "Why, Mr. Kapostoulos," she said. "How nice to see you."

He smiled. "Please call me Kap. All my friends do."

Kapostoulos had sidled up to us—sidled up to my mom, I should say—and was smiling a bit too much for a man whose best friend had died just three days before. I struggled to remember his first name—heck, I would have struggled to remember what "Kap" stood for. But Mom sure remembered.

"Nice to see you again," I lied.

He nodded acknowledgment. Wearing a navy blazer, khaki-colored pants, and a blue striped tie, he looked more like a cruise director than someone in mourning.

"Enjoying our beautiful sights?" he asked, but before we could answer, he continued. "Have you been to the Lincoln Memorial yet?"

"Not yet," Mom said. "Is it as pretty as this is?"

"Each of the sights near here has its own beauty," he said, with a meaningful gaze at my mom. "It's worth spending time getting to know them all."

I wanted to roll my eyes, but there was no one to appreciate my discomfort. Nana had stepped closer to him, and I could tell she was sizing him up. I was disheartened by the deepening smile lines on her face.

"We should get going," I said. "Lots to do, you know."

"Perhaps I could accompany you," Kap said, moving toward me. "It has been a while since I have had time to appreciate the magnificence of this area."

"I thought you lived here," I said.

"But I've been out of town for a long time."

I couldn't help the brusqueness in my tone. "I would think you'd be spending time with Ruth and Joel Minkus."

My mom shot me a look from behind Kap. It was meant to reproach, but I didn't care. Who was this guy? And why was he bothering us?

"Although Carl and I knew each other for many years, there is no love lost between me and Ruth." He held out his hands as though in supplication. "But Joel and I get along very well. In fact, he informed me about how Ruth treated you yesterday when you saw her at Arlington."

I started to scoot away, but Mom and Nana didn't move.

"I would like to offer my apologies," he said

"For what?"

"On Ruth's behalf. She's under considerable strain, and I'm sure she didn't mean—"

"First off, no apology necessary," I said. "Families in the midst of shock and grief aren't always responsible for what they say"—I didn't let him interrupt—"and second, I think it's rather presumptuous of you to apologize on behalf of someone who you just admitted doesn't care for you very much."

He smiled. That bugged me.

"Now," I continued, "we have to be going."

"Ollie!" Mom said. She looked like a seventeen-year-old who was just informed of a ten thirty curfew.

"We have a lot to do," I said.

"But if Kap wants to come along with us, I think it would be nice," Mom said.

Nice?

As if given a great gift, Kap's smile grew. I wanted to ask my mother what was wrong with her all of a sudden, but the words died on my lips. Kap pointed to something in the distance, which immediately captured Mom's full attention. They started walking south, and I fell in behind them with Nana.

"What the heck just happened?" I asked.

She leaned in toward me. "Your mother's been going through a tough time."

"She has?" I stared down at her. "What kind of a tough time?"

Nana linked her arm through mine. "I'd call it a delayed midlife crisis, but that sounds too pat. She's been moved out of the counselor job she loved at the women's shelter into a position that's far below her skills. They're downsizing, or so they say. What's really happening is that they're pushing the older, well-paid workers out or into lesser jobs so that they get disgusted and quit. She used to be excited to go to work every day—to help people. Now she just sits at a desk and makes phone calls to raise money."

"They made her a telemarketer?"

Nana nodded.

"She never told me."

"Of course not." Nana slid a look at the two of them in front of us. "And on top of it all, she's been lonely, Ollie. Very lonely. I'm not the most exciting company, you know."

"Nana . . ."

"It's true. I'm still pretty active and I still volunteer at the hospital, but when your mom comes in from work I can see the dejection in her eyes. There's nothing for her to look forward to anymore."

"She has friends . . ." The image of Mom sitting in a dark room lit only by the flickering television flashed through my mind. "Doesn't she?"

"Most of them are married, and they do couple things." Nana shrugged, and then answered my unasked question. "Even though your mother has been on her own for a long time, things have changed for her now. It's as though when she lost her job she lost a part of herself."

I didn't know if I could talk around the hard lump that had suddenly lodged in my throat.

Ahead of us, my mom laughed. Kap laughed, too, their heads leaning toward each other.

There was something about him that didn't seem authentic, but I couldn't put my finger on what it was. The two of them laughed again and my mom smiled at Kap in a way that made her look ten years younger.

Nana whispered—close to my shoulder. "This trip out to see you, Ollie, was all your mother talked about for weeks. It gave her something important to look forward to."

I nodded, not knowing what else to say.

"In some ways, it's nice that you don't have to work while we're here."

I felt the now-familiar stab of disappointment. For fleeting moments, the horrible specter of Minkus's death disappeared. But then it all came rushing back with a sharpness that made me suck my breath. "I wanted so much to show you the White House."

"Your mother wants so much to spend time with you. Maybe all this is working out for the best."

Nana's arm in mine felt small, yet it was a comfort. She patted me. "Sometimes we just need to wait and see. Time will tell and before you know it, you'll be back in the White House kitchen again, and everything will be back to normal."

I bit my lip. Weren't those the exact words I'd used to reassure Bucky just this morning?

"Thanks, Nana," I said.

MY MOM HUMMED AS SHE MADE US A LATE LUNCH BACK AT MY apartment. I'd offered to do the cooking—after all, that was what I did for a living and I wasn't doing much of it these days—but she insisted. Said she wanted to take care of me while she still had the opportunity to do so. A pointed look from Nana warned me not to argue.

"So what did you and Mr. Kapostoulos talk about, Mom?"

He'd accompanied us to the Vietnam Veterans Memorial and to the World War II Memorial, which Nana had particularly wanted to see. He spent most of his time chatting with my mom, leaving me and Nana to wonder about their conversation. At the World War II Memorial, after we'd walked around the expansive structure, he thanked us for sharing part of our day with him and he spoke briefly to my mom, alone.

"He prefers to be called Kap," Mom said.

"Right." I wondered if my smile looked as disingenuous as it felt. "So what *did* you talk about? Did he want to know all about your life history?"

"Not yet, not all of it," she said with a sly smile. "But he did tell me that he encouraged Ruth to call and apologize to you for her outburst at Arlington yesterday."

"He didn't."

"It seemed important to him." She glanced at her watch, then at her purse on the counter.

"That's all I need," I muttered. A thought occurred to me. "Did he ask for your phone number?"

"Ollie. I don't even have a phone number here. He knows I live in Chicago."

"You have a cell phone."

She turned away and went back to humming. Nana warned me with her look to stop asking questions. But I couldn't let it go. "Did you give it to him?"

Finally, Mom turned. Her hair was pulled back, and her face was flushed, but she was smiling. She looked so pretty, so vivacious and so full of life. Kap had put that sparkle in her eyes just by paying her some attention. I sighed, knowing I should let it go. But I couldn't.

"Yes, I did," Mom said in a tone that dared me to object. She placed three bowls of tortilla soup on the table. They steamed with freshness and a hint of spice. I started in on mine and was immediately rewarded with a taste of home. "Do you have a problem with that?"

Nana kicked me under the table. I took another sip of soup and pretended not to hear.

Mom waited. Nana kicked me again.

"Nope," I lied. "Not at all."

"Good, because he and I are going out Friday."

I opened my mouth in protest, but a third swift kick to my shin shut me up. Bending my head, I concentrated again on my soup.

"That's wonderful, Corinne," Nana said. "Where is he taking you?"

"I don't know yet."

"Mom," I said, putting my spoon down, "we don't even know this man. How do you know it's safe to go out with him? He could be a masher."

"A masher!" She laughed. "I used to use that line on you when you were a teenager."

"Mom, I'm serious. You know nothing about him."

"He was good friends with Carl Minkus," she said. "A very famous NSA agent."

"Yeah, and that famous agent is dead."

She shook her head, but kept smiling. "You sound like an overprotective parent."

"But you just met him."

"In fact," she added mischievously, "I think you'd make a great parent." She fixed me with a glare. "Exactly when do you plan to give me grandchildren? I'm not getting any younger, you know."

She always knew what buttons to push to circumvent an argument. I'd only finished about half my soup, but I stood up. "I'm sorry, this is great, but I'll have it later. I promised to stop by Bucky's house, and then I have dinner plans with Suzie and Steve." I carried my bowl to the side to cover with plastic wrap before placing it in the fridge. "And I need to call Tom."

Excusing myself, I blew out a breath. My mother knew we were on dangerous ground here. Marriage and babies were not something I cared to discuss. Not now at least. Maybe not ever. I didn't see myself toting around tots anytime soon. My chosen career was in a male-dominated field and while all the rhetoric claimed that women could have families and maintain careers, too, I knew that in this extremely competitive arena I needed to hold tight to every edge I could wrap my enthusiastic fingers around. I'd been top chef here for a relatively short time. And as soon as the next administration took over, I could be out of a job. Kids were not on my horizon. The topic wasn't open for discussion, and Mom knew it.

Her bringing it up when I pressed her about this Kap fellow was her attempt to strongarm me into silence. For now, it worked. But I'd figure out a way to talk with her about him. There was something about the guy I just didn't trust.

I thought about my upcoming visit with Bucky. He and I would have to discuss the situation. If the Easter Egg Roll were to be permanently canceled, the press would have a field day. There would be no way to recover from such a public-relations nightmare. I thought about calling our contact at the American Egg Board, Brandy. Effervescent and eager to help, she was just the sort of person who could get things rolling.

I started to look up her number, but stopped myself. Tom would probably consider that "meddling" in the situation. Anger rumbled up from deep in my throat. I was thwarted, no matter which way I turned.

I dialed Tom's cell but hit "end" when I heard my house phone ring. Geez! I hadn't gotten this many phone calls at home in the past year. I picked up the kitchen phone because it was closest. "Hello?"

A woman asked, "Is this . . . Olivia?" Familiar, but I couldn't quite place the voice.

"Yes."

"I . . . that is . . . this is Ruth Minkus."

Fortunately I was right next to a chair. I sat. "Hello," I said, and because I couldn't come up with anything better, "How are you?"

She sucked in a breath, but didn't answer. "My husband's 'friend,' Mr. Kapostoulos"—her emphasis on the word "friend" dripped with sarcasm— "suggested I call you."

My face must have conveyed my pure shock because both Mom and Nana stopped eating to stare at me. Mom pantomimed, "Who is it?"

"He suggested you call me?" I echoed into the receiver. Then pointing into it, I mouthed back, "Ruth Minkus."

They exchanged looks of horror and both started mouthing questions at me. I couldn't follow them and pay attention to Ruth at the same time, so I averted my eyes. I chose to stare at the ceiling, hoping its blankness might aid my concentration. My brain couldn't absorb the fact that Ruth was calling me. And, based on the stammering on the other end, she didn't quite believe it, either.

"I suppose I mean to apologize for my behavior yesterday."

I was quick to interrupt. "There's no reason to—"

"Kap said I offended you."

"Kap's wrong," I said, with more than a touch of vehemence. Movement from my right caused me to look over. My mom made a face and got up to work at the stove. Nana stayed put, watching me. I returned my gaze to the ceiling. "I was not at all offended. I understand completely. You're going through a lot of strain right now."

"I am," she said in a tiny voice. "It's been so much pressure. I've been working hard to help my son, Joel, in his bid for the senate seat and now this . . . I don't think I'm handling it very well."

I felt for her. She had just lost her husband and was being bullied into making unnecessary apologies. Embarrassed to have been pulled into this, I said, "I am very sorry for your loss."

"Thank you."

I was about to make another pleasant, innocuous comment—one that would allow me to segue into an excuse to get off the phone—when she said, "Joel thinks I was wrong to accuse you, too."

"As I said, Mrs. Minkus, there's no need—"

"Were you planning to come to Carl's wake tomorrow?"

"Ah . . . no, I wasn't."

She made a *tsk*ing noise. "That's because of my outburst, isn't it?"

"No," I said. "I didn't—" I was about to say that I'd never had *any* intention of attending her husband's wake, but realized how rude that might sound. Softening my response, I tried a different approach. "I know this has to be a very stressful time and I wouldn't want to compound that tension. I'm sure my presence at the wake would be distracting."

"Distracting? How?"

"Because . . ." I groped for a quick explanation. "My staff is still banned from the kitchen."

"Oh, I didn't know that," she said. "I confess I've been trying to avoid reading the papers. It's just too much, you know?"

I did know. "I want to express my sympathy again, Mrs. Minkus."

"I would appreciate it if you would reconsider."

"Reconsider?"

"It would mean a lot to me if you would come tomorrow night," she said. "I feel just terrible about my behavior yesterday. In fact, I feel terrible about everything these days. I can't go around burning bridges just because my life has fallen apart."

I heard her voice crack. I didn't know what to say, but she continued. "I mean, I have to think about Joel. He needs me to be strong right now. And I made him ashamed yesterday. Would you please come to the wake? Even if the rest of your staff can't make it, it would go a long way to proving to Joel that I didn't mess things up." She sighed deeply. "I may not always agree with Kap, but this time I think he's right. Please come, Olivia." Her next breath seemed to shake, and I sensed she was close to tears. "I'd better go now." With that she hung up.

I stared at the receiver for a long time. What in the world had that been about? Kap had forced her hand, no doubt about it. But to what end? And why would Joel care whether his mother offended the executive White House chef? I was about to tell Mom about this bizarre conversation, but realized she had left the room.

Nana pointed to the guest bedroom, where I found my mom at the computer. "That was Ruth Minkus," I said.

She turned toward me, arranging her body to block the screen from my view. "What did she want?"

"To invite me to her husband's wake."

Mom twisted, quickly minimized the window, and then returned her attention to me. I'd seen a tiny bit of the page she'd been viewing. "Were you reading the *Liss Is More* column again?" I asked.

Nervous laugh as she stood. "Why would I read that trash?"

"Then what were you reading?" I felt like a parent who just caught her teenager visiting inappropriate sites.

"Just silly stuff," she said, trying to guide me out the door. "Nothing worth mentioning. Let's go see what Nana's up to."

"Mom—"

Her shoulders dropped. "I wasn't reading that crazy man, Liss," she said. "But I found out that his articles are reprinted on the Internet and people can write in and make comments on what he wrote."

"And?"

"There are some very odd people in the world," she said. "I mean, I thought Liss was out of his mind, but people go off on the strangest tangents and say very mean, very cruel things."

"Let me see," I said, moving toward the computer.

She blocked me.

I laughed. "Mom, you can't keep me from reading what's out there."

She suddenly looked so sad, my heart hurt.

"Did someone mention me?" I asked.

"Not exactly." She bit her lip. "It's just that people were asking about the Easter Egg Roll, and I knew how worried you were about that. I didn't want you to see all the questions."

"That's not all you didn't want me to see, is it?"

"Some people don't know what they're talking about."

I made it around her and maximized the browser window again. I sensed her resignation both from her deep sigh, and from the hand she placed on my shoulder as I scrolled through the comments.

There were, indeed, a lot of strange people in the world. I wondered if these were the same folks who, for kicks, sent out indecipherable spam in their spare time. I started at the top—the most recent commentary—and worked my way through several screeds that had more to do with battling the writers' own demons than Carl Minkus's death. Seemed to me that the earliest posts stayed on topic and the more recent ones were lame attempts to discredit earlier posters.

"What about the Easter Egg Roll?" asked Theda R. from Virginia. "My kids have been looking forward to this all year! Can't someone just boil a few eggs so the kids won't be disappointed?"

From Sal J.: "What do we care if another bureaucrat is dead? He got what he deserved, if you ask me. Minkus was screwed up and whoever took him out deserves a medal."

Yikes.

"These people have too much time on their hands," I said, continuing to scroll. I stopped when I saw the next one. Blood rushed out to all my extremities, rendering me light-headed.

"That girl the president hired to cook for him—that Ollivia Parras—she's nothing but trouble since she took over the job. She can't cook worth a nikcl and she can always try seeing how she can get in the headlines. It's all her fault your poor kids don't get to roll their eggs this year. I say the president should fire her butt and fast!"

No matter that the writer of this little diatribe—R. I.—spelled so many things wrong, including my name. No matter that he, or she, was grammatically challenged. The message was clear.

"I can so cook," I said unnecessarily. But the accusation stung.

"You see, this is all garbage," Mom said. "I shouldn't even have been reading it."

I wanted to shake it off, but my eyes were scanning again. There were more postings questioning whether there was any way to keep the Egg Roll on schedule, a few that talked about Minkus and who might have wanted him dead, and a couple more that called for my immediate dismissal.

"Cheery stuff," I said, trying to swallow a hot bubble of disappointment.

"They don't know what they're talking about."

She was probably right, but the attacks were brutal. And they hurt.

I'd been on enough Internet pages like this to know that at the bottom there should be a form available to add your own commentary. But this time, no little box appeared. Instead, in red italics were the words: *Please allow several minutes for your comment to post.*

I spun. "You didn't."

Mom blushed, waving a hand at the screen. "I couldn't let them talk about you like that and not do anything."

I dropped my head into my hands, took a deep breath, and hit "refresh."

CHAPTER 12

OF COURSE THE PAGE TOOK FOREVER TO LOAD. OF COURSE. SOME-times my connection was blazingly fast, and times like this—when I really wanted information quickly—the computer became uncooperative and petu-lant, like I was still on dial-up.

While I waited for the Liss commentary to blink back into existence, I chanced a look at my mom. "Just tell me you didn't mention me by name."

She opened her mouth but no words came out.

Just as the website popped up to tell me that it was temporarily unavailable, my cell phone rang.

"Aargh!" I took a look at the display. Tom.

"Did you try to call me?" he asked when I picked up.

"I started to, but then Ruth Minkus called."

"She called you? Why? Did she start accusing you again?"

"No," I said wearily. I didn't feel like explaining. Over the past few days all I'd done was explain. What I wanted—what I *needed*—right now was to be back in the White House kitchen, working on the Egg Roll. We were already three days behind schedule. "She called to apologize," I said. "Long story."

He waited a beat. "So, what's up?"

Was it my imagination, or was there a lilt of impatience in his tone? "The White House Egg Roll," I began.

"We've been over that."

"No," I said carefully. "You said you expected they would cancel it. But they can't."

"They 'can't'?"

"You know what I mean." I grimaced at the pleading tone in my voice. "I think it's a mistake to cancel the Egg Roll."

"Oh you do?"

"Yes I do," I said, getting my back up. "Who can I talk to about it?"

"I'll look into it for you."

"No, Tom," I said, regaining a little composure. "You're responsible for my actions, remember?" Without waiting for him to answer, I pressed on. "That means that you have a conflict of interest. You believe keeping me out of the kitchen will keep me out of trouble. Or," I added, with a smidge of sarcasm, "your perception of trouble. I think it makes more sense for me to talk with someone else about this. Do you have Craig's cell phone number handy?"

"You would go over my head?"

I wouldn't really, but I was desperate and I didn't want him to call my bluff. Even though we occasionally got angry with one another, we knew our limits. Calling Craig would push things and I truly didn't want to cause irreparable damage to our relationship. Even if this *was* turning into my career versus his career. "Maybe Craig isn't my best option. How about if I talk with Paul Vasquez?"

Seconds ticked by without my being able to read his mood. Why were so many of our conversations so antagonistic lately?

"That might be a good idea," he finally answered and I sensed conciliation in his words. "I do understand how important this is for you."

"I know you do, and I also know you're in a tough position."

We were both silent for a long moment.

"I'm probably less likely to get into trouble if I'm at work," I said.

He made a noise that might have been a laugh. "You may be right." Shifting gears, he asked, "Anything else new?"

I debated telling him about Bucky having the Minkus file on his home computer, but decided to hold that back for now. No need to get Bucky into trouble unnecessarily. "I'm planning to go over every step of dinner preparations. I'll make notes of anything that might be helpful to you."

"Sounds like a plan."

"Thanks for helping out with Suzie and Steve earlier. They're having me over for dinner tonight to thank me for getting the newshounds off their front lawn."

"Nice. I do all the work, you get the reward."

"Want to come with?"

"Some other time." He made a sound—like he was sucking his bottom lip. "Until this investigation is complete, it's a good idea if you and I aren't seen out together."

That stung, too. Even more than the Internet postings had. "I guess you're right."

"Try not to talk about the case with your SizzleMaster friends, okay?"

"Pretty hard to do after reporters showed up on their front lawn."

He was silent again. "Just try to keep a low profile."

"I did just think of something."

"Uh-oh."

"I know we're under suspicion, and so are Suzie and Steve. But what about the other guests at dinner that night? I mean, Carl Minkus's second-in-command sure stands to gain now that his boss is dead. And what about Alicia Parker? Or her husband? They were there, too."

Tom's long, deep breath wasn't quite as annoyed-sounding as I'd expected it to be. "First off, people don't just go killing one another to get job promotions. At least not usually. Sure, you'll be able to quote some news story where that happened, but in the real world, most people just don't operate that way."

"What about—"

"Alicia Parker?" He laughed. "She's too big for even you to touch, Ollie. Alicia Parker is a cabinet member. I'm sure there are people looking into her background, but this is one hot wire you don't want to even get near. Trust me."

He was right about that. I'd only met Secretary Parker in passing once or twice, although I'd seen her interviewed on TV fairly often. She came across as strong-minded, honest, and brave. "Yeah," I agreed. "And anyway, she strikes me as the type who—if she wanted you dead—would just come straight up and shoot you. I don't see her sneaking poison into an eggplant entrée."

"Keep in mind, Ollie," Tom said, and the warning was back in his tone, "Minkus might have died of natural causes."

"Natural causes could also mean a food allergy," I said. "And if the medical examiner proves that, then I'm out of a job for sure."

"I'm sorry," he said, the gentleness in his tone catching me off-guard. "With this new directive from Craig, I haven't been very supportive recently, have I?"

"You have," I said, remembering that he picked up my family from the airport and stood by me while I was being interrogated. "I shouldn't be so difficult. You're under a lot of pressure."

"I am. And I hope you can understand that."

"I do," I said. And I did. Mostly.

MY MOM CORNERED ME WHEN I GOT OFF THE PHONE TO LET ME know that Mrs. Wentworth and Stanley had invited us out to dinner. I declined because of my meeting with Bucky and dinner plans with Suzie and Steve. Mom and Nana had, however, jumped at the chance to see more of the area, and I was glad. Knowing they were in good hands with my neighbors allowed me to feel a little less guilty leaving them.

I called Paul on the way. Although I was lucky enough to get to speak with him directly, he was running late for a meeting. When I pressed him about letting us back into the kitchen, he hedged. But that was better than saying no. Plus, they hadn't yet canceled the Egg Roll. I took that as a positive even as I got him to promise to get back to me. But when I hung up, I realized he hadn't said by when.

Bucky's Bethesda home surprised me. I'd never been inside, and except for the recent trip in the limousine when the Guzy brothers dropped him off, I'd never even known exactly where he lived. This was a cheerful little neighborhood, with lots of shiny cars outside tidy front lawns. Parallel parking on residential streets was never difficult for a native Chicagoan, and I tucked my little coupe into a tight spot between two SUVs.

Although this was an old neighborhood, every town house on this street and the next sparkled like new. I'd heard that this section had undergone major renovations in the past decade. I could see the allure of living here. The trees were mature, the homes well-tended.

Bucky met me at the door, wearing a wide cotton apron tied over pale legs. It gave him the appearance of not wearing any pants, and I breathed a sigh of relief when he turned around to gesture me in and I saw his blue cutoff shorts. "It's warm in here, sorry," he said. "I'm working on a new quiche. Just drop your jacket anywhere."

Sniffing the savory air, I shut the front door and followed him through the pristine living room toward the kitchen. My stomach growled as I picked up the scent of baking cheese. "How long have you lived here?" I asked.

"Eleven—no, twelve years," he said, raising his voice so I could hear him. Whatever he was concocting in the kitchen must have needed his immediate attention, because I heard him clanking things in and out of the oven, even as

I peeled off my jacket and draped it over the back of a purple couch. I ran my hand along its back pillow. Suede. Not at all what I would have imagined in Bucky's home. "You should have seen this place back then." He peeked his head around the corner. "Took a lot of work to get it to where it is now."

"It's gorgeous." I wanted to ask if he lived alone, but I held my tongue. Bucky and I had never been friends in the sense that we discussed personal lives, and my being here suddenly seemed like an intrusion.

The living room was painted ecru, with matching crown molding and bare maple floors that shone, but didn't squeak. Lights were on everywhere and I stopped on my way to the kitchen to admire some black-and-white photographs on the dining room wall. The shots had an Ansel Adams look to them, but the photographer's name was listed as "B. Fields."

"Did you do all the remodeling yourself?"

"With the hours we work at the White House? Are you kidding?" Back out of sight again, his voice was muffled. "I did do a lot, though. It's invigorating."

I joined him in the kitchen. What must have once been a tiny galley kitchen had been updated and expanded into a huge space that made me salivate. With gleaming pots hanging over a center island, not one, but two built-in stovetops, and two double ovens, this was the sort of kitchen I hoped to have in my own home some day. While my apartment's small space was serviceable for my personal needs, I knew that if I ever settled down somewhere permanent, my kitchen would look just like this.

"Wow," I said. "This is amazing."

"We like it."

Time to bite the bullet. "We?" I asked. "I didn't know you were married. Are you?"

He gave a small smile. "Not yet."

"Kids?"

This time he fixed me with a glare, though not an unfriendly one. "Do I really seem like the type who would have kids?"

"Whatever you're making smells wonderful," I said to change the subject.

"Good. I know we're not going back to the White House anytime soon, and I don't want to get rusty."

"Bucky," I said sincerely, "I doubt that could ever happen."

He wiped his hands on a towel and removed his apron. "There. Everything's good for now." He set a timer. "Let's go into the living room and take a look at that dossier."

* * *

BY THE TIME THE LITTLE CLOCK DINGED, WE'D COME UP WITH almost nothing, dietary-wise, that we couldn't have recited from memory.

Bucky pulled out a gently browned spinach quiche.

"Looks great," I said, coming close to breathe in the aroma. "Smells wonderful, too."

"Want some?" he asked.

"I'd love to, but I have dinner plans."

His reaction was small: a slight drop of his shoulders, the quick twist of his mouth.

"But boy, it really does smell good," I amended. "Maybe just a small piece?"

"Sure," he said without reacting. But when he sliced a generous portion onto a piece of black and gold rimmed china and placed it in front of me, his eyes were bright with anticipation. "Let me know what you think."

"Fancy plate," I said.

"Why save the good stuff for special occasions?"

I forked a piece of the pie-shaped slice and pronounced it heavenly. If I hadn't had plans to meet with Suzie and Steve in the next hour, I would have asked for seconds—even after this generous first serving. The quiche was so good, in fact, it was all I could do not to request a sample to take home to share with Mom and Nana. "You'll have to give me this recipe," I said.

"Already on our books." He smiled, and it dawned on me what an unusual sight that was. "I plan to include it . . ." Stopping himself, the smile faded. "I should say, I *planned* to include it in the next set of samplings for Mrs. Campbell to taste."

I patted his hand. He flinched but didn't pull away.

"Well, that's just another reason why we need to work hard at getting back into the kitchen. I don't see anything in Minkus's dietary profile that could have had such disastrous consequences, do you?"

Bucky had started to clean up the area and I marveled, again, at how pristine the place was. At the White House, when we were in the midst of preparing a state dinner, or other big event, the kitchen got a little cluttered. Although we had help and we cleaned up as we worked—there really was no way around that—at home I was not quite so fastidious. Bucky, however, was.

"You know," I said, "we read over the rest of his dossier but we really didn't digest it."

He half turned. "What do you mean?"

"Here, for instance." I pointed. "Minkus was appointed to his position during the prior administration. He worked hard to make a name for himself as a terrorist fighter. But he also held a position as a counterintelligence liaison to China."

"So?"

"So isn't that a little weird? Kind of a strange combination, I think."

Bucky didn't seem as interested in my musings as he was in putting his quiche away. "Who appointed him to the liaison position?" he asked.

"Don't know. Obviously there's a lot in his file we wouldn't have access to. They only provided us this top-line information. Stuff that anyone could probably find in an Internet search, if they knew what they were looking for."

"Hmph," Bucky said, bustling around the kitchen as I pored through the file.

I mused aloud. "And what about Phil Cooper?"

"That's the guy who reported to Minkus, right? Another security official."

I pointed again, but Bucky just worked around me. "Exactly. Cooper worked for Minkus for about two years. It doesn't say much here about him, except to mention that he's part of Minkus's staff."

"You're not thinking Cooper killed Minkus just to get his job?" Bucky scowled. "People don't usually do that. At least not in the real world."

Almost word for word, Bucky had just echoed Tom's sentiment.

"What about China?" I asked. "Didn't they just have that double-assassination in Beijing? The one that's been in all the headlines."

Stopping mid-stride on the way to his stainless steel double refrigerator, Bucky cocked his head. "Yeah. Wasn't that the day after Minkus died?"

"Do you think it's related?"

"Like . . . some Chinese official sneaked poison into Minkus's food? Yeah. Sure."

"Think about it. According to rumors, the Chinese had insider spies in the United States. Maybe Minkus discovered who that spy was who was selling our secrets. Maybe a Chinese operative got to Minkus before dinner."

"An operative." Bucky snorted. "You sound so official. Like a character in a movie, figuring out a global conspiracy."

Put like that, it sounded ridiculous. I felt stupid for seeing patterns where there were none. For suspecting people like Phil Cooper when I had no reason to do so. I closed the file and placed both hands on top of it. "You're right," I finally said.

Wiping his hands after putting the food away, Bucky shrugged. "If some-one did get to Minkus before dinner, then I guess we just have to be patient. Let the medical examiner figure out what killed him. God, I hope that's it. I'm not saying I'm glad he's dead, you understand. But now I care less about that, than about how it happened. I just hope they find out what—or who—killed him. Until then, no matter what we say or do, we'll always be known as the killer kitchen."

Oh God, I thought. The killer kitchen.

SUFFICIENTLY FULL FROM MY HEALTHY HELPING OF QUICHE, I nonetheless headed to the studio where Suzie and Steve filmed their *Sizzle-Masters* television shows. I hoped for two things: that whatever they served would be light, and that the newshounds who had been staking out their home had given up. After my day of interruptions, the last thing I needed was to deal with the media.

The directions they'd provided were perfect and I pulled up to the studio five minutes early. From the outside it looked like a typical industrial building, but once inside, I felt as though I'd just stepped into someone's home.

"Ollie, thank goodness," Suzie said, giving me a quick hug hello. Hugging her was like being enveloped by a favorite aunt, all soft and smooshy, and smelling like White Linen cologne.

"How are you doing?" I asked. "Were you able to lose the reporters?"

Suzie was the type who didn't understand the principle of "personal space." She held my hand as we meandered through a waiting area that felt more like a cozy living room: two softly glowing lamps, red walls, jewel-toned accents. "Thank you so much for helping us out," she said, her face close to mine. "I thought Steve was going to lose it."

"Lose what?" he boomed from behind a thick wall. The side door was open to the filming portion of the studio and I stepped in and then up onto the raised portion, blinking into the high illumination.

This room was peculiarly lit. While the stage area was hyper-bright, the audience section was dark. I could make out rows of seats, rising toward the back of the studio, guaranteeing everyone a good view. From the looks of it, there were six rows in two sections. Maybe a dozen seats per row. Things sure looked bigger on TV.

"We're keeping the lights off in the outer portion so that no one knows we're here," Suzie said as though I'd asked the question. She squeezed my hand. "I'm so glad you were able to come."

Her voice held a strange quality. Not relief. Not a shared understanding of what we were all going through.

"Is there something else going on I should know about?" I asked

They exchanged a look. Suzie let go of my hand. "Like what?"

I gave an exaggerated shrug. "Nothing. Anything. I'm just trying to make sure you haven't been bothered any more."

"No," Suzie said, leaving my side to tend to a pot on the stove. She kept her back to me. "Everything has been really quiet since we got here."

"So your filming went well?"

"Very," Suzie said.

Steve nodded. He stood in front of the central countertop, which faced the cameras. A large overhead camera pointed down, the better to show the folks at home precisely how items should be prepared. Before him was a heaping mound of grilled vegetables—peppers, onions, zucchini, mushrooms. I wondered how many people they were planning to serve.

The two of them worked at their stations with their backs to one another. Very straight, very tense backs. The pressure in the room was so thick I could swim in it.

"So why here?" I asked.

Steve lifted his head, but his eyes didn't focus. "Hmm?"

"Here? You mean at the studio?" Suzie spoke over her shoulder. "Oh, we just thought you'd like to see it."

"Come on, guys," I said to their backs. "Something doesn't smell right and I can tell you it isn't the grilled portabella."

Suzie said, "How about we eat first, discuss business later?"

"Business?"

"Suze," Steve said, finally turning to face her. "There is no business to discuss. Remember?"

Now my curiosity was piqued.

Suzie turned. Her smile showed too much teeth. "I thought we decided—"

"Yes." His smile was an almost perfect mimic of hers. "We decided to have a nice dinner and then give Ollie a copy of the DVD."

Surprised, I asked, "You have a copy?"

"Of course," Steve said. "We're co-producers."

As if that explained it to non-TV-savvy me. But that didn't matter. "Where is it? Can I see it?"

He flung a derisive look over his shoulder and said, in a too-casual voice, "Sure. That's the whole reason we wanted to have you for dinner tonight. But let's eat first."

We made our way to the table. "I'm very glad to hear about the DVD." I carried a basket of fresh-baked sesame rolls, which warmed my hands. "I had asked our chief usher about getting a copy, but he didn't know if we could."

They exchanged another look.

The dining area was beyond a half wall—sliced vertically—that made it seem as though we were in an entirely separate room. Open to the cameras yet again, this part of the stage was decorated with homespun accessories, giving the area the feel of a middle-class American home.

Suzie gave me a funny look as she gestured me into a chair. "Why do they want a copy of the DVD?"

Steve speared a perfectly grilled ribeye and placed it on my plate. "Medium-rare okay with you?"

"Perfect." I turned to Suzie. "I was hoping to use the DVD to prove that nobody in the kitchen could have added anything to Minkus's plate before it went out. Your crew was still filming right up to the end, remember?"

She nodded, but stared down at her own steak. She looked ready to cry.

"What's wrong?" I asked.

She shook her head. "I should have served the soup first."

"I make the finest grilled vegetables in North America," Steve said, leaning over to spoon a helping onto my plate. "Say when."

But I was looking at Suzie. Her downcast expression was not soup-related. Of that I was certain.

I reached over to touch her hand. "Suze?"

Vaguely aware of a steamy scent wafting upward, I heard Steve say, "Should I keep going?"

I glanced at my plate, alarmed at the pile of vegetables he'd mounded there. "When—when!" I said, jerking my hands up. The quiche in my stomach shifted. "I'll never be able to eat all that."

"Sure you will," Steve said with over-the-top ebullience. "I'm telling you, you've never tasted better."

I twisted my head from side to side, to keep an eye on both of them. "What's really going on here?"

Suzie sniffed.

Steve sat. "Eat," he said. It was more an order than invitation.

I tried to manage my impatience by slicing off a small piece of ribeye. Steve had, in fact, grilled it to medium-rare perfection. Popping it in my mouth, I savored its tenderness. "This is wonderful."

"Don't forget your veggies."

I couldn't possibly forget—not with him constantly reminding me. I speared a green pepper. The vegetable's skin, shiny with marinade, was cross-sected with grill lines and topped with an ingredient I assumed was chopped garlic. Waves of heat tickled my lips as I took my first bite.

I froze, mid-chew.

It was all I could do to keep from violently spitting the pepper out onto my plate. It tasted like nail polish remover. Or at least what I imagined nail polish remover might taste like. My eyes widened—I didn't have any idea how to remove this vile thing from my mouth with Steve watching me. Waiting for me to proclaim his creation fabulous.

"Mmm," I said, grabbing desperately for the napkin on my lap. Damn. Cloth. I needed paper.

"What do you think, Ollie?" Steve asked, his eyes glittering. "Bet you've never tasted anything like it."

I stood.

All of a sudden, it hit me. What if Suzie and Steve *had* poisoned Minkus? Were they now trying to get rid of me? I raced out of the stage area, ducking into the washroom, where I yanked the wastebasket to my face and spit the offensive vegetable out.

Was my light-headedness because I'd jumped up so quickly—or was I about to die just as Minkus had? I gripped the countertop and looked into the mirror. The lights were still off, so I couldn't see much. My lips tingled. My tongue was numb.

Just like Minkus.

I had to get out of here.

"Ollie, what's wrong?" Suzie asked, following me into the room. Blocking my exit.

Suzie's careworn face had paled. Steve stood behind her, looking grim. Why? Because their plan had failed?

"Sick," I said, my tongue sluggish and swollen. "I better go."

Steve shook his head. "I'll drive you home."

"No!" I shouted. "My car is here. I'll be okay."

Now it was Suzie shaking her head. "I won't feel comfortable with you driving alone. Is there someone we can call? Maybe I'll drive with you and Steve can follow us."

She reached over and felt my forehead. "You're clammy."

No kidding.

"Come on," she said, taking my arm. "Let's sit for a few minutes."

I tugged away. "Gotta go."

"But what about the DVD?" Suzie asked. "You really wanted to see it."

Not at the expense of my life, I thought.

She pressed. "Come on back to the table. I'll get the DVD and then we'll figure out how to get you home safely."

Working my way to the door, I tried to still the thudding of my heart. Was its extra-speedy beat from that single bite of green pepper? Was I about to go into cardiac arrest?

Ready to run, I looked at Suzie and Steve. Really looked at them. These two had been my friends for several years. Why was I suspecting them of murder?

Because they'd been acting like weirdos leading up to dinner. That's why.

"My purse," I said, hurrying back to the table. I chanced a look at Suzie's and Steve's plates. Neither had taken the grilled vegetables.

My stomach churned and I put a hand over my mouth.

Suzie beat me to the table and picked up my purse but didn't hand it over. Steve told me to wait while he got the DVD.

Would he come back with a meat cleaver?

"I told my mom and nana that I was coming here tonight," I said.

Suzie looked distracted. "Will they be able to come get you?"

"No—they don't have a car." I held out my hand for my purse.

She stepped back, out of my reach. "I don't know if you're safe to drive." Worry wrinkled her forehead. "You seemed fine until you started eating."

"No . . . I've not been feeling well."

The platter of vegetables sat directly in front of Suzie's plate. She eyed them, then looked at me. "It's too bad," she said. "Steve was so excited to have you try this new marinade."

I'll bet.

Eyeing the veggies again, she leaned forward and picked up a piece of grilled portabella. If she tried to force-feed me, I was going to run for the door.

She surprised me by taking a big bite. "Oh my God," she said, around the mouthful. She looked around wildly, but didn't run away, as I had. Instead she grabbed the cloth napkin off the table and spit into it. "My God," she said again. "That's horrible."

"Found it!" Steve said, emerging from the back area. No meat cleaver. No gun. He held a DVD in a jewel case near his head. He waved it triumphantly.

"Steve," Suzie said, pointing at the vegetable platter. "What did you do to those?"

He looked from his wife, to me, to the platter, and then back again. "What's wrong with them?"

"They're disgusting. What's in that new recipe you used? This is the worst thing I've ever tasted. I swear, if I didn't know better, you were trying to poison us."

Suzie's hand flew to her mouth as she realized what she'd said. Then: "My tongue is numb."

Steve's smile dissolved. Anger and disbelief took over, as he leaned over the table to grab one of the grilled veggies. He threw two peppers into his mouth and began to chew vigorously. But not for long. Within seconds he was gagging.

Steve spit out the veggies, just as Suzie and I had. "What the hell?" he asked.

"Should we get to a hospital?" I asked. "All of us?"

Frantically wiping at his tongue with his napkin— a truly unappetizing sight if there ever was one—Steve shook his head. "I can't imagine . . ."

He slammed the DVD onto the table and ran out of the dining room back into the stage-kitchen. We followed.

Digging out an olive oil container, he smelled the top of it. "Seems fine," he said. Then, with a look of dawning realization, he pulled a plastic bowl from the refrigerator and removed the top. He stuck his face close to its contents. He then tipped a finger into the mix and touched it to his lips, grimacing at the taste. "Dear Lord," he said.

"What?" Suzie asked.

Overhead lights were still pouring brightness down onto the stage and the two of them looked like characters in a play—characters that had just been delivered very bad news.

Perspiring heavily, Steve shook his head. "This isn't garlic," he said. "This was supposed to be a tomato-garlic topping."

Suzie and I looked at each other in silence. Steve stared up with confusion on his face. "How could I have not noticed?" He touched the chopped-up substance.

My heart resumed its trip-hammer beating. "Maybe we should try to figure out what it is," I said, feeling like the only voice of reason in the room. The two of them were staring at the bowl, perplexed. "We may have to call the poison control hotline."

Still grimacing, Steve said, "This doesn't even smell like garlic."

"I get it," I said. "It's not garlic. How about we try to find out what it is?"

"How could I have made this kind of mistake?"

Since Steve's lament was rhetorical, I turned to Suzie. "Do you have a list of inventory? Stuff you've ordered? You have a lot of assistants here, right?"

She nodded, staring at Steve.

"I'm guessing one of them made this mistake. And since this is probably a food item, I'm sure we're all going to be okay."

She nodded again.

"Can I have your lists?"

Luckily, their computer was on and in minutes we had accessed their inventory, and meals planned for the next several days' shoots. "What's this?" I asked. "I thought you guys didn't do desserts on the show." The item I pointed to was a persimmon-and-lemon cookie.

Suzie looked over my shoulder. "Oh," she said. "We thought it might be fun to branch out, to start including desserts, too. We have a one-hour show coming up where we prepare everything from soup and salad to dessert. This was going to be one of our experiments."

The light was beginning to dawn. "This calls for persimmon pulp," I said. "Where would that be?"

She rummaged around the kitchen, then held up a finger and headed to the rear of the studio. Steve had been paying attention. "Oh geez," he said. "You think this is chopped persimmon?"

"Unripe persimmon," I corrected. "If you have an assistant who confused persimmon with garlic, I think you need a new assistant. It makes sense though. The bitter taste. The numb tongue."

Suzie returned. "According to our records we received a shipment of persimmon. But there's nothing here."

"Ollie," Steve said, "I can't tell you how embarrassed I am."

"At least we know we're okay," I said, thinking the fruit in the bowl had to be *very* unripe. Nothing else could taste that vile and still not kill you. Tannins in unripe persimmon made the fruit unpalatable. And that was being kind.

There was a stool next to the counter. Steve backed up onto it. "Oh my God," he said. "Can you imagine if this had happened in front of a studio audience?"

Unripe persimmon wasn't toxic in such a small dose. And though it had the potential to cause bezoars, nasty masses that can accumulate in the esophagus or intestines if consumed in large quantities, I doubted anyone would ever eat enough to allow that to happen.

I rolled my tongue around in my mouth, willing the taste away. "Do you have anything to drink?" I asked.

"Sure, of course," Suzie said, hurrying toward the refrigerator. "I could use something, too." Over her shoulder, she stuck out her tongue. "Ick."

"I'm so sorry," Steve said, for about the fifth time. "I can't understand how this happened. I mean, the assistants know that I keep my garlic in that bowl. I always use the same bowl for garlic." He looked about to cry. "But this time it was supposed to be a tomato-garlic combination. How could they have made such a stupid mistake? And why didn't I notice it?"

"Let's just be glad it wasn't anything really bad for us," I said, relief making me ultra-chatty. "For a minute there I was wondering . . ."

I stopped myself. Did I really want to tell them that I'd felt threatened? That I'd been ready to dash out the door? Wouldn't that make it obvious that I suspected them in Minkus's murder?

"Ollie!" Suzie said. The look on her face was one of incredulity. "You didn't think we were trying to—"

"No. No, of course not," I lied.

"It's all my fault." Steve placed both elbows on the countertop and buried his face in his hands. "I made this mistake because I was preoccupied. What other mistakes am I liable to make?"

We both looked at him.

"This isn't going to go away," he said.

"What isn't?"

"We didn't have anything to do with Minkus's death," he said, looking up. "I swear I didn't. Neither did Suzie."

"I didn't think—"

Suzie placed a hand on my arm. "Yes, but the Secret Service probably does think so."

"Why?"

"The NSA, Suze," Steve said. "I think the NSA will be the first on our tails." He lowered his head into his hands again. "But they won't be the last."

CHAPTER 13

THE WORRY LINES ON BOTH THEIR FACES TOLD ME THEY WERE terrified. "What are you talking about?" I asked.

Steve seemed to have aged ten years in the past five minutes. "Want to finish dinner?" He tried a small smile. "I promise I won't make you eat your vegetables."

It was a lame attempt at levity, but I think we all needed some sort of relief. "It's okay," I said. "I'm really not all that hungry. I'm sorry about wasting such a nice steak. Can I take it home?"

My request cheered them up. Professional chefs hate to ruin meals. Asking for the remaining steak told them I liked the dish, and that I trusted them.

"Of course!" Suzie said. "As soon as I pour you something to drink, I'll get the steak wrapped up for you."

The iced tea was sweet and I let it pool in my mouth to help rid myself of the persimmon aftertaste. Within minutes, the dining room table was clear. Suzie put down a fresh tablecloth and we all leaned forward over our glasses of iced tea to talk. At the center of the table was the DVD. What I wanted most of all were answers. The DVD might hold some. But I had a feeling that Suzie and Steve held more.

"Tell me why you think the NSA will be 'tailing' you."

They exchanged a look.

"Come on!" I said. "Just tell me. Spit it out."

Suzie fingered her neckline. "Are you still dating Tom?"

The question startled me into silence. "Uh . . ."

"Because, first, you have to promise you won't tell him."

Alarm bells rang in my head. And they weren't from eating unripe fruit. "I can't promise that."

They exchanged another look. "They probably already know anyway," Suzie said.

"But what if they don't? What if the files are lost right now? Or maybe they put all of Minkus's stuff in limbo. Then we'll just be opening up a can of worms."

Their argument zinged my curiosity into high gear.

Speaking very slowly, I asked them again, "Tell me what's going on." I stared at Steve—a warning not to beat around the bush any longer. "If you mistook chopped raw persimmon for garlic, there's got to be something weighing on your mind."

"A long time ago," he began, blinking sandbaggy eyes, "back in college, in fact, Carl and I were friends. Roommates freshman and sophomore year. He was a political science major. I was . . . well"—Steve gave a wry grin—"I was undecided for a long time."

I'd had no idea that Minkus and Steve had ever known one another. "Why didn't you say anything while we were preparing dinner Sunday?" I asked. "You obviously had a copy of our guest list. You should have mentioned something."

"Well . . ." Steve dragged the word out. "He and I didn't exactly part on the best terms."

I chanced a look at Suzie. From the encouraging expression she was plastering on her husband, I knew she'd heard this story before.

"Go on," I said.

"There was this girl . . ."

Uh-oh, I thought. Isn't there always? "And you both fell for her?"

Steve shook his head. "I wish it were something like that. No."

I waited.

"She was a nice girl. Mary. She was on full scholarship and she worked really hard to keep at the top of her class. Going to college meant everything to her. She lived on the floor above us."

I took a look at Suzie. She was squinting, like she knew this would be hard to hear.

Steve took a deep breath. "Mary was actively involved in student government, and was president of the honors fraternity."

"She sounds like a real go-getter."

Steve's mouth twisted. "She was my good friend."

"Was?"

"More iced tea?" Suzie asked.

At first I thought it was an odd time to interrupt, but when I noticed Steve having a hard time maintaining composure, I took a big drink and said, "Thanks, that would be great."

When we were all settled again, Steve squared his shoulders. "By the time we were juniors, Mary had become a powerhouse on campus. She was destined to do great things—we all knew it. And we all supported her. She was one of those people who had a thousand things on her plate, but who always could make time for you, if you needed a hand, or help with studying, or advice— whatever. Mary made you feel like you were the most important person in her life at that moment. We all adored her."

I was starting to have a queasy feeling. "And Carl Minkus?"

Steve spat an expletive. "Carl was a drunken idiot. He and I wasted a lot of our freshman year. By sophomore year, I got tired of the constant partying. It was time, you know?" He looked up at me.

I nodded.

"Carl's father had been the president of Zeta Eta Theta—the same fraternity Mary was now president of. And Carl was jealous. He was under pressure to bring his grades up." Steve gave an unhappy laugh. "There was no way he could even qualify for membership, let alone be an officer, but that didn't stop him."

This story seemed like something that couldn't have anything to do with dinner last Sunday, but I let him continue.

"The elder Minkus pulled some strings and—what do you know?—Carl was initiated into Zeta Eta Theta. He called me to brag. Like this was some kind of real achievement." Steve made a face. "Mary's hands were tied."

"He and Mary didn't get along?"

"Not at all. She was upset about having to initiate Carl. She fought it, hard, because she believed in preserving the integrity of the organization. But once he was a member, she didn't make waves. She was like that. She fought as hard as she could for what she believed in, but when the battle was over, she gave in graciously."

Now Steve was squinting. He cleared his throat. "That wasn't good enough for Carl. He wanted to be president, just like his old man. He had a lot of money, but Mary had brains and guts. She was the epitome of grace under pressure. He made her life difficult but she outclassed him in every way. And then he snapped."

"Over a fraternity presidency?"

Steve rolled his glass back and forth between his hands. "You have to understand. At the time, this was a very big deal. Every Zeta president since the chapter's inception had gone directly from college into a solid, lucrative position, thanks to elder 'brothers' in the business world. Mary had a spectacular future in front of her."

"But?"

"Carl kept me updated. With the benefit of hindsight, I think he was doling out just enough information to keep me off track. He told me he had given up his craving for the Zeta presidency and that he had offered Mary an olive branch. He said he would stop badgering her if she'd meet him for coffee to talk about it. She agreed."

I waited.

"That was the night she disappeared."

I sucked in a breath so hard and so fast that it made me cough. "What?"

"We never saw her again."

"But . . ."

He held up a hand. "Carl said he waited for her for hours at a coffee shop. Lots of people there—lots of witnesses. The barista commented that he was surprised Carl didn't float out of there after all the coffee he drank that night."

I shook my head. This wasn't making sense. "You're trying to tell me—"

"I believe Carl had something to do with Mary's sudden disappearance."

"Are you saying she's dead?"

He closed his eyes for a long moment. "After a few days we heard from her. She left. Went back home. Said she was giving up school for personal reasons—and not to contact her again. But you had to have known Mary to realize this was the last thing she would do. Attending the university was everything to her. She would never have gone without a fight. Something happened that night. I know it. But knowing something and proving it are two different things." Steve's eyes welled up. "Kids began calling her a dropout." Another expletive, this one under his breath. "She was carrying a four-point-oh on a full-ride scholarship. No way would she just drop out.

"All sorts of rumors started—ranging from her being gang-raped to having had a nervous breakdown." He blinked, and swallowed. "I never did find out the real story, but I knew Carl was behind it."

Aware that anecdotal stories didn't prove a person's guilt or innocence, I was hard-pressed to offer any consolation. But if Steve's suspicions were right, it certainly made it seem as though Carl Minkus was a poor choice for the NSA. "I don't know what to say." I also didn't know exactly how this impacted Minkus's death investigation.

"Here's the thing, Ollie," Steve said, his voice shaking. "I pushed it. I went after him. I told him I knew he'd done something to Mary."

"What did he say?"

"What do you think? He told me I was nuts because I had a crush on her and that I couldn't face the fact that the campus sweetheart had up and left us. He told me that she told him she'd met a guy the week before and she was considering running off with him. A biker. Yeah." Another bitter laugh. "But the school believed him."

"What about her family?"

"I called them, once, about a month later." Steve swallowed and I could tell it hurt. "Mary killed herself. This bright, wonderful girl had taken her own life. I couldn't believe it. Her father was angry I'd called and told me never to bother them again." He shrugged. "What could I do? I was a kid. There was no way to make the administration listen to me. And even if they didn't believe Mary dropped out on her own, they weren't going to give me the answers I wanted. It was all Carl's fault. One time, I grabbed him and told him I swore I'd see this through until we discovered the truth."

"What happened?"

Steve's eyes were bright red. "Nothing. But Carl—maybe he wasn't school smart—was street smart. He didn't give up anything that might point to him. And after a while I just couldn't do it anymore. I gave up. Eventually I discovered the culinary arts. I started working hard in my major. I didn't forget about Mary, but I just stopped pushing."

I patted his hand.

"You don't understand," he said, jerking away. "I got a great job out of college." He stared at me and spoke slowly. "A great job."

"That's good."

"No," he said. "I got it through Carl's father. He made sure I landed well. He made sure I had everything I needed." He shook his head. "He bought me off."

Suzie looked ready to cry. "I'm sure it was just coincidence."

Steve slammed the table with a fist. "No. It wasn't."

I sat back, unsure where to go from here.

Steve wiped his eyes. "I stopped looking for answers. I failed."

"I'm so sorry," I said.

"There's more," Suzie said.

I glanced at her, then back to Steve, who picked it up again. "Everything went quiet for a long time. We all worked hard, all graduated. Carl moved into bigger and bigger positions of power, and eventually got to his position at the NSA." Steve wagged a finger at me. "I always made it a point to keep up with his career. Just in case. I figured Carl forgot about me. Well, at least until Suzie and I got the TV show. Then, all of a sudden, we're stars." He smiled. "Small stars, but, you know, kinda well known."

I nodded.

"Out of the blue, Carl calls me. About a month ago, I think. Wasn't it?"

Suzie was biting her lip. She nodded.

"He starts out like we're old friends, but pretty soon he's gloating, saying that he remembers what his dad did for me all those years back. He tells me that he never had anything to do with Mary leaving school or killing herself, but he always resented the fact that I believed he did. And that's when he tells me that our positions had been reversed."

"What?" I was totally confused.

"He says that now that he's in charge of NSA investigations, he's going to take a look into my file and see if I've ever been involved in any terrorist activities."

My mouth opened. I didn't know how to respond to that.

Suzie spoke up. "We didn't know who the guests were going to be before we scheduled the White House shoot. If we had, I can tell you that we wouldn't have picked that particular day."

"I've never been involved in any terrorist activities," Steve said. "But my father was a salesman who traveled extensively to the Middle East. Minkus found that interesting. He said he was going to see me hang."

"Literally," Suzie said.

Steve fixed her a look. "Even if he didn't find me guilty of terrorism—and I don't know how he could—he could kill my career." To me, he added, "I think that's what his ultimate goal was. To see me ruined."

"That's a terrible story," I said.

"And that's why we think the NSA might be looking at us now that Minkus is dead," Suzie said. "We had a motive."

Steve stared at the table. "I say: Good riddance to bad rubbish."

"Wow." I knew it would be a while before I could take it all in.

"Don't tell your boyfriend, okay?" Steve asked. "I mean, just in case Minkus was bluffing. Maybe he wasn't looking at me at all. Maybe he was just playing mind games. He was always good at that."

"I don't know what to say."

"Please, just keep this to yourself," Suzie said. "For now. The news says they're working really hard on determining the cause of death. As soon as they figure out it wasn't something he ate"—she tapped on the DVD case—"and they see we didn't do anything to poison his meal, we should be okay. I don't think it would be in anyone's best interests to bring up all this old history."

I licked my lips, realizing that the feeling had come back to my tongue. Now only my brain felt numb.

CHAPTER 14

ON MY WAY HOME, I CALLED BUCKY AND TOLD HIM I'D GOTTEN a copy of the DVD. He and I made plans to go over it the next day and he said he'd call Cyan to include her as well. While I was on the phone, Tom beeped in, and I hung up with Bucky to take the call.

"Hey," I said. "Busy night, but I'm finally heading back. What time were you planning to stop by?"

"Ah . . ." he said. "Looks like plans have changed."

"You're not coming over?"

"No."

"But you mentioned that Craig wanted me to have a look at something. What about that?"

"Craig changed his mind."

"Do you want to stop by anyway?"

He hesitated.

"Forget I suggested it," I said. "Never mind."

"I just think it's best if we aren't seen together too much. At least until this investigation is over."

"Yeah, you said that before." What I wanted to say was that coming over to my apartment was hardly "being seen" together.

"Well," he said awkwardly. "I guess I'll talk to you later."

"Yeah," I said. But my heart wasn't in it.

When I finally made it to my apartment, I was completely worn out from the day's craziness. Voices—more than just those of my mom and nana—and the scent of fresh bakery met me as I unlocked the front door.

"Ollie, is that you?" Mom called.

I tossed my jacket to the side and put my keys in the front bowl. "Sorry I'm so late."

"You hungry?"

I was. After the story Steve had told, we were all so drained that Suzie had forgotten to give me my leftover steak. "What smells so good?"

Mrs. Wentworth, Stanley, and Nana were sitting at my kitchen table, all drinking coffee. Stanley stood up. "Here, you sit down."

I waved him back and poked my nose into the refrigerator.

"I made pork chops," Mom said. "With that topping you like. Want some?"

Having my mom here made me feel the comfort of being a little girl again. She seemed to enjoy bustling about, and as I took a bite of her homemade pork chops, I thought nothing had ever tasted so wonderful. I must have made a noise of pure pleasure, because they all stopped and looked at me.

"Rough day?" Nana asked.

Mouth full, I nodded.

"The news is saying that the president won't be able to make it to Carl Minkus's memorial service," Mrs. Wentworth said. "They're having the wake tomorrow."

Stanley didn't like the fact that the president wasn't planning to attend services for a man who had died under his roof. "Not right," he said. "Sure, I know he's got a country to run, but would it kill him to take a few minutes out to pay his respects?"

None of us answered him. I took another bite.

"Your mother says you were visiting with the SizzleMasters," Mrs. Wentworth said. "How did that go? Do they have any idea what might have gone wrong at dinner?"

Stanley gave her a stern look. "Now you're making it sound like you know for sure that whatever killed Minkus came out of the kitchen. For all we know, he did himself in. He was in the NSA. Maybe he took one of those suicide pills."

Mrs. Wentworth raised a skeptical eyebrow.

"All's I'm saying is that we can't go jumping to conclusions or nothing. We have to wait until somebody finds the answers. Like Ollie here." He turned to me and smiled.

I looked away, but found Mrs. Wentworth staring at me the same way. "I think it's up to you now."

For the second time that night, I nearly spit my food out. This time, instead, I held a hand up in front of my mouth and chewed quickly. "What are you talking about?"

My two neighbors wore twin "Are you a simpleton?" looks on their faces. Mrs. Wentworth patted my hand. "Just do what you've done before. Try to figure out who did it. Before long, you'll have the whole thing solved. And you'll make the headlines again."

"I appreciate your faith in me," I began, "but I think that's exactly what the Secret Service *doesn't* want me to do."

Mrs. Wentworth snorted. "They're just jealous."

The sudden warmth that suffused me had nothing to do with the temperature of the room. It was something much more. I was home, fed, comfortable, and surrounded by family and neighbors who cared about my well-being. And, on top of that, they were convinced I would be able to figure out what the medical examiner, Secret Service, NSA, and other professionals could not. I patted her hand in return. It was nice to feel appreciated.

"Thanks."

UNFORTUNATELY, THE WARM AND FUZZY FEELINGS WERE SHORT-lived. When my newspaper arrived the next morning, I spread it out on the kitchen table, and sucked in sudden panic when I turned to the *Liss Is More* column. Reading the first line reminded me—with the subtlety of a gut-punch—that I'd forgotten to revisit Liss's Web version yesterday to see what comment my mom had left. With the flurry of activity, the plethora of interruptions, and so much on my mind, I'd simply forgotten.

"Oh my God," I said.

Today Liss Is More says: "Thanks, Mom!"

Faithful readers will be interested to know that it seems this lowly column has touched a high-pressure nerve. We caught a live one yesterday. One of our "Anonymous" submitters posted the following (reprinted in its entirety from the Web):

Dear Mr. Liss,

Your column only exists to appeal to the lowest, most base of human interests. Why would you suggest that those working in the White House kitchen might have had anything to do with Carl Minkus's death? Don't you have better things to do? Olivia Paras runs that

kitchen with energy, pride, and dignity. It's your column and the
garbage you and your followers spew that's keeping her from being
able to return to her job. Stop blaming her for canceling the Easter
Egg Roll. It's your fault. You, and people like you, only want to sell
newspapers, rather than find the truth.

Sincerely,
An Angry Reader

My, my. Angry Reader indeed. She asks (and I use the pronoun "she" with confidence) if I have nothing better to do. Well, today I want to say, "Thanks, Mom," because after reading your letter, I did find something very interesting to do. I took a closer look at our country's executive chef and discovered that Ms. Paras's mother and grandmother are currently in town visiting their famous progeny. You, faithful readers, will recall that Olivia Paras has already made a name for herself (can you say "notorious"?) while in our nation's employ. Earlier this week, I broached the idea that Ms. Paras may have gotten bored and played Russian roulette with dinner with no thought to its disastrous consequences, but I gave up that idea after White House press agents suggested I lay off. Fair enough. But yesterday's entreaty by Ms. Paras's mother (and can there be any doubt who wrote that?) now urges me to take a closer look.

Does Ms. Paras care to tell us why she spent so much time meeting in secret with Suzie and Steve—the SizzleMasters—last night? After all, they, too, are under suspicion. Stay tuned, faithful readers. In coming days *Liss Is More* may have more to share about SizzleMaster Steve's history with the dead agent Minkus.

Let's all take this time to look up the word *collusion* in our respective dictionaries, shall we?

"Oh my God," I said again. What had she done?

"What's wrong?" Mom asked, coming in to the kitchen, still in her nightgown.

I expelled a hot breath and had about one second to decide my next move. "Nothing," I said. I shut the paper.

"You look like you've gotten some terrible news, honey." Moving toward the countertop, she started to pour herself a cup of coffee.

"Why don't you shower first," I suggested. "I made that a while ago and it's probably stale. I'll make fresh."

She gave the pot a curious look. "There's plenty in there."

"Yeah, but it's a little weak." I grimaced, lifting my half-filled mug. "You and I both like it stronger. I'll put some of the weaker stuff in the carafe for Nana."

Mom didn't seem entirely convinced that I gave so much thought to our morning coffee, but she shrugged. "All right. I won't be long. What are we doing today, anyway?"

"I have to make a few phone calls," I said. That was an understatement. All I wanted at this moment was for her to leave so I could start damage control. "But I have a few ideas. We'll talk about it after your shower."

Finally, she left the room.

Tom answered on the first ring. "So meddling runs in the family, eh?"

"Oh my God," I said, for the third time. "What am I going to do?"

"*You* are going to do nothing at all," he said. He gave a short laugh, which I thought was inappropriate, given the circumstances. "I guess it's like they say: The apple doesn't fall far from the tree."

"What do you mean by that?"

"The next time I chastise you for getting involved in situations you should stay out of, just remind me it's in your DNA." He laughed again. "Your poor mom. I know she was just trying to help. How is she taking today's new twist?"

Nana came into the room. She helped herself to a cup of coffee.

"She hasn't seen it yet."

"Are you going to show it to her?"

Nana settled down across from me. She squinted over the top of her mug.

"I don't think so."

Tom made a noise. "Do you think that's best?"

I had no idea what was best. I had no idea which way was up at the moment. I said so.

"Listen," Tom said, using his serious voice. "This Liss character is nothing more than a pain in the ass. Don't give him another thought, okay? You got that? People read his column for entertainment, not for news. By next week, they'll have forgotten all of this."

"Not if the Egg Roll is canceled." I was morose and felt like spreading it around. "Then nobody will ever forget. When was the last time they canceled an Egg Roll?" I asked. "I mean, except for weather, or world wars?"

"Ollie." Still the serious tone.

"Liss paints me as a lunatic chef who would risk her guests' safety for another shot in the limelight. Doesn't he understand how much I hate making the front page?" My voice had gone up. Turning my ear toward the hallway, I relaxed when I realized the shower was still running. Nana continued to stare at me, her eyebrows tight.

"Okay," Tom said, more soothingly than I had any right to expect. "Let's just take this slowly. I suggest you ignore Liss. He's the least of your worries right now."

I groaned.

"You called me for a reason," he prompted.

"I have a copy of the DVD from Suzie and Steve," I said. "They gave it to me."

Instead of being pleased, he got angry. "You couldn't get a copy from me, so you went out and got one on your own? Ollie, what did I ask you about staying out of this investigation?"

"That's why I'm telling you. They want me to go over it—heck, they want *you* to go over it—because they believe it will prove that no one in the kitchen could have done anything to Minkus's food."

"First of all . . ." I sensed a lecture coming on. "We aren't going to be able to tell anything from the recording. Give me a break. How would any of us watching know whether that was salt—or arsenic—someone is adding to a dish?"

"Don't you think the fact that we're all willing to make the DVD public is proof of innocence?"

"Hardly proof. No matter how much you, or the SizzleMasters, want to get involved, nothing you say or do will be of any help right now. This death has to be investigated step by step. All options will be kept open until we're able to eliminate—"

"Listen," I said, interrupting him. "There's a reason Suzie and Steve want you to see the DVD."

A heartbeat of silence, then, "A reason."

"I can't tell you what it is, but I—"

"Ollie."

"Trust me here, okay?"

I heard him give an exasperated sigh. "I asked you not to get involved."

I said nothing.

Tom broke the silence. "What did Suzie and Steve tell you?"

Although I wanted to honor Steve's request to keep the information about

Mary and her history with Minkus to myself, Liss's column today intimated that it wouldn't be long before the whole world knew. "They told me something in confidence," I began. "They specifically asked me not to tell you about it."

"And you don't find *that* suspicious?"

"I would, except I know what they're keeping to themselves. Everyone has secrets, Tom."

Another exasperated sigh. "You just can't stay out of things, can you?"

"You told me to go about my business like normal. You told me it was fine to keep in touch with my friends. These are my friends," I said. My voice had gone up again, just as I heard the shower turn off. Nana still listened.

"These are my friends," I said again, more quietly. "And if I have to, I will tell you the story they told me. I don't believe they could have done anything to Carl Minkus, but I do believe there are other reasons they might come under scrutiny."

Sounds came through the receiver that made me believe Tom was scratching his face. "So what am I supposed to do?"

"For one, you can appreciate that I'm keeping you updated on all this, just like you asked me to," I said with a little snap. "I'm not getting involved, but as information comes to me I'm sharing it with you. I think that's fair."

He didn't comment.

"I'm going to take a look at this DVD," I said. "I'll have Bucky and Cyan take a look at it, too. If we see anything weird, I'll tell you immediately."

"Ollie," Tom said gently, "if anyone in that kitchen had intended to kill Carl Minkus, don't you think they would have made sure to do it off-camera?"

Frustration worked its way into my voice. "What am I supposed to do? Just sit on my hands until that medical examiner finally gets off his duff and tells the world it wasn't my fault? This is my career we're talking about."

"I know," he said. "And you know I can't share information with you. What I can tell you is that we're working around the clock to get this thing settled. The best advice I can give you right now is to find something to keep you busy. To take your mind off of the problems."

I blew a raspberry into the phone.

"I understand this isn't easy. Use this time off as a gift. You've got your mother and grandmother there keeping you company. I suggest you enjoy your time with them."

When we hung up, Nana's mouth twisted sideways. "Who hasn't seen what?" she asked.

Hoping my mom was still busy in the bathroom for a few more minutes, I opened the page to Liss's article and turned it to face Nana. I let her read a little bit before explaining, "Mom sent in a comment to his website yesterday. I don't think she realized what a Pandora's box she would open."

Nana put a finger on the paper to hold her spot. "What does Tom say about this?"

"He wants me to ignore it. Pretend it doesn't exist."

Nana kept reading.

I stood and began pacing the small kitchen, thinking about how Bucky's space was so much more the sort of kitchen I should have at home. Quick pang of jealousy. Why was it that when things were bad, suddenly *everything* seemed negative? Why did my tiny kitchen bother me today? It had never bothered me before. But I'd never been served up on a silver platter before, the way Liss was doing—with my mother's help. "How can I ignore that when he's clearly skewering me? I mean, this is personal!"

"What's personal?" Mom asked, as she came into the kitchen. Her hair was still wet, but she was dressed and made up.

Nana answered before I could. "That damn medical examiner."

She gave me a look that warned me not to contradict.

"Why?" Mom asked, making her way around the table to read over Nana's shoulder. "Did he say something more in the paper today?"

As unflappably as anything, Nana turned the page before Mom could see Liss's article. "No, there's nothing in here today about that. We were just talking about Ollie not getting back into the kitchen yet."

Mom gave me a funny look when she noticed the coffee hadn't changed. "I thought you were going to make fresh."

I apologized. "I wound up talking with Tom for quite a while. Sorry. I'll make some now."

She waved me away. "Don't worry about it."

Nana and I shared a conspiratorial look. She pushed herself up from the table, and tucked the newspaper under her arm. "I guess I'll get in the bathroom next."

Mom pointed. "I haven't read that yet."

Nana unfolded the paper, and dropped a few sections back onto the table. "Here's the weather, the fun stuff . . ." She rattled off a few more. "You're lucky I feel generous today," she said with a wink. "Usually if you snooze, you lose."

My mom rolled her eyes good-naturedly, and didn't seem to notice at all that Nana had tucked the front-page section back under her arm.

I did a few morning chores, checked my e-mail, then called Bucky and Cyan.

Mom and Nana were at the kitchen table looking ready to go, when I approached them with an idea. "How about you two come with me to Bucky's place?"

At their confused, expectant looks, I explained.

"First of all, I really wanted you to meet my team, and although this isn't the most optimal of circumstances, I think it could work."

"You've got a funny glimmer in your eye," Nana said.

I pointed to her. "That's because I want to put you both to work. Bucky, Cyan, and I are convinced that Paul Vasquez—he's our chief usher and in charge of just about everything at the White House—will eventually tell us that the Egg Roll is back on. I want to get started on boiling eggs."

"Should you do that?" Mom asked. "Until the medical examiner—"

"This isn't that *CSI* TV show. It may be months until we get a definitive answer." I shuddered at that thought. "I just have to do something. I mean, if the Egg Roll is canceled then we're stuck with a roomful of eggs. I get that. But what if they decide that the event will go on after all? What if they decide that on Sunday afternoon? Then what? We'll never get enough eggs boiled in that amount of time."

Nana said. "I'm up for it."

Mom nodded. "Me, too."

"Good. Bucky's expecting us there later this morning. If we work all afternoon, we can still quit in time to come back here and change before going to Minkus's wake tonight." The idea of going in there by myself was unpleasant at best. And if my family was with me, I figured I could make a polite and fairly quick exit after paying my respects. "You are both planning to come with me, aren't you?"

My mom's face went red. "Of course. I wouldn't want you going alone."

Nana laughed at her. "And you wouldn't want to miss the opportunity to pay your respects to—or should I say flirt with—Kap, would you?"

Darn. I'd forgotten about him.

"At a wake?" my mom asked with a touch of indignance. "I wouldn't do anything like that."

I could have kicked myself for forgetting about Kap. "I can go alone."

"No," Mom said, too quickly. "We wouldn't want you to have to face those Minkuses on your own, honey."

I swallowed my reply.

CHAPTER 15

CYAN PULLED ME TO THE SIDE MOMENTS AFTER WE'D ARRIVED AT
Bucky's. "Did you *see* this place?" she asked gesturing around the rooms with
her eyes. "It's gorgeous. I don't know what I expected, but it sure wasn't this."

Bucky was still near the front door, hanging up coats, making small talk
with my family.

"I know what you mean. I was here the other day for the first time—which
is why I knew his place was perfect for our project. But"—I ran my hand along
the living room sofa again—"purple suede?"

"Is he married?"

We were still talking in whispers. "I asked. He said, 'Not yet.'"

"Lots of work ahead of us today," Bucky said, clapping his hands together.
He seemed unnaturally cheerful, and completely at ease with the four of us
just hanging out at his house. "Let's get started."

Again, he was dressed in shorts, with an apron over. He ushered us all into
the back of the house and his expansive kitchen. Mom and Nana exclaimed
delight when they stepped into the bright, professionally appointed space.
Cyan's mouth dropped and she turned in a slow circle, taking it all in. "Wow,"
she said. "If they ever decide to renovate the White House kitchen, I think you
should design it."

Bucky glanced at me quickly—almost as though he was fearful that I would
take Cyan's comment as a slam against me. "Yeah," I agreed. "Bucky, if they
ever give us the money to redesign the kitchen, you're the man. I can't imagine
anyone doing it better."

He gave a half smile, which was an odd sight. It didn't last long. He clapped his hands again. Bucky was ready to work, and in this domain, he was clearly the boss.

"I arranged for the eggs to be delivered here," he said.

Cyan had opened his super-sized refrigerator and turned to us with a pained look on her face. "This is nowhere near enough." she said. "Looks like maybe ten dozen or so."

My stomach dropped. Bucky had assured me he could handle the egg acquisition, and I'd trusted him to do so, without any double-checking. Bucky shook his head. "The rest are downstairs," he said. "I'll show you."

Nana opted to stay on the main level, but the rest of us traipsed down the steps into the dungeon-like cellar. "Wow," Cyan said, her voice echoing off the stone walls. "It's cold down here."

At the head of our little troupe, Bucky turned. "Exactly," he said. "I keep it at about thirty-six degrees." He opened a heavy door and pointed to a thermometer inside. Flicking on the light, he kept talking, even as the rest of us gasped. "Here we are."

He wasn't kidding. There were eggs . . . everywhere.

"This is almost as big as our storage at the White House," Cyan said in awe. "You could start your own banquet business out of your house."

Bucky winced. I wondered if his fears about our losing our White House positions were working on him. He stepped forward and rested his hand on one of many stainless steel carts filled, top to bottom, with fresh eggs.

"I talked with our friends at the American Egg Board," he said. "They're sympathetic to the situation and after a little coaxing, they agreed to let me hold on to these for transport." He turned to me. "But I had to promise that they'd get them back as soon as the Egg Roll was over."

"No problem," I said. "Bucky, you're a miracle worker."

Again, the half smile. "Have you talked with Paul recently?"

"I called him just before we left," I said. "No updates yet."

"So, we could be doing all this work for nothing?"

"We could."

Bucky nodded. "Well, you're the boss."

"And I think this is a great idea," Cyan said. "It sure beats staying home waiting for the phone to ring. At least we're doing something."

Upstairs, we settled ourselves into an assembly line of sorts. We estimated we had approximately six thousand eggs on site. "That's a great start," I said.

"If we can get these done, then maybe in the next few days we'll be able to pick up the rest, and by the time Monday rolls around, we'll be all set."

Cyan and I were the runners. We went up and down Bucky's back stone steps, carrying large square crates of eggs. Mom and Nana made sure to gently place each and every one into giant pots of cold water, easing them in to prevent cracking.

Once the eggs were boiled, Bucky ran them under cold water, then dried and placed them back into their cradles. "Why do you bother to dry them off?" Nana asked. "I never do that. The heat makes the water evaporate."

He pointed into one of the crates. "If they're not dry, they tend to drip and then the eggs sit in little puddles of water." He shook his head. "I don't like that."

"But when we dye them, they'll just get wet again." Nana said.

"And I'll dry them again," he said patiently. The caustic, angry Bucky we knew from our White House kitchen was surprisingly gentle with my mom and nana. "You see, if we let them sit in the crates wet"—he wadded up a cloth and dipped it into one of the egg holders—"we would have to then go in one by one and dry out these spaces out. If we don't, we'll wind up with little round water spots at the base of every colored egg." He wrinkled his nose. "Not nice."

While each new batch of eggs boiled, Nana, Mom, Cyan, and I took each and every dried egg by hand, and dipped them into vivid pinks, blues, greens, and yellows.

Eggs, eggs, and more eggs. I was going to dream about eggs tonight. After so many hours surrounded by steam, heat, dripping dye, and eggy smells, I started feeling just a little bit punchy.

"Hey Bucky," I said. "You did an *eggcellent* job of getting all this together."

He rolled his eyes. Cyan laughed.

Mom said, "Relax. It's just a *yolk*."

Nana held up a pink-dyed egg. She giggled. "Isn't this an *eggsquisite* color?" This time we all groaned.

Bucky glanced up at the clock for about the third time in as many minutes. Cyan noticed, too. She and I exchanged a look.

He turned to us. "How many more eggs are left downstairs?"

Cyan stood. "I'll go check."

"No," he said quickly. "No, that's okay. I just was wondering."

Again he checked the wall clock.

"Are you *eggspecting* someone?" Cyan asked.

While the rest of us smiled at her attempt, Bucky frowned. He wiped his hands on his apron. "I think we should start wrapping up for today, don't you?" Without waiting for an answer, he poured out the boiling water, even though the eggs still had another minute to cook. "It's getting late and I know you wanted me to take a look at that DVD tonight. You made me a copy, right?"

"I thought . . ." I gestured to encompass myself and Cyan, "We were all planning to watch it together."

"I lost track of time," he said without apology. "Did you make an extra copy? Can you leave it with me? I'll get to it tonight."

"No, I didn't," I said, bewildered. "I didn't think we'd need any extras." Mom and Nana stood and started to clean up.

"No, no," Bucky said, stopping them. "I'll take care of it."

"You're acting a little weird all of a sudden," I said.

"Is it so strange to have another commitment?" he asked, the old crustiness back in place. "I told you I lost track of time and I'd rather not . . ."

Bumping sounds from the back of the house silenced us all. There was the unmistakable sound of a door opening, closing, and of footsteps coming up the back way. I turned to Bucky. He looked miserable.

A clear voice called out, "Buck?" Female voice. Slightly familiar. "Can you give me a hand?"

He'd gone red in the face. "Hang on," he called, then bolted for the back door.

We heard low conversation, all of us leaning closer to the door to hear better. They weren't having an argument, but Bucky's lower-timbered voice sounded terse. A moment later he came through the door carrying two eco-friendly shopping bags jammed with groceries, wearing a look of resigned indignation.

He stopped in the doorway and I got the impression that he intended to stay there, blocking our view. "Buck," the voice said, from behind him. "Can I get through?"

She was tall, with clear Irish skin, long red hair, and a smile as wide as the Potomac. Recognition kicked in a half-second later. "Brandy?" I said.

She placed the bags she carried on the nearest open countertop and came over to greet me. "How are you, Ollie?" With a glance around the kitchen, she said, "Looks like you've gotten a lot done today." Long-limbed and bright-eyed, she always wore an aura of confidence that allowed her to carry off such an unusual moniker.

Mom and Nana were looking at me, mildly perplexed. Cyan was wide-eyed. "Brandy," she said. "How are things going?"

I introduced my family, relying on my autopilot politeness to carry me through. When Cyan and I exchanged a glance a moment later, Brandy caught it. "Yeah," she said, tossing her head back in a laugh, "I'm the big secret." She held up her fingers to make air-quotation marks, then pointed at the back door. "Can you believe he was trying to convince me to tell you I was just making a delivery?" She laughed again. "Sorry, honey," she said, kissing him on the cheek. Even though he was obviously uncomfortable, he didn't seem entirely displeased by her display of affection.

Brandy had been our liaison to the Egg Board for as long as I'd been working at the White House. She was great. "How long have you two . . ." I gestured to encompass the house.

She glanced at Bucky, whose lips were tight. Then she winked at me. "Long time."

Inwardly, I groaned. I think I'd actually tried to set her up with another White House staffer some time ago.

Little had I known. About Brandy—about my colleague Bucky. To me, he'd always been a crochety older guy, brilliant in the kitchen, but difficult to deal with. Brandy was about five to seven years older than I was, and suddenly, next to her, Bucky seemed much younger. Talk about a paradigm shift.

"Hey," I said in delayed realization. "No wonder you were able to get all these eggs delivered here."

Brandy flung a grin at me. "It pays to have friends in helpful places."

"*Eggsactly!*" I said.

Mom and Nana were confused, but rolling with the punches. The same couldn't be said for Cyan. "You mean," she said, "all this time we've been working together, you two have been able to keep a secret relationship going?"

Bucky made a face, then turned his back to us. "Better than some people."

I felt my face redden. Brandy patted Bucky on the shoulder as she passed him to get to the fridge. "How is your handsome Secret Service boyfriend?" she asked.

I shook my head. "Minkus's death makes things a little rocky."

Brandy wrinkled her nose. "Yeah, I can imagine. Tough times. But Tom's a great guy. You'll be fine."

I nodded, not entirely sure I believed her—and at the same time amazed that she even knew that Tom and I were together.

Bucky had stopped cleaning up. "Seeing as how we're all here now, we might as well finish the job."

"Is anybody hungry? I can order in," Brandy asked. "I would offer to whip up something—heck, I've got plenty of groceries—but the fact that I've got not one, but three chefs here, is a little intimidating."

I was about to demur, but Bucky mentioned an ethnic carry-out place he liked. "If we have something delivered, we'll all be able to check out that DVD."

For about the fifth time that day, Bucky made my jaw drop.

TWO HOURS LATER, WE HAD GOTTEN MORE EGGS BOILED, THE kitchen cleaned, and the DVD started. Bucky maintained control of the remote and we fell into a rhythm of watching, then stopping, then discussing, all aspects of the dinner preparation.

Nana, on the purple couch next to my mom, had fallen asleep shortly after Bucky hit "Play" for the first time.

"This is all great," I said, when we'd finished dissecting our performances and had restarted the tape from the beginning, "but the camera people were more concerned about angles. Look." I pointed toward the screen, where Suzie was arranging salad greens on a plate. "Even though there are a bunch of cameras rolling, most of the angles are artsy, keeping focus on the plated food and our faces. All the busy preparation is going on in the background. There's no way to see if anyone dropped something into Minkus's food."

Bucky, looking thoughtful, pointed the remote at the television, but didn't press any buttons. Cyan stared at the screen as though waiting for it to tell her something. Brandy asked my mother if she'd like more iced tea.

"Maybe," Bucky said, "we should be looking at who's staying off-camera."

Together we accounted for everyone in the kitchen staff, including Suzie and Steve. Occasionally someone left the room—to get something from storage, or from the refrigerators, or for any number of reasons. With everyone in constant motion, there was no way to determine any unnecessary off-camera forays. Even after studying the outtakes.

"If there was anything in Minkus's food, I doubt it was in the salad," I said. "Everyone had that. Same with a few of the sides, and dessert. It had to be the entrée. Otherwise there would have been too much chance that he didn't get the right one."

As soon as the words left my mouth, I sat up.

"You don't think that maybe it was the salad—or the dessert—and it was meant for someone else?" Cyan asked.

The thought was too terrible to contemplate. Had someone targeted President Campbell and missed? I shook my head. "Let's not get crazy here. Let's just deal with what we know."

"We know squat," Bucky said.

Mom and Brandy got up and went into the kitchen. After another five minutes of futile food-prep-watching, I took a look at my watch and realized we were running much later than I'd expected. "I have to go to Minkus's wake tonight," I said, standing.

Cyan and Bucky both said, "What?" so quickly, it startled Nana awake.

I gave them the lowdown on Ruth Minkus's phone call.

"That's a little odd," Cyan said.

Mom was still out of the room, so I lowered my voice. "Not when you understand the back story." I told her about Kap and about his efforts to smooth things over between Ruth Minkus and me. "Probably just because he's attracted to my mom."

Nana had roused herself enough to add, "He sure doesn't try to hide it."

"So, you're actually going to the wake?" Cyan asked disbelievingly.

"I hate those things," Bucky said.

I gave him a look. "Like anyone enjoys them."

I had no desire to visit a funeral home tonight, but I hardly felt able to refuse. Ruth had asked me to come. And though I barely knew the woman, I had to believe she would not have taken the time to call me if she hadn't felt compelled to. Who's to say how different people deal with grief? Maybe I represented closure for her.

After stopping back at my apartment to shower off the day's egg smell and to change into appropriate clothing, my family and I drove to the funeral home in a Maryland suburb.

"Don't they usually have services in the Capitol for big shots like Minkus?" Nana asked.

I smiled at her in my rearview mirror. "I think they save that honor for presidents," I said. "Besides, this place is probably near the Minkus home. I'm sure Ruth made the final decision on where her husband would be waked."

"Took them long enough," Nana said with a sniff.

"They had to wait for the autopsy," I said. My heart did that speed-beat thing it always did when I thought about how much my career hung on the medical examiner's findings. I knew things moved a lot more slowly than they did on television, but it had already been four days.

My mom was riding shotgun and was staring out at the scenery as we drove. "You okay?" I asked.

She had been twisting the rings on her fingers. "Fine, fine."

I waited.

"I was just thinking about your dad."

"Still miss him?" I asked.

"Every day."

CHAPTER 16

RUTH MINKUS HAD CHOSEN THIS FUNERAL HOME WITH CARE. The parking lot was expansive, and the venue stately. I offered to drop Nana off under the huge canopy-covered entrance, but she snapped good-naturedly, "What, are you saying I'm too old to walk?"

I shook my head and parked in one of the last available spots, about a half block from the front door. We walked past dozens of dark government-issue sedans and shiny, expensive imports, my pumps making lonely taps on the sidewalk. Outside, people mingled. Men and women in business suits stood around in small groups. A few of them smoked, and all of them looked up to see who was arriving. Just as quickly, they returned to their conversations, dismissing us as unimportant. I was okay with that. People didn't often recognize me without my tunic and toque. Tonight, I was grateful for the measure of anonymity.

There had to be a hundred floral pieces in the chapel, all sadly bright and all giving off that peculiar scent that let you know you were at a funeral, even if you were blindfolded. The newspaper obituary had requested donations to charity in lieu of flowers, but apparently lots of mourners didn't get that memo. Either that, or this was yet another place where even politics didn't die. An impressive floral arrangement might not provide the family much solace, but it had the potential to say a lot about the generosity of the giver.

Well-dressed individuals waited in line to pay their respects to Ruth and Joel Minkus—there were at least fifty people in front of us. As we inched forward, I took the opportunity to read the cards on some of the floral sprays. Two huge red, white, and blue arrangements with gold ribbons flanked the casket. My mom raised her eyebrows, obviously impressed. "Those are probably from the White House," I said. Then, "Hey, look at this."

They leaned close. "It's from his health club." The three of us exchanged a look of amazement. "Geez, when a big shot dies, everybody sends flowers, huh?"

Over the course of the next ten minutes, we read all the other gift cards within our reach, but we hadn't moved more than a few feet.

"Maybe we can just sign the book and leave?" I suggested.

If my mom had been hoping to see Kap tonight, she clearly was dissuaded by the press of the crowd. "Maybe that would be best."

Nana was scanning the room, eyes sharp. "Where's the shrine?" she asked. We both looked at her.

"You know—the poster board with pictures of Minkus. Milestones. Birth, marriage, vacations, his kid being born and growing up." She made a 360-degree turn, twisting, as she did, to peer around the gathered family and friends.

I pointed to a table on the room's far left where a silver-framed computer monitor stood. "No homemade poster," I said. "Nowadays people opt for a digital display."

She fixed me with a skeptical look. "You mean the family doesn't sit around and laugh and talk and cry as they make the posters and remember all the good times together?"

"Sure they do," I said. "But now, instead of messing up the original photographs with tape or glue, the funeral home scans them and presents them as a slide show."

"This I gotta see," she said. And she was off.

"Don't they have those in Chicago?" I asked Mom.

She shrugged. "Maybe the rich folks do."

I guided her out of line and sought out the line for the guest book. "With this crowd, Ruth Minkus wouldn't have even noticed us. I'm sorry to have pulled you and Nana out for this."

"Don't worry about it, honey. I'm just happy I raised a girl who does things right. I'm proud of you for coming here even though you didn't feel like it."

"Olivia Paras?"

I turned. A short gentleman extended his hand to me. Like all the other men here, he was wearing a suit, but unlike the other mourners, he wore a smile. "I'm very glad to make your acquaintance," he said. "I'm Phil Cooper. This is my wife, Francine."

I shook his hand and that of the knockout blonde woman next to him.

"I'm very sorry for all the trouble since Sunday's dinner," he said. "And, if

I may say so without sounding crass, I truly enjoyed the meal you prepared for us." He gave a self-conscious shrug. "I was enjoying the entire evening up until . . . well . . ."

He turned toward the casket for emphasis. He didn't need to do that. We all knew what he meant.

"Thank you," I said, not entirely certain that was the proper response.

Francine sidled up to her husband and tucked her hand through his arm. "It really was a wonderful meal," she said. "It was my first time visiting the White House—you know, as a guest. Can you believe it? I've lived here in D.C. my whole life, but I've only done the normal tours. I was so excited when Phil and I got invited." Her face was pink with animation and she smiled much more brilliantly than one should at a funeral home—no matter what the circumstances. "I had such a nice time. It's unbelievable."

"Thank you," I said again, this time wondering what, exactly, she meant by "unbelievable." Dinner at the White House or the fact that her husband's boss had dropped dead after the meal? Nodding acknowledgment, I searched for an excuse to step away. I was near enough to the end of the guest book line, so I stepped in, hoping it would move quickly and we could get out of there.

Phil stepped a little closer to me, speaking quietly. I had to strain to hear him over the din of conversation surrounding us. "Have you heard anything more about what happened that night?"

I shook my head, thinking it was an odd question for a security agent to be asking the executive chef. "Have you?"

"Not much," he said, glancing around. I got the impression he was making sure no one could overhear us. "What's happening with the Egg Roll Monday? And what about your staff? Any idea when you might be cleared?"

Since when did federal agents care about the kitchen staff? "We're still waiting for word."

The conversation was beginning to sound like something from a bad spy movie. It got worse when Cooper gestured with his eyes. "Look who's here."

I glanced over to the corner, near the back, where an elderly man hunched over his cane. "Who is he?"

"You don't recognize him?"

I looked again. "No."

Cooper came closer, so that he and I were now facing the same direction. His wife had disengaged herself from his arm and was now talking with my mom. "That's Howard Liss."

Instinctively I gasped, resisting the overwhelming urge to march over and tell him off. Not good form at a wake. "What's he doing here?"

"He likes to 'immerse himself' in his stories. At least that's his claim. Personally, I see him as a vulture, circling and hoping for some new tidbit to exploit." Cooper winked at me. "I just wanted to let you know because you seem to be on his radar lately."

"Thanks."

"Rumor has it he's targeting me next."

"Where did you hear that?"

Cooper didn't answer. "It was very nice to meet you, Ms. Paras. I wish you the best of luck."

He left as Nana returned.

When we finally made it to the front of the book line, I wrote my name and address and then turned away to allow the next person access. "Aren't you going to take a holy card?" Nana asked.

"No."

"Hmph," she said, as she reached in to snag one for herself. "I'll take it then."

"I think we can sneak out now," I said, speaking quietly. I told them both what Phil Cooper had told me. The three of us stole peeks at Howard Liss.

"He looks like a bad person," Mom said. "I can tell these things."

I thought he looked rather benign. I don't know what I expected, but it wasn't a slim, white-haired, distinguished fellow leaning on a carved cane. His photo in the newspaper must be at least a decade old, I decided. Instead of a hard-hitting reporter who may or may not twist the facts to suit his journalistic fancy, this guy looked like a college professor. Somebody who taught economics, maybe. Or philosophy. And definitely nearing retirement.

"Let's get out of here before he sees us," I said.

We had just made it to the chapel doorway when we stopped short.

"Corinne!" Kap said with a bit too much pleasure for my tastes.

My mother said, "Kap!" with about the same expression.

"I'm so happy you were able to make it," he said. Turning to me, he squinted. "How was Ruth to you tonight? Did she seem better?"

"Ah," I said, hedging. "We didn't get a chance to talk with Ruth one-on-one." I gestured vaguely in the direction of the casket and the crowd of people surrounding it. It dawned on me that I hadn't even gotten a glimpse of the deceased. "The line is so long . . ."

"We can't have that," he said. Taking my mother by the arm, he smiled down at me. "It's so hard for Ruth to talk to everyone she intended to. She would be very upset if you left."

"I don't want to bother—"

"No bother at all." He leaned down to speak close to my ear. "As a matter of fact, Ruth wants to ask you something."

The skepticism must have shown on my face, because he was quick to add, "I don't know what it is. She seems to be pushing for answers when there are none."

"I hope there are answers soon," I said, my impatience with being trapped at this funeral parlor with no clear means of escape showing through. "I don't blame her a bit. As soon as they vindicate the kitchen, I'll be able to get back to work."

Kap's reaction surprised me. "They haven't allowed you back yet?"

This was in the news almost daily. I wanted to ask the man if he lived in a cave, but politeness won out. "No. Not until the medical examiner clears us."

Howard Liss had sidled up to us and had heard most of our conversation. "Hello," he said. "You're Olivia Paras, aren't you? I'm—"

"I know who you are."

He didn't extend his hand. Thank goodness, because I would have refused to shake it. He tilted his head with a sly smile. "I see you've been reading my column."

"Yes," I said. "And I suppose I have you to thank for all my time off."

"That's one way to look at it." His eyes lasered in on mine, like Arnold Schwarzenegger's in the first *Terminator* movie. "You haven't gotten word that you're allowed back in the kitchen yet?"

"No," I said, keeping my voice light. "But if we were to be allowed back in, I'm sure you'd be the first to know."

His mouth twitched. Like he was enjoying this.

Which meant it was time for me to leave. "If you'll excuse us," I began.

"And you must be Olivia's mother," Liss asked, ignoring me and turning to my mom. "A pleasure."

I touched her arm. "Mom. Let's go."

Kap insinuated himself between them. "Why are you here, anyway?" he asked Liss.

They were about the same age. Both tall and white-haired. But where Liss had a cane, and the milky-white complexion of a man who spent his sunshine in front of a glowing computer screen, Kap was olive-complected, fit, and muscular. He looked like a poster boy for Viagra commercials.

Liss pulled himself up to full height, which was about an inch shorter than Kap's. "I was going to ask Ms. Paras the exact same thing." Again, the laser eyes. "I don't understand," he said, then a corner of his mouth curled up. "What is your connection to the deceased?" he asked. "Other than the fact that you fed him his final meal?"

Tiny Nana, with her big heart—and suddenly loud voice—thrust her holy card into Liss's hand. "You know what this means? You are at a wake, mister. If you can't behave properly, I think maybe you should go home."

People around us began to take notice.

Liss smiled down at the card in his hand. He pointed to Minkus's death date on the back of the picture of Saint George. "See this?" he asked. Without waiting for us to answer, he said, "This isn't right. Carl Minkus wasn't destined to die on *this* date." He shook his head. "And if you had anything to do with it, Ms. Paras, the world needs to know that."

My mom muttered, "You're despicable."

"Maybe so," he said. "But it's people like you who read my column." He smiled. "And when you respond so predictably, you keep me comfortably employed."

Much to my dismay, Ruth Minkus spotted us talking with Liss. She immediately made her way over to us, Joel at her side.

I desperately wanted to run.

"Olivia," she said, as she drew closer. "How kind of you to come."

If she recognized Liss, she didn't show it. She didn't even acknowledge Kap. I took Ruth Minkus's hand. "I'm sorry."

Biting her lip, she looked away. Liss's eyes narrowed and his gaze bounced among us all. I released Mrs. Minkus's hand, expressed my condolences to Joel, then turned my body to exclude Liss from the group. Mom and Nana came in around me, and Kap followed, effectively closing Liss off from our conversation. "I don't want to keep you from your guests," I said to Ruth.

She glanced toward Kap, fixing him with a cool stare. "Would you mind? I need a moment alone with Olivia."

My mind screamed, *"No!"* I wished we had never come to this thing, no matter how much Ruth had entreated. "We really should be going."

Ruth turned to Joel, who seemed torn. "Go mingle," she said, giving his arm a little shove. "Your father would want you to talk to everyone here. To thank them."

Reluctant to leave his mother, he tried to argue.

"I'm fine right now," she said. "And this is important. Go on."

Joel left.

I wasn't keen on leaving my mother in Kap's clutches, but she was a savvy, grown woman. There wasn't much I could—or should—do to stop her. Plus, Nana was with her. I wondered for a moment if this was how parents felt when their children started dating: worried, protective, unwilling to let go. I blew out a breath and followed Ruth to the far left of the room. We were near the digital display where the slideshow of Carl Minkus photos played. The current shot was one of him in uniform.

Ruth's eyes clenched shut and she looked away.

This side of the room had at least as many—if not more—floral arrangements than the other side had. I tried not to breathe in the sickeningly sweet scent as I read the gift cards in an effort to give Ruth a chance to compose herself. After a moment, she spoke. "I really have to get back to greet everyone who came here." Her eyes widened and she again looked ready to cry. "But I needed to ask you something."

"Of course."

In the space of the seconds it took for her to speak again, I wondered what was hardwired into our brains that prompted us to forgive transgressions and promise cooperation to those who grieved. Ruth Minkus had been horribly rude to me not two days earlier. And yet, here I was.

"I read Mr. Liss's column," she began. "And I know you're friends with Suzie and Steve."

I waited.

She blinked a few times. "There was something about Steve my husband didn't care for."

I still waited.

"Do you . . . that is, would you have any idea what the bad blood is between them?"

Time for my best defense—deflection. "What makes you believe there was bad blood between them?"

Her eyes were glazed as though reflecting on old memories. Whatever she found there made her mouth tighten. "Carl wouldn't tell me. And I knew better than to press." Blinking again, she stared at the front of the room, where her husband lay in repose. I knew she couldn't see him through the throng, but her breaths became short and shallow. Looking away, she suppressed a shudder. "If I would have known the SizzleMasters were in the kitchen that day . . ."

"You don't really believe that they could have had anything to do with your husband's death?"

Ruth Minkus's face flushed and I could see how much of a toll this conversation was having on her. Her entire body trembled. "Did they say anything to you? Did they do anything suspicious the day of the dinner?" She put both hands on my forearm. "Please, if you can think of anything that can help me make this go away, please do."

My logical brain wanted to tell her that nothing would make this sorrow go away except time, but I knew that victims, and families of victims, sometimes needed closure in order to begin the grieving process. With the suddenness of Minkus's death, Ruth needed anything she could to help her hold on. That's what she was searching for. I couldn't blame her.

"I'll do what I can. But right now, you probably have to get back."

She nodded. "Thank you for coming, Olivia. May I call you Ollie?"

"Sure," I said. Unable to resist my natural impulse, I again took her hand. "If there's anything I can do, please let me know."

WE HADN'T GOTTEN A HALF BLOCK AWAY FROM THE FUNERAL home when Nana piped up from the backseat. "Odd," she said.

I glanced at her through the rearview mirror to see her staring out the side window, with a look of concentration. Like she was trying to work something out in her head.

My mom twisted in her seat. "What's odd?"

"The photos on that digital whatchamawhoozis."

Relieved to be away from the place, and finding her choice of words humorous, I smiled. "What was wrong with them?"

Nana shook her head. "Not 'wrong' exactly." She made a face. "Just incomplete, somehow."

I hadn't spent much time checking out the digital display, and had only caught that one quick glimpse of Minkus in uniform.

"I mean," Nana continued, "when I go to these wakes, I always see pictures from the person's childhood—and college pictures—and wedding pictures."

She resumed looking out the window. "The only pictures here were recent ones. Or political ones. I mean, I think there were three different shots of him with presidents."

"Maybe that's what Carl Minkus would have wanted," Mom said.

I nodded. "I'm sure it is. He was climbing the ladder, no two ways about it."

"By making enemies along the way."

I glanced again at Nana in the backseat. She was thinking about Joe McCarthy, I could tell.

"Who was that big military guy with all the medals on his uniform?" she asked.

There had to have been a dozen well-decorated military types in attendance. "Which one?"

She described him well enough for me to recognize. "General Brighton. He's another big hot shot," I said. "Why?"

"He was talking with your boyfriend."

"What?" I asked. "Tom was there?"

A half-second later I realized I'd jumped to an erroneous conclusion. Nana tapped Mom on the shoulder. "No," Nana said to me. "He was talking with Kap. For quite a while."

"Washington is a small place," I said, trying to process that "boyfriend" comment as it related to my mother. "Almost everyone knows everyone else."

"Something about their conversation," Nana said.

"You eavesdropped?"

"Don't I wish! I couldn't get close enough to really hear everything they were saying."

I was reminded of Tom's comment about the apple not falling far from the tree.

"But you heard something?"

"They both used words like China and classified," she said, clearly proud of herself.

She must have caught the look on my face, because she added, "I *did* hear them say that. They were about the only words I could make out, but they were clear as day. Of course, they also said Minkus's name. Several times." She held up a finger. "The thing is—I could tell from their body language that whatever it was, it was really important."

When we got home I decided to leave a voicemail for Paul Vasquez, and I was surprised when he personally picked up his phone.

"Good to hear from you, Ollie. How are you holding up?"

We talked for a while before I hit him with my big request. "Is there any way at all we can get back into the kitchen?"

I heard him take a breath, as though preparing to let me down, so I interrupted.

"This may sound stupid, Paul, but at the Minkus wake tonight nobody really seemed to pay me any mind. I think the big theory suggesting the kitchen staff had anything to do with Minkus's death has just about died down."

"You attended Carl Minkus's wake?" There was uneasiness in Paul's voice. "I didn't realize you knew him."

"I didn't," I explained hastily. "I met Ruth Minkus for the first time just a few days ago at Arlington, and she insisted I attend."

He was silent for a moment. "If it were anyone else, I wouldn't believe it. Odd things seem to happen around you, Ollie."

"I know," I said. "I'm trying to change that."

He was silent for a heartbeat. "What about Suzie and Steve?"

I knew what he wasn't saying: that even if it hadn't been any of our staff members, we were—that is, I was—still responsible for every plate that left the kitchen. If Suzie and Steve were guilty of poisoning Minkus, my head wouldn't just roll. It would bounce down the stairs.

"I don't think they had anything to do with it."

"Oh, Ollie," he said with resignation. "I wish I could make the decision this minute to bring you and your team back, but my hands are tied. I'm sorry."

"Do you know if there has been any progress at all?" I asked, wanting to prolong the call. It was my only tie to the White House right now, and it seemed a lifeline. The longer we talked, I reasoned, the better the chance that an aide would rush in and tell Paul the ban had been lifted. "Are we expecting any news soon?"

Another resigned sigh. "You know I would tell you if I could."

"Yeah," I said.

"I'm working to get you back here," he said with the first glimmer of cheer I'd heard all night. "But I hope you're not planning to stir anything up."

I thought about my promise to Tom. "Don't worry. I'm behaving myself."

But I wondered if Tom realized how much that was killing me.

CHAPTER 17

BACK AT MY APARTMENT, OVER MILK AND COFFEE CAKE, I CALLED everyone to order. "Listen," I said, "remember when those kids bullied me when I was little?"

Mom and Nana nodded.

"And remember how you told me that by giving in to my fears, I was allowing them power over me?"

Again, they nodded.

"Well, isn't that what Liss is doing?" I asked.

Mom nodded. "That's exactly right."

"Let's promise ourselves not to read his articles anymore," I said. "Let's refuse to let him have power over us."

"I like that attitude, Ollie," Mom said.

Nana yawned. "Me, too. As of right now—no more Liss."

IN THE MORNING, WHEN MOM ASKED, "ANYTHING NEW IN THE headlines?" her tone was light, but her eyes asked if I'd cheated and peeked at what Liss had to say.

"More unrest in China," I said, not rising to the bait. "Can you believe this?" I pointed. "The Chinese government is now claiming that the United States is responsible for the double-assassination."

Her interest was piqued. She leaned over my shoulder as Nana came in, freshly showered and dressed to go out. We both looked up. "Where are you going?" I asked.

"I have a very good feeling about today," she said, patting her fanny pack. "I want to be ready."

"Good," I said. "Maybe I can take you to see more of Washington."

"Wow," Mom said, scanning the article. "According to this, the two men who were killed had been wanted for questioning by the United States. The Chinese government is now saying it was the Americans who assassinated them instead."

"That doesn't sound right."

"Read it yourself."

I did. The story was written by a U.S. correspondent clearly attempting to distance himself from any factual inaccuracies. He repeatedly talked about his sources and suggested, more than once, that presented facts should not be taken as true until proven. But, he also discussed the wild claims of the Chinese government and what it might mean to the United States if their allegations were true.

"So," I said, slowly, trying to distill the information down to its key points. "They're saying that they sent spies here and once we discovered them, we went over there to kill them? That seems so wrong." I shook my head. "That can't be the whole story."

Mom and Nana looked at me.

"Think about it. If they have two spies who have given them information on the United States—and God help us if they got anything important—why would there be any need to kill them? The two men were back in China, for some time. I'm sure they had been debriefed. What possible motive would the United States have to kill them at that point?"

"You know as well as I do that our government does plenty of things in secret," Mom said.

"True," I acknowledged. "But this seems pretty far-fetched. Now, if those Chinese spies gave their government bad information"—I shrugged—"There might be repercussions from above. But they shouldn't blame us for it. The United States gets enough bad-mouthing as it is."

"Other countries are just jealous," Nana said.

We both smiled at her.

"You two seem pretty chipper this morning," she continued. "I take it that means neither of you read that *Liss Is More* filth."

"You would be right," I said.

A knock at my front door. Being on the thirteenth floor in a building that required a buzz-up limited the possibilities of who it could be.

"I'll get it," I said, and wasn't surprised to see Mrs. Wentworth.

She held today's newspaper aloft, her arthritic right hand clamped around its edge, her other hand gripping her cane. "How come you're still here?"

I was about to ask what she meant when she pulled her cane up and used it to move me out of the way. "Looks like your friend Liss scooped everybody this time."

Before I could stop her, she'd tottered into the kitchen. "Good morning, ladies," she said. Then, catching sight of the newspaper on the table, she turned to me with a glare of impatience. "How come you didn't tell me you already saw it?"

"What are you talking about?" I asked. "Liss? No way we're reading him anymore. The lies he prints—"

She made an impatient face. "The guy is good." Waving away my protestations to the contrary, she said, "Yes, yes, I know what he's been saying lately. And I know he's been taking pokes at you. But if you don't look at his conjecture—if you just look at his facts—he's been pretty damned accurate so far."

"Accurate?" I started to protest. "I don't think so."

"Well, you better hope he is this time."

She splayed the newspaper out before us. Standing back, she smiled at us expectantly. "Nice to be the bearer of good news for once," she said.

Curiosity got the better of me, as it usually does, and I leaned forward. I scanned quickly, looking for what might have spurred Mrs. Wentworth to come knocking at my door. And then I found it:

And You Read It Here First

We join the White House in saying, "Welcome back!"

Liss Is More has learned that the White House kitchen staff has been officially cleared of suspicion in Carl Minkus's unexpected death. Word is that the staff will be notified shortly and will be expected to return to work immediately. *Liss Is More* also has it on good authority that the president and First Lady have had their fill of food prepared by well-intentioned but ill-trained Secret Service personnel. I know my good friend

Executive Chef Olivia Paras will be delighted by this new turn of events, both for herself and for her staff.

Side note to Ollie: See? You can stop blaming me for the cloud of suspicion that hung over your head. I just report the facts. I don't invent them.

"'My good friend'?" I asked, fuming. "How does he come up with this stuff?"

Mrs. Wentworth tapped the words. "It sells papers, kiddo."

"Yeah, well, maybe I'll cancel my delivery." As angry as I was at Liss in general, I was mostly furious at his assertion that my staff and I had been welcomed back to the White House. "Accurate? I don't think so. If he were accurate, wouldn't I have heard from our chief usher by now?"

At that moment, a phone rang. The sound was faint and the tune wasn't the one I used for my cell phone, but I instinctively turned toward the little device and picked it up. "Not me," I said.

My mom got a split-second quizzical look on her face, then jumped up. "That's mine," she said, clearly surprised. "I don't get many phone calls, so I didn't . . ."

We missed the rest of her words as she turned into the bedroom. We heard soft scuffling sounds, then the tune ended and my mom said, "Hello."

Two seconds later, she shut the bedroom door.

"A gentleman caller?" Mrs. Wentworth asked.

Nana snorted. "And I think I know exactly who that gentleman caller is."

"Kap," I said. I had forgotten about their "date" today.

"Now don't get all worked up, honey," Nana said, patting my arm like I was a four-year-old. "Your mom is allowed a little bit of fun while she's out here."

Her words hit their mark. I had wanted to make this trip the best Mom and Nana had experienced. I'd wanted to make them love Washington, D.C., as much as I did—by showing them the White House from the inside. By letting them walk the halls—not like tourists, but like insiders. Instead, the vacation had been sliced to ribbons by Minkus's untimely death, and my obsession with getting back into the kitchen.

I had to face facts: The only real highlight this entire trip for my mom was her flirtation with Kap. In less than a week, Mom and Nana would be back in Chicago and Kap would still be here. Why was I behaving like an overprotective mother, trying to thwart my mom's happiness? If she wanted to spend time with a man her age, a man who was clearly interested in her, then why shouldn't she?

I argued both sides in my mind even as Nana and Mrs. Wentworth carried on a separate conversation. I had just about convinced myself that Kap's phone call was a good thing for my mom's ego when she emerged from the bedroom, her face flushed.

"Mom," she said to Nana in a voice that held slight urgency, "you won't mind if I take some time this afternoon, will you?" Almost as an afterthought, she turned to me. "You don't mind either, right?"

Nana spoke before I could. "'Course not, Corinne." She slapped the back of her hand against my forearm. "Right, Ollie?"

Mrs. Wentworth asked the question. "Kap taking you out?"

In that instance, I felt a resurgence of fear. All the arguing I'd done with myself went out the window. There was something not right about Kap. I sensed he was not all he appeared to be, and if there was one thing I knew, it was to trust my gut. I couldn't let my mother go out with him. Not alone. It was all too convenient that he'd popped into our lives just at this time. What was he really after?

"Yes," Mom said. "He and I are going to dinner. But we plan to tour more of the National Mall first."

"I thought we were all going to do that today," I said, petulance creeping into my voice. "I thought we were all going to go together."

Mom smiled. "I know how busy you are, Ollie . . ."

"Why isn't he at the funeral?" I asked. "Shouldn't he be with the family today?"

"I asked him that, actually."

"And?"

"He said that Ruth and Joel preferred to keep the interment private. Family only."

A teensy bit of spite from me. "I thought he was as close as family."

Mom gave me a chastising glare.

"Hey," I said. "Why don't we go with you? Nana and I." I turned. "And you, too, Mrs. Wentworth, if you want."

Mom's eyes widened.

"I'm not up for that today," Nana said. "In fact, I think it might be just a little too cool outside for these old bones. Thanks anyway, honey."

Mrs. Wentworth pierced me with a shrewd look that, in one second both berated me and mocked my attempt. "Sorry, dear. Stanley's coming by later. We have plans."

The idea of my tagging along with Mom and Kap by myself was unappealing, to say the least.

The phone rang—my house phone this time—preventing me from making that suggestion. "Hang on," I said, reaching for the receiver. "Before you give him an answer—"

"I'm going with him, Ollie." Mom said. "I already told him he can pick me up at two."

A thousand thoughts flew through my brain as I picked up the phone without checking Caller ID. "Hello?"

"Ollie, it's Paul."

Like a rerun of Monday morning, our chief usher was calling me at home—what could have happened now?

"Yes?" I said dumbly.

"I take it you've seen the Liss article?"

"Just a minute ago."

Paul sounded angry and resigned at the same time. "I don't know who leaked the story to him. It's a pretty sad day when our staff learns that they're back to work through the newspaper rather than through official channels."

My mom's plight momentarily forgotten, I caught hold of what he was saying. "We're back? We can come back?"

"Right away. The sooner the better."

Relief washed over me, rinsing away the crustiness of fear. "Thank you so much, Paul."

"Don't thank me," he said. "The president and First Lady moved mountains to get the medical examiner to rush his decision. It's because they want to get to the bottom of this mess, of course."

I sensed he wasn't finished talking.

"But it's not just that. There's another tidbit Liss got right in the story," he went on. "The first couple is plenty tired of Secret Service food. How soon can you get here?"

There wasn't a lot of choice, really. I couldn't stay home—not when I was needed back at the White House. As much as I didn't want my mom heading out for parts unknown with the mysterious Kap, there was little I could do to stop her. In the end, I left Mom and Nana with a spare set of keys and strict instructions to call me if anything came up or if they had any trouble whatsoever.

"What sort of trouble do you expect, Ollie?" Mom asked with a little too much glee.

"None," I said. "Of course. But, you know, just in case."

Nana looked up at me, a twinkle in her deep-set eyes. "So, no wild parties while you're gone?"

A HALF HOUR LATER FOUND ME READY TO BOARD THE METRO for my first trip back to the White House since Minkus's death. My head was everywhere but where it should have been—aware of my surroundings.

I entered the mostly empty train car and didn't pay any attention to the man who followed me in until he sat in the seat next to me. He wore an old-fashioned brown felt hat pulled low, and his overcoat was turned up at the collar. Except for his leather-gloved hand atop a cane, there was nothing distinctive about him. He smelled of too much aftershave.

In one instant, I berated myself for letting my guard down, but I'd been in situations more touchy than this one, so I didn't hesitate. "Excuse me," I said, and got up to change seats.

"Olivia," he said.

About to take an aisle seat kitty-corner behind him, I turned. "What?"

"Come back. Sit down. We have to talk."

He lifted the brim of his hat just enough.

I was about to exclaim, "Liss?" but he placed a finger across his lips. "*Shh*," he said, then tapped the seat next to him. "Sit down. Quickly. We don't have much time."

"What are you, some sort of conspiracy theorist?" I asked, not caring at all that I spoke loudly enough to be heard by other passengers. "Oh wait." I snapped my fingers. "That's exactly what you are!"

I turned my back and headed to an aisle seat even farther away.

He turned and glared at me. Though I could only see his eyes and nose out of the top of his collar, I could feel the heat blaze. I wished I had a paperback or something to read. Instead I turned my head to the window. Unfortunately, we were underground and there really wasn't much of a view, so I kept eye contact with my reflection, drawing from it a little sense of empowerment.

Liss scuffled to his feet and made his way over to the seat in front of me. There were a handful of other passengers in the car and they started to take notice. Not that I cared.

"I was right about you getting back into the White House today, wasn't I?" he asked.

I didn't bother to answer. I stared at the window.

"I have sources," he said.

"Let me guess. Is his name Deep Throat?"

I felt his gaze rake me up and down. "Isn't that a little before your time?"

"Facts," I said, biting the word out, "and history are important to me. And should be to all of us."

I was feeling pretty good about holding my own against this despicable man. He had already hurt me—and my mother—with his vicious column. I had nothing to lose here. I almost wished he would keep at it, so I could knock him to his knees.

He lowered his voice and leaned closer. "What if I told you I have facts that would rock the country's very core?"

"I'd say you wouldn't know a fact if it bit you on the—" Stopping myself in the nick of time, I cleared my throat. "I'd say you were bluffing."

He raised a white eyebrow. "So you are a temperamental chef, after all."

Placing my hand on the back of his chair to boost myself, I stood to change seats, yet again.

"Please wait," he said, placing his hand over mine. "I apologize."

I yanked my hand out from under his. "You will never be able to apologize enough."

When I sat four seats forward, across from an elderly woman who gave me a worried glance before staring at the floor, I expected him to follow. He didn't.

He stayed in his seat for the entire ride to McPherson Square. As the train pulled into the station, I stood to disembark.

Just as the train slowed, Liss stood up. He made his way over. Seconds before the doors were to open, he leaned close to my ear.

"There was trouble in the security office," he whispered. "It has to do with China. Minkus was about to investigate Phil Cooper, his second-in—"

I turned to him, and spoke in a clear voice. "I know exactly who Phil Cooper is. After everything you've written, so does the entire population of Washington, D.C."

Shock registered in his eyes and he looked from side to side, like a spy from a 1940s movie. "Not so loud—"

"Don't tell me what to do," I said. "And why are you bothering me with this anyway? I don't have time to listen to your crazy conspiracies. If you believe you have some burning scoop, why not publish it in your column? Why accost me on my way to work?"

By now the entire train was paying attention.

He whispered, "Because I think you can get me information on Phil Cooper and his anti-American activities." His teeth were clenched, his body was rigid, but his eyes didn't leave mine. "From your Secret Service boyfriend."

How did he know about Tom? Speechless, my mouth moved, but nothing came out.

He took the opportunity to lean in again. "You want me to go public with your romantic dalliances? I'm sure that headline will sit very well with MacKenzie's boss."

The car's doors opened. "Climb into that little hole of yours and dream up more of your nasty lies," I said. "It's what you're good at."

I stepped out and didn't look back.

CHAPTER 18

MY ANGER AT LISS DIDN'T DISSOLVE, BUT MY MOOD LIGHTENED the moment I stepped into the White House kitchen. It was clean. One of our crews had evidently put everything back in its place after the investigators finished. And the smell was exactly right. Dash of yeast, a sprinkle of coffee, and hint of cleaning solution. Although the scents were faint—we'd been banished for four days— they were strong enough to make my heart race with possibility. I closed my eyes for just a moment to breathe it in. "Oh," I said quietly. "It's good to be home."

"It is, isn't it?"

At Cyan's voice, my eyes opened. "As much as I've been enjoying my family, I really missed coming to work."

She tied an apron around her waist and lifted her chin to say hello as Bucky entered the room. "I have so many friends who complain about going to work," she said. "Some of them really hate their jobs. I almost feel guilty because I love this place so much."

"We're blessed," I said.

"Yeah, but for how long?" Bucky wondered.

Cyan and I had the same reaction to Bucky's question. We both stared at him with puzzled expressions.

"This isn't over," he said. "I heard what that medical examiner said this morning."

"I didn't know he was on TV today."

Bucky's downturned mouth let me know that whatever Dr. Michael Isham had had to say wasn't particularly good news. "Yeah. After Paul called, I flipped on the news. The medical examiner's office isn't clearing us of anything yet. He said that results are still pending."

"Then why are we here?"

He shrugged with exaggerated motion. "They can't have the Easter Egg Roll without us, I guess. They can trust us to hard-boil a few thousand eggs for the kids to play with. But I wager they won't allow us to work on the food for the event." He held up a finger in emphasis. "I *guarantee* they'll come up with a reason why we won't be serving food on Monday."

"We always serve food at the event. That's part of the draw," I said. "I'm sure now that we're here, everything will start getting back to normal."

Bucky shook his head, scowling. As he turned away, Cyan's expression asked me where the pleasant fellow from yesterday had gone.

Paul greeted us from the doorway. "Welcome back."

We spent the next few minutes exchanging greetings and comments about being glad to be at work again. I mentioned to Paul the need for the kitchen to bring on a couple of SBA chefs and expressed my preference to have Rafe, and our recent recruit, Agda, as part of the team. With our workload, we would need a few more temporary chefs, too.

"Ah," he said. "Other than the three of you, and Marcel and his staff, we're not bringing 'unknowns' into the kitchen until the entire Minkus investigation is complete."

My mouth opened in disbelief. While we could handle the day-to-day meals with ease, we could not—by any stretch of the imagination—handle Monday's anticipated crowd by ourselves. "How are we going to feed all the partygoers at the Egg Roll?" I asked. "Rafe and Agda have worked here before. They're not exactly unknown. And even with them we'll be severely shorthanded."

Paul waved away my concerns. "I understand. Let me explain. There has been a change in plans."

Bucky gave me a look that said "I told you so."

Paul took a deep breath. "After much discussion, the president and First Lady have decided that it would be in the best interests of all if we limited Monday's events. We will hold the Egg Roll as scheduled, but no White House party afterward."

If a person could look smug and unhappy at the same time, it was Bucky.

"But . . ." I didn't know what else to say. "Why?"

"Coming on the heels of Carl Minkus's death, the aspect of a formal party that evening might be construed as unseemly. In bad taste. But no one would disagree with keeping the Egg Roll for the benefit of the children."

Bucky's warning made me believe there was more to it than keeping up appearances. For his part, Bucky had turned his back while Cyan and I waited for Paul to finish.

"You have to understand that the president and First Lady believe in all of you. They wanted you back here as quickly as possible. This"—he held his hands aloft—"is a testament to their belief. Don't underestimate it."

We nodded, but were silent. Paul patted me on the shoulder on his way out. "Things will start to get better soon. I'm sure of it."

He left, and we set to work on dinner, eventually settling back into our comfortable rhythms. When I signed onto the kitchen computer, I found a note from the First Lady:

> Welcome back, Ollie—to you and to your staff. My husband and I are very much relieved to know you're back in charge. Thank you for your patience during these trying times.

I shared the note with Cyan and Bucky who, respectively, were cheered and unfazed. Tonight's dinner, capitalizing on the fresh veggies from my garden on the third floor, boasted a little Italian flair. We were serving a spring greens salad, bruschetta, and pasta primavera with chicken, asparagus, cherry tomatoes, and baby squash. Marcel, I knew, was planning the big finish of warm Brie with walnuts and maple syrup, garnished with fresh berries.

After we got the bruschetta topping started, I turned to Bucky. "I haven't spoken with the Secret Service yet about picking up the eggs."

He raised his head in acknowledgment but didn't respond.

"I'll talk to them as soon as we're settled here. But I'm sure they're going to want specifics. Do you have a good time I can ask them to be there? Will Brandy be home?"

Bucky's head snapped up. He made an imperative, unintelligible noise—halfway between a gasp and a *"Shh!"*

"What?" I asked, not understanding.

He gestured the two of us closer, his eyes wide with anger. "Do *not* say another word," he said, his voice menacing. He looked about the kitchen but there was no one else around. Keeping to a whisper, he said, "You will not refer to her in any way that might bring notice to our . . . our . . ."

"Relationship?" I prompted.

His glare darkened. "It does not exist."

"Uh . . ." Cyan ran her fingers over her lips. "What?"

Again the unintelligible noise. "The relationship you refer to is private. It does not exist"—he jammed a finger onto the countertop—"here. You will not refer to it, or to her, in that regard. We refuse to make ourselves a spectacle."

Perhaps reading the expressions on our faces, he quickly added, "We want to keep things private."

"Sure," I said, but his words hit me in a way I hadn't anticipated. As I went back to preparations—cleaning the asparagus and baby greens—Liss's not-so-subtle threat to make my relationship with Tom public sent a shooting pain of fear up the back of my throat.

"What's wrong, Ollie?" Cyan asked. "You're pale."

To tell the truth, I felt pale. A sadness I couldn't reach sickened me. And I knew this queasy dread wouldn't go away until I could make things right. The question was, how? I took a deep breath. "I need some air," I said. "Give me a minute."

Even as I strode out of the kitchen, I was pulling my cell phone out of my pocket. I made my way outside into one of the courts that flanked the North Portico. "Tom," I said when he answered.

"What's wrong?"

The fact that he could tell so quickly that something was wrong was not lost on me. He and I had gotten to that point where we could often anticipate what the other would say. Comfort. We'd had that. For a while, at least.

I wanted to talk. But I knew this wasn't a conversation for the phone. "Something's come up."

"Are you all right?"

"Yes, yes." Gosh, I was not handling this very well. "Everyone is fine. But Liss—Howard Liss."

"You're back in the White House, aren't you? I heard you got the all-clear today. I wanted to call, but I'm in training today."

"Oh, you're busy?"

"We're on a break right now. Your timing is phenomenal."

"At least something is."

"Talk to me, but make it quick. We're being called back in for the next session."

There was no way to put this in a thirty-second conversation. "Just do me a favor and call me when you get out, okay? Call me first before you do anything. Will you do that?"

"What's going on?"

"Nothing." I cringed. That was a lie. "It will keep until you call me." I hoped that was the truth.

"Ollie, you're making me nervous."

"Don't worry. I'll tell you later. But it'll be okay." I felt a swift stab in my heart. "I have it all figured out."

He gave a short laugh. "I don't know if that's good news or bad news. But I do have to go. I'll call you later."

"As soon as you get out, right?"

"That very moment."

I rolled my shoulders but didn't feel any better. That queasy sensation was still there. I stared up at the sky from between the court's side walls. Overcast today. I shivered. It was cold outside, but I just noticed it now. My sorrowful mood did not have its genesis in Liss's threat. Liss had only exacerbated an awareness that was already there. I knew what I needed to do. But I wondered if I had the strength to do it.

The sky above held no answers, so I made my way inside to the kitchen's warmth, where life always felt safest.

MARGUERITE SCHUMACHER, THE WHITE HOUSE SOCIAL SECRETARY, met me in the hallway. "I was just coming to talk with you." Pert and dark, she had limitless energy, and a tenacity that I admired. "Have you heard about the plans?"

I told her I had. "I'm just disappointed that they're canceling the post-party. Everyone always looks forward to that."

She wrinkled her nose. "I have to tell you, at first I thought canceling the party portion was a bad idea. But after talking with Mrs. Campbell, I understand where she's coming from."

"Having a party just a week after Minkus's death wouldn't look good?"

"That," Marguerite agreed, "and . . ."

"What else? What are they not telling us?"

She placed a finger on her lips. "Don't share this with anyone else."

I felt my heart skip a beat. "What is it?"

For the third time today, the person I was talking with looked both directions before speaking. Anyone else might have started to develop a complex. But I understood. That's part of the world I chose to live in.

Something else clicked in that moment. That realization that I was always in the middle of things. That's who I *was*.

"You remember our last big holiday?" Marguerite asked.

"How could I forget?" The days leading up to the official White House holiday open house had been eventful, to say the least.

"Mrs. Campbell doesn't want to take any chances this time. She wants the children to have their event, but, in her words, doesn't want 'to tempt fate' by entertaining all the adults later that evening."

"'Tempt fate,'" I repeated.

Marguerite nodded. "At least until the Minkus investigation is completed."

"So she believes Minkus *was* murdered?"

"I really can't say."

I watched her reaction. "You don't know, or you don't want to tell me?"

She gave a Mona Lisa smile. "I really can't say." Then, deflecting my question, she brought me up to date on the expected guests, and explained that there would be additional security—more than usual—on the grounds that day.

"But they never considered canceling the entire event?"

Marguerite gave me a weary look. "You're damned if you do and you're damned if you don't. Canceling the kids' events would be such a disappointment. There are families who look forward to this all year. Some come from across the country just for the chance to participate. Mrs. Campbell doesn't want to let them down."

"What about the clowns and the book readings and the magic shows?"

"Of course. We'll still have all of that."

"But there will be added security."

"A *lot* of added security."

"And the guests aren't going to notice?"

She grinned. "In an effort to keep people from feeling uncomfortable, the extra Secret Service agents will be in costume."

I raised an eyebrow. "Not bunnies?"

She laughed. "Some of them. Others will just be dressed like regular partygoers and will mingle in the crowd."

"Good plan," I said. "Thanks for the update, I'll let my team know."

A glance at my watch reminded me that my mom and Kap were probably on their date right now. I considered calling my mom's cell just to check in, but nobody likes a buttinsky, and that was exactly what I would be. I thought about calling my apartment. Maybe Nana would be able to give me an update on the situation.

I made sure to refrigerate tonight's bruschetta topping before making the call. Just as I pulled my cell phone out again, Bucky grabbed my arm, then let go almost immediately, as if surprised by his own action. "They want me upstairs."

"Who does?"

"The Secret Service." He swallowed. "They say they have a few more questions for me. Oh my God, they think I did it, don't they?"

My number one assistant, I was discovering, went from zero to sixty in the space of a heartbeat. I'd never known anyone who flipped from emotionless to panicked with such speed.

"Bucky," I said, with intense calm, "if they thought you did it, would they have allowed you back into the kitchen?" I extended my arm out toward our workstations and all the items we had in progress. "Would they allow you to cook for the president of the United States of America if they suspected you of murder?"

Bucky held his hands to his head. "We haven't served the food, have we? No. They just brought us here for more questioning."

"Why are you so afraid?"

My question seemed to stun him. "Why aren't you?" he asked, stepping back. "This Minkus situation gives them the right to poke their noses into our private lives."

"Yes, but—"

"What will happen if they find out that I'm living with . . ." He widened his eyes as if to say "You know who." Rubbing his hands over his face, he groaned. "I could lose my job. I could lose . . ."

He didn't have to finish the sentence. Personally, I thought his fear was over the top. I didn't believe for a moment that his relationship with a member of the Egg Board would cause any conflict of interest whatsoever. If it did, then what would be said about my relationship with Tom?

That thought dried my mouth. Thoughts of our talk later today sent pillars of fear driving down into my stomach. There was nothing I could say to Bucky to reassure him. And I wished there was because maybe then I could reassure myself.

But before I could even attempt, one of the Guzy brothers came into the kitchen. "Buckminster Reed?"

Bucky lifted his head.

"Come with me."

Cyan and I tried to smile as Bucky left—an effort to make this sudden summons seem like no big deal—but he wasn't buying it. His lips tight, he gave us a long, meaningful stare before following Guzy boy out of the room.

"He'll be okay." Hearing myself say the words actually made me feel a little bit better as though by virtue of will I could make everything okay. Weren't we back in the White House? That was a step in the right direction, for sure.

Cyan said, "Yeah," but her tone was unconvinced.

In addition to preparing dinner, we worked ahead. It had been so long since we'd been in the kitchen that there was a lot of catching up to do. Cyan and I barely spoke as we cleaned out old food that had gone bad and began chopping, cleaning, and slicing items we knew we would need going forward.

Just as we finished, Bucky returned. His pale face was covered with a sheen of perspiration. "What happened?" I asked.

His eyes were glassy. "The dossier," he said.

Minkus's. "What did they say?"

"They're considering suspension."

"That's not right," I said, untying my apron. "Let me talk with them."

Bucky's hands came up. "Don't."

"What have I got to lose?" I asked, anger making me reckless. "They're probably going to call me up there next and tell me I'm suspended, too."

Cyan wasn't understanding. "What dossier? Why will either of you be suspended?"

I explained about Bucky sending Minkus's dossier to his home computer. "Bucky made me a copy. So we're in the same boat." I cast a glance at the doorway. "Probably just a matter of minutes before I'm summoned, too."

"I didn't tell them that you have it," he said.

Taken aback, I could only ask, "You didn't? Why not?"

Bucky boosted himself onto the stool we kept near the kitchen computer. He leaned his elbows on his knees and lowered his chin into his hands. "Why get us both into trouble?"

Never in a million years would I have expected this show of unity from Bucky. I patted him on the shoulder. "Thanks."

He nodded absently. "We have to worry about the eggs," he said. "If they suspend me, they sure as hell aren't going to want to use the eggs I have stored at my house."

That had the potential to become a problem. "Unless we work through Brandy," I said quietly. "She might be able to use other channels to bring them here."

I expected him to react—to scold me again about bringing up her name—but he just blinked. "Yeah."

"When will you know?" Cyan asked. "I mean . . . whether they're suspending you or not."

He shook his head. "No idea."

"I'm still going to talk to them." I folded my apron and placed it on the counter. "You know this is all for show—to make it look like they're running the most thorough investigation they can. If it were up to Mrs. Campbell . . ." I stopped myself before finishing the sentence.

"What were you going to say?" Cyan asked.

Bucky glanced at me with the most curious expression. Half-cynical, half-hopeful. This man was a walking contradiction.

"Just that I believe the investigators aren't seeing the forest for the trees."

"Huh?"

"Never mind," I said. "I'll be right back."

I caught Paul in his office. "Ollie," he said, not smiling. "I think I know why you're here."

"They can't suspend Bucky."

He shook his head. "My hands are tied."

"We all take paperwork home. It happens all the time."

"But guests don't usually die," he said, then added, "Thank God for that."

"You mean to tell me that if Minkus hadn't died, and yet the Secret Service had found out Bucky forwarded that document to himself, they wouldn't raise an eyebrow?"

Paul made a so-so motion with his head. "That's impossible to tell, but I have to believe they're cracking down especially hard in this case. There's no textbook on what to do when a White House visitor dies—or is killed—while at dinner with the president."

"What can I do to vouch for Bucky?"

Another so-so motion; this time Paul's eyes looked sad. "I don't think that will do much good at this point."

"My support wouldn't count for anything, would it?"

Paul looked away. "It's not that."

"Sure it is." I heard the bitterness in my voice and then I couldn't stop myself. "Doesn't anyone care about what might have really happened here? Why is everyone so suspicious of us? And why bring us back if the Secret Service isn't going to trust us? If they're so leery about us being here, how can they be so sure we won't try to poison someone else?"

My voice had gotten louder and even I realized I was approaching panic. Not very professional. I toned down immediately.

"Sorry," I said. "I guess I just don't understand any of this."

"As I mentioned," Paul said, "you—and your staff—are back because the First Lady requested it. When the word comes down from that high up, the Secret Service has no choice in the matter."

The thought that had occurred to me earlier sprang back into my brain. "Thanks, Paul," I said.

"Is there anything else you need?"

"No," I said. "Not unless you can prove that Carl Minkus died of natural causes."

He opened his hands. "I'm sorry there's not much I can do."

I forgot about calling home to check with Nana until I was back in the kitchen. I would have pulled out my phone, but I caught sight of Bucky removing his apron with a look of abject defeat on his face.

"They didn't . . ." I said.

He didn't make eye contact. "One of those twin agents—Guzy—came by to tell me. Said I could finish out the day, but I figured why bother?"

When he finally looked up at me, his eyes were glassed over and held such weight that I could barely stand to look at him.

"Don't go yet," I said. "Please."

"Why?"

"I have an idea."

He started to shake his head—to argue—but I stopped him.

"Just a couple more hours, okay? Just trust me."

The words fell out of my mouth and with them, I realized I was almost promising him I'd fix the situation. But could I? Did I have the support I needed to pull this off?

"Come on, Buckaroo," Cyan said, with a lightness so forced I felt her pain. She pointed to the clock with a floury finger. "It's only a couple more hours and we could sure use the help."

"Don't know what good I'll be here," Bucky said, but he tied his apron back on.

"Let's just worry about planning next week's menu," I said.

"Being suspended and all, I probably won't even be working here next week. They didn't even say how long I'd be off. Maybe indefinitely."

His tone was gruff, as might be expected, but yet again Bucky's vulnerability caught me by surprise. He'd always been my loudest critic and biggest annoyance. To say I'd been tempted to serve him notice—more than once—was an understatement, but recently I'd begun to see him in a different light. What had happened to cause him to be so contrary all the time? What made him so difficult? I was just grateful to know that apparently Brandy had been able to pierce his armor. At least he had some sunshine in his life.

I had an idea. A good idea, I thought. But it had the chance of coming back to bite me, too.

"Okay," I said. "We have no major events next week after the Egg Roll, so we can probably bring out a few of the family's favorites while tossing in a couple of new items. Any suggestions?"

We discussed the menu at length and I was encouraged to note Bucky getting into it—crabbing at me when I disagreed with him. Bucky's complaints actually made me feel good. Almost like we were getting back to normal.

When we had the week's worth of meals planned, I headed to the computer to put it into our standard format before submitting it to the First Lady. Behind me, I heard Bucky sigh.

"So, that's it, huh? I guess I should get going."

"Did you refill our tasting spoons?" Cyan asked him. "We sent the ones that had been sitting here over to the dishwashers, but they haven't brought us any clean ones back. Would you mind checking on that before you leave?"

Bucky rolled his eyes, but complied.

As soon as he was out of the room, Cyan sidled up next to me. "He doesn't want to leave."

"If I have anything to do with it, he won't."

She peered over my shoulder, then whispered, aghast, "You aren't."

Not looking at her, I shrugged, returned to the e-mail I'd been writing.

"We all do our part," I said. A couple of keystrokes later, the message was sent. "Now, let's keep our fingers crossed."

At least I was doing something. My spirits buoyed, I took a deep breath and reveled in the joy of moving forward. But that feeling was short-lived.

"Olivia Paras." Peter Everett Sargeant III's pronouncement was not an inquiry. More like a command.

I turned, dismayed by the unexpected arrival of our sensitivity director. "Yes," I said. "What can I do for you?"

He stared at me through hooded eyes. "We need to talk."

"I am up to date on all the schedule changes, Peter," I said. "And since we are no longer serving dinner on Monday, we no longer are dealing with 'sensitivity' issues with regard to meal planning. The Egg Roll menu was approved a long time ago. If whatever it is you need to discuss can wait until next week, I would prefer we do so."

He tilted his head in his inquisitive yet condescending way, but I caught the underlying glee in his eyes. "I wish it were that simple," he said with a smile. "But I'm afraid this matter is much more grave than that."

I couldn't imagine anything more serious than canceling a White House event, but I took the bait. "Fine. Let's step—"

Wrinkling his nose, he turned to Cyan. "You will excuse us."

She looked to me. I nodded. "Sure," she said. "I'll be downstairs."

He watched her leave. "Why do you keep her on staff?" he asked. "For one thing—"

"I don't believe you came here to discuss my staff," I said, interrupting. "So if you don't mind, let's get to the heart of the matter, shall we?"

As it always did when I dealt with Sargeant, my posture became more rigid, my speech pattern more formal. There was nothing casual about this man. Perhaps subconsciously, in an effort to facilitate more efficient communication, I parroted his terse, prim demeanor.

He began: "You are incorrect in your assumption."

I startled, and it bugged me that he noticed.

His smile grew broader. "This is most certainly about one of your staff members. I am here to discuss the immediate dismissal of Buckminster Reed."

Whatever I'd expected, it wasn't this. Gathering my wits, I searched for a comeback. "Bucky doesn't report to you. He isn't even within your chain of command."

"Which is why," he said with exaggerated patience, "I am coming to you first. It is unfortunately true that I have no authority where Mr. Reed's continued employment is concerned. But I heard what he did, and I find that wholly unacceptable." The smile never wavered. "As should you."

"Bucky did nothing wrong."

Sargeant raised both eyebrows. "You can't possibly *sanction* the willy-nilly distribution of confidential documents?"

I took a breath, but before I could respond, he continued.

"I hope this doesn't mean that a closer look into your habits would turn up evidence of such irresponsible behavior."

"Studying a dietary dossier at home does not constitute irresponsible behavior."

"Perhaps not." His mouth twitched. "But you are seen as a 'golden girl' by this administration, and hence, none of your transgressions are ever seriously investigated. I would very much like to see that changed."

I was still processing that little mention of "golden girl" when he spun on his heel and turned away.

Stopping at the doorway, he examined the ceiling for a moment, before directing his attention to me. "Eventually President Campbell will finish out his term. And then the spell you have on him—and the First Lady—will come to a crushing end." He wrinkled his nose, speaking in a conspiratorial whisper. "I look forward to that day."

Cyan found me still staring at the empty doorway when she returned a few minutes later. "Is Mr. Cheerful gone?"

I bit the insides of my cheeks.

"What happened?" she asked.

I couldn't find it in me to explain. "He's a piece of work, that one," I finally said, shaking my head. "We need to watch our backs."

Bucky returned with several stainless steel bowls of tasting spoons, which he put in prime spots around the kitchen. He stood for a moment with his arms akimbo, surveying the scene. "You two are going to have a lot of work by yourselves."

"I know," I said. "I am not looking forward to that at all. What are we going to do without you here?"

Bucky gave me a look that told me he appreciated my words, even as he maintained the scowl. "Maybe I should make room in the refrigerators for all those eggs."

"That's a great idea," I said. "While you do that, I'll—"

I was silenced by the unmistakable sound of a new message on the computer.

Cyan, standing closer to Bucky, obviously didn't hear it. "You'll what?"

"Give me a minute," I said, turning my back.

They headed to the refrigerators while I opened my inbox. The note was brief and to the point.

Thank you for the information, Ollie. That is, indeed, sad news. It is my hope that Mr. Reed will be cleared soon to continue in our kitchen.

My heart sank. I don't know why I hoped for more from Mrs. Campbell—or why I expected an immediate turn of events—but I had. I supposed I should be happy to know that the First Lady had received my message so quickly. The menu I'd sent included a quick summary of what was happening with Bucky, and a polite entreaty asking Mrs. Campbell to intercede on his behalf. I had clearly overstepped my boundaries, but when one of my employees was in trouble, what else was I to do?

"You two should be able to handle it from here," Bucky said when he and Cyan returned. "I'm going to take off."

This time there were no tasks left to assign—and no way to logically argue for him to stay. I no longer held out hope that Mrs. Campbell would stay his suspension. We were out of options. "Keep in touch," I said.

"One of us will," he said. "About the eggs."

He untied his apron, and I could almost see the weight on his shoulders as he shrugged into his jacket and fixed a baseball cap on his head.

Impulsively, I said, "I'm going to do whatever I can to get this fixed."

One corner of his mouth turned up. "I know you will."

And then he was gone.

"We'll never get through a whole week without help," Cyan said after a long minute. "They're not letting us hire any SBA chefs and now without Bucky . . ."

I had been thinking the same thing. Best-laid plans. When I had arranged for my mom and nana to come visit, I'd done so with the belief that with a contingent of help and our full staff, we would be in fine position to get everything done on time. But there was no way to get through an entire week with just the two of us, unless we were both willing to spend every waking hour here.

I sighed. Mom and Nana would be on their own for the next three days, at least. Maybe longer. This was not how I'd planned their visit.

I reached for my cell phone and dialed my apartment. Glancing at the clock, I tried to gauge how long it would be before I headed home. "Hi Nana," I said. "Can I talk with Mom?"

"She's not back yet."

I looked at the clock again, as though it might have lied to me a moment earlier. "She went out hours ago."

"They must be having a nice time."

"But it'll be dark soon."

Nana laughed. "You sound like your mother did on your first date."

"But that's different. This is Washington, D.C. She doesn't know her way around yet."

"I'm sure Kap does."

That's exactly what I was afraid of. "Has she called?"

"Did you call us on your first date?"

"Nana," I said, my tone serious, "aren't you worried?"

"No. And you shouldn't be, either. Your mother's a big girl."

"When do you expect her back?"

"When the sun comes up."

"Nana!"

She laughed. I made an exasperated noise. "Do me a favor—call me when you hear from her, okay?"

"I might be hard to get ahold of," she said merrily. "Your neighbor's teaching me a new card game, so I'm going over there now. Good thing you called when you did. Five more minutes and I'd have been gone."

When I hung up, I stared at my little cell phone.

"What's wrong?" Cyan asked.

It took me a minute to put it into words. "When I left my family to pursue a career, I guess I figured they would always just stay the way they were." I looked up. Cyan shook her head, not understanding. "I mean, I knew I was changing, but I never expected them to do anything, or be anything different than my mother and my grandmother. But they are. They've grown—they've changed."

"And that's a bad thing?"

"No," I said. "It's a good thing. I'm just not adjusted to it yet. It's my problem. Not theirs. I think I've been holding on to my memories of them—kinda like holding on to a bit of childhood. But now I'm realizing that's gone."

"I understand," she said. And by the look in her eyes I knew she did. "Just remember to appreciate every moment you have them with you."

* * *

I CALLED TOM ON MY WAY TO THE METRO STATION, JUST A LITTLE bit perturbed that he hadn't called me back like he'd promised.

"Ollie!" he said with such relief that my anger immediately dissolved.

"What's wrong?"

"I was called in to a special meeting immediately after the seminar. And then after that, Craig needed to talk with me."

The heaviness in his voice made me ask: "About?"

"Can't say. I was going to call you in about ten minutes. But now that you called me, let's talk. What's on your mind that's so important?"

I swallowed, but didn't break stride. "Can we get together?"

"Tonight?"

I didn't like the mild peevishness to his tone, nor did I look forward to what I knew would be a difficult conversation, but I persisted. "I think that would be a good idea."

"Sounds ominous. What do we need to talk about?"

"I haven't gotten to McPherson yet," I said, avoiding the question. Thinking quickly, I tried to come up with a place that would afford us a little privacy. "If you're nearby, we can meet at that martini bar you've always wanted to try."

"You want to go to a martini bar? What about Froggie's?"

I didn't want to tell him that I wanted to protect Froggie's. That we'd had a lot of good memories there. I didn't know exactly what I planned to say, but I did know that a conversation like this was best held elsewhere. "The martini bar is closer. I can be there in a few minutes."

He made an odd noise. "I guess I have no choice."

I DIDN'T ORDER A MARTINI. I OPTED FOR COFFEE INSTEAD. TOM looked over the tiny leather-bound menu and asked the waitress for a Sam Adams.

"I thought you were looking forward to trying something new," I said.

We were seated at a tall table in the dark bar's front window. He leaned forward on his arms. "So . . . why are we here, Ollie?"

All day I had been rehearsing options. How I would open, how I would progress, what I might expect Tom to say. How I would answer. But all my preparation went out the nearby window. I turned to watch a couple across the street. Arm in arm, they laughed. Little puffs of air curled in front of them as they turned the corner and strolled away.

Tom touched my arm. "Ollie?"

It didn't help to look at him. Actually, it made it worse.

"This is hard," I said.

"What is?"

Was that fear in his eyes, or just the reflection of a passing car's headlights? I took a breath.

"Ollie, don't do this." He reached out and grabbed my hand. "I know you're upset about my comments recently. I know you think I don't understand you—"

"You don't."

He squeezed. "But I do."

I tugged my hand back. "I want you to tell Craig that he can stop threatening you."

He leaned back, looking hurt. "I'm not afraid of Craig."

"I'm afraid of what he can do to you. And to your career."

Tom waved his hand as though brushing away a fly. "I can handle him."

"You're not going to have to."

The hurt look came back.

My stomach flip-flopped, and my heart raced with panic. My words came out fast, almost as though I was afraid that if I took my time, I wouldn't have the courage to say them. "I want you to tell Craig that we've broken up." I swallowed. "I want you to tell him we're not a couple anymore."

He was shaking his head. "This is all wrong," he said, staring out the window. "We can't let Craig—or even this investigation—dictate how we live our lives." He made eye contact again. "We have to be true to ourselves."

I nodded. "That's the other part of it."

He looked confused.

"I can't be the person you want me to be."

He said nothing.

I folded my hands on the table then dropped them to my lap before continuing. "I can't let this go."

"You can't let us go?"

"No," I said sadly. "I can't let all these kitchen accusations continue without doing anything. Without defending myself."

"But, Ollie. You're not authorized—"

"I know I'm not," I snapped. "And I never intended to throw myself into the middle of the investigation, but I can't just stare in from the sidelines, either. Every move I make, I worry: Will this be construed as getting involved? Am I putting Tom's career at risk? Will Tom get mad at me because I talked with Ruth Minkus? Because I met with Suzie and Steve? Because I studied Minkus's dossier? It's making me crazy."

"Where did you get Minkus's dossier?"

Now I waved him off.

The coffee grew cold and the beer warm as I told Tom exactly how I had been feeling since he made me promise not to poke my nose into the investigation. "I never intend to get involved in these things. You know that. But I can't keep second-guessing myself. I can't keep worrying that I'm stepping out of bounds somehow." I met his gaze. "I have to be who I am, Tom. I have to be true to myself. And our circumstances are such that I can't be myself—not really—if you're part of my life."

He pursed his lips, not meeting my eyes. Finally, when he did, he said, "That's it then?"

"Is there anything you want to say? Anything else you want to talk about?"

His expression grew tight. "No. I think you made yourself clear." With that, he pulled out his wallet, tossed cash on the table, and stood up. "Do you want me to walk you to the Metro station?" he asked with no emotion whatsoever. "It's late."

I had expected questions, even hoped for him to argue me out of it. But instead, my now-former boyfriend stood next to the tall table, waiting for me to alight from my chair. "That's okay," I said. "I'll be fine."

He pinched the bridge of his nose with his fingers. "Let me rephrase that. I will walk you to the Metro unless you tell me I can't."

"Thank you," I said. When in doubt, always be polite, my mom advised. A sad thought flashed through my mind. Mom was on a first date—and I was on a last. "I appreciate it."

We walked in silence the entire way. Tom didn't accompany me down into the station, and at the top of the stairs, I was prepared for an awkward good-bye. But when I turned to him, he had already started away. "Tom," I called to his back.

He waved a hand, and half turned in acknowledgment. But he kept walking.

CHAPTER 19

I STARED OUT THE WINDOW OF THE METRO TRAIN, SEEING NOTHing. My conversation with Tom replayed itself in my mind, like a wretched scene from a sad movie. I analyzed every movement, every nuance. Not that there was much to decode. Once I'd told him what was on my mind, Tom had made it clear he couldn't get away from me fast enough. Had I done the right thing? Was I inadvertently punishing him for not supporting me? Was I being selfish with my need for the freedom to poke my nose where I wanted to poke it?

My heart seemed to beat more slowly than it ever had, every lub-dub a crushing ache. The relationship might have ended, but that didn't mean my feelings for Tom had. I still cared deeply for him, and probably always would. I wondered again if I'd made the right decision. But Tom had been asking me to be someone I wasn't. He wanted a girlfriend who would follow the rules of life that made sense to him, but were anathema to me.

In his life, he was right—just as I was in mine. No fault to be assigned. But no happy ending, either. I looked out into the darkness.

I sighed again. Just because this was the right thing to do didn't make it easy.

"You're back," Nana said when I came through the door. Her face was bright with excitement, but I couldn't find it in me to smile back.

"Where's Mom?" I asked.

"She had a wonderful time," Nana went on, unmindful of my mood. "They only got back about a half hour ago."

Instinctively I looked at my watch, but the time didn't register. Still, I knew it was late. "Just a half hour ago?" I asked, still standing in my little foyer. My mind was slow to process her words. "But it's after midnight."

Nana grinned.

"Whatever," I said. My conversation with Tom was still fresh in my mind, and still stung. I wanted to crawl into my bed and sleep away my disappointment. I desperately wanted to be alone.

"Ollie," Mom said, coming in from the kitchen. She, too, looked at her watch. "I thought you'd be home by now."

Looking away, I said. "Lots of catch-up work."

Nana continued to beam at her daughter, but my mom was staring at me. "Is there something wrong?"

Making a face that said, "Nah," I lied, shaking my head. "Just a long day. That, and the fact that they've suspended Bucky."

They chorused their disapproval and started to ask me questions, but I really couldn't handle explaining everything right then. Cranky, tired, and feeling as though my hands were tied, I realized it was better to let someone else talk for a while. "How did Kap behave?" I asked.

"Behave?" There was levity in Mom's voice, but I could sense her displeasure at my choice of words. "Perfectly, of course. We went to a lovely restaurant for dinner." When she told me about the upscale seafood restaurant, I interrupted.

"You have that chain in Chicago. I've seen at least one of them downtown. And in Schaumburg. Probably Oak Brook, too."

Mom's smile faltered only slightly. "You may be right, but this was a new experience for me."

"It's a decent restaurant," I said against rising anger I knew I should contain, but couldn't. "But why not take you somewhere unique to D.C.?"

She blinked. "The restaurant didn't matter. What mattered was the company."

"The company of a man who was on a date with you instead of at his best friend's funeral?"

"Olivia!" Mom snapped.

"I'm sorry," I said. Although I meant it, I was not able to stand there and talk a moment longer. I didn't blame her. I blamed myself. But that didn't mean I had control over my emotions right now. I wanted to find a familiar hole and hide, letting the rest of the world go on without me. Every thread of my soul panged with disappointment. All I wanted was to be alone.

The looks Mom and Nana gave me were less of anger and more of concern. "I'm sorry," I said again.

"Something *is* wrong, isn't it?" Mom asked.

One thing about people who have known you since birth: You can rely on them to be your strongest allies when times get really tough, even if they don't fully understand. I knew they would cut me the slack I needed tonight. And despite my desire for solitude, I was glad they were there. "There's a lot wrong," I said finally. "But right now I better go to bed before I make things worse." I tried to smile, but I wasn't fooling anyone. "I'm going to put an end to this horrible day, and start fresh tomorrow."

Nana and Mom exchanged glances.

"That's probably best," Mom said.

I lay awake for a long time, staring up into the darkness until my eyes adjusted and everything in the room seemed clear again. *If only life were like that,* I thought. Look at something long enough, and see it for what it really is.

Mom and Nana sat in the kitchen, talking. I couldn't make out their words, but the soft murmurings—which I knew were full of concerns about me — reminded me of nights in my bed when I was a little girl at home and the comforting sound of their quiet conversation lulled me to sleep. Oh that I could return to those days, just for an instant . . . Just for tonight.

Sleep continued to dance in the darkness, just out of reach. As I stared at the ceiling and reshuffled my last conversation with Tom, I watched the dull luminescence of the clock. Its digital numbers inched upward with painful precision.

Tomorrow would be a better day, I promised myself. Until I realized it was already tomorrow.

CHAPTER 20

DESPITE MY PRONOUNCEMENT NEVER TO READ *LISS IS MORE* again, the man's appearance on the Metro yesterday spooked me enough to check if he had made good on his promise to "out" my relationship with Tom. Just wait until he found out we were no longer a couple. I'd scooped him on one story at least. But there was no joy in it.

I scanned the page quickly. Today's column made no mention of me, and none of Tom, thank goodness. Today, Liss seemed focused on Carl Minkus's next targets. He wrote extensively about Alicia Parker and Phil Cooper and why Minkus might have had reason to suspect them of consorting with terrorists in their free time.

Happy that he hadn't targeted me again, and convinced that Liss was certifiable, I shoved the newspaper away, and decided that this was a very positive omen. A very good way to start the day.

I made coffee, started breakfast, and resolved to beat away any negative thoughts—if not for myself, then for my family. I owed them that much. My behavior yesterday after Mom's date was inexcusable.

Homemade waffles, topped with bananas, strawberries, and blueberries would make a good start, I decided. The mixed scents floated above my head, and I knew—with a kitchen as small as mine—it wouldn't be long before the delicious aromas woke up my sleeping family.

A few minutes later Mom wandered into the kitchen. "What's the occasion?" Still in her bathrobe, she blinked at the kitchen clock. "You're up early."

"I have to be at work in about an hour," I said. "But I wanted time to visit before I left."

She looked at me quizzically. "Need any help?"

"No," I said. "Sit. Let me take care of you this time."

She sat, and turned the newspaper around to read. "Anything I should be aware of in here?"

"We're flying under the radar today," I said in a cheery tone. "So far, so good."

I poured her a cup of coffee and set out the half-and-half. "So . . ." I said.

She dragged her attention away from the newspaper. "So?"

I was at the counter, half facing her. Taking a breath, I messed with some of the waffle fixings and said, "I was out of line yesterday."

She nodded, but didn't say anything for a long moment. Then: "Yes, you were."

"I am sorry. Truly sorry."

"I know," she said, turning back to the news. "And you should be."

I sprinkled powdered sugar over a strawberry-topped waffle and placed it in front of her. "Did you want blueberries? Bananas?"

"No. This is just perfect."

Strawberries were always Mom's favorite. At least some things hadn't changed. "Whipped cream?"

She laughed. "You trying to fatten me up?"

"No, just trying to apologize."

"Sit."

I grabbed my own fruit-topped waffle and joined her at the table.

"Ollie," she said, gently, "I had a wonderful day out yesterday."

"I'm glad to hear that. Really, I am," I said. "I don't know what—"

She shushed me with a look. "You and I both know that when this vacation comes to an end, Nana and I will be headed back to our trivial lives in Chicago."

"Trivial?" I shook my head. "You do so much—"

"Shh," she said with force. "My life is good, for me. But it's . . . little. I'm not surrounded by the most important people in the world like you are. You see and hear and do things most of us only dream of."

"That doesn't make what you do unimportant."

"True, but what you don't seem to understand is that while I'm here, I get to share a little bit of your life. And Kap . . ." Her eyes went all dreamy for a moment. "He's part of that. He's interesting—different." She laughed. "And sexy."

I felt my face redden.

She laughed again and playfully tapped my hand. "All I want is to have fun," she said. "I don't get a lot of fun back home."

I nodded. Regret at my attitude from the day before soured my stomach.

I looked down at the uneaten waffle and changed my mind about it. "I really am sorry," I said again.

"And you're forgiven," she said. "I do understand, you know. I remember when Nana went out on a couple dates."

"Nana dated?"

As if summoned, my grandmother appeared in the doorway. "Damn right I did," she said, sniffing the air and eyeing my plate. "Maybe someday I'll tell you about all the ones that got away."

"Ones?" I asked. "Plural?"

Nana lowered herself into the chair opposite mine. "You going to eat that, or you going to stare at it all morning?"

I pushed the heaping plate across the table. "For you."

She dug in as I stood up. With a hand on my mother's shoulder, I reached down to kiss her cheek. "Thanks, Mom."

MUCH TO MY RELIEF, HOWARD LISS WAS NOT ON THE MORNING Metro train. Not that I'd expected him to be up and about this early. Most people weren't.

That's why it was such a surprise to get a voicemail beep when the train came aboveground at Arlington Cemetery. My phone had been off overnight but I'd turned it back on before leaving the apartment. That meant that whoever called had done so in the past few minutes. Maybe it was Mom or Nana.

The train slowed, then stopped to load new passengers at Arlington. As a lone person boarded the car in front of the one I was in, I took the opportunity to access my message: "Olivia," came the breathless voice. "This is Howard Liss. You must call me as soon as you get this. I'm sure your phone has a redial feature, but don't use that one. Use my private line." He provided the number, but I didn't even consider writing it down. At the same time, the Metro started moving again. "This is of the utmost importance." I heard him take a breath, before repeating: "*Utmost*. I know you think you should not contact me. But if I don't hear from you by mid-morning, I will move forward to make public that relationship we discussed. I know you—"

And just like that, I lost the signal.

I swore.

The two other riders in my car looked up.

I lifted a hand in apology. "Sorry."

One returned to his newspaper. The other leaned against the window and closed his eyes.

Just what I needed. More Howard Liss. Why on earth was he contacting me, anyway? What good could I possibly do him? "That relationship we discussed . . ." The creep. He was lucky I couldn't get a signal. Otherwise I would have called him back immediately just to burst his little bubble.

The train ride to McPherson Square took an interminably long time. I'm usually the kind of person who stews about something before issuing a retaliatory response. Tom used to call me a little volcano. By the time I made it to the street level and pulled out my phone, I'd built up such a head of steam that I could barely contain myself. Somebody had to zip this guy's mouth shut, and I felt like just the person to do it.

I punched the redial button. He answered on the first ring. "Howard Liss."

"This is Olivia Paras," I said briskly. I had rehearsed a whole slew of powerful opening lines, but what came out was: "How dare you threaten me?"

He made a gurgling noise. "Oh, yes. Hello."

I pressed the phone tight against my ear. "All you can say is 'Hello'? After leaving me a threatening message, you can only say, 'Hello'?"

He dropped his voice. "You weren't supposed to call on this number."

"Oh, yes," I said loudly as I strode south toward the White House. "That, too. What do you think I am, some simpleton? Just because I was involved in a couple of"—I lost my intensity for a moment, thinking about my involvement in other situations—"incidents at the White House, doesn't mean that I care to participate in your crazy schemes. And I don't—"

"Please," he said, interrupting me. "Can you call me back on that other number?"

What the heck was wrong with this guy? Convinced he was even more touched in the head than I'd originally assumed, I was tempted to hang up. But I couldn't. No matter the state of his mind, this fellow held the power to mess up my life. And Tom's career. Before I hung up, I knew I had to impart one very important piece of information.

Using the same name for Tom that Liss had when he accosted me on the train, I said, "You need to know that 'MacKenzie' and I are no longer involved."

Dead silence.

"Liss?" My footsteps made soft scratches on the sidewalk as I kept up a quick pace. "Are you there?"

A click and then my phone went dead. I muttered an angry expletive as

I dialed my voicemail account and listened to his message again. This time I memorized his "preferred" phone number and dialed it as soon as I terminated the call.

"Olivia?" he asked when he answered. "Thank goodness."

"What is wrong with you?" I asked. "I have no intention of turning this into a chatty phone conversation. So just listen. The 'relationship' you threatened to make public is no longer an issue."

Dead silence, again.

If this unscrupulous, unprincipled blabbermouth hung up on me a second time, I swore I would march down to the newspaper office to confront him personally. He surprised me by whispering, "Hang on one second."

Moments later, the quiet background on his side of the connection was replaced by the sound of traffic and wind. "You there?" he asked.

"Not for long." I wasn't exaggerating. I'd made the trek from the station to the White House gate in record time. Anger does that for me.

A crowd lined up along the White House fence startled me for a moment, and I slowed my pace. But then I remembered what day it was. Egg Roll tickets would be handed out today and hundreds of people were already lined up—some of them having camped out overnight just for the chance to be part of Monday's festivities. Bundled up against the morning chill, they sat in small groups—in lawn chairs, or huddled in sleeping bags on the cold sidewalk.

"Listen," Liss said.

"No, *you* listen. Did you not hear what I just said about my relationship with Tom?" I clenched my eyes shut. I'd been careful not to use his first name in this conversation. Too personal. But I'd gotten so worked up with all the interruptions that I'd lost that small measure of control. I coughed and clarified. "I am no longer involved with Mr. MacKenzie."

"That's too bad," he said. "I'm sorry."

This man was definitely crackers. "The heck you are," I said. "If it weren't for you threatening to make it public—"

"That's not what I want to talk with you about."

I was within thirty feet of the gates. I kept my voice low to prevent eager ticket-seekers from overhearing my conversation. But most looked too sleepy to care. "In case you didn't understand me the other day, I have no desire to talk with you. About anything. And now that you no longer have Mr. MacKenzie to hold over my head, our conversations are finished."

"But don't you want to know who killed Minkus?"

I stopped walking. "Like you have that information. Give me a break. If you knew, you'd tell the world."

"Knowing something and proving it are two completely different things. You've learned that, haven't you, Olivia?" Now that he was standing outside his office building—an assumption I made based on the ambient noises and his intense desire for privacy—his voice took on a condescending air. "Wouldn't it help you—and help your assistant Bucky—if the real guilty party were brought to light?"

"When I find out," I said, "and I say 'when,' not 'if,' it will be through proper channels, not through some delusional journalist's mad ravings."

He made a noise that sounded like, *"Tsk."*

"Have a good day," I said, for lack of a better send-off.

"Wait."

"I don't have time for this."

"Well then maybe your mother does."

My hand tightened on the phone. "Don't you ever—"

"She really likes that Zenobios Kapostoulos, doesn't she?" he asked. "But I believe you know him better as Kap."

I was stricken silent until I remembered that we'd all been in the same small group at the Minkus wake. "You are mistaken," I said. "Yet again." I resumed walking to the gate.

"Am I?" His voice resumed its playful arrogance. I hated it. "Then I assume your mother didn't tell you about her dinner date last night."

"How the hell—?" I stopped myself, took a deep breath, then continued. "Don't you have anything better to do than to poke into my family's life?"

"Your mother's friend Kap is involved with Minkus's death."

"What?" I asked. "How?"

"Oh, so now I have your attention." I heard him lick his lips. He must have covered the mouthpiece, because suddenly the background noises grew quiet and hollow. "I don't know precisely. Yet."

My mind raced as I tried to piece things together. "Kap wasn't at the dinner Sunday. He couldn't have done it."

"You sure about that?"

"I'm sure he wasn't at the dinner."

He chuckled. "That's not what I meant and you know it. How sure are you that he didn't do it?"

I wasn't. "Then why don't you tell me how he did?"

"I can't. But what I can tell you is that Kap isn't working alone. And I don't even believe that's his real name."

I glanced at my watch. I needed to be in the kitchen posthaste. Not standing out in the chilly morning, listening to outlandish scenarios. This moment held a peculiar sense of déjà vu.

I started toward the gate again. "I gotta go."

"Wait," he said, so quickly and forcefully that I stutter-stepped. "Phil Cooper."

"What about him?"

He heaved a huge sigh. "I didn't want to get into this right away, but I'll tell you."

"Then hurry up."

"I have reason to believe that Phil Cooper committed the actual murder."

"You just said Kap did it."

It sounded like he licked his lips again. He'd be chapped before he knew it. Good.

"I said Kap was involved. Listen, please. The two of them are meeting today." He started talking very quickly. "I have a source."

"Why tell me?"

"Because another one of my sources trusts you. And through you—through your mother, to be precise—I can gain access to Kap."

This was getting totally out of hand. I would not allow him to involve my mother. "I'm done," I said loudly. I excused myself to make my way through the line of waiting people, then slipped my employee ID through the card reader at the gate. "Good-bye."

"Kap and Cooper have ties to the Chinese government. They took Minkus out." His words were tinctured with an air of desperation. "I have a source that can prove this. I know I'm right. And you'll be reading about it in my column soon. Why not help me? You like all that attention, don't you?"

I passed the guard in the front gatehouse, who had been watching my animated movements with a look of concern. Giving him a little wave, I said into the phone: "No, I don't. And to be perfectly frank, I'm convinced that Liss is *not* more."

Before he could say another word, I hung up.

"SORRY," I SAID, STRIPPING OFF MY JACKET AND DONNING AN apron. "I meant to get here sooner."

Cyan waved me away with a mixing spoon. "You're hardly late. I just got here myself."

"What are you working on?"

She brought me up to speed on breakfast preparations. She had gotten almost everything done already—so her protestation that she'd only just arrived really didn't ring true. I gave silent thanks for having such a reliable staff to depend on, then felt the immediate crush of disappointment when I remembered Bucky's situation.

"Howard Liss called me this morning," I said as I pulled an asparagus and artichoke frittata out from under the broiler. I eased it onto a serving plate and looked up just in time to see Jackson walk in.

The head waiter smiled. "Ready to go?"

"Just about." Cyan sprinkled a little cinnamon onto the president's French toast. He and his wife had completely different breakfast favorites. While he preferred basic fare such as scrambled eggs, hash browns, and French toast, his wife had a more adventurous palate. Today's veggie frittata wasn't exactly exotic, but it had been considered "unusual" the first time we served it to her. Now it was one of her favorites.

With all the recent upheavals, I thought that it would be nice to treat them to their particular comfort foods this week. I garnished the plates with fruit and edible flowers. "There you go."

Jackson took off, plates in hand, and Cyan and I cleaned up. "Howard Liss called you?" she asked. "Why?"

I tried to summarize his ramblings as best I could, but in the end all I could say was, "The man has crazy ideas. I'm ashamed to say I stayed on the phone with him as long as I did. I should have hung up immediately."

"You're just too polite, Ollie."

"And it gets me into trouble."

Cyan laughed. "Tom wouldn't argue with that."

My breath caught.

Her voice lowered. "What happened?"

I shook my head and started to pull out recipes for the next day's meals, but she stopped me with a firm hand on my arm. "Talk to me."

"We have a hundred things to do before Easter dinner tomorrow, and before the Egg Roll on Monday."

"And we're ridiculously short-staffed until Bucky comes back," she agreed. "But we can still afford a couple of minutes to talk. Tell me what's going on."

"It's over," I said simply. "I ended it."

Cyan had chosen violet contact lenses today. Her purple gaze unnerved me, so I kept talking. "Tom's job was on the line because of me. Craig Sanderson believes that pitting boyfriend against girlfriend is an effective deterrent to poking my nose into official business."

"Sounds like it was more effective in driving a wedge between you."

I gave an unhappy laugh. "It's been a hell of a week."

Cyan bit her lip, and I could tell she didn't know what to say.

I patted her on the shoulder. "We'll get through this."

"You and Tom?"

"No. Our kitchen." I settled myself on the stool in front of the computer screen. I needed to e-mail Brandy. "First things first. We have to arrange for getting all those eggs here. Even though we got a lot done already, we still have more to do."

"Speaking of tons to do, we have two extra guests for lunch today."

I clicked an open document. "It's not on the schedule."

"Paul called down here before you got in. I didn't get a chance to update the file yet."

"I'll do it." Hunching over the keyboard, I asked her for specifics. She dug a scribbled note out of her apron pocket and I turned to wait. "Phil Cooper and..." She shook her head. "I'm going to massacre this name. Zee...Zeno..."

"Zenobios Kapostoulos?" I stood up.

"How in the world did you know that?" Cyan stared at me.

Speechless, I replayed the tape of my conversation with Liss in my head as I paced the small area. He had been right—again. "They're meeting with the president?" I asked. "Here? Today?"

Cyan nodded.

Liss hadn't mentioned the president, but he had known about the two men meeting. What else was Liss right about? That Kap had been instrumental in Minkus's death? The same guy who had taken my mother out on a date? My knees wobbled, and I eased myself back onto the stool.

Cyan, obviously shaken by my sharp reaction, kept asking, "What?" but I didn't answer. She brought her face close to mine. "You're scaring me, Ollie."

I tried to put everything together, but I was coming up woefully short.

"We have Cooper's information in our files," Cyan said. I could tell she was trying to understand me, and when she couldn't she tried throwing more information, hoping for a hit. "Paul says he'll have this Zeno guy's stuff sent down ASAP."

"Good," I said. "I can get a look at his dossier."

"Who is this guy?"

"Kap," I said. "The guy who's dating my mother."

"He's coming here?"

Time was ticking and the longer we sat around talking, the worse things would get. Rather than answer her, I said, "We need help."

She waited, frustrated dimples framing her mouth.

"I'll tell you everything," I said. "But first we have to get those eggs delivered here, and we need another set of hands in the kitchen."

"But Paul won't let us—"

"Call Paul. See if he'll bring Henry back. Just for a couple days."

Cyan grinned. "Ollie, you're a genius! I'm sure Paul will agree to that."

"Just remember, tomorrow is Easter. Henry may not be able to make it."

Her cheer dimmed only slightly. "Well, there's only one way to find out."

CHAPTER 21

LUNCH PREPARATION AT THE WHITE HOUSE SHOULD NOT BE fraught with worry. But here I was, dropping utensils, spilling raspberry sauce, forgetting where I left the container of almonds, and having to re-confirm the oven temperature three times before I trusted I'd set it correctly.

We received Kap's dossier. His occupation was listed as "consultant" and he was apparently self-employed. I wondered exactly what sort of consulting he did that brought him to the White House today.

It wasn't just the fact that Liss had predicted this meeting that threw me off my game. And it wasn't because of Kap's alleged involvement in Minkus's death—although I had to admit that was a big one for me to get my head around. I was upset, worried, and uncharacteristically frantic because we were serving a meal in the White House to Phil Cooper. Not only had he been one of the individuals present at Sunday's disastrous dinner—according to Liss, he was one of the prime suspects. Like him or not, and I certainly didn't, Liss had an uncanny knack for being able to find things out.

I could not let anything go wrong—not with the food—this time. But what if Cooper had bigger game in his sights? But I couldn't go sounding the alarm to the Secret Service based on vague, unsubstantiated innuendo from a questionable journalist.

Cyan and I worked in almost total silence. In between lunch preparations, she and I also did our best to work ahead for tomorrow's Easter dinner. But when I dropped yet another one of our tasting spoons, she gave out a strangled cry. "You're making *me* nervous now."

"What did Paul say about Henry?" I asked.

She stopped long enough to look at me. "That's the fourth time you've asked me." She glanced at the clock. "In the past two hours."

I rubbed my forehead with the back of my hand. "I just can't seem to concentrate."

"You're going to have to, especially if Henry can't make it. Paul said he would call him personally. He'll let us know when he gets an answer."

"Of course," I said, realizing I *had* heard this information already. "But I can't stop thinking about how this luncheon meeting could go bad." I swept my hand out, encompassing the room. "We have to make certain that nothing happens to the president's food between the time we prepare it and the time it's served."

"How do you intend to do that?"

I shook my head. I didn't know. "Where are they serving?"

Cyan gave me a look that made it clear I'd asked that question before, too.

"Oh, yeah," I said, remembering. "The President's Dining Room." I stared down at the greens before me, looked up at the door, then studied the clock. "That will make it difficult."

"Make what difficult?"

"What if we accompanied our creations?" I was thinking out loud here, but the more I talked, the better the idea began to sound. "We can tell the wait staff that we need to prepare this tableside—"

She looked shocked. "But we don't."

"Who's going to argue with us?"

"The President's Dining Room is in the West Wing!" she said, although she clearly knew I was aware of that fact. "Are you nuts?"

"No, listen." I held up both hands, excited now. "The butlers will serve—just like normal. But we would be right outside the dining room, plating the courses just before they go in."

"That's crazy," Cyan said. "What do you think you can possibly accomplish?"

"We'll be able to ensure that the president's food is safe. That's paramount. There will be no chance for anyone else to have access to the food before it's served."

"You don't trust our wait staff?"

"I do," I said. "But call me paranoid. Something went wrong on Sunday, and we still don't know what it was. All I know is that I'll feel better if the chain of custody isn't compromised. The only way I can be certain of that is to be there myself."

"'Chain of custody'? You're starting to sound like a TV cop show." She shook her head, but I noticed the glimmer of possibility in her eyes. "We'll have to clear this with Jackson."

"Not only that," I said, my mind in hyper-drive, "we can maybe even get a sense of what's going on in there. I mean, why are they meeting with the president anyway?"

"Ollie!" Cyan's expression was one of utter disbelief. "You know that's none of our business. Besides," she added, her tone softening, "they'd never let us close enough to actually overhear anything. Not in the West Wing."

"You're right," I said. "But maybe we can find out what Kap is doing here."

She gave me a skeptical look. "Is that what this is all about? You're playing detective because of him cozying up to your mom?"

"No," I said. And I meant it. "I don't know what the guy's story is, but I can't help feeling that we need to be there. Liss swears that Kap and Cooper were responsible for Minkus's death. If he's right, then our president will be dining this afternoon with two assassins."

I didn't understand Cyan's sudden sympathetic expression. "Ollie," she said. "I know you're taking this Minkus death personally. I understand that. I feel it, too. But there's really not a thing either of us can do. It's completely out of our hands."

She had a point. The heightened tension I'd felt from making elaborate plans fell suddenly away. I picked up the greens I'd been working with. "You're right."

"Plus we have so much work to do . . ."

"What's this?" came a booming voice from the doorway. "Are we standing around chatting or are we working?"

"Henry!" I dropped the greens and wiped my hands on my apron to give him a big hug. "You came!"

"I left home the minute I received Paul's call." He reached out to hug Cyan, too. "How could I resist? He said you needed me."

A lump lodged in my throat. It was so good to see Henry—so good to have him here. His face was ruddier and more wrinkled than I remembered, but he had slimmed down, and—did I imagine this?—had developed significant muscularity. "You look great," I said. "What have you been doing?"

"I added a secret ingredient to my diet," he said with a wink. "Powerful stuff."

Cyan teased: "You should consider sharing your secret ingredient with the world. You'd make millions."

"No sharing," he said, wagging a finger, his smile bigger than I'd seen it in all the time we worked together. "Nope, nope, nope."

"Secret ingredient, huh?" I put my hands on my hips. "Okay, Henry, 'fess up. What's her name?"

"Now what makes you think that a woman is responsible for my . . . renaissance?" His eyes twinkled.

We waited.

"Her name is Mercedes. And now, you two astute detectives, tell me what needs to be done."

We brought him up to speed on all menu decisions and discovered that Paul had already briefed him on the Bucky situation. "We are most certainly under the gun," he said. "But this kitchen has been in dire straits before. We shall prevail, as we always have." Finished with his proclamation, he turned to me. "Ms. Executive Chef, I am at your command."

WITH HENRY ON OUR TEAM, WE FLEW THROUGH TASKS, THE three of us so comfortable and confident with one another that we required minimal discussion to get things done. Even better than having two extra hands and an extra brain in the kitchen, Henry boosted our morale by his very presence.

Lunch was due to be plated in about thirty minutes and I still hadn't completely given up the idea of finagling a way into the West Wing to ensure President Campbell's food made it to him safely.

Swinging past the computer, I noticed I had a new e-mail. "Excellent!" I said aloud as I read it.

"What's up?" Cyan asked.

I turned. "Brandy says she'll be able to help us with . . ."

I stopped.

At the opposite end of the counter, carving cherry tomatoes into tiny flower-shaped garnishes, Henry looked up. Cyan tried to prompt me. "With what? The eggs?"

"I've got it!" I said.

They shared another quick glance. "Great. Got what?"

"Brandy managed to get all the eggs transported back to a staging warehouse," I said, talking quickly. "This is perfect."

Cyan nodded, clearly dubious.

"I need to arrange to have the Secret Service pick up all the eggs. Which means I have to coordinate with Craig Sanderson. How about if I head over to the West Wing when the butlers come for the president's lunch? I'll be able to make sure that the meal gets there safely and while I'm there, I'll try to snag a few minutes of Craig's time."

"Lame," Cyan said.

"Maybe, but I don't trust Cooper or Kap. I have to do this."

"I know you do."

Henry had been watching us, his eyebrows raised. As I started to explain, he held up a hand. "Maybe it's best if I don't know."

MORE OFTEN THAN NOT, PRESIDENT CAMPBELL HELD CASUAL LUN-cheon meetings in the White House Mess, which was the navy-run kitchen and dining room in the basement of the West Wing. The fact that he had requested today's lunch brought in from the residence kitchen, and the fact that he was choosing to dine in the President's Dining Room, told me that whatever this meeting was about, it was important enough to warrant privacy.

Jackson kept his eyes forward, not saying much for most of our passage across the residence. The lack of conversation was okay by me. I was salivating. But that was more from curiosity than from the delicious aromas drifting upward from the cart the butler pushed.

He and I took a roundabout path to the basement of the West Wing and when we finally arrived at the elevator that would take us to the main floor, Jackson gestured with his chin. "Secret Service office is that way."

"I know."

He waited a beat. "You aren't here just to talk with Sanderson, are you?" He flicked a glance down toward the covered plates and accompaniments. "You're making sure this food stays safe."

I nodded.

"If I didn't know you as well as I do, Ollie, I'd take offense."

"Jackson, I don't think for a minute . . ."

He held up a hand, but was interrupted when the elevator opened. We got in, Jackson backing the cart in so he could exit gracefully at the first floor. When the door closed again, he said, "I know you're not thinking about me doing something bad to the food." He pointed. "Brand-new salt, brand-new pepper. Freshly sterilized flatware. Everything here is clean."

Each diner was always provided his own set of everything, including condiments—to prevent the inexcusable "boarding-house reach." I nodded. "I'm sure it is."

His nostrils flared. "You're wondering about Cooper."

Astonished by his astuteness, I nodded again.

The elevator opened and we made our way out, the cart's contents clanking softly as we traversed the carpeted floor. "I guarantee you I am not going to turn my back on this cart for one moment." He nodded solemnly as we walked.

"Thanks, Jackson. You're the best."

We'd both lowered our voices. In this wing of the White House, I was always awestruck. This was the epicenter, the heart of the free world—at least, in my unabashedly patriotic way, that's the way I saw it. I knew from firsthand experience how much time and effort went into every decision here. While I certainly wasn't privy to classified information, I knew the people who were. I saw the toll the weight of responsibility took on each and every member of the administration. These were good people, making the best decisions they could, every single day.

We stopped our trek just outside the President's Dining Room. To my left was the Roosevelt Room, and straight ahead, through a small angled corridor, the Oval Office. Even after working here for so long, being in this part of the White House made my skin tingle.

With so many people navigating the hallway, Jackson wheeled the cart into the empty Roosevelt Room. Across the hall from the President's Dining Room, and with access to the Oval Office, the windowless space housed a long table that comfortably sat sixteen. President Nixon had named the room to honor both Theodore and Franklin Delano Roosevelt. Sitting Republicans traditionally displayed Teddy Roosevelt's *Rough Rider* painting over the mantle, and sitting Democrats traditionally displayed Franklin Delano Roosevelt's portrait.

President Campbell, who expressed great admiration for both men, opted to feature both paintings in the room and instructed the staff to alternate the artworks' positions so that they equally shared the position of prestige.

"Good thing you're here," Jackson said. "I can use the help." There were butlers he could have called, but we had an unspoken agreement: The fewer people involved, the better we could keep our suspicions under wraps. Although

I knew this was probably overkill, neither one of us wanted to leave anything to chance. "I'll be right back," he said.

While he disappeared into the dining room across the hall, I waited near the Roosevelt Room's doorway, the serving cart directly behind me. I knew Jackson was preparing the dining table for the meal. Seconds later, he emerged, dodging several staffers in the hall as they walked past. "We may serve."

Usually, at dinner, the butlers handled no more than one plate at a time. In fact, at the most formal affairs, all guests are served at the same moment by individual butlers. It's quite a sight. Since today's luncheon was informal, however, Jackson carried in one plate of baby greens with raspberry vinaigrette dressing for the president, then came back for the other two plates.

I maintained my presence near the doorway, the cart safely stowed behind me. Now that I was in the heart of the West Wing, I tuned in to passing conversations. I caught a few vague references to headline topics, but nothing about Minkus. Until Jackson returned.

"I will check back with them in a moment. They will be ready for the entrée shortly," he said. "Right now, it's quiet. I don't think they plan to do any serious talking with their mouths full of your famous salad."

I shrugged, feigning nonchalance.

"What were you hoping to overhear?"

"Me?" I asked. "Nothing at all."

"Yeah, like I believe that," he said with a smirk, then lapsed into the folksy speech that he probably reserved for times when he was relaxing with friends. "Don't you be trying to pull one over on old Jack."

"Okay," I said. "The other guy . . . not Cooper . . . goes by the name Kap." Jackson must have detected the disdain in my voice because his eyebrows raised. I frowned. "He took my mother out on a date."

The look on Jackson's face would have been enough to make me laugh if the situation hadn't been so serious. "Well, that's about the last thing I expected to hear."

"Not only that, he's a good friend of the Minkus family. I have to believe there's a connection now that he's chumming up with Cooper."

Jackson glanced at the dining room door. "You wait here," he said.

As he continued to serve, he provided me with a play-by-play of the conversation going on in the dining room. "Just discussing that assassinations in China," he said. But then he shook his head. "Cooper, I understand why he's here. But not that other gentleman. I wonder what his story is."

I thought about Liss's allegations. I wondered if Kap could have poisoned Minkus before dinner—I thought about how much Ruth Minkus despised the man. Did she have a sense about him? I would probably never know.

Jackson came in, his eyes bright. "You want the scoop?" he asked. He scanned the room and lowered his voice. "President Campbell took a call while I was in there. From the medical examiner."

I swallowed. Waited.

He whispered, "And he shared this information with the other two men."

"Well?" My throat was so dry I could barely ask, "What did he say?"

Jackson's brow furrowed. "You aren't going to like it."

Visions of heads rolling—mine, Bucky's, Cyan's—made my legs weak. "Just tell me."

"They figured out what killed Minkus."

I held my breath.

"It was a toxin."

Oh my God, I thought. It couldn't be. "Like . . . botulism?" I asked.

Jackson shook his head. "Don't know. President Campbell wrote it down while he was on the phone, but I couldn't get a look. Soon as he got off the phone, he showed the note to the other two. They didn't say it when I was in the room, but they did say 'toxin' a couple of times."

I prayed it wasn't botulism. It couldn't be. I took great care in my kitchen to keep food safe. That was part of my responsibility. It just couldn't be. It couldn't be.

"I have to find out," I said.

Jackson looked as upset as I was. "Don't know how you can."

"They aren't going to announce it?"

"No, ma'am. All three agreed to share this on a 'need to know' basis until . . . something—don't know what—can be verified. They're keeping mum. Heck, the president won't even say it in front of me and you know we're usually invisible." Jackson's face was creased with worry. "I probably shouldn't have told you that much."

"Don't worry, it won't go anywhere." I closed my eyes for a long moment. "That means the kitchen is under suspicion again, doesn't it?"

"I can't answer that, Ollie," he said. "But I can tell you that they aren't sharing this information with the media yet, so . . ." He held a finger to his lips. "Okay?"

My brain was on hyper-drive. "If it was botulism . . ."

Jackson grimaced. "For your sake, hope it isn't."

I nodded. I supposed I'd find out soon enough. I hated waiting. In this case, however, I had no choice. He left me again.

Moments later, Jackson came back into the Roosevelt Room.

Followed by Cooper.

My shock at the agent's unexpected appearance rendered me speechless.

"Hello," he said pleasantly. "It's nice to see you again, Ms. Paras."

I murmured a polite reply, not understanding this turn of events. Jackson intervened. "Mr. Cooper needs this room to make a private phone call," he said with just the proper eloquence to usher me out. He followed me into the hall with the now-empty food cart.

Already dialing, Cooper offered absentminded thanks.

As soon as we were in the corridor, Jackson pointed to the dining room. "Come on, let's get in there."

"In?" I asked. "Where?"

He brought a finger to his lips. In hushed tones, he urged me forward. "President Campbell was called away by his secretary. It's your chance, Ollie. Take it now or . . ."

He didn't get to finish his sentence.

I stepped into the President's Dining Room, Jackson behind me. He began clearing the plates around the room's sole occupant, Kap, who was leaning on the table, his head propped up with one hand.

"Good afternoon, Mr. Kapostoulos," I said.

He looked up immediately. "Ollie," he said, standing and closing his portfolio as he did so. "It's good to see you again."

Making small talk while I helped clear the tabletop, I forced a smile. "You, too. I happened to be over here, with Jackson"—I gestured out the door—"and I took the opportunity to stop by and say hello."

"I'm glad you did." But he didn't look glad at all.

In record time the table was clear except for coffee cups, a few ancillary items, and three leather portfolios. All closed. Darn it.

"How is your mother?" he asked.

"Great," I said. "She really enjoyed dinner the other night."

"I'm glad."

Calling on moxie I didn't know I possessed, I said, "Small world. I'm surprised to run into you here at the White House."

"Yes, I imagine you are." He glanced down at the table, as though eager to get back to work. "And it was nice to see you again."

I took the hint. I was being dismissed.

"I don't want to bother you any longer, but . . ." Acting on whim, I blustered forth. "If you wanted to stop by the kitchen before you leave, I would love to show you around."

Kap looked up from his papers, regarding me with a bit of wariness now. "That's very kind of you. I may take you up on it."

Was he as eager to find out more about me as I was about him? I hoped so. That would give me an opportunity to figure out exactly what this man was after.

Jackson was finished in here. And so was I.

As we left Kap sitting there, I worked up my most welcome smile. "I really hope you stop by."

WITH THIS NEW TOXIN INFORMATION RUNNING THROUGH MY frenzied brain, I almost forgot my Secret Service mission. No longer encumbered by the wheeled cart, I took the stairs just outside the Cabinet Room down to the lower level.

I was glad to find Craig in his office. As much as I didn't want to talk with him directly, I knew I had to. I waited in the anteroom for his assistant to announce me, and was shown in at once.

"Do you have a minute?" I asked.

Craig would be so much more handsome if he smiled once in a while. He had been writing longhand when I walked in, and he was slow to pull his attention from the paper before him. Slower still, was the drawl in his question. "What can I do for you, Ms. Paras?"

I pasted on a cheerful face. "Two things."

His eyebrows arched and he placed his pen on the blotter, carefully arranging it exactly parallel to the blotter's edge. "You may proceed."

"First, I need to arrange to have the eggs delivered to the kitchen. Our Egg Board liaison has our supply ready. I just need the Secret Service to coordinate with her."

He nodded, pulled out a fresh sheet of paper, and wrote on it. "Specifics?"

I provided Brandy's name, phone, e-mail, and the location of the eggs. He recorded it all.

"Consider it done," he said. "And second?"

This was the hard part. "It's about Agent MacKenzie."

His expression utterly neutral, he blinked slowly, waiting for me to continue.

"You need to be aware that Agent MacKenzie and I . . ." I faltered. Biting my lip, I tried again. "There is no need for you to . . ."

Again, the slow blinking. "Ms. Paras, exactly what are you trying to communicate about one of my agents? Are you reporting improper behavior on his part?"

"No!" If it were anyone but Craig, I might think he was trying to make a joke. But this guy was all serious, all the time. My voice naturally rose, but I struggled to lower it, cognizant of others in the anteroom. I stepped closer and spoke quietly. "Tom and I broke up, okay?" When there was no reaction on his part, I clarified. "We are no longer in a relationship. You got your wish."

His brow creased. "And you are telling me this, why?"

He knew exactly why, but I took another step closer to his desk. "You can no longer hold Agent MacKenzie responsible for my behavior," I said. And then I said the words that hurt most of all. "He is no longer part of my life."

I didn't wait for Craig to respond. I turned and hurried out the door and didn't stop walking until I was safely back in the haven of the kitchen.

"You okay?" Cyan asked.

I nodded. "Mission accomplished."

She and Henry wore expressions that said they didn't believe me, but we had so much work ahead that neither of them pressed me for more.

CHAPTER 22

"HERE COMES TROUBLE," CYAN WHISPERED.

In the midst of chopping chives, I looked up.

"And this is the kitchen staff," Sargeant said, sweeping his arm forward to encompass all of us. "Although I confess I'm stymied as to why you wished to visit this part of the residence. Are you, perhaps, an aspiring chef?"

Standing a head taller than Sargeant, Kap halted in the doorway before entering. He ignored Sargeant's question and addressed me. "I hope I'm not interrupting you, Ollie."

"No, not at all." I wiped my hands on my apron and stepped forward.

Nonplussed, Sargeant attempted to regain control of the conversation. He glared at me. "I wasn't aware you and Mr. Kapostoulos were acquainted."

I opened my mouth to form a vague reply when Kap said, "Ms. Paras and I have friends in common." Kap looked at me. "Good friends, wouldn't you say?"

Well, wasn't that a little presumptuous. "Yes," I said, more to annoy Sargeant than agree with Kap, "very good friends."

Sargeant sniffed. "I have a list of questions for you, Ms. Paras. They came from the president himself. We are very concerned with sensitive food issues that relate to religious observances and belief systems. In fact, when Mr. Kapostoulos expressed his desire to visit the kitchen, the president suggested I accompany him. He believes that this way I can kill two birds with one stone, as it were."

The hairs on the back of my neck stood up, but Sargeant poking his nose into the kitchen was nothing new. Doing so in the presence of Kap, however, made it odd. "Of course," I said. "Let's get started."

I watched Henry and Kap size each other up. They were about the same height, about the same age. Henry resembled a kindly uncle, while Kap could have graced a senior edition of *GQ*. Henry offered to show Kap around, but our visitor declined and politely suggested Sargeant carry on.

At that, Sargeant opened a portfolio and clicked his pen. Kap's dark eyes visibly hardened, almost as though the irises had swallowed up the pupils. He fixed his laser gaze firmly on our sensitivity director.

Sargeant asked, "What sort of delicacies do you generally prepare for the president and his guests?"

"There are many," I said. "That's a difficult question. Is there something specific you want to know about?"

"No. No." Sargeant smiled, but I could tell it was just for show. "I just need to clear up these loose ends." He consulted his notebook. "For instance . . . have you ever served truffles?" He looked up at me.

"Yes."

He wrote that down. I got the feeling he was gauging my truthfulness. But why would I lie? "Foie gras?"

"The president doesn't like it. So, no."

"Caviar."

"Yes."

"Puffer fish."

"No," I said, aghast.

He watched me as I answered. "You have never served puffer fish?"

"Of course not. It's too dangerous."

With a prim smirk, he nodded and wrote that down.

A moment later, he continued with the questions, finishing off a list of about ten items, most of which we had served at one time or another. But never puffer fish. It wasn't worth the risk. The skin and organs contained deadly toxins.

I looked up at both of them.

"What is it?" Kap asked.

I lied, "Nothing."

"You're sure?"

"I . . . I have a lot to do for tomorrow. I just thought of something I forgot."

Sargeant wrinkled his nose as he shut his notebook. "I suppose that will be enough for now. I'm no longer needed here." He waited, as though hoping we'd correct him. We didn't.

"It was a pleasure to meet you, Mr. Kapostoulos," Sargeant said with a little bow. He ignored the rest of us and left the room without looking back.

Kap turned to us. "Who hired *that* . . . gentleman?"

Cyan laughed. "We haven't been able to figure that one out yet."

Kap smiled at her and at Henry. "Would you mind if I borrowed your boss for a few minutes?"

My heart gave a little thump of disappointment. I didn't know what he might want to talk about, but it was probably about my mom, and not something I wanted to hear. I steeled myself and followed him out. He led me into the Center Hall. "I don't want to worry you, Ollie," he began.

"I'm not worried," I said. "My mother is a smart, strong lady."

"She is," he agreed. "And her daughter takes after her."

Blatant flattery always made my teeth hurt. I clenched them. "What was it you wanted to talk about?"

"I would appreciate it if you didn't mention my visit here."

That seemed like a peculiar request. "Your visit to the kitchen?"

"My visit to the White House."

"Who would I tell?"

"Your family?" He shot me with that laser gaze again. "Howard Liss?"

"What?" I laughed my disbelief. "Why do you think I would have anything to do with that repulsive—"

"He hasn't contacted you?"

The question shut me up. "How did you know that?" I asked. "What kind of consultant are you, anyway?"

"Let's keep my visit to the White House between us, okay?"

I didn't understand. "But other people have seen you here." I held up my fingers, one at a time. "Henry, Cyan, Jackson, Peter Everett Sargeant III, not to mention everyone in the West Wing."

"I'm not worried about the other staff. They're not on Howard Liss's radar." He ventured a smile. "Please, let's just keep this between us, shall we?"

The minute he left, I headed for the computer. "So that's your mom's boyfriend?" Cyan asked.

I didn't think it was a good idea to look up my Internet question while Cyan stood next to me. "Just while she's in town."

From behind us, Henry grunted. We both turned.

"He's here to stay," Henry said.

"What do you mean?" I asked.

Henry stopped chopping scallions to look up at us. "He's got the look."

"What look?"

My former boss waved his knife at me. "You're not going to get rid of him very easily."

"Great," I said.

Cyan patted me on the shoulder. "He's very good-looking."

"So was Ted Bundy."

Cyan laughed, but at least she headed over to the other end of the kitchen. I was free to surf the Net. Sargeant's inquiries—with Kap at his sleeve—were too suspicious to be the routine questions he claimed. The first thing I typed into my browser was "Puffer fish," then, "Enter."

And there it was.

Tetrodotoxin. Extremely deadly. Could cause death in as little as twenty minutes. This *had* to be the toxin Kap and Cooper were discussing at lunch today.

Puffer fish was considered a delicacy, but much too dangerous for me to consume myself, let alone serve to the president. But if my hunch was right, it was this toxin that killed Minkus.

I signed off and sat there for a minute, closing my eyes against the fear. Puffer fish poisoning was serious. No wonder they suspected the kitchen. I had no idea how to deal with the onslaught of publicity this revelation was certain to generate.

All day, with this new tetrodotoxin information floating around, I had expected the Secret Service to swarm the kitchen and kick us out again. That hadn't happened. Instead, the eggs arrived just as Craig had promised; preparations moved forward for the following day's holiday meal; and Cyan, Henry, and I made great strides on the Egg Roll preparations.

When I finally left the White House that night, it was late. The Metro was still running, fortunately, so I set off for the McPherson Square station, hoping the brisk walk would help clear my head. Just outside the East Gate, I pulled out my cell and was surprised to see I had two missed calls. The first one was from Tom. "Call me when you can." I looked at the phone, waiting for more. But that was the extent of the message. Time-stamped about two hours ago.

The second call was from Liss. Of course. My new buddy. Despite Kap's best efforts, Liss had probably gotten wind of the ME's report and wanted a news scoop for tomorrow morning's edition, about how often we served puffer fish to the president. I listened to his message. "Olivia—I understand that the two men we discussed have indeed had their audience today. You may be interested to know that when they left their meeting, they went straight to visit the 'late agent's' office." He paused, as though allowing me time to let the information settle in. "What do you think they are looking for?"

He'd made it sound like one of his scandalous headlines. The lunatic. I ignored his call and instead steeled myself before dialing Tom. He answered right away. But rather than say hello, he asked, "Why did you tell Craig we had broken up?"

"He *told* you?"

"Why did you do that, Ollie?"

"So he could no longer hold you responsible for my actions."

Tom made a noise of complete exasperation. "You didn't think I could handle it?"

"I didn't think you should have to."

He was silent a moment. "Let me guess: You're running your own investigation."

I shook my head, even though he couldn't see me. "I'm just trying to clear the kitchen's name."

"Well, you can quit right now. You've been cleared."

"What about Bucky?"

He didn't have an answer for that.

I pressed my luck. "Can I ask you something?"

"Shoot."

"They know what killed Minkus, don't they?"

He hedged. "This is a discussion for another time."

"Was it really tetrodotoxin?"

"Where did you hear—?" Agitated, he nearly shouted, "How do you know that? No one knows the name of . . ." His voice trailed off but his anger was still palpable.

I was at the mouth of the McPherson Square station, but I didn't head underground, where my signal would be lost. "I just heard some things, okay?"

Tom's irritation manifested itself in a series of restless noises. "My God, is nothing safe from your damn snooping?"

I started to answer, but he cut me off.

"We're on cell phones. Stop talking. Now." He blew out a breath. "Where are you?"

"Just about to get on the Metro to go home."

"You're at the station?"

"At the top of the stairs."

"Wait there," he said and hung up.

I didn't much care for the idea of hanging around waiting for Tom, especially when he sounded so aggravated. It was dark out, and standing alone outside a Metro station made me believe I was asking for trouble. But he arrived in less than five minutes. Pulling up in a government-issue sedan, he popped the locks and waved me in.

"First of all," I began, even before my butt hit the seat, "I work in the White House. I hear sensitive things all the time."

He pulled away the moment my door was closed. "Do you usually broadcast them over your cell phone?"

"No one is listening in on my cell phone."

"You sure about that?"

I shrugged.

His mouth was tight as he asked, "You ever think they might be listening in on mine?"

"I thought yours was secure."

He made an exasperated noise. "You and I work in the White House. *Nothing* is as secure as we'd like it to be."

"Second," I said, "if this puffer fish toxin is what killed Minkus, why in the world is the kitchen cleared of suspicion? I would think this would make us look more guilty."

"Puffer fish isn't the toxin's only source," he said.

"I know that. But that doesn't mean the kitchen should be cleared."

I had no idea where we were going. From the arbitrary turns Tom took, it appeared he had no idea, either. "You don't want to be cleared?"

"Of course I do. I just don't understand it."

There was a parking spot open, just a few cars ahead of us. Tom was silent as he pulled into it and shut off the engine. "Why do you need to understand? Why can't you just accept the facts as presented to you?"

"Because they don't make sense."

He stared out the windshield for a long moment. We were on a deserted street not far from the expressway, and I could see the lighted Washington Monument in the distance. At least I recognized where I was, in case he made me get out and walk.

I took in his profile, and knew that would never happen. For all our miscommunication and differences of opinion, Tom was an honorable guy.

"Now, listen carefully, Ollie," he said, still staring straight ahead. "I am going to tell you something that is not classified information. But it's close. This may not answer your questions, but if you listen . . . carefully"—he turned to face me as he repeated the directive—"you should be satisfied. And maybe then you'll be able to stay out of the Secret Service's business. For once."

I was about to protest that I hadn't actually done anything wrong this time, but the look in his eyes warned me to keep quiet.

"Hypothetically," he said, "special agents who have done field work . . ."

"Like Minkus?"

He held a finger to my lips. Despite my resolve to distance myself, I felt a familiar tingle at his touch.

"Special agents who have done field work," he repeated, "may, and I repeat—*may*—have acquired the necessary means to . . . dispatch . . . hostile individuals who intend to harm the agents."

"Dispatch meaning . . . kill?"

He nodded.

I thought about that. At dinner on Sunday Minkus and Cooper were the only two present who had ever done field work. "Okay."

"Tetrodotoxin," he continued, assuming a bit of a teacher-tone, "which can be extracted not only from the puffer fish, but from the blue-ringed octopus, and several other species as well, is very effective in killing humans." He raised his eyebrows. "Because tetrodotoxin is an unusual substance, a medical examiner would not know to test for it. At least not initially."

"I'm with you," I said.

His eyes registered sadness. I wished I'd chosen different words.

"It is not unreasonable to assume that a field agent could have such a substance in his or her possession."

"So you think Cooper did it? You think Cooper spiked Minkus's dinner?"

Tom's eyes narrowed. He didn't answer, but I could tell that wasn't the conclusion he wanted me to draw.

"If we take our hypothetical agent as an example . . ." he said.

Okay, he meant Minkus.

". . . and that agent believed he was being targeted . . ."

"For what?"

"*That* is classified."

I nodded. "Go ahead."

"If the hypothetical agent was under pressure from outside forces . . ." Tom gave me the evil eye. "Strong forces, say from hostile foreign governments . . ."

I nodded again.

". . . we think it is likely that such an agent might have been prepared to protect himself."

"Then how did *he* end up dead?"

He shrugged. "That's the million-dollar question."

"Could he have committed suicide?"

"That is one of several scenarios we are looking into."

I held Tom's gaze for an extended moment. "That's a nice, tidy answer," I said. "But there's more, isn't there?"

He licked his lips and shrugged. "All I can tell you is that agents all over the world—some from other countries—have the same means of killing at their disposal. It's also possible that our hypothetical agent was assassinated by another country's operative."

"China, most likely," I said. "Right?"

Tom leaned back, and it was then I noticed how close he had been. "That's as much as I can say."

"I take it from your reaction over the phone that this revelation about tetrodotoxin won't make the evening news."

He shook his head. "We can't let that out. Not yet. No one knows except for the president, a couple of trusted advisors . . ."

I thought about Cooper and Kap. Were they the trusted advisors Tom referred to?

" . . . and those of us on the PPD. I gotta tell you, Ollie: I never expected the chef to be party to this information."

"I overhear a lot."

"Sure," he said, clearly not believing me. "Just don't tell anyone else, okay? We're not even telling the Minkus family, yet. Until we know for certain whether he was targeted—or whether he took his own life—we can't let even a hint of this get out."

We sat in silence for a moment.

One thing still bothered me. "What makes the medical examiner so sure this toxin didn't come from the kitchen?"

Tom shifted in his seat. "Hypothetically, again?"

Could he use that word any more times tonight? "Of course."

"Toxic substances are tightly controlled by the government—as you might expect." He squinted into the night. "But occasionally the government experiences a breach. And sometimes a breach isn't discovered until an inventory is taken."

"The NSA is missing a supply of tetrodotoxin?"

Tom's jaw worked. "It may have simply been misplaced."

It all made sense now. "That's why the ME knew to test for it."

He didn't answer that. He didn't have to. "Whether an individual acquired it from the government supply, or whether this is a mere clerical error, there are serious issues at stake. And a lack of competence we find unacceptable." He looked at me. "There are already measures in place to discover what happened and to prevent any such mix-up from happening again."

"Wow." There really wasn't much else to say. "This is real, isn't it?"

He looked at me.

"I mean, we hear about espionage . . . but there are real people who use toxins against one another. On purpose." I shuddered. "I don't like it."

"Necessary evils."

"Maybe," I said.

Again we were silent for a long moment. I broke the silence. "What are you doing for Easter tomorrow?"

He shrugged. "Family stuff."

"I'm cooking at my place," I said, by way of conciliation. "At four. In case you're interested."

His eyes were unreadable. "I . . ." His voice made a tiny little catch. "Ollie. I think maybe we need this break."

I felt my heart wrench.

He looked into my eyes. "Can I ask you something?"

I swallowed hard and nodded.

Tom inhaled audibly. "Last night you said that you can't be yourself with me. Do you really believe that?"

My mouth went dry. I wanted to avoid answering, but he stared at me with an intensity that would brook no lie. "I do, actually."

The expression on his face looked like somebody had punched him in the gut, but he nodded and glanced at his watch. "The Metro probably isn't running anymore. I'll drive you home."

"Thanks."

We made small talk as we drove, and I waited until he pulled up to my building to say, "I'm sorry."

He sat in the darkness for about ten seconds, staring straight ahead until he finally shook his head, and said, "No, I'm the one who's sorry."

CHAPTER 23

THE FIRST FAMILY HAD ATTENDED SERVICES THE NIGHT BEFORE, and had no other official plans beyond entertaining their family for dinner at noon. An easy day, as far as we were concerned, and we planned to start preparations for the Easter meal just as soon as the morning rush was over. Cyan and I finished garnishing the breakfast plates just as Henry strode in. "Happy Easter," I said.

Uncharacteristically grumpy, he pointed at me. "Do you know Howard Liss?"

"I wish I didn't."

"He accosted me on my way in to work." Henry tied on an apron and consulted our schedule as he continued, working and talking at the same time. "The man is stalking the White House. When he saw me, he wanted to know why I had been brought back here to work."

"That's none of his business."

Henry's face flushed. "I wanted to tell him that, but you know reporters—they'll make it sound like you're hiding something. I just told him that I was happy to be able to help out as we prepared for Monday's big event."

I sensed there was more.

Henry's eyebrows bunched together. "He asked about you. Specifically, he asked if you had any connection to Phil Cooper."

"He did?"

Henry nodded. "Liss seems to believe that Cooper has a hidden agenda. He didn't accuse the man of killing Minkus, but he came close enough for me to smell the suspicion on him. This Liss is a wild card."

"You're telling me. I don't know where he gets his information." I voiced a tidbit that had been bothering me. "Don't you find it odd that he never publicized the fact that Bucky is suspended?"

Cyan shrugged. "Maybe he doesn't know. The newspapers didn't even mention it. I think Paul kept that information in-house."

"I wish all information was kept in-house," I said.

Henry continued, undaunted. "Liss is determined to get Cooper fired."

"He told you that?"

"Close enough. I quote: 'Our country can't afford to clean up any more of Cooper's messes.'"

I shook my head. "We can't worry about Liss. Or anyone else, for that matter. Our job today is simple: Easter dinner for the First Family, then the last-minute preparation for tomorrow. The sooner we get it all done, the sooner we can all get home to our own families. Now, let's do our best to provide our president with the best dinner ever, shall we?"

Henry's smile was wide. "You have become the leader I expected you to, Ollie."

MONDAY MORNING I WOKE UP EARLIER THAN I NORMALLY would. I couldn't sleep, knowing how much we had to do. I had been through Easter Egg Rolls before—but this one loomed large. Short-staffed, behind schedule, and still suspected by the public, we were nonetheless expected to put on the biggest, best Egg Roll event ever. My family must have felt the same charge in the air because Mom and Nana got up with me, and bustled me out the door with good wishes for a successful day.

"You remember how to get there?" I asked them for the tenth time.

Mom sighed. "Yes, and before you double-check again, we do have our tickets. We will be there, Ollie. We wouldn't miss it."

I couldn't take the Metro this early, so I drove in, trying my best to enjoy the dark morning sky and the promise of possibility. I usually loved early mornings—the air smelled fresher and the world sparkled with newness—but today my worries kept me from being able to enjoy any of it.

Once in the kitchen, there was very little chatter. After preparing the First Family's breakfast, we set to work on everything else planned for the day. My mind was on Tom. And Bucky. And getting everything done just right and on time. The annual Egg Roll was a major Washington affair. I remembered the huge crowd waiting patiently for ticket distribution on Saturday. No one wanted to miss it.

Activities were scheduled—and food provided—all day. In addition to the actual rolling of the eggs, there would be a kid-friendly band playing pop hits; famous politicians reading books to youngsters; tours of the gardens; and, of course, visits from the Easter Bunny and other familiar characters.

By eight in the morning, we were ready.

"Let's roll 'em out," I said.

Henry began the arduous task of getting the hard-boiled eggs out to the South Lawn. Although he had lots of help from the wait staff, it was still a major production to get the eggs out with minimal breakage, and into place in time for the festivities to begin. We'd boiled about 15,000 eggs in total, dyeing a large portion of them. The remaining undyed eggs were set up at tables where children were offered supplies and the opportunity to decorate their own eggs, if they wished.

The pre-dyed eggs were used in the races. Marguerite Schumacher's team not only provided giant spoons to push the eggs down their grassy lanes, her volunteers kept order—inasmuch as that was possible—running and timing the races, and naming winners. On a day like today, however, everybody won.

It was nice not to have to worry about that part. Once the boiled eggs were out of my kitchen, I breathed a sigh of relief. They were a huge responsibility and I was happy to deliver the precious eggs into Marguerite's capable hands. Major hurdle number one: complete.

But then I remembered Bucky. He had worked so hard to get these eggs done—to get them delivered—to make sure everything went smoothly. For all his complaining, the curmudgeon should be here to appreciate the fruits of his efforts. I missed him.

With a grunt, I hoisted a lemonade dispenser onto a wheeled cart. We provided soft drinks and snacks all day. Keeping items cold, and others warm, was one of our biggest challenges. Another important concern was inventory. We wanted to have enough so as not to run out of anything. As Henry and the wait staff wheeled the third and fourth carts of eggs out the back of the White House and toward the South Lawn, I went over the menu again with Cyan. She and I had been alternating outdoor and indoor duty as we confirmed our strategy to replenish the buffet tables at regular intervals. We'd be keeping our runners busy.

On my final trip back to the kitchen, I ran into Cyan on her way out. "We're good to go," I said. "Perfect timing. I was just coming to get you."

Together we headed to our station, just south of the East Wing. The morning was bright, the dew just beginning to evaporate. I wished for a touch more warmth today, and I was hopeful for it. The forecast called for a surge from the south. I rubbed my arms. Five more degrees would do it.

In addition to the official Easter Bunny, who was easily recognized by the massive, beribboned basket he carried, there were at least a dozen other costumed characters strolling the grounds. But most were not ordinary rabbits. Pink-, blue-, and purple-furred, I knew these were actually Secret Service agents in disguise. Cyan and I had seen several of them donning their outfits in the Map Room—the Guzy boys among them. One of the monstrous brothers lumbered by me. With a bulletproof vest and the bright, thick hide, it had to be extra hot in that costume. And no way to even wipe his brow without removing the headpiece. Poor guy.

"The Eagle has landed," Henry said when he joined us. "Or should I say, the eagle's eggs have landed?"

There were two long buffet tables set up in the grass, about twenty feet apart. The way we had it planned, Cyan and Henry would each handle one and I'd float between them, overseeing the entire food service, allowing them breaks when needed. It would be a long day, but we'd been through this before. To be honest, we enjoyed this particular event. No one wanted to miss even a minute of the kids' excitement.

The buffets were set up identically. We offered simple fare—cheese sticks, salads, veggie burgers, and fruit, among other barbecue staples like grilled chicken and hot dogs. We had, in fact, worked hard to keep the menu uncomplicated but sufficient to satisfy as many tastes and dietary needs as possible.

"Here they come," Cyan said.

I looked up at the wave of humanity rolling toward us. Within minutes, the lawns were packed and veteran egg-rollers made their way to the South Portico, waiting for the First Lady to make her appearance on the Truman Balcony.

I wished I could stand up there, too, just for a moment. I wanted to be able to overlook the grounds. There were tents—giant three-pole monsters, and little one-pole pavilions—set up in strategic spots all over the Ellipse and South Lawn. The large exhibition areas would serve as main stages for the featured tween bands, and the small ones for political dignitaries who'd volunteered to read picture books aloud. There were craft tents, too. Some offered egg dyeing, others allowed kids to create cardboard bunny ears for themselves. With flowers and streamers and balloons against the backdrop of the springy green lawns, this was truly a most beautiful event.

We always had a huge contingent of volunteers. Most of them were local teens, some were members of the Egg Board, but all were easily recognized by their white aprons and big smiles. The sun warmed my bare forearms. But I still felt an unhappy chill.

Cyan and I were putting our finishing touches on the buffets when the music strummed to life. I heard the beginning strains of "Easter Bonnet," and looked up to see two full-sized yellow bunnies accompanying the First Lady on the Truman Balcony.

Those of us on staff had been told what the visiting public had not. All yellow bunnies were performers. The rest of the "hare" staff, aside from the official "Easter Bunny," of course, were Secret Service agents in disguise. They would keep in character by mingling and interacting with the kids, but in case of trouble, the pink, purple, and blue rabbits were on call.

The yellow bunnies on the balcony were pretending to conduct the band while the families on the ground stared up, enjoying the beautiful music and crisp spring day. When the song ended, Mrs. Campbell stepped to the microphone. She gave a short speech of welcome and reminded everyone that the races would begin when her husband blew the whistle.

From that moment on, it was a whirlwind. My team and I worked the grills, barely getting time to look up and enjoy the show. When we did, during the infrequent lulls, I watched the little kids run around in bouncing bunny ears while happy parents looked on. Next to us, a kiddie band played nursery rhyme songs, and in spite of all I had on my mind, I found myself humming the ditties by early afternoon. Catchy little buggers.

At some point soon, the Marine Band would be called upon to play. I thought how much Mom and Nana would be thrilled to hear them.

I checked my watch. They should be here by now. After a quick confirmation that things had slowed down and everything was under control, I asked Henry to oversee the process while I went to find my family. "I'll be back in a minute."

He waved a spatula at me. "Take your time."

I made my way down the gentle slope toward the Ellipse, where guests were still arriving. I had told Mom that I would be stationed near the East Wing, so I hoped to find them somewhere in the approaching crowd.

"Ollie!"

I turned. Nana was waving—her smile as bright as the day had turned out to be. I changed directions, and was about to ask where Mom was when Nana closed the distance between us and grabbed my arm. "Guess who we ran into?"

"I have no idea—"

"Ollie!" Kap called as he and my mother made their way around a group of stroller-pushing parents. "Wonderful party."

I gave him an auto-pilot response: "Thanks." Then collected my thoughts. "What are you doing here?" I asked. "Do you have grandkids participating?"

He laughed. "No, unfortunately. I have a little business to take care of today." Well, wasn't that cryptic. "It's amazing what events you can attend when you pull a few strings. But I am delighted to see you again." At that he tugged my mom's arm tighter into his. "This has been a most pleasant surprise."

Nana nudged me. What she wanted me to say or do, I had no idea. "Mom, I want to be able to take you inside later," I said, and then turning to Nana, "Both of you." So as not to appear too rude to Kap, I added, "My family has never been inside the White House."

"Then you are in for a treat," he said. He looked about to say more, but his eyes tightened. I followed his gaze. Phil Cooper and his wife had just struck up a conversation with Ruth and Joel Minkus. Why Kap should be distressed by this, I had no idea, but I read his concern as clearly as if there were a neon sign above his head advertising it. "Will you excuse me?" he asked. With that he turned and walked away.

"That was strange," Nana said.

The Coopers and the Minkuses looked to be engaged in lighthearted conversation, but when Cooper leaned forward to say something to Ruth, she instinctively leaned back. Body language rarely lied, and I wondered what vibe she'd gotten from this man that made her want to keep her distance. No matter. I found it more interesting that when Kap approached, all conversation stopped. So, why not join the happy little party to find out more?

"Let's go say hello," I said, and led Mom and Nana closer.

"Good to see you, Ruth. You, too, Joel," Kap said, shaking Joel's hand. Ruth murmured politely.

Kap held a hand out to Cooper and introduced himself. Cooper obliged and both men acted as though they had never met before. What was up with that?

Kap shot me a look that reminded me of my promise not to mention his presence at the White House the other day. But none of this made any sense. D.C. was a small enough town. They could have run into one another any number of ways—and they had both been at Minkus's wake. Their charade made me curious and the hairs on the back of my neck began to prickle.

"It's good to see you, Ollie," Ruth said, placing a hand on my shoulder. "This event is so cheerful. And we needed something to cheer us up. We're very glad we came, aren't we, Joel?"

Joel put his arm around her. "Very glad." He turned to me. "My mom needed a break. She's been staying in the house by herself all the time."

"Look over there," she said excitedly. "Senator Fredrickson. Go say hello." He shook his head. "I'm here for you today, Mom."

I was close enough to hear her whisper, "And the whole reason we came out was for you to network. So get going. You will never win that senate seat without help." She pushed at him. "Go on."

He obliged, clearly under duress.

"Now that the crowds have died down, maybe you ladies would like something to eat?" Kap asked. "How about we sample these lovely buffets?"

"That sounds wonderful," Mom said. She and Nana joined Kap. And, much to my surprise, the Coopers and Ruth followed.

"Help yourselves," I said, "while I make sure everything is under control."

I checked in with Henry, who waved me off. "We're doing fine," he said with a wink. "I have done this before, you know."

Cyan called me over. "Henry is enjoying his time in charge again. Take advantage of it. Go enjoy your family. We're fine."

Mom and Nana had gotten in line in the right-hand buffet behind Ruth Minkus and Francine Cooper. Kap and Phil Cooper went to the left. As I passed behind the two men, I heard Cooper whisper, "I told Ruth we were getting close."

Kap's reply was tense. "You didn't tell her what was missing?"

"No, of course not. She still thinks it was an inside job."

"She doesn't suspect?"

Cooper almost laughed. "I think she suspects *you*."

Kap kept his voice low. "She despises me. But I understand why. And if Joel has political aspira—" He stopped himself when he saw me. "Ollie, what can I do for you?"

"I was about to ask you the same thing. Are you finding everything you need?"

Kap gave me a puzzled look. I could tell he was wondering whether I'd overheard them. What did Ruth not suspect? That her husband had been poisoned by some missing tetrodotoxin?

Cooper seemed unfazed by my sudden appearance. He smiled, and brought his face close enough to mine that no one nearby would be able to hear him. "Thank you, Ms. Paras, for not mentioning our visit the other day." He glanced around. "At least not to those outside the White House."

"I will be the first to admit I don't understand," I said. "But—"

"Yes, thank you," Kap said, cutting me off.

Just then Mom and Nana joined the group, looking for a place to sit. "When you're finished," I said to them, "I can take you on that tour."

Because I didn't think it appropriate to sit and eat with the guests, I meandered over to watch an egg roll race, reflecting on how this was exactly the sort of family event that our nation was famous for. I talked with a couple of volunteers and then made my way back to the buffets. Ruth was waiting for me. "Why is Kap sitting with your mother?" she asked.

I shrugged, not thrilled about the situation myself. "They've been seeing each other," I said. "Socially."

Her lips tightened into a thin line. "I don't trust him. I don't think you should, either."

"Why not?"

She gave me a meaningful look. "He is not who he seems to be."

Instinctively, I moved closer. "What do you mean?"

"I shouldn't tell you this," she said, her eyes wide. "Because I'm not even supposed to know . . ." Her words came fast, as though she were afraid she might get cut off. "But my husband found out that Kap"—she gestured toward the crowd with her eyes—"was selling U.S. secrets to China."

My heart skipped a beat, then began to race. Ruth grabbed my arm. "Kap only pretends he was my husband's good friend now that he's dead. But Carl saw through him."

"Do you have proof?"

She squeezed my arm hard. "No, of course not. Don't you think I would come forward if I did?" Looking morose, she glanced to where Joel was chatting up a senator from Illinois. "Carl had proof. He told me he did. And Carl was about to blow the whistle on Kap." She swallowed, glancing around yet again. "So Kap had him killed. And Cooper was the one who did it," she said. "Right under my nose."

"Why are you telling me this?"

"I need your help. And Howard Liss trusts you."

Liss, I thought. That's when the light dawned. Ruth was the confidential source he kept talking about.

"Ollie!" Nana called to me from about twenty feet away. "We're ready."

I waved. "I'll be there in a minute." I was trying to process Ruth's revelation. "What does Liss have to do with this?"

"He knows the whole story," she said. "He's the one who figured out the connection between Cooper and Kap. Howard Liss has been following this story from day one and keeping me updated. I help him, too, a little bit. I trust him. And he trusts you."

I shook my head. "I *don't* trust Liss."

"Whether you do or not," she said, "we need your help. We need to uncover their treason before they kill anyone else."

Nana called me again. "I really have to get going," I said, inching away.

Ruth's eyes narrowed as she looked at me. "Don't you care about your country?" she asked.

That irked me. "Of course I do," I said, with more than a little spirit. "But if you're depending on Liss for your information, I want no part of it."

She looked stricken, then resolute. "Listen," she said, talking quickly, "Kap plans to kill Cooper. Did you know that?"

I didn't want to continue this conversation and tried again to make excuses, when she said, "You didn't believe that those two just met today, did you?"

So she knew. Stunned silent, I waited for her to continue.

"Cooper and Kap pretended they didn't know each other. That was for my benefit," she said, pointing her finger hard into her chest. "Cooper killed my husband. Now Kap needs to get rid of that loose end. He's going to do that by killing Cooper."

I waved to Nana and Mom, who were still waiting. Next to them, Kap stared at me with an odd expression on his face. I turned to Ruth. "What do you need me to do?"

CHAPTER 24

RUTH WAS ABOUT TO ANSWER, BUT KAP TOOK THAT MOMENT TO steer my mom and nana over. "We're ready for our tour," Nana said cheerily. "If you have a few minutes."

What I wanted to do, more than anything, was show my family the China Room, the kitchen, and take them into the heart of the White House. But here I was, asking them—again—to wait just a little bit longer. "I'm sorry," I said, "something came up."

"What's going on, Ollie?" Mom asked.

Ruth excused herself, shooting Kap a hateful glare as she left.

Kap watched her leave before speaking. "You were talking with her for quite a long time there."

I nodded. "She's having a tough day. Holidays, you know."

"Anything else?"

"Why do you ask?"

Kap's expression was unreadable. "Just making conversation."

Oh, sure, Kap. Claim you're striving for inane conversation while the world crashes down on me. Ruth's allegations were nothing short of explosive, and I needed to sort facts from conjecture. "Hang on one minute," I said, and raced over to where a giant pink bunny leaned over to pat an adoring toddler on the head. When the bunny righted himself, I sidled up. I was pretty sure who was inside this suit. "Agent Guzy?" I whispered.

The bulky head turned toward me, blocking my view of anything beyond its fat fuzzy grin. I tried to look behind the screen-printed eyes, but couldn't see inside the darkness. The head moved up and down slowly, nodding. I knew that bunnies were instructed not to talk to the children, but I hoped he could hear. I whispered, "I need your help."

Waving a pink-pawed good-bye to the children who had gathered around him, the Guzy Bunny followed me away. As we walked, I explained what little I could. "Listen, I don't know exactly what to expect, but the gentleman I am about to introduce you to may bear watching."

Guzy Bunny leaned his giant head close to mine. One of the bent ears grazed the side of my face. His voice was nearly inaudible. "What do you need me to do?"

I leaned up, pulling the plaster and fur face closer, hoping to be heard over the high-pitched squeals of children playing tag nearby. Hoping to not accidentally tug his head off.

"Just keep an eye on this guy, all right? I'll hurry back as soon as I can with more information."

The big head nodded again. Guzy Bunny followed me to the table's edge.

"Look who came to visit," I said with forced cheer.

Mom and Nana looked up at me, painfully unimpressed. Detritus from the day's event littered the tabletop, and the other empty chairs were tilted and angled, as though their occupants had just tumbled out of them. Kap sat on the edge of his folding chair and studied the grounds, looking ready to bolt at any moment.

"This is . . ." I thought fast. "Fuzzy. He's going to take you around the grounds and show you the gardens."

Mom shifted in her seat. "We don't mind waiting for you, Ollie."

Nana patted the big pink paw. "No offense, Fuzzy."

Fuzzy Guzy stayed silent, obviously waiting for them to stand and join him. When that didn't happen, he lowered his cotton-tailed bulk into the nearest empty chair—right next to Kap. Without saying a word, the big rabbit patted the table in front of him, and folded his paws one on top of the other. "Thanks," I said. "I'll be right back."

"Ollie." Kap started to get up. "Do you need help?"

"No, not at all," I said and sprinted away before he could argue.

Leaving Mom and Nana with him seemed wrong somehow. Ruth had said that Kap wasn't who he pretended to be, and I believed that. In fact, I'd sensed that from the start. But in this crowd, with all of those kids running around, and with Fuzzy Guzy watching over them, I didn't know how much safer they could be.

I spotted Ruth about a hundred feet away. She was leaning against a tree trunk, in conversation with Phil and Francine Cooper. Damn. Another delay. "Ruth," I called. She turned and waved. I hadn't expected her to be with Cooper. Could she be warning him about Kap's alleged plans?

I slowed my pace, striving to appear casual. "Did you all have enough to eat? How was the food?"

Francine smiled and told me how wonderful everything tasted. Cooper distractedly agreed. Ruth made eye contact with me and raised her brows. What did that mean?

"When you have a few minutes, Mrs. Minkus," I said, "I wouldn't mind a chance to finish our conversation."

"Maybe later," she said. "I'm not feeling so well."

Phil Cooper was instantly solicitous. "Do you want to sit down? Can I get you something?"

The offer seemed to stun her. "No, I'm just a bit unsettled," she said, her voice shaking. "I'm not used to eating—I haven't had much appetite over the past several days. Please don't trouble yourself. I'll be fine."

As though drawn by the tug of a magic umbilical cord, Joel rushed over from out of nowhere. "Mom, what's wrong?"

She smiled up at him. "Nothing, honey. Maybe you should call for the car. Would you, please? I'd like to go home now."

Joel ignored her request and instead grabbed the nearest folding chair, pressing his mother to sit. As Ruth lowered herself onto the seat, she shooed Phil and Francine Cooper away. "I'm fine," she said. Her voice seemed to have regained its strength. "You two don't need to worry about me. Joel is here now." The Coopers left, albeit reluctantly.

One of our volunteers came over and asked if there was anything she could do. Although Ruth tried to assure us all, I knew it was too late. This was the White House. No one got light-headed around here without it becoming a federal case. This little incident—forgettable in most any other environment— had just shattered my hopes for continuing our conversation.

When one of our on-site paramedics arrived "just to make sure," I left Ruth in good hands and decided on the best approach to extricate my mom from Kap's company.

Phil Cooper saw me walking rapidly across the lawn, and changed his trajectory to intercept me. "Is she okay?"

"I think she'll be fine," I said, slowing. "The medic is checking her out. And Joel's there."

Phil nodded. Francine joined us. "She seemed okay five minutes ago," she said. "It's like something came over her all of a sudden."

I turned back to look at Ruth again. All of a sudden? Like . . . Carl Minkus? Oh my God.

"What was she doing right before I came up?" I felt panic rise up in my chest. Ruth's rantings about Cooper's involvement in her husband's death started to solidify. But I couldn't stop myself from asking, "Did she eat anything?"

Cooper looked at me like I had bay leaves shooting out my ears. "We all ate," he said, clearly confused. "And it was very good."

"Did she complain about tingling in her lips?"

Phil had unscrewed the cap of his water bottle and drained what was left before he answered. "No, she didn't complain about anyth—" In that instant I knew he understood the nature of my question. His face lost all expression and he stared at the area where the medics were now talking with Ruth. "You don't think her food was tainted . . ."

My limited research on the toxin led me to understand that victims had tingling mouths and numb tongues, which quickly spread into paralysis of the diaphragm. Unless the victim was given immediate and constant CPR, the toxin led to death.

"She said she was feeling light-headed. That isn't what Carl Minkus complained of, is it?"

Cooper touched his fingers to his lips. "No," he said. "Carl was different. But . . . I can't help thinking . . ." He scanned the crowd.

"What?" I asked.

From behind us, Kap appeared, deftly moving into the space between me and Cooper. "What's happening?" he asked. Turning to the large pink bunny behind him, he said, "Get away from me. Go find some kids to entertain."

Cooper was pale. "They might have struck again. Let's get over there."

Without a backward glance to me, Kap and Cooper headed toward Ruth Minkus, the pink bunny trotting faithfully behind. Ruth was seated on the grass now, surrounded by her son, a medic, and several volunteers. I heard her protesting that she was just fine and that she and Joel would like to leave.

"She sure sounds better," I said.

Francine's pretty face twisted with concern. "Ten minutes ago she was hurrying around—busy. In fact, I thought it was strange that a woman still grieving for her husband should be shuttling food and drinks for other people."

That got my back up. Guests should not be working at this event. "You mean she fixed a plate for Joel," I said for clarification.

"No," Francine said. "Actually, it was kind of strange. Phil and I were getting ready to leave and she came over with a couple bottles of water. She said we looked thirsty." Unscrewing the bottle in her hand, Francine took a swig, emphasizing her point.

Francine had used the word *strange* to describe Ruth, twice in the same conversation. The back of my neck and shoulders began to prickle again. Thoughts began to formulate. I excused myself and jogged toward the small group gathered around the woman on the grass. Francine followed me.

"No, really," Ruth was saying in a voice much stronger than I expected. "I'm just fine." Without another glance at those around her, she grabbed her son's arm and stood up. "Joel—let's go. Now. Please. Get the car."

Joel took off like a shot. As soon as he was out of sight, Ruth boosted herself to leave. What prompted me to stop her, I don't know. But I needed to. She had the answers, and there was no time to lose. "Ruth," I said, "just a minute."

She didn't answer. She kept walking. Very fast.

I started to follow, but Cooper grabbed my arm. His empty water bottle dropped next to my feet. Sweaty and pale, he held fingers to his mouth. "My lips," he said thickly. "I can't feel them." He looked around with wild eyes.

Cooper let go of me long enough to grab Kap's arm. "Not China," he said. Then his knees gave out and he collapsed to the ground. "It was her."

In an instant, I understood.

I dropped to the grass next to Cooper and pointed to the direction Ruth had taken, "Stop her," I said to Kap. Then to the medic, I shouted, "This man needs help!"

The medic responded at once, calling for assistance as she closed the distance between us. "What have we got?" she asked.

"Tetrodotoxin," I said. "It's what killed Carl Minkus."

A second medic relayed that information into his radio as he knelt on the ground next to me. "He will go into respiratory failure quickly," I said. "His diaphragm will be paralyzed. You *have* to keep him alive."

I bolted to my feet and ran to catch up with Kap, looking back long enough to see Francine standing terrified next to the emergency response team. She sobbed as she watched them work on her husband. I wanted to be there for her, but I had to follow Kap. I could see him in the distance, looking both ways; it was obvious he had lost Ruth. Behind him, Fuzzy Guzy looked ready to pounce on his quarry. My mom was about halfway between the two, looking both ways as well.

For a moment I wondered where Nana was, but I didn't have time. I ran, full out.

I didn't get far.

"Ollie!"

I turned.

Ruth stood behind one of the abandoned balloon sculpture tents, the right half of her body hidden from view. She peered out around the corner, struggling with something I couldn't see. "You need to get me out of here."

I said the first thing that came to mind. "You killed your own husband? My God, why?"

"Get me out of here. I know you can do it."

Whatever she had behind the white canvas made her recoil.

"Get me out of here now." Her teeth gritted. "Before it's too late."

Several hundred yards away, Kap turned to look around. I started to call to him.

"Don't," she said.

And then she jerked her quarry into view.

I started to scream, but clapped my hands over my mouth. If I drew any attention to the three of us . . .

Nana fought her captor, but Ruth was twenty years younger and ten times stronger. She'd shoved fabric into Nana's mouth, and had her wrapped in a bear hug from behind. "Shut up," Ruth said, but her voice was ragged from exertion. Then to me: "Get me out of here or your grandmother gets dosed."

My mind telescoped to the small vial in Ruth's left hand. She held on to it so tightly, I could see the whites of her knuckles straining her skin. Nana kicked and tried to scream. Ruth rocked sideways, maintaining control of my grandmother's writhing form.

"Don't mess with me, I'm warning you. You have to get me out of here. You *know* how to do it."

Secret Service agents were busy with Cooper and with Kap. No one took notice of three women by this vacant tent. I took a step closer. "Give it up, Ruth."

"You want Grandma dead?"

Nana kicked, and although Ruth grimaced, she didn't let go.

Working to tamp down the panic crawling up my throat, I pleaded. "Listen to me. Let her go—I'll get you out. I will."

"She comes with." Ruth gave the area a quick glance. "No one is going to question us if we're helping your grandmother. She stays with me until I'm out."

My mouth was dry, and I couldn't think—couldn't begin to figure a way out of this one. "Nana," I said.

Ruth tugged Nana in a vicious Heimlich maneuver. Nana's muffled gasp tore at my heart. She slumped, unconscious.

"Nana!" I cried, starting toward her.

"Get back!" Ruth said. "Damn." Tightening her hold around my grandmother, she pulled her hands close enough to start unscrewing the vial. "Get me out now, or I swear . . ."

"Okay." My fear made it almost impossible to breathe. "Keep the bottle closed. Please."

She looked both directions. "Which way out?" she asked. Then, as I started to move toward her, she yelled at me to stop again. "I don't trust you."

At that moment the trees behind Ruth parted and a giant purple bunny emerged. But this one was headless. The second Guzy brother held one finger on his lips as the other reached into the side of his costume. I prayed he was going for his gun.

"You can trust me," I said, talking quickly. "You can. There is a way to get you out. I know how to do it."

Ruth shook her head. When she let Nana's body go, it dropped almost soundlessly to the ground. My heart dropped with her.

"No," she said. "You *won't* do it. You're one of those bleeding-heart patriots." Her words came fast. "But . . ." She glanced at the vial, then at Nana's prone form. "I can make sure you won't follow me." She bent, intending to pour the liquid onto Nana's face.

I rushed her, just as the Guzy behind Ruth shouted, "Stop!"

Her head jerked up.

The split-second delay was all I needed. I hit Ruth in a full-body tackle, grabbing her bony wrist, dragging it away from Nana as far as I could. Ruth and I twisted together as we fell to the ground. She gurgled her surprise, but recovered quickly and began fighting me, hard.

Her face contorted with effort, she yanked her arm. I felt her wrist slipping out of my grasp but the bottle flew from her hand. Time seemed to move in slow motion as the vial somersaulted about six inches above her face, about six inches below mine. I clenched my mouth and eyes shut until I heard the dull thud of the glass hitting bone. It had bounced off her cheek, spilling its contents all over her face—some in her eyes—with the bulk running down her cheek and into her open mouth. I immediately let go and jumped away from her, feeling my own face for any vestige of the deadly liquid on me. Dry. Thank God. Ruth sat up and spit, crying out for help as she clawed at her eyes.

I whirled to grab my grandmother by her shoulders. "Nana?"

She blinked up at me. "Are we safe now?"

None of the liquid had landed anywhere near my grandmother. I breathed a deep sigh of relief.

"Are we safe?" Nana asked again.

"Yes," I said. "What about you? Are you okay?"

"Help me up," she said.

"Maybe we should wait for the paramedics. You shouldn't move around so fast."

She boosted herself on one arm. "Help me up," she said again, this time forcefully. "You think I didn't do that on purpose?"

"You faked passing out?"

"Dead weight is always harder to work with," she said as she got to her feet. "Figured you needed some assistance on this one, honey. Glad your old nana was here to help."

We gave Ruth and Guzy wide berth as he came behind her, pulling out his handcuffs from within his fuzzy costume. "Careful," I warned. I pointed to the vial and to Ruth, who was sobbing into the soft grass. "Tetrodotoxin."

The headless rabbit spoke into his microphone as he knelt next to her.

The emergency staff quickly surrounded us. Joel broke through. "Mom?" He scanned the crowd before kneeling at his mother's side. "What happened? Who did this?"

Ruth had begun to hyperventilate, screaming about a conspiracy, but I noticed her gasping for air. I couldn't watch. And I didn't want Nana to see any of it, either. I walked her away from the crowd. "Let's get you inside," I said. Secret Service agents swarmed the area, and we made a slow trek toward the White House. Within seconds, Mom joined us.

"What's going on?"

"I'll tell you later. Where's Kap?"

She pointed back in the direction we'd come. "He's checking on Mr. Cooper. Ollie, what just happened?"

Nana held my mom's hand. "Corinne, we figured it out. Me and Ollie. We figured out who killed that Minkus fellow." She looked up at me. "I don't understand why, though. Do you know?"

I shook my head. Even if I had suspicions, I wasn't ready to share them aloud.

"See, Corinne," Nana continued, "it's just like I always say. She takes after me." Reaching up to pat my cheek, she said, "The apple doesn't fall far from the tree, eh?"

CHAPTER 25

CRAIG SANDERSON CIRCLED MY CHAIR FOR THE THIRD TIME.
This small office in the East Wing—the same one where I'd waited to be interrogated by Secret Service assistant deputy Jack Brewster last week—was cold. I kept my hands together between my knees for warmth, but shivered involuntarily. Craig smiled at my discomfort, and tried to share the enjoyment with the only other person in the room, Agent Snyabar.

Snyabar stared straight ahead. Totally impassive.

Craig started in on me again. "You told the medic on the scene that Agent Cooper had ingested tetrodotoxin."

It wasn't exactly a question, so I didn't answer.

He rubbed his chin, feigning thoughtfulness as he continued to pace around me. "I have to wonder how you knew which toxin killed Carl Minkus."

Still not a direct question. I bit the insides of my mouth.

"Not that we aren't grateful, mind you. Agent Cooper is in intensive care, but is expected to make a full recovery." He stopped and looked down at me. "I'm sure he's very appreciative of your intervention. And your prescience. How did you know what he'd been poisoned with? Oh wait! I forgot just who we're dealing with here—the White House chef who feeds the First Family and saves the world in her spare time." A frown contorted his face as he glared down at me. "Like a special agent in disguise. Talk about delusions."

Silence hung in the air between us. I stared at the walls.

Craig cleared his throat. "Ms. Paras, you made a special effort to inform me that you and Agent MacKenzie were no longer . . . in your words, 'in a relationship.'"

I looked up at him.

His eyebrows arched upward. "Why?"

"I told you why. So that you could no longer hold him responsible for my actions."

He made a sound like, "*Tsk*."

"What?" I asked.

He exhaled loudly. "This is an unfortunate turn of events. However, the ends do not justify the means."

"What are you talking about?"

Craig's smile was just as nasty as his frown. I wanted to slap it off his face. "While I'm sure Agent Cooper is indebted to you for saving his life, it is clear to me that you could not have known about the toxin unless Agent MacKenzie breached security by telling you."

I jumped in my chair. "He didn't tell me."

"Oh, I suppose you guessed?"

"Yeah, kind of. I figured it out."

Craig seemed to find that funny. He looked up at Snyabar again. The other agent kept his eyes forward. "And how—exactly—were you able to figure out something so incredibly obscure?"

I bit my lip. I couldn't mention Kap. Late yesterday, I had been debriefed to the extent deemed necessary. Kap was, indeed, not the man he appeared to be. A covert CIA agent, he and Cooper had uncovered Carl Minkus's deep secret. It was Minkus who had been selling intelligence to China for years. Cooper and Kap were on the verge of being able to prove his treason—but then Minkus died. In the White House.

"I hear things, and I can put two and two together." Sitting up a little straighter, I added, "That's a talent that comes in handy, don't you think?"

"Two plus two," he said. "In addition to being a culinary genius, the chef is a math whiz." His eyes narrowed and his jaw tightened. "You will be interested to know that I have taken steps to dismiss Agent MacKenzie from the PPD."

I caught my breath. "You can't do that."

"I most certainly can, Ms. Paras." He lips widened in a mean, straight line. "Unless you care to share any more of your mathematical skills with us . . ."

I waited. I had no idea where he was going.

"For instance, if you tell me specifically how you 'deduced' the name of the toxin . . . if," he continued, raising his voice, "you were to cooperate—fully—I *might* be convinced to refrain from transferring Agent MacKenzie to the uniformed division."

During yesterday's debriefing, which had not included Craig, I learned that both Cooper and Kap had suspected Chinese operatives from the start. They were, however, stymied as to how the assassination had been carried out. Never did they suspect Ruth of slipping the toxin into her husband's dish.

I wasn't supposed to talk about it. I had given my word. But I thought about Tom—he had worked his entire career to become a member of the elite PPD. And now Craig, with no justification, planned to strip him of that. "I can't talk about it," I said. "But I can tell you that Tom did absolutely nothing wrong. He did not breach security." I sighed. "He never does, even when it costs us both."

"Not good enough. Who else could have possibly told you about the tetrodotoxin?"

Desperation ran through my mind. Then, I had it. "I did get the information from someone here at the White House."

Craig's eyebrows raised again. "Who?"

I took a deep breath. "Peter Everett Sargeant the Third."

"The sensitivity director?" His face contorted. "How would he know anything?"

I shrugged. "He came in and started grilling me about puffer fish on Saturday. He asked, repeatedly, if I'd ever served it to the president. It wasn't much of a leap after that. Like I said, two plus two . . ."

"Nice try, Ms. Paras, but—"

The door opened. Craig's boss, Jack Brewster, walked in, followed by one of the Guzy brothers and Tom. "Excuse us, Ms. Paras." He gestured me out. I stood, making eye contact with Tom, but his expression was unreadable. Just as I made it to the doorway, Brewster added, "You are released."

I stood still as the door closed behind me.

It had been suggested—strongly—that I take some personal time. And now that I had agreed, I had no responsibilities in the kitchen until late next week. Bucky was being reinstated, and I knew that my team, especially with Henry there, would handle everything just fine. Although I longed to go down there to see my staff, I knew it would be best if I went home and spent time with Mom and Nana.

But something made me stay. Exhaustion? Fear for Tom? Whatever it was, I stopped at a chair in the hallway and sat down.

The last I'd heard yesterday, Ruth was in intensive care. No word on her condition today. But she had talked—some. From what the authorities discovered, she had known about her husband's treasonous activities for a long time.

He had even shared with her his fears about being found out. He knew Kap was onto him and he planned to take Kap out.

Aware that Carl's treason would be brought to light at any moment, Ruth could no longer take the pressure. Worse than her husband being a traitor was the effect Carl's arrest might have on their son's political aspirations. Reasoning that Carl would be put to death for his actions anyway, she did her best to prevent him from ruining their son's life by squelching the ugly truth before it came out. When Carl revealed his plan to kill Kap, Ruth saw an opportunity to save her son's career. She used Carl's own supply of toxin to kill him, in effect hoisting him by his own petard.

All to save Joel from the stigma of being the son of a traitor.

I thought about Nana's observation at the wake. No happy family pictures on that digital slideshow. My guess was there were more issues in Ruth's life—but those we might not ever know.

So deep was I in thought that I didn't hear the door opening until Craig emerged. He shot me a look that would kill a less sturdy woman. But I stood.

He stormed down the hall.

I scrambled to get out of the way when Jack Brewster came out a moment later, talking genially with Tom. Brewster saw me and walked over. "I don't condone your involvement in sensitive activities, Ms. Paras. Remember that." He turned to Tom and shook his hand. "I'll see you later."

Guzy and Snyabar followed Brewster, but as they passed, Snyabar turned to me and winked.

"What happened?" I asked Tom.

His eyes held a look I hadn't seen before. Excitement tinged with sadness. "I've been promoted." He looked down the hall where Craig had gone. "I've got Craig's job. He's been assigned to a field office."

It took me a moment to find my voice. "How?"

"Someone—a high-ranking someone whose name I have not been provided—came to your defense. Craig tried very hard to get you fired and to get me reassigned. Instead, it backfired on him."

I thought of Craig's gloating smile as he was grilling me. "Good."

Again Tom looked down the hall. "He was just trying to do his job, Ollie. Protect the president."

Suddenly I felt very small. Craig *had* just been doing his job. I shouldn't be taking any glee in the fact that he'd been demoted. "Yeah, you're right. I'm sorry."

He turned toward me. "I am, too. This is not how I wanted to be promoted. If Craig hadn't tried so hard to get rid of you . . ." He gave me a look that I didn't understand. "You have friends in high places and you came out on top. Again."

"Then why do I feel just the opposite?"

"That I can't answer. But I feel it, too."

Our eyes locked for a few seconds. He didn't smile. Instead he mumbled that he needed to go, and left me standing in the hall.

I stared after him for a long moment, before heading home.

CHAPTER 26

"HOW DID IT GO?" MOM ASKED THE MOMENT I CAME THROUGH the door.

"Confusing." And far too much to discuss just now.

"You still have a job?" Nana asked.

Mrs. Wentworth and Stanley were in my kitchen, looking up at me with anticipation. I said hello. "I still have a job," I answered. "Although I don't know how I managed it."

Nana patted my hand as I pulled up a chair to join them. "You did good," she said.

There were cookies in the middle of the table, and within seconds of my sitting down, my mom had poured me a cup of steaming coffee. I glanced at the clock. "It's still morning," I said. "I feel like I've been gone for days."

"Why do you folks have all the fun?" Mrs. Wentworth asked. "Your grand-ma's been here for a few days and she gets all the excitement. Just once I'd like to be involved in one of your adventures, Ollie."

I shook my head. "Believe me, they're not all they're cracked up to be."

"Did you see the morning paper?" Mom asked. She must have known I hadn't, because she pulled it out and folded it to Liss's column. "Read this."

Today, *Liss Is More* gives credit where it is due.

I glanced up. "Oh no. Am I in it?"

"Keep reading." Mom said with a smile.

Yesterday's fun-filled extravaganza on the White House South Lawn—the annual Easter Egg Roll—was marred by two unhappy incidents.

"He shouldn't be reporting this!"

"Keep reading," Mom said again.

Not one, but two attendees were stricken by illness and had to be taken to nearby hospitals. Agent Phil Cooper suffered a massive heart attack. He is expected to make a full recovery thanks to the quick intervention of medics on the scene. Not so lucky was Ruth Minkus, widow of the recently deceased Carl Minkus. She was believed to have suffered from a ruptured aneurysm in her lung. Although she was rushed to emergency surgery, she did not survive. Our sympathies are with Joel, who has now lost both parents in little over a week.

In the middle of it all, once again, was White House Chef Olivia Paras, who appropriately gets in more hot water than a tea bag. (This reporter made several attempts to reach Ms. Paras for comments, only to be rebuffed.) This time, however, she is credited with alerting paramedics and is to be thanked for her presence of mind as well as her heretofore unknown ability to triage.

"I can't believe this."

Nana chuckled. "You shouldn't. Most of it isn't true. Except for the part where you should be thanked."

My family and neighbors knew part of the truth, though not all of it. They didn't know about Minkus's treason. They knew Ruth killed her husband, but they didn't know why. They didn't know Kap was an undercover spy—although I believed my mother suspected as much. All they knew, and cared about, was that we were all safe, here, and in one piece. And I still had my job at the White House.

I turned my attention back to Liss's article.

It is too bad that Mrs. Minkus died before the medical examiner released his findings. She would have discovered that her husband died of natural causes after all. Unfortunately, she went to her grave believing someone had murdered him. I am sad for her, but even more so for Joel Minkus—this week has been the worst of nightmares.

And today I announce my vacation. An extended vacation. Effective immediately, I am suspending this column. Indefinitely. This week has been too much. Even for a crusty old newsman like me. As they say, Liss Is More, but sometimes less Liss is better. At least for the moment.

Carry on.

"Wow." That was about the only thing I could say.

"Yeah," Mom said, folding the paper neatly. "I'm keeping this."

"What for?"

Nana slapped my hand playfully. "Souvenir, what else?"

THE PHONE RANG WHILE MRS. WENTWORTH AND STAN WERE still at my kitchen table. It was Suzie and Steve calling, this time with happy news. Apparently the FBI had cleared them, just as the Bureau had cleared Bucky. They were grateful to me for the reprieve, despite the fact I insisted I had nothing to do with it.

Later that afternoon, I offered to take Mom and Nana anywhere they wanted to go, but they insisted I relax. "Too much excitement," they said. "You need a break."

I had just dozed off on the couch with my family reading and watching TV next to me, when the apartment phone rang. I rose to answer it and sucked in a breath when I saw the Caller ID—"202."

This was exactly how this whole ordeal had started a week ago.

My heart pounded, but I answered.

It was Marguerite Schumacher.

Mom and Nana stopped what they were doing to watch me. I listened to Marguerite, answered in the affirmative several times, and with a great sigh, hung up.

"What was that about?" Nana asked.

Mom had gotten to her feet. "Is everything okay?"

For the first time in days, my heart was light. "Remember that White House tour I promised you?" I asked.

They nodded.

"We're on for tomorrow at noon."

I watched relief flood their faces.

"Oh, and wear something nice," I added.

They both looked at me in puzzlement. "Why?"

"The president and his wife," I said, "have invited *us* to lunch."

EGGCELLENT EGGS

EGGS ARE ONE OF THE MOST BASIC INGREDIENTS IN THE KITCHEN. They're great on their own, whether coddled; scrambled; fried; boiled; or simply accented in omelets, quiches, and custards. They serve to bind savory ingredients together, as in meat loaf, meatballs, croquettes, and so on. They make baking possible, forming a protein base for everything from cookies to cakes to pancakes to crepes to soufflés and beyond. Eggs are probably the single most versatile ingredient a cook works with. They're also fast-cooking, full of nutrients, and easily digested protein, and delicious. What more can any chef ask for?

I work long hours, so I frequently fix myself breakfast for dinner after a long day in the kitchen. There's just nothing better than a fried egg sandwich for a late-night meal when I don't feel like rustling up something complicated to eat. I refuse to apologize for it these days. Whenever I mention my little secret of eating breakfast food at night, my friends all confess to loving breakfast for dinner, too. It's even become something I deal with in my job, because the First Family actually asks for breakfast for dinner about once a month, so I've added it to the official White House First Family Meal Rotation. I never thought my secret fetish for breakfast at night would become a job requirement. But eggs are comfort food, so I can see why they remain perennial favorites, especially in the White House.

Here are a number of good egg recipes to try for yourself, ranging from the simple to the refined. Eggs don't have to be confined to breakfast or brunch. Try them for dinner. I bet you'll find, as I have, that the people you're feeding will love them. Happy noshing!

Ollie

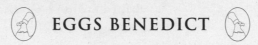 EGGS BENEDICT

8 eggs

4 egg yolks

2 tablespoons cream

Juice of ½ lemon (around 1 tablespoon)

½ teaspoon kosher or sea salt

Pinch cayenne pepper or paprika (optional)

1 cup (2 sticks) butter, melted and still hot

4 English muffins, fork split, buttered and toasted

8 slices warm Virginia ham (or Canadian bacon, if you prefer) cut to
*   fit the muffins*

Chopped parsley to garnish (optional)

Serves four.

Bring a medium saucepan full of salted water to a rolling boil. Reduce heat to a gentle simmer. Crack 1 egg into a small bowl, taking care not to break the yolk. Gently slip the egg into the saucepan filled with hot water, and repeat with 3 more eggs. (You can usually fit 4 eggs at a time in the hot water. Too many, and the eggs won't poach correctly.) Gently coddle to doneness, about 3 minutes, until the whites are set and the yolks remain runny. Remove the eggs from the hot water with a slotted spoon. Set on warmed plate to hold. Repeat with remaining 4 eggs.

Make Hollandaise Sauce: This blender recipe takes a lot of the angst out of the process of making the sauce the traditional way, which is over a double boiler with a wire whisk. I find it's a lot easier for home cooks to get perfect hollandaise sauce this way. Place egg yolks in a blender container. Add cream, lemon juice, salt, and a pinch of cayenne or paprika (optional, but it adds a nice bite). Cover and pulse on low until blended. Remove the middle insert from the lid, and while continuing to blend on low, slowly and gently add the hot butter to the egg mixture, in a gradual stream. The sauce should thicken and smooth about the time the last of the butter goes in. (The hot butter cooks the egg yolks and the blender emulsifies the lemon juice and melted butter with the yolks.)

On warmed serving dish, top each toasted English muffin half with a warm slice of Virginia ham. Place a poached egg gently on top of the ham. Pour hollandaise sauce over eggs. Sprinkle with paprika and chopped parsley to garnish. Serve warm.

This recipe sounds a lot more complicated than it is, and it's a restaurant favorite because it used to be a lot harder to make at home. In fact, eggs Benedict used to be a bear to make—especially getting the sauce right. Doing it on the stove, the sauce had a tendency to curdle in inexperienced hands. Thanks to the wonder of modern blenders and a good stove, you should be able to have this on the table in less than 20 minutes.

 ## HERBED SCRAMBLED EGGS

6 eggs
2 tablespoons olive oil, divided
3 tablespoons chopped chives
1 clove garlic, smashed, peeled, and minced (see note, below)
1 teaspoon fresh thyme leaves, or ½ teaspoon dried thyme leaves
1 cup fresh spinach, washed, de-stemmed, and patted dry
Kosher or sea salt and pepper, to taste

Serves two.

Break eggs into a bowl. Stir with a fork or whisk gently to break up, but not to blend totally. Set aside.

Heat a large skillet over medium heat. Add 1 tablespoon olive oil and gently rotate the pan to coat the bottom. Add chopped chives, garlic, thyme, and spinach. Stir until spinach wilts and the garlic cooks through and softens, about 2 to 3 minutes.

Transfer mixture to warmed serving plate.

Add remaining olive oil to the same skillet. Gently rotate the pan to coat the bottom. Pour beaten eggs in oiled skillet. Allow bottom to set. Bring in the edges to the center, letting the remainder of the uncooked eggs pour across the pan to cook. Add cooked herbs and greens. Stir slowly until eggs are cooked and the greens and herbs are roughly incorporated, 1 to 2 minutes. Top with salt and freshly grated pepper, to taste. Slide onto warmed serving plate. Serve warm.

The easiest way to deal with fresh garlic is to place a clove on a cutting board, place the broad end of the blade of a chef's knife over it so the blade is parallel to the cutting board surface, and smash your fist against the smooth metal of the knife— carefully! Don't let your flesh get too close to the knife's cutting edge—kitchen accidents are bad. The pounding will smash the garlic and burst the clove free of its papery wrapping, which you can pull off and discard. You can then chop the clove easily.

 ## CINNAMON FRENCH TOAST

4 eggs
1 cup half-and-half
2 tablespoons brown sugar
1 tablespoon cinnamon, plus extra for serving
1 teaspoon vanilla
1 small loaf French bread, raisin bread, or whole wheat bread, sliced
½ cup (1 stick) butter
Maple syrup
Confectioner's sugar
Fruit to garnish (optional)
Ice cream or whipped cream (optional)

Serves four.

Preheat oven to 200°F.

Break eggs into a flat-bottomed square casserole dish. Whisk until uniform and yellow. Stir in half-and-half, brown sugar, cinnamon, and vanilla. Whisk till blended. You will need to whisk lightly before each dip; the cinnamon tends to float.

Dip slices of bread into the egg mixture, one at a time, on both sides.

Heat griddle over medium-high heat. Place pats of butter on griddle, one for each space on which you plan to cook a slice of toast. Place dipped bread slice on top of each pat of butter. Cook until browned, about 2 minutes. Top with another small pat of butter. Flip slices onto butter to cook other side of toast until browned. Remove to warmed serving plate. Place completed toast slices in oven to keep warm while you continue cooking.

Plate slices onto a small pool of maple syrup. Sprinkle with cinnamon and confectioner's sugar. Add a side of fresh fruit to garnish. Serve with more maple syrup on the side.

For true decadence, serve with ice cream or whipped cream.

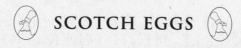

SCOTCH EGGS

This is a hearty recipe that is the old Scotch equivalent of a modern breakfast sandwich—portable, easy to eat on the run, and filling enough to see a working person through a busy morning. This is not diet food, but it is amazingly tasty.

> *6 eggs*
> *1 pound breakfast sausage, thawed*
> *1 cup seasoned bread crumbs*

Serves three.

Preheat oven to 350°F.

Hard-boil the eggs: Place the raw eggs in a saucepan with enough room-temperature water to cover about 1 inch over the top of the eggs. Bring the water to a boil over medium-high heat. Remove from heat and let sit for 15 to 20 minutes. When the pan, water, and eggs have cooled enough to safely handle, pour off water. Rattle the eggs in the pan to bash the eggshells against the side. This will break them and leave the eggs easy to peel. Peel off eggshells and discard.

Divide breakfast sausage into 6 pieces. Roll each piece into a ball and flatten it. Put the sausage patty on your hand, place a hard-boiled egg on the sausage and gently roll the sausage around the egg with both hands until it is covered in an even layer of sausage. Roll the sausage-covered eggs, one at a time, in seasoned bread crumbs. Place the crumb-covered eggs on a cookie sheet or in an uncovered casserole dish and bake until sausage is cooked through, about 25 minutes.

To serve, cut each egg in half lengthwise. Lay the two halves on a plate, side by side, cut side up, to show layers of crumbs, sausage, egg whites, and egg yolks.

Serve warm.

A FAT-FREE, CHEESE-FREE, YOLK-FREE, HIGH-FIBER OMELET

Given that almost every recipe in here is likely to send a cardiologist into palpitations, here's the exception.

> ½ cup broccoli florets, cleaned and chopped
> 1 cup fresh spinach leaves, cleaned and de-stemmed
> ½ cup fresh mushrooms, thinly sliced
> 1 plum tomato, chopped

1 green onion, rinsed and thinly sliced
¼ cup fat-free ham, cubed
1½ cups egg substitute
Salt and pepper, to taste

Serves two.

Coat a nonstick skillet with nonstick cooking spray and place over medium heat. Add the vegetables and the ham to the skillet. Sauté until the veggies are cooked through, the spinach has wilted, and the broccoli is tender, about 3 to 5 minutes. Remove from heat to a warmed plate and set aside.

Rinse and dry the skillet. Spray again with nonstick cooking spray. Add egg substitute to pan. Roll the pan around, spreading the egg substitute evenly across the skillet surface. Reduce heat. Cook over medium heat until bottom is well set, about 2 to 3 minutes. Flip egg in pan to cook other side. Place vegetable-ham mixture on half of the egg's surface. Fold cooked egg round gently over veggies. Slide out of skillet onto warmed plate.

Season with salt and pepper, to taste. Serve warm.

DEVILED EGGS

6 hard-boiled eggs
3 tablespoons Dijon mustard
½ small onion, very finely minced
1 tablespoon white wine
2 tablespoons mayonnaise
Paprika, for garnish
Chopped chives, for garnish

Serves four.

Cut hard-boiled eggs in half lengthwise. Scoop out yolks into a medium bowl.
Set whites aside on serving tray. Refrigerate. Whisk the egg yolks with Dijon
mustard, onion, white wine, and mayonnaise. When well blended, pipe or
spoon the egg yolk mixture back into centers of cooked whites. Sprinkle with
paprika. Top with chopped chives. Serve chilled.

AIOLI
(GARLIC MAYONNAISE)

3 egg yolks

4 cloves garlic, mashed, peeled, and very finely minced

1 tablespoon Dijon mustard

¾ cup olive oil (not extra virgin)

1 teaspoon white wine vinegar

½ teaspoon kosher or sea salt

¼ teaspoon white pepper (You can use black pepper if you don't have
this, but you'll see the flecks of it in the finished product. It gives
it a rustic look, which isn't all bad.)

Juice of 1 lemon

This is a blender recipe, to take all the stress out of getting it to emulsify.
Place the egg yolks, garlic, and the mustard in the container of a blender. Cover
and pulse to blend completely, about 1 minute. Remove the center of the lid,
and begin to pour the olive oil into the container in a thin stream, still running on slow. When the mixture comes together and looks like mayonnaise
(usually about when half the oil is incorporated), stop pouring oil and add in
the vinegar, salt, and pepper. Blend. Add in another thin stream of olive oil
while blending. Stop when about 2 tablespoons of oil are left to add. Add a
splash of lemon juice. Blend. Adjust seasonings to taste. Add the rest of the oil
if needed. The sauce should be thick, creamy, and rich, with a lovely tang of
garlic.

If you don't want to use raw eggs for this, don't worry. Start with a cup of good-quality regular mayonnaise. Whisk in ½ cup olive oil, 3 cloves finely minced garlic, and the juice of 1 lemon. It won't be as good, but it's close, and you won't have to worry about using raw eggs.

 # SPINACH QUICHE

¼ cup butter

3 cloves garlic, smashed, peeled, and finely minced

1 small onion, trimmed, peeled, and finely chopped

1 pint fresh mushrooms, cleaned and thinly sliced

1 (10-oz.) package frozen chopped spinach, thawed and drained

4 ounces herbed feta cheese, crumbled

8 ounces good-quality cheddar cheese, shredded, divided

½ teaspoon kosher or sea salt, or to taste

¼ teaspoon ground black pepper

1 deep-dish pie crust, unbaked

4 eggs

1 cup milk

Serves six.

Preheat oven to 400°F.

Melt butter in a large skillet over medium heat. Add minced garlic and onion. Stir gently and cook until onion is soft and slightly browned on the edges, about 5 minutes. Add mushrooms and stir until warmed through and reduced, about 3 minutes. Add spinach, feta cheese, and half of the cheddar cheese. Add salt and pepper, to taste.

Place mixture into unbaked pie shell.

In a medium bowl, whisk eggs until blended, add milk, whisk to combine well. Pour into pie shell over vegetable mixture.

Place filled pie shell on cookie sheet to keep it from overflowing.

Place into preheated oven. Reduce oven heat to 375°F. Bake for 20 minutes. Top quiche with remaining cheddar cheese. Return to oven and bake for and additional 30 to 40 minutes. Quiche is done when the eggs are set and firm in the center.

Remove from oven and let sit for 10 minutes. Serve warm.

 # CHOCOLATE SOUFFLÉ

Soufflés, by definition, are temperamental. If something goes odd, or somebody bumps the oven wrong, or the phone rings at the wrong time, the thing can deflate like a kid's balloon. So go into this knowing that it will taste good, even if it doesn't look good. But it's actually pretty easy to make—it just isn't always goof-proof.

But it will usually look fantastic, and it will impress your guests like almost nothing else will.

3 tablespoons unsalted butter, softened
½ cup sugar, divided use
6 egg whites
4 ounces best-quality dark chocolate, chopped
½ cup very cold water
⅓ cup cocoa powder
Confectioner's sugar, for garnish (optional)
Berries, for garnish (optional)

Preheat oven to 350°F.

Coat the insides of 6 individual soufflé dishes completely with ½ tablespoon butter. Refrigerate until the butter is set, about 3 minutes. Place a teaspoon of sugar into each dish. Shake and turn the dishes until sugar completely coats the butter. Tip out any excess. Add more sugar if needed.

Place prepared dishes on a baking sheet and set aside.

In a very clean mixing bowl (any fat will keep the eggs from whipping well), beat the egg whites on medium to high speed until foamy. Gradually add the remaining sugar a little at a time, and beat until eggs are glossy and soft peaks form when beaters are lifted. Set aside.

Place a large metal mixing bowl over a pan of simmering water. Place the chocolate into the bowl, and stir until melted, glossy, and smooth. Remove from heat. Add the water and the cocoa powder. Stir until smooth. Let cool 1 minute.

Add about ⅓ of the egg-white mixture to the cooled chocolate mixture, folding together gently.

Add the folded mixture to the remaining egg whites. Fold together gently.

Spoon into prepared dishes. Using a straight-edged knife, level the egg mixture in the dishes even with the tops of the dishes. Wipe the edges of the dishes with a dampened towel to clean them.

Bake until soufflés puff up and are cooked through but still moist in the center, 12 to 14 minutes.

Sprinkle with confectioner's sugar and garnish with berries, if using, and serve immediately.

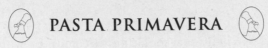 PASTA PRIMAVERA

6 ounces bow tie pasta

2 tablespoons olive oil

2 cloves garlic, smashed, peeled, and minced

2 chicken breasts, de-boned, skinned, and chopped into 1-inch cubes

½ pound of asparagus, trimmed, washed, and sliced into 1-inch
  pieces

½ pound cherry or grape tomatoes, rinsed and halved

½ pound baby squashes, rinsed, trimmed, and halved

¼ cup fresh basil leaves, julienned

Kosher or sea salt, to taste

Black pepper, to taste

¼–½ cup freshly grated Parmigiano-Reggiano cheese, or to taste

Serves four.

Bring a large saucepan of salted water to a boil over high heat. Add bowtie pasta and cook according to package directions.

While pasta is cooking, place olive oil in a large skillet over medium heat. Add garlic and chicken to the pan, cook until garlic is soft and chicken is browned, about 5 to 8 minutes. Add vegetables and cook until vegetables are warmed through and beginning to soften but still retain a little bite, about 6 to 8 minutes.

Stir in fresh basil and remove mixture from heat. Season with salt and pepper, to taste.

Drain cooked pasta. Toss chicken and veggie mixture with pasta. Top with cheese. Serve warm.

WARM BRIE TOPPED WITH WALNUTS, MAPLE SYRUP, AND BERRIES

This looks great, tastes better than it looks, and takes almost no effort.

1 small round Brie, at room temperature
1 cup peeled, chopped walnuts
1 cup good-quality maple syrup, divided
1 quart rinsed berries, any type
Assorted crackers

Serves four.

Preheat oven to 300°F.

Cut the top rind off a small circle of Brie. Place on an oven-safe serving platter. Top with walnuts and ½ cup maple syrup. Turn oven off. Turn broiler on high. Broil cheese until nuts are toasted and cheese is soft. This is something you'll have to watch closely—the nuts can burn quite quickly. Remove from oven.

Add remaining syrup. Surround Brie wheel with alternating pools of berries and crackers. Serve immediately.